D1151121

The
Elizabeth Omnibus

THE LADY ELIZABETH AS A YOUNG GIRL.
By kind permission of the late King George VI.

The
Elizabeth Omnibus

MARGARET IRWIN

Published in Great Britain in 2008 by
Allison & Busby Limited
13 Charlotte Mews
London W1T 4EJ
www.allisonandbusby.com

Young Bess first published in the UK in 1944 by Chatto & Windus, London.
Previous editions published by Allison & Busby in 1998 and 2007.

Elizabeth, Captive Princess first published in the UK in 1948
by Chatto & Windus, London.
Previous editions published by Allison & Busby in 1998 and 2007.

Elizabeth and the Prince of Spain first published in the UK in 1953
by Chatto & Windus, London.
Previous editions published by Allison & Busby in 1999 and 2008.

A CIP catalogue record for this book is available from
the British Library.

10 9 8 7 6 5 4 3 2 1

ISBN 978-0-7490-7982-6

Typeset in Sabon by
Terry Shannon

The paper used for this Allison & Busby publication
has been produced from trees that have been legally sourced
from well-managed and credibly certified forests.

Printed in the UK by CPI Bookmarque, Croydon, CR0 4TD

MARGARET IRWIN (1889–1969) was a master of historical fiction, blending meticulous research with real storytelling flair to create some of this century's best-loved and most widely acclaimed novels, including *The Galliard*, *The Stranger Prince* and *Young Bess*.

Young Bess

'Such incredible fierce desire'
Nan Bullen

To
Lucy Bell

My thanks, 'first and foremost on the list,' to JRM.
And to Lady Helen Seymour for the lively help she gave me,
with the papers and household books of the Seymour family.

CHAPTER ONE

She had been allowed to come out to the royal flagship, and had been eating cherries and strawberries dipped in wine. All round her the sea was a flaming white glitter, the air was hot high summer, the wind in a mad mood; she was twelve years old, and Tom Seymour, who was Admiral of the Fleet and her favourite step-uncle, was talking to her as though she were rather more; he was joking and chaffing her, but then he did that with all women, even with the Queen.

And he went on talking to her, looking down at her with wickedly merry eyes half shut against the sunlight, watching her as though he really wanted to know how she would answer.

'And what will you do when England is invaded?' he asked her. 'Will you raise a regiment and ride at the head of it? Will you be Colonel Eliza or Captain Bess?'

'England won't be invaded. She never has been.'

'Not by the Normans?'

'Five hundred years ago! And they were us, or they couldn't have done it.'

'There speaks the proud Plantagenet!'

She stamped like a wilful pony and tossed her head, and the wind seized a strand of her smooth hair and pulled it out from under her little jewelled cap, tossing it like a wisp of flame, teasing her just as he was doing; but it was a bad joke to mock the thin strain of royal Plantagenet in the Tudor blood – and with her father on board.

'It's lucky for you I'm no tell-tale-tit.'

'No, you'll never be that.'

'How can you tell what I'll be?'

All her egoism was agog. What would she be? At twelve years old anything was possible. And so he seemed to think as he scanned her, and the wind flicked the wisp of hair into her eyes and made her blink.

'How can I tell what you'll be? You may become anything. Elizabeth the Enigma. Will you be beautiful? Will you be plain? You might so easily be either. Will you have a pinched whey-face and carrot-coloured hair and a big peeled forehead like a pale green cooking apple? Or will you suddenly be mysteriously lovely, with your hair aflame over that white face, and that quick secret look of yours? What will you become, you strange secret little thing?'

'I *will* be beautiful, I *will*!'

But how astonishing that he should dare to talk to her like this. The man could be afraid of nothing.

He saw her thought and laughed again. The light reflected from the sea rippled up and up over them in a ceaseless wavering pattern. Their faces were still in that moment of silence, and their eyes looked steadily at each other; but all the time the flickering movement went on, a current of sea-light weaving its web over them both, over their bright, stiff clothes, the golden point of his beard, the red lights in her hair, the soft gleam of her bare neck and shoulders. For the moment they seemed quite alone on board the *Great Harry* on the summer sea, the sails soaring above them like big white clouds, and the other ships careening and skimming past them, trailing their blue shadows over the sparkling water. They were here to defend the English shore, the long line of emerald downs behind them, and in front the golden shimmer of reeds that surrounded the Isle of Wight.

At any moment the enemy fleet might heave into sight out of the blue distance, the biggest fleet ever gathered together against this country. It was, as she had frequently heard of late, the most fateful moment in all their history. And she had been allowed on board the royal flagship! So great was the privilege, so lovely the day, so bright the air, so dangerous the moment, that perhaps it really did not matter what one said. She gave a swift glance behind her; no one was near. She said, very low, the thing she must not say; she spoke of the person who must never be mentioned.

'My mother – was she beautiful?'

The air still quivered in the sunlight, the deck shone smooth as satin; even the flighty wind had dropped for the moment as if to hold its breath. But her step-uncle still stood and looked at her; he did not turn away muttering some excuse to leave her as fast as possible; he did not even turn pale nor pull at his elegant little foreign-looking beard. He answered, without even lowering his voice, as though it were quite natural that she should speak of her mother.

'No, she was not beautiful. But she was clever enough to make anyone think so whom she wished.'

The child drew a deep breath as though they had stepped past a precipice.

'Well, I am clever, so all my tutors say. I too will make people think I am beautiful.'

'Who do you want to think it?'

She looked up at him and a deep mischievous smile stole over her pale little face. Tom Seymour was certain that the answer would be one swift monosyllable – 'You!' But it was not. With an odd mixture of childish coquetry and passionate sincerity she replied, 'Everybody!'

'What! Do you want the whole world for your lover?'

'Yes, or at least the whole country. I don't mind so much about foreigners.'

He flicked her cheek. 'What a wanton! And I thought you a modest little maid. There's another puzzle. Will you be good? Or will you be naughty – like your mother?'

There again. Yet the deck did not open and let him fall straight into the sea.

'You remember her?' she just breathed.

'As if I had this moment heard her laugh. "Ha, ha!", that was how all the Londoners read it when your father had his initial and hers intertwined over the gateways. H.A. – HA HA! They read right, for she laughed at everything and everybody.'

'Even at—'

'Yes, even at him. She was clever, but not wise. She danced herself into his favour and laughed herself out of it – to her death. And she went laughing to that death. The Sheriff was shocked.'

He fell silent, hearing once again across the years an echo of the shrill mocking note, clear as the call of a bird, and as wild and void of human meaning, that had made men call Nan

Bullen a witch. Well, she had used her witchcraft on the King, enslaved him, scorned him, held him off from her for six long years, while to suit her plans he wrecked the whole structure of the English Church, and built it up anew with himself as Pope in England. The King himself said he had been seduced by her sorcery to marry her, but that was after little Bess was born and no boy for heir, and the King had by then turned to Tom Seymour's meek little sister, Jane. Plain Jane her brother rudely called her, though she was pretty enough, but with a prim mouth and pale eyes and no charms that could vie with Nan's, except the charm of being wholly unlike her. Unlike Nan, she was a gentlewoman by behaviour as well as by good, though not noble, solid county family birth.

That had brought Bess's first step-uncles on to the scene; the eldest, Edward Seymour, newly created Earl of Hertford, tall, sparely built, keen-faced, of the kind that goes on being called a rising young man even when rising forty; fiercely and coldly intellectual in his pursuit of his ideals, or, some said, of his ambitions. He had married one sister to the King, another to the grandson of a blacksmith, but both, it was thought, to the same purpose, for the blacksmith's son had been Thomas Cromwell, the King's greatest minister, and his heir a catch even for a rising earl.

His second brother, Henry, flatly refused to rise. He had heard enough of public life to prefer to remain a simple country squire, declining all honours and even invitations to Court.

The youngest, Tom Seymour, acclaimed the handsomest man in England, was the complete opposite of Edward – a wild rascal whom no semi-royal responsibility could sober, and with a proficiency in swearing so picturesque that he had said it was his chief qualification for the post of Admiral of the Fleet. That he had others was evident from the work entrusted to him at this dangerous crisis; he and his ships had been stationed at Dover to defend the Kentish coast against the French invasion, and had now joined up with the main fleet, under his command, at Portsmouth. Soldier, sailor, and foreign diplomat, Tom Seymour had had a brilliant career in all three professions, and had started it well before his sisters' marriages had helped on the family. He had been abroad for the best part of the last seven years, on embassies to the French Court, to the King of Hungary, and to Nuremberg; he had been in Vienna for two years and seen a good deal of the war against the Turks; he had exchanged the job of Ambassador to the Netherlands for that of Marshal of the English army fighting against Spain, and done it so well that he was appointed Master of the Ordnance for life in reward for his military services.

His reckless courage had given rise to a score of wild stories; so had his attraction for women. His good looks were the least part of that attraction; it was his careless talk, his great infectious laugh, his good-humoured gaiety and utter lack of premeditation or caution, in a Court growing paralysed with these things, that made him irresistible. Though nearing the middle thirties, he had managed to evade all his matrimonial pursuers, and they were many. The Duke of Norfolk's beautiful daughter had been desperately anxious to marry him for years, but her brother, the young Earl of Surrey, declared the Seymours were upstarts and wouldn't hear of it. His father, the old Duke, was as harsh and intolerant an aristocrat as his son, but not when it suited his self-interest, and he had rather favoured the match, since the Seymour brothers were now the most powerful men in the country, next to the King; it was not merely that they had provided him with one of his wives, but that she had provided him with his only male heir, Edward, the little Prince of Wales. There were no 'steps' in that relationship; they were the flesh-and-blood uncles of the undoubted heir to the throne. Prince Edward was legitimate by all counts and all religions, whereas nobody could be quite sure how the King's two daughters stood; so often had their father bastardised them by turns. 'The Little Bastard' had been the most frequent informal title given to the Princess Elizabeth at her birth; nearly three years later her father had himself endorsed it by Act of Parliament.

And now the Little Bastard herself asked about that title. Standing by Tom Seymour, leaning over the gunwale, the light from the water rippling up under the soft childish chin, her head turned sideways towards him, her eyes, so clear and light, taking their colour from the sea, fixed themselves upon his face. She said in a voice that he could only just hear above the creak of the ropes and the wash of the waves against the boat's side: 'The women are no use. They answer what they think one ought to think. Can you tell me who I am? I once heard my sister Mary say to another woman that she did not believe I was even the King's bastard – I was just like Mark Smeaton, the handsome musician that was beheaded with my mother – and the woman laughed and said there was choice enough, since three other men had been beheaded too, and one of them her own brother.'

Tom Seymour gave a startling exhibition of his choice of oaths. 'Your sister Mary is a sour old maid, poisoned with hate and jealousy of your mother.'

'But she doesn't hate me – or at any rate she is very kind to me. She did not know I was listening.'

'And well whipped you should have been for it – and would have been, had I been there. But never mind that, or her. I tell you, by God's most precious soul, you are the King's daughter every inch of you, and none could doubt it who looks at you. Can you doubt it yourself, standing here on his flagship, the *Great Harry*? And by God,' he muttered on a sudden drop in tone, 'here comes Great Harry himself.'

Yes, here he came, rather like his own ship, she thought, as he swung portentously into their line of vision, a ship with huge bellying sails ('bellying' is good, she thought, with a pert snigger concealed behind the grave mask of her face as she sank to the deck in a deep curtsy), his silks and jewels flashing in the sunlight and his great hot red face beaming and glistening like a painted block of wood carved on a ship, while beside him Edward Seymour, Earl of Hertford, stalked earnestly like a lean shadow.

Now the King was in front of her, towering over her, blocking out the sunlight, with his silly little flat cap squat on top of all that bulk, and his finger and thumb, hot and sticky as a pair of sausages and yet with surprising force beneath all their fat, pinched her chin and pulled her upright from her curtsy; now she must look him in the face and smile, for he couldn't abide sullen, scared children; they should be frank and fearless as he had been himself. So she stood straight and looked him squarely in the eyes and gave him a charming, ingenuously admiring smile, while he playfully tugged at the loose strand of her hair, and tucked it back under her cap, and she thought: was this enormous being before her, man or monster or god?

He himself did not quite know, for with his arm flung round the nervously smiling Chancellor Wriothesley he was talking of his last Chancellor, jolly Tom Cromwell, and lamenting that he had not got him here now – a pack of rascals had schemed against 'the best of his servants' and so brought him to the block, the more's the pity. Terrible, jovial, at his nod the greatest heads in the kingdom fell, struck by Jove's thunderbolt – and then he seemed astonished and annoyed that he was not sufficiently a god to put them on again. She had seen him weep brokenheartedly over his first wife, 'the best of women', over his last one, Cat Howard, 'the lovely little wretch' – he'd done them both to death but he still loved them. (But no one had ever heard him mention Nan Bullen since her death.)

His present wife, Catherine Parr, had been a widow almost as often and as briefly as King Henry had been a widower. One could not imagine her without a husband, it would have been such a waste of gentle, humorous, infinitely tolerant benevolence. She put a hand on Elizabeth's arm as the child stood there watching the Ship of State surge on, having laid his grappling arms on Tom Seymour now; you could almost hear the young man's wiry frame crack as that obese giant flung his free arm round his shoulders.

'Why so pensive, Bess my sweetheart?' asked Queen Catherine's pleasant smiling voice.

Bess said demurely, 'I was thinking, Madam, of the story

of the fisherman my nurse used to tell me.'

'And what was that?'

The royal procession was well past now.

'Oh, there was a flounder in the sea that promised the poor fisherman three wishes, and his wife made him go down night after night to ask them, though the wind rose and the waves roared and at the last he had to bellow through the storm:

> *"Flounder, flounder in the sea*
> *Come and listen unto me.*
> *Come, for my wife Isabel*
> *Wishes what I dare not tell."*

For she made him ask first to be King, and then Pope, and then God.'

Catherine shook her head, but the little face remained as blankly innocent as a baby's. You could not even see that she was frightened, but she was. ('Dear God, have I gone too far this time again? No, not this time, not with nice soft Pussy-Cat Purr. She'll see no further than's good for me – or her.')

The two were great friends. Elizabeth had a pretty knack with stepmothers. The four that she had known had all been fond of her, one after the other; she had written letters to them in French, Italian and Latin, and this present one made as much a companion of her as if she were grown up. They read French and Latin together, and with little Edward, so much younger than Elizabeth but already the cleverest of the family, and with Mary, so much older, but, in Elizabeth's opinion at any rate, so much the stupidest. Catherine Parr, a born homemaker, was in fact succeeding almost miraculously in

making a real home for the King's three ill-assorted children
by different mothers.

Family life was a difficult affair with a father who had
repudiated two of his six wives, beheaded two others, and
bastardised both his daughters; yet Catherine managed to
bring to it some sense of coherence and even security. She
rescued Edward on the one hand from being utterly overlaid
by tutors; and on the other, instead of discouraging Mary
from reading in bed at night as did everyone else because it
was bad for her very weak eyes, she suggested her translating
Erasmus's Latin treatises. The poor girl, no longer a girl,
badly needed other occupation than fussing over her clothes
and other people's babies, and it might flick her pride to read
in Udall's preface the praises of modern learning in
'gentlewomen who, instead of vain communication about the
moon shining in the water, use grave and substantial talk in
Greek or Latin.'

There had been no such need to flick little Bess's mental
energy into action. Last New Year's Day the child had given
her latest stepmother a present of a prose translation she had
made herself of a very long religious poem by the present
Queen Marguerite of Navarre, sister to King François I, that
brilliantly learned and witty lady. Yet she could perpetrate the
'Mirrour of a Guilty Sowle,' which ran, or rather limped, to a
hundred and twenty-eight pages of the Princess Elizabeth's
childish but beautifully clear and regular handwriting, and of
Queen Marguerite's edifying sentiments expressed in a
profusion of confused dullness. But no one could doubt the
suitability of the little girl's choice; it would never have done
to present a new stepmother with a translation of one of the

merry and improper stories in Marguerite's *Heptameron*. Nor were learning and propriety the only qualities displayed in the gift; Elizabeth had made the canvas binding of the book and embroidered it with gold and silver braid and silken pansies, purple and yellow, and one tiny green leaf; it was the part she had most enjoyed doing – at first; though she got tired of it long before the end, and the stitches went straggly.

She liked to make her own presents, and had always insisted on her own choice in them. At six years old she had flatly refused to give her baby brother Edward any of the jewels or elaborate ornaments that were offered to her as suitable gifts for his second birthday; no, she would have none of them, though tempted momentarily by a bush of rosemary covered with gold spangles, which, however, on reflection she decided to keep for herself. And she carried out her determination of making the baby a cambric shirt.

A small girl so practical and independent was wasted in a royal household, the women decided; Bess was clearly cut out to be a good wife and mother in a poor household with a host of children. But Bess did not agree, though she did not say so. Even at six years old she had become something of an adept at not saying things, though she could not always keep it up, for she was also an adept at pert answers. And nothing could alter her quick and imperious temper, which had shown itself so masterfully before she was quite three years old that her distracted governess had written long garrulous letters to the Lords of the Council about the difficulty of controlling 'my lady's' princely demands for the same wines and meats that her grown-up companions were having at table. Bess's state had been far from princely then; her clothes were all outgrown and there were no new ones for her; she had been sent away into the country with no provision made for her, and her governess at her wits' end as to how to clothe and feed her.

Yet only a very short time before, her father had tossed her up in his arms, and crowds of gorgeous strangers had thronged round her, uttered ecstatic little cries at the sight of her, bowed down to her and pressed glittering toys into her hands.

There was a winter's evening when she was just two and a half years old (she always remembered it, though people said she could only have remembered hearing of it) when that enormous figure, not nearly as stout as now but seeming even taller, and dressed from top to toe in yellow satin like a monstrous giant toad, hoisted her up on to a vast padded shoulder, where she clutched at the white feather in his flat cap, and carried her round at that dizzy height, showing her off to everybody, shouting, 'Thank God the old harridan is dead! Here is your future Queen – Elizabeth!' And all the courtiers shouted back, and the dark crowds in the street below the window where he stood with her, in a terrifying exciting roar, 'God save the King! God save the Princess Elizabeth!'

'The old harridan' was her father's first wife and her half-sister Mary's mother, Queen Katherine of Aragon, that noble Spanish princess who had been hounded to death at last by her husband's six-year persecution. That was at the end of January, and by the following May Bess's mother too was dead, her head cut off by her father's orders; and by the next morning he was wedded to Jane Seymour.

Bess did not know that at the time, only that she went away into the country, that there were no more crowds nor shouting for her, that her clothes grew shabby and uncomfortably small for her, and no one was in the least excited or pleased to see her.

'*Here we go up, up, up,*
Here we go down, down, down,'

so the children sang, playing on the see-saw on the village green, but she was not allowed to play with them either. The time of neglect and poverty passed; she went up again, though never to the dizzying height of her first two and a half years; she went back to Court, where, however, a new baby, a tiny boy, was now the centre of all the swaying, bowing crowds, carried aloft on that towering shoulder.

It was he now whom the giant King would dandle and toss in his arms by the hour together, and stand at a window showing him to the crowds below; and their roars would surge up in rugged waves of sound, 'God save King Hal!' 'God save the Prince!' 'Long live Prince Edward!'

The baby's mother, Jane Seymour, was not there. She had died in giving birth to him – 'my poor little Jane,' the King said occasionally with a sob.

He did not seem to like Bess now, he was odd and uncomfortable with her; sometimes she would catch him looking at her with a strange intent gaze, and then when she looked back he would turn away and talk to someone else. And he never again called her Elizabeth, but only Young Bess, which should have sounded more affectionate, but did not.

Long afterwards she guessed that he had ceased to feel her worthy of the name, for he had bestowed it on her in memory of his mother, that gracious and beloved princess, last of the royal Plantagenets, who had given him his most legitimate claim to the throne.

But at the time Bess only knew that she must be very good and quiet and not thrust herself forward. Her half-sister Mary, a grown-up woman, said: 'It is your turn now to learn to be silent, as I have done.'

She said it on a note of acid triumph, for she had been forced to agree to the Act of Parliament that declared her mother's marriage illegal and herself illegitimate, forced to acknowledge this baby sister's prior right to the throne over herself, to let her take public precedence to her everywhere, and even to serve as maid-of-honour to her. That had been when Elizabeth was 'up, up, up'; now she too had been bastardised and was 'down, down, down,' where Mary had been for many years now. She looked cowed and dull. She was a good woman and did not seek to revenge herself on her small half-sister for the agonies and humiliations she had had to suffer on her behalf; instead she tried hard to be kind to her, but Bess knew she did not like her.

The King talked about finding a new mother for his poor motherless children, and then something opened in Mary's dull face: in one instant it had shut again, but in that instant Bess felt she had seen into hell.

It was not so easy a task by now to find a new Queen for England. The foreign princesses were growing wary. A Danish one said that if she had two heads she would be delighted to lay one at the English King's disposal; a French one, tall and stately, of the House of Guise, was told that Henry wished for her as he was so big himself, he needed a big wife; and she replied, 'Ah, but my neck is small.' And Mary of Guise had the effrontery to marry his nephew instead, that young whippersnapper King James V of Scotland. Then Tom Cromwell, the 'best of his servants,' engineered a German Protestant alliance and a marriage with the Bavarian princess, Anne of Cleves, whose portrait was very pretty, but not, Bess decided, as quick and chic and merry-looking as that of her own mother, Anne.

But when the new bride arrived, and all the Court went to meet her with the King (Bess, now six years old, by the side of her twenty-five-year-old sister, Mary), then everybody saw with a shock that the bride was not pretty at all. Fat 'Crum' was bustling about with a staff in his hand, sweating with energy and anxiety – 'just like a post boy,' Tom Seymour whispered wickedly, though Bess thought him much more like a panting ox. He acted as interpreter between the King and the large raw-boned German princess, who beamed effusively and said 'Ya, Ya,' for she was as stupid as she was plain, she could speak no language but her own, to the shocked amazement of Bess, who had never heard of a princess who couldn't speak at least six languages including Greek and Latin. Crum remarked to the King that she looked 'very queenly,' but he did it timidly, 'as though he were offering a coin to an elephant,' said Tom Seymour.

The elephant rejected it; he shot one red glance at the best of his servants and trumpeted two words: 'What remedy?' In six months he had found it; annulled his marriage with Anne, and beheaded Cromwell.

Elizabeth heard of it a month before her seventh birthday, while she was stitching at the shirt for her baby brother. She knew by now that this ox, who could pounce like a tiger, had got her mother beheaded, after making her Queen; and now he was beheaded himself. 'Here we go down, down down.'

Anne of Cleves lived on in England; she said she would 'always be a sister' to Henry, she was kind and friendly to his daughters, and she did not even mind (perhaps she was relieved) when he married Cat Howard, an enchanting creature not quite eighteen.

Mary was cold and haughty to Cat, a flighty girl, seven years younger than herself, who had scrambled up to womanhood in the careless modern fashion among a host of boys and girls as wild and reckless as herself. She said Cat was of inferior rank and not at all fitted to be their father's wife. In her scorn of Cat, Bess could see what this daughter of the Spanish kings had felt for Bess's mother, Nan Bullen, whose family had lately started to spell their name Boleyn to make it sound grander. They were relations of the Howards – but of far less noble stock, and Nan was the granddaughter of a mercer and Lord Mayor of London, as Mary once blurted out to the child when provoked by her to one of her hysterical rages.

It was perhaps the worst shock to her self-esteem that Bess had received in her childhood. There was no disgrace in having some of your family executed; it was a thing that might happen to anybody, and frequently did; and under the Tudors, the more noble the family, the more likely it was to happen. But a mercer, a Lord Mayor! She flung an inkpot at Mary, called her a liar, and rushed screaming with fury to her beloved governess, Mrs Ashley, who soothed her with reminders of her mother's Howard uncle, the great Duke of Norfolk, of one of the oldest families in the kingdom. But Bess was not impressed; she thought her great-uncle Norfolk a vulgar old man who said very rude things, and she had heard that he was always ready to do the King's dirty work for him; this she imagined to be something to do with cleaning his horse or his boots when on an expedition together.

Mrs Ashley was worrying about something more important; Bess must be very careful never to quarrel with her half-sister, the Lady Mary, 'for one never knows – And she had good reason to hate your mother, Queen Anne, who was, God forgive her, very unkind to her and to her poor mother, Katherine of Aragon – and *she* was a saint if ever there was one.'

Bess said mutinously, 'Well, I'd rather have a witch for my mother than a saint – and an Englishwoman than a Spaniard – and anyway, why should Mary turn up her nose at Cat Howard?'

She adored the lovely warm impulsive creature, the Rose without a Thorn the King called her, who insisted on giving Bess the place of honour next herself, as she was her cousin. She brought gaiety into all their lives; she coaxed the King with such endearments as 'her little pig,' for he was growing very stout; but, determined to defy it, he rose at five or six and rode and went hunting and hawking with her every day and often all day, sometimes tiring out nine or ten horses in a single hunt. King François's sister, the fascinating Marguerite, kept asking flatteringly but tactlessly for his portrait, and he hoped to give Holbein a chance to show how young he'd grown in body as well as heart – but alas he was still 'marvellously excessive in drinking and eating', so people noticed; and also that he often held quite different opinions in the morning from those he held after dinner.

And the months went on passing and Cat gave no sign of bearing a child.

But on the whole he was in a sunny humour, so much so that he quite forgot his awkwardness with Bess and treated her once again as his especial favourite, so that the child came under his wayward, extraordinary spell, and saw how it worked on others; they might be baffled, thwarted, exasperated, even terrified or loathing, but, when he chose, they could not resist him. Nor could Bess. She tingled with triumph when he laughed at her bright answers and quoted them to the Court as remarkable specimens of childish wit. It was a thrilling sport, this answering back; she knew that she must go about it as warily as if 'offering a coin to an elephant,' for she could never be sure if the offer would be accepted with a slap of his thigh that sounded as though he were thumping a cushion, and a delighted roar that he would write and tell that to old Foxnose François himself, by God so he would! Or else a sudden terrifying knitting of those infantile eyebrows, a pursing of the little slit of a mouth, a narrow glance like the thrust of a stiletto, and the sharp command to get out of his presence for an impudent little bastard. 'By God you go too far!'

There came a dreadful day when she went so far that she never came back for a whole year, and never knew what she had said to put him in such a lasting rage. But that was after he had become indifferent again, sunk in gloom and fat, his cheeks grey and flabby, and had a horrible tendency to burst into tears in front of everybody – for it was after he had had Cat Howard beheaded for adultery.

'It is no more the time to dance,' they told Cat when they came to arrest her, and sent away her musicians. They took her to the Tower, the royal palace, fortress, prison, where she had slept before her Coronation, as her cousin Nan Bullen had slept before hers; but this time she went in by the Traitors' Water Gate, as Nan Bullen had done the second time she went there, and like Cat, left it only for the block.

'It won't be hard to find a nickname for me,' Nan had giggled with desperate gallantry. 'I shall be called Anne Sans-Tête!' and she had put her hands round her long slender throat and promised the executioner an easy task. 'They might make ballads of me now,' she said, 'but there is no one left to make them now they've killed my brother. Oh yes, there is my cousin Tom Wyatt – but he is in the Tower too.' There had been a vein of wild poetry in Nan herself, a living echo to the art of her brother and cousin.

But the people did not make ballads of her, they did not like her enough. Their legends of her were not pretty; they said she had tried to poison the Princess Mary; that she had a rudimentary sixth finger on her left hand, though so tiny that few ever noticed, and that it was a teat to suckle her devil's imps who told her how to bewitch the King. In any case, she was an upstart who had worked and schemed and waited for six years to oust the Good Queen Katherine of Aragon and her daughter Mary, the true heir to the throne; she had been hard and sharp and tyrannised over everyone, even the King;

had loved to crack her whip at him and show her power; she had met him at a dance, and a pretty dance she had led him ever since – so they said when, for her too, it was no more the time to dance.

She had been unpopular, and that was the real reason she died; and her daughter knew this by the time her gay, kind-hearted cousin Cat Howard met the same fate, while still in her teens.

Bess was eight when this happened; nine when she offended her father and was sent away from Court; ten when she returned again at the entreaty of yet another stepmother, another Queen Cat, no wild heedless kitten this time, but her motherly Pussy-Cat Purr, as Bess instantly called her.

Would this one stay? Bess passionately hoped so. She had stayed two whole years by now, a record in the child's experience. She never flirted with anyone else, she was wise and kind and tactful, but could anyone ever be tactful enough with the King? She had found that she herself could not; and Bess had a good opinion, and with reason, of her own tact. And Queen Catherine had given no sign of bearing him an heir, and everyone hoped for a baby Duke of York to follow the little Prince of Wales – 'in case.' It was the lack of direct male heirs to the throne that had torn and ruined the country with the Wars of the Roses in the last century. To secure the Succession, Bess knew this to be the one unswerving purpose behind her father's murderous philanderings.

She had noticed the sudden hush, the shiver of excited apprehension that seized the gay rollicking girls of the Court when the King's gaze fell on one of them a trifle longer and more weightily than it was wont, 'Was the King about to seek a new wife?' The whisper would run like wildfire through the Court, and following it in the minds of all, though unspoken – how soon would yet another Queen be told that 'it was no more the time to dance'?

She watched her stepmother with a solicitude that was positively maternal; she was watching her so now, on the deck of the royal flagship, as they walked up and down in the wake of Great Harry. The men were talking of the danger of invasion – a nice safe subject, she considered; one could hardly go wrong over that. In fact, it put all the men in a good humour, as usual. Her magnificent Howard cousin, the young Earl of Surrey, the soldier-poet, blazing in scarlet from head to foot, was saying in his cool insolent drawl that all the men between sixteen and sixty had been called up along the coasts, and could be called out at an hour's notice; his father, the Duke of Norfolk, that lean old wolf, was snapping his jaws in a hungry grin as he told how all his stout fellows of Norfolk had sent a deputation to him begging him that 'if the French come, for God's sake bring us between the sea and them that we may fight them before they get back to their ships.' God's body, that was the spirit!

Tom Seymour said it was sheer folly of the French to bring galleys from Marseilles, and barges – they would all be boarded as easily as jumping off a log. At which Edward Seymour drily remarked that they had three hundred tall ships as well.

Tom flung back his head and shouted with laughter, 'D'you think I'd forgotten their tall ships? They'd no reason to forget ours when I sailed slap through their blockade and re-victualled our garrison at Boulogne under their noses.'

'Braggart!' muttered Edward, and for an instant the two brothers looked daggers at each other; but just then the King's voice boomed out like a foghorn:

'We whipped them by land and sea last year, and by God we'll do it again.'

Certainly an invasion was the best thing to talk about. And next to that, the Scots. The King had beaten them last year too. But the Scots were not quite so good, for they would not stay beaten. He (or rather Norfolk) had smashed their whole nation years ago at Flodden, where his brother-in-law, King James IV, had got killed together with most of his nobles; he had smashed them again about a couple of years ago at Solway Moss when his nephew, young King James V, died of a broken heart from his defeat; and since then Edward Seymour, Earl of Hertford, had destroyed Melrose Abbey and Dryburgh, and 7 monasteries, 5 market towns, 243 villages, 13 mills and 3 hospitals in one district alone. But still the unspeakable villains would not stay smashed; though ruled only by James's French widow, Mary of Guise, that very same tall lady who had had the effrontery to refuse King Henry's offer of marriage with an unseemly joke about the smallness of her neck, and to prefer his red-headed rascal of a nephew to himself. She was now refusing his offers of marriage for her infant daughter Mary to his little son Edward, or rather (for she would have agreed to the marriage without his conditions) she was refusing to send her baby away from her to be brought up at the English Court under the charge of her great-uncle who had caused the death of that baby's father and grandfather; such ungrateful, unnatural, unwomanly behaviour made Henry purple with rage every time he issued orders to his armies to raze Edinburgh and all the Border cities to the ground, exterminate every man, woman and child in them, and above all seize the person of the infant Queen of Scots. But she had not yet been caught, although she had had to be hurried away into lonely mountain fastnesses to escape. It was early to begin adventure, very early to be a queen, almost as soon as she was born. Elizabeth felt a thrill of envy for the tiny mountain princess whose mother was guarding her so indomitably.

Here came the gentle Archbishop Cranmer, his heavy sagging cheeks more yellow even than usual, for he had just been seasick. Bess detested his soft voice and nervous eyes, even as her mother had done. He had helped Nan Bullen to the Crown, but done nothing to hinder her from the block; his 'former good opinion of her prompted him to think her innocent,' so he wrote to the King; but then 'his knowledge of the King's prudence and justice induced him to think her guilty.' Such balanced casuistry had echoed down the years, even to Nan's little daughter.

Henry flung out a great wave of charm at the Archbishop's approach, and a padded arm like a silken bolster round his shoulder, sweeping him in his stride ahead of the others.

'Aha, my chaplain, I've news for you. I know now who is the greatest heretic in Kent!'

The Archbishop's eyes seemed to bolt out of his head like a startled rabbit's. For an instant Bess thought he was going to be sick again, on the royal sleeve. And no wonder, for Henry, watching him sideways with some amusement out of the poached eyes set flat on his cheeks, was twitting him with his own words; had he, or had he not, burst out to his Chapter at

Canterbury, 'You will not leave your old Mumpsimuses, but I'll make you repent it!'

'Old Mumpsimuses,' the King pointed out, was not the way an archbishop ought to refer to the ancient holy forms of religion; it was small wonder that the Chapter had retaliated by sending out an accusation of heresy against him and his chaplains. And from the very sleeve that was now enfolding the victim's neck in the affectionate grip of a grizzly bear Henry produced the paper of the accusation, while in a jocular aside he reminded his friend that three heretics had lately been burnt alive on Windsor Green: 'And what do you say to that, my old Mumpsimus?'

Cranmer had so much to say that the King quickly cut him short, and Norfolk seized his chance to cut in. He shared Bess's feelings about the Archbishop. Cat Howard had been Norfolk's niece as well as Nan Bullen, he had worked for her marriage to the King as hard as he knew. And then that sneaking Lutheran fellow, who had picked up a wife in Germany, as well as a lot of these poisonous new revolutionary notions, had gone and destroyed all his work by getting poor Cat beheaded, just as Nan had been, and the whole family had shared in the disgrace for a time.

'For my part,' he growled virtuously, 'I never read the Scriptures and never will. It was merry in England before this new learning came up, but now every ploughboy thinks he's as good as the priest – and maybe he is, seeing what some priests are!'

He glared at the Archbishop, who weakly averted his gaze. Henry, cocking an amused little gooseberry eye at Norfolk, called out, 'Paws off there! Down – good dog, down! You got

your teeth into a Cardinal when you shogged off Wolsey –
must you worry an Archbishop too?'

'God's body, Your Majesty, I only meant that I wish
everything were just the same as it used to be in the good old
days. New ideas indeed!' His glare had swivelled round on to
Edward Seymour, who was of the advanced party and eager
for reform in politics as well as religion. 'New ideas – and a
brand-new peer to lead 'em! All this fine talk of the rights of
the people – rank revolution, that's all it amounts to,' he
snarled at Seymour, but the King clapped a hand on his
shoulder.

'No more of that now, or you'll be giving us one of your
Council speeches till we all get lost in your thirdlys and
fourthlys.' He turned to his anxiously waiting Archbishop,
but only to deal him some heavyhanded chaff about his wife.
Was it true that Cranmer had had her smuggled from
Germany into England in a packing-case which some careless
porter had placed upside down, so that she had had to scream
to be rescued? 'There's a fine tale of a wife tails up! Well, well,
I owe a couple or so of my wives to your services, so no doubt
you think I should wink at yours, but it's a big wink that will
cover an archbishop's wife boarded up in a box. Old Wolsey
had as fine a mistress as money could buy, but that was all
correct and above-board – not under the boards!'

Cranmer became incoherent in his denials and
protestations; he would not dream of evading the law against
married clergy, he had never seen his wife since he came to
England to be Archbishop – at least, not, not—

'Not in a packing-case, hey? Or did you send her packing?'
Like some huge cat with a shivering mouse, he played with

the terrified little man, enjoying his discomfiture and the roars of laughter from Norfolk and the others. Just as Cranmer was certain that the blow would fall on him both for heresy and illegal matrimony, Henry suddenly returned to the former charge and rumbled out, 'That little matter of your Chapter's complaints is easily handled. I'll appoint a commission to examine the charges – and put you at the head of it! *And* help you with the answers. I've not forgotten my theology. That will cook their goose for them. So whichever goose roasts, it won't be you.'

His hearty friendliness made Cranmer almost blubber with thankfulness; it made his small daughter grow thoughtful. The Queen was still with the two men, though Henry had outstripped the rest of the company, but he had beckoned her on, so he must wish her to hear this conversation. Bess they did not notice; she was, indeed, at some distance and looking out to sea as though absorbed in the other ships, but her sharp ears had been listening acutely. Why was her father so kind to old Mumpsimus? (Yes, that was the perfect name for him and his meek bag face – a mouse with the mumps!) Henry had, as it happened, a warm and affectionate respect for Cranmer's disinterested love of learning and his lack of ambition, but as these qualities did not appeal to Bess, she discounted them. And the King had been angry enough, so she had heard, when he had first received the accusation of his Archbishop's toying with heresy. But then someone had said Cranmer was too useful for the King to lose him. How useful?

Was it because he had already got rid of three wives out of six for the King, and might be required to get rid of a fourth? The notion came to her on a sudden heartstop of dismay as she realised what prompted it, for she could hear her father's and stepmother's voices – arguing! How could the Queen be such a goose? 'Whichever goose roasts' – the King always said he liked nothing so well as a good theological argument; that he liked women to be intelligent – but surely anyone would know that he only liked an argument when he got the better of it; and however intelligent a woman might be, she must be less so than himself. Queen Catherine was arguing the case for translating the Bible into English; Henry was shouting that, in consequence, 'that precious jewel, the Word of God, was being disputed, sung, and jangled in every alehouse and tavern,' which showed how he was getting the worst of it, for he was only quoting from his last speech in Parliament, since he could not think of a fresher answer.

Catherine evidently began to get some sense of her danger, for without any crude change of subject she adroitly introduced some flattery on the great and beneficial changes Henry had made in England's religion. But that wouldn't do; couldn't she see that the King had never wanted to introduce any changes in religion, that he was as ardent and conservative a Papist as anybody – with this one exception, that he alone was to be Pope.

And behind all Bess's anxiety was the terrifying fact that the Queen's friend, Lady Anne Askew, had been arrested for denouncing the Mass, and had been tortured in the Tower more than once. Was it an attempt to make her implicate the Queen? Whatever happened, Catherine must not plead the cause of her friend now – let her be tortured, racked, burnt, but if the name of Anne Askew were mentioned now, it would be the death-knell of Catherine Parr.

It didn't look as though Catherine would get the chance to mention it, for Henry was doing all the talking now, watching her out of the corner of a hot, intemperate eye while he threw out some ominous chaff: 'So you've become a learned doctor, have you, Kate? You're here to instruct us, we take it, not to be instructed or directed by us?'

Kate quickly protested, but, unheeding, he began to roll his great head and mutter, 'That's a pretty business when women turn clerics; a fine comfort for me in my old age, to be taught by my wife!'

It was going to happen – it was happening now – nothing could stop it. Bess shut her lips tight to keep from screaming aloud. Could nothing else happen to prevent it? Why couldn't the French sail up *now* and attack? More fervently than any stout fellow of Norfolk, she prayed silently for a sight of their foes. 'Oh God, let them come and invade England *now*, quick!'

'Anne Askew!' The fatal name had been spoken, it crashed on the air like the crack of thunder. But it was not the Queen who had uttered it; it was the King, accusing her of having sent the condemned woman money and promises of help, of having received heretical books from her in times past, of – would the next word be – 'Treason!'?

Bess opened her lips and screamed.

They all turned towards her, hurried towards her, cried out what was the matter. Now she would have to find an answer. Had she twisted her foot? Seen a mermaid or a sea-serpent? She would only be scolded and sent below, and the King's rage increased by so momentary an interruption. She screamed again, on a high note of childish excitement, and pointed:

'The French! Their ships – far out to sea – coming up like clouds!'

So intense was the conviction in her voice that for an instant they believed her. Then, as no confirmation came from the crow's nest, they said she must have imagined it and taken the white clouds on the horizon for the sails of the French fleet. Her best retreat would be to look childishly stupid and sulky, admit she had been frightened, perhaps even shed a few tears. But she decided to brazen it out. 'I *did* see the ships – for a moment. They've disappeared now. Perhaps they saw us and sailed away.'

Henry's infantile eyebrows puckered in his vast face. His just anger had been interrupted by this false alarm, and now surged back, redoubled. 'The girl's lying!' he roared. 'The French have been reported miles away. She could never have seen them.'

He looked at his daughter and saw her mother's face, the big forehead, the clever bright eyes, the silly little rosebud of a mouth that had smiled so sweetly at him – and at others. 'Take the little bastard away!' he shouted,

But at that moment Elizabeth had one of those stupendous strokes of luck that were enough to accuse her as well as her mother of witchcraft.

A shout came ringing over the sea and was echoed by another. The alarm had been raised in good earnest, the French fleet sighted, sailing straight towards Portsmouth.

CHAPTER TWO

Elizabeth was disappointed in her first invasion. She had thought they would stay on the flagship, that she would have a first-hand experience of a sea-fight, that somehow she would manage to dress up as a sailor and save Tom Seymour's life. Then for once he would take her seriously, he would take her hand, and look deep into her eyes and say – what *would* he say?

It didn't matter, for it didn't happen, none of it happened.

That glittering July sea and the proud ships floating over it all vanished like sea-spray as far as the royal family party were concerned; in no time they all bustled off the flagship and on to a very fast pinnace and made for the shore and then inland. It was not Bess's idea of the way to take an invasion. She had seen her father ride off to the French wars last year, in a suit of armour that two slight young men could easily have got into together, and hoisted on to an enormous dapple-grey Dutch stallion, seventeen hands high, with white feathered hoofs and flowing white mane and a little angry red eye, not unlike his rider's. They had needed no army behind them, she had thought, to strike terror into the foe.

But now – was this the way he had fought when he got there? She was told that Kings and Queens must not adventure their persons like common soldiers and sailors. She was not convinced. She told Tom Seymour with a sniff that the flagship had better be re-christened 'The Great Hurry'!

He scrutinised her narrowly. 'How could you, on deck, have seen the French fleet before any lookout in the crow's nest had seen it?'

'I don't know. My eyes are better than theirs, I suppose.'

'Even your bright eyes couldn't see them before they came up over the edge of the horizon. Haven't your tutors taught you that the world is round?'

'Then they must be wrong, and the world is flat.'

'So that's flat. You'd shape the whole world differently to suit yourself!'

'Why not? My father does.'

'You're his daughter, no doubt about that!' he chuckled.

'*I'd* have stayed and seen the fight,' said Bess. 'I'd not have let the French land on the Isle of Wight.'

But the French accomplished nothing by that; they soon had to take to their ships again, and after a short engagement were driven back out to sea. The fortune-tellers were now saying they had known all along that this was not the invasion England had to fear; her real danger, worse than any she had faced since the Normans landed, would not come for more than forty years, in the summer when there would be four noughts in the date, for an 8 is a double nought, one on top of the other, so the year '88 would be quadruply unlucky. Bess asked why the unlucky noughts shouldn't be for the invaders. 'Anyway it's naught to me,' she said, for who cared what would happen more than forty years hence, when she would be an old woman, if indeed she could bear to live as long as then? And anyway there could be small danger from foreign ships since the great French Armada had such poor success; everyone was boasting of England's security behind her sea-walls; a blunt fellow even said as much to the Emperor Charles V in Spain, and his son, that cold, formal youth, Prince Philip.

'Young Cheese-face,' Henry still persisted in calling the Emperor, the nephew of his first wife, ever since Charles's visit to England, to be betrothed to the Princess Mary, then a pretty child of six, who had not shared her father's view of her prospective bridegroom's long pale face and wedge-shaped chin, very like a slab of cheese. She had given an ardent hero-worship to her cousin, the young monarch on whose lands, her mother had told her, the sun never set; and who, still more important, was a very devout Christian. But the betrothal came to nothing; all that was over twenty years ago, and now the Emperor Charles was mobilising against the Protestant princes in his Empire, so that, in spite of his confidence in England's splendid isolation, Henry was finding orthodoxy advisable, and the Queen's broadmindedness untimely. (Besides, she had not borne him an heir. 'Impossible! she is so virtuous!' said the wags.) So Anne Askew was burnt for denouncing the Mass; though the following month Henry tried to get the King of France to join with him in abolishing it. Bess found politics difficult to understand. Anyway, they were now at peace with France, and the King spoke so beautifully on charity and concord to his Parliament that they all wept.

But Parliamentarians' tears, and the King's charity and concord, did not lessen Bess's anxiety one jot, and there came a moment in the garden when the confirmation of it stared her in the face, stared up at her from the path, a sickly white paper scrawled with black writing which told her at one glance that the King had finally given over his faithfully devoted wife to the power of the beast. It was an indictment of Catherine Parr, and Henry had set his name to it.

No sooner had Bess seen it than the Chancellor Wriothesley, who had been Chancellor Cromwell's secretary and helped work his fall, came hurrying back between the clipped yew hedges.

'A paper!' he panted, 'a scrap of paper – has Your Highness seen it?'

Bess shook her head, lifting wide blue eyes to his, and pointing at what she had apparently all this time been staring – a butterfly that had perched on her bright shoe, mistaking it for a flower.

'Oh, you have disturbed him!' she exclaimed reproachfully as it flew away. 'A paper, did you say? Is it important?'

Mr Wriothesley had already stuffed it into his sleeve, violently cursing the tailors who could not invent any safer receptacle in men's clothes, while women went hung round with pockets.

He departed as fast as, or rather faster than courtesy permitted; a beast padding away in his soft broad velvet slippers, and the little slits of satin over the toes like claws in the sunlight, Bess thought, standing there stock still until he disappeared.

The garden was all still round her, cut into sunlight and sharp shadows, and the bees hummed loud, or was it the blood throbbing in her ears?

Then, with a glance to right and left of her, she picked up her skirts and ran, ran into the Palace to her stepmother and gasped out what she had seen.

Catherine Parr sat stunned; she neither moved nor spoke nor wept. Bess despaired. No silent grief would move the King. At last, through blue lips, Catherine moaned, 'What shall I do? What shall I do?'

Bess told her.

'You must cry, cry, cry, and loud; so that he'll hear, so that he can't hear anything else. Do it in the room next his. Shriek. Be hysterical, mad. Go on for hours and hours and hours.'

Catherine did. A clamour of weeping and howling next door disturbed the King; he sent to stop it, but it went on; he sent to ask the reason for it, and was told the Queen was distressed because she feared she had displeased him.

That brought him himself; he told her he could not bear her to cry, which was true, especially after three hours. But he spoke kindly; he got her to stop; then, after a little more comforting, he went on with their last theological argument. But the mouse avoided the cat's paw this time; his wife would not discuss religion; she referred it and all other questions to his omnipotent wisdom; if she had ever seemed to do otherwise, it had only been to pass the time and take his mind off his bad leg.

'Then, sweetheart, we are perfect friends again!' said Henry; and the Chancellor was sent packing with a flood of abuse when he called about the Queen's arrest. There was no arrest. The crisis had passed, and Henry yawned, when he did not swear at his bad leg. Perfect friendship is not as stimulating as discussion.

Life was growing dull and depressing. Old enemies were dying, and that is often worse than the death of old friends. Martin Luther died, far away in Germany. When Henry was a brilliant young man he had written a theological treatise confuting Luther's heresies, and the low fellow had replied with his usual bad taste. 'Squire Harry wishes to be God,' wrote the miner's son, 'and do what he pleases.'

The Pope, on the other hand, had shown his appreciation by giving Henry his title 'Defender of the Faith': 'F.D.' He thought of putting it on all the coins of his realm. Now there was no one to confute – except the Pope, whose latest title for him was the 'Son of Perdition and Satan.'

Worse even than Luther's death, they said François I of France was dying. Ever since he could remember, Henry had been an envious rival, a frequent foe, an occasional boon companion of Foxnose François. It was impossible to imagine life without this peppery stimulus.

Worse still, François was three years younger than Henry, was as tall and strong, had lived as well (though it was doubtful whether he or any other man had ever eaten as much), and yet here he was, petering out, surely long before his appointed span of years, like a feeble old man, a premature death's-head warning at the feast of life. For if life were not still a feast, what was it? Luther was dead, François might be dying, and he wasn't feeling very well himself; but thank God there was still good eating and drinking, and not all his doctors could keep him from it, especially when it came to the Christmas and Twelfth Night feasts.

All the Royal Family were together for these festivals, and most of the cousins too, with one notable and, to Henry, infuriating omission. The Queen of Scots, four years old this December, was still absent from the hospitable board of her great-uncle who had offered his only son in betrothal to this fatherless brat, Queen of such a beggarly kingdom that his Ambassador had nearly burst out laughing at the poverty of the baby's coronation in Stirling.

But there was one bit of news from Scotland that had put Henry in high good humour; the new Scots leaders of the Reformed Religion had at last succeeded in murdering the great Cardinal Beton, the right-hand man of the French Queen-Dowager, the Regent of Scotland. Henry had been giving advance payment for this work for years; now at last, in his palace of Greenwich just before Christmas, he heard from the murderers' own lips how they had stabbed the enemy of Christ as he sat in his chair, and hung his body over the wall of his castle at St Andrews.

Henry, as he made his final payments, reflected that it had been well worth the money. Much as he disliked these 'ministers of the true religion,' they would work for Scotland's alliance with England against the age-old Franco-Scottish alliance favoured by Cardinal Beton and his Regent of Scotland, that damned obstinate, suspicious-minded Frenchwoman who would not entrust her little daughter to his tender avuncular care.

Edward, now nine years old, a pretty boy with smooth flaxen hair, did not want to be betrothed to a baby. He would rather, if he had to have a cousin, marry the Lady Jane Grey, a year older than himself, though much smaller, who often helped him with his lessons. But Jane in her turn thought him more suited to one of her little sisters. She was undergoing a rather solemn adoration for Elizabeth, so much older, by three years, than herself, and wearing her cleverness with so gay and insouciant an air.

Jane was King Henry's great-niece, standing in the same relationship to him as the baby Queen of Scots. For Henry had had two sisters, the Tudor Roses they were called when in the splendour of their sumptuous white and red, their blue eyes and golden hair. The elder, the Princess Margaret, had married that strange, beautiful tortured creature, James IV of Scotland, and made a few gallant efforts, but only briefly, to live up to it. When he was killed on Flodden Field, her son, James V, was a year old; when he in his turn died broken-hearted from defeat by the English, his daughter Mary had become Queen of Scots at five days old.

Henry had been much fonder of his younger sister, Mary Rose, who was lovelier and merrier than Margaret, and did not grow too fat like her; nor did she plague him with long tearful letters and demands for money. For all that, he had made Mary Rose, at eighteen, marry the invalid old French King Louis XII instead of the man of her choice. But Mary had the Tudor way of getting what she wanted; in a few months she had danced the adoring old Frenchman into his grave, avoided the proposals of his young successor, François I, and married her beefy English duke.

Her granddaughter Jane Grey had inherited none of the glowing colours and bouncing vitality of the two Tudor Roses; she was tiny and pale, with some fair freckles on her straight little nose, which her mother unavailingly scrubbed with all sorts of concoctions, but they remained, with something of Jane's own persistency. Her eyes and forehead gave promise of a certain grave beauty, and beneath it an unexpected force of character.

Her younger sisters, Catherine and Mary, were so small that their mother was afraid they might be dwarfs.

Taking Elizabeth's hand before the banquet, Jane whispered as demurely as if she was saying grace, that thank God her parents were away, for it was hell when they were at home. Many children might think it dashing and modern to refer to their parents' company as hell; not so Jane, that best of all good little girls. Elizabeth was as startled as if a mouse had sworn. 'The creep-mice' was her name for the three little Grey cousins; could this one be a shrew-mouse? She looked down at the meek little face under its smoothly parted hair, and saw it set and tense.

'Your mother is very strict, isn't she?' Bess whispered back sympathetically.

'She never stops scolding, pinching, and slapping me. However hard I work, it makes no odds. You are lucky to have only a stepmother.'

And a murderously inclined father? Yes, on the whole Bess thought she was, since he forgot about her for long spaces together, whereas Jane's mother never forgot her eldest daughter; in fact, the Countess of Suffolk never stopped thinking; it was a mistake. The Grey mare, Tom Seymour called her, and said she stood two hands higher than her little weak mule of a husband – also broader, for she had the Tudor tendency to fat, and hunted like fury to escape it, and not, like her uncle, King Henry, for love of the sport. But nothing that she did would be for its own sake. She rode ambition harder than any horse, and had great plans for Jane, that was evident. No doubt she had determined to marry Jane to Edward and make her Queen of England, thought Bess with a sharp twinge of exasperation that she had not been born a boy. For then she would be King before Edward or Mary, who had been put back into the Succession, after Edward, a year ago; and then, too, her mother would not have been beheaded, 'and *she* would not have slapped and pinched me, especially if I had been a boy.'

Aloud, she told the younger child to come and look at the Christmas present Mary had given her – five yards of yellow satin to make a skirt, and Mary was keeping it to have it made up. 'It cost seven and sixpence a yard,' said Bess proudly, and then winced at the sound of her own words; would Jane recognise in them the tang of the Bullens' draper grandfather?

But Jane was far too nice a little girl to do anything of the sort; she smiled with unenvious pleasure, while her younger sister Catherine, hugging a doll almost as big as herself that Mary had given her, uttered rapturous squeaks at sight of the shining stuff.

But the person it gave most pleasure to was Mary as she showed it off to the children; she loved children, and fine clothes, and she loved giving presents; nearly all her allowance went in these three things. Her room was strewn with patterns of glowing carnation silk and blue and green brocades for yet more dresses, and a roll of some spangled Eastern stuff to which she had already treated herself, and a dozen pairs of fine Spanish gloves. 'When *will* she wear them all?' Bess wondered, and wondered more that at thirty years old a woman should care what she wore.

'I have something pretty for you too,' Mary said to Jane,

pleased that the little girl had evidently not expected anything for herself; and she stooped to put a gold and pearl necklace round the thin childish neck. 'It's a very little neck,' said Mary as she fastened the ponderous clasp, and Bess repressed a faint shudder, for wasn't that what her mother had said in the Tower, when she put her hands round her slender throat and laughed that the executioner would have an easy job?

She turned her attention hastily to the present moment; it was her chance now to feel envious, and she promptly took it. Why should Mary give anything so gorgeous, and worth far more than five yards of satin even at seven and six a yard, to their small cousin, who did not at all appreciate it? She was too young and too much of a bookworm to care about clothes and jewels, and was even rather critical of Mary's doing so. She had said Mary overdressed; probably she had heard her mother say so, but anyway it was a foolish thing to say.

'Anything might happen,' Bess's governess had said, warning her to keep friends with Mary. But the 'anything' might be Jane marrying Edward and becoming Queen of England; in which case it was sensible and far-sighted of Mary to give her the necklace, so Bess finally excused her – though indeed she could not believe in Mary being sensible and far-sighted.

But she forgave her even this lack when Mary paid up the forfeit Bess had won from her at 'Bonjour, Philippine' last week. A gold pomander ball with a tiny watch dial in it was a fascinating prize, as curious as it was magnificent. All Bess's careful respect to her elderly half-sister exploded at the sight of it, and she flung her arms round her neck.

'My ball, my golden ball! I will carry it always at my girdle and never be late. I could never have got anything half so beautiful for you if you had won. But you will win next time, won't you?'

'Oh no,' said Mary with a rather bitter little laugh, 'you will always win.'

There was a moment's uncomfortable pause. Why *did* Mary say these things? There was no answer one could make to them.

But Queen Catherine, looking in to tell them to come and play Blind Man's Buff, made everything seem happy and smiling again, as her dear Pussy-Cat Purr always did. She discussed Mary's patterns and advised the goose-turd green rather than the brilliant new colour, popinjay blue, that Mary hankered after. 'The goose-turd would be far more becoming to your delicate fair skin,' she said tactfully, and they all giggled when Mary wrinkled up her round button of a nose and objected that it had a stinking name!

Catherine took her arm as they left her room and chaffed her about all those gloves. Had the King of Poland sent them? He was the latest suitor for Mary's hand; King Henry was encouraging him, and the Queen was really hopeful.

But not Mary. There had been too many suitors ever since her early childhood: the Emperor Charles; James V of Scotland; François I, who had gallantly preferred her to the Princess of Portugal 'with all her father's spices'; even her own half-brother, the illegitimate Duke of Richmond, suggested by the 'advanced' Pope Clement as a means of securing the Succession – but found Henry less broad-minded. And now there was the danger that a foreign Papist husband would press her claim as the Papist heir to England: but still her father used her as bait. 'A bride in the hand is worth two in the bed,' he said.

'As long as he lives,' she broke out, 'I shall be only the Lady Mary, the most unhappy lady in the world.'

She burst into tears, dragged her arm away from her stepmother's, ran back into her room and slammed the door.

'Poor woman!' said the Queen, and turned to Jane and her small sister Catherine, who were looking profoundly shocked. 'I pray you will never know such unhappiness as your cousin's,' she said. Something told her that it was no use saying anything of the sort to Bess, whose little pointed face had shut itself up in an inscrutable expression. 'Come,' she cried gaily, 'we mustn't miss the Blind Man's Buff. The Lady Mary will join us at the banquet.'

The Blind Man's Buff had already begun, and Tom Seymour was Blind Man. Staggering and groping absurdly, his black sleeveless coat, lined with cloth of gold, swinging in a wild circular movement from his shoulders, he swooped and swirled and spun round on his heel, round and round like a gorgeous spinning-top, and the men thumped him on the back and then dodged away, and the girls pulled his coat and then fled shrieking as he darted on them. Bess flung herself into the game, plucked at his sleeve, then, more daring, pinched his hand and ran away, but he was after her; so directly that he must be cheating; she nearly called 'A Cheat! A Cheat!' but why should she? She wanted him to catch her, and in spite of her dodging he did. Now he had to guess who it was in three guesses; his hands stroked her face, her hair, her thin bare shoulders; he was an unconscionable time in guessing.

'The Lady Mary,' he said, and there was a shout of

laughter, but it was not too absurd, for Mary was short and Bess was already the same height. 'The Dowager Lady Dorset!' he said, to a louder yell of laughter, for the Dowager was past seventy. He must make very sure now or he would lose his guess. He pinched her ear, and gave a tweak to her nose. 'The Lady Elizabeth!' he said. 'I'd know that nose in a thousand.'

And he pulled off his bandage and tied it round her eyes while she said low, 'You are a poor Blind Man not to have caught anyone before.'

'Ah, but you see I didn't want to – before.'

Now it was her turn to clutch at the air, and swing round and run while hands pulled and touched her and voices called and tittered all round her.

The King sat in his great chair with the new seat embroidered by his daughter Mary for his Christmas present. The seats of Henry's chairs were apt to wear out; this one was so ample that the materials had cost Mary £20. He was spread over every stitch of that labour of filial love as he sat staring at all those glittering young figures prancing, dancing, running here and there. Usually he chuckled and cheered them on, but now he stared without seeming to notice them; only, once or twice, his poached eyes rolled round between the folds of his cheeks to follow the antics of the pretty young widow of his old friend Charles Brandon who ran with tittering shrieks to escape the blindfolded pursuer.

Would she be his seventh wife? It had been whispered. But there was another whisper that said the King would never have a seventh wife.

Now came the real importance of the evening, and his flat

eyes opened with the gleam of a hawk's as a host of silver-clad pages carried in long tables and set them up on trestles in the hall; roasted Peacocks in their Pride with spread tails and swans re-invested in their snowy plumage were perched on them, waiting to be carved, and a few of the lately discovered turkeys brought to breed in Europe from the New World by a Spanish adventurer, Pedro Nino. 'But it will take more than Nine Pedros to make us English take to such poultry, tasteless as wood,' proclaimed King Henry, who, however, liked to show these novelties among the old Christmas dishes; mince pies in the form of the Christ Child's manger, boars' heads whose jellied eyes glared between their tusks as fierce as in life, shepherds and their flocks made of sweetmeats, and flagons of cock ale, a mixture of ale and sack in which an old cock braised with raisins and cloves had been steeped for nine days and the liquid then strained and matured.

Henry was hoisted by four men out of his chair and into one that fitted his stomach more accommodatingly against the table.

The buzz of talking and guzzling rose higher and higher as the wine circulated; when it had soared almost an octave, music took up the note, and the voices of choristers clear and piercing sweet. They sang a song that Henry himself had composed, words and music, when he had just come to the throne, a youth of eighteen, in the full flush of his cherubic beauty and athletic vigour, 'rejoicing as a giant to run his course.'

'Pastime with good company
I love, and shall, until I die.'

The little eyes blinked and closed; the vast padded figure in the chair sat like a dummy, apparently insensible, as he listened to what he once had sung. It was still true, he told himself, it always would be; pastime – good company – none had had better. Odd that of all that brilliant company it was only those that he had enjoyed long ago who now stood out vividly in his mind, so much more vividly than all these scattering, chattering young apes he had just been watching, even that brisk young widow of Charles Brandon's – the half-Spanish girl – what was her name? He could not trouble himself to remember. The notes that he had once plucked out for the first time on his lute were teasing him with older memories.

Charles Brandon himself seemed nearer now than his widow, so did all those other vigorous young men with whom he had once played games and practical jokes and exchanged low stories with roars of laughter and thumps on the back: that young rascal Bryan whom he had nicknamed the Vicar of Hell – Buckingham – Compton – Bullen – all dead; some, it is true, by his orders, but that didn't make it the less pitiful for him that there were now so few of the old faces round him, so few to remember him as he once had been.

There was that tough old ruffian Norfolk, of course, he'd always been there from the beginning of time – where *was* Norfolk? He stared at all these new young upstart whippersnappers, seeking Norfolk's grizzled peaked beard and wiry hair, still black, somewhere among them. 'Where—' he began aloud, then checked; he had remembered, just in time, that Norfolk was in the Tower, awaiting sentence of death. He had already signed the death-warrant for Norfolk's son, the Earl of Surrey; in a day or two now the insolent conceited lad would lay on the block the handsome head that had dared compose verses against his King.

> *'Whose glutted cheeks sloth feeds so fat*
> *That scant their eyes be seen.'*

Was it possible young Surrey had intended that for his Dread Sovereign? But anything was possible with these Howards. Two nieces Norfolk had wedded to him, and both had to be beheaded. Now Cranmer and Ned Seymour said that he had conspired to put his son on the throne. He denied it, of course. 'When I deserve to be in the Tower,' he had exclaimed, 'Tottenham will turn French!'

Just like old Norfolk! Told George Lawson once that he was as good a knight as ever spurred a cow! Useful fellow, Norfolk, always ready to run and pull down whoever he was set on; how he'd chased Wolsey from town, swearing he'd 'tear the butcher's cur with his teeth if he didn't shog off!' Pity you couldn't tell with the best wolf-hound when it mightn't turn and bite its master.

He took a deep drink, with a glance at his watchful physician. 'Let every man have his own doctor,' he wheezed. 'This is mine.'

This was a good song of his. Surrey, the lazy cub, was writing verse without rhyme and calling it a new invention, blank verse. Blank it was. His own was the real thing.

> *'Youth will needs have dalliance,'*

sang the choristers.

His youth had had all that youth ever dreamt of, once his dreary lonely boyhood had passed, and his stingy old father in the shabby fur cloak had died, and young Prince Hal found himself one of the richest kings in Europe. He had turned everything to gold with his Midas touch; the foreign visitors could not believe their eyes, they had to finger all the tassels and cups and jugs and horses' bits, to be convinced that they were solid gold. He had been the most splendidly dressed king in Europe. What feasting there had been, unequalled by Cleopatra or Caligula, the ambassadors said; what spiced game and venison cooked in sour cream, what flowing of fulsome wines.

It was the same now, but it had tasted better then, after his father's diet of porridge and small beer; and with the zest of youth, an appetite as voracious for fun as for food, that pie he had carved, full of live frogs that leapt out over the table and floor, making the girls scream and jump on the benches, lifting their skirts above their knees – what a roar of laughter from him and all the other young fellows had volleyed and tumbled round the hall, echoing back to him now after all these years.

The lids of those lowered eyes just lifted; the grey lips moved. 'Another cup of wine,' they mumbled.

'Every man hath his free will,'

sang the choristers from Henry's early song.

What masquerades there had been then, what pranks and dressing-up as Muscovites or Saracen robbers, surprising the Queen and her ladies into delicious alarm and then laughter! What dancing, he himself leaping higher than any, and long,

long into the night, and then after he had played a hard game of tennis, wrestled in bout after bout, run races and leapt with the long pole, or been in the saddle all day riding at the gallop after hounds, riding in the lists and unhorsing all his opponents. There was no one could beat 'Sir Loyal Heart', the name he always took in those tournaments of his youth, when he cantered up on his great war-horse with his wife's Spanish colours on his sleeve in defiance of the fashion (for a knight should wear some other lady's), into the pavilion that was all spangled with gold Tudor roses and the pomegranates of Aragon, and H.K. intertwined.

H.K. everywhere for Henry and Katherine.

'As the holly groweth green and never changeth hue,
So I am – ever have been – unto my lady true.

For whoso loveth should love but one,
Change whoso will, I will be none.'

That was another song of his, but he never cared to hear it sung after the 'H.K.' was all changed everywhere to 'H.A.' for Henry and Anne. 'HA HA!' shouted the rude Cockney boys, and they were right – the common people always were in the long run – right to mock and distrust that accursed whore who bewitched Sir Loyal Heart and led him into captivity, unrewarded for six long years. What torture of desire he had undergone for her, what abject letters he had written her – and then the reward, good God, another girl!

He blinked down the table at the girl, as lithe and whippy as a greyhound puppy, and the light glinting on her red-gold hair. 'Nan Bullen's brat!' he muttered to himself, 'a wheyfaced scrap of a thing like her mother, a green apple, a codling,' he drooled on, regarding her with a fixed and menacing eye.

She looked back at him; for one instant he saw himself reflected in the dreadfully dispassionate eyes of a very young girl. But the image was quickly blurred; the light seemed oddly dim tonight, as it had been in his father's day when they cut down the number of candles and saved the candle-ends.

What did that girl matter – or all the other girls either? – though it was enraging the way the Tudor stock had run to seed in a crop of females: first his own two daughters; and then the only grandchildren of his two fine strapping sisters were those three diminutive Grey brats, and the baby in Scotland who might well become the most dangerous person in Europe.

But he had the boy, his son Edward, yes, he had got a legitimate son at last. He turned his great stiff head slowly and stared at the pale child beside him; nothing like as big and strong as he himself had been at his age; he was much more like what Henry's elder brother Prince Arthur had been, but that Henry could not bear to recognise; for the slight boy whom he could scarcely remember had died at fifteen of a consumption. No, Henry would see no likeness to Arthur in Edward; for one thing, Edward was far cleverer, already he knew more than lads twice his age. 'I wish I had more learning' Henry had sighed when a youth, as greedy for the beauty of great minds as for rich food and drink, for pleasure and sport and glory and conquest.

He had welcomed Erasmus to his Court, he had been proud to count him as a friend; and witty ironic Thomas More too, with whom he had walked so often in More's garden at Chelsea, watching the river flow past and the seagulls swoop and swirl, while they discussed everything under heaven and in it too as they walked up and down, his arm round his friend's neck. But his friend had betrayed him, defied him, tacitly refused to recognise the righteousness of his divorce from Katherine of Aragon, turned stiff-necked in resistance to his will, until there was nothing for it but to cut off his learned and witty head. Tom Cromwell had urged him to it. 'More must go,' he had said; and then in his turn Crum had to go. Crum was a knave if ever there was one: when Henry held a knave in his hands at cards he used to say 'I hold a Cromwell!' But he was a witty devil and a good servant.

The best of friends, the best of his servants, the best of women, how was it that all had failed him? He needed friendship, he needed love, he needed a wise, tender, infinitely understanding companion who, while giving him all the glowing admiration that was his due, would also know just where to throw out a hint in guidance of his judgment, where to encourage and where to still the doubts that often stirred deep down within himself, so deep that even he did not always recognise them until too late.

But he had never had such a companion; never since— Was there a strong draught that made the candles gutter and sway, and the smoke swirl in wreaths from their flickering flames? Through the blue and shifting mist he was seeing pictures he had not seen for over forty years – a fair Spanish princess of sixteen, all in white, with long hair down her back, seated in a litter hung with cloth of gold, and himself riding beside her, a cavalier of ten, entrusted to escort his brother Arthur's bride through the roaring, cheering flower-strewn streets of London. He, who was never allowed all his boyhood to be with any girl except his sisters, had then his first taste of the pageantry of chivalry that he adored in the romances; and was so intoxicated by it that, that evening, to show off to Katherine, he danced so hard that he had to tear off his hot coat and caper in his small-clothes. And after Arthur had died a few months later, and Henry had married his widow a few years later, he went on showing off to Katherine, finding her the perfect audience, through twenty years of marriage – until he found to his rage that she too claimed to take a part in the play herself.

Muttering something to himself, he reached forward to take another helping of sugared marchpane, felt the marble edge of the table pressing into his belly, and squinted down at it resentfully. How long had he been in labour with this huge paunch? Tonight it seemed so short a time had turned that splendid young athlete, with flat hard stomach and limbs clean as a whistle, into this mountain of pain and disease, in labour with – was it death? The choristers sang:

'To hunt, sing, dance
My heart is set.
All goodly sport
To my comfort
Who shall me let?'

There was no one to offer let or hindrance to his pleasures; except himself. '*Every man hath his free will,*' but what use was that? Since a vast aching body told one, as sternly as any gaoler come to arrest a quaking girl, that 'it is no more the time to dance.'

There was no pleasure now left to that body except to cram it further with food, with deep stupefying draughts of wine, cloying the palate, mercifully dulling the senses. He reached forward for his cup. '*Who shall me let*?' Neither his anxious-eyed physician nor his fearfully watching wife dared offer let or hindrance.

And suddenly he began to talk. His great voice swayed gustily to and fro, a storm wind rising and falling in the hall that a moment since had been full of music and pattering chatter, and now was paralysed into silence with the resurgence into life of the figure-head, monstrous and moribund at head of the table.

He talked of the French and how he had so lately beaten them; he had made the Narrow Seas English for all time; no other foreign invaders would ever dare come sailing up the Channel. Once indeed he might have turned the tables the other way and conquered the whole country of France after winning a yet more glorious Agincourt; he had in fact conquered and now held Boulogne. When only twenty-two he had taken the Chevalier Bayard prisoner and shown them that an Englishman could be every bit as much a 'very perfect gentle knight' as any bowing Frenchman. ('Now,' thought Bess, playing with the nutshells on her plate, 'now he will say, "Stout fellow, Bayard, a very fine fellow."') Sure enough he said it, and with episcopal authority – 'Old Gardiner showed sense, for a bishop, when he said Bayard is a stout fellow.' He always had to say that when he mentioned Bayard, to remind himself that he did not really bear the noblest man in Europe a grudge for knighting François on the terrible battlefield of Marignano when the young French King and his armies had fought 'like infuriated boars.' Henry had never been in a battle like that; even now, when François too had grown old and cautious, it irked him to think how the Foxnose had once fought his own battles, where Henry had only paid the Emperor to fight them.

Well, it was something to have had an Emperor in his pay. And once he had planned to make himself Emperor when his servant Wolsey had aimed to be Pope – Wolsey the butcher's son, a fellow that had once been put in the stocks for a brawl at a fair, but whom he had raised to be the greatest priest and statesman in England, and, almost, in Europe. Yes, he had brought England back into the Continent, he had made her a power to be feared and courted.

'Look at the Field of the Cloth of Gold!' he shouted suddenly. *That* showed Europe was at his feet – and with what a show! The English had outvied the French at every point; François alarmed at the competition, had sent anxiously to him beforehand to ask him to forbear making so many rich tents and pavilions. François had shown him with great pride a portrait of a woman called Mona Lisa that he had bought from the old painter Leonardo da Vinci who had died the year before; he had paid four thousand florins for it, a ridiculous sum for a picture, and of a rather plain woman too.

Henry could retaliate with Holbein, whom he had honoured with his patronage and an income of £30 a year (less £3 for taxes) apart from the sale of his pictures. The new Dutch School was coming far more into fashion than those old Italians.

They said François was as tall as Henry, but it was only because the Frenchman's wretchedly thin legs made him seem taller than he really was. If only he could have matched his knightly prowess against François in the tourney, which cautious royal etiquette forbade, he would have proved himself the victor, he was sure of it. He had overcome all his opponents in it, and killed one of his mounts from sheer exhaustion (François had overcome all his too, but they had probably thought it wise to let him win). Henry had excelled even his crack English archers at the long bow; the French had gasped with admiration of his aim and strength. Certainly he would have been more than a match for François.

'Remember how I threw him in the wrestling bout?' he chuckled. 'What a to-do there was! Kings mustn't be thrown! Why, Kate, you and the French Queen had to pull us apart, d'you remember, hanging on to our shirt-tails like a couple of fishwives parting their husbands in a brawl!'

The hall seemed to rock to the sound of that mighty guffaw, and echoed it back in a frozen silence. No one knew where to look, what to say. The King heard and saw the emptiness all round him, a herd of sheep staring, but not at him, not at anyone, a wavering cloud of white foolish faces, scared and averted, and among them a very young redheaded girl playing with the nutshells on her plate. Who was that girl? She was always cropping up, baffling, frustrating, charged with some hideous memory.

The scene grew thicker, more confused. 'Kate!' he called in sudden terror, '*Kate*!' A woman was hanging on to his arm, imploring him something. She seemed to think it was her that he had called – why, he did not even know who she was! Some fellow was loosening his collar, the woman put water to his lips.

He stared at the red-headed girl and knew now she was his daughter – but not by Kate. There had been other Kates, Annes, Jane – but the Kate who could remember him at the Field of the Cloth of Gold, as King and bridegroom at eighteen, as a child of ten riding beside her, that Kate had gone for ever, and would never come back.

Not Katherine of Aragon hung on his arm, but Catherine Parr, who knew him only as an obese, sick old man.

He made a mighty effort and guffawed again. 'Why, how I've scared the lot of you!' he gasped out. 'Who do you think I took you for, Kate? I was asking only if you remembered hearing the tale. You were only a little girl when it happened.'

But he spoke with difficulty and his lips had gone blue, as had his twitching hands where the great jewelled rings were sunk in fat.

Bess, holding on to her nutshells so tight that they cut into her hands, stole a glance at him under her down-dropped eyelids and thought his face looked like a glistening suet pudding. Then, even as she glanced, it sagged, a deflated bag, turned a greyish purple, and a tight smile twisted it as though trying to hold it together; the eyes opened for one instant in a puzzled, frightened stare – and then the crash came. He fell forward over the table, into clattering plates and knives and cups, and a great red pool of spilt wine pouring over and drip-dripping on to the floor like drops of blood.

Women shrieked, men sprang up, Edward Seymour rapped out a sharp order, and servants surrounded the King, bent over him, more and more of them, until at last they succeeded in hoisting the inert mass into a poled chair, and staggering off with it through the wide-opened doors.

Bess unclenched her hands and saw the palms were bleeding. She looked at Tom Seymour, and saw he was looking at her. She looked hastily at her brother Edward, and saw he was finishing Jane's marchpane. Edward liked sweets.

She slipped out and found her governess, Cat Ashley, who had already heard all about it.

'But, Ashley,' said Bess, 'I though it was François who threw the King.'

'Sh-sh-sh,' said Ashley.

CHAPTER THREE

The king lingered nearly a fortnight. His mind did not again wander. With Herculean courage he bent it to his will, though his face had gone black with agony, and his legs, which had had to be cauterised some time before, were plunged in a perpetual fire. Yet he forced all those last hours of his long torture to the service of his son, and the constitution of the government that might best safeguard his minority.

There was no time now to brood on the past; that company of long-forgotten comrades that had stepped forward as he began to lose his grip on life were driven ruthlessly back into the shadows. They were dead and done with; there was nothing to be done about them. With the hand of death heavy on him, every nerve and impulse in that fast decaying body reached forward to the future. His dying urgency was fiercer far than that of youth and hope.

For thirty-eight years he had worked tirelessly to secure his kingdom both on and from the Continent; to secure it at home in England, both from Papal interference and the revolutionary dangers of the New Ideas; and to secure its uncertain sovereignty over Wales, which now he had definitely incorporated with England by Act of Parliament ten years ago; over Ireland, where the sovereignty was far more uncertain; and over Scotland, where, he had to admit in rage, it still did not exist.

With failing, gasping breath, he urged on his brother-in-law Edward Seymour, Earl of Hertford, the necessity of his completing Scotland's conquest, as the first work to be done in the new reign.

Edward Seymour, as Prince Edward's uncle, would be on the Council of Regency which Henry appointed; and with him fifteen of the wisest of his Ministers: a judicious mixture of the 'New Men' who inclined to reform, and conservative elements to act as a brake; such as Chancellor Wriothesley, a heretic-hater, to pull Cranmer's lawn sleeve when it flapped too urgently at 'Old Mumpsimuses' – so he said with the ghost of a smile before it twisted into a grimace of pain. And he added Edward Seymour's younger brother Tom to the Council, a lively fellow after his own kidney, with none of Edward's priggish and possibly dangerous earnestness; he might act as a check on it, for the two brothers couldn't abide each other.

Henry knew that Edward Seymour, beneath his stern exterior, was white with eagerness for him to die. He had accused Norfolk and Surrey of aiming at the sceptre – well, the pot may have accused the kettle. One could trust no one. The nobles were always ready to conspire, the commons to rebel. The nation itself had a proverb that the vice of the French was lechery, but that of the English, treachery. He had to leave his life's work to a child of nine – and to what busy and ambitious schemers? What chances of treason and murder? 'Woe to the land whose King is a child' – woe also to the child! The skeletons of his own boy-uncles, murdered sixty years ago in the Tower by their uncle, Richard III, would raise their little heads through his fever to warn him how near the fate of Edward VI might be to that of Edward V and his small brother. But *this* uncle, Edward Seymour, virtuous, high-principled, was no Richard Crookback – or was he?

Anyway, he could do no more. And he had to see about dying. He left command that he should be buried at Windsor beside the body of Jane Seymour, his third wife, the only one who had given him a son. And that his soul was to be prayed for, and masses said for it, to release it the sooner from Purgatory. He had abolished Purgatory – he had intended to abolish the Mass – but no matter, one might as well be on the safe side. Henry had never learnt that he could not eat his cake and have it; there was no time to learn it now.

Bess spent the days in terror lest she be summoned to his sick-chamber. But he did not send for her, nor for Edward. It had become indeed no place for children. He sent for his wife Catherine, and for Mary, separately. They both came out weeping uncontrollably.

Bess gazed in wonder at her stepmother. She would be free now and unafraid, yet she was crying as if for the loss of a child. Had he been sorry? What could he have said to move her so? He had said, 'It is God's will that we should part.'

Bess could recognise the simplicity of greatness; and its practical quality. It was no good looking back; he had looked forward, told Catherine he wanted her to keep all the jewels and ornaments he had given her, and not to hand them back to the Crown, and that he had 'ordered all these gentlemen to honour you and treat you as if I were living still.' Yes, Bess conceded inwardly, as she listened to her stepmother, it was something for Catherine Parr to have been made a Queen.

And Mary, of course, was always ready to cry.

Mary had, in fact, cried so much at the interview with her father that he could not bear it, and had signed to her to leave him, for by then he could speak no more.

He had tried to talk to her of the councillors he had appointed, but she would only beg him not to leave her an orphan so soon. To which he made no answer. But presently with deep earnestness he had asked her to try and be a mother to her brother Edward, 'for, you see, he is little.'

It was that last request that tore her heart. Catherine Parr owed him royalty, honour and jewels. Mary's debt had been otherwise; she had been dispossessed from her royal and legitimate inheritance, and dishonour cast on her birth and on her mother; she owed him years of loneliness, sometimes imprisonment; insult and ill treatment both from himself and his servants; worst of all, separation from her adored mother all the last years of Katherine of Aragon's life; a refusal even to be allowed to go to her when she was dying and afraid, as even her stout heart admitted, that she would have to die alone and abandoned, 'like a beast.' Did Mary not remember how she had been forbidden her mother's death-chamber, when she came out of her father's, sobbing as if her heart would break?

So Bess asked herself with the clear-cut logic of thirteen, and a horror of the father who had killed her own mother four months after he had at last worried Mary's to death.

She could not guess how much else Mary remembered.

The huge decaying body Mary had just seen had not appalled her as the corruption of his soul had done, long years ago, when he became rotted with power and the lust of life.

The thirty-year-old woman who met the child's astonished gaze, all her pent-up passion in these repressed years broken loose by an agony of pity and desire for what might have been, had one of her violent irrational impulses, and tried to tell her what her father had been; like the Sun himself when he 'cometh out of his chamber like a bridegroom.'

'You never knew him as I did,' she burst out, 'you never saw him as a young man, glorious, gay, doing everything twice as hard as other men. He made everyone else seem a ghost. You should have seen him as I did when I was a child, on board his ships in a common sailor's dress, short trousers and vest but all of cloth of gold, and blowing a whistle so loud it was like a trumpet. But he was kind and tender too, tender even in teasing.'

A flood of tears choked her as the memory swept over her of his pulling off her hood at some solemn State function, so that her hair came tumbling over her shoulders. The schoolboy prank had been partly due to his pride in her long fair hair – she had known that, even at six years old. He had loved to show her off to the grave courteous foreigners who had come to ask her hand for their Sovereigns of France or Spain. 'This girl *never* cries,' he had told them proudly.

'She has made up for it since,' Bess thought, in acute discomfort at her half-sister's emotion. It only made her hate her father worse than ever; why couldn't Mary be sensible and hate him too, and then she would be glad instead of sorry that he was dying?

'You will be able to marry now,' she said in desperate attempt to comfort or at least turn her thoughts, 'and then you'll have your own children instead of just Jane and the other silly little Greys – you know you said that as long as he lived you'd only be the Lady Mary.'

But Mary's re-discovered appreciation of Henry could not go so far as to admire the forward-thrusting mind he had bequeathed to Bess. She only wanted to look back, to forgive, and if possible excuse her father.

'He would have arranged a marriage for me if he could,' she said eagerly. 'He spoke of it to me just now and how sorry he was that fortune had prevented it. You are too young to understand – but you will – how difficult and dangerous a thing is a royal marriage. The fate of a whole nation may depend on it.'

Her eyes narrowed; her face grew strained and terrible. 'The fate of a nation,' she repeated. 'Yes, and its soul, its living soul. That is what one marriage may destroy.'

She was thinking how the King's marriage to Nan Bullen had done that; had torn the nation's soul away from Christ's Church to the pagan worship of the State; had imposed a revolution from above on to the people, so that they were persecuted, not for a new idea, but for believing in the faith of their fathers; had robbed and desecrated the tomb of Saint Thomas à Becket who for three hundred years had been a national saint and hero and was now declared a traitor for having opposed his King, his bones thrown on the common dust-heap by royal command. Henry had, in fact, pulled down the whole structure of the Church just as he had pulled down and robbed the monasteries, and built it up anew with himself at the head of it – in order that he might marry Nan Bullen.

And of Henry himself, and 'the terrible change' that the foreign ambassadors had noticed in him at that time, Mary could only think as of the destruction of a soul. Only a year or two before, they had reported that 'Love for the King is universal...for he does not seem a person of this world, but one descended from Heaven.'

But so had Lucifer descended from Heaven, to become Lord of Hell. Mary had seen her gay affectionate father, a conventionally pious man, disintegrate before her eyes into an irresponsible ogre; or else, even more disillusioning, into the ridiculous figure of a man driven between two women, living for a long time under the same roof with them both, helpless, angry, even frightened.

Yes, he had been frightened of his Nan; she had taunted him and told him what to do and what not to do.

She had told him not to argue with Katherine of Aragon, for he 'would always get the worst of it'; not to see his daughter Mary when he went to visit his baby daughter Elizabeth, for his 'weakness and instability' might let him soften to her.

Once – it was on an autumn morning and all the fields and trees were gold under the wide still sky – Mary had met him by chance walking in the open country, and he stopped and spoke kindly to her, telling her he hoped he would soon be able to see her more often, and then, abruptly, he moved away, and she saw it was because two of Nan's servants were sidling up to overhear.

Mary knew that her desperate loathing and jealousy of Nan was not only on her mother's account; it ran like a withering fire through her veins. The image of Nan had burnt into her eyelids so that whenever she closed them she saw the slight supple figure enthroned in the amazing black dress that her daring French taste had dictated. It had cost more than five times the amount of Mary's dress allowance for the whole year; thirty-two yards of black satin and velvet, and the King's jewels gleaming out of all the blackness; and framed in it a thin white face, bold forehead and scarlet lips and black eyes that sparkled and, the ambassadors said discreetly, 'invited conversation.' 'The Night Crow,' Wolsey had called her; the She-Devil, Mary called her, as did all decent women, knowing the danger of her and her like to safe, ordered matrimony; she had been chased by a mob of women several thousand strong who yelled their curses on 'the goggle-eyed whore,' – and Nan had told of that herself, with shrill shameless laughter.

Would Mary ever forget her laugh? Never, never, never, she told herself in agony when she woke in the night to hear it ringing in her ears, hearing that laugh alone, and everywhere else the night-long silence. No more the sweet familiar sound of bells from the chapels where the monks had prayed for men's souls at their appointed hours, the bells that had always comforted her childhood when she woke afraid of the dark. That laugh, ringing down through the years, had silenced them, it seemed for ever.

It was on an evening in early spring that it had sounded their doom; when the wind and slanting sunlight were sharp as thin steel and all the little thrusting flames of the crocuses in the garden at Hampton Court were tossed this way and that with the light shining through them, and out swept 'the Lady' (not wife yet, nor Queen) from the Palace, into the bowing, curtsying company on the terrace, out she swept all in one flashing movement, chattering and calling, greeting first one and then another, and cried to Sir Thomas Wyatt, whom all the world knew to be mad for love of her, 'Lord, how I wish I had an apple! Have you such a thing about you, my sweet Tom? For three days now I have had such an incredible fierce desire to eat apples. Do you know what the King says? He says it means I am with child. But I tell him "No!" No, it couldn't be, no, no, no!'

And then out rang her laughter, sharper, wilder than the early March wind; and her thin nervous hands flew up like fluttering white birds to peck and clutch at the King's pearls round her throat, pearls bigger than chick-peas, and she stared at all the shocked dismayed faces, and suddenly turned and fled from them, still laughing, back into the Palace, leaving only a ringing, mocking, frightened echo in the appalled hush she had created.

Now everyone knew. The six-year siege that the King had laid to Nan had been raised at last, the fortress yielded, which she had held through all his furious importunings while living under the same roof, his showers of gifts and titles, even through the general belief that she had long since been his mistress. It had been yielded at the exact moment when, his patience strained to snapping point and his resentment mounting to fury at the way she treated him, it had become necessary to apply the final spur.

Now Henry and his new servant Cranmer would have to stir themselves in good earnest to get Nan's child born in wedlock. They did.

On the last day of that March of 1533 Cranmer was consecrated Archbishop of Canterbury and had to swear allegiance to the Pope before the high altar – but, four days earlier, he arranged another and more private ceremony before the altar of the Palace Chapel in Westminster, where he forswore this sacred oath in front of a notary and other witnesses, declared that he put the King's will above the Pope's, and that whatever he would have to swear at his consecration was only an empty formula. He did not like being consecrated in deliberate perjury, but Henry had another word for it, which was 'compromise.'

It took Cranmer under two months of the Sacred office thus achieved to find the marriage of Henry to Katherine of Aragon to have been 'null and void from the beginning.' That was just before the end of May, and on the first of June he crowned Nan Queen of England; King Henry was excommunicated that summer; and on the 7th of September Elizabeth was born.

Just when and where Nan's marriage to Henry occurred in this sequence nobody quite knew: but Cranmer pronounced it to have been 'good and valid.' Its lack of ceremony was made up for at her coronation, when all London was draped in scarlet and a conduit ran claret and white wine through Cheapside all the day – but, so the seventeen-year-old Mary heard with delight, in all those gaping crowds there were few heads bared, and fewer still to shout 'God save the Queen.'

But Nan still held her head high, and did so until just three years later she laid it on the block. That altered nothing – to Mary. Nan had won.

In twin birth with her child, Elizabeth, the Church of England was born; and the break with Rome, with the Pope and the monastic orders, made complete. The bells were silenced.

Nan had won. Her daughter would win. Mary's despondent nature was certain of it. But one comfort she could clutch to herself; she had been born of a woman who loved the King, and Elizabeth had not.

She looked up from her brooding reverie to speak to Elizabeth, perhaps to say that very thing – she did not want to, but often words came out of her mouth and hung on the air for her to hear them, aghast, before she knew she had spoken them.

But it did not matter now if she spoke them or not, for Elizabeth had tiptoed softly away.

Bess went to find Edward. He was reading St Paul's Epistles in Greek with Jane Grey, while their tutor, pretending to correct their exercises, snored murmurously near the fire, its light flickering upwards over his finely cut nose.

She sat down on the bench beside them, and the three fair heads bent together over the book and talked in whispers.

'They've sent for old Mumpsy-mouse,' said Edward in his even little voice. (Bess's nickname had at once become the children's name for Cranmer.) 'He'll be coming down by water. That means he's not likely to last the night, and I shall be King tomorrow.'

Bess, callous enough herself about her father's death, was startled, not for the first time, by Edward's lack of feeling, for Henry adored his son. She longed to tell him he was an ungrateful cub, but one doesn't say these things to a boy who will be King tomorrow. Probably Jane had influenced him, since she openly hated her parents.

But Jane was not interested in current affairs; she was wrestling furiously with a tough passage of Greek prose. 'I think,' she said, 'Paul got it wrong himself.'

'Very likely,' said Bess. 'Pope Clement told the theological students at Rome never to read him, as it would spoil their style.'

Both the younger children froze at mention of the Pope. It was not done. 'Have you been talking to Mary?' Edward asked severely.

'Yes, but not about religion. She is very unhappy at the King's dying.'

'Why should she be?' said Edward. 'I shall see to it that she is properly treated, even though she is a Papist.'

'If we don't finish this epistle,' said Jane, 'we shall be whipped tomorrow.'

'I shan't,' Edward reminded her. 'Barnaby might.'

'Yes, Your Highness has a whipping-boy. It isn't fair,' she added under her breath.

'What is the day of the month?' Bess asked suddenly.

'The 27th,' they told her, and knew why she had asked. If the King lived till tomorrow morning, the Duke of Norfolk would die. His execution had been fixed for dawn on Friday, January 28th. But if the King died tonight, then Norfolk would live. His son, Henry Howard, the Earl of Surrey, had been beheaded nine days ago, after a speech of furious defiance when, like a stag at bay, he had stood and gored the King and Council with his words.

None of the children spoke of him, for they had worshipped him from afar as a scornful god who had scarcely noticed their presence; they had yelled with shrill delight as they watched him at tennis, winning game after game, or in the tilt yard, charging down on his horse White Cherry, as he wrote himself, on

> 'The gravel-ground, with sleeves tied on the helm,
> On foaming horse, with swords and friendly hearts';

they had sung his songs, all in the modern Italian manner which made other verse seem so tame and old-fashioned; and envied the Irish girl, Fair Geraldine, to whom he had written them.

But his father Norfolk, a grumpy fierce old man, they did not like; it was therefore possible to discuss his chances.

'Mary will be sorry if he lives,' said Edward, who had heard how Norfolk had tried to bully her into submission to her father's divorce. 'He told her once that if she were *his* daughter he'd knock her head against the wall till it was as soft as a baked apple.'

'It's that already,' said Bess, and they all giggled. Somehow it was irresistible to make a butt of Mary when they got together, but she felt guilty and uncomfortable in doing so; poor old Mary, it wasn't fair, especially just after she had been talking to her almost like a sister – well, a half-sister.

'Why are you always rubbing your nose?' Edward asked his sister suddenly.

'I'm not,' she said indignantly, and then in self-contradiction, 'it tickles.'

Ever since Tom Seymour had tweaked it in that game of Blind Man's Buff she had felt anxious about her nose. Why did he say he'd know it in a thousand? Did he think it would be big or bony? She could feel just the faintest hook in the bone, but then all the heroines in the romances had aquiline noses. Still—

'You'll make it red if you go on,' said Edward, and buried his own in St Paul again.

Silence fell on them all except for the gentle rhythm of Mr Cheke's faint snores and the sudden spurts and crackle in the fire.

It was a wet windy night. The draught blew the wood-smoke down the chimney and the candle-flames this way and that. Bess noticed a winding-sheet of wax forming in one of them; was it for her father or for Norfolk? She shivered, and glanced at the others, but they had noticed nothing; they were deep in their Greek. 'They're only children,' she thought.

Mr Cheke woke with a snort as a puff of smoke blew into his face; he jerked up, saying, 'Well, well, well!' and tried to pretend that he was exclaiming at something he was correcting in the exercises and that he had not been asleep at all. The little girls smiled slyly at him; they had a great admiration for him – Jane because he was the best Greek scholar in Cambridge; Bess because he was so handsome and aristocratic looking that no one would guess his mother kept a small wine-shop in a back street there.

'A forfeit!' she cried, in what Jane thought a very pert way. 'Whoever falls asleep must tell a story!' And instead of reproving her, as Jane thought he would and should (again it wasn't fair), he laughed in a shy pleased way as though she had paid him a compliment. So they all sat beside him, hunched on the hearthrug, with their hands held out from their wide sleeves to the spluttering blaze of the logs as the rain fell down the great chimney, and he told them the story of Saint George of Merry England and the Dragon. He told it well and dramatically, making Saint George speak in Latin in a very grand voice, and pointing out a great dragon with fiery eyes that they could all see in the fire. The girls listened with grave attention, but Edward startled them all by bursting out laughing. It was the more astonishing as no one had ever heard him laugh before; a pale little smile was the most he had ever achieved. Nor could he tell what he had found so funny in the story; he just went on laughing in that shrill childish treble, to their consternation, for no one in the Palace should do it on the night the King was dying, and for Edward of all people to do it was so odd as to be uncanny.

Jane said in her sedate fashion, 'They say Crassus laughed only once in his life, and that was at an ass eating thistles.'

'But St George isn't an ass,' said Elizabeth rather sharply.

'Hee haw! Hee haw!' brayed Edward weakly, wiping his eyes; then began to laugh again.

Was he bewitched? He looked as though he had been suddenly transformed into a goblin, with that small mouth stretched from one to other of the immensely long ears that peaked up above his straight hair, and the little round button of a chin turned to a sharp point. Was he really a changeling? Bess asked herself with a twinge of childish fear.

Mr Cheke in his kind way said he was over-tired, excited, he had got another of his colds, and had better go to bed and he would tell Mother Jack to bring him a hot posset to drink. Mrs Jackson had been Edward's nurse 'as a child,' he would explain gravely, but he still called her Mother Jack and got her to tuck him up in bed on every possible excuse; Bess said it was why he had so many colds.

She decided to go to bed too; it was better than doing nothing. She left the room with exaggerated grace, for she thought Mr Cheke was looking at her.

But in bed she could not sleep. She lay watching the firelight through her bed-curtains, hearing the rain drip-dripping, and all the time the minutes too were dripping past; old Mumpsy-mouse was slipping along down the black rain-drummed river in his barge, landing at Westminster, coming up to Whitehall Palace, coming into that awful room where the King lay already unconscious, the greatest King England had ever had, people said, and there he lay, a rotting hulk, with the life drip-dripping away from him.

She shivered and huddled the blankets more closely round her. All the warmth imparted by the silver warming-pans seemed to have gone chill; the sheets were cold as cere-cloths to wrap the dead in, so she told herself with an almost enjoyable thrill in working up her own fears.

The great clock outside tolled out midnight: one, two, three, four—; if that hulk still kept its fierce hold on life, by eight o'clock tomorrow old Norfolk, listening to the rain, and the minutes dripping past, would then be beheaded. Would they go down to hell together, the King's hands gripping his servant's throat?

She did not care for old Norfolk, but he was in 'that very narrow place, the Tower, from which few escape except by a miracle,' and that place exercised a terrifying spell on her imagination; was it because of her mother's last hours there? Or because – because somewhere in the unwritten future she might find herself floating down the rain-drummed river to the Water Gate that is only opened to admit traitors?

Past and future, death and life, the air all round her was full of forces struggling together in the dark, and behind them, flowing on endlessly, relentlessly, the dark river of Time, bearing them all away.

With a sudden panic-stricken movement she leapt out of the bed, pulled on a long, fur-lined bedgown, thrust her bare feet into a pair of heelless embroidered slippers, and went hastily, stealthily out of the room.

The Palace was alight, silent, waiting. She ran along the passage and paused as she saw at the end of the long gallery the armed halberdiers standing at attention like statues against the tapestry that moved in the wind so that its patterned figures looked more alive than they. What use were they? They could not hope to bar Death from stalking down the gallery, in through that door at the end. She slipped back behind the corner of the passage as she heard the faint sound of a voice, very low, but fast, urgent, almost desperate, coming near, then further away till lost in silence, then back again, up and down, up and down the gallery. She peeped round the corner again and saw Edward Seymour, Earl of Hertford, walking there with his friend Sir William Paget, the Secretary of State, and talking, talking as if he would never stop, flinging out his arm every now and then in an abrupt, angry gesture. Sometimes Paget would lay a hand on it as if to restrain him, and once he spoke, clearly, 'Too many irons in the fire,' she heard, but that was all, and indeed he had little chance to speak through that low persistent torrent of words. Their shadows ran up against the wall as they advanced, Paget's thick nose and two-pronged beard sticking out of his great fur collar in absurd exaggeration, while Edward

Seymour's face ran into a long narrow point; the shadows grew, then dwindled, then came again, then away.

The clock boomed out a single note. It was one o'clock, it was morning, it had only to strike seven more times and then—

The door at the end of the gallery opened. The two men walking up and down stopped dead, their faces turned towards the open door and the little close-knit group of figures that came out of it, walking very slowly with bent heads and a faint intermittent murmur of voices, just as though they were mumbling in church, Bess thought. Old Mumpsy-mouse was in the middle of them, his face yellow and glistening with sweat under the waving torches; and, yes, with tears; he drew his sleeve across it and mopped it as he came up to Seymour and his friend, and said on a beautiful low yet clear note, like the toll of a bell:

'All is over. His Majesty has died in the faith of Christ.'

They were all coming on now down the gallery towards her. Bess had slid back behind the shadowed corner of the passage and now fled noiselessly down it. Had they seen her, were they coming after her? She dared not look back, she turned down a little stairway of only three or four steps, sped along another corridor, swung round a corner and fell against a man. She began to sob and gasp something about a nightmare.

'Steady now, steady. What's all this?' said Tom Seymour's voice.

She looked up wildly into his face with incredulous relief, and flung her arms round him. He pulled her back through a doorway into a little bare room where the firelight flickered on new wooden panels all over the walls and ceiling. He thrust a taper into the fire and lit a couple of candles on the table, took her by the elbows and turned her face to the light, while she stared, fascinated, up at those square, humorously cocked eyebrows, so unlike his brother's fretted brows, and saw how his short hair curled towards them at the side of his head.

'Now,' he said, 'what's the to-do?'

'The King is dead.'

Tom Seymour drew a soft whistle through his lips.

'So-o-o! I've won a thousand crowns.'

She swung sharply from him. 'How dare you bet on the King's death?'

'Not so, my Princess. I bet on old Norfolk's life. Always said there's no axe long enough to reach him.'

'Yes, he'll live. I'm glad.'

'Are you fond of your great-uncle?'

'No. But I'm glad that someone who has gone to the Tower will get out again.'

He nodded, with understanding. 'Tell me, how did you know this of the King?'

'I heard old Mumps— the Archbishop himself say it. He came out of the King's rooms and told your brother – he was there walking up and down, talking, talking, talking.'

'Trust Ned for that!' he exclaimed with an unpleasant laugh, and added eagerly, 'Did you hear what he was saying?'

'Only one word – "Liberty."' ('Oh, *that*!' said Tom contemptuously.) 'He was talking very excitedly – like this,' she imitated the sawing movements of Seymour's arm and the fierce solemnity of his face, in a way that made his brother chuckle – and she added, 'but very low.'

'Can't trust his own shadow as usual – that's the worst of these damned virtuous fellows, they never dare speak out. Well, he's got his chance to now – it'll be a great day for him and all his new notions. May he ride 'em safely, that's all – and maybe he won't!'

He had forgotten her, his handsome angry face was sparkling with malicious interest as though he were looking on at some play she could not see; but suddenly he turned from it, looked sharply at her and asked:

'What were you doing running about the Palace in your shift?' and gave a pull at her bedgown, which she quickly hugged round herself again.

'I was frightened. I heard the clock strike. I had to know – or anyway do something.'

He bent suddenly forward, paused, then put his arms round her, kissed her swiftly on the chin and cheeks, and at once let her go as she struggled.

'I'm thirteen and a half,' she said indignantly. 'I'm too old to be kissed.'

'Too young, more's the pity. Now run back to your room, or to your maids if you're frightened, but don't say you met me. Child, are you crying?' He cursed softly under his breath. 'I daren't keep you here, it's too dangerous, for you as well as me. Go to your Mrs Ashley.'

She shook her head, gulping back her tears. 'I don't *want* women. I don't *like* them. They always say the correct things and expect one to say them too. I shall say them all tomorrow, I shall cry then for my father. I am not crying for him now – I don't know who it's for – me, I think.'

He took her by the shoulders, very gently this time, and

began to shove her out of the room, but she twisted round to look up at his face. 'One thing I must ask of you before we part,' she said earnestly. 'I may never have so good a chance again.'

'Ask away then, but quickly.'

'How is it you'd know my nose in a thousand, and just by feeling it?'

'By feeling it,' he replied, and kissed her again, this time on her nose.

CHAPTER FOUR

Next day Bess waited to hear the news of her father's death as if for the first time – but nobody told it to her. Nobody seemed to know of it; the doctors went to his room as before, the guard was changed outside his doors, all just as though he were still alive. The Palace was full of whisperings and hurryings, the street outside of troops marching; on the day after, Saturday the 29th, Parliament met, but still nothing was said and no one announced the King's death.

Bess had to nurse her secret knowledge until Monday the last day of January, when Edward Seymour, Earl of Hertford, with a long, grave, anxious face, told her and her brother together that their father was dead, and that he would now be a father to them. The Council had appointed him the King's guardian and Lord Protector of the country.

So that was why he had delayed the news – in order to make all his arrangements safely first, and take the supreme power before the country knew what had happened. Bess, mustering her tears, and gazing up at his noble countenance (he had a finer head even than his brother Tom's, but few noticed that), swiftly calculated what steps he must have already taken.

So that was what he had been talking about with Paget in

the midnight gallery, with their shadows going up and down, up and down – no wonder Paget had tried to restrain him! 'Too many irons in the fire' – how many?

Even little Edward, without her clue to his uncle's actions, could see something of what had happened; he began to cry and say he didn't want a Lord Protector, and if he must have one he'd rather have Uncle Tom, and where was Uncle Tom? Edward Seymour looked grim at mention of his brother and did not answer; when he spoke again it was about something else and in a severe, repressive voice.

Edward began dimly to realise that he would never see his father again, and that nobody else would ever make so much fuss over him; he put his head down on his arms and sobbed: 'I don't want Protectors, I want – I want my father.'

Bess, who had begun to cry dutifully for her father, found herself doing so in good earnest. She put her arm round the little boy; they clung together and ignored their uncle, who hovered uneasily over them, trying to find something comforting to say, and failing, even to his own ears. It was odd, he reflected scornfully, his delicate eyebrows shooting up into his already worried-looking forehead and making a sharp network of new wrinkles – it was very odd how much better his rascally younger brother would have succeeded. Children must be as undiscerning as women, for they all alike adored Tom. But he had more important things to see to, and at last, to their relief, he went away, and as everybody else seemed too busy to attend to them at the moment, they were left alone.

Sitting there huddled together like a couple of forlorn fledgelings, they heard the trumpets sound outside and the long strained shout of the heralds: '*Le roi est mort. Vive le noble roi Edward.*'

'I don't want to be King,' sighed Edward, his flaxen head still tucked into Bess's shoulder.

She gave it a little shake. 'Yes, you do. You're going to be a great King like your father. Uncle Edward won't last long. You'll grow up soon and do what you want, and not what he wants.'

'He wants me to marry that baby, the Queen of Scots, and she, Aunt Anne, wants me to marry Janet, and I don't want either.'

'How do you know?'

'Janet told me so herself. She heard them talking when they thought she was asleep.'

Janet was Edward Seymour's pretty, clever little daughter, and Bess was not at all surprised that her mother planned to marry her to the King. Edward grumbled on, 'All these cousins – all these nasty little girls – I don't want any of them. Janet is not royal, she's my subject. When I marry, I'll have a princess, a foreign one, well stuffed and jewelled.'

'Stuffed?'

'With money, silly, and lots of fine clothes, and perhaps a province or a navy. I'm not going to be fobbed off with a cousin and no proper dower. The Seymours are a beggarly lot, they haven't enough clothes to go round. They can't have, or they wouldn't have taken Surrey's when they got him beheaded.'

'What *do* you mean?'

But it seemed it was true. Edward had heard that too from Janet (in whose company he had been thrown by her mother), that her parents had seized not only the dead Earl of Surrey's house and possessions and splendid horses – 'Yes, even White Cherry whom he would never let any one else ride'– but all his clothes down to the very caps and stockings. A vision rose in Bess's mind of the gorgeous scarlet dress Surrey had worn on board the *Great Harry*, and she broke into horrified, hysterical laughter at the thought of it on Edward Seymour, who always wore the plainest dark clothes. It wasn't possible. Of course it must have been his wife, their Aunt Anne, who had done this horrible thing – a vulgar rapacious woman, as handsome as an Arab hunter, but with an eye like a gimlet and a mouth like a steel trap. It was all the more horrible because Surrey, though hating Edward Seymour as an upstart, had been attracted by the flashing vigour of his wife and paid her attentions which she prided herself on rejecting; he had written her an ode, 'On a lady who refused to dance with him,' a title that fascinated Bess, for how could any woman have refused to dance with Surrey?

She was their thin aunt; Jane's mother, the Lady Frances, their fat aunt. Sometimes they argued which was worse; Bess thought she knew.

But thank heaven there was no more time for thinking. Edward had to be dressed in his best clothes and ride in state through the city to the royal Palace of the Tower, where all new Kings had to stay for the few weeks before they were crowned. And as soon as he had ridden off on his white pony, looking very small and solemn among all the attendant nobles, the Queen pounced upon Bess, and carried her off with her, with hardly any preparation or packing, to the Manor House at Chelsea, which King Henry had had built as a nursery for his children and then presented to Queen Catherine.

Oh the relief of getting there! Catherine and Bess hugged each other and ran straight out into the garden to see if there were an early snowdrop – 'after all, it will be February and spring tomorrow!' said Catherine, on such a note of ecstasy that you would have thought she had been longing for the spring all her life – as indeed she had.

At Whitehall, the King's body lay in state. Bishop Gardiner had a hot encounter with Lord Oxford's company of players, who were going to act a grand new play at this unsuitable moment; he advised a solemn dirge instead, and finally had to appeal to the Justice of the Peace, swearing that if he couldn't prevent the play he would at least stop people from coming to see it.

The players in revenge chalked on the walls of his palace:

'As Gardiner such he is,
He spoils so all our plants
That justice withers, mercy dies,
And we wronged by their wants.
A priest only in weeds
And barren all his seeds.'

But they had to give in, grumbling, illogically that if only Old Hal were alive he'd be the first to tell them to go on with the play. Much *he'd* have cared for a solemn dirge! What bluff King Hal liked was a good show with plenty of dancing and jolly songs, and a fine performer he'd been in them himself when he was younger; so all the older players reminded each other, shaking their heads over their mugs of ale and complaining that nothing would be the same now Old Hal was dead. There'd never be another King like him – a bit hasty maybe, chopped off heads like cabbage stalks when he'd a mind to – but they were generally the nobles' heads, mark that, and no doubt they deserved it. He kept those proud bullies in their place, made them kneel when they addressed him as 'Majesty', a grand new title for a King, but the common people always found him as jolly and friendly to talk to as one of themselves, and almost as easy to get the chance to talk to too – you only had to step out beside his horse when he went riding and pull off your cap, and he'd rein in and chat with you as though you'd known him all your life.

Pity he couldn't have lived till the young one was in the saddle, instead of their having one of these new jumped-up nobles as Protector, a strange new-fangled title, though very old men like Martin Whitehead, who was kept in the Company to work the fireworks in the jaws of the Hell-fire dragon, could remember the time when there had been a Protector before in England. For that was what Crookback called himself for a few weeks before he called himself King Richard III – until he got killed by Old Hal's father.

And at the Crookback's name they all said 'A-ah' and took a deeper drink, for which they had to pay, although this very day the Protector had led the little King in a grand procession through the city and everybody had turned out to cheer them and run along beside their horses up Tower Hill. But not a drop of free drink did the Protector order for them, and no pipes of wine were laid in the streets; he rode along beside his nephew, looking very fine and noble but cold as a statue, and harried-looking too; he might take all he could get, but he'd never get any pleasure of it, nor would anyone else.

'Old Hal would have given us a drink,' grumbled the young ones as they turned away in disappointment: 'Young Hal gave us a drink,' mumbled the old ones, remembering that golden youth riding in triumph to the Tower, and added, 'God rest his soul!' with more feeling than Bishop Gardiner, whose sonorous voice was saying daily masses for his dead master, while his indignant mind absorbed the discovery that he had been cut out of his Will.

Seven other bishops assisted him in his thankless office, and Archbishop Cranmer was present though he would not celebrate High Mass, which showed the way the wind blew and that the new Government would now go all out for the new austerity in worship. But until the old King was buried, his masses had to be said, and they went on for a fortnight in Whitehall Chapel, where the King's body lay in state, and all day the nobles and gentry filed past it, and the ladies of the Court sat up in a separate gallery to pray.

The King's widow, the Dowager Queen Catherine, came up to Whitehall from Chelsea, and at first she brought the Princess Elizabeth with her to the Chapel, in her purple mourning, holding her new pomander firmly to her nose. It contained a dried orange stuck with cloves and impregnated with other perfumes; the watch set in the filigree case also served its purpose since she could watch the time without seeming to do so.

But she quickly discovered that she had a cold, and did not come again before the coffin was moved in the middle of February to its burial at Windsor. She made up for her

remissness by a very stilted letter in condolence in beautiful
handwriting to her young brother, which tied itself up in such
tortuous expressions that she herself could not quite make out
what she had meant to say; but they greatly impressed
Edward, who wrote back compliments on the elegance of his
'most dear sister's' style. He added that there was evidently
'very little need of my consoling you' and 'I perceive you think
of our father's death with a calm mind,' which made his most
dear sister give a rather lary eye at the paper. Such common
paper too! Was Edward Seymour going to be a skinflint
guardian?

Bess liked being at Chelsea better than anywhere else. The
house was a pleasant, fair-sized mansion, with no pretensions
to a palace, built in the modern fashion of red brick with
chimneys and turrets clustering together, and plenty of tall
windows so that the rooms were filled with light and one
could watch the endless busy movement of the boats sailing
up and down the river and hear the cries of the watermen. She
felt safe and snug as a kitten being looked after by two
motherly cats: her stepmother, Pussy-Cat Purr, and her
governess, or rather her lady-nurse, Cat Ashley, whom her
royal charge regrettably called Ash-Cat, a nickname which it
must be admitted suited Mrs Ashley, a thin sallow woman
with a casual strolling air and a roving eye always ready to
twinkle with entertainment over any scraps of news she might
pick up, and they were many.

She told her charge, sitting in the window-seat looking out
on the river, something of what she had heard at Whitehall of
King Henry's last hours, how he had stared into the shadowy
corners of the room and muttered 'Monks! Monks!' But none

knew whether in remorse at having turned them out of their monasteries, or because at the eleventh hour he had wished in vain for their ministrations. And at the end, when he had lost consciousness and none had thought to see him move even a finger nor hear him speak ever again, he had started up in bed so that all were amazed at his strength, and cried out in a clear voice, 'Nan Bullen' – 'Nan Bullen' – 'Nan Bullen.'

'Yes, three times he called her, and his eyes wide open, staring as if he saw her there, standing before him, and that's the only time he's ever said her name since – since—' and Cat Ashley's eager voice broke on a sob.

Mr Ashley was related to the Bullens, and his wife, dazzled from the first by that lively, go-ahead, essentially modern family, had been as devoted to Nan as she now was to her daughter.

Now at last it was safe to speak of her, now that King Henry, having spoken, had died.

And after his funeral, followed by a procession four miles long, had left for Windsor, Cat Ashley picked up a grisly tale of the coffin having burst the night before the burial and how the plumbers had to come and solder it up again; and this she knew for a fact, for one of them was engaged to her own chambermaid, but of course it was kept quiet, and scarcely any knew of it who attended the magnificent ceremonial next day when Bishop Gardiner preached his most moving sermon on 'the loss to both the high and low of our most good and gracious King'. 'As well he might,' the Ash-Cat declared, her twinkling black eyes rolling round at Bess, 'seeing that it's meant the loss of all his hopes from the Will!'

Bess sat hugging her knees, staring at the rain-scuds flying down the river from the west, feeling very grown-up to be told so many things that she knew she should not be told. But one of them startled her worse than even the horrifying tale of the coffin, and that was when Cat Ashley, pulling a long purple thread through some mourning garment she was making for her, said lightly, 'It's my belief your stepmother will be a widow for even fewer days this time than the last. She must make haste with all her mourning clothes if they're to be ready before she's ordering her wedding dress for the Admiral.'

Bess's knees went taut as whipcord in her grasp. If she did not hold on to them tight she would be springing up to fly at the Ash-Cat, shake her and scream that she was a liar.

She kept silent. Cat Ashley, disappointed in her lack of interest, said, 'Well, and I thought you would be pleased. He'd be your step-stepfather then, and your guardian as like as not.'

'I don't want him as a stepfather,' said Bess, loosening her grip on her knees with a jerk. 'I don't believe the Queen wants him as a husband either. Why should she?'

It was a good move, for Mrs Ashley at once poured out a protesting flood of all the reasons, among them some very flattering to the Admiral, which Bess heard with little painful stabs of pleasure – the finest man in England, so handsome, tall and splendid in his bearing, with none of his brother's cold stateliness but all the more imposing just because he didn't trouble about it; there was a careless magnificence about him, like that of a man born to be King. Fierce as a lion in battle, yet as merry as a schoolboy, and that grand voice of his, it would put courage into a mouse.

'But the Queen – isn't she rather old for him?'

'*That* she's not, at just thirty-four, and he a year or two older, though they neither of them look it. Besides – this had to be a secret while your father lived – I don't know that I'd better even now—'

'Now, my Ash-Cat, hand up your titbit; I'll never stop twisting your tail till you do.'

Bess had seized Ashley's little finger and was pulling it round and round. Laughing and jerking her hand away, Ashley disgorged the titbit; Catherine Parr and Tom Seymour had been privately betrothed before her marriage to the King. When he signified his choice of her as his sixth wife, there was nothing for her to do but to give up Tom, for to have married him against the royal will would have only meant utter ruin and probably death for them both. She had been a faithful wife and devoted nurse to Henry for three and a half years, and he had been the third elderly widower she had had to marry.

Now at last she was free to take her own choice and still young and pretty enough to enjoy it. She had already been having some confidential meetings with the Admiral in London even before the funeral – though that was all quite correct and above-board, since he had been a member of King Henry's household and was now one of the Council of Regency, and had many things to discuss with her about her royal charges. 'But depend upon it, they've found time to discuss their own affairs too, and what I say is, the sooner the merrier: she's a sweet kind creature and deserves her luck, and I wish it with all my heart – don't you too, my Lady Bess?' she added, suddenly surprised by the child's grave silence.

But Bess, having got all she wanted out of Ashley, was quick to assume a reproving air. 'It's a serious matter,' she said, 'and you oughtn't to talk of it, Ashley. Oh, to *me*, yes,' she put in quickly, at Ashley's indignant movement – besides, she might want Ashley to talk again. 'But not to anyone else. The Council may not approve, and I know Edward Seymour hates his brother—'

'So do I, *and* I know why. Jealous!'

'Jealousy is a dreadful thing,' said Bess virtuously.

Ashley gave a quick look at the demure face. 'That's too good to be true. Are you mocking me, my Lady Mischief?'

'No, only myself,' murmured Bess, but went on rapidly, 'At the least, they'd make a horrible scandal if it were talked about so soon after the King's death.'

'Talk? *I* talk! It was only to please Your Highness, and I've found you are to be trusted. You can be sure I would never talk to anyone else, never, on any dangerous matter.'

'Can I, Cat? Can I?' She said it slowly, reflectively, and those clear, light-coloured eyes of hers seemed to Cat to be looking right through her. Was it a child who spoke and looked thus? It was more like some ageless Sibyl.

Cat had flushed to the roots of her hair; she took her young mistress's hand in both of hers and said, as though she were giving the oath of fealty, 'I swear to Your Highness, you can be sure of me.'

Bess leapt up, flicked Ashley on the nose, cried, 'Silly old Ash-Cat, what are you so solemn about? Look! the shower is over and the sun's come out!' and dashed into the garden.

CHAPTER FIVE

It was a large and charming garden, enclosed within its high red brick wall that was only ten years old, but already mellowed to a warm rosy hue, and had small fruit trees splayed against it. Some old trees and shrubs had been allowed to remain, though they interrupted the symmetry of the formal rectangular flowerbeds and knot gardens and paths edged with box hedges a few inches high. In the wall at the far end was set a postern gate which opened on to the reedy marshy fields, bare of hedges but with outcrops of scrub and forest, that spread away into a blue distance of low wooded hills, the heights of Highgate and Hampstead.

And across this open country, by the single road that led through the village of Chelsea to the Manor, Tom Seymour came riding this windy stormy sunny afternoon in late February.

He saw the bright sails of the boats on the Thames scudding as if on dry land beyond the trees, which were still bare and purple-black, but flushed here and there with the palest glimmer of gold; it might have been the willows budding, or only wet twigs in the sunlight. The square stone tower of the church on the riverbank looked almost white against a blue-black stormcloud, for the sun was shining on it, and the golden weathercock flashed through the tossing branches as if some exotic bird had strayed up-river with the seagulls that squalled and swirled around it, making wheels and arrows of white light.

He came to the new red wall of the Manor garden, dismounted and gave his horse's bridle to the groom that rode with him, opened the postern gate with a key that he pulled out of a little purse in his belt; and there he stood for a moment, quite still. The formal flowerbeds were glistening with wet earth, but along the borders crocuses pierced them with little flecks of coloured light. Some hazel shrubs dangled their catkins in the wind in a shimmer of faintly yellow tassels, and a blackbird shouted its early song as it balanced itself precariously on the topmost twig of a taller tree, swinging and bowing to the wind. The small stone fishpond reflected the sunlight in a mirror of gold. Round and round its edge a childish figure in purple silk was running, dancing, leaping, tossing a golden ball high into the air, and catching it again. A gleaming cloud of hair blew out from under her cap as she danced, and she shrieked as the wind blew her ball all but into the pond, retrieved it in a wild, sideways leap, and all but fell in herself, laughed on a note that seemed to answer the blackbird's, and pranced on.

At first glance it was as though one of the crocuses in all its sheen of purple and gold had sprung into human stature and movement. Crocuses and the early song of birds, and a laugh as shrill and wild, and those darting movements, erratic as a dragonfly – what was it they were all bringing back to him? In an instant he had it – an evening in early spring just fourteen years ago, as vivid as if it were this month, and Nan

Bullen's slim form flashing out upon the terrace at Hampton Court, swirling and trailing her bright plumage as she turned from one to another – and then laughed. 'Lord, how I wish I had an apple!... Such an incredible fierce desire to eat apples! Do you know what the King says? He says it means I am with child. But I tell him "No!" No, it couldn't be, no, no, no!'

And again that laugh that had rung on and on in his ears, so that he still seemed at times to hear it, especially on these cold spring evenings so like herself – sudden, harsh, brilliant, changeful.

Thus unceremoniously had the advent of this girl, the Princess Elizabeth, been announced to the world six months before her birth – in a woman's 'No'; not meant to be believed.

And here she was herself, dancing on the verge of womanhood, and till this moment he had not perceived it.

Suddenly she saw him standing there, stopped dead, letting her ball fall to the ground, while she stared as if at a ghost, swooped to pick it up in an action like the plunge of a long-legged foal, and then at last advanced slowly towards him.

'How did you get there?' she asked, almost in a whisper. 'The garden was empty, and now – you've appeared.'

'By magic. You were thinking of me, and I obeyed your wishes.'

'I was *not*!' she exclaimed indignantly.

'No need to toss your head. All those golden catkins on it are tossing hard enough without your help.'

'I call them lambs' tails.' She flung away from him and broke off a couple of their branches. He noticed how abrupt and angular her movements had become again as soon as she ceased to dance, and yet there was still something of that wild grace in them. But what had happened to her manners, and was she angry just because he had startled her? He at once became the magnificent courtier, sweeping his hat to the ground in a low bow.

'I implore pardon for not recognising Your Highness earlier. I took you for a wood nymph and now I see my mistake. You are a great princess – are you not?'

She swung round to him again, her face flaming.

'I won't be mocked,' she said, 'I won't, I won't!' and stamped her foot, all the more like a wilful colt.

He put a hand on her shoulder. 'What's the matter, child? Here's a nice welcome for me after these weeks! I'd hoped day after day to see you at Whitehall, but no, you had a cold and had to keep your bed – your flowerbed I should say,' as she stepped back from him inadvertently over the little box hedge. Even Bess's indignation had to break up in laughter as she shook the wet earth off her heel.

'It was only a church cold,' she said.

'Now do you know I guessed as much! What's your golden apple, my Lady Atalanta?' and he took the pomander ball from her hands. 'Remember that if, like her, you embark on a race for glory, you must never turn aside, as she did, for golden apples.'

Turning it round, he saw the watch-dial set in it and exclaimed, 'Is this how you kill time?'

'It won't go anyway. It stopped' – she paused and stole a look at him under drooping white eyelids, then finished on a note of exquisite melancholy – 'on the night my father died.'

'What a shocking little liar you are! Do you ever say a word you mean, or that you mean anyone to believe?'

'Not often. What is the use?'

He put the pomander back into her hand and his own hand over hers, holding it and the golden ball together, and she shivered at the warm strong grasp. His voice too was warm and strong; what had Ashley said of it – that it would put courage into a mouse? But it did not put courage into her; she wanted to burst into tears, to fling herself into his arms, to fasten herself tight up inside his coat and never have to face the world again; and go on feeling those deep tones tingling through her like the throbbing low notes of a harp.

'What has hurt you, little Princess?'

She struck away his hand and ran from him, turned at the edge of the pond and flung her pomander at him with all her force.

'Catch!' she cried on a high, merry note, but her face was that of a little fury, and she had thrown the hard gold ball to hit, not to be caught.

He dodged it and dashed after her, seized her by the shoulders and swung her round to him. 'You little wild cub!' he exclaimed, laughing, but like her his face was in earnest. And he held her a moment before he spoke again.

'Are you so much a cub after all? It won't be long before you're grown up. Bess, will you marry me?'

'You're laughing at me again.'

'And why not? Can't one marry and laugh?'

'Then you've only just thought of it this moment.'

'What of that? Everything has to have a beginning.'

'It's monstrous, why you're—' No, she must not say she had just heard he was practically betrothed to her stepmother. She finished, 'You're nearly three times as old as me.'

'But in ten years I'll be only twice as old.'

'Ah, you *have* thought of it before! You couldn't have done that sum in your head on the instant.'

'Witch! Will you have me?'

'No.'

'Why not?'

'I'm too young.'

'Not yet husband-high?'

'Oh, as to that!' She had nearly said, 'I'm already as high as the little Queen,' but she changed her ground. 'I shan't think of marrying for years yet, if ever, and I'm in mourning for my father – for two years at least,'

'Tell that to the Merchant Venturers!'

She was casting wildly for her reasons. Suddenly she remembered what she had said to Ashley of himself and the Queen – an objection of even more force in her own case. 'I couldn't marry without the Council's consent – I'd lose my place in the Succession.'

'As much as your place is worth, hey?' He was grinning, but not very pleasantly. 'And why shouldn't they consent?'

'Oh well, there's your brother—'

'There is indeed my brother. I'll see about that. And now answer for yourself. Wouldn't you like me for a husband when you're a little older? Wouldn't you, my tawny lion cub? No claws out now!

"*Noli me tangere*, for Caesar's I am,
And wild for to hold—"'

'Who said that?'

'Tom Wyatt, of your mother. And now another Tom is saying it of you. God's soul, it will be a work to tame you!'

'I'll not be tamed by you or any. I'll be myself alone, always, I—'

He put a hand under her chin and forced it up to shut her mouth. Then he bent slowly, his eyes laughing down into hers, his face came nearer and nearer, she knew he was going to kiss her on that forcibly closed mouth, and she stopped trying to move her head this way and that; she stood breathless, her whole body stiff and taut in expectation.

A woman's voice came ringing out into the garden, soaring on a clear high note of happiness, calling to them, laughing at sight of them, winging towards them, and Queen Catherine came running into the garden.

Bess wriggled furiously, trying to get her chin free of that grip of his finger and thumb, but it held like a vice and the Admiral never stirred.

'Come here, my Pussy-Cat,' he called, 'and tell me how to deal with this vixen of yours.'

He had even taken her nickname for the Queen! Bess was aghast at his impudence – and his duplicity, for here he was laughing with Catherine and telling her practically all he had just been saying to herself, as though it were nothing but a joke, or – far more horrible thought – was it *not* duplicity? Had it really all been only a joke, which she had been fool enough to take seriously?

'I've been asking if she'll have me for a husband when she's older, but she'll have none of me. What's more, she's flung her watch at me – there's a fine way to pass the time!'

He let go of her at last and strolled over to pick up the pomander and show the broken watch in it to Catherine, and Catherine scolded Bess lightly for her carelessness with her possessions, just as though she were a child. But then she was a child again now; they both seemed to think so; they did not mind her being there while they chatted together with gay, friendly intimacy that sometimes dropped on to a tender note and sometimes pranced into flirtation. Yet Catherine did not want her to leave them, she kept her arm round her as they walked, and though she did not bother to bring her into the conversation, she turned to her sometimes with a smile of such happy goodwill that it gave Bess a throb of awed envy, not for what Catherine possessed, but for what she was – so naturally good and kind and unsuspicious, as she herself could never be.

The wind was too cold for sauntering; they went indoors, and Catherine gave the Admiral a posset of mulled wine and spices to warm him after his ride, and still would not let Bess leave them. So she sat on a cushion by Catherine's chair near the fire and played with her new greyhound puppy, and listened to their assured, easy, grown-up voices as they talked on and on, forgetting her (yes, he had even forgotten she was there), and felt unutterably miserable that she was only thirteen and a half.

They talked over Edward's coronation last week. Thank heaven, Catherine said, that Mr Cheke had shown some sense, in spite of being a great scholar, by insisting that the service in the Abbey should be shortened so as not to exhaust the child more than was necessary: as it was, he had been sick from sheer nervousness all over his beautiful pearl-embroidered white waistcoat, even before the procession had started; and after it was all over he had had to go straight to bed instead of sitting up for the splendid banquet Tom Seymour had given to all the Court in his grand new house at Temple Bar – and here she went into a fit of giggles.

'I can't help it,' she gasped out, 'it looked so funny, you and your brother sitting on either side of his empty throne like a couple of watchdogs and glowering at each other across it! My Lord Protector had reason to glower, certainly,' she added with quick tact, 'for you outshone him completely in the procession. What a shout they raised as you rode by. It was like the roar of the sea.'

Tom looked pleased. 'Ah, he laid down plenty of wine for them in the fountains this time, but they'll never shout "Good Old Ned!" for him as they did for "Good Old Hal!"– nor for the boy either,' he added without even troubling to drop his voice, which made Bess certain he had forgotten her presence, for surely even he could not be so incautious as to criticise her brother in front of her?

She had stuck her two branches of lambs' tails into a silver jug on a table and was watching the ghostly shadow of their dangling tassels that the pale sunset light had thrown on the wall. She thought of Edward being sick on his gorgeous Coronation dress – why couldn't he have waited for a basin? Boys had no control. So they wouldn't ever call him 'Good Old Ned.' Would they ever shout 'Good Old Bess' for her? But she didn't like the sound of that – it would be better if it were 'Beautiful Bess' or 'Our Glorious Bess.'

The city children would dress up as angels for her then, and sing, as they had done for Edward:

'Sing up, heart, sing up, heart,
Sing no more down,
But joy in (King Edward) that weareth the crown.'
        (Queen Bess)

It had reminded her of the children playing on the village green at Hatfield:

'Here we go up, up, up.
Here we go down, down, down,'

and she thought that one day her turn might come, and she would be up, up, up, not on a see-saw but on a white pony riding to her Coronation, and a tinsel-winged angel would come flying down (but you could see his wire ropes in the sunlight) from a triumphal arch in Cheapside and give her a purse of a thousand gold pounds, and *she* wouldn't just drop it like a toad as Edward did because it was so heavy. But even Edward had shown pleasure at the tightrope dancer who greeted him with such amazing antics on a cord slung from St Paul's Cathedral to the Dean's door. It was grand sport being crowned; but her envy was the more painful for a throb of pity that Edward had been too tired to enjoy it as she would have done.

Her elders had settled down into a rich comfortable grumble; it was comfortable because they were sharing it so wholeheartedly, but they were both angry and indignant; Tom kept exploding into more and more surprising references to different parts of the Deity's person, and Catherine kept beginning her sentences with 'I should have thought—'

All the arrangements for the new regime seemed to have been just what the late King did not intend. The Council of Regency that he had ordered was being set aside as a completely subservient body to Edward Seymour, who had at once taken supreme power as Protector and got himself created Duke of Somerset, while Tom had been fobbed off with a couple of empty titles, for he was now Lord Sudley and Lord High Admiral – 'God's beard, what's that to me who have been Admiral of the Fleet in good earnest?' And of what account was an extra title or two at a Coronation when everybody got them? Even his bashful second brother, Homely Harry, had had to accept a knighthood to bring him slightly more into line as one of the King's uncles.

But Tom had been given no working share in the Government nor personal control of the King, although, or no doubt because, the King liked him far better than his Uncle Edward. Catherine too had had good reason to expect a share in the Government, for King Henry had once appointed her Queen Regent during his absence in France; the only time a Queen Consort had had the title formally conferred on her. But what she really wanted was to be made personal guardian to the King; she had looked after him more closely than anyone these last few years, nursed him through illness and read his lessons with him; she knew how fond he was of her in his odd way, and that King Henry would have wished her to continue her charge of him.

'It isn't what Hal wished that counts now,' said Tom, 'it's what our precious pious Ned wishes.'

'I should have thought he's pious enough to carry out Hal's wishes. He was there when the King told his nobles to treat me always with as much honour as when he was alive – when he said I was to keep the jewels he'd given me.' And suddenly she gave a sharp cry, 'Oh, the jewels! I've just thought! I left them at Whitehall.'

'God's blood, why didn't you keep a hold of them?'

'I didn't think of them, or anything else except getting here as fast as we could. I could hardly wait for my maids to pack. All those horrible whispers at Whitehall—' she shuddered and hid her face in her hands. 'You know they say the King was dead three days before—' She broke off and laid a hand on Bess's shoulder.

'Yes, I knew that too, Madam,' said Bess, and looked across her in cool challenge at Tom Seymour.

So he had not told Catherine how she had met him on the night the King died. But he paid her no attention; the jewels were worrying him far more.

'You were mad to leave them behind,' he said. 'I'll get them for you at once, before my sweet sister-in-law puts a claw on them.'

'She *could* not, Tom. They're the King's jewels.'

'Couldn't she! You don't know our new Duchess, our Lady Protectress! She'd say she's protecting them for *this* King. And Ned would back her.' His blue eyes were brilliant with anger under their dark brows; he sprang up, swearing torrentially, and looked round for his cloak.

'Where are you going?' she cried in distress.

'To Whitehall and the whole Protectorate pack. I have a deal to say to them.'

He strode over to Bess and patted her head. 'What else shall I say to them, my Lady Bess? Shall I ask them for your hand?'

She swung up her arm with a slap at his face, and he caught it by the wrist.

'So here it is, you've given me it already.'

He lightly kissed her hand and then the top of her head, and in another moment he was gone, Catherine pattering out beside him, plucking at his sleeve, begging him to be cautious, her tone half laughing and wholly loving.

Bess was left alone. She raised her eyes to the wall and saw the shadowed pattern of her branches fade fainter and fainter as the light died, until it disappeared and the wall was blank.

CHAPTER SIX

Four days later, Catherine told Bess that she and Tom
Seymour would marry as soon as it was possible for her, so
recent a royal widow, to do so. They had just become
formally betrothed, with rings and a written contract of
marriage, but this would have to be kept the closest of secrets
while Tom set about getting the consent of the Council to it.
She had written to him to wait two years, but he had
scratched out 'years' and changed it to two months.

She looked anxiously at the wooden little face in front of
her, pale, with the mouth set in a determined line and the eyes
regarding her so steadily yet blankly; Catherine could not see
what lay behind them. Surely she liked Tom; Catherine could
not imagine any woman of whatever age failing to do so, and
he was so charming with her, teasing her so gaily, and really
fond of her too. She did want this odd difficult girl to be glad
of their marriage, to know that her home would be with them
for as long as she wanted it. She said this last, and Bess
thanked her, and then remembered to smile and said she could
not imagine any home as home without her Pussy-Cat Purr on
the hearth. Catherine, feeling baffled, admitted that it was
indeed extraordinarily soon for her to be planning her next
marriage, only a month after the King's death had been made

public; she told her of her previous betrothal to Tom and how all thought of it had had to be laid aside at the King's command to her to be his wife.

Bess thought, 'Why does she tell me all this, and of her betrothal now, when if I were foolish or treacherous it might bring ruin to them both?' How silly women were, always telling each other things, however dangerous! She would never tell any woman anything; even if it were not dangerous, what was the use? You never knew what the other might be thinking about it. Here was she thinking all sorts of angry, contemptuous things about Tom Seymour, while her stepmother prattled on in her artless fashion about his wonderful loyalty and constancy in having waited for her these long three and a half years, and never wanting to marry anyone else, though he might have made such brilliant matches.

'Such brilliant matches,' thought Bess, 'to a King's daughter and second in succession to the throne'; yes, he had wanted that; and if she were as foolishly girlish as her stepmother she would now be telling her so, and causing all sorts of mischief for all of them.

But had Tom really wanted it, or had he only been playing at it?

Her questions tormented her. Catherine, looking down at her shut face, asked her what she was thinking.

'That I should be happy, Madam, ever to find a tenth part of the happiness you deserve.'

It was far too good to be satisfactory.

Catherine with a sigh went over to her little Italian escritoire and began to write to Tom. Within three minutes she had forgotten that odd difficult girl as she scribbled in hot haste, her face flushing and her breath coming faster in delicious excitement.

'I pray you be not offended with me in that I write sooner to you than I said I would, for my promise was for but once in a fortnight. Howbeit, the weeks are shorter at Chelsea than in other places.' She smiled broadly at the excuse, and indeed she had a better; she must tell him that his brother Edward had said he would answer all her requests about her jewels, etc., when he came to see her, which he had said more than once he would do, and had not done. 'I think his wife has taught him that lesson, for it is her custom to promise many comings to her friends and to perform none.'

Then, having signed it in a hurry, she remembered all the things she really wanted to say, and a P.S. followed, longer than the letter, telling him how she had always wanted to marry him, 'before any man I know.' She had had to give up her will, and now God had given her it again – 'God is a marvellous man.'

And then she remembered that she must tell him if he visited her here in secret he must come so early in the morning as to be gone again before seven o'clock when anyone was about, and to come always by the postern gate in the garden and the lonely marshy road across the fields over the footbridge that was ominously named Bloody Bridge from the number of murders committed there by highwaymen – a terrible precaution, when he must ride alone in the dark hours to preserve their secret, but the danger from highway robbers to such as Tom was nothing to the danger of the Council – and the Duchess, his brother's wife.

But God would protect him, God was a marvellous man, the birds were singing their mating songs high and glad through the sunny window, and Catherine felt no fears as her quill pen scratched on; and behind her her stepdaughter sat on her low stool with her face cupped in her long hands, and listened to that scratching and the songs of the mating birds and wondered whether, if she had been a woman grown, Tom Seymour would have deserted his loving Catherine for herself.

The weeks were short at Chelsea, and elsewhere. Everything seemed to move twice as quick now the old King was dead and men dared to put their plans into action as fast as the changes in nature. The spring rushed on, the flowers rushed on, the birds picked off the heads of the crocuses, but the daffodils shot up in their place, the birds built nests, and the nobles houses.

Edward Seymour decided that as Lord Protector and Duke of Somerset he must have a London palace worthy of himself, and pulled down the north aisle of St Paul's Cathedral (which contained the elder Holbein's pictures of the Dance of Death), the Priory of St John of Jerusalem at Clerkenwell, and a couple of Inns of Court, all in order to furnish space and materials for Somerset House.

So of course his brother Tom was not going to be outdone in the housing matter, which had hitherto given him no concern, for he had always preferred to live in lodgings when in London, changing them frequently, but always taking his adoring old mother to keep house for him wherever he moved. But now he too decided that his dignity as Lord Sudley and Lord High Admiral demanded a fine house in his name, though characteristically he could not wait to build one. His brother for once was really sensible and pleasant about it, for 'good old Ned' promptly turned a bishop out of his house and confiscated the best part of his property, so that Tom should have a huge mansion all ready to hand, with stables, tennis-courts and bowling-greens in the Strand, orchards and meadows and terraced gardens leading down to the river, and call it Seymour Place. He was already installed in it a fortnight after the proclamation of Henry's death, and the whole vast place was humming with activity and gaiety, banquets, sports and water-parties.

Spring was in the air; even tutors and bishops, even vice-chancellors, even archbishops, bore testimony to it, and with them half the clergy. Bishop Parker, Vice-Chancellor of Cambridge, rode off to get married to the young woman who had waited patiently for him for seven years. For Cranmer had at once pushed forward Parliament's edict to legalise matrimony for the clergy, and produced his German Frau in the open, to everyone's rather malicious curiosity. It was extraordinary how difficult it was to avoid references to packing-cases in her presence. Tom Seymour did not try; he at once asked her what she thought of that little box of a palace at Lambeth.

Curates and parish priests all over the country were rushing to get married, but the results were not always as happy as the bridegrooms, for their parishioners frequently sent in complaints of their choice: that these new young wives were either too frivolous and got their husbands into debt, or else they poked their noses into the affairs of the parish, in which they should have no business. Finally it was decided to pass another edict, declaring that all clergymen's prospective wives should first have to be passed as suitable by a bishop and two Justices of the Peace.

It was well they had not also to be approved by the Duchess, for her antagonism to poor John Cheke's new wife would have lost him his place as the King's tutor had he not written letters that fairly crawled in apology for her, both to the Duke of Somerset and his exigeant lady.

Among all these mating and nesting plans, those of Tom Seymour, both for himself and others, threatened more upheaval than those of all the clergy. For a boy-King's uncle who married the Queen Dowager of England would form a great counter royal house which might well bring about another civil war. His elder brother had already taken on a practically royal authority, given himself powers to act independently of the Council's advice, used the royal 'we' even in his private correspondence, and alarmed everybody by his presumption in addressing the new French King as 'Brother'. (For Foxnose François died at the end of that March, having been as much dashed by Henry's death as Henry had been by François' dying illness; the lifelong rivalry had ended without either of them finally succeeding in getting the better of the other.)

Somerset House and Seymour Place already looked like dividing not only half London but all England between them. 'You *must* go warily,' Queen Catherine told Tom Seymour, who wagged his finger against his fine nose and promised he would be as wily as the serpent and as gentle as the dove – which gave her more amusement than hope.

But he was being more wily than she knew. One proof of it,

though not to her guileless eyes, was that little Lady Jane Grey came to stay at Seymour Place with her tutors and her servants and her personal possessions, in charge of Tom Seymour and his mother. Catherine was delighted, for this would mean her having the charge of Jane's tuition as soon as she was openly married to Tom; the child was far from happy at home; the country air of Chelsea with the sea-breezes coming up the river, and the companionship of her gay playfellow Elizabeth, would do her a world of good. In fact, Jane had already grown a whole new crop of freckles in her first week at Seymour Place, and her small nose was quite covered by them, so much more time did she spend out of doors.

Jane's freckles were not Tom Seymour's prime motive; nor, when Catherine demanded with ingenuous admiration how he had managed to persuade Jane's parents, did he confide to her that he had paid Jane's impecunious father a lump sum down of £2,000 as an extra inducement to place his daughter in Tom's care.

And he had bigger bait than that to offer: the opportunity and influence he would have as Edward's favourite uncle to push forward a match for him with Jane Grey. The Protector might succeed at any moment in marrying the boy either to his own daughter Janet or to the little Queen of Scots; nobody was sure which he favoured most; he was indeed not quite sure himself, for his desire for England's peace and prosperity and unity with Scotland was sometimes almost as strong as, sometimes even stronger than his desire for his own personal advancement.

So, as Tom was quick to point out to Jane's anxious father,

with the odds against them on not only one but a pair of fillies for the matrimonial stakes, they must move quickly to get Jane into the running. He would work it with the boy, he could do anything with him, he told Henry Grey, a nervous pallid little man, overshadowed by his stout Grey mare, the hard-eyed, hard-riding Lady Frances, with the red hardening to purple in her fat cheeks (King Henry's niece, so that it was she who gave Jane her claim to the throne, and never let her husband forget it). He trotted along in the terraced gardens by the river in vain effort to keep step with the Lord High Admiral's long strides, and peered up at the wagging point of his burnished beard, at the gay blue eyes, and warmed himself in the ringing confidence of that great voice; while Tom, looking down at the thin moustaches, the long nose and absurdly high collar, longed to tell his fellow-conspirator that he looked like a seedy mule peering over a wall.

The Admiral's first step was to introduce a valuable servant of his own, not inappropriately named Mr Fowler, into the King's household, and was pleased to hear that Edward often asked about him and when Fowler thought he could see him. Fowler, under instructions, asked if the King didn't think it strange that his younger uncle had never married. Edward, not having thought, did not answer. Fowler then asked if he would like him to marry.

'Oh, very much,' was the bored reply as he tried to tie his spaniel's ears over the top of its head.

Well, then, to whom?

'Anne of Cleves,' said Edward automatically. It was always a safe answer.

The spaniel yelped. So did Mr Fowler, almost. 'Your royal

father called her a Flanders mare,' he said reproachfully.

'What's wrong with a Flanders mare? I wish I had one. I'm tired of ponies.' Then an impish gleam came into his eyes and he swung round from the spaniel, who at once leapt up for more teasing. 'No, d'you know what? I wish he'd marry my sister Mary and get her away from her old Mass.' And he gave a shrill crow of unaccustomed laughter that suddenly robbed him of his chill bewildered royalty and turned him into a mischievous schoolboy.

'Poor brat!' Tom exclaimed in a burst of pitying affection when he heard of it. '*I'll* make him laugh when I get at him!' He could do anything with his nephew – if he could get at him. But that was the difficulty. Edward was being kept at his lessons harder than he had ever been kept before. Even when he was not at them, the Protector or one of his most trusted intimates was always with him; his own sisters could hardly ever see him by himself, and to Elizabeth, on one of the very rare occasions when they managed to give his guardians the slip, he burst out in fretful annoyance that he was scarcely ever alone for as much as half a quarter of an hour. And this particular occasion was won only by a glorious adventure.

She had been allowed to come and see him, but an excuse had been found to prevent Queen Catherine coming too to visit her stepson as she had wished, and Mrs Ashley was in attendance on her. The two children conversed solemnly in front of her and a couple of under-tutors (not Mr Cheke) and a major-domo of the Protector's. Then Elizabeth showed off for a bit in Latin, and Edward first matched her easily in it, then branched off into Greek, at which she fell rather behind and made an attempt to catch up in Hebrew, but again the honours were easy, so she shot into Italian, wherein she was really fluent and Edward far behind. The tutors, applauding her, excused themselves for the King's backwardness by declaring that they had nothing to do with his Italian lessons and made no pretence themselves of proficiency in the language.

On this assurance Bess slipped in a sentence or two in a 'little language' that they had long ago made up together out of a mixture of baby-talk, private slang and Latin or Italian-sounding endings to the words. It would not carry them far, but enough for her to ask him if they could not talk alone, and for him to tell her that he might manage it with his fellows if she would get rid of Mrs Ashley. He then said in English that he would like a game of shuttlecock with her, and they went out into the courtyards at the back of the Palace. He would not play in the closed-in tennis-courts; it was a lovely evening and he wanted to be out of doors. On the way there Bess had whispered to Mrs Ashley, who now said she had a cold and must not dawdle about in the raw evening air and went indoors. The major-domo had not come out, and the tutors walked up and down discussing the scandalous innovation of the modern pronunciation of Greek which Mr Cheke, as Greek professor at Cambridge, was bent on introducing. It was said that Archbishop Cranmer backed him up – that showed what excesses Reform could lead to!

Suddenly Edward drove the shuttlecock far over their heads into a tree, and then found it was the only one he had brought.

'Fetch me more,' he shouted to the tutors, who began to call to a page who was passing, but Edward stamped his foot and roared, 'Fetch them yourselves! You'd have done it fast enough for my father.'

That sent them scurrying, each trying to outrun the other, and as they whisked out at one end of the courtyard Edward seized Bess's hand and ran out at the other, into a yard where there was a mountainous woodpile. He clambered over it, she followed unquestioning, and into a hollow that had been cleared among the logs, where they squatted down completely hidden.

'I've come here once or twice with Barney,' he told her. Young Barnaby (Barney at home) Fitzpatrick, three or four years older than Edward, was the son of an Irish peer, Lord Ossory; he had left the wild hills of Donegal some years before and become Edward's favourite school- and play-fellow, and on rare occasions his whipping-boy. The gay coolness and lack of resentment with which the Irish boy took the beatings that were beneath the dignity of his royal master seemed to Edward the perfect example of knightly valour and endurance; it was entirely fitting that Barnaby should have been chosen to bear the banner of King Arthur, riding in a black coat, as one of the nine youthful henchmen at King Henry's funeral.

'I hope Barney won't mind my showing this place to you,' he continued rather doubtfully, to Bess's surprise, for he was not wont to be so careful of the feelings of others, 'but anyway I am glad you made me think of it. I am sick of being treated like a baby—'

'Like a prisoner,' said Bess.

He shot her a quick look. 'So it is. Let them wait, that's all. I'll show them something when I'm really King.'

'You're that now. Look how you sent those Peeping Toms packing. It was just like our father.'

He flushed with pleasure. The ogre for whom even Edward had felt some fear and repulsion as well as unwilling fascination was already becoming a legend, a symbol for superb power. 'You think I'll ever be like him?' he asked wistfully.

'Not as fat, I hope!' she laughed.

'Hush! Someone might come near enough to hear you. Oh Bess, it's good to hear you laugh again.'

'Why, at Chelsea we are always laughing, and so would you if you were there. Why shouldn't you be allowed to see your own sister?'

'Or my stepmother or my own uncle?' he capped her, with an indignant wriggle that had disastrous consequences, for a bole in the wood caught and tore his beautiful silk trunk-hose, but they neither of them bothered about that.

'Look,' he said urgently, 'the Admiral often goes to visit the Queen at Chelsea, doesn't he?'

'Oh, once or twice he's been, think,' said Bess airily.

Edward took this very coolly. 'I expect he goes, and you must see them there, so when next you do, give him this. It's surer than sending it by Fowler as I'd meant to do. You can read them.' And he thrust into Bess's hand two rather crumpled, dirty scraps of paper on which he had scrawled in haste, unlike Edward's usual tidy writing, except for the upright precise signature, with the flourish like a whip at top of the final 'd':

'My Lord, send me per Fowler, as much as you think good. Edward'; and

'My Lord, I thank you and pray you have me commended to the Queen.'

'Better,' he observed, 'to send 'em per you.'

'Perhaps.'

'Oh well,' he chuckled, 'I've made good use of old Fowler, leaving notes to the Admiral for him to find under the carpet in the dining-room.'

It struck Bess that it was the Admiral who was making use of Fowler.

'Does he send you money by Fowler?' she asked, trying not to sound astonished.

'Yes, it was he who thought of it – my Uncle Tom, I mean. Oh, I know it doesn't seem very kingly,' and the boy's fair face went a deep pink, 'but am I treated like a King? I've so little pocket-money, I've none to give presents to my servants – not even to Barney when he gets a thrashing for me. Why, do you know what the Admiral said when he heard that, the first time I had a chance to talk to him? He laughed and said, "It's a very beggarly King you are! Not a penny to play with nor give to your servants!" And he handed me forty pounds straight off.'

'How like him!' exclaimed Bess, glowing.

'Yes, he's given me a deal more. And I've shown him favour in return. I've insisted he shall attend me sometimes at Court, and I'm going to see him when I wish, by myself, and I will not be interrupted.'

The royal favour seemed of a dubious nature to Bess if his interviews with his uncle were only to produce pocket-money for himself. 'That will make the Protector jealous of him,' she said. 'You may have to stand up for one uncle against the other.'

'I am doing so,' said Edward magnificently, and suddenly she was struck by the significance of that second bit of scrubby paper. Edward had written a message for the Queen expressly for the Admiral to give her; then had the Admiral confided his secret plan of marriage to the child so as to get his backing for it? It was an odd conspiracy, between a man of thirty-five and a boy of nine and a half. She wished she knew how much Edward knew; but she would at least be on safe ground if she spoke of Queen Catherine's love for Edward himself, how she missed him, wished she were still supervising his lessons and seeing to it that he did not work too hard. Edward conceded placidly that he knew the Queen was very fond of him; he added that he was very fond of her, and would much rather be with her than his Aunt Anne, the Duchess, who was always saying nasty things about her, and about the Admiral too.

They had been talking very fast, but now already they heard voices in the distance calling in search of them, and Edward spoke still more quickly, gripping his sister's knee with his thin little hand. 'I want Uncle Tom to be my guardian instead of Uncle Edward, and to be Protector too. He'd be a much finer one. Then I could live with him and the Queen when they marry, and do as I like. Why shouldn't I? I'm the King.'

'When they marry...?'

'Yes, it's my wish. I told him so and he seemed quite willing. Then I could live with her and him and you, and we'd all be together and I could get rid of Uncle Edward. Don't you think it a good idea of mine?'

'Very good,' said Bess rather soberly, 'if it can be done.' So the Admiral had been clever enough to make Edward suggest the marriage himself and think it all his own plan!

He was evidently preening himself as a match-maker. '*I'll* help them and stand by them. *They* are sure to try and stop it. How dare they, if I give my consent? Tell her I give it, that I want her to marry him. I'll write to her when I get the chance.'

Bess wondered how she could warn him tactfully to be careful. The Admiral did not seem to have done it at all.

'The Protector is very powerful,' she said.

Edward suddenly flared up. 'Who is he, I'd like to know? Just Edward Seymour, that's all. He'd be nobody if he wasn't my uncle; everything he's got is through me, and yet he behaves as though he were King and I nobody. Nothing is as I want, only as he wants. I'll show him who he is some day, by God's soul I will!'

Nothing could have more displayed the influence Tom Seymour had already won over the child in his brief stolen interviews than his favourite oath piping out of the prim little mouth. Edward swearing was like Jane talking about her parents' company as hell; people were often oddly unlike themselves. An Uncle Tom's Edward might become something very different and, to Bess anyway, far more attractive than the Uncle Ned's Edward, even though in revolt, which was all he had the chance to be at present.

The seeking voices had died away, calling in the distance. Edward cautiously reared his head above the logs. 'The coast's clear. Better take our chance before the search thickens. We'll go by Barney's secret way.'

Bess clambered after him; they crept along by a wall, climbed in through a little window, ran along a passage, her heart thumping at the sound of scullions' voices in the kitchens, and her ironic sense telling her that it was an odd entry into his palace for the absolute monarch that Edward had just so proudly shown himself.

A minute later they were seated on the window-sill of the room where they had first met, and, as the door opened, conversing brightly in Latin on the advanced views of Bishop Hooper of Gloucester, that surplices, like copes and chasubles, were 'the rags of the Harlot of Babylon'.

It was not only the tutors who entered and Mrs Ashley, sniffing atrociously, either in continued pretence of her cold or in genuine tears, for with them was that redoubtable lady the Protector's wife, the new Duchess of Somerset, her fine eyes snapping in fury and alarm, her tall elegant form wiredrawn with agitation. To her torrent of angry questions Edward replied calmly that he had wearied of waiting for the shuttlecocks and returned to the Palace for a little religious discussion 'with my sweet sister, Temperance'.

The Duchess only just suppressed rapping out one of the oaths that were familiar to all who knew her in the hunting-field, and demanded the reason for this preposterous new name for the Princess Elizabeth.

'It suits her,' said Edward. 'Temperance is a fair and godly thing in women. I would more of them had it.'

Bess held her hands together to keep from clapping. The Duchess's thin face was nearly purple, all its hard beauty had gone from it – 'she looks like a meat-chopper,' thought Bess – and then the Duchess's voice rang out on a new icy note of rage as she enquired if it were in godly conversation that the King had torn his stockings? Edward looked down at his legs, baffled, but his sister came to his defence.

'There is a nail sticking out on that chair,' she said. 'That is why we came over to the window-seat.'

The nail could not be found. The Duchess fumed. Bess, watching her in delight, said in a voice of soft concern, 'Perhaps, Madam, the King my brother might wear some of the late Lord Surrey's stockings?'

'And now,' she sobbed out to Queen Catherine, when she had got home and told her adventures and already counted the cost of that delicious rapier-thrust, 'now she will never allow me to see him again if she can help it.'

Edward did write to his stepmother, who between tears and laughter showed the letters to Elizabeth. They were extremely fatherly; they gave his blessing on her marriage and exhorted her to 'persevere in always reading the Scriptures, for in so doing you show the duty of a good wife and a good subject'; they thanked her heartily for her gentle obedience to his royal advice to accept the Admiral as a wooer, and assured her that 'he is of so good a nature that he will not be troublesome to you'. And he promised the lovers his protection and to 'so provide for you both that if hereafter any grief befall, I shall be sufficient succour to you'.

'And he will not have his tenth birthday for four months yet!' exclaimed Catherine.

In contrast with his elderly style, the Princess Mary's blunt refusal to the Admiral to use her influence in their favour seemed quite schoolgirlish.

'I refuse in any way to be a meddler in this matter,' she wrote to him, though glad to help him in anything else, *'wooing matters set apart, wherein, being a maid, I am not cunning'* (even the emphatic underlining suggested the raw girl). She showed very plainly that she was both shocked and hurt that Catherine could contemplate marriage so soon, undeterred by 'the remembrance of the King's Majesty, my father...who is as yet very rife in my own remembrance'.

That was Mary all over, prudish, sentimental, clinging to the past, blind to facts (for no one had better reason to know what horror the remembrance of the King held for his widow), but doggedly honest. No one would ever get a promise out of Mary that she did not mean to keep. 'Poor lady,' sighed Catherine while her lover swore at Mary for a rude old maid: '"To be plain with you"! – hardly necessary to tell us that, when she can never be anything else!' he growled.

Mary maintained her tone when at last the marriage was made public by the end of June, and presently wrote to Elizabeth begging her to come and live with her at her manor-house of Kenninghall in Norfolk, so that the two royal sisters should join together in showing their disapproval of the behaviour of their father's widow.

Elizabeth giggled. Nothing would induce her to leave the delights of her homes in or near London, now grown so gay and exciting with the Admiral as their acknowledged head, for the dank marshy misty place in the wilds of the Norfolk fens, with her strict elderly sister in charge of her instead of the easy-going Catherine. But whatever happened, she must not offend Mary; every time Edward had a cold or a bad headache, the behaviour of the Court to Mary, as heir to the throne, showed her that.

So she had to pass her first real test in diplomatic

correspondence, and settled down to it at her little escritoire with such lively enjoyment that her tongue kept stealing out all the time she was writing, and curling round the corners of her smiling mouth so that, as the Admiral declared on coming into the room, she looked like a sly sandy kitten licking her lips over stolen cream.

'And what is it you're writing? Your first love-letter, I'll be bound, to make you so smug! Come, confess, which of the pages have you seduced?'

He looked over her shoulder, but she had put her hands over the paper; he pulled them away, the inkstand overturned, she shrieked in indignation, snatching up the precious letter, and he chased her round the room for it. Catherine came running at her cries and scolded them both like a pair of naughty children, and the Admiral defended himself, saying he had got to supervise their ward's conduct and how could he, if she carried on a clandestine correspondence with the grooms?

'I don't!' shrieked Bess. 'The letter's to my sister Mary.'

'Tell that to the Beef-eaters! Would anyone write to your sister Mary grinning all over their face? Let's see what merry jests you've put in it!'

'No, no, the jest's to me only. No one else can see it. No one *shall* see it. Give it back, give it me!'

She was chasing him now, for he'd snatched the paper out of her hand and was holding it at arm's length above his head far out of her reach while he dodged round the furniture and finally behind the Queen, darting out first on one side of her, then the other, while Bess put her arms round her stepmother's plump little figure to try and catch him behind it.

'Ouch! You're squeezing me to death between you,' Catherine gasped out, laughing. 'Stop teasing the child and give her back her letter.'

'Read it yourself then first, Cathy, or I'll not be responsible!'

'No, *no*!' shouted Bess, stamping her foot in a real rage by now. 'She's *not* to, nor you. It's my letter. Give it back.'

He fluttered it above her head, making her jump for it like a dog; at last he let her snatch it from him and she fled from the room clasping it to her breast. He turned to Catherine, suddenly dropping his fooling.

'Is it safe to let her send it without our reading it? We've got to be careful with Mary – so has Bess. It's a ticklish position.'

'Dear heart,' said Catherine, smiling at him as though he were a cross between God and her imbecile child, 'I'd trust Bess to deal with a ticklish position rather better than yourself!'

Bess, reading her letter in the beautiful flowing handwriting that her tutors had taught her, would have concurred. She had pretended entire agreement with her 'very dear sister' while refusing to do anything she asked; shared her 'just grief in seeing the ashes or rather the scarcely cold body of the King our father so shamefully dishonoured' by their stepmother's marriage. (Yes it would have been awkward if Catherine had read that! though she would have understood why Bess had to write it.)

And now came the cream of the jest, though, as she had just said, for herself alone: 'I cannot express to you how much affliction I suffered when I was first informed of this marriage.' (True enough that, in all conscience! No wonder she had grinned as she wrote in amused appreciation of her insincere candour.) Sincerity broke in also when she wrote of the Queen's 'so great affection and so many kind offices' to herself, but these were advanced only in excuse for Bess having to 'use much tact in manoeuvring with her for fear of appearing ungrateful for her benefits'. It was the nearest she dared get to reminding Mary that she, too, owed her stepmother gratitude for her kindness.

But she did manage with consummate aplomb to warn her 'dearest sister' (why did that look so much more affectionate when it came in the middle of a letter?) of the folly of 'running heavy risk of making our own lot much worse than it is; at least, so I think. We have to deal with too powerful a party, who have got all authority into their hands, while we, deprived of power, cut a very poor figure at Court,' – a pathetic picture of two royal Cinderellas that made its writer, in the midst of a whirl of festivities, chuckle happily.

And here Bess did make a bad slip, carried away by her own worldly advice to the woman of over thirty. 'I think, then,' she wrote, 'that the best course we can take is that of dissimulation... If our silence does us no honour, at least it will not draw down upon us such disasters as our lamentations might induce.'

The letter was a perfect piece of diplomacy – if only it had been addressed to the right person. But a letter is a joint affair, depending almost as much upon its reader as its writer. The determined honesty, the loathing of compromise, that Mary had inherited from her mother, without any of her mother's tact, made her quite incapable of taking warning from Bess's reminders of the harm her protests might do to herself.

But the warning she did take was of Bess herself, that inscrutably smiling girl, just on fourteen, who could so complacently accept it 'if our silence do us no honour'; who could so cynically plan, 'the best course we can take is that of dissimulation'.

And Mary would remember that warning to the end of her life.

CHAPTER SEVEN

Young Edward, not content with writing good advice and assurances of his patronage to his elders, and terse demands for cash to be slipped under carpets, also kept a Journal.

It was Mr Cheke's idea, and it gave him a pleasing sense of importance to write it, sitting at his little desk which was covered with black velvet, so as not to show the inkstains (an economical notion of the Duchess); it contained fascinating inner compartments and secret drawers where he could store his treasures; some buttons of agate and gold, some strange new instruments that showed the signs of the zodiac and the movements of the stars (Edward liked stars); a cormorant's egg which Barnaby had brought him from the Donegal cliffs; and half a dozen dog collars of red and white leather, a present from Cuthbert Vaughan, his Master of the Dogs.

There he sat in 'the Kynge's secret studie' at Westminster, the only place where he could feel himself in undisputed command of a kingdom, looking out on the busy river and on the further shore the gardens and towers of Lambeth Palace where Archbishop Cranmer sat writing, just as busily as himself, at the new English Prayer Book, that staggering innovation that was to make a new religion, a new England, and all the great men in the land would contribute something to it; Edward would himself. Already his only title for it was 'the Book of my proceedings'.

Meanwhile he wrote his Journal. And on the same page as his account of the 'great preparation mad to goe into Scotland' by the Lord Protector and other great nobles, to carry out King Henry's dying wishes to have the Scots finally and thoroughly smashed, he put the briefest of records of his uncle Tom Seymour's marriage to the Queen, 'with wich mariag' (spelling was not yet stabilised, especially Edward's) 'the Lord Protectour was much offended'.

But as the Scottish campaign was carrying the Lord Protector away from this domestic scene of action, he had at first to leave hostilities to that keen lieutenant, his wife. The Duchess instantly attacked with full batteries of abuse which did not spare even that national monument the late King.

'Did not King Henry marry Catherine Parr in his doting days, when he had brought himself so low by his lust and cruelty that no lady that stood on her honour would venture on him?' Whereas she herself was not only the wife of the Duke of Somerset and Lord Protector of England, but the great-great-granddaughter, on her mother's side, of the tenth son of Edward III. It was nothing to her that the progeny of that enormous family would soon make it quite difficult for any gentry *not* to be descended from Edward III; she looked on herself as the one and only Plantagenet, and it was a gross personal insult that she should have to bear the train of the Queen Dowager who was really only Catherine Parr, a nobody, 'now casting herself for support on a younger brother. If Master Admiral teach his wife no better manners, I am she that will.'

And that Impossible She proceeded to teach her new sister-in-law manners by jostling her in the doorway at State functions and fairly stampeding out of the room so as to take precedence of her and avoid bearing her train. 'Exceeding violent' was the verdict of the astonished witnesses, and, in the opinion of one sly observer, this business of the Queen's train was kicking up so much dust that it might well end in smothering both their husbands.

For Tom could also be exceeding violent; he swore with loud and terrible oaths that 'no one should speak ill of the Queen, or he would take his fist to the ears of those who did, from the lowest to the highest.' Which gave to many a reasonable hope of seeing him box the Duchess's ears, or perhaps even the Duke's.

The Court was beginning to take sides, and furiously. Nearly everybody there was finding the Duchess's 'many imperfections intolerable, her pride monstrous'. Ned Seymour had always been an almost oppressively upright and conscientious man; but no one could trust a man ruled by such a wife, and many said that in his quieter way he was becoming almost as bad. He had set aside the conditions of the late King's will almost before the breath was out of his body and taken his supreme power by a *coup d'etat*; he was destroying churches, even parts of St Paul's, to build himself Somerset House – the churches did not matter, they were fair game and everyone was doing it, but St Paul's was more than a church, it was the City, it was London itself; and Somerset House was more than a house, it was a palace bigger than anybody else, even a King, had ever had.

Worst of all, the fellow would make speeches; beautiful

speeches, which nobody could make head or tail of; speeches about liberty and freedom of speech for all men, about religious toleration and free discussion as the best way to settle all problems, and not merely of religion either. He had not only repealed all the laws against heresy but most of those against treason too; a man might now even impugn the Royal Supremacy in speech, though not in writing. It was plain asking for trouble and rebellion, and as if this were not enough, he was actually going against his own class, encouraging discontent among the common people, for that was what would come of his taking their side against their landlords in his attempts to give them back their common lands. For centuries they had been allowed to graze their sheep and cattle on them, but they had now been enclosed for the use of the big landowners, who were bristling like hedgehogs at the idea of giving them back to the people.

Let him try out his fool notions on religion if he must; but property, that was another matter, that was sacred.

And now here he was doing his youngest brother out of the property that was rightly, even legally, his and his wife Catherine's. A fellow that could trick his younger brother out of his own, that showed you what the fellow was really like.

For in the midst of all these mutterings and growlings was heard that magnificent voice of Tom Seymour.

'My brother is wondrous hot in helping every man to his right, save me! He makes a great matter of preventing my having the Queen's jewels, which you see by the whole opinion of the lawyers ought to belong to me, and all under pretence that he would not the King should lose so much – as if it were a loss to the King to let me have mine own!'

Even the Queen's wedding ring had been robbed from her, he told Fowler as he sat drinking in the privy buttery; and Mr Fowler sighed piously and said (or said afterwards that he said), 'Alas, my lord, that ever jewels or muck of this world should make you begin a new matter between my Lord Protector and you!' At which my lord roared for his boots and rode away.

And his wife Catherine, who had been so careless of the 'muck of this world' when she had fled the Palace of Whitehall in those haunted days of last January, was now as eager and indignant about the jewels as he. To her they were no capricious gift of King Henry's doting days, but her just wages for three and a half years' devoted service as his sicknurse, a job that few women would indeed have willingly ventured on.

And it was not only the jewels, and not only King Henry's gifts. Catherine's favourite country manor of Fasterne had been grabbed by methods even more flagrant. The Protector, or again his Duchess, had without its owner's consent, coolly installed a tenant in it who paid the bare minimum of rent (and presently ceased doing even that) and refused even to allow her to graze her cattle in its park, so that she had to pay farmers for their pasturage – and this at the same time that the Protector was proposing to reform the grievance of the enclosures and to give the grazing lands back to the people! Charity, or rather justice, should begin at home, said Tom loudly; and even his gentle Cathy wrote to her husband that it was lucky his elder brother was away at the moment, 'for else I believe I should have bitten him'.

But she fully intended to utter all her rage against the

Protector to him in front of the King, 'if you do not give me advice to the contrary,' – as if it were likely Tom should ever give her such advice! Now that she was married to him she was so deep in love that she was coming to rely utterly on him in all matters, with the abandonment of a woman entirely happy and satisfied for the first time in thirty-five years and four marriages. Any doubts she had ever felt as to his perfect moderation in temper or judgment had been cast to the winds; she was now young for the first time, young and foolish, glorying in feeling so and in looking up to the finest man in England as her arbiter in all things.

Others did not altogether endorse her opinion; that of the more discriminating of his fellows was that 'the Lord Sudley was fierce in courage, courtly in fashion, in personage stately, in voice magnificent, but somewhat empty in matter.'

But he was extremely popular with them; they agreed that his little wife, after all she had been through, deserved her luck, for it was plain that they were really lovers. And if all the world loves a lover, it also loves a younger son, who has to make his own way in the world, as Tom had done triumphantly, and no thanks to his elder brother. And now that that supremely fortunate elder brother was actually trying to hinder him, it was not only base, it was unnatural.

They all liked the little Queen and they liked Tom, even if he did brag and wag his beard a bit – in fact, all the more for doing so; he was so wildly, gloriously indiscreet, generous not only with his money and his sumptuous entertaining, his royal banquets, his gaming parties and water parties and sports of every kind, but also with himself, talking so freely and openly without any shadow of suspicion or even caution of his hearers, taking them all for granted as his friends, certain that they would feel just as he did about the wrongs he had to endure from his brother, and quite reckless lest such talk might lay up occasion for yet worse wrongs. And, however angry, he was never tedious nor doleful, would shrug it off with a laugh and 'Oh well, "more was lost on Mohacs' field," as they still say in Hungary!'

The common people too adored him. Every time he went out they roared for him as they had done for King Hal when at the height of his popularity, and there were many who said he was more like that King when young than the pale little Prince ever showed a sign of becoming – as kingly, and with a finer beauty than even that giant had once worn; and the hearty carefree laugh that rang out from him as he scattered coins among the crowd sounded in all older ears as the echo of that great laugh of Bluff King Hal in his golden youth.

Free with his money he was, like Hal, and saw to it that the conduits ran wine in the Strand when he gave some grand show at his house there – which was more than his elder brother did, for all that he called himself the Protector. Solemn as a judge *he* was; he might talk big about reform, but reforms never did anybody much good, there was always a catch somewhere, and the rich managed to make themselves richer by them while the poor came off worse than before. A lot of fine talk cost him nothing, and did nothing for anyone else; hot air never warmed anybody – but what everyone could see and hear for themselves was that he was busy feathering his own nest, with hundreds of workmen hammering all day at that vast new house to be called by his name.

Altogether, Tom had good reason to be pleased with the way things were going. The Protector went up to Scotland at the head of his army and left his younger brother as his Lieutenant-General in charge of the South Ports, and this gave him more scope. Which he used rather mysteriously when he went to dislodge a notorious pirate called Jack Thompson who had seized the Scilly Isles, and came back apparently well satisfied although he had not dislodged him. Was it because he had agreed to share the swag with Mr Thompson?

His friends chuckled and said they always knew Tom was a born buccaneer; but agreed it looked serious when he protected pirates even in the Admiralty Courts, and complaints began to come in from foreign Powers of the loss of their ships.

He was playing with fire, too, among papers, hunting up all the old records he could find to prove that when a boy-King had two uncles, one of them should be Protector of the Realm and the other the Governor of the King's Person. There was no doubt that the King himself would eagerly welcome it. 'If only he were five or six years older!' Tom would exclaim, 'then it would all be plain sailing.' Still, he had got the boy eating out of his hand, eating up a lot of cash certainly, but it should pay good interest.

In his brother's absence he now had more chance to see him by himself, though they still had to resort to the underhand tricks of truant schoolboys to get in touch, but that too was all to the good, since it was breeding in Edward a contained fury of discontent against his present guardians. Nor did it seem to be only self-interest that bound the child to his younger uncle; he was obviously dazzled by him and would stare, almost awed, when he heard his jolly laugh, as at something so alien to his cold restricted life that he did not know how to meet it.

For his stepmother his feelings were simpler and more certain; for four years she had taken the place of the mother he had never known, and as naturally and lovingly as if she were indeed his mother. He missed her badly, and deeply resented that he was still being kept apart from her except for the briefest of formal visits. Even when she stayed at St James's Palace and he at Whitehall within a stone's throw, he found he could only write to her although 'I was so near to you and expected to see you every day'.

But the Admiral promised he would make it all come right. The Admiral said it was ridiculous that he should have to sit at his books all day. A King ought to be a good fellow, and mix with other good fellows – 'Look at your father, he was hail-fellow-well-met with everyone at sight and it served him a deal better than writing treaties against Luther and getting dubbed Defender of the Faith by the Pope,' – an unfortunate example, for the small face beneath him at once looked huffy and his nephew hastened to say that *he* was writing a comedy against the Pope, called 'The Whore of Babylon'.

'Very sound, very sound,' said his uncle, 'though you'd do it better later when you know more about—'

'I know all about the Pope.'

'—more about whores then.' But he found it safer to step off the subject, for Edward took his position as Supreme Head of the English Church very seriously. So he talked to him of his other duties as King. He ought to go on board the splendid ships that his father and grandfather had built, and tell the sailors that he would build more, to down the Spaniards and conquer the New World beyond the Western Ocean. All true Englishmen were growing sick and tired of sitting at home, watching the smoke of their firesides, now that they no longer went out in every generation to fight in the wars in France. Agincourt was now only an old song –

'Our King went forth to Normandy
With grace and might of chivalry' –

and England had shrunk from a Continental Empire to a little island (and only half of that). But a fine navy might still make her a world power.

And Edward ought to go hunting and hawking and prepare to lead his armies in the field; in Hungary a man did not count himself a man unless he were on a horse.

'Yet the Turks beat them at Mohacs,' Edward interpolated – odious child, he knew everything; but his uncle had a better answer this time.

'And well I know why, as Master Gunner of England, who am seeing to it that it shall never happen to an English army. The Turks were the first to use this stinking new artillery in full force, and the finest chivalry in Europe went down before it. It happened once, it will happen again, but not to us while *I'm* in command of the Ordnance – if I have the right backing.'

'*I'll* back you,' said the child, suddenly lighting into enthusiasm.

'You'll be a fine King,' said Tom, patting the fair head, but again came the petulant jut of Edward's full under-lip, that so reminded one of his father.

'I am King now,' he said.

'You ought to be more of one. You can't always be tied to your Uncle Ned's leading-strings, you know, and he's a bit of an old woman, far too old for you anyway.'

The under-lip stuck out further in a ferocious pout. 'I wish he were dead,' it said.

This was going further than Ned's brother had dreamt of. Edward saw his uncle's astonishment, sucked in his lip so that his mouth became a tiny red button, and repeated with cold, considered obstinacy, 'It would be better if he died.'

It was too much for the hardy buccaneer, who had only been tentatively feeling his way to the suggestion of a joint guardianship with his brother, and now felt a slight shiver at this 'sweet gentle child', as everybody called him.

He told his wife that he was a little monster, whereat his Cathy indignantly told him that he did not understand children and that it was all because Edward had been taken away from her own motherly care. Tom scoffed at the notion that he did not understand his nephew; anyway, the boy understood *him* and what he wanted, which was the important thing. Edward was going to write out a list of his complaints against his Uncle Somerset, and sign it with the royal signature, telling exactly what he felt about being kept so strictly in hand and so short of cash, and so entirely unsuitably for a great King who had just had his tenth birthday. Tom was going to read it out at that autumn's Parliament, 'And,' said he, 'if they don't do as I want about it, then by God's teeth I'll make it the blackest Parliament ever known in England!'

Even Cathy was startled into alarm and begged him not to oppose his brother so openly; but he only laughed at her fears;

and then, before the scheme was ripe, the Protector, Duke of Somerset, came home from Scotland in the autumn, a conquering hero, his position greatly strengthened by his having won a tremendous victory at some place with the absurd name of Pinkie. The soldiers said it was really his second-in-command, John Dudley, Earl of Warwick, who won it. In any case, everybody said that this time the Scots would certainly never be able to lift their heads again; though a few seemed to remember much the same thing being said five years ago after the battle of Solway; and some old croakers went so far as to remember that there had been even more reason to say it over thirty years ago, after Flodden.

The conquering hero himself felt his success oddly clouded, though it was only by a dream, which he recounted to his secretary Mr Patten on the morning of the battle as they walked on the ramparts, looking towards Scotland; and told him to write it down, though, as Mr Patten objected, it was only an idle dream.

'Dreams should not be idle,' said his master. 'They should be the busy servants of those statesmen who have the courage to dream wisely.'

So the secretary shrugged imperceptibly and noted down how the Protector had dreamt of his triumphant return to Court after the campaign, and the hearty thanks expressed to him by the King and all the country: 'but yet he thought he had done nothing at all in this voyage – which, when he considered the King's Highness' great costs and great travail of the great men and soldiers all to have been done in vain, the very care and shamefast abashment of the thing did waken him out of his dream.'

What could be the point in noting such moonshine, thought Mr Patten, when it had been directly followed by his winning a stupendous victory in which he had killed thousands of the enemy, laid waste their country and destroyed their harvest; and his troops, mainly hired mercenaries from Germany and Spain, had kindled such furious hatred among the Scots that there was no hope of their accepting his very reasonable and conciliatory offer of peace and union.

He omitted all King Henry's arrogant claim to Scotland as a vassal state, and based it only on an equal union through marriage of her Queen and England's King, with Free Trade between the countries, and both England and Scotland to be renamed together with Wales as Great Britain; an island empire 'having the sea for a wall, mutual love for a garrison, and no need in peace to be ashamed, or in war to be afraid of any worldly power.'

Which put it beautifully; but, as Tom said, it wasn't much use to preach mutual love when you'd let loose the German *landsknechts* and Spanish ruffians under the Italian *condottiere* Malatesta to loot and rape, burn and murder through the countryside. With their aid he'd won the war but lost the peace, for Scotland was more determined than ever to get their little Queen over in safety to France and betroth her to the Dauphin before she should be captured by force and taken to England. A French fleet had been known to have been hovering off the Scottish shores this summer; now they would have to wait for the spring, since no good seaman would trust so precious a freight to the dangers of a voyage between St Simon's and St Jude's Day and Candlemas, when storms were at their worst, and by seaman's law no ships should then sail the Northern Seas. But they were only biding their time, and then Scotland would be driven deeper into the arms of France than ever before, and England would have to face the prospect of encirclement on south, north and west by France, and by French armies in Scotland, with Ireland as a third base for invasion, easy to capture from Scotland – the very danger that Somerset had recognised and striven so hard to avoid.

It was his fate to have to work by force when he would far rather use persuasion. He tried to use it now, and set in train an immense invasion of another sort – to wit, thousands of religious leaflets and hundreds of Bibles in English, printed in Geneva. For he saw clearly that Scotland could only be united to England if she shared her new Reformed Religion, and that this was the best lever to use against her alliance with Roman Catholic France.

Another propaganda weapon lay in the prisoners he had taken, who were to buy their freedom, also pensions and promises of important marriages, by undertaking to work for English interests in Scotland. The Scots Lord Chancellor himself was one of these, the Earl of Huntly, a fat, talkative fellow who thought he ruled Scotland; and the fickle flimsy Fair Earl of Bothwell, tall and stooping rather from his slight shoulders, very vain of his delicate colouring that betokened consumption, and of his wavering blue eyes. He insisted on marriage to either of the Princesses, Mary or Elizabeth (he hadn't seen either and didn't mind which) as his price; and was fobbed off instead with the usual promise of Anne of Cleves – a promise that nobody, least of all the lady in question, intended to keep. The Fair Lord Francis had a wife at home (and a schoolboy son, James, as dark as he himself was fair), but he had just managed to divorce her, having had the intention of marrying his own Queen-Regent, the mother of the little Queen of Scots. A royal marriage was evidently his *idée fixe*.

The citizens of London wanted to express their loyal gratitude to the victorious Duke of Somerset by giving him a triumphal procession through the city, but this he modestly refused – to their annoyance, for if one had the expense of a war, one might as well have the fun of it. But the eldest Seymour's lonely spirit was too aloof to see how a gorgeous spectacle and free drinks running in the gutters would enhance his popularity – just as he never saw that his modesty was first credited as parsimony, and then hypocrisy; for he now placed himself in Parliament on a throne high up and apart from all the other lords, to their intense exasperation.

If *this* were modesty, give them Old Harry's pride! Their offended dignity was only aggravated by his piety, for in his prayer at the opening of Parliament he spoke of himself as 'called by Providence to rule' – but Providence never offered him that upper seat!

The newly self-made Duke then complained of his parvenu Council as a lot of 'lords sprung from the dunghill'; after that, a good many of them said they would prefer Tom as Protector. And Somerset put the final edge on Tom's own grievances against him by writing him a long and solemn letter urging him 'to receive poor men's complaints, that find themselves injured or grieved, for it is our duty and office so to do'.

Tom's roar of rage as he read it brought his household running to hear his blasphemously and indecently expressed opinion of an elder brother who had never helped him to anything, but withheld his wife's possessions, down to her wedding ring, and then lectured him on brotherly duty to his neighbour!

His furious laughter went rolling and roaring through the house; he kicked a chair across the hall and picked up another and broke it in his hands; he swore he would go and see our Pulpit Ned on the instant and ram his canting letter down his throat; he would ask him how he had the face to talk about the Rights or Wrongs of the poor, when he had done his own son and heir out of his inheritance and was now cheating his own brother out of his goods; he was an unnatural father and an unnatural brother, in fact there was nothing natural about him, and he accused his own mother, as she came tottering and quavering down the stairs, of having conceived him of the Devil.

A birdlike little old lady, usually spry and dapper as a water-wagtail, Lady Seymour now twittered about the hall, fluttering her hands and uttering disconsolate chirps such as 'Now, now, now!' 'Another quarrel!' 'Not again!' 'Always fighting as boys, I thought they'd kill each other, and now, now—'

His wife sobbed, the servants peeped awestruck round doorways, Bess took a gallery seat at the top of the stairs to watch the row, and little Jane Grey peeped over her shoulder and wondered if all grown-ups were mad.

The quarrel raged its way into the Protector's palace, and as usual it took the Protector some time to understand what

Tom was making all this noise about. He had been meaning himself to get in first with his own grievances.

His nervous eyebrows went fidgeting half-way up the furrowed dome of his forehead as he complained how he had to cut short his campaign in Scotland to hurry home and enquire into all manner of disturbing reports of his brother. Surely the welfare of the State mattered more than petty personal affairs, women's toys, trinkets.

What was this about the Lord High Admiral countenancing piracy? It had even been suggested that he meant to establish a naval base for himself in the Scilly Isles.

But here the Admiral blew away the suggestion like a gale at sea.

'Piracy, pooh! The pirates of today are the pioneers of tomorrow. You'll see! England will owe more to her pirates than to her Protectors.'

The Protector hastily abandoned pirates. Tom had been unsettling the King's mind, taking him out hunting when he should have been at his lessons, thrusting himself into his favour—

'God's blood, and isn't he my nephew as much as yours? Why should you have the right to work the poor little brat to death at his books when his head's spinning so that he can hardly see? I'll swear you don't even know that his eyes are weak and have to be bathed with Mother Jack's foul mixtures—' (The Protector didn't; nor did the Admiral till his wife had told him.) 'Suit you finely to have a blind King, so that you can carry on your Protection – God save the mark!'

The younger brother shouted; the elder compressed his

lips; the Duchess swept in and told Master Admiral what she thought of younger brothers and their wives, and the Admiral told her what he thought of her; the Protector slid away to compose a prayer to 'the Granter of all peace and quietness, the Defender of all Nations, who has willed all men to be accounted as our neighbours, and commanded us to love them as ourselves; and not to hate our enemies, but rather to wish them, yea and also to do them good if we can…to give unto all men a speedy wearisomeness of all war, hostility and enmity…and grant in Thy days Thy great gift of unity'.

It was perhaps the most moving and perfect prayer ever addressed on behalf of a conquered enemy, for it was a prayer for Union with Scotland; but, for once, 'petty personal affairs' may have also tinged those austere desires for the welfare of the State.

The brothers' quarrel was patched up somehow, as it had to be to avoid a hideous open scandal. The Lord High Admiral's income was increased by £800 a year; and then the Duke of Somerset settled down with a sigh of relief to the enormous but congenial burden of the reform of religion and organisation of the Church as an efficient branch of the Civil Service; the direction of all England's foreign diplomatic correspondence (with only two secretaries to help him); the supervising of every meeting of the Council and of Parliament; and a host of far-reaching but not always practicable schemes for the freedom of speech and the Press, and for social reforms to check the rise in prices and the debasement of the currency, to stop land-grabbing by the New Rich and unemployment of the poor; he even had a Court of

Requests set up in his own house so that the humblest suppliant who came to complain of any wrong or oppression might get the ear of the great Duke himself, the Good Duke, as the poor now called him.

But the Duchess still wore the Queen Dowager's jewels.

CHAPTER EIGHT

The Admiral lost his chance to make that autumn's Parliament the blackest ever seen, not because of the power of the greatest statesman in England, but because of the intractability of a small boy.

Edward had never supplied him with that signed list of complaints that was to win him his freedom and his Uncle Tom's ascendancy; instead, he had asked his tutor about it, and 'Mr Cheke said I had better not write it,' he said in his cool little even voice, as dispassionately as if he had been let off writing a Latin prose.

For the second time the reckless adventurer felt a slight shiver as he looked down at the pretty, rather mulish little face. *Did* he – or anyone else – understand children, their secret and incalculable life, governed by no one knew what obscure impulses and caprice?

Young Edward had certainly seemed to resent his elder uncle's domination even to the point of hating him and wishing his death; but now he appeared to have forgotten all about it, or at any rate did not wish to be bothered with it, but only to be left alone.

This was indeed something of the case, for Edward's weak vitality had begun to shrink from his overpowering younger uncle; he vaguely felt that he could never be the sort of King that Uncle Tom expected him to be – but if he couldn't be a mixture of Christopher Columbus, Richard Coeur de Lion and Saint George (silly, that story of Saint George, he was sure there had never been any Dragons in England), at least he could be the wisest, most learned and most religious King England had ever had. A deal of people thought he would be, too.

The learned refugee, Dr Bucer from Germany, said how lucky his subjects were to have a philosopher for their Prince. (Dr Bucer was lucky too, for Edward had sent the cash for him to have a German stove in his house at Cambridge as he couldn't get warm with the English open fires.)

But his Uncle Tom wouldn't think anything of a philosopher King. His Uncle Somerset would.

The Admiral could tell him exciting stories of the heathen Turks, how their janissaries dipped the horsehair plumes of their lances in blood as a sign of war, and for years now those lances were pointing further and further into Europe; the Sultan's dashing incendiaries had plundered Austria and hammered on the walls of Vienna while his Crescent still flew from the citadel of Buda Pest, where Tom himself had feasted and talked with him in his dark gleaming coat of mail, with heron plumes waving in his turban, fastened by a diamond named the Eye of Heaven.

Edward listened with interest, but considered that the Turk was still a long way off, and Europe wasn't England, there was all the sea between; and moreover England was his, and Scotland ought to be too, his father had always said so; and his Uncle Somerset was fighting this Scottish war, not just for Europe or Christendom, but for *him*.

So that it was with a thrill of personal pride that he wrote in his Journal a full account, almost as clear and vivid as if he had been there himself, of the battle of Pinkie, how 10,000 Scots were slain, and 1,000 lords (he wrote 2,000 in his first enthusiasm but punctiliously altered it to the more modest estimate); how the Scots strove for the higher ground 'and almost gott it', but Somerset rallied the English horse so that 'the Scotts stood amasid'; how Somerset was challenged by the pompous Earl of Huntly to single combat but refused him for the excellent reason that he was in charge of so precious a jewel as the governance of his King's person, and how John Dudley, Earl of Warwick, chased that plump Scottish braggart and was almost taken prisoner himself by riding slap into an ambush, but was rescued by a French knight Berteville who got 'hurt in the buttok', but, as Edward finished with a flourish that turned his final 'y' into a horsewhip, 'the ambush ran away'.

And he rubbed his eyes, which were smarting again, and sent for Mother Jack, who clucked like an angry hen at all these books – 'Aren't there enough in the world as it is and enough trouble caused by them?' (she disapproved of the new English Bible) 'But you too must go scribble, scribble, scribble?' – and delicately painted his sore eyes with a feather dipped into a precious water compounded of fennel, rue, pimpernel, sage, celandine, honey, and fifteen peppercorns, boiled in a pint of white wine to which was added five spoons of 'the water of a man-child that is an innocent.'

But the precious water didn't do as much good as usual, and Edward swore at his nurse with a few of the Admiral's thundering oaths, and the Protector, who never used a brutal or coarse expression in the whole of his life, heard them and demanded which of the King's playfellows had taught him those shocking words. Edward was just going to tell their origin when young Barnaby Fitzpatrick, rolling up his blue eyes with the look of a repentant cherub, admitted to having taught his King to swear.

'And why did you so abuse your trust?' demanded the Protector sternly, while Edward stared, too astonished to speak.

Barnaby was plainly perplexed, but only for the instant. 'I thought,' he said presently, now casting down his eyes in an even more specious humility, 'that it was the proper thing for a King to do.'

There was a moment's hush in which all there seemed to hear the echoed roar of King Harry's monstrous blasphemies. Then the Protector hurriedly ordered the Irish boy to be whipped in Edward's presence, and rubbed it well into his nephew that the same should be done to him too if he were not the King. Edward, white and sullenly furious, watched his friend's punishment, and as soon as they were alone, demanded indignantly why he had courted it.

'Ah, and why wouldn't I?' said young Barnaby carelessly. 'You don't want another fight between your uncles, do you?'

'I have too many uncles,' said Edward ominously.

Christmas brought the first full reunion of the royal family since their father's death. Even Mary accepted the invitation to Court, though it involved her in long arguments with the Protector, who attacked her right to have Mass said privately in her own house; and she counter-attacked the way in which he was setting aside all the terms of her father's Will.

Somerset's attempts to prove that his late Sacred Majesty's intentions were entirely Protestant landed him in a mass of self-contradictions; it was the Admiral who, as he crudely said, 'took the cow by the horns' and pointed out to Mary that King Henry's words and actions had been so inconsistent that it was impossible to base a settled policy upon them. Oddly enough, the Princess seemed to prefer this to his brother's justifications; in spite of the snubbing she had given Tom over his marriage a few months before, they grew very friendly together over music; and when she sighed over her lack of practice in the virginals he lent her his best musician to give her lessons.

He had brought a band of gipsies from Vienna who delighted both the Princesses by playing to them the music they considered appropriate to their charms; Elizabeth's was a wild Hungarian dance, and Mary's a tender mournful ballad about the wanderings of the Magyars in search of their Promised Land, which brought tears to her eyes.

She was in a genial mood, very new to those who had not seen her since she kept her own household, free of the Court and her father's domination. Even her religion seemed to be sitting more loosely on her, for she lost a bet of £10 to Dr Bill, one of the leading theological lights of the Protestant Church; and could not refrain from going a pleased pink when told that her translation of Erasmus's Paraphrases of St John had been issued to all the churches in England as a companion volume to the new English Bible.

'We'll be having you as good a Protestant as any of us,' Tom said, and she only gave her great gruff laugh that reminded one of her father and sounded so oddly from her small, rather shrunken figure. As usual, it was much too showily dressed; ermine stripes ran in every direction like an erratic zebra, and the shoulder-puffs on her sleeves reached her ears, her face poking forward between them, shortsighted, peering, vaguely bewildered but determined.

The dances and romping games, the fooling and practical jokes were as fast and furious as they had been a year ago under the glazed eye of the huge figure that had sat glittering and moribund in the chair worked by his devoted daughter. This was not because the Protector had the same simple enjoyment in games of Snapdragon, Forfeits, Kiss-in-the-Ring, and Hunt-the-Slipper (indeed, he was barely conscious that they were going on), but because the Admiral had by common consent been appointed Lord of Misrule.

Even the little King took part in a Masque of Cats, and was gravely pleased with his tabby coat and furry mask with whiskers a foot long. He had to enter on the shoulders of John Dudley, the Earl of Warwick, dressed as a dog, according to the curious Natural History of masques. The famous soldier capered about behind the scenes, barking beautifully, then ducked before Edward, but the boy, small even for his age, looked round for a stool to help him to mount; there was none, so Tom placed a massive brass-bound Bible on the floor, but his nephew was shocked at the idea of standing on the Word of God.

'Half the fellows at Court have risen by it,' said Tom with a wink at John Dudley, but the joke went too near home, for the new Earl had made an enormous fortune out of the

Reformation and the sale of Church lands, and had testified
to the new piety *à la mode* by christening one of his sons
Guildford, the first time anyone had been christened after a
town and not a saint. Since Henry's death, with the
Reformation coming out into the open, he had risen rapidly.
So he naturally found Tom's joke in the worst of taste. 'A fine
figure of a man,' he drawled in an audible aside. 'Pity it wants
a head – may do so in earnest before long.'

There would have been a duel had not the Protector been
determined to put down that 'heathenish custom'. Tom told
him he was a fool to be so scrupulous as to miss a chance to
get Dudley out of the way. 'He's a dark horse and will be in
the running against you before long, you can take my word
for it,' – nor did it strike him as odd to expect his brother to
take his word for it, when he himself had so openly entered
the running against him.

Elizabeth had lost a forfeit to the Admiral; she was indignant,
for he had taken the unfair advantage of bursting into her
room in the morning, putting his head through the bed-
curtains and shouting 'Bonjour, Philippine!' before she was
awake. He was always up early and generally looked in on his
way from Catherine's room before Bess was up, or he himself
more than half dressed. 'Now then, Slug-a-bed!' he would
call, and pull off the bed-clothes and tickle or smack her to
make her get up, and tell her she was an idle slut and sing:

> 'See-saw, Margery Daw
> Sold her bed to lie upon straw.
> Wasn't she an idle slut!'

Bess found these sudden surprises very exciting, sometimes rather alarming, but even that was pleasant. One moment she would be sound asleep, and then crashing into her dreams would come a deep gay voice, a thrill of expectation – what was it that was going to happen? – and she woke to see his face laughing down on her, and this time it was saying, 'Bonjour, Philippine! And now what forfeit will you pay me?'

'Bread and cheese! You've got everything you want.'

'Not everything. Pay me a kiss to start with.'

She had kissed him often, leaping up and flinging her arms round his neck, but now suddenly she shied at it, slid out at the other side of the bed, and ran through the open doorway into the next room where her maids were preparing her bath. He gave chase, there was a wild scurry and giggling, she dodged behind first one girl and then another, she ran round the wide tub of porphyry and he leapt over it, dropping a slipper splash into the steaming scented water, stubbed his bare foot against the marble side of the tub, sprawled forward, dealt her a resounding smack from behind, caught at the flying skirt of her shift and gave it a tug which pulled her backwards plump into the bath with a mighty splash that emptied half the water on to the floor, drenched her hair and all the furniture near. The laughing shrieks brought Mrs Ashley running; she shrieked a little too, in camaraderie, but not with the same conviction; she was shocked at the Admiral's deshabille, at his bare foot, at his romping with the Princess and her maids in her bedroom. People might talk, they might even blame herself.

She pointed this out to him later and asked him to stop his morning visits: she owed it to herself, as she was in charge.

The Admiral did not care what she owed to herself, an interfering cackling busybody, making a storm in a possetcup! He was genuinely astonished, for he not only swore, to show the purity of his intentions – 'God's precious soul, where's the harm? I mean none, so I'll not leave off!' – but he actually burst out that if there were any more of this meddling he would tell the Protector how he was being slandered – as certain of Ned's partisanship as if they were still at school, and Ned the much elder brother who would lecture him gravely on his faults but be sure to take his side against anyone else.

So the Admiral did not leave off, and out of bravado made the fun even more outrageous; sometimes Bess ran from him among her maids, sometimes hid from him in the bed-curtains or cupboards and was punished with a slap or tickling that made her wriggle and giggle and hit out at him and shriek for mercy or for help from the giggling maids, and enjoy it all thoroughly. All very well, thought Mrs Ashley, to say it was nothing but a childish frolic, but there were none of these frolics with the child Jane Grey – indeed, one couldn't imagine her, though only eleven, taking part in them. But there was no question of it, for she had her separate apartments, servants, and tutors.

Mrs Ashley, not the wisest of women, and terrified of tackling the Admiral again, tried warning her charge, reminding her that she was now nearly fourteen and a half, and growing very like her mother in some ways, and ought to begin to behave with the dignity and decorum of a young lady.

'Did my mother?' asked Bess demurely.

Her governess wished she had the Admiral's privilege of smacking her. She said she was very pert and silly, that men were fools in not recognising when a girl was no longer a child, but that they did not really like hoydens, and that of all people a Princess should not behave like a romping milkmaid.

This began to go well; Bess felt uncomfortable and looked furious; but Mrs Ashley, afraid of provoking one of the girl's rages, which always reduced her to a shaking fit of nerves, then spoilt all chance of real effect from these snubs by making mysterious hints.

Bess's mother, Nan Bullen, had driven men mad for her; she had been betrothed when only fifteen to the poor young Percy, Lord of Northumberland, who had never got over it, 'and your eyes are like hers, though they were black as sloes – but I'll swear the Admiral sees it too. If you knew all I could tell you, you'd see I'm not making a fuss for nothing, but there are things you don't know and you must take my word for it, and be very careful with that man.'

Thus darkly nodding and pursing her lips, Cat Ashley overshot her mark, and knew no peace till Bess had coaxed and bullied the secret out of her.

'The Queen was only second-best to him; he'd have had you if he could. But the Council wouldn't hear of it, so he fell back on his old sweetheart – oh, he's very fond of her, all the world can see that—'

Yes, Bess could see that; but she was seeing other things too; the garden at Chelsea nearly a year ago, and the Admiral standing watching her as she played at ball with her pomander; he had asked her to marry him, he had taken her chin in his hand, he had been just going to kiss her, and not, she was sure, in the casual hearty way he had so often kissed her since, as one kisses a child – and then his Cathy, her Pussy-Cat Purr, came out, and he turned it all into a joke. Watching them together, straight on top of that moment in the garden, she had been quite sure it had only been a joke; and then within four days had come the dreadful damning confirmation of it, when Catherine told her she had just been formally betrothed to him. Bess had shrugged it off, of course, she owed it to herself (but she owed the phrase to the Ash-Cat, she realised in sudden annoyance at its vulgarity). She had laughed and played with him all this year; but, as she was now suddenly aware, all the time her heart had been broken.

She made up her mind to be very grave and dignified with him, rather distant, but not in obvious displeasure, only wistfully aloof. The result was that the Admiral asked her if she had a stomach-ache. And it was impossible to go on being wistfully aloof when you were tickled almost into hysterics.

Mrs Ashley had to look round for a third person to whom to complain; and ended, where she had better have begun, with the Admiral's wife.

Here naturally she dropped no dark hints (she had indeed been doubtful of their prudence the moment she had uttered them to Bess), but based her warning on the danger of tittle-tattle from the maids; people would say she oughtn't to allow the Admiral to come into her young mistress's room in his bedgown and with bare legs, and the Princess herself in bed. She knew, of course, that he saw no harm in it; she knew what sailors were; she knew – but she did not need to know any more, for Catherine at once agreed quietly and said she would see to it.

It was very tiresome, Catherine thought; she had been so delighted with the jolly easy friendship between Tom and Bess, who had almost stopped being that odd difficult girl since he had come into their household, and become more of a real child than Catherine had ever seen her; indeed, that was why she had failed to realise that she was beginning to grow up.

Now she looked at her with awakened eyes and saw how much taller she had grown lately and prettier, and how the curves of her breasts just showed like small apples above the stiff front of her bodice. The girl was in her fifteenth year – and she herself was thirty-five. That gave her a shock, for it was the first time she had ever thought of comparing herself with Bess.

A plague on these women and their solemn unctuous airs, they spoilt everything. It was not that Cat Ashley had spoken any evil, nor probably thought any, but she had made her conscious of herself, of her husband, of Bess. Once a thing was thought, you could not stop it; it was like throwing a stone into a pond, the ripples went further and further out and must go on till they reached the very edge.

And what should she do? What *could* she do that would not look suspicious, jealous, the very things she most hated? 'Nothing will ever be the same again,' she told herself miserably, as she held her mirror close to her face and wondered if it had not begun to look thinner lately, even rather hollow under the eyes. But there might be a happier reason for that than her age; it might well be that at last, after all these years, she had begun to be with child. The hope restored all her happiness and confidence, and she knew suddenly what she should do.

Next morning when the Admiral came into Bess's room Catherine came too, and together they woke her, laughing, together they tickled and teased her while she defended herself with the bolster and there was a brief pillow-fight.

But it was not nearly so exciting for Bess.

After that, Catherine was nearly always there as a third partner in the romps, and a very lively one, even destructive on one bright morning in early February, when Bess came out with great dignity towards them as they walked by the little fishpond in the Chelsea garden, came slowly, like the tragedy Queen Herodias, down the terrace steps, attired in a black silk dress.

Her mother, she knew, had had a penchant for black; it was French and chic, and emphatically grown-up; it would remind the Admiral both of Nan Bullen, who had driven men mad for her, and of her own advancing age.

But it did not seem to do any of these things. He stood with his legs apart and his thumbs in his belt and rocked backwards and forwards roaring with laughter, until at last he had breath enough to ask her why on earth she was play-acting in that hideous dress. And Catherine said, 'It doesn't suit you at all, my darling. Do go and take it off.'

She stamped with rage. 'I won't. It's a most suitable dress. Why shouldn't I wear black? I'm in mourning for—' but black was not the royal mourning, and the Admiral finished it for her. 'For your poor dear husband, I'll be bound. You look a brisk young widow.'

Bess went more tragic than ever, for it was all too true. She was indeed a widow, in mourning for the husband she had never had. How heartless and obtuse he was not to see it!

Instead, he snatched the scissors that dangled from his wife's girdle, and chased her round the pond, swearing he would cut that preposterous frumpery into ribbons. All her indignant sorrow went to the winds; she picked up her solemn skirts and ran squealing, plump into Catherine's arms, who in fits of laughter held her while Tom slit up the dress this way and that.

'Now go and take it off, you monkey,' said Catherine, kissing her, 'and put on your prettiest colours for this spring day.'

She ran back into the house, laughing now as much as they, to meet Cat Ashley's horrified exclamations and scoldings at the damage to her new dress, 'and such beautiful stuff'.

'It's not, it's hideous,' said Bess airily. 'And anyway it's not my fault. It was two against one, for the Queen held me while the Admiral cut it up.'

'*Well*!!' said Mrs Ashley, looking unutterable things and then apparently swallowing them, for she jerked her head back, then forward, like a hen with a large pea, and pursed her lips tight as if to prevent anything ever escaping through them again. What did at last emerge was a very dry thin note: 'The Queen knows her own business best, I suppose.'

'She does,' said her charge, suddenly flaming. 'And that business is not yours, you prying, prowling old Ash-Cat. Get out of my sight, I'm sick to death of your mimsey face.'

Her governess took the hint.

CHAPTER NINE

The stone had fallen into the pond, the ripples were spreading, and not all Catherine's gallantry could stay them.

But she did not know this at once. For her hopes of being with child had become certainty and Tom's delight was uproarious. He was very careful of her and gave her tender instructions as solemnly as a village midwife, so she told him, mocking him with equal tenderness. She must go walks every day to strengthen their boy (they never doubted it would be a boy and all his names were chosen), but she must not get tired, and plenty of country air would be good for her. So they moved about from house to house, and Bess went too.

She too was delighted that there would be a new baby step-stepbrother for her to play with, and she would embroider a shirt for him too. She kept Catherine amused, reading Italian romances to her or playing her lute or the virginals; she had a real ear for music and a delicate light touch. Then, suddenly bored and cramped with sitting still, she would spring up and go running down the garden paths with her greyhound and break into the steps of a gipsy dance, she and Catherine both singing the tune.

Tom, hot and dusty after riding back from London, Court life, and a fresh quarrel with his brother, would come upon some such idyllic scene and reflect anew on the advantages of domestic life among the Turks. 'When I was in Buda Pest' became a rather frequent note of nostalgia. They managed these things better in Hungary; it was reasonable and natural for a man to have at least two wives, so as to amuse himself with the one while the other was occupied with bearing his child. He adored his Cathy, there was no other woman like her, but Bess was not a woman, she had all the contrast of crude, budding girlhood, the sharp sweet flavour of a not quite ripe apple. 'Lord, how I wish I had an apple! Have you such a thing as an apple about you, my sweet Tom?' He had such a thing about him, and he must not taste it.

One evening at Chelsea when a soft gusty wind was tossing the pear blossom over the red brick wall, and the new moon had just begun to show like a ghostly flower caught in the topmost branches, he came back from Westminster in a teasing mood that had a tang in it of bad temper, and chaffed Bess on her matrimonial prospects. Had she any fancy for a cold climate, for sleighing and skating, and a moody young Northern giant for a husband?

For the Protector had decided to marry her either to the Danish or Swedish prince. 'Good for trade,' said Tom; also of course she must take a Protestant, and that narrowed the field; best of all, it would get her out of England and lessen her chances of ever becoming Queen of it.

Catherine looked up, startled, for no one spoke of those chances; the loyal notion was that Edward, though possibly rather delicate, would grow up, marry and have children; and even if he did not, there was Mary. But Bess took it very coolly. She only said in a low tone as though to herself, 'I shall not leave England, however many husbands I may marry.'

He tweaked her ear. 'Here's a large-hearted lass. How many are on the list?'

'I've no list. It's you, my Lord Admiral, who should have a wife in every port.'

'And a port in every storm?'

'Not you! But you make a storm in every posset-cup.'

'She's put you down!' exclaimed his wife.

'If I put her, she'd give birth to vixens. Her tongue's sharper than a tooth, even her hair's aflame with malice. Go and quench that foxy red brush of yours or I'll cut it off and hang it in the hall as a trophy among the other wild beasts' heads.'

It flashed on Catherine that people were sometimes rude like this when they had begun to fall in love but did not yet know it – yes, and looked at each other like that, with a curious new awareness, their eyes casual and mocking on the surface, yet with a stranger lurking in their depths, intent, watchful, defiant, as though a challenge had gone out between them and had been accepted.

There was nothing she could do; she sat stunned, feeling a little sick, and did not dare look at them again. She heard nothing more that they said; her mind was talking too loud to herself, arguing, disputing.

'But he loves me, I know it. He loves me *now*, not merely in the past, nor in the future as the mother of his child.'

'Fool! That man could love several at the same time, it's his nature to make any number of women happy. And at the moment you are not his lover, only the mother of his child.'

'But she's not fifteen yet, not for five months.'

'Fool! She's older at times than you have ever been. Do you

ever know what she's thinking, feeling, deep down beneath her pert chatter, her budding airs and graces? They are those of a child pretending to be a woman; but all the time beneath them there is a mind at work, the mind of a woman pretending to be a child.'

A wave of hysteria was surging up over her; in another moment she would scream her thoughts aloud, make wild and horrible accusations. Whatever happened, that must not. She murmured that it was getting chilly and slid away.

Tom did not notice her going. Bess did, and thought that she ought to run after her, but had an odd fear of doing so. She had not seen Catherine's face, but had felt that someone quite different had risen silently from the bench beside her and stolen away into the chill evening air.

She shivered and told herself that she did not want to go after her, so why should she? She was sick of doing what she ought to do, of being the good little girl. Besides, she was no longer a little girl; princes were making offers for her hand; they had done so since she was a few years old, but then it had not mattered personally to anyone; now it did. It mattered to Tom Seymour, she was sure of it; and it mattered much more to herself. Her pert answers to his banter had served to gain time while she turned this new project over in her mind and discovered what she thought of it. She discovered that it had put her in a smouldering rage. Not for worlds would she show this to Tom, who had so lightly betrayed his own anger at the plan; so she appeared to consider it with pleased curiosity, while she longed to order the Protector to the block for daring to dispose of her without even consulting her first. How dared he, or any man, treat her as a mere property of the

State, an appanage of the Crown, a bargaining asset? It was what all princesses were, as a matter of course, yet her knowledge of this made no odds to her; *she* was different.

But to Tom she only laughed when he said she might as well marry a turnip as a Swede. 'And why not?' she said. 'There ought to be roots in matrimony. Perhaps I'll strike mine in new soil after all, and see the world.'

He looked quite hurt as he answered, 'But you said just now you didn't want to leave England.'

He had taken that to mean that she didn't want to leave him! A delicious new sense of power thrilled through her as she realised it; she too could tease him, then, more exquisitely than he had ever teased her, and she flung back her head and laughed.

He stared; a slow flush was mounting to his forehead; she had never seen him look like this. He said, 'You are like your mother when you laugh.'

'*Oh*!' came on a pettish note of disappointment. 'Was all the world in love with my mother?'

'Half of it was. The other half hated her.'

'Will that be like me too? And you—?' She paused, looking at him sidelong in desperate coquetry, then said breathlessly, 'Of which half are you? I think you do not hate me.'

'No, Bess, I don't hate you.'

His voice sounded thick, he looked at her as though he did not see her, the Bess he had always known, but some thought of her that lay within his mind. And it was she who had done this, had laughed and looked and spoken so as to make him lose hold of that moment; she too, then, like her mother, might drive men mad for her, and had begun even earlier to do it. She felt drunk with triumph. This moment was hers; he should do what she wished with it.

She stood up, with a gesture of command rather than invitation, and said, 'You were going to kiss me once, in this garden – it was over a year ago. Will you do it now?'

Did he hear her – see her even? It seemed he was staring too hard to see her. Her heart thumped furiously against the whaleboned case of her bodice as though it were trying to get out; panic swept over her, it was all she could do to keep from turning and running headlong into the house. But no, she must not, she would not lose this moment, it was hers, and she clenched her hands together as if to clutch it to her.

But it was no use, she was going to lose it, she was losing it, something was happening that would tear it away, a sound, a movement seen in the tail of her eye.

Little Jane Grey was walking sedately down the path towards them, her freckled face composed into a set pattern of solemnity.

'I have just returned from Westminster,' she told Bess on a note of anxious awe, 'and have a message for you from the King. Mr Cheke is very ill.'

Bess slipped her a look full of loathing. 'Is that all?' she said.

'But it's Mr *Cheke*. He's ill.'

'Well, I can't help it. Why have you got to come running to tell me at once? You're always thrusting yourself in everywhere – little nuisance!'

This brutal attack on top of her cousin's astounding heartlessness was too much for Jane.

'It's not fair – I *wasn't* running – I *don't* thrust in – I'm always trying to keep out of everybody's way—' Two large tears rolled down her cheeks.

'Cry-baby! You'll always say everything isn't fair – you'll never love anyone but old dons and tutors – you – *Ow*!' she ended on a yelp, for the Admiral had lunged forward and dealt her a thumping smack, and there was nothing exciting or tantalising about it. It hurt.

'You young bully,' he roared, 'I won't have you unkind to my Jane.'

He sat on the bench and took the little girl on his knee, and she put her head on his chest and sobbed. Bess knew he had fallen clean out of love with her; she was only a child to him again, and an unpleasant child at that. She could have killed her small cousin.

Jane conscientiously raised her tearful face from the Admiral's waistcoat and gave Edward's message: 'The King told me – to tell you – "Tell my sweet sister Temperance," he said—' Pause for effect, Bess was certain, but again unfairly, for Jane was choking back her sobs. 'The doctors thought Mr Cheke will die, but Edward has prayed for him and knows his prayer will be answered. He asks you to pray too.'

She drew a deep sniff and laid her head down against the Admiral's arm.

'There, there, my pretty,' he said. 'All will be well, you'll see. God's sure to listen to our sweet sister Temperance.'

Bess walked past them with her nose in the air, and as she passed gave a vicious tug at Jane's long hair that hung over the Admiral's arm, then ran for her life.

* * *

She would never speak to her cousin again, nor the Admiral; she would marry the Swede or the Dane and leave England for ever and never see any of them again; and when she heard Catherine was feeling ill and had had to go to bed she was not a bit sorry. Catherine had the Admiral to love her and would soon have a jolly baby to play with, his baby. Catherine had everything, it wasn't fair. But no, only silly little girls thought that, and she wasn't going to be a cry-baby, so she only sulked like a thundercloud all the next day, until suddenly she remembered that there was going to be a banquet that evening, and scampered off to choose her prettiest dress for it.

It was a grand affair, though informal; Tom was entertaining the King and all the important people at Court, to commemorate another reconciliation with his brother. Catherine came down again for it, looking so gay and pretty that Bess was sure she had only been shamming, until she was close enough to see that she had put on more rouge than usual.

Edward came up the water-steps in a white and yellow suit by the side of his uncle, like a canary under the wing of an eagle. The Duke was looking very noble and forgiving this evening. The Duchess looked like a peacock, her handsome head poised above her glittering robes. But her face was ravaged, insatiable. Surrey would not write poems to her now. She was with child again, as though even in that she must enter into rivalry with her sister-in-law.

The food was delicious though strange, for among all the usual great roasted birds and pies the Admiral's Viennese cook gave them goulash and thin slices of pumpernickel dotted with little white and scarlet toadstools made of cream cheese sprinkled with red sweet peppers, and radishes cut in the shape of Tudor roses; and they drank a rich golden wine of heady sweetness which their host had brought from the sun-baked mountain plateau of Tokay. Even Somerset thawed under it and told his brother with a complimentary bow that it was like drinking liquid sunshine.

The music was always good at the Admiral's house, but tonight his gipsy players and singers seemed to have Tokay in their veins (as in fact they had); their strange tunes were as intoxicating as the wine, and when they played behind Bess's chair the music appropriate to her charms, they chose this time, not a lively dance, but a love-song with a wild call in its refrain that came again and again, tingling and throbbing through the hot buzz of talk and smell of food and wine. Why had they chosen this for her tonight? Was the little dark-faced monkey of a man, capering in his gorgeous embroidered coat behind her chair, a magician as well as a musician, with power to see into her heart?

Or had the Admiral told him to play this? The second possibility was even more exciting, for if it were so, he had then forgotten their quarrel – not forgiven it, for Tom would never bother to forgive, though he might easily forget – which was far better. Then he did not love Jane best, '*his* Jane' indeed! He did not think herself an unpleasant child, he—

'Why do they play this tune for you?' said Edward, who as usual sat with his sister, the next highest in the land (since Mary was absent), on his right hand. 'It's not a bit like you.'

'What tune *is* like me, then?' she demanded tartly; she was sure he had no idea, and had only said that to be tiresome.

Edward replied promptly, 'Jumping Joan.'

His friend Barnaby, coming forward at that moment to serve him on bended knee, gave a sidelong glance of adoration at the Princess Elizabeth and wondered why she looked so cross.

After the banquet they danced, and after they had danced the formal Court dances that everybody knew, Tom said he would show them something new, and as old as the Magyars' Covenant of Blood, and that was the Palace Dance.

His Bohemians thrummed out a rhythmic measure in which there was hardly any tune but an endless throbbing, drumming movement, as compelling as if it were the procession of a sacrificial victim; they led the way ahead of the company, Tom gave his hand to his hated sister-in-law and told her to give hers to the gentleman of her choice, and so on, each taking a partner by the hand and pacing, slowly at first, then faster and faster, following those little dark foreign men who were dancing, prancing, fiddling, twiddling ahead of them, through the hall and the great staircase, down the long passages, up the odd little flights of stairs and down others, through room after room of the rambling manor-house, 'upstairs and downstairs and in my lady's chamber,' laughing and talking and glittering they went, and all the time some couples kept dropping out, getting left behind, while the rest linked up to new partners.

And so, for a few moments, Barney's dream came true, and he danced hand-in-hand with the Princess Elizabeth.

She did not look cross now. She smiled at him with seraphic ecstasy induced by the Hungarian music and Tokay; the torches knocked bright sparks out of her hair; and to his bewildered delight she swung him out of the procession to an alcove in one of the downstairs rooms and sat on a window-seat while he leant against it. Even her explanation for this, that her new shoes were too tight, made as she kicked them off, could not dim the romance of such a moment to Barney, who remained silent with awe, even about the shoes.

She said casually, 'We are cousins, aren't we? You are a connexion of the Butlers of Ormonde, I think, and my mother's grandmother was one of them – I very nearly was myself.' And then as the boy stammered with astonishment she told him how the Bullens had tried to marry Anne to the Earl of Ormonde of that day but she had flatly refused. 'Think of it! If she had not been so staunch, I'd have been born in Kilkenny Castle, and my only glimpse of town life a visit to Dublin!'

He burst out laughing at thought of this radiant creature among the thatched roofs of that primitive city. It was easily seen how such a prospect had driven her mother, that gay Frenchified coquette, to the perilous pursuit of King Henry that ended in her death. But he naturally did not speak this thought aloud, only: 'Kilkenny! After six years at the French Court! Your Highness's mother could never have stood that!'

'I wish I could see the French Court,' sighed Bess.

'And I,' said the page. 'I mean to, too.'

'Do you, Barney? You must not mind me calling you that, for you see my brother always does when he speaks of you.'

'Mind!' When the flattery of her using his intimate home-name sent his blood tingling into his head!

She saw it with delight. So she could use her power on him too, a boy she had scarcely spoken to before. But he was only a boy, perhaps no older than herself, though already so tall (and, yes, he was very good-looking) and shy, so she was careful not to show that she saw it, but asked him with easy friendliness why he wanted to go to the French Court. Barney in a burst of confidence told her that it was not the Court he wanted to see, but something of the French wars. 'But I wouldn't know how I can leave himself, not till he can shake a loose leg a bit more—'

'Shake the Protector off his back, you mean!'

And she laughed with delicious, daring camaraderie, for well she knew she was mad to speak so of Somerset, 'but not to you,' she said, and he drew nearer in the proud joy of sharing an indiscretion. It was not the only one they shared, for she had put up her hand with that half appeal to him, and he had taken it in his, and she did not know how to draw it away, though she knew she ought to; she was of the blood royal, second in succession to the throne of England, and more, she was in love with the most magnificent man in the kingdom, a man three times the age and ten times the power and experience and worldly knowledge of this young page, the son of an Irish Chieftain, who came from the hills and bogs of a savage country where no Englishman went, except to lose honour and die.

'I may never hold your hand again,' he said. 'I may never look at you again except from across the hall and I carrying some pompous dish that no one wants to eat, and you with some great English lord looking into your eyes the way he'd drink the honey from them as if they were the blue flowers of heaven itself. But this moment is mine, and not even God can take it from me, that I'm holding your slight hand in mine, and your eyes are looking at me. I'll never ask it of you again. I ask only this, to be true to you and yours from this hour on. Wherever I am across the seas, whatever I am doing there, I swear to leave it on the instant that I know I can be of service to you or yours, so help me God and His Mother.'

He bent his smooth dark head and kissed her hand, so hard that it hurt. As he looked up, Bess flung her arms round his neck and kissed him.

Behind her the window was open to the soft spring night, and she heard the faint crunch of gravel on the path. She swung round, but the steps had passed on. Frightened, she put on her shoes, caught Barney's hand and swung him back into the procession and they danced on.

There was another break in it, and this time her hand was in her brother's; it was hot and clammy as it pulled her aside.

'Let's stop a moment,' he said, coughing. 'Look, here's a cool corner. Did Jane give you my message?'

'What message?' ('the blue flowers of heaven itself' – had Barney really said that about her eyes?).

'About Mr Cheke?'

'Oh – that!'

'What do you mean? Did you forget to pray as I asked?'

'Oh no,' said Bess with glib haste, 'I prayed – hard.'

'It didn't really matter.' Edward's voice sounded rather smug. 'I'd done it, and God heard me. I knew He would. I told them all so, this morning when I came down to breakfast, and it's happened just as I said it would. At midday he took a turn for the better. The doctors say now he will live.'

'Flounder, flounder in the sea—' sang Bess, to her brother's astonishment. 'Do you too think you are God?'

'Of course I don't,' said Edward, hurt. 'God heard me, that's all. Don't you believe in prayers?'

'Not half as much as our sister Mary does, and yet you are dead against her.'

'She,' said Edward with masterly simplicity, 'prays in the wrong way.'

'How do you know which is the right one?'

'The best brains in the kingdom are finding out. Listen, I've just heard this from the Archbishop, it's to be the final blessing to the service of Communion – that's what it's to be called now, you know, instead of the old Mass. Cranmer won't truckle to that.'

'Well, *he* ought to know all about truckling – perhaps even how to avoid it!'

'What do you mean?' demanded Edward sternly, but was too eager with his information to wait to reprove her. 'He's made everything perfectly clear in it. "The piece of God, that passeth – all understanding." You see? Who wants to tear God's flesh in his teeth and drink His blood? The blood and wine are only a symbol of remembrance – a piece of God that passes through men's minds, all men understanding that it is but a symbol. Do you understand?' he added anxiously, for women, even the cleverest, were sometimes curiously obtuse.

Bess was thinking it out. At last she said, 'I should give more attention to spelling and less to theology if I were you. I believe it might help.'

But as she looked down at the flushed face and saw through it into the childish, precocious, literal mind that was so determined, like his father's, to build for himself a cast-iron set of theories that should prove himself always in the right, a sudden trembling wave of pity caught her up. Why should he not think himself in the right? He was so small and frail, he might not have very long in which to do it. Something of Barney's protective passion for his little King had communicated itself to her, though she could not know, as did his constant companion, how much he needed it; only that, where his father's sense of self-rightness had blazed like the sun at noonday, Edward's was like a pale slip of moonlight, steady but cold, cold and lonely.

A great heat had gone out of the world with the passing of King Henry, stupendous rascal as he may have been. That vehement and earthy heat seemed to have burnt out all the life round it; both Edward and the Protector were shadows in comparison, conscientious, earnest, cold.

The music was dying away through the house – a long tingling sigh, and then it ceased, as if giving up the competition with the enormous buzz of voices that drummed from every corner of the manor like the humming from a monstrous hive. The noise converged from every side and surged into the hall; the guests were gathering together and taking their leave in order of precedence; the Duke of Somerset approached his royal nephew respectfully and reminded him of the speech of thanks he must make to his other uncle; the King came down into the hall with his sister, and his gentlemen-in-waiting lined up behind him. His page Barnaby Fitzpatrick came forward with his monarch's fur-lined cloak over his arm to protect him from the night air on the river, bent to put it round the younger boy, then straightened himself, stood back tall and slim and dark behind the fair child, and his glowing eyes fastened once more on his Princess.

She thought he looked like a supple water-reed among all these stiff-coated cabbages. She gave a swift glance round; no one that she could see was looking at her; and placed the tips of her fingers to her lips.

They were all going away down the water-steps; the King had entered his royal barge, the rest were following. Catherine said, 'I cannot stay on my feet one moment longer. I am going to bed,' and her husband tenderly pressed her to do so.

'I'll see to the rest. There's no need for you to worry. Go to bed and sleep sound. I'll not wake you by coming in to say good-night.'

Catherine went.

Bess stayed beside Tom, still saying goodbye to all the lesser guests. He turned to her in a pause between the leave-takings and said, quick and low and furious, 'I must speak to you, tonight. Come out on the water-steps as soon as all these poultry have clucked away. I'll have my barge ready; we'll go on the river.'

'What am I to say to Mrs Ashley?'

'Tell her to go to the devil along with the rest of these old hens. Do I need to tell you what to say?'

'No,' said Bess.

She ran upstairs. Cat Ashley was waiting for her, laying out her night-shift.

'Go away,' said Bess.

'But—your Highness!'

'Didn't you hear what I said? Well, if you must stay, give me my cloak – *any* cloak, woman! What are you havering for?'

'A cloak – *now*? A *cloak*!'

'Stop clucking! I'm accompanying His Majesty on his barge.'

'The royal barge left a quarter of an hour ago,' said Mrs Ashley, slowly stiffening.

'What the devil do I care? Give me my cloak.'

'I dare not.'

But in a paroxysm of nervous agitation Mrs Ashley had already reached it down. Bess snatched it from her, dealt a resounding smack on her governess's cheek which sent her staggering into a chair, and whisked out of the room.

Sitting up, a little stunned, her hand groping doubtfully, unbelievingly, to her face, Mrs Ashley heard the bedroom door being locked on her.

CHAPTER TEN

'I tell you I looked in through the window as I passed, and I saw you fling your arms round a man's neck and kiss him.'

'I have kissed no man tonight,' said Bess.

Well, it was true, wasn't it? Barnaby Fitzpatrick was no man yet; he was probably no older than herself. But it was delightful that the Admiral should think she had kissed a man tonight, a real grown man; that he should mind so much that she felt a delicious qualm of terror as to what he might do next.

He could not do much, he reflected. Not with his watermen rowing the barge within a few yards of them, and their heads facing the canopy under which he and the girl sat on their cushions. Fortunately, the fellows could not understand English, or so he chose to believe. He slipped his arm round her under her cloak and pressed her lithe young body against his own. There was nothing tender or yielding in it, but he felt it tingling with life.

'God's living soul!' he breathed in her ear. 'If only you were not a virgin!'

In answer came a shocked gasp that turned to a desperate little laugh, and then a whisper: 'How do you know?'

'You devil's strumpet! Have you given your body to any

man? Who was that fellow tonight? *Answer* me!' he commanded, while his hand gripped her arm.

But she did not cry out. 'Now I shall have to hide my arm from my waiting-women,' she breathed softly.

'Only from your women? Has no man seen them?'

'Oh yes!'

'Which? You witch! You bitch!'

'Who? Tu whit, to whoo! Why you! you!' she gave back on a mocking call that answered the big white owl as it went skimming past them over the dark waters to its nest in the old trees round Lambeth Palace.

Bess leant forward from the canopy to watch its flight. The moonlight fell on her face, a pale oval in the darkness; it glittered on her eyes. Her lips parted in a smile of ecstasy that chilled the man beside her as though he had no part in it, for it was self-contained, the bliss of suddenly awakened vanity. She had no room at the moment to think of Tom himself; she was too full of the discovery that can only come once in a lifetime, if it come at all, the discovery that she, like her mother, was the kind to drive men mad for her. Barney had been mad to speak to her as he had done tonight, the Admiral was mad to take her out in his barge, and she herself mad to box her governess's ears and rush out to join him. 'This is the happiest night of my life,' she told herself, for never before had a man told her that he loved her, and tonight two men – well, a man and a boy – had done so.

The river flowed past below them, gleaming dark and pale together, the ripples lapping and hissing against the sides of the barge; rippling in secret laughter, it flowed on beside them, past them, away into the darkness of the sleeping city, a river tireless as time itself, bearing on its shores this mighty stream of human life all unknowing of its future, even as she was of hers, with all her life rippling away before her into the undiscovered darkness.

'London is breathing all round us,' she said.

'Its breath stinks, then,' said Tom.

But he could not prick her ecstatic bubble. Of course the river smelt, but so did the ghostly shapes of white may trees flowering on its banks. The dark towers of Whitehall Palace glided past them, and she giggled in delight to think what the Protector and his wife, shut up there in the stuffy dark, would say if they knew who was outside in the barge. The jagged unfinished walls of Somerset House rose beside them; the old houses on London Bridge flung a dark pall shadow upon them as they shot one of its arches; in the distance a lighted window shone out high up among the trees.

'There is a light in Lambeth Palace,' said Bess on a pious note. 'My brother says the Archbishop is working night after night at this new religion.'

'There's something in it,' said the Admiral reflectively. 'Some of these Reformers suggest making it legal to have two wives.'

'I'd never make one of a pair!'

'Not you! You'd be as jealous as the Sultan.'

'Or as yourself. Some of them say a woman should have two husbands, but you don't mention that!'

'God's death, who *was* that man?'

'There *was* no man.'

'Liar!'

Bess hugged herself with enjoyment. 'What will you

become?' he had once asked her, and this was what she had become: a woman with the power to tease him into a rage while she kept her head. She spoke in a cool detached voice, only spoilt by a slight breathlessness. 'Some of them want to do away with marriage altogether. It isn't only religion is in the melting-pot, it's the whole of society. Nobody knows what will happen – to any of us – but then – nobody ever did.'

And her unusual philosophic speculation relapsed into a high-pitched giggle of excitement.

It exasperated him. Why the devil had he been such a fool as to bring her out? Virgins were raw as unripe fruit. She was not yet ripe enough even to be excited by a man, only by the admiration and desire that she excited. She was a pert affected chit – not a patch on her mother, and never would be. He told her so, and she longed to scream with rage but became very grown-up and distant and told him it was nothing to her that he had plainly been in love with her mother – as no doubt it had been nothing to her mother either.

He roared to the boatmen to turn about and take them home.

Bess sat stiff with fury. She told herself she cared less than a hoot of the white owl what the Admiral thought of her, or any other man. She would never care for him, or any man. What pleasure was there in seeing them get hot and excited, beyond the pleasure that she could make them do so? That was all they should ever be to her – tributes to her power.

The river flowed against them now, the ripples flopping louder against the barge as they were rowed up-stream, the rowlocks giving their steady rhythmic click in answer. The sleeping houses slid past again, but the awe she had felt of the stream of unknown life was now tinged with both pity and envy – so many little humdrum lives sleeping all round her, people going home from work every night, maids that she had seen this morning hanging out their summer smocks to bleach in the sun, lads she had seen last week in the dawn of May Day bearing green branches from the woods to deck their homes, hovels though they might be – all these people lay sleeping helplessly round her, poor, pinched, and ugly perhaps, yet all had been intent on getting home to something or someone that made it home to them. But for whom was she going back, in Catherine's house?

She would not think of Catherine.

The moments were slipping past them in the dark, sliding along as fast as the ripples below them. The river-bank rose beside them; tall reeds swayed in the night breeze and shadowy willows drooped towards them; wild swans lay asleep like patches of moonlight, and the white saucer shapes of hemlock starred the darkness. They passed the square stone tower of Chelsea Church, they were just coming to Chelsea Place, the moments were slipping away faster and faster, and she had wasted them all in teasing; this was the happiest night of her life and she had thrown it away, she had driven away the man who sat beside her. She tried desperately to recall him. In a sudden jerky voice she said:

'Soon it will be strawberry-time again. Do you remember them dipped in wine on board the *Great Harry*? I was a little girl then.'

'You are now,' he replied sourly. 'The more fool I for wasting time on such a flutterpate!'

It was no good. The barge had stopped. He was holding

out his hand to help her out on to the water-steps. She had let it all slide past her, instead of telling him how she loved him. Next time she would tell him.

She huddled her cloak round her and pretended to yawn. 'And now I must let out my governess,' she said. 'Heigh-ho for hell let loose!'

CHAPTER ELEVEN

'Hell let loose!' said the Duke to himself, looking sideways across the velvet counterpane at his Duchess. He had been thinking it some time. Aloud he said in a carefully gentle tone, 'Well, it's time we both got some sleep.'

It only started her off again. Up sprang all the different heads to her wrath, as many as the hydra-headed monster's.

Imprimis: Her brother-in-law's party this evening; its showy, its sumptuous, its positively vulgar display, for there was no state, no dignity about it, a hoydenish romp led by a pack of prancing foreigners. And where did he get the money for it, a mere younger brother? By all sorts of vile practices, she'd be bound: commerce with pirates, taking bribes, false coinage – there was a deal of debased money going about.

'King Henry started debasing it long ago,' the Duke murmured. The Duchess kicked the sheet.

Item: Her sister-in-law's appearance this evening, its showy, sumptuous, positively vulgar, etc., as before. Far too much rouge, which only showed up how wan and peaked looking her face had grown. The folly of starting a first child at her age! And if she did succeed in bearing it, 'Look at the danger to *us*! A son and heir of theirs starting a rival royal house!'

'Well, I can't prevent their having one,' said the Duke.

'When did you ever prevent anything? You should have prevented the marriage. But you can't even prevent her taking precedence of me.'

'You did that, my love.'

The Duchess actually hooted. The Duke thankfully forbore to tell her how the guests had grinned and nudged each other as the two ladies, both great with child, had collided and all but stuck in the doorway.

Item: On the same matter of this treasonable marriage. Yes, it was sheer treason. For it had taken place so indecently soon after the King's death that if Catherine had had a child at once by the Admiral it might have been in doubt as to whether it were not by the late King – and so treasonably, have endangered the succession to the throne.

'But she didn't, so it couldn't,' he replied.

'But she might have, and then it would have,' was the answer.

The Duke gave it up.

Item: 'Another matter.' (The Duke drew breath in relief. He drew it too soon.)

'This matter of my eldest son – our eldest son. It is he who should be heir to your titles and estates.'

'You ask me,' said the suffocated voice in the rosy gloom of the bed-curtains, 'to set aside my legitimate eldest son and heir by my first wife, for no other reason than that you want your own to inherit. It is impossible, and you know it. The law—'

'Pah, don't weary me with lawyer's stuff. I know that you can do what you like with the laws. You are altering them and bringing in fresh ones every day to suit yourself. King Henry himself never did such preposterous things as you are doing. *He* would never allow the clergy to marry – he always said they'd breed like rabbits and over-populate the island. Besides, look at Mrs Cheke!'

'Cheke's not a clergyman.'

'A tutor then, it's all the same. But why are you dragging in clergymen—'

'I was not.'

'—when I'm talking of my son – our son – whom you want to dispossess? Don't you love me better than you did your first wife? You must, or you wouldn't have divorced her for me.'

He supposed he had. He really couldn't think now how it had happened.

'Well then,' continued the inexorable voice, 'while you're fiddling with the law to please your own whims, you can do this one little thing for me.'

He *could* not do it.

But he knew that he would.

Item: They must have more than empty titles and lands to leave to her son – their son. Would those lazy hounds of workmen never finish Somerset House? And the mansion he proposed to build near his old home, Wolf Hall, barely started! No really suitable place of their own to live in when in town, Richmond and Sion House so out of the way. Master Admiral had *his* town house all ready; being only a younger son, he would of course get Seymour Place and the best of everything, while they themselves at this moment were boxed up in this untidy rabbit-warren of Whitehall.

'It was good enough for King Henry.'

'That old man! So old-fashioned. Never minded even about water laid on.'

'If a conduit 1,600 feet long and 15 feet deep will satisfy you,' came an exhausted whisper, 'the foundations for it are already laid down at Wolf Hall. I had a letter from my brother Henry about it this evening, just before we started for Seymour Place. I believe I have it in this room.'

His voice had quite revived at the hope of finding something to stave off the other. He got out of bed, and turned up the lamp. It was a warm night. He padded barefoot across the room and drew back the window-curtains and saw the light up the river in the Archbishop's study, as Bess had seen it from the Admiral's barge. But he did not draw the same pious conclusion.

'Cantuar is going the pace. There he is sitting up at cards again. Last week when I supped at Lambeth Palace I won thirty-five shillings off him. A lot of money for an Archbishop.'

'But you lost one and fourpence to the Bishop of Rochester at his shooting-match at Guildford yesterday,' came an accusing reminder from behind him.

The Duke hastily turned to the table where he had left the papers concerning the new place he was going to build near his old home of Wolf Hall. His brother Henry, the stolid country squire, was seeing to it all for him; it was all he was good for. And he lived now at the old timbered house of Wolf Hall; it was all it was good for. Not worth adding to – a poky little place, his Duchess had called it; and when his sister Jane had married King Henry they had had to convert the great barn into a banqueting hall for the festivities, since there was no room in the house for all the Court. King Hal in high good humour, having just beheaded Nan Bullen, had twitted Jane with their marriage revels in a barn, like any pair of gipsies. She had smiled dutifully. But her eldest brother had felt it deeply.

Now he was making up for it. Neglecting Wolf Hall itself, he had bought up vast new estates all round it. The mere names of the manor-houses on them filled nearly three columns. He had dissolved a priory near Pewsey to furnish himself with a country house, but that would only be temporary. An enormous palace would rise on the two wooded hills of Bedwyn Brail, already cleared of trees for the purpose, commanding a spacious view of the Vale of Pewsey. He had enclosed huge parks for hunting and stocked them with game. He had ordered caravans of Purbeck stone to be quarried in the Isle of Purbeck and brought all those miles in an endless procession of straining oxen carts. He had (or Henry had) got the brickmakers digging clay for ninety thousand bricks. Four hundred workmen had been at work on the place for a year.

And today had come from Henry the magic message: 'The plumber is getting ready.' He read it out in triumph.

'Is that all? What of the new lake?'

'He says, "The pond, thanks be to God, will hold water."'

'As it should at a cost of £43. 15s. 10d.'

'But he won't compass the bottom.'

'Whose bottom?'

'Ramphries Bottom. If that's brought within the compass of the pond—'

'Lake.'

'Yes, lake – "Then," he says, "the Tenants of Wilton should

have no maner of common for their rudder beasts, which would be to their utter undoing, for they kept before this tyme in their common, as they say, 180 rudder beasts, and if the whole wood and bottom aforesaid shoald be taken from them, then they would kepe none. And as it is an Old Saying, 'Enough is as good as a feste,' I pray God so we may finde urne."'

'What in the name of God are "rudder beaste"? And "urne"?'

'Urne is "ours" – "ouren," as he would say. And rudder is the rude Saxon word, "hruther" or "hryther," for horned cattle.'

The Duchess lay back on the satin pillows apparently in a dead faint, from which she presently recovered sufficiently to demand of her lord how this rustic had been begotten in his family, and what had given him the notion that he could so identify himself with the Lord Protector as to speak of "ouren," "urne," or "ours"? Lecture him with old sayings? And consider the interests of the cottage tenants as of superior importance to the Lord Protector's?

The Protector tried to point out that it would not look well for him to enclose common grazing land that had belonged for centuries to the people, merely to enlarge an ornamental lake, and at the very moment that he was bringing in an Act of Parliament against the enclosures of the Common lands. But his difficulty in doing so made him wonder, not for the first time, whether any man could be a reformer who was not a bachelor.

He beat a retreat to Henry's letter. Henry had stocked Fasterne Park with 500 deer, a piece of news that gave the

Duchess some satisfaction, for the Admiral and Catherine were still vainly petitioning for Fasterne, her family property, to be restored to her. The Duke had not told that to Henry. Nor did he tell his wife that he had not told him.

Encouraged by her approval, he handed on Henry's information that 'the work will get on faster if God send fayre wether, as hitherto we have none, but always extremity of rayne.' 'Curious thing,' added the Duke. 'He told me the workmen say it's never stopped raining since Thomas More was beheaded. You wouldn't think they'd still care about the death of a scholar.'

The Duchess didn't care what they cared about. She remarked that Henry was 'a proper hayseed, always grumbling about the weather!'

'He grumbles about more than that.' The Duke got back into bed, pulling back the curtain for the light as he added, 'Barwick seems to be a slack paymaster. Henry asks me to write to him direct to pay the wages punctually – "or els" – where is it now? Oh yes – "or els shure our men will not aply ther works so well as els: for the poor men here do much complayn—"'

'No news in *that*!' barked the Duchess, but he went on unswervingly, '"although they be delayed but from Satterday to Monday next following, yet somewhat it hyndereth and the poor men can not forebeare, because they must take the advantage of the market, or els they can not live with their wages; for where an ox selleth for XX nobles ther will but small penyworths arise, and when it is bought out of the market then it is worse. This do the poor men alledge unto me with such an exclamacion that I can do no lesse than write the same unto ye."'

The Duke laid down the letter, 'How like Henry!' he said indulgently.

'*Just* like Henry! Making their exclamation to him indeed! That shows what sort of master he makes. They can speak to him as to one of themselves.'

'That is how it should be, surely.'

'Oh, leave all that for your speeches! You are not in Parliament now. We'd best go down and see to it or nothing will get done.'

'But – the press of my work! I have five new Bills to introduce at this session.'

'Surely you can manage a "Satterday to Monday next following"?'

'Well – it would be very pleasant.'

But would it? He wasn't sure. Nor was she. Last time they had gone, a herd of little pigs had been cluttering up the drive just as she was alighting from her coach, and when at her command the Duke had complained to his brother, Henry had only grinned and held up one of them in his arms. "A pig can look at a Protector," he had said. That was Homely Harry's idea of a joke. No, she decided, they would not go down for a Satterday to Monday.

'Pray Heaven he never come to town again to disgrace us!'

'He never will, you can rest assured of that. It was hard enough to make him come up for his knighthood at the Coronation – and then complained his new boots were too tight and that he'd rather be fox-hunting.'

'That plebeian sport! He might at least make it hares. The upkeep of that old house at Wolf Hall is absurdly expensive. £2 a year for the Chaplain – the same wage as the Grubber. It is simply throwing money away, as we are never in residence.'

'But Henry is, on my account.'

'Then let him pay it, if he has need of one, which he has not, for I'll swear he goes to the village church with the other yokels. Has he no more to say?'

'Only that he ends as usual, "Praying you that I may be most hartely commended unto my good lady your bedfellow."'

The Duchess yelped. 'Of all odious coarse old-fashioned expressions! Is it not enough to have a scoundrel for one brother-in-law but I must have a simpleton for the other?'

He tried to soothe her with a sleepy laugh that ended abruptly in a yawn.

'But, my dove, you *are* my bedfellow.' And he put an arm round her to demonstrate the fact, but his dove clawed it. Pained, he withdrew it.

'My first Duchess would never have dared do that. And she was a Fillol.'

'I am a Plantagenet.'

'Only on the distaff side.'

'What odds? At least it ensures legitimacy.'

'She was no bastard,' he said haughtily.

'And no duchess either. You forget how raw your title is.'

'And you, that I gave you yours.'

'What need have I of your upstart Tudor titles, I whose mother was a daughter of the great-grandson of a son of Edward III?'

'The youngest son – of thirteen. In a few generations there'll be precious few of our families who can't claim descent from a son of Edward III.'

The Protector always took long views. But his tact in propounding them was short-sighted. The storm that followed raged hysterically over every cause for grievance he had ever given her.

'I am wretched, wretched, wretched,' she cried. 'I don't know what is wrong – only everything in the world. I only know that I am the most wretched creature alive and I wish I were dead.'

He tried desperately to comfort her, while he wondered how he had ever become enslaved to this strident woman. She reminded him that she was with child by him, of all the painful symptoms of her condition, of her certainty that she would not survive its birth, for she had never felt as bad as this time.

But she would survive it; she would survive him; she would live to be nearly a hundred, and marry again and make others as wretched as himself. He knew it all. He could not escape. He could only agree to all her terms of unconditional surrender.

'You will make my son your heir?'

'Yes,' he said faintly.

'You will never give in to the odious woman and her demands for Fasterne?'

'No,' he said fretfully.

'Nor for her – for the King's jewels?'

'No.' It was almost a whisper by now. He added after a hesitant pause, 'Not even – don't you think we might send back her wedding ring?'

'Most certainly not. It's the principle that counts. Admit that she has the right to one thing, then she has it to all.'

He saw the conclusion only too well. He even agreed to it. But not aloud.

The voice continued: 'You will look into those extraordinary practices of the Admiral – piracy – false coinage – his quite open working up of a party against you? And his seduction of the Princess Elizabeth.'

'What!' The exhausted voice was startled into life again.

Oh yes, the Duchess had had it on the best authority from her maid. Or, at least, if the Admiral had not already seduced the Princess, he soon would. An offence not merely against morals but against the throne.

Her tongue darted hither and thither. If he could see it (but he had put out the light) it surely would be forked. It hissed the word 'treason'.

'Do you understand what you are demanding of me?' he said. 'You are wishing me to prove my own brother guilty of high treason. To condemn him to the block.'

'It would not be you. It would be the law.'

'Which you have already asked me to twist to your purposes.'

He did not hear her answer. He felt he was suffocating. And it was now near morning, and if he got no sleep, how could he work tomorrow? He promised to do all she had asked, and at last her tongue was still, and they lay still, the woman still within the man's arms, taut, wide-awake, staring with hot eyes into the dark.

A consuming envy seemed to burn away her vitals; envy of her hosts this evening, who had been so much in love that they could not wait to marry at the prudent time; of the Princess Elizabeth sitting upright and bright-eyed beside her brother at the banquet, so very young; of the way she had looked across the table at the Admiral's genial jokes, meeting his quick glances, startled yet unaware, her eager childish hands stretched out so greedily to life, all unknowing what they might take.

So she herself had been – once.

What had happened since to make everything so different? If she had had a man in love with her like the Admiral, scoundrel as he might be, would she not be different now? But he hated her, as she hated him, hated, hated.

Her life was nothing. She too had clutched at it with both hands, and it had crumbled in them to dust and ashes. All her beauty, her radiant strength of will and purpose, strength to love or hate (it was the same thing really) all wasted on this man beside her, a fine figure, but only a figure, a figurehead rather, dry as dust, cold as ashes; while his youngest brother glowed and vibrated with the warmth and splendour of life. And she had wasted herself on this poor weak creature, whom she could twist round her little finger.

Yet in her despair she turned and clung to him like a thing drowning.

He had fallen into an uneasy dream, and felt she was dragging him down, down, into the uttermost depths of what black and icy sea?

He floundered this way and that in those dreadful waters, dragged down, down, down by his frantic burden, floundered and floundered. A huge fish floated towards him and stared at him with gaping mouth and eyes.

'Flounder, flounder in the sea,' he heard his mother say, and through the black engulfing water all round him he could see her perched by his little carved wood bed in the old nursery at Wolf Hall, telling a bed-time story to him alone; when he was still the only boy, and no interloping baby brothers as yet, only docile, adoring sisters. He could see his mother's peaked cap, her small hands gesturing as she told the story; he tried to reach her through the choking waves, to call to her to save him. 'Come to me,' he shrieked. 'Come and save me.'

But she never saw nor turned her head; only her voice went on inexorably:

'Come, for my wife Isabel
Wishes what I dare not tell.'

CHAPTER TWELVE

The light burnt all night in Lambeth Palace, where Archbishop Cranmer sat, writing the new English Prayer Book that was to make a new land of saints from this old sinful England.

He wrote in his window, never seeing the soft spring night outside, but only the balancing phrases that took shape on the blank paper beneath his fingers, phrases that responded to each other, built themselves up like the rungs of a ladder up to heaven, into the most perfect prose ever yet written in English.

And it was he who was writing it, he who was creating this great work, imperfect, tremulous man that he was, an arrant coward, as he had always known whenever he had entered the presence of that Sun of Man, that majestic, rollicking, bewildering, baffling Master, who had passed away only a little over a year ago, though it seemed like three or four centuries, and left the world this tired dim place, peopled by shadows.

He fingered the two grey prongs of straggling beard that were growing as long as a gnome's in a German fairy-tale.

He had never cut nor trimmed it since King Henry died. His Gretchen did not like it. She did not see why he should look like an old goat as a protest against shaven priests – nor as a token of affection to his late master. Women had no sense of loyalty. They had no sense of proportion. She was mistress of Lambeth Palace, she was wife of the Archbishop of Canterbury, a thing no woman had ever been before.

Yet she could worry about his beard. Was it, after all, a mistake to combine the clerical office with matrimony? He had never intended to do so himself; in fact, he had intended neither.

He had been frightened from women as a young man when he had been tricked and bullied into marrying the bouncing black-eyed niece of the landlady of the Dolphin Inn at Cambridge, and had therefore had to resign his new-won Fellowship. It had been a bitter pill to swallow along with the 'raw, small and windy ale' that Erasmus had so complained of as they sat and drank together at the Dolphin.

Lucky for him, said his friends, that his Black Joan died in childbed within the year, and he was promptly re-elected as Fellow. He also took Orders, a safeguard against further assaults. And ever after at Cambridge he frequented only the White Horse, where there were no dangerous women though plenty of dangerous talk; for the inn was so well known as a meeting-place for Lutheran reformers that it was nicknamed Little Germany.

But when much later he visited their headquarters in Germany itself, he fell in love, at forty-five, with the daughter of a scholar at Nuremberg, a maiden as fair, pliable and docile, as devoted to himself, as Joan had been dark and flashy and shrilly intent on her own way. He felt safe with Margarete Hosmer – Gretchen she liked him to call her – who was young enough to be his daughter, but cared and cooked and sewed for him as though she were his mother. After more than twenty years the widower remarried, intending never to settle permanently again in England, certainly never to hold office there.

But no sooner had he acquired a wife than King Henry required him to help get rid of his; no sooner had he resolved to slip quietly into retirement than King Henry ordered him to become Archbishop of Canterbury. He was plunged into action for the first time in his life, and in middle life. His friends showered congratulations on him; he would be the King's greatest servant, as Wolsey had been, now cast away. But Cranmer did not want honours and preferment and riches; he wanted peace and quiet.

Henry promised it to him; he even liked to share it; often he would come to visit him at Lambeth, look at his books, ask to see what he was writing now, and walk with him in the garden, even in winter, where as he said he could find rest as nowhere else, in its 'singular quiet.'

The Archbishop's hand paused in its writing as the rhythmic thumping click of rowlocks floated up through his open window at this late hour. He went to the window and his eyes absently followed the dark form of a barge gliding past; then turned and rested on the moon-washed spaces of the lawns directly below him, the black shapes of trees, the ghostly bushes of white may that wafted their scent out on the cool air.

It had not always known peace. He could see the sharp shadow cast by the little shed where Sir Thomas More had sat and awaited the verdict of the Commissioners that was to be his doom; while at a little distance 'boisterous Latimer' had walked up and down with various doctors and chaplains, joking and jollying them, flinging his arms about their necks.

And there was the pretty summer-house that Cranmer himself had built, now turned to a glimmering temple by the magic rays of the moon. He used to love to sit there, sometimes dozing a little in the sun; until that night in May before Nan Bullen's execution. Then he could find no sleep in his bed, and wandered out into the garden, up and down, up and down, remembering how More had prophesied this very thing: 'her sporting and dancing will spurn our heads off like footballs, yet it will not be long before hers will dance the same dance.'

It had not been long. Just a year after the King beheaded More to secure the legality of his marriage to Nan, he ordered Cranmer to prove the marriage illegal: and struck off the lovely head for which he had spurned the wisest and noblest in England.

'Is there in good faith no more difference between you and me,' More had asked her, 'but that I shall die today, and you tomorrow?'

The question had echoed in Cranmer's heart ever since, but addressed to himself.

Never since that night had he been able to find rest in the little summer-house where at last, worn out by wandering aimlessly up and down, he had sat breathing in the scent of the white may, while the birds began their first faint songs and the dawnlight turned the river pale as a corpse; and he knew that his love for his great master was full of horror and fear.

Yet this love was somehow enhanced by it. The King had

never been cruel to *him*, so that his adoration had in it something of the pride of a favourite pupil. He needed that, for his schooldays had been tortured by a savage bully of a master who, as Cranmer frequently explained, had 'dulled and daunted the fine wits of his scholars.' Every time he forgot anything he said this, lamenting that he had lost 'both memory and audacity' from his cruel treatment and could never recover from it. Every time he did so he knew his old complaint was boring his friends, who thought it high time to outgrow his childish troubles; and what was there to complain of anyway, since More himself had been astounded by the subtlety of Cranmer's mind?

Surprisingly, it was a master still more savage who restored his self-respect by making him his friend. And absorbing the singular quiet that Henry had loved like himself, Cranmer felt that he alone knew what it was to miss the King.

CHAPTER THIRTEEN

'I love you. You think I am a child, that I don't know what that means, but I do, I *do*. I want to be yours, now, wholly and for ever.'

'Bess, you're mad, we're both mad I think—'

'Does my Lord Admiral preach sanity, safety to me now? Will you of all men trim your sails to the wind?'

'You devil's brat! You've bewitched me clean out of my senses.'

'But I want you too. I am longing – oh, for what? I do not know, and if you do not give it me, I shall never know.'

'Child!' he cried, but it was no child he held in his arms.

The wind outside the little arbour in the pleached alley was tearing the clouds and the fruit trees and flowering shrubs to pieces; long strips of white scudded across the brilliant sky, clouds of blossom blew up in the air, separated into pink and white snowflakes to be tossed here and there over the prim walks; butterflies were blown as helplessly as the flying petals, and a pair of blackbirds went fluttering up, this way and that, as light as scraps of burnt paper in the wind, screaming and chattering because their nest had been blown over and their silly fat fledgelings were now each opening a squawking orange beak and rolling an indignant eye in so many different parts of the garden. The boatmen were shouting to each other on the river beyond the garden walls as their slight craft drove headlong before the half-gale; from their cockney, jeering cries one could not guess what danger they were in, but certainly they were trimming their sails to the wind.

Which the Admiral, of all men, could not do. He looked down at this young witch that had flung herself across his knees, a thin scrap of a girl whose arms felt brittle enough to break in his grasp.

How on earth, or in hell rather, had she come to get this hold on him? He had thought he was amusing himself with a little girl, crude, yet sharp as a small stiletto, and sure enough she had stabbed him to the heart.

Her face looked up at him, all the lines immature, yet a white flame in the red of her hair; he bent his head to quench it, and kissed her.

There came another sound among all the crying noises in the wind, a crunching sound on the gravel of short high-heeled steps that kept hurrying and then checking, steps that were accustomed to be faster and lighter than they now had to go. Catherine came down the pleached alley, stopped dead, turned round as if to go back, then turned again, and came slowly on to them.

Quickly the Admiral gave Bess a shake, told her jokingly to get to her feet for a brazen hussy, told Catherine he'd been scolding her, for he'd looked through the window and seen her kissing some man, but now all was forgiven.

Bess babbled nervously. 'It's not true. What man could I have kissed? I never see any man alone but my tutor, and *would* I kiss Mr Grindal?' She finished on a frightened giggle.

But neither of them was listening; nor looked at her, and Catherine's face staring up at her husband was grey and pinched. She opened her mouth to speak, but no sound came out; she was twisting her hands together and suddenly she flung them open as though throwing something away, and turned and ran back down the pleached alley, ran blindly, clumsily, heavily, so differently from her usual light dancing step that Bess saw for the first time what it must be to her to be carrying the burden of a child.

The Admiral brushed straight past her and ran after Catherine.

She was left standing alone in the flickering pale green light under the leaves. She felt that she would now be alone for ever.

'You must go away,' said Catherine. 'What else can I do? I am responsible for you, and if any harm comes to you while under my charge, I should have betrayed my trust.'

'Madam—' began Bess, but Catherine put up her hand.

'I know what you would say, and I too, that my lord intends you no harm. But we have to think of harm in other terms than those of actual fact. The harm done you by gossip and slander might endanger not only your reputation but your whole position in the country, perhaps even your life. And I am certain that, if no bad twist should happen to your fate, you will one day be Queen of England.'

She spoke so quietly, casually almost, that Bess wondered for a moment if she had indeed heard her, or if it were her own voice that had at last uttered this thing that she had said to herself so long: 'You will one day be Queen of England.'

She had never believed that she would ever hear anyone else say it, and now here was the Queen herself saying it, at the very moment when her pain and humiliation were so acute that she could not believe she would ever outlive it; all her life she would be standing in front of her stepmother, staring down at the black and white marble tiles, unable ever again to lift her eyes and look Catherine in the face.

Yet Catherine had not spoken harshly; there was a distressed, almost an apologetic note in her 'I *must* send you away,' as though wondering whether she were wrong in doing so, whether there were anything else she could possibly do, or have done in the past. 'I have thought of you as a child,' she said, 'but you are that no longer. You have great responsibilities and dangers ahead of you, and I should only add to them if I kept you here. What are you thinking?' she added suddenly, for there had been no change in the masked face since she began to speak to her. But now at last Bess raised those long white lids that veiled her eyes, and looked full at her.

'That you said, Madam, I should one day be Queen of England.'

She must hear her say it again. Not till then could she believe that she had already heard her say it. Elizabeth of England – how impossible it was that she should ever be called that! Why, there had never been a Queen of England in her own right before, except that one unfortunate example, four and a half centuries ago, of Queen Matilda (enough reason in herself why there had never been another), and even she had to share her title with her enemy cousin King Stephen.

Yet Catherine's quiet voice was considering the matter as

coolly as if it were the most ordinary thing in the world.

'I think it very likely. Your brother is delicate, more so than those now in charge of him trouble to consider. Your sister would never hold the people as you could do. For, remember, that is the whole crux of the matter. Kings here in England do not rule by divine right but by the will of the people. It was the people who put your grandfather on the throne when he defeated and killed Richard Crookback. Your father never forgot that, not even after thirty-eight years of such power and popularity as an English King has not known for centuries. "Would I be such a fool as to kick away the ladder that mounted my family to the throne?" Yes, he said that to me. But now it is the third generation, and neither your brother nor sister will, I think, keep that same sense of what the goodwill of the people has done for their family; or of what it may cease to do, if they are not careful of it.'

'I thought my father ruled more absolutely than any King has dared do here for generations.' Bess spoke eagerly, snatching at this generous chance that Catherine had given to get both their minds away from her present disgrace.

Catherine was indeed determined she should think of the future rather than the present. Her conviction of what that future would be had come to her long since. 'But don't you be the little fool I was when my future was told me as a child,' she said, with a gallant effort at her old gaiety. 'For when a fortune-teller told me I should one day sit on a throne and wear a crown, I refused to do any more sewing, for my hands, I said, were reserved for royal actions – and well slapped I got for it.'

'But it came true,' said Bess. The future is already written for those who can read it in the stars.' She yearned to consult an astrologer, but even in this unguarded moment of relief knew she would be scolded for saying so. But Catherine saw her wish clear enough; she leant forward and took her hands, speaking again with an urgency that sounded rather desperate even to herself, for why should she have to say everything now at this moment, as though there would never be another chance to do so? And suddenly it came into her mind that there might never be one, and that she loved as her own child this girl who had given her more bitter agony of heart than ever her cruel father had done; and that that love mattered more to both of them, and would last when the agony had long since passed away.

'The future is written,' she said, 'but it's in our hands to blot it if we will. The future is for you to make, as you will. The people of England will never keep a wanton for their Queen. They hated your mother as one; it may have been unjustly, but whether so or not, that hate brought her downfall. Their love will bring you greater strength than any army. Treasure it as you would your life, for it will be your life. Why do you cry?'

'You speak so strangely – it's as though we were never to meet again.'

'I did not mean to frighten you. We shall meet again – yes, of course we shall. But how can one count on anything as certain among "the changes and chances of this mortal life" – have you heard that phrase of the Archbishop's? He should be one of our famous poets, yet no man will know what share was his in this Book of Common Prayer – common to all England, its writers unnamed, with all the holy beauty of their words in common.'

But what was the use of her going on about old yellow-faced Mumpsy-mouse and his precious book, when she had spoken as though they might never meet again, as though she might die? 'I cannot bear it,' sobbed Bess, crying as Catherine had never seen her do, 'to go away, and you ill, and it is all my own fault.'

'Not all,' said Catherine sadly.

That obscure and sudden disease, the sweating sickness, was killing off people within a few days of their getting it. Edward's tutor, Mr Cheke, had recovered, but Bess's tutor, Mr Grindal, had caught it and died, and there was all the question of a new tutor for her. Her repentant mood did not lead her to any meek acceptance of her guardians' choice; she flatly refused to learn from the Oxford scholar whom both Catherine and the Admiral wished to appoint. Oxford was old-fashioned, behind the times; all the Princess Mary's tutors had come from Oxford; and Bess insisted on a Cambridge man.

Mr Roger Ascham had been Greek reader at St John's, had set all Cambridge reading and acting Greek plays; he had been Mr Cheke's favourite pupil and supported his theory of modern Greek pronunciation, which was denounced at Oxford as rabidly as heresy. Greek was in itself a kind of heresy; religious reformers based their authority on the newly discovered Greek texts and manuscripts; and this rage for the New Learning had all the excitement of revolt against the tedious old Latin that the monks had used and everyone was tired of.

If you read Greek you were not only clever, you were

modern, you were advanced, you were in the fashion.

And Bess was as determined to flaunt the New Learning as new clothes; she would have this coming Cambridge man, and nobody else. She had already started a correspondence with him, in Latin of course. He was as eager for the post of her tutor as herself. He pulled wires, he wrote charming letters to Mrs Ashley and sent her a silver pen of exquisite Italian workmanship. In the end, as usual, Bess got her way.

This triumph gave a fillip to her departure and took away a little from the uncomfortable sense of being sent off in disgrace. Catherine had done her best to avoid that; but she was deep in love, ill, and frightened, and could not always control her temper. It would flash out at moments in little sub-acid remarks, and then she would be sorry and try to make up for it, and that made it worse.

And Tom had gone off on one of his frequent sudden expeditions to some island or other – Wight or Lundy or the Scillies – murmuring mysterious boasts in his beard: 'Easy to run down the office of Lord Admiral as a show-title, but I tell you it means something. I've now got the rule over a good sort of ships and men. It's a good thing to have the rule of men,' he had added, glowering rather belligerently at his household of women and little girls, and off he had gone without even saying goodbye to Bess. But it was certainly easier with Catherine when he had gone.

Before he came back, Bess too was gone, in the week after Whitsun, riding off down the sun-baked rutted white lanes with the dust rising in clouds under her pony's hoofs and powdering the round pink faces of the campion on the hedges, swirling up over the white clusters of heavy-scented may, up, up, as though to chase the larks that soared, shrilling their songs into the blue sky.

It was good to be riding away from disgrace and scoldings, however gentle; yes, and even from the Admiral and the storms he brewed. All her life lay before her on this springtime journey. Anything might happen. She might run away with Barney, and Edward would make him Lord of Ireland, and she would wear a green kirtle and coat of cloth of gold, such as her mother had so nearly done, in a painted palace built of clay and timber where on winter nights one could hear the howling of wolves on the wind.

She might run even further westward, sailing for months towards the sunset, towards the strange lands that had lain there undiscovered since the beginning of time and now were newly opened to them. The Admiral sometimes spoke in his wild half-joking way of ousting the Spaniards there and founding an empire of his own – and then his eyes had rested on her, and she knew now that when he saw himself as its King he had thought of her as its Queen. Why hadn't she known it at the time? Not even when he told her once that she wore the sunset in her hair and the barbaric gold of the Incas!

She drew in her breath sharply at the memory, then jerked herself awake from her daydreams. Anything might happen, but these things would not happen.

But no, what might really happen was that she would be Queen of England.

She had flatly refused to sit in the stuffy coach with Cat Ashley, declaring its jolting made her sick. But there was another reason beside her enjoyment in the ride, and that was the strange new pride thrilling up in her, that she was riding through the country, showing herself to the people, *her* people – so she had believed, and now Catherine had said they might be one day.

At the least, she could smile and flourish her whip as they ran from their fields and barns and cottage-doors to stare at the young Princess Elizabeth riding by in her white dress with the sunlight on her hair; at the most, she could find some pretext to stop and talk with them, pretended her pony's shoe was loose, or that she wanted a drink of new milk from the pail that some sturdy bare-armed girl was carrying home ('How enchanting to be a milkmaid!' she said, while the girl's shy glances told her how enchanting she would find it to be a princess).

Her escort found it impossible to hurry her through the little country towns, especially if a market were going on, or a travelling fair; then she must buy this or watch that; it was all they could do to stop her getting her fortune told, and always she would talk with any and everybody, however unsuitable. 'Why not, if my father did, and he was King of England?'

Old men told her that it would never be a merry England again till they heard the church bells ringing through the day and night at the hours of prayer, reminding the sick and sorry that they could always go up to the kindly monks for a bite and sup. Bess listened sympathetically to them; as also to the young men on the extreme left of Reform, who insisted that God Himself should be abolished; and that the country would never be right till ruled by 'communistic law'.

But what everybody told her, and far more eagerly than matters of religion or politics, was that in spite of the new laws wages were sinking, since men would work for next to nothing to avoid unemployment; prices were rising, for, though fixed in name, one could always pass something under the counter; and that for all the money you spent you only got rotten imitation goods – leather falsely curried and tanned; 'feather' beds stuffed with rubbish; and even, worst of all, beer made without true malt.

Things were bad, but they might be worse, and one mustn't grumble, said they, grumbling hard, but generally finding something they could make a joke of.

This, and the dogged courage of their patience, made her feel akin to them, though she did not recognise it, only that she was interested and pleased, especially in that they liked her.

She saw a rabble of beggars, alarming as a troop of marauding robbers – which indeed they were; her escort closed in round her, church bells clashed out a warning, and the gates of the little country town she had just left clanged to against them.

> 'Hark, hark, the dogs do bark,
> The beggars are coming to town.'

She saw a little boy led by a chain, and a man with an iron ring round his neck and the letter S branded on his forehead to show that he was his master's slave for ever, to be sold or bequeathed at his will; for the new law against unemployment had made it legal for vagabonds and their children to be sold into slavery. This then was what lay behind the cheerful remark 'might be worse'.

A chill fell on all her high spirits; she rode under the great oaks of Hatfield Park knowing suddenly, irrevocably, that she must not love Tom, nor Tom her, that she was going away where she would not hear his jolly laugh nor deep teasing voice, nor look up at the swaggering shoulders and catch his mocking glance, that had lately grown heavy with desire as he looked at her.

How could she, even half in fun, as a game of 'Let's pretend', have imagined herself with the boy Barney in his remote and savage island? If she could not love Tom, she would never love anybody else, never, never.

But she must not love Tom, and, almost worse than this, she might not have her Pussy-Cat Purr's loving tenderness round her any more.

Nonsense, Catherine had said, of course she would see her again, and very soon; wait till her child was born, and then everything would be the same as before. But would it? Bess could not quite believe it. She too had had her glimpse, though she tried not to recognise it, into what was written in the stars.

In this sudden depression at the end of her long ride she sat down to write her departed-guest letter, giving thanks for the manifold kindnesses received from her late hostess. With an unusual and pathetic humility she assured Catherine that 'Although I answered little, I weighed it all the more deeply when you said you would warn me of all evil that you should hear of me. For if you had not a good opinion of me, you would not have offered friendship to me that way at all. But what may I more say than thank God for providing such friends to me?'

CHAPTER FOURTEEN

The new tutor was a success, especially in his pupil's opinion. At thirty-three, Roger Ascham was one of the foremost Greek scholars of the day, but he was by no means only a scholar; he was an accomplished musician, and a keen and knowledgeable sportsman. Bess remembered her father's pleasure in the Treatise on Archery which the young Cambridge don had published and presented to King Henry shortly before his death; it was in English, which showed his originality and freedom from pedantry; in fact, he valued the writing of good English prose as highly as that of Greek or Latin, and foretold a magnificent future for it. The new Bible, the new prayers in the churches, showed, as the poets had already shown, what the English language could do. But it must not stay only in the pulpit, nor in poetry; it must come down into the world and express the common life and simple pleasures of humanity – yes, not only of the science of the long bow, that backbone of England, but of such lesser sports as cock-fighting. And his mild brown eyes glowed as he sketched his plans to the Princess for a Book of the Cockpit which should be his best offering to English sport and prose.

He was full of praise for Bess's own writing, the simplicity and directness she could command when she chose, letting the style grow out of the subject. Unfortunately she was apt to forget this when anxious to write brilliantly, and would never quite believe him when he told her that good style knew no tricks.

He encouraged her dancing and music, which previous tutors had condemned as a waste of time, played and sang duets with her, taught her to shoot with the long bow as her father had taught her mother; and of course, when she discovered from Mrs Ashley that Nan Bullen had had a special shooting-costume made for her, she had to have one too and a saucy green hat with feathers and long elegant shooting-gloves. He told her of cockfighting matches and dicing parties at Cambridge in which he had so nearly made his fortune, but managed instead to lose all his spare cash. All this was surprising in so learned and gentle a scholar, but was very far from meaning that lessons were neglected.

She worked at Greek with him in the mornings and at Latin in the afternoons, on his system of double translation, turning the originals into English and then back into Greek and Latin; she even worked a little at what he called, rather contemptuously, 'Euclid's pricks and lines', since mathematics were also fashionable, though they could never, he assured her, be of the same value to human intelligence as the classics. And he was enchanted with her skill and speed and the fiery intentness of her concentration. Bess collected compliments on her brains as greedily as her mother had done those on her charms. Not but what she would have liked those too. But that would come.

There were encouraging signs of it even now, when Mr Ascham sought to inflame her with his own passion for this new world of ancient Greece, to which her own nature was, he suggested, as much akin as if she were a nymph or goddess born anew from that shadowless tireless dawn of the world, with the dew of that dawn still glistening on her brow, and the spear of the huntress Diana poised in her hand. Indeed, the fancy sometimes affected him almost with fear, as he watched her across the study table, her face, intent and pale in the bright aureole of her hair, lighting suddenly into a smile that was not of any christened soul, but inscrutably aware of her strange power.

So had he seen a marble goddess smile, made by a man who had never heard of Christ.

In excuse for these pagan fancies he would remind himself and tell his pupil that the world was coming out of its old dark cramped preoccupation with Heaven and Hell, with the Earth wedged unalterably between them; that Copernicus had proved the Earth to be no longer the centre of the universe but one of a myriad stars circling round the sun, 'like courtiers round their Sovereign,' said he, thinking of a vast red face and a hot hand that had slapped him on the back, and a mighty voice saying his treatise on archery had scored a bull's eye! 'And as they will circle round your royal father's daughter, should Divine Providence ever place you on the throne.'

Bess's smile was certainly pagan now. It was all very well for an upstart Protector to make a modest claim for Providence putting *him* in power, but when she got there she would know what to thank for it – her father's blood and her own wits.

At present those last were well occupied, and she herself content to stay quiet and work, but not as her cousin Jane was working with her grave young tutor Mr Aylmer, a scholar of the conventional pattern and no sportsman, for the sheer disinterested love of abstract learning. For Bess never lost sight of the aim and object for which she worked: to make herself as fit to be on the throne of England as ever her learned young brother would be.

And in the meantime Mr Ascham's admiration (was it perhaps, sometimes something more? She had caught him looking at her rather oddly across the study table) was a faint compensation for the Admiral's exciting companionship; it served to pass the time, and it provided her with useful counter-thrusts against Cat Ashley.

That much-tried governess was not unnaturally in a twitter of nerves at their expulsion from Catherine's household, and the construction that might be put on it; she was for ever warning Bess against making eyes at men, against making pert answers, against a score of new-found faults in her behaviour.

Never before had Mrs Ashley seen so clearly, in watching her charge, that her mother had not been a lady. What was it that Queen Nan had said when Cat Ashley was going to see the Princess Mary? 'Give her a box on the ears now and then for the cursed bastard she is!'

No, much as she had admired her husband's cousin, even in her flashes of dangerous temper, Mrs Ashley could not but reflect on looking back through the years that that had not been the remark of a lady.

'How can you hope to be Queen', (the girl had let that out) 'when you chatter with every stable-boy and take no care of your dignity?'

'Mr Ascham says my dignity and gentleness are wonderful.'

Or – 'Women should be modest and remember their weakness. They can't be the equal of man.'

'They can, and I am. Mr Ascham says my mind has no womanly weakness, and my perseverance is equal to a man's.'

Mrs Ashley began to think her silver pen rather dearly bought. At this rate there would soon be no holding her young mistress. It was clear that she had captivated her new tutor as she had the last, and the greater the scholar, the less his sense.

The sight of Bess preening herself on her dignity and gentleness, who so short a time ago had locked her into her room while she went gallivanting on the river at night alone with the Admiral, was the last straw.

'I tell you what it is, my young Madam,' she flared out, 'you are like the cat in the fairy-tale who was turned into the form of a lady and could behave as such perfectly – as long as she did not see a mouse! Mice or men it's all the same – the moment you catch sight of one, hey presto! Away go all your fine manners and you must pounce!'

And the scolding ended in fits of laughter from them both.

But Bess was not entirely as confident as she seemed. She was anxious about Catherine, who she heard was not at all well, and at last realised that it was a serious matter for her to be having her first child at thirty-five. And Catherine's generosity made her ashamed and embarrassed; she had actually encouraged her husband to write to her, and sent messages by him as she did not feel up to writing herself, and told Bess how she missed her companionship and wished she were there with them at Sudley Castle, where they had gone for her to bear her child in the peace and quiet of their Gloucestershire home.

Determined to be as prudent as possible, Bess wrote her answer to Catherine, not Tom, but asked tentatively that he should continue to 'give me knowledge from time to time how his busy child does', and added with a sad little attempt at a joke, 'If I were at his birth no doubt I would have him beaten for the trouble he has put you to.'

'Him' and 'he'; no one thought of the coming baby in any other terms. Catherine made his sex a particular point in the petitions she offered up for his safe arrival, in the family prayers that she held for her household – a new development which her husband complained was adding fresh revolutionary terrors to the Reformed Religion, since the servants would be wanting their wages raised for having to troop into the hall and pray twice daily. He himself generally found he had to attend to some earnest business at the bottom of the garden at just those moments, and would stroll off, singing a popular street song in parody of the New Religion, which, he declared, was one of hate.

'Hate a cross, hate a surplice,
 Mitres, copes and rochets.
 Come hear me pray
 Nine times a day
 And fill your head with crochets.'

Pity the best of women had to have crochets, he told Cathy, laughing at her pet preachers and her enthusiasm over the higher education for women. She was only a little hurt, for she knew she would not like her Tom any the better if he held advanced views like his brother. She told herself they were so happy that they could afford the jolts that might have broken a more brittle happiness – differences of opinion, downright quarrels, even bitter moments of jealousy.

Until, when it came to that last: the image of Bess's darting glance, the dragonfly swiftness of her turn of head, would rise before her, and she could not feel her happiness so secure.

But her child would safeguard it.

Tom did his own part towards the coming event by visiting all the best astrologers and fortune-tellers, and they all gave him certain assurance that his child would be a son – just as they had done to King Henry before his daughter Elizabeth was born, but nobody was going to remember that now. It would make all the difference to Tom's position, his ambitious hopes and intrigues, if he had a son and heir to be their focal point for the future.

At the end of July, just a month before Catherine's time was due, the Duchess gave birth to a son. 'And let *that* spur you to a strapping boy!' Tom told his wife. He was full of gay confidence, and as long as he was there she was too; but in his absence she drooped and was beset with nervous fears and melancholy. That was easily remedied, he told her; he would not leave her till the child was born and all well again.

He refused Somerset's offered command of the fleet in this summer's campaign against the Scots armies who had been annihilated last summer at Pinkie. But in spite of that, the Protector had to appeal to the Emperor for help, and march against his conquered enemy with the German troops, paid for in advance – a difficult matter with the Treasury bankrupt from the debts and debased coinage left over from the old King's reign; and Somerset could not help thinking it an uneconomic measure, when thousands of unemployed Englishmen were wandering homeless on the roads, and the magistrates could find no remedy except to flog and imprison them for their failure to find work. Though they knew well that no work was to be had, since they themselves were mostly employing one shepherd boy to mind their new flocks, where their fathers had given work to fifty ploughboys and farm labourers.

Still, there was no doubt that unemployed men quickly became unemployable, and these wretched vagrants would be no use as soldiers compared with the German mercenaries; moreover, they were apt to fraternise with the Scots, and particularly, as fellow-peasants, to dislike firing their harvest and ripening crops.

The German mercenaries had no such scruples; they were a race apart, bred only for war, heavy and inhuman as their armour: 'Find some means of making it move without 'em inside it, and you'd never know the difference!' said Tom, who hated the Germans from what he had seen of them in Hungary where they had spied and wormed their way in for centuries, and now treated the Magyars like slaves in their own country, holding them to the law passed over a hundred years before, that no one should have any position of importance unless he could produce a testimonial of Purity of Race, proving that all his four grandparents belonged to the ruling German nation.

Ned asked what the – he nearly said 'the devil' but changed

it to 'on earth' – the four German grandparents had to do with his mercenaries?

'Why, this, you fool – yes, you can look down your long nose at me and think you're always right, but you don't know everything, nobody here knows what the Germans are like. Ask the Magyars. Ask the Poles. Ask that old fellow I met in Cracow – only he died last year – you know who I mean – old fellow with a beard like a furze bush and a bumpy nose turned up at the end from poking it so high into the heavens – God's light, what was his name? – who wrote that the sun doesn't move but that we all go whizzing round it instead.'

'If you mean the Polish heretic Copernicus—'

'Why heretic? He dedicated his book to the Pope, who accepted it. Are you Reformers going to be more pernickety than the Pope? But whatever Copernicus wrote of the stars, he was sound on the Teutons, and the way they've ravaged Poland year after year. He told me himself, "We can scarcely dwell in our own houses for an hour." And all because the Germans think they are made by God to conquer the world. Their Emperor is not the Emperor of Germany, he's the German Emperor – of the World. But you'll never understand that here, you think it's just an empty traditional title. One has to have lived on the Continent to see it. And it's this Master Race of mechanic monsters that you're bringing into this island to fight your battles for you, against fellows who speak the same language as ourselves – and to do the dirty work you can't get Englishmen to do. You hire German hogs while our decayed yeomen rot in idleness on the roads. And *then* you complain that the Scots won't listen to your fine speeches about brotherly love and Free Trade!'

His elder brother said that Tom entirely failed to understand the Scottish question. Extreme measures had unfortunately been made necessary by this final outrage of the Scots, for they had at last shipped off their little Queen safely to France. Even Tom's shallow brain should grasp the danger to England of a Scottish-French encirclement.

But Tom only howled in exasperated boredom. He said that a lot of long words didn't alter facts; that Ned thought he could make the Devil himself sound respectable by speaking of his 'extreme measures'; that the Scots ought not to object to having their people slaughtered, their wives ravished in their sight, their fields burnt, their churches, towns and villages razed to the ground, as long as he left the words 'English Sovereignty' out of his peace terms; that in all his life Ned had never grasped a single fact – only words, words, words.

The argument, as so often happens in the inconsequence of family quarrels, wandered far afield in a furious comparison of the 'ordered and disciplined' German rulers in Hungary with the dispossessed Magyar nobles who, having been left no other means of subsistence, would swoop down from their mountain fortresses on the market-place and carry off goods or, better, someone for ransom – preferably a Jew, for that was worth a bag of ducats where even a rich merchant would only fetch a reasonable sum. Good fellows, those Robber Knights, and no one in the world so handy with horseflesh.

Tom, glowing with nostalgic appreciation, wondered whether it wouldn't be a good plan to kidnap his royal nephew and ransom him for his own Protectorship of him. It was a bright notion and would be thought nothing of in

Hungary, but here in England everyone was so conventional.

He swung off to visit his nephew and consider him from the point of view of this possibility. He found Edward ruffled as an angry kitten because Mary had written to him (on the eternal vexed question of having the Mass in her household) that 'although he was of great understanding, yet experience would teach him more yet'; an elder-sister touch far more irritating than the friendly equal arguing and wrangling between him and Bess. He showed his uncle with some pride his prompt retort to Mary that *she* 'might have something to learn, and no one was too old for that!'

But what chiefly infuriated him was that the German Emperor, her mother's nephew, was throwing out hints that if Mary were not allowed her own way, he would withdraw his Ambassador.

'Just because he is her first cousin and was once betrothed to her, how dare he think that gives him any right to interfere with *me*? I'd have declared war on him by now, only my Uncle Somerset is such a slug and won't set about it.'

Tom heartily encouraged him to 'pull the Emperor's nose' – in spite of the fact that he had always said it was a shame to bother the Princess Mary about her private worship, and that 'Live and let live' was the only sound course in religion. He disliked the Reformers, if anything, rather more than the priests; he complained that they made far more fuss about religion in their determination to prove themselves in the right; in fact, he had only joined them for professional purposes, since it was politically necessary to be on their side, and also because, like the rest of the nobles, he had made a good thing out of the plunder of the Church lands and property.

But questions of consistency never troubled him. It was enough that his brother was letting in an advance guard of the Emperor's troops, that the Emperor wanted to interfere in England as he had done practically everywhere on the Continent, and worst of all, that he was the Princess Mary's first cousin.

'The Hapsburgs don't need to fight – they marry. They've got a hold over half Europe by that, and they'll get it here if we don't look out. Peaceful penetration – allies in the family – paid troops to fight our battles and act as spies in our country! Show him you won't stand any of it.'

'I will,' said Edward, squaring his elbows and clenching his inky fist round his pen as he bent over his black velvet desk to write a belligerent letter to the terrible Charles V, Imperator Mundi.

Tom, standing behind his chair, suddenly swept him up out of it, tossed him up in his arms just as though he were a baby, and hugged him. 'You're the living spit of your mother – just Jane's prim little determined air!'

'Put me down!' exclaimed the King in a squeak of astonished indignation. 'I'm like my father – they all say so.'

'Oh, you're old Harry's own, sure enough, a chip off the old block. By Christ's soul, you'll make a King to match himself, and not all these canting snivelling book-learned old women shall keep you from it! I'll get you away from them, never fear.'

'Put me *down*!'

At last Tom heard him, put him down and knelt to him with exaggerated deference, humbly craving his dread Sire's pardon for his familiar treatment of him. Edward pulled down his waistcoat, smoothed his hair, and said in aggrieved tones, 'Now I shall have to get it brushed again.'

It wasn't until he had left that Tom remembered the prime motive of his visit, which was to consider his nephew's kidnapping.

Well, that could come later.

CHAPTER FIFTEEN

The Good Duke sat looking down his long nose at the letter, in Latin, of King Edward of England to the Emperor of the World. There were three mistakes in the syntax. It was time young Barnaby was whipped again. It was the only thing that had any real effect on Edward. He made a note of it and leant across the table to stick it in a stand.

His eye fell on his last letter from his brother Henry at Wolf Hall.

'Further ye sent us downe such a lewde company of Frenchmen masons as I never sawe the lyke. I assure you they be the worst condicyoned people that ever I sawe and the dronkenest; for they will drynke more in one day than 3 dayes wages will come to, and then lye lyke beasts on the flore not able to stande. They are well nigh XXXs in debt for beer, victuals and other borrowed money. Praying you that I may be most hartely commendyed—' but here the Duke's eye instinctively averted from the fateful word 'bedfellowe'.

What a welter of things he had to see to, and all himself, for no one else ever did them properly. Was it even worth the trouble, all this accumulation of vast estates which he never had time to ride over – of palaces spreading over the earth, towering to the sky, which he might never live even to see finished?

But this would never do. He made a shuddering guess at what his Duchess would say if she had heard his thought. He was not building for himself (nothing that he did was for himself) but for his son – and hers. Not for his eldest son, by Katrine Fillol; *he* had already been dispossessed of his birthright and his younger stepbrother was to inherit his father's titles and estates. The Good Duke did not care to think of that.

It was narrow to consider one's own flesh and blood, or even one's own countrymen, as of prime importance. His public prayer to the Defender of All Nations showed a new and nobler view. And he had given practical testimony to it by opening a settlement of Flemish weavers, exiled for their religious beliefs, on his own estates at Glastonbury; the Somerset Weavers they were called, after him, a lasting tribute to his tolerance and foresight.

He took long views, in private as well as public matters. It was a fine instinct that made him take his pleasure, not in momentary self-indulgence, but in planting great trees that he would never see full-grown, in building palaces such as Somerset House that would dominate the untidy huddle of London's wooden buildings like an eagle brooding over a nest of sparrows.

The only idle moments he knew were those in which he stood watching his workmen, as busy as a swarm of ants, at work on that enormous ant-heap. He even sometimes watched them during sermon-time. The new Scottish preacher, Mr John Knox, whom he had imported as the latest of the Royal Chaplains, had actually dared raise complaints about it.

But then Mr Knox raised complaints about everything. His first sermon at Court had been a frenzied diatribe against the iniquity of kneeling at Communion. The Archbishop thought it went too far. The Duke had appointed him for his Protestant zeal, to which he had earlier testified by his share in the murder of Cardinal Beton in Scotland. King Henry had rewarded that deed with good money; but the French had imprisoned him in their galleys for it. You would have thought that after two years as a galley-slave the man would be pleased with the post of King's Chaplain in the now most firmly Protestant country in Europe. But he spent most of his time in bitter quarrels with his fellow-Reformers, with half the Court officials, and even, when he could, with his new patron the Protector. It was plain he could bear no authority but his own. Yet the Duke hesitated to get rid of him. The fellow was a powerful preacher. He had a vein of shrill nagging invective that was all the more telling because of its feminine quality – in fact, it had something in common with the Duchess's.

'What do you think of the new Chaplain – John Knox?' he demanded abruptly of John Dudley, Earl of Warwick, who had just entered, twirling a minute nosegay of single clove pinks, lad's love and balm of Gilead, in a slender silver flower-holder.

'Neither grateful nor pleasable,' replied the Earl promptly. He strolled over to the window and looked out. 'Besides,' he added over his shoulder, 'he called me Achitophel in his last sermon.'

The Duke exclaimed 'Tsa!' so violently that it sounded like an oath. 'It's sheer blasphemy to use the Bible as a stalking-horse for opposition to the Government!'

'He'll always be in opposition to any Government.'

'Yes. He's best as a revolutionary agent. I might send him later into Scotland to stir up revolt against the Government there.'

'Must it be later?'

The Earl's voice was low and pleasant; it sounded always as though he were smiling, though he did not in fact often smile. His hair and slight fringe of beard were cut very short, his moustaches very thin in a curved pencilled line. He did not look in the least like a famous soldier, but a fastidious dandy; his clothes of exquisite simplicity, almost monastic in style, no jewels, not even a ring; his delicate eyebrows and fine eyes fixed in a cool stare that held a hint of mockery.

Nor did the new Earl look like one of the 'Lords sprung from the dunghill', as the new Duke had unkindly stigmatised him and his fellows. As a matter of fact, his remote ancestry was rather more illustrious than the Duke's; and his air of patrician calm would never lead one to suppose that his father, Edmund Dudley, had been a clever shady lawyer who made a lot of money for King Henry's father by hunting up obsolete old laws and imposing huge fines on all who were, quite unconsciously, breaking them. Henry VIII, on coming to the throne as a bright lad of eighteen, had promptly executed him, as a popularity measure; but there was no ill feeling about it. Edmund's son, John Dudley, had risen steadily at Court; Henry had a high opinion of his ability, created him Viscount Lisle, appointed him Lord High Admiral, and nominated him as one of the Lords of the Council of Regency for his son. On the King's death, when most people moved one up, John Dudley was created Earl of Warwick and handed over his post as Lord High Admiral to Tom Seymour, then Admiral of the Fleet.

He was by far the most important figure on the Council after Somerset, and had managed the Scottish campaign rather better than he, but the Duke felt no uneasiness on that score; he had long ago labelled him in his mind as an old friend, and his labels were apt to remain unchanged.

But he was annoyed by the fellow's idle air; here he was lounging into his room, apparently only to sniff at his posy and remark on the stifling August heat and the stinking steam of the vapours exhaled by the river that wound like a decaying dragon below the open windows. With a curious glee in his gentle voice he called Somerset's attention to the oily glitter on old Thames' dark scales, too sluggish for ripples, a slimy pewter colour under the thunder-grey of the sky.

'Look at the old serpent gliding down to Tower Bridge and Traitors' Gate,' he said, 'so rotten that she is phosphorescent, and faugh!' He twiddled the miniature bouquet at his nose, 'Yet she's swallowed finer bodies than yours or mine, and will swallow more yet, that old serpent.'

The Good Duke flung down his pen. 'Your fancies may be poetic,' he rapped out in the tone of an irritable schoolmaster, 'but I have no time for them. Can you not see that I am engaged on business of the State?'

Dudley flicked a glance across the writing-table; it came to rest on the note Somerset had just written and stuck up in the stand before him 'Barnaby to be whipped.'

A slow bluish flush crept up above the Good Duke's beard. 'The King's learning,' he said, 'is the prime business of the State. We can't have him writing to foreign princes with mistakes in his Latin syntax.'

He tossed Edward's letter over to Dudley, who read it with an eyebrow up. 'We can't have him writing to foreign princes with declarations of war either,' he remarked softly.

'Oh – *that*! I shall tear it up, naturally.'

'Then why trouble about the syntax?'

The Good Duke groaned. It was impossible to explain a principle. Nobody but himself was capable of understanding one.

He curtly offered his visitor a seat, in the manner of one who has made up his mind to endure interruption, and demanded the reason for it.

'An unwelcome one, I fear,' said the suave voice by the window. 'The House of Commons has just thrown out your Act against the Enclosures of the common lands.'

The Protector was silent. Then he reached for his copy of his Proclamation on the Enclosures and began to read it out. John Dudley sat down. He had heard it before. The pitiful complaints of His Majesty's poor subjects left him cold. In what far Eden had they not complained?

'"In time past,"' read the Protector, '"ten, twenty, yes and in some places a hundred or two hundred Christian people have inhabited and kept household, to the replenishing and fulfilling of His Majesty's realm with faithful subjects for its defence, where now there is nothing kept but sheep and bullocks. All that land which heretofore was tilled and occupied with so many men is now gotten by insatiable greediness of mind unto one or two men's hands and scarcely dwelt upon with one poor shepherd. Men are eaten up and devoured and driven from their houses by sheep and bullocks."'

'Not original,' murmured Dudley. 'Sir Thomas More wrote back in the 'twenties that sheep are eating men.'

'Even that tax I put on, of 2d. on every sheep owned, hasn't stopped it.'

'You can't put back the clock. The wool trade's been going on "in time past" for a long time. And it gave England her wealth.'

'What's the use of wealth?'

The Earl of Warwick cocked an ear to listen to the hammering of the hundreds of workmen engaged on the building of Somerset House. The Duke of Somerset heard it too. He tapped nervously on the table as though to cover the sound. The Earl coughed sympathetically.

'Look at the final result!' said the Duke. He picked up his Proclamation again. Dudley hastily agreed that the final result was deplorable. Hoping to forestall a renewed reading, he remarked that one result was the shortage of man-power in this Scottish war; but the Duke instantly capped it from the Proclamation, '"This realm must be defended against the enemy with force of men, not with flocks of sheep and droves of brute beasts."'

'The Italian and German troops make a good substitute,' soothed Dudley.

The Protector, mindful of his talk with Tom, said curtly, 'I've had quite enough of that.'

'Let's hope the Scots will too.' Dudley got up and added

sympathetically, 'It has not been a lucky session for all of your Reform measures.'

'For not one of them! The House of Commons have thrown out my Bills to provide for poor children in each town, and to prevent farmers being unjustly turned out of their own land; while the House of Lords reject my Act to prevent the decay of ploughing and growing of crops. Most important of all, my project for the Reform of the Common Law didn't even reach a second reading in the Commons. Every one of my schemes to provide for the poor has failed.'

'You are forgetting your Act of Slavery.'

The Protector's eyes rolled round at him with the look of a wounded stag.

'Yes. The only one to be passed unanimously by both Houses! The only way in which Parliament would consent to provide for the unemployed.' And he began to quote his Slavery Act, by heart.

The Earl pulled a scrap of paper on the table towards him and drew a gargoyle face. 'I know,' he said, 'but there have been slaves here in England before now.'

But the Duke went on quoting. The Earl began to scribble.

The Duke never noticed it. 'At least,' he said presently, 'it only applies to the able-bodied. The Act provides for the aged and impotent by collections in church every Sunday. *They* are not slaves.'

'They'd be no use,' said the Earl. In a minute or two this fellow would argue himself round, as usual, into self-justification.

But instead, 'Liberty, liberty!' cried the Duke in a great voice. 'Is this to be the end of all my hopes to make England a land where nothing can be profitable that is not godly and honest; nor nothing godly and honest whereby our neighbours and Christian brethren are harmed? But these fat newly rich fellows in Parliament care nothing for their brethren. Is there indeed one honest man amongst them except myself? And you,' he remembered to add.

'Parliament represent the rich. Why should they care about the poor?'

'Then by Heaven!' (the Protector had actually made an oath) 'I will not rest until the poor too are represented. I will reform Parliament so that the yeoman, yes and his labourer, shall find a mouthpiece in it.'

Dudley repressed a shudder of that contemptuous distaste with which one recognises symptoms of an abnormal state of mind. Really, Somerset was becoming a public danger as well as nuisance. Reform always led to revolt. And the fellow was working the Duke himself into a frenzy.

With lips white with rage, the Duke burst out, 'In spite of the devil, of private profit, self-love, money, and such-like devil's instruments, *it shall go forward.*'

'Would you go against your own class?' Dudley asked in carefully gentle reproof. 'The new landed gentry are making still stronger distinctions between rich and poor. Even the universities are becoming conscious of rank; they are growing so expensive that the yeomen and labourers can no longer afford to send their sons. Absurd as it may seem, I believe that very soon Oxford and Cambridge, yes, and even Eton, will be only for the sons of gentry. Regrettable, but one can't put back the clock. Your hopes for the future are really only dreams of the past, when any labourer's son could get the learning that is now the privilege of the rich. But we must forget all that and live in the present.'

The Duke sighed heavily. There was no time he liked so little.

'Whatever makes the past or future predominate over the vulgar present,' he pronounced, 'advances us in the dignity of thinking beings.'

Dudley laid a friendly hand on his shoulder. Poor old Somerset, he should have been the celibate Master of some college, a thinker, dreamer, idealist.

'You drive yourself too hard,' he said. 'There are limits to what one man can do, though you will never recognise it. Think less of your brethren – and more of your brother.'

Somerset started as if stung. 'What of my brother? I've had enough of him and to spare. He was here just now, haranguing me like a tornado.'

'It's in the family,' thought Dudley, and aloud 'Will he take the command of the fleet you've offered him?'

'Not he! Nor would I urge it now after the fantastic way he's just been talking to me about the Scots, as though it were a crime to lead foreign troops against them. You'd think they were his brothers!'

'That's dangerous.'

'When was Tom ever anything but dangerous? Well, he can't do much harm now, for he's gone back to his wife – says he'd rather stay at home to make merry with his friends in the country.'

'Hmm. I don't like that. Sounds as though he means to go on working against you in your absence. He's getting up a stout following among the squires and yeomen – a following of ten thousand if one's to believe his own boast. Old Squire Dodrington has been up in town for the lawsuit on his lands, and tells me that Master Admiral was mighty sympathetic telling him how *he* would get him justice; this when Tom came to dinner at Dodrington Hall bringing a couple of flagons of good wine and a venison pasty and roast sucking-pig or two – no wonder he's a popular guest! He does it all round the country, dining with his inferiors, but not at their expense. Tells his friends to do it too. At least half a dozen fellows in the House have told me of it.'

'It isn't treasonable to be a good diner-out,' said the Duke uncomfortably.

'Depends on the after-dinner talk. He makes no secret of his discontent, that he is not allowed his share of power – meaning, no doubt, the lion's share. He has always been accustomed to it, hasn't he – at home?'

The Protector winced. So it was common knowledge that Tom had always been their mother's favourite! He tried to think of some scathing reply that would show his complete indifference to the matter; but Dudley, with an airy flick of his flower-holder, had already passed on to another. What of the pirate, Jack Thompson, and the Admiral's obscure dealings with him? Fishy he called them, very fishy – 'Have you taxed him with them?'

'I have,' said the Protector shortly. He had heard enough of pirates and their virtues from his brother.

Dudley then spoke of this notorious scandal about the Princess Elizabeth.

The Protector said nothing. He had heard too much of the Princess and her vices from his wife.

'The whole country knows why she was sent away from the Queen's household. There are some who say they know more – that it was because she was found to be with child by him.'

The Good Duke looked at him. 'She won't be fifteen till next month.'

'It is still possible.'

Even the Good Duke noticed something of ironic pity in the other's cool gaze. In another minute he would be telling him the facts of life. He was determined to snub him.

'You talk like a woman,' he said in pained disgust.

The Earl recognised his mistake in entering into competition with the Duchess. But he stuck to his guns on the practical issue. The Princess is only second heir to the throne, but it's not a bad second, with a delicate child and a sickly woman in her thirties between. An heir to her and the Admiral would put him in a paramount position.'

'A bastard would not be an heir.'

'It's not so long since the Princess herself was referred to as the Little Bastard, even by her sire. It's a position easily remedied nowadays, when divorce is becoming so common – and so respectable.'

The Good Duke cleared his throat. He had had a divorce himself. The Wicked Earl (as some were inclined to think him) was, on the other hand, a faithfully devoted husband and father to twelve children. He was walking up and down the room on a soft measured tread, his hands behind his back twirling that miniature bouquet like a budding tail.

'It's not any one particular prank of the Admiral's that makes me anxious,' he said slowly, as though considering aloud. 'It is that everything he does, kissing that little red-haired wretch, currying favour with the King and telling him you're too hard a task-master, dining with country squires, encouraging pirates – in all this he is helping to rock the ship of State – and that in foul enough weather already, God knows. The whole country's in a smoulder of discontent, any breeze may blow it into a fire of revolt. Even at best there is only a quivering quiet. Remember those attempted risings this spring in half a dozen counties. They never gathered head, for they were not united. They may yet unite.'

'The base ingratitude of the people!' Somerset exclaimed. 'I've done more for them in eighteen months than the old King in the whole of his reign. Do they *want* tyranny? Do they *hate* liberty? I have given them freedom of speech – of opinion—'

'One has to be full fed to care about opinion.'

'I have swept away all the monstrous new Treason and Heresy Acts of the last reign, that Act of Six Articles which they called the Whip with Six Strings. Royal Proclamations can no longer become law of themselves. I have removed the restrictions on the printing of the English Bible.'

'Do they care about the Bible?'

'What in God's name *do* they care about? I have minimised executions, refused to employ the torture-chamber. Do they care nothing for that?'

'No one cares if others have been tortured and executed. Those who have been, aren't alive to thank you.' And Dudley turned on his heel with a flourish of his flowery tail.

Somerset slammed his hands down on the table. 'You are telling me that all they care about is hard cash. It's not my fault the Exchequer was bankrupt at King Henry's death. That the only thing that's cheap is labour. I've brought in laws to raise wages, to lower prices, to prevent the markets being flooded with trashy goods. But no laws can make good men. Men have never been so mad as now to make money at the expense of their neighbour. But that is not a cause, it's a consequence. Debased coinage, debased goods, they're the result of debased ideas. All the old ways are gone. The world is in the melting-pot. We have the chance now to build a far greater and happier State than ever before. But they cannot take that chance; they cannot even see it. They are blind with greed. They are like wasps in a honey-jar, never seeing that their neighbours' deaths lead only to their own.'

Dudley led him gently but firmly back to the point. 'Very true. The country is ripe for revolution. I know the tenderness of your feelings for your mother. But in such a case surely your country should come first.'

'What do you mean by speaking of my mother?'

Dudley did not appear to notice the question. 'Those risings this spring failed at the outset because they had no leader. What if they should find one? I would rather your brother were anywhere this summer but at home in Gloucestershire.'

'Where under heaven then should he be, unless he were dead?'

Dudley was silent.

The Protector glanced at him, then looked away.

The silence thickened. It weighed on the room like a thunder-cloud.

Dudley began to whistle a nonchalant tune. 'Well,' he said, 'I must not delay your work for the State any longer.'

He took his leave. The Protector watched him go. He in his

turn now walked up and down the room, which had grown even more oppressively hot. He could not settle his thoughts; they chased each other round and round like rats in a trap, chasing the things that Dudley had said, had not said, had looked.

Could he have meant what he looked?

He thought of Tom, that perpetual nuisance of a youngest brother who had always given trouble at home; even as a baby he had been a sturdy rogue, grabbing the others' toys, trotting through the Ladies' Garden and picking off the heads of the flowers, and never smacked nor even scolded by their mother; then later playing truant from his lessons, robbing the apple orchards in Pound and Broom Close and the cherries in Ladelwell-pound; later still, making friends with such low rascals as Gorway's son the shepherd boy and young Wynbolt the undergrubber and going poaching with them at nights. What an uproar there had been when the red-faced old keeper of the Home Park (what *was* his name? Something like an apple – Quince? – no, Vince) had complained to their father, gobbling with rage! And Tom at last got the thrashing he so richly deserved, but only chuckled in triumph because he had padded his breeches with rags. Tom, later, getting into that mess with Edie of the dairy-house and her fellow Audrey Cocks with the bold black eyes (how was it he still remembered *their* names – a couple of dairymaids?). Getting into debt; getting into all sorts of mischief when he went to the French Court in the train of Bryan, whom King Henry had nicknamed the Vicar of Hell – 'and this young rascal is his best chorister there!' old Foxnose François had said, pinching Tom's ear, so that he only swaggered about his scrapes.

And it was the same with the Hapsburgs in Hungary; and in the Netherlands with the Emperor's sister, the Regent there; and even with that grave and dignified Oriental Potentate, Suliman the Magnificent. It was the same everywhere; people only liked him the better for being a showy daredevil adventurer. And most of all, King Henry.

With a sudden unhappy little yelp he began to move things restlessly about on his table as he remembered that enormous laughter of their royal brother-in-law while he read out bits of Tom's letters from the Turkish wars.

Henry had made endless use of 'Good Ned', had worked him to death and barely grunted his appreciation.

But he would stand anything from Tom. When privately betrothed to their sister Jane (with Nan Bullen still alive), he had proudly told them how she was working the tapestry pictures for their nuptial bed-curtains herself, and Tom had asked with that impudent cock of his eyebrow, 'What's the subject? Bathsheba?'

That would have been the end of any other man. Yet the King had still liked Tom best.

And always their mother had loved him best, her precious youngest boy, the mother's spoilt darling, and had taken his side in the furious quarrels of his boyhood (the Wolf Cubs at Wolf Hall the neighbours had called them); and when their father was away, told Ned he must take care of his little brother and be like a father to him, which was impossible and unfair, for she never told Tom to treat him with the respect due to a father, or even to a so much elder brother. She never backed up his authority for all she kept saying, 'You're so much older and wiser, dear Ned'; she only said that to coax him into pulling Tom out of his scrapes; it was all he was there for.

And Tom himself thought it quite enough reward to clap him on the shoulder with that insufferably jolly air and say, 'Good old Ned, I knew you'd always stand by me.'

Yes, he'd always stood by him; he supposed he would always have to, even now, even though Tom was now deliberately working against him, undermining his authority, disloyal to the core, imperilling all these disinterested, far-sighted schemes of his – any one of which was worth a deal more than that young Tom Fool.

Yet all were imperilled by this braggart, this *farceur*, this unnatural brother, whom he had got to try and get out of the trouble he was making for himself, as though that, and that alone, were his perpetual job in life.

He would not think of that. He would think of his plans for the future of the people, which would, which *should* go forward, in spite of the devil, or private profit, self-love, money, and such-like devil's instruments – yes, and in spite of Tom.

So he tried to think of all he was doing for the people, and of what he must do next; but always he kept seeing that raw foggy night in his boyhood when he and Tom had been out shooting birds in the Forest of Savernake with their crossbows. They had lost their way in the sudden thick mist, and had met a wild boar face to face and he had struck up Tom's bow just in time to prevent the young ass stinging it up with an arrow. And he had driven off the boar and at last found their way and brought them both safely home. And as they came near Wolf Hall their little mother came flitting out of the broad lighted doorway like a frightened bird, and down into the dark towards them, crying, 'Tom! Tom! Is he there? Is he safe?'

She had thanked and praised him afterwards, explained that she had asked first for Tom 'because, you see, Ned, he is such a little boy.' But it made no odds: she had not cried out for him; and that raw foggy night had struck a chill damp on his spirit ever since.

The stifling smelly mist from the river was creeping into the room, dulling the light. How long had he been pacing up and down, doing nothing?

His restless eye, roving over the floor, caught sight of a small white object. It was a tight paper ball. He remembered now that Dudley had scribbled something on a scrap of paper which he had been crumpling in his hand as he talked, and must have dropped. He picked it up, smoothed it out, saw a rough drawing of a gargoyle head, and some lines of verse. He read:

'*Observe; 'tis the mild Idealists*
Who plan our social Revolutions;
Then come the brutal Realists
And turn them into – Executions!

And, first and foremost on their lists,
Appear the mild Idealists!!'

CHAPTER SIXTEEN

So the Duke went up to Scotland with his German troops and without his brother, and people said that for a fighter like Tom to choose to stay at home with a sick wife at this juncture looked extremely sinister, and his friends warned him to become 'a new sort of man, for the world began to talk very unfavourably of him, both for his slothfulness to serve and his greediness to get.'

The joke of it to Tom was that for once, in the burning August heat, he was really eager to escape from the stifling smelly town, and to ride back to Gloucestershire through cornfields splashed with scarlet poppies, back to the cool gardens of Sudley, where for the moment all his care was to cheer and hearten his Cathy and plan with her the nurseries for their child.

He had hung her room, where the baby would be born, with new tapestries showing the story of Daphne; even the wet-nurse's bed was to be decorated with gay colours 'to please the babe.' The day nursery led out of it, all ready furnished even to the minute chair of state upholstered in cloth of gold where the baby should receive his first visitors when he was old enough to sit on a chair at all.

Jane Grey helped with all the preparations in grave delight, and Bess nearly cried with envy when she heard of them, to think that Jane was there and not herself. However badly she had behaved, Catherine had always liked her best, she was certain, and would rather have her there now than her good little cousin.

And her other little cousin, Mary Queen of Scots, now five and a half years old, had eluded all the efforts of the English fleet to capture her, and arrived in France, where the King and his wife, Queen Catherine de Medici, and, far more important, his *maîtresse en titre*, Diane de Poictiers, all declared her the loveliest child they had ever seen, and treated her publicly as the prospective bride of their small son, the Dauphin. So she would be Queen of France some day as well as Queen of Scotland – a very convenient base for her French armies to undertake their long-planned invasion of England.

For Bess never forgot for long that summer day on board her father's flagship when the French Armada, three hundred strong, was sighted sailing towards Portsmouth.

She never forgot that her father had called the baby Scottish Queen the most dangerous person in Europe; and now that Mary was in France, playing with a still younger baby boy, Bess understood why. And her precocious fear of her was sharpened by childish envy, as of her cousin Jane; for if Jane were safe and happy, cosseted by Catherine and planning baby clothes and nursery furniture with her, Mary was surely the luckiest child in the world, the most important, with a life already as adventurous as a fairytale, and now the spoilt and petted guest of the glittering Court of France.

But she herself, the eldest of the three cousins, was left out of everything, out of cosy domesticity and thrilling triumph alike; banished, disgraced, and with no one to admire her but Mr Ascham.

On the last day of August, hot and still and bright, when the Cotswold hills lay as soft and purple as ripe plums in the hazy sunshine, Catherine's baby was born, and it was a girl.

The midwife, being the best that money could hire, was the one who had helped the Princess Elizabeth into the world, and had had to break the news of her sex to her expectant sire. Never would she forget the tremendous figure striding up and down the gallery at Greenwich Palace, stopping short at sight of her, swinging round and stiffening taut as a lion crouched to spring, in the suspense of his unspoken question. She had felt her answer freezing on her lips, could hardly herself hear the words she faltered, 'Your Majesty – a beautiful little – daughter.'

The bellow of a maddened bull had replied. Yet even that moment, which the midwife had thought her last, had not been as terrifying as the one a little later when the King had stood by his wife's bedside, looking down at the infant Elizabeth, stood in silence worse than any roar of rage, and said at last in a low and dreadful voice, 'I see that God does not wish to give me male children.'

Now it was all to do again. Now it was Tom Seymour, Lord High Admiral, striding up and down the long gallery in that castle of pleasant golden Cotswold stone at Sudley, and to him too a male child had been promised by prophecy, as important to his reckless gamble with ambition as ever it had been to the Tudor dynasty. And to him too went the now doubly nervous midwife, taught by experience what the disappointed sire was like.

But there was never any counting on Tom. Yet again the midwife stammered, 'A beautiful little – daughter.' But he seemed to have forgotten all about the sex question, he demanded only how the mother and child were doing, and he rushed up to see them as soon as he was allowed; and when he was given a glimpse of the daughter that had as shockingly betrayed his trust in God as ever King Henry's had done, he was as delighted and proud as if a daughter had been just what he had hoped and prayed for from the beginning.

He even had to dash off a letter at once to his brother the Protector with a full description of the baby's beauties and asking him to rejoice with him, quite forgetting that this was just what Somerset and his Duchess were certain to do, since the birth of a mere daughter rendered him so much less dangerous.

Clearly Ned had been right to call Tom shallow, but what a mercy it was to find him as shallow as this! It thawed the elder brother, who had just finished writing a long and well-deserved lecture, into adding a very kindly postscript, congratulating him on the birth of 'so pretty a daughter.'

In his relief he found he could take real pleasure in the latest news from his other brother; in the furzes that Henry had planted in the new hare warren; 'the wild bore and 500 dere shal be sent next week; there be pasture ynough for them, for the grounde was never so well before-hande yn grasse thys tyme of the yere as yt is nowe.'

The Duke even pulled a philosophical smile over Henry's

explanation that 'It was not possible to devyde the bucks from the rascalls, but we wyl put all yn together.' It was a forester speaking of the difficulty of dividing the full-grown deer from the lean and inferior – but so perhaps God might speak of men.

And he did not fall into one of his fretful storms of nervous rage with the messenger when he read that the lewd company of Frenchmen 'be departid and stoln away like themselves'; for his head was full of the old days when he and Henry and Tom used to go hawking in Collingbourne woods and hunting the wild boar in Savernake Forest, and, when the day of reckoning came round, toss a penny for who should pay the necessary fourpence to buy hempen halters to bind their quarry's legs to a pole and carry him home in triumph.

> 'Gear may come and gear may go,
> But three brothers again we'll never be.'

But they would be. They would leave their womenfolk behind and all three go hunting together as in the old days.

Brotherly love was once again possible – even between brothers.

He was so far carried away that he sent a message from his Duchess (there was no need to be too literal in going to get it from her lips) assuring Tom of both their hopes that now his wife had begun so well she would bear him many more children, sons as well as daughters.

It was a venturesome tempting of Providence. But anything might happen before then.

It did.

By the time that letter reached Gloucestershire all Tom's pride and joy were being dashed to the ground. Catherine had become dangerously ill with puerperal fever. It came on her with such appalling swiftness that it was difficult even for those in attendance on her to grasp what had happened. One moment she was smiling contentedly at her husband's delight and amusement at this absurdly tiny scrap of flesh that waved its pink fists so helplessly in the air; the next, she was frowning and tossing her head from side to side on the pillow and speaking in a high peevish voice quite unlike her own, speaking things that no one, not even herself, had known she thought.

For they did not grasp at once that she was delirious when she complained to her husband that he was really wanting her to die, so that he would be free to marry the Princess Elizabeth.

He did not know how to comfort her, for he soon found that his words could not reach her understanding; he consulted with her friend Lady Tyrwhitt, who was in charge of the sickroom, and as he stood with her in the window, looking anxiously towards the bed, that strained unnatural voice called out, saying he was standing there laughing at her misery, and that he had given her 'many shrewd taunts.'

Was this the end of all their joking and playing, all his teasing of her, and her calling him brute and bully in fun – that it should be thus monstrously translated?

'Christ's soul!' he cried, 'I cannot bear it. Cathy, Cathy, my sweet fool, when did I ever want to hurt you?'

He flung down on the bed beside her and took her in his arms, pushing her hair back from her hot face with furious tender hands, until at last his love communicated itself to her, and she lay quiet.

Presently she recovered consciousness enough to say that she would make her will, leaving all her lands and money to her husband and 'wishing that it were a thousand times more in value.' But she never mentioned the baby on which all her thoughts and hopes had been set for so long; she seemed to have forgotten its very existence; and her ladies shook their heads over this, taking it as a sure symptom of approaching death.

They were right, for two days later she was dead.

CHAPTER SEVENTEEN

The first Protestant royal funeral took place in England with the Lady Jane Grey as chief female mourner, and Mr Coverdale, the translator of the Bible, to preach the sermon and explain that all the alms and offerings given were not 'to benefit the dead, but for the poor only'; nor were the prayers and lighted candles for 'any other intent or purpose than to do honour' (but no benefit) 'to the deceased.'

'The new Church,' said Elizabeth bitterly when she heard of it, 'deserts her children at the grave.'

Jane Grey, who was visiting her on her way to her home at Bradgate in Leicestershire, was shocked at her cousin's attitude. 'It is illogical and impious,' she said, 'to pray for the dead.'

'Would you say that if you yourself were at the point of death?'

'I would, and shall. I shall ask people to pray for me as long as I am still living, but the moment I am dead it would be wrong.'

Yes, she would hold by that. Whatever Jane said, she would stand by. Bess gave a laugh which startled the younger girl, who had, however, some glimmering of what she was feeling.

'She often wished you were there,' Jane said. 'She would

rather have had you with her than me, I know. She has left you half her jewels.'

Bess turned sharply away, and Jane, looking sadly after her, wondered why her cousin could not take her grief in a more Christian spirit. It seemed to make her harsh and mocking.

Jane had been so looking forward to her comfort and guidance; and Bess had just had her fifteenth birthday, which made her practically a grown-up woman. Jane would not have her twelfth for three weeks yet, but her parents seemed to think that made her one also, for they were saying it was not suitable for her to stay on in the Admiral's household now that his wife was dead. She thought this absurd, for her great difficulty was to make the Admiral realise she was as old as she was. He still gave her dolls and spoke to her as though she were about six, and when she protested, said it was her own fault for being so small, she grew downwards like a cow's tail.

But Bess, instead of agreeing how silly and tiresome Jane's parents were being, only said that she wasn't going to answer for the Admiral. And finding her so unsympathetic, Jane could not bring herself to tell her real sorrow; which was that it was the Admiral himself who had sent her away.

So shocked and stunned had he been by his wife's death that all his far-reaching plans and ambitions had gone clean out of his head; he would not even keep his household, but talked of dismissing the lot and going right away, he did not know nor care where; and packed Jane straight off home to her parents as though she were a puppy he had tired of training.

And now Bess said she was lucky to have parents and a

home to go to, where she would be safe and be told what to do. Really she must be ill!

Mrs Ashley also thought her charge's behaviour odd; the girl had been utterly bewildered and aghast at first at the news of Catherine's death, yet seemed even more angry than sorry, and went about with a white face and shut set mouth when she did not fly into sudden and unreasonable rages.

The Admiral's servant who brought the news told them of his master's passionate grief; but Bess showed no sympathy, and when Mrs Ashley told her it would be only right and proper for her to write him a letter of condolence, she flew out at her governess like a spitfire and snapped out, 'I will not. He doesn't need it.'

Mrs Ashley told her she was monstrously unfeeling. What was worse, it looked so marked. *Someone* from the Princess's household must write; 'If Your Grace will not,' she said in coldly formal remonstrance, 'then I will.'

So she did, but when she showed the letter, Her Grace gave it an indifferent glance and said not one word about it, one way or the other.

Mrs Ashley's conclusion was that the Princess did not believe in the Admiral's grief for his wife; perhaps did not wish to believe it.

'Your old husband is free again now,' she said lightly one evening, when the girl's fierce tension had for some time relaxed and she had flown suddenly into a wildly silly mood that seemed to welcome chaff and badinage – and whatever she might welcome, Mrs Ashley must try and give. 'Oh yes,' she continued, nodding her head, 'You can have him if you will, and well you know it. If the Protector and the Council give their consent, would you be so cruel as to deny him? You were his first choice, you know…'

Bess had clapped her hand over her governess's mouth. 'If you don't stop talking,' said a small clear deadly voice, 'I'll thrust you out of the room.'

One could never be sure what she would welcome.

But certainly she listened with both ears when people spoke to each other, not to her, about the Admiral – especially if they spoke praise, which made her flush with pleasure. Mr Parry the cofferer, who kept all the household accounts, was a great friend of Mrs Ashley's, and the two of them would casually remind each other, in front of their young mistress, what a great man the Admiral was clearly born to be; how he had begun to win position and notice entirely on his own merits, as a younger son, and before any of his sisters had made important marriages; how the sumptuous state he kept abroad for the honour of his country came as naturally to him as to any of the great princes of the House of Valois and of Hapsburg, and how his popularity with them had made his success as a diplomat.

'A King among kings, he was their fellow from the first,' Mrs Ashley declared, rolling up her eyes, and Mr Parry, turning his down modestly, said, 'Ah, but what did he care for that, whenever there was a chance to prove himself a man among men? Off he dashed in the middle of all his success and splendour at the Hungarian Court, to fight in their quarrel against the cruel Turk. "A lion in battle," so the King of Hungary wrote of him to King Henry.'

Mrs Ashley took up the antiphony.

'And as great a sailor as soldier – look how he drove off the

French Armada when they outnumbered us by five to one!'

'And I was there!' Bess thought, hugging herself, while her eyes glowed in the firelight like a cat's.

But she could not contain in silence her pride and glory in that towering figure on the deck of the *Great Harry* as the enemy sails hove into sight over the edge of the bright sea. She laughed aloud, yet her laughter had a secret sound; they pressed her for its reason, and then she said in airy tones, 'Three hundred tall ships sailing to invade England – and then "Pouf! the wind blew them away!" That was all that happened, so the Admiral said; "We'd the luck of the wind." What would have happened if the wind *hadn't* changed just then? But no, he was certain that England would always have luck, and the wind, on her side – on his side too,' she added tentatively.

Mrs Ashley quickly assured her that the Admiral was born to be lucky, the youngest son of three, as in the fairytales. Hadn't he proved himself lucky in Court and camp, and, she hoped, (with a sly look) in love? Bess leant forward and nonchalantly touched a log of wood. She thought nobody would notice, but the tutor did.

Mr Ascham's brain was whirling in a vortex of emotions; jealousy was shot through with pride, and a new awareness of what he himself was capable, as well as that bold and handsome conqueror of his Princess's thoughts. Yes, they were both of them men of this new many-coloured, fast-moving age, when a man was not content to be one thing merely, but was often courtier, soldier, statesman, sportsman, all in one.

He had just had a grave warning from his former tutor that

his passion for dice and the cockpit would be his ruin. But would it? He had put his best writing into this new book he was doing on the Cockpit; he was making English prose, a new thing, the thing that Englishmen would write in future instead of the old monkish musty Latin.

Those two bawds were chuckling now over the Admiral's pranks that had made him the favourite of King Henry and the playboy of Europe; 'but of course his elder brother can never understand that. *He* can only see him as the bad boy of the family!'

The tutor unexpectedly chimed in on an acid note; only Englishmen were so stupid as to think that to be solemn, dull and unpleasant was a sure criterion of solid worth and intellect. King Hal had known better, because the joy he took in living had been more French than English, and the keenness of his wits more Italian than either. 'He was not content merely to govern with a strong hand such as England needed; he has made her excel in music, in singing and dancing above all other countries, and encouraged plays to be written in English – light and transient toys they are called by the solemn dullards, but there's no knowing what those plays might become in the hands of some great poet. He wrote himself, was musician and composer, dancer and draughtsman, the best of our sportsmen – and our greatest ruler!'

'And *my* father,' Bess murmured.

They spoke of King Hal, while she thought of the Admiral, and Mr Ascham of himself.

'Man is a microcosm,' he cried. 'The full man should take all life for his province.'

'What's this about a full man?' came a great voice from the

doorway. 'Here's one that's empty as an old can.'

Bess half rose from her chair, then sat down again, gripping its arms. All the resentment that had been surging in her against the Admiral these past weeks was whirling away. She tried to clutch on to it. She had forgotten Catherine while she listened to praise of him; now she told herself, 'Catherine is dead and he doesn't care. Catherine is dead, and he and I made her unhappy. Catherine is dead, and it's her I loved, not him. Oh God, make me go on loving her and not him.'

It was no good. He was there at the end of the hall flinging off his cloak, he was striding across to her, lifting her hand to kiss it, and how warm and strong his grasp was round her fingers, how warm and strong his voice. His eyes were laughing into hers again – how dared he ever laugh at her again? She had told herself she would never laugh with him again – you might as well tell the grass not to grow nor the birds sing. She raised those drooping white-lidded eyes and looked full at him.

'Why have you come, my lord?' She tried hard to make the question sound casual and matter of fact.

'Don't you know, my Lady Bess?'

There was no attempt to make the answer sound casual.

Tom in fact had recovered. Which does not mean that he had never been sick – sick unto death, for that was what his soul had been, a ship that had lost its rudder and was veering wildly to the winds of despair and utter weariness of all ambition. He had been within an ace of killing himself in the days that followed Cathy's death.

But his body simply would not let him stay sad; the

unthinking high spirits of sheer physical vigour would keep tingling through his veins, reminding him even in the very midst of his stormy grief that it was good to be alive. Being miserable was no use to anyone, least of all to Cathy. If he did not kill himself he must go on living; and if he went on living he must be busy, active, make plans, take chances, run risks, or he would be blue-moulded with misery. He must have bustle, music, the flickering light of hundreds of candles and torches, the noise of people coming and going, of people talking, courting him, discussing gay and desperate ventures, and of his own voice laughing away their fears.

He caught again at all the old schemes that he had begun to let fall through his fingers in the first shock of his despair; countermanded the disposal of his household; sent for his everwilling old mother to come and take charge of the female part of it; and wrote off to Jane's parents to have her returned to his care and his mother's chaperonage, explaining that he had only sent her away because he had been 'so amazed that I had small regard either to myself or my doings.'

They hesitated; the Admiral was still dangling that prize of the Crown of England for their daughter, but *was* he a suitable match-maker? There were all sorts of stories about him and Elizabeth even while his wife was alive and the Princess a schoolgirl under his roof; and now he was a widower, with only old Lady Seymour to hold him in check – and when would she ever do, had ever done such a thing?

Their timid half-denials put more life into the bereaved widower than all the beautiful letters of condolence he had received. Now he had something to do; he must ride off on the instant and put some spunk into these Grey creep-mice, and off he went to lead Henry Grey once more up and down the garden path. He told the old gentleman that if he backed out now he would lose all hope of ever getting a King for a son-in-law. Since there was no longer any chance of marrying the little Queen of Scots to King Edward, the Protector had now the single aim of pushing forward his own daughter, Janet Seymour, as his bride; Tom had certain knowledge of this, he declared, thumping Henry Grey's top waistcoat button as the little man hummed and hawed and Tom had to bite his lip to keep from whistling 'How shall I make this ass to go?'

In fact, he only agreed to 'go' after the irresistible argument of ready cash. Tom paid the more pressing of his debts; and Jane Grey was told to write a nice letter to the Admiral telling him she would be glad to return to his guardianship.

She needed no telling; the Lady Frances, reading her daughter's letter, felt that Jane had rather overdone her 'thanks for the gentle letters which I received from you' and 'your great goodness toward me...as you have been unto me a loving and kind father, so I shall be always most ready to obey your godly monitions and good instructions.'

'God's blood, I hope not!' rapped out her anxious mother, slapping her riding-whip against her fat thigh. 'And why sign yourself his "most humble servant during my life"?'

'Because I could not be it after my death,' said Jane. The logic was unanswerable. And since even the threat of a whipping would not make Jane write her letter again, or even scratch out the last three emphatic words, it was despatched 'this 1st of October 1548.'

Through the great woods that spread for miles round

Bradgate the Admiral and his retinue again came riding, the golden leaves falling round them; again he dined and wined, walked and talked, hunted and made merry with the Greys. But this time when he left, Jane rode back with him to his house in the Strand – a long ride, they had to stop at more than one town *en route* for cold beef and beer for themselves and their numerous escort, and Jane was astonished at the gusto with which he ate it, and, for the matter, at her own. On this lovely changing autumn day the world seemed to be beginning all over again.

Yet only a month ago she had followed Queen Catherine's corpse to the grave, her long black robes trailing behind her. And this splendid figure in the sunlight beside her, filling the keen air with his talk and laughter, had then been a great dumb beast, his face the dark shadow of what it now was. And Catherine would not be there to run out with little cries of greeting when they reached Seymour Place.

'Oh God,' Jane sighed to herself, 'if only everything could always stay the same!'

But in one respect change was welcome; her cousin Bess would not be at Seymour Place.

Jane was only a side-line. Bess was the Admiral's main ambition – and unfortunately for him, not only an ambition. He knew that to pursue her in haste was to imperil all his hopes, not only of her but of personal safety for them both; yet he could not help it. He was mad, but not blind; seeing the danger, yet remembering only the warmth of her lithe body tucked down beside him in the barge, of her pointed face dimly white in the luminous darkness of that night last

May; of her evasive mocking answers to his furious questions.

She had never told him who the man had been that he had seen merely as a shadowy form against the light as the girl leapt up to it, her arms outflung in a wild movement of childish abandon. She was growing up so fast; who was she seeing, falling in love with perhaps, even at this moment? There could be no one but the tutor; but these tutors were dangerous fellows, they were there all the time, and this one was young, a sportsman who taught her to shoot and play and sing as well as read Greek.

Never trust a music master – he knew! He'd given music lessons himself, though not for money. But he'd got his reward. Was this Mr Ask'em (that's bad) – Mr At'em (that's worse) getting his?

The possibility took him headlong down to Hatfield.

The sight of Mr Ascham's pleasant smile and square shoulders (a bookworm ought to stoop and frown) did not encourage him; nor did the way he sang praises of his pupil when the Admiral, as was right and proper, enquired about the Princess's progress in her lessons. Sang was the word, for Mr Ascham became positively lyrical when he mentioned the beauties even of Elizabeth's handwriting – true, he was forming it himself. And when he spoke of the grace and 'grandity' of her deportment, the Admiral, amused by this odd tribute to her budding queenliness, was seriously alarmed by the light that glowed in those mild brown eyes as they turned to follow the swift and resolute movements of his pupil. She went past them in the stiff embroidery of her clothes as though walking on Mount Gargaros on 'new grass and dewy lotus and crocus and hyacinth' bringing sunshine in her wake. Aloud, the tutor spoke the words of the old blind poet, and the Princess, turning her head, flashed him a smile and called something back as if capping his quotation. This Greek, the Admiral decided, gave them an unfair advantage.

And of course he could get nothing out of Elizabeth when he questioned her. Yes, Mr Ascham was charming; he made her lessons much more interesting than poor Mr Grindal had done; yes, it was an advantage that he was not only learned but a keen sportsman and musician.

It was not the first time he had been baffled by this impertinent chit. Would he ever get the better of her till he held her in his arms and made her his own? Would he even then?

He took her by the elbows and told her he was mad for her; and she looked up into his eyes and laughed.

'You need not be so coy,' he said. 'The report goes now that I am to marry little Lady Jane.'

She tore herself out of his hands and whisked away like a whirlwind. 'So you've two strings to your bow! Then you'll never shoot straight.'

He gave a roar of delight at her sudden white fury. 'You little fool, it's a joke, that's all. I'll not have her if you'll have me.'

'Nor my sister Mary? Nor that unfailing stopgap, Anne of Cleves? Report has married you to both these lately. It says indeed that you don't care whom you marry as long as it's a princess and her dowry.'

'So much the better,' he answered casually, 'The more

they guess, the less likely to guess right.'

'Is that why you've been making enquiries into their lands and inheritance as well as mine?'

'Of course. Has it made you jealous? It has! Come, admit it!'

'I'll admit nothing,' she cried in rage. 'It's nothing to me whom you marry.'

'Not if it's yourself?'

'I won't marry you, or anyone. I'll not be tied and bound. A wedding ring is a yoke ring.'

'Not between friends. Aren't we good friends?'

'Very good.'

'And don't you love me?'

'I love a friend as myself. But I should love a husband more than myself, since I should be giving myself to him.'

'And will you not give yourself to me?'

He caught her to him, he kissed her again and again until she took fire from his lips and kissed him back suddenly, savagely, then tore herself away, darted across the room, picked up a comfit-box and started cramming her mouth with sweets as if to besiege it against further kissing, and mumbled with her mouth full, 'You can't marry me without the Council's consent, or you'll marry nothing. And that you'd never do.'

'Would *you*?'

Almost – when he looked at her like that, and his voice dropped onto that deep note – almost she thought she would give up anything she had to be his. Anything she had, yes perhaps – but anything she might have? Even that future that had been written for her in the stars? One could alter that future, for man had free will to disrupt his own fate if he would. Would she?

She looked at him, and her eyes were not mocking now, nor angry; they were clear and blank as water in a glass. She swallowed hard, gulping down the last of the sweets.

'No,' she said.

CHAPTER EIGHTEEN

The Admiral decided to attend to business. He had already been doing so on the lines that had annoyed Elizabeth, enquiring into her lands and income and, disappointed with the results, comparing them with those of the other female legatees of King Henry's Will, to make sure that she was not being cheated. He also tried to set about an exchange of her lands for those in the same area as his own in the west, and suggested to her that she should ask the Duchess to help work this with the Protector. Bess could hardly believe her ears. *She* ask the Duchess for anything?

'I will *not*. I'll not begin to flatter and sue now.'

It was awkward. He could not explain that he was already fortifying his castle of Holt in Cheshire in case of a possible revolt, and that in that case it would be well to have her lands in line with his. A female conspirator just fifteen was not a good choice of ally.

He fell back on his friends, and he had plenty of them. He asked them about their lands, how near they marched with his own, what power they had in them, urging them to increase it, and not merely with the gentry – 'for *they* are not the fellows that count, they're too cautious and heavy; the little they have hangs round their necks like a millstone, they're for ever fearing they'll lose it. No, the men for my money are the yeomen, the true leaders of the countryside, in touch with all the peasants as we can never be. Shake hands with the yeomen of England, and you have your hand on England itself.'

And he urged on his friends those Rules for a Perfect Guest that had alarmed the Earl of Warwick: to take your own wine and victuals and leave them to your hosts while declaring their tough mutton and home-brewed ale and cider the best you ever tasted. By these simple means he would soon have the best part of the country with him; and as Lord High Admiral he had the sea, with the islands as naval bases at his back.

When he had all that power in his hands, the Council would have to consent to his marrying Elizabeth. And of her own consent he was now pretty certain.

Even he knew that he must not go and see her too often at this juncture, but the Ash-Cat was working steadily for him, and Parry, the cofferer and steward – 'stout fellow Parry,' and loyal to the bone to them both.

He wrote frequently to her and gave the messengers orders to wait while the Princess wrote her answers; and write she did, always very properly and circumspectly: but she did not keep the messenger waiting. And he felt he could read between the lines.

'I am a friend not won with trifles, nor lost with the like.' What a queer solemn assurance from the chit who had just been flirting so lightly with him!

And to assuage (or was it to arouse?) his jealousy at some fresh plan of the Protector's for a foreign alliance for her: 'It has been said that I have only refused you because I was thinking of someone else. I therefore entreat you, my lord, to set your mind at rest on this subject; up to this time I have not the slightest intention of being married, and if ever I should think of it (which I do not believe is possible) you would be the first to whom I should make known my resolution.'

His head jerked back in a crack of laughter as he read that. He would indeed be the first, and not so long now, to whom she should make known her resolution.

As for those coy protestations about never marrying, she was an absurd minx to think them worth the writing.

He had to ride down just once more to tell her so, and had the luck to meet her out riding through the beech-woods round Hatfield that dull late November afternoon.

'What do you know about marriage?' he said as their servants promptly dropped behind. 'Or about yourself either? You're a child, though an intelligent one – too much so, one would think, to write such stuff.'

'I've learnt about marriage from my stepmothers,' she said, sliding a look at him.

'God forbid! D'you think, then, we all play Old Harry with our wives?'

'You've not all got his opportunities.'

'No, but seriously—'

'Seriously, my lord, my first stepmother, Jane, died in childbed, and so was the only past wife he spoke of with respect; my second, big Anne Cleves, he shoved out of the way for my pretty cousin Cat Howard, whom he beheaded – and my last one gave me a step-stepfather,' she finished, and this time she did not look at him.

He stared at the white profile against the grey misty beech-trunks, their horses' hoofs squelching the thick wet fallen leaves of the road through the woods. There was no colour anywhere except in her hair, which flamed like a belated autumn leaf beside him. They said red hair showed a passionate nature; she had shown him that too. But how much else was there in her that she did not show?

They were having her portrait painted now, a stiff unchildlike thing (pity old Holbein was dead) and not much like her except for the childishly thin erect shoulders and beautiful hands, carefully displayed, and the level eyes that could look at you so coolly with that wicked little hint of mockery in one of them – he'd always told her they didn't match! The lips were shut tight, compressed into a thin line as if to let no secret escape them. 'Cross at being made to stand still so long, weren't you?' he had chaffed her as he looked at it. But yes, there *was* something in it that was like her, the gaze so direct, yet baffling.

'Elizabeth the Enigma,' he had once called her years ago when she was quite a child, called her that to tease her as he had stood watching a pattern of wavering watery light flickering up under her soft yet resolute little chin. Where had that been?

It did not matter. His name for her had come true. He never could be sure of her.

'Say it!' he roared suddenly. 'Why do you never say what you think?'

'I do not say all that I think. But at least I never say anything I do not think. What is it you wish me to say?'

'All – yes, all that you think. What is this grudge, or fear against me – why the "stepfather"? Catherine is dead and I cannot help that. I loved her.'

'And loved me.'

'I could not help that either. Nor could you.'

'Nor may you help loving others. And that would be hell on earth to me.'

She whipped up her horse and galloped ahead. He rode after her, he caught at her rein, his eyes were blazing with anger, he said he would never love, never had loved, any woman as he loved her. Still holding her bridle, he leapt from his saddle and pulled her down from hers, letting her horse go.

'I'll show you how I love you,' he said between his teeth as she fell forward into his arms and they closed round her, hugging the breath out of her.

His startled horse veered round and began to canter back down the ride. A heavier, more regular thudding of horses' hoofs came towards it. 'God's soul!' Tom exploded in incredulous fury that their escort should dare to catch them up.

But the gaunt old man with the long white beard flowing over his chest now riding through the woods towards them, like the approach of winter, was none of their escort. It was the Lord Privy Seal – Father Russell – as Tom always called him.

'I feared frost and here's snow,' said Bess to herself.

CHAPTER NINETEEN

'My Lord Admiral,' said the Lord Privy Seal that evening, 'there are certain rumours about you which I am very sorry to hear.'

'What are they?'

'That you mean to marry with' – he coughed a little – 'the Lady Mary, or else – ahem – with the Lady Elizabeth.'

'Oh, *that*!' observed Tom casually. 'Surely you'll throw in Anne of Cleves?'

'That too is said,' said Russell stiffly, 'and the Lady Jane Grey has also been mentioned. It makes little odds which of them it is, since all are royal; except that, naturally, the King's sisters are the most royal of all.'

'Father Russell, you are very suspicious of me. Who's been telling you these tales?'

Father Russell would not say, except that those who had done so were the Admiral's very good friends and advised him, as he himself did, 'to make no suit of marriage that way,' as though it were too dangerous even to repeat the names of the prospective brides. But Tom showed no such caution.

'Even a King's sisters may marry,' was his modest answer, 'and better for them to marry within the realm than outside it; so why might not I, or any other man, raised by the King their father, marry one of them?'

It sounded a fair and honest question. But Father Russell's face was nearly as long as his beard as he replied to it.

'My lord, if either you or any other within this realm shall match himself in marriage either with my Lady Mary or my Lady Elizabeth, he shall undoubtedly procure unto himself the occasion of his own utter undoing – and you especially, being of so near alliance to the King's Majesty.'

A deep silence followed the warning. Their steps went on and on, up and down, heavy, padded, measured steps in velvet slippers on the black and white marbled flags of the hall floor, while the rain fell outside the shuttered windows that rattled and creaked in the wintry gale.

Tom's Austrian boar-hound pricked an ear and stirred in his sleep by the fire as a gust and spatter of rain blew down the wide chimney and hissed on the burning logs.

He raised his head and listened to the footsteps going up and down behind him. His master was not wont to walk so, in silence, with any man. He rose heavily, stretched himself and shaking off the dreams of hunting that had been enchanting him as he lay in blissful warmth with his nose to the fire: he went and walked beside his master, up and down, up and down, to tell him that he was there, and that if he uttered the word he would be delighted to fly at the throat of this skinny man who smelt old and dry, who walked cautiously, who spoke coldly, who had made his master silent.

And he gave a preliminary yearning sniff at his bony ankles.

'What's your dog doing?' asked the Lord Privy Seal. 'Reminding me that there are better friends than humans,' said the Lord High Admiral.

It was Privy Seal's turn to sniff.

'And what would you get out of it?' he asked suddenly. 'How much do you think you'd have with either of them?'

'Three thousand a year,' said Tom coolly.

'You're wrong. Not a farthing more than ten thousand down, in money, plate and goods – and no land. And what's that to a man who's got to keep up the estate of a Princess's husband?'

'They *must* have £3,000 a year as well,' said Tom.

'God's body, they will *not*.'

'God's soul, they will! God's life, I tell you—'

'God's death, I tell you, *no*.'

The Lord High Admiral, outsworn by that aged and venerable man, Lord Privy Seal, was silent again. Only his hound gave a hungry yawn.

Upstairs in her little closet, with the firelight winking on the silver candlesticks and the gilded carving of the ceiling, and the icy rain drumming against the windows where padded blue velvet curtains shut out the draughts, Mrs Ashley was having a long cosy chat with Mr Parry, the steward, over a nice hot brandy posset of her own brewing.

'Oh, it's true enough,' said Mrs Ashley. 'There's – well, what shall I say? – put it at its lowest, there's goodwill between the Lord Admiral and Her Grace – but I had such a charge of secrecy in it that I dare say nothing about it, except that I would wish her his wife of all men living. And I dare say he might bring off the matter with the Council well enough.'

'But do you think he will with her?' asked Mr Parry. 'I once was bold enough to ask her whether she'd marry him if the

Council liked it, and all she would say was, "When that comes to pass, I will do as God shall put into my mind."'

'That's Her Grace all over,' chuckled Mrs Ashley. 'Fobbed me off too, she did – or tried to. "What's the news from London?" she asked after my last visit. "Why," said I, "the voice goes there that you are to marry the Lord Admiral." Such a look she gave me – and then laughed – you know her laugh, clear as all the birds in the air. "Get out!" said she, "That's only London news!" Oh, she's deep – deep as a well, but she'll never take *me* in. I know too much.' And she took another sip at her posset and wagged her head, then two or three more sips and wagged her head two or three more times; then set down the empty cup and pursed her lips as though not another drop nor word should pass either way.

It was clearly incumbent on Mr Parry to do something about it. He leant forward and filled her cup with a carefully steady hand, then sank back with a comfortable sigh and said, 'Ah, she's got a true friend in you.'

'That she has,' said Mrs Ashley. 'Too true, maybe. I've tried to shield her when it's done no good to her, but harm to me. *That* woman, the Duchess, I mean, must have as many eyes in her tail as a peacock. The things she's nosed out!'

'What things?' enquired Mr Parry, as his colleague showed further signs of pursing.

'Things that I never breathed to a soul – and never will.'

'Come, if the Duchess knows them, what matter who else does?'

'She doesn't know all, thank heaven, and what she does is all crooked, like her own nasty mind. Told me I wasn't worthy to have the governance of a King's daughter! Because I permitted – *permitted*, mark you! – that's a nice one, if she only knew! – *permitted* my young lady to go out at night on the Thames in a barge with the Admiral. And other light parts.'

'Which parts?'

'Just parts,' said Mrs Ashley vaguely.

'Well, there's no harm in a barge,' said Mr Parry. 'Can't be, with the oarsmen facing the canopy. If it were a gondola, now! I knew a man who'd been in Venice,' he began reminiscently.

The spur acted quickly. Mrs Ashley, determined to prevent his anecdote, hastily assured him that there were other light parts besides barges. There were garden walks, benches in pleached alleys, and there the late Queen Catherine had come on her stepdaughter in her husband's arms.

'No!' said the steward.

'*Yes*!' said the governess.

'And that's why,' said the governess with finality.

'Why what?' asked the steward.

'Why we had to go away and have a separate establishment for Her Grace. It wasn't the first time the Queen had been jealous, I'm sure of that, and she was getting near her time, which made things worse.'

She emptied her cup absent-mindedly.

'What was I saying?' she asked.

'That it made things worse.'

'What things? Oh yes, the Queen's jealousy, poor soul. I can tell you, Mr Parry, it's been no easy business among the lot of them.'

Mr Parry made sympathetic noises and filled up his own cup.

'No easy bus-i-ness,' repeated Mrs Ashley, determined to get those s's quite distinct. It was the consonants that were the trouble. She would talk more freely if there weren't so many tiresome consonants in the words she wanted to use. No one could say she was drunk. She had seen Nan Bullen reeling about the room and swearing, but *she* was never like that. She might not be a queen, but she was a lady. And Mr Parry was a gentleman, a nice safe quiet dependable gentleman. It could not matter what one said to him. He understood.

'Women,' said Mr Parry.

'Yes, women,' said Mrs Ashley, 'and one of them hardly a girl, but the most difficult of the lot. After all, she's—' she rushed her consonants, '—she's old-Harry's-daughter.'

'Eh?' said Mr Parry.

'Red hair,' explained Mrs Ashley. 'Not pretty, but—'

'Ah,' said Mr Parry.

'The Admiral was always wild for her. Only married the Queen because he couldn't get the Princess.'

'Oh!' said Mr Parry. He filled up both their cups.

'And then,' said Mrs Ashley, looking at her cup, surprised to find it still so full and sipping a little to rectify this, 'then, of course, with her in the house, there was the devil – ahem! shall I say, Old Harry? – to pay!'

She laughed, and so did Mr Parry. After all, it was a long time since she had had such an enjoyable evening, such a companionable evening. She wanted to say so, but companionable was a difficult word. It was better to stick to facts.

She stuck to them. All that about the Admiral coming into the Princess's room in the mornings. Bare legs. Bed-curtains.

Smacking. Tickling. They were all quite simple words. And didn't mean any – he hadn't meant any harm. He had sworn so, on God's mosht precioush shoul. But when Queen Catherine had found her alone in his arms – well that was another matter.

Mr Parry quite agreed.

'Well, all that's over now,' said Mrs Ashley. 'Poor lady! He's free now. And I'd wish her his wife of all men living. For it's my belief, if she doesn't marry him, she'll marry no one.'

She sighed deeply and picked up her cup, but it was empty. Mr Parry leant forward again.

But he never filled the cup. He sat there with his eyes on Mrs Ashley, and hers on his, and between them a cry went shivering through the air, splintering up that cosy friendly warmth into thin particles of ice, a cry that froze them both sober, a cry not of this world nor of any that they knew.

Mrs Ashley sprang up, knocking the jug out of Mr Parry's hand over her gown and never noticing it; she picked up her wet skirt, never noticing that it dripped with brandy posset, and ran, straight as a die, to the room of her charge, the Princess Elizabeth.

She burst open the door and drew the bed-curtains. The light of the candles and the fire poured into the dark cave of the curtained bed, over a slight figure sitting bolt upright, and red hair rippling over the bare shoulders, and a small white face aghast, with staring eyes and open, shrieking mouth.

'My lamb,' cried Mrs Ashley, 'my sweet, my treasure, what's the matter? There's no harm near you, there's nothing here, I tell you, nothing but your old Ash-Cat.'

She hugged the staring face to her thin bosom, stroking the

rough hair over and over, feeling the young bones of the skull beneath, and now feeling, almost with relief, the long sobs that came welling up, shaking the childish shoulders.

'You've been dreaming, my lamb, that is all, a hateful dream. You've been riding the night mare – where to? Tell your old Ash-Cat. It's better to tell and have done with it so.'

'Oh Cat, my old Ash-Cat, you're right – if only I could tell it, Cat, my Ash-Cat.'

What was it there at the end of the corridor that had been so terrible, so strange, yet somehow familiar? The rain on the roof, the icy winter wind, they had drummed in her sleep now for years – no, only two – the years since her father died. The night he died, just two years ago, she had got out of her bed in the Palace at Whitehall and run along the corridor, until she fell plump into the arms of the Lord Admiral. Ever since she had dreamt of running along the corridor, into his arms.

Tonight again she had done so, but this time the door at the end of the corridor was closed. She had hammered on it with both fists, knowing that if it did not open at once she would be too late – too late for what? Too late for her life, or his, or both?

The door would not open, but she could see through it.

She saw the Admiral sitting on a stone bench in a small bare room, taking off his shoes. He was looking into them, plucking something out of them, and then beginning to write with it. He was writing to her. But whatever he wrote she knew she would never see it. She tried to call to him through the door. But he could not hear her, and she could not see what he was writing.

'I shall never see it,' she cried to Cat Ashley, 'I shall never, never see it!'

The dream was fading. Even as she thought of it, she could not think what had so terrified her. The things that had affected her conscious mind came forward instead. So that all Cat Ashley heard of what she had *not* dreamt was this: 'What reproaches did Queen Catherine whisper to her husband on her death-bed? What misery did she know through marrying the man she loved?'

Said Cat Ashley stoutly, 'She knew great happiness with him. Let that content you, as it did her. There was no bitterness in her end.'

Bess answered her, 'Because there never was in her life. It would not be so with me. If my husband did not love me alone, it would be worse than death, it would be perpetual hell.'

'Sweetheart, is this the dream that troubled you so?'

'No,' said she. 'I dreamt of the Admiral taking off his shoes.'

Her laugh terrified Mrs Ashley more than her cries had done.

Suddenly the girl sniffed long and searchingly. 'Fie, Ash-Cat,' said she, 'how you stink of brandy!'

Bess was asleep. Light tawny eyelashes lay on the pale cheeks like two ruddy half-moons in a summer dusk. Mrs Ashley whispered to her charge, waited, heard no answer but long regular breathing, and the rain drumming on the roof.

She ran back down the passage to her own little closet. The candles were low in their candlesticks. The fire was dim and red. Mr Parry, that silent fat man, lay stretched in his chair, his hands folded piously across his stomach. He looked extremely dependable, even in his sleep.

'Mr Parry!' said Mrs Ashley.

Mr Parry sat up. He kicked a log. A bright flame-light filled the small room. All the gilded carving in the ceiling leapt to life, the silver candlesticks gleamed red.

'Mr Parry!' said Mrs Ashley, and there was agony in her voice. She had forgotten all about her consonants. It did not matter how she spoke, as long as she said what she must say. 'Mr Parry, I spoke unwisely just now. I wish I had not said all that I said to you of her Grace the Lady Elizabeth and the late Queen and the Lord Admiral.'

'You can depend on me,' said Mr Parry. 'Not another soul shall ever hear of it, not if they were to drag me in pieces by wild horses. No,' said he, sitting up and looking straight before him with solemn unctuous eyes at the winking silver candlesticks, and then all round him on the small room filled to the ceiling with bright firelight, 'not if I were dragged in pieces – by wild horses.'

CHAPTER TWENTY

His mother and little Jane Grey were in the house when they came to arrest the Admiral.

Old Lady Seymour did not twitter and flutter, nor even cry. She stood like a small statue of grey stone; her lips moved a little but no one heard what she said, except Jane, who thought she was praying and crept to her side to join her. But the words she heard, over and over again, were: 'I knew it. I knew it. I knew it. One of them would kill the other.'

The frightened tears began to run in silence down Jane's face.

But the Admiral was as gay and unworried as if it had been a summons to Court.

'You'll see me back again in no time, never fear,' he told them. 'They'll never dare do anything really against me. And if they did, Ned wouldn't let 'em.'

But even as he said it, an uncomfortable echo sounded in his mind from Ned's last solemn warning and lecture, uttered after Father Russell's had so signally failed. 'I may not be able to save you,' he had said. 'Only yourself can do that now for certain.' And he had begged him – yes, his urgency had really amounted to that – begged him to go on a mission to Boulogne to see to the defences there – to get him out of

England, that was patent; but for the first time Tom wondered if Ned hadn't after all been sincere when he pressed it on Tom's account rather than his own.

He had so nearly gone to Boulogne. He had even begun to pack for it. And then – Mr Parry had come up from Hatfield. He had brought a letter from Elizabeth; nothing much, as usual, to be got from that. But he could tell the Admiral a deal about her, and his plump smiles and sympathetic glances had told still more.

The Princess changed colour very noticeably if the Admiral were but mentioned; and if anything praising or admiring were said, 'she drinks it in as a flower does the rain, lifting her head to it, and you can see the little pulse in her throat throbbing with pride.' He had then remarked discreetly on the arrangements for a town house for her so as to visit the Court and her brother this winter.

'That won't be till after I've gone to Boulogne – they'll see to that!' said the Admiral bitterly.

And after Mr Parry had left he had sat trying to think out his plans, but he could only think of the pulse throbbing in that childishly bony little hollow at the base of her long throat – a pulse that throbbed even at hearing him mentioned. He thought how he could make it beat; how he could make every inch of her body tingle with longing for him, as it had never yet known that it could do.

His steward had come in with a pile of papers for him to sign, giving powers to various persons to act for him at home while he was in Boulogne.

'Take them away,' said the Admiral. 'I'm not going.'

And so now he was not in Boulogne, he was in his own

house of Seymour Place in the Strand, and they had come to arrest him. A stupid business, he'd never forgive Ned for frightening his mother like this. Ned had got frightened himself, that was why he'd done it; he was as nervous as a cat, and cowards were always cruel.

'They can't do anything,' he told his mother. 'They've got nothing really against me. You'll see me back sooner than if I'd gone to Boulogne. Give me your blessing, little Mam.'

As he knelt to receive it, the sense of that hurried muttering whisper struck chill on his heart.

'I knew it. I knew it. One of them would kill the other.'

He sprang up and flung his arms round her, swept her up from the ground and tried to kiss warmth into that cold old face.

The Captain of the Guard reminded him that they must go. He went, not looking back. A small figure came pattering after him.

'My lord, my lord,' cried Jane's voice. 'Say goodbye to me too!'

He stooped and kissed her, and she clung to him. 'You are going to the Tower!' she said, and shuddered.

'What of that? You'll go to the Tower too one day.' And he whispered, smiling at her, 'The night before your Coronation, when you marry the King.'

'That is different,' sobbed Jane. 'I shan't go by the Traitors' Gate.'

'Don't be too sure,' he chaffed her. But she would not be coaxed into a smile.

'You have been a true father to me,' she said, 'better than my own.'

'That's easy!' He added hastily, 'To such a daughter. Come, you must stop crying or your eyelashes will fall out. Look after my mother and make her laugh.'

And then he went.

CHAPTER TWENTY-ONE

Sir Robert Tyrwhitt dismounted at Hatfield House at the head of a considerable body of servants, and demanded to see the Princess Elizabeth. He was told that she was at lessons and could never be disturbed till they were finished. Sir Robert, tugging at his short scrubby greying beard, showed an order signed by the Council.

He was promptly ushered into the study, where Bess sat opposite Mr Ascham and a maid-in-waiting yawned over her embroidery-frame in the corner. Usually this was Mrs Ashley's occupation, but she had had to go up to town in answer to another summons from the Duchess, and departed with many wry anticipations of another wigging, slightly mollified by the company of Mr Parry, who was making one of his rather mysterious visits to the Admiral. So a young girl sat in Ashley's place and pretended great interest in the lesson, until she found she could not catch Mr Ascham's eye.

Mr Ascham shut his books slowly, looking across the table at his Princess. He saw terror leap at the back of her clear eyes, and then they seemed to cloud over, deliberately, as though she were pulling a veil across her face while she summoned all her forces of courage and deception beneath it.

The thought flashed through his mind: 'Is this perhaps the last time I shall see her?'

Then he had to go, and she was left alone, facing the little man who had always disliked her and had now suddenly become a powerful enemy. What could have happened to place him in this position?

'The Lord High Admiral,' said Sir Robert slowly, and then waited a moment, watching her intently, as a cat watches the mouse just beyond its paws. She knew it, and though a sick cold wave crept up over her flesh, turning everything dark round her, she did not stir a hair's-breadth, and her eyes faced his, still veiled and inscrutable.

'The Lord High Admiral,' he repeated, 'has just been arrested by order of the Council and taken to the Tower.' She still did not move, nor did her eyes flicker.

It was unwomanly, inhuman. He had banked everything on this first shock. But he had others in store.

'Mrs Ashley and Mr Parry,' he began, and again paused before finishing his sentence, 'are also under arrest.'

Still she stared, and her eyes looked more blank than before. Then suddenly they flashed open in a green flame, she leapt forward, her hand swung up and out, and she would have struck Sir Robert full in the face if he had not stepped back so abruptly that his heel slipped on the marble tiles and he sat down on them suddenly and painfully.

A gleam of delight shot through the Princess's eyes as she looked down on him, her clenched fist still raised so that he fancied she was going to hit him as he sat on the floor; but she thought better of it, put her hand resolutely behind her back, and shouted in a voice that surprisingly resembled her father's, 'God's death, how dare you arrest *my* governess and steward?'

Sir Roger got up, carefully refraining from feeling himself behind. His face was crimson, his eyes glazed with fury. He said, 'Mr Parry, the pandar, and your bawd are in the Tower by now, giving a full account of Your Highness's relations with the Admiral, and how you plotted to marry him against the will of the Council.'

She laughed, at first wildly, on an unmistakable note of hysteria. Tyrwhitt heard it, hopefully, but she heard it too and controlled it, though now shaking all over, and went on laughing – but deliberately, scornfully.

'Take care,' she said. 'You are not very wise. I am second to the throne.'

'Ha, you've thought of that, have you?'

'I am neither an idiot nor a child.'

'Married to the Admiral, you thought you would be able to take the throne for yourself.'

'By God,' she cried, 'you go too far.'

'Not as far as I may yet go. It is said that Your Grace is with child by the Admiral.'

She was silent, staring at him; then, 'You will answer for this with your head,' she said softly.

'Ah! Already you think you have Sovereign power. I advise Your Grace to remember your honour, and the danger you are in, for—' he paused again, and then said with ominous weight. 'You are but a subject – as was Your Grace's mother.'

All colour seemed to drain from her eyes; the pupils narrowed to pin-points like those of a cat – or a lion about to spring. At last she spoke wildly, in terror as well as rage.

'I appeal to the King my brother. I appeal to the Protector. I will go to them and answer any charges made against me. I will not stay here to be abused so traitorously.'

She made for the door, but he stood against it. 'I have to inform Your Grace that the Protector's orders are that you remain here under strict watch.'

'Am I a prisoner?' Her voice faltered at that.

'Virtually. Your Grace will not be put to the indignity of being under lock and key – unless it becomes necessary.'

He bowed low, went out and shut but did not lock the door, then waited. She did not rush out. He ducked down, looked through the wide keyhole, and had the satisfaction of seeing that unwomanly inhuman girl fling herself on the floor in a passion of frantic weeping.

But that moment of pleasure died in him as he walked thoughtfully away to write his report to the Protector. He would have to admit that he had got absolutely nothing out of the Princess. Shock tactics had proved useless. It looked as though he would have to change them.

'She has a very good wit,' he wrote, 'and nothing can be gotten from her except by great policy.'

He would have to try it.

He did. Next day he sent a respectful message asking the Princess to grant him another interview, which of course she had no power to refuse; and then apologised, frankly and humorously, for having lost his temper in such an unwarrantable fashion – it was all because he had sat down so hard and she had looked so pleased, he said, smiling ruefully as he tenderly felt the part affected.

Then he began to coax and excuse her. She had not always

behaved as properly as a young lady should – come, she must admit that, for everybody knew that she had been sent away from Queen Catherine's household because of her conduct with the Lord Admiral.

'If Queen Catherine were here *she* would answer for me,' Bess interpolated on a strangled sob, and then the forlornness of her position broke her down. She had no heart now to defy Sir Robert. He had told her she was but a subject – as her mother had been; had hinted that as her mother had died, so might she. Was it true that he had only spoken so in a rage? Certainly he seemed gentler now, and he grew still gentler when she cried.

So she cried a good deal.

He was then very fatherly; he patted her head and even to like doing so, for he went on stroking her she gritted her teeth to keep herself from shaking he told her she was not to worry too much. young,' he kept saying, and it was not really he as that of her elders who ought to have taken better; if only she 'would open all things and the and shame will be ascribed to them, an into consideration by His Majesty, th and her eyes, whole Council.'

But she would only open her mou Robert's eager after rubbing them, just in time to glance at her as she seemed about d, 'what's the odds?

'Come, come,' he said as she it cannot matter what Your servants have told everyth you say.'

Then why should he wan to say it?

She said a great deal, but nothing that Tyrwhitt wanted.

Again he had to write to the Protector: 'In no way will she confess any practice by Mrs Ashley or the cofferer Parry concerning my Lord Admiral.'

It was infuriating: what sort of a fool would his master think him that he could not force the girl to speak? He dug the pen into the ink so angrily that it splashed on to the paper, and added:

'Yet I do see it in her face that she is guilty, and yet I do perceive that she will abide more storms ere she will accuse Mrs Ashley.'

He tried more storms. He tried gentle persuasion and complacently assured the Protector that he was 'beginning to grow with her in credit' – but unfortunately he could give no tangible proofs of it.

He tried a formal commission to put her under cross-examination and take down her evidence.

He tried a false letter from the Protector to himself which agreed that he should show her as if at some danger to himself with a great protestation that I would not for £1,000 . . . of it'; this confidence trick, to make her confide in him, produced much polite gratitude for his trust who had notwithstanding, I cannot frame her to all points.'

poems to her friend, the Lady Browne, née Fitzgerald, women had not 's Fair Geraldine, and Surrey had written the Fair Geraldine so he had to the Duchess. His taste in said a thousand symp-ood as in dress; so Bess decided after which nevertheless left B- axed and condoled with her, and teasing, complimentary things with only one consideration –

what was it exactly that she had said to Lady Browne?

She had seen no one of her own household since Tyrwhitt's arrival, but only him and his accomplices, his wife and her servants. Lady Tyrwhitt's affection for Catherine made her take a very hard view of the bright young girl who had disturbed Catherine's married happiness. Bess was not bright now, but neither was she humbled, nor conciliatory, nor frank. She regarded Lady Tyrwhitt with more undisguised hostility than she had dared show any of the others; her tone to her, prisoner though she was, speaking to her gaoler's wife, flicked a whiplash of contempt. Yet she was well aware how desperate was her position.

Parry had rushed to his wife when he heard he was to go to London and be questioned; had torn off his chain of office, wrung his hands and thrown away his rings, sobbed out that he wished he had never been born for now he was utterly undone; and several servants had witnessed his panic.

They told this to the Princess, who spat. Certainly she needed a new governess, said Lady Tyrwhitt. But Bess knew the stakes were for more than that. In this struggle, which might be for her life, and, as she was beginning to understand, was most certainly for the life of the man she loved, she had no one whose advice she could ask; no one to whom she dared speak without guarding her every word, her every look; no one near her who was not her enemy, watching, listening, waiting to trap her unawares.

The hard frost that was imprisoning earth and air outside her windows, so that sometimes as she stood staring out through them she saw a starved bird fall to the ground like a stone falling, was shutting down on her spirit. Did they mean to freeze her too to death, with terror?

She turned with a shudder from the window and crouched down by the fire, holding out her long hands to the warmth which glowed through them, showing the pink flesh translucent and the shadowy thin bones encased in it. So easy would it be to become a skeleton; already you could see its narrow framework. Instinctively her hands went up and round her slender throat: 'I have a little neck,' her mother had said, 'It will not be hard work for the executioner.'

There she sat with her fingers round her throat, staring into the fire. There was a fox in the fire, a flaming red fox in a black cave, peering out at her with winking glowing eyes, the wicked eyes of a fox caught in a trap, but they were the eyes of a fellow-conspirator, perhaps of herself, and they bade her beware.

Lady Browne came flurrying in and knelt down beside her and flung her warm arms round her. 'My child,' said that soft imploring Irish voice. 'My darling child, I've run here to warn you. Sir Robert is on his way to you – he has the statements, signed statements made by your servants in the Tower – they have confessed everything.'

'*What* have they confessed?'

Lady Browne, already in tears, became rather incoherent, but kept on urging, 'No time to lose – he's on his way here. Think what you'd better say and tell me quickly, then I'll tell you if it's safe to say to him.'

Bess was crying with fright. Her voice could just be heard in a thin squeak.

'Have they confessed? What have they confessed?'

'Everything. I've told you, everything. Their statements are here, signed by them. It was Parry did it first.'

'Parry! The traitor!'

'Yes, yes,' agreed Lady Browne eagerly.

'The liar!'

'Oh,' said Lady Browne more dubiously. She waited, but nothing more came from the girl, and she ran back to Sir Robert and told him what the Princess had said. Sir Robert noticed rather what she had not said. But he hoped more from the signed statements.

They were thrust into her hands, while he and two or three other gentlemen hovered round her, hunched uneasy shadows hanging over her, at which she dared not look. She choked back her tears.

She looked down on the papers and at all the black marks of the writing that wriggled and squirmed over them like small black snakes. They would not keep still. She could not read what they said if they would not keep still. She heard a voice that sounded a long way off: 'Look! She is going to faint!'

If she did that, it would be a sign of guilt. If she did that, she might say something incriminating while she was unconscious. She dragged her senses back under control, focused her eyes until the snakes became still. But that was worse, for now scattered words and sentences swam up from the paper and struck at her eyes so that she reeled under first one blow and then another.

Humiliating things they were, all written down for everyone to see, and looking so much worse in words. She turned her head to avoid seeing them, but she *must* see them, everybody here knew what they were, and was watching to see how she would take them. Those morning romps when Tom would swing into her room and if she were up, 'strike her upon the back or buttocks familiarly and so go forth' (how low it sounded, but nothing in it – they must see there was nothing), 'and sometimes go through to the maids and play with them and so go forth.' (Well, that proved there was nothing.) But here was something about her being in bed, and how 'he would open the curtains and bid her good-morrow and make as though he would come at her, and she would go further in the bed so that he could not come at her' – and more about his chasing her and her running to her maids and getting them to hide her. It all looked so shocking written down in solemn words, read by these shocked solemn elderly faces all round her – a herd of old bearded goats, she longed to call them. She *could* not read further with all their wall-eyes on her. She must gain time somehow, hold up some sort of mask.

She tried to say, 'How do I know these are not forgeries?' but her breath would not come, nor her voice except in a ridiculous squeak; her face was flaming hot while all the rest of her body seemed to be turning to ice, and her heart hammered so loud against her stiff bodice that surely everyone there must be hearing it.

It seemed a long time before she managed to gasp out that she must examine the signatures carefully to make sure they were genuine.

Tyrwhitt took this insulting suggestion very coolly and saw its intention.

'Your Grace knows your governess's and steward's signatures with half an eye,' he remarked scornfully.

But Bess was not to be stampeded. She pretended to pore over the signatures while her glance shot here and there over the papers, taking in the worst that she could see.

Parry's was the danger-point; Cat Ashley would never give away anything that he had not; and so it was his report that she scanned in swift sweeping glances. It seemed to be all about a long gossip he had had with Cat Ashley full of 'she saids' and 'I saids'; and Parry had evidently seized his chance to curry favour with the Protector by abusing the man whom he had been serving so assiduously as go-between, for he had written: 'Then I chanced to say to her that I had heard much evil report of the Lord Admiral…and how cruelly and dishonourably he had used the Queen.'

This from Parry who was always trying to get kind messages out of her for the Admiral and running up to town with them as often as he could! Parry the pandar – Parry the traitor!

And out of all this tittle-tattle there were other sentences sticking up like swords – 'I do remember also that she told me that the Admiral loved the Lady Elizabeth but too well, and had done so a good while: and that the Queen was jealous of her and him. "Why," said I, "has there been such familiarity indeed between them?" And with that she sighed and said, "I will tell you more another time." But afterwards she seemed to repent that she had gone so far with me and prayed me that I would not disclose these matters, and I said that I would not. And again she prayed me not to open it, for Her Grace would be dishonoured for ever and she likewise undone. And I said I would not; and I said I had rather be pulled with horses.'

The silence was filling the room. She would have to speak.

She said, still gasping for breath, and every word seemed to come with a gulp, 'This man – has proved himself false – through and through. I do not believe – my governess ever said such things to him.'

Tyrwhitt answered her. 'She denied them and would say nothing on her own account, until they were brought face to face, and Parry stood fast to all this that he has written. Then she burst out against him and called him a false wretch and reminded him that he had promised he would never confess till death. That proved his words.'

Again the silence came creeping out of all the corners and crannies of the room. The eyes round her were boring through her like screws, further and further inside her head, until soon all inside it would lie open for them to read.

At last she looked up; she stared full at Sir Robert with eyes that did not shift, though everything at which they looked seemed to waver.

She spoke in a voice that no longer shook. 'It was a great matter for him to promise such a promise, and to break it.'

CHAPTER TWENTY-TWO

Sir Henry Seymour rode to London for the second time in his forty years of life. The first time had been just two years ago when Brother Ned had made such a pother about his going up for the Coronation to be made a knight because his little nephew was being made King; though for the life of him Henry could not see what that had to do with him. He had flatly refused to be made a peer; if they must make a fool of him they must, but they should not carry it on to his children.

Though he knew, of course, that it wasn't always Coronation-time, he had ever since pictured London as a crammed shrieking whirligig of a fair-ground, where people drank and danced in the streets and sang and shouted like madmen and jostled and trampled each other into the mud, and you couldn't see the sky because of a lot of mummers and jugglers played their foolery on platforms or ropes high over your head; and he'd got a cricked neck looking at them, and his ears dinged with noise till they buzzed, and his pocket was picked. Nothing in his life, he thought, would ever get him to London again.

Yet here he was on Dapple's back, going at a steady jog-trot down the long wintry rides of Savernake Forest, with the brown interlacing pattern of the bare branches overhead, and the crackling of the horse's hoofs through the frosty crust on the mud underfoot, jogging once again to London town, to see Brother Ned.

He rode through some of Ned's vast new estates, past his splendid mansion that was rising higher and higher, brick by brick, till all the ninety hundred thousand of them should be placed on top of each other; and even then it would not be the summit, for dozens of newfangled chimneys were to go on the roofs, wriggling up higher and higher as if to vie with the Tower of Babel.

Henry didn't fancy all the bright red brick and white stone facings and windows wide as walls, glittering with brittle glass. To his mind, the shining surfaces of the modern houses were harsh and garish, like the modern people who live in them, all for show. Even the land was for show nowadays, a desecration in Henry's eyes equal to blasphemy.

Rich tradesmen were buying country estates so that their sons should be brought up on them as gentry! And those who already had land must have more. But the more land they got, the more they lost touch with it, and with the people on it; cut off from it by their own climbing ambition, climbing after fame and gold, climbing to the top of the tree, spending their vast new wealth only on fine feathers and feathering their own nests with them, never caring what other nests crumbled and fell to the ground.

'Charity died when chimneys were built,' the villagers said, for the poor never got such good fare under them as they had been given in the smoke-raftered, draughty old halls of the old gentry.

Had Brother Ned also lost all sense of charity as his chimneys rose? Well, he would soon see.

But he did not, for he did not see Brother Ned nearly as soon nor as easily as he had imagined. The Lord Protector sent word that he would be glad to see his brother Henry as soon as his press of business gave him a moment's leisure; as soon as that happened he would send word again.

But word did not come. It was Henry who sent word again, and got the same answer.

Henry began to hang about the precincts of the Duke's palace. Others were doing the same thing, quite a crowd of them. He talked with them in the casual manner with which he talked with neighbouring farmers at a cattle-sale, and found they were waiting to enter the Court of Requests which the Good Duke had set up in his own house to hear the complaints of the poor who could not afford the expense and delay of the law courts, or who had already tried them and been dissatisfied with the results.

For the Good Duke often overruled the decisions of the magistrates, and made them repair the wrongs they had done, so they told Henry gleefully. 'The law is ended as a man is friended' – that was true enough of most of the judges, since if a man could not afford to bribe he had better not go to law at all; but it wasn't true of the Good Duke. He was told the case of the poor widow who had been defrauded of her lands by Paulet, Lord St John, and how that great lord had been forced to redress the injury done her. 'The Good Duke doesn't only bring in laws against the rich, he sees to it that they're carried out. That's how he makes the mare bite their thumbs,' they chuckled. 'He sees that justice is done and the wrong righted.'

Very good, thought Henry, as long as Brother Ned were always right himself. But it struck him as an extraordinary instance of arbitrary power to reverse the magistrates' decisions entirely on his own judgement.

And he heard other things, not so much to the credit of the Good Duke. He learnt how he had pulled down two parish churches, St Mary-le-Strand and Pardon Church, and a chapel, to provide further building materials for his Somerset House, and had begun to pull down St Margaret's Church at Westminster as well, but there the cockneys themselves rose in protest and prevented it by mobbing his workmen and driving them away.

''Tisn't right,' said the waiting suppliants. 'Pulled down part of St Paul's too, he did. Might as well pull down Westminster Abbey next.'

'Ar,' said Henry.

He made no claim to priority through his kinship to the Protector, gave his name simply as Squire Seymour (he pronounced it Semmor, and Wolf Hall as Ulfall) and waited his turn in the queue of plaintiffs.

Waiting never troubled Henry. He could stand for an hour or more leaning over a gate staring at his pigs or his brood mares. Here he sat stolidly on a bench along with the other clods of English earth, waiting patiently for his turn and staring at the floor or at his fellows, who stared back at a man like many of themselves, dressed in simple country clothes, a leather jerkin, and long heavy riding-boots, and his face ruddy, wrinkled and tanned, itself a square of weather-beaten leather within its tawny fringe of short beard, like the yellow lichen on a red brick wall. His eyes when he raised them from the ground were as clear and direct in gaze as those of a boy.

You might think that no thoughts stirred behind those placid brown orbs – and perhaps they did not stir much; but they were there, lying deep and still, reflecting the things that he heard spoken round him, reflecting others that he had heard before.

Strange things he had heard told in dropped tones over the wassail cups of this Christmastide, things that sounded like the old wives' tales told by his nurse in his childhood, and so for the most part he believed them to be – rehashed and served up in a modern setting.

A wise woman, a midwife, living in a neighbouring county, not a hundred miles from London, was awakened on a night of this winter by a strange horseman who wore a mask of black velvet. She was made to mount behind him and ride off with him through the night. Before reaching their destination, the horseman put a bandage over her eyes and tied her hands that she might not raise it. He then lifted her down from the horse and led her into a house which must, she knew, be very large, for she counted her steps going through the hall and then up one staircase, down another, along one, two, three passages, then into a very warm room where the bandage was taken from off her eyes and she saw an enormous fire blazing on a great stone hearth. A carved and gilded bed hung with bright tapestry was at one side of the room, and by it stood a very tall man, richly clothed, and he also was masked and said no word.

In the bed lay a very young and very fair lady, her red-gold hair falling loose over the pillows, who was in labour. The midwife helped her bear the child, all things being put there necessary, and all the time not a word spoken. When the baby was delivered, the tall man took it from her hands and threw it on the fire. She was then given a bag of gold, her eyes bandaged as before, and she was taken back to her cottage, the horseman making her swear never to say what she had done that night.

But while she had been at work on her task she had contrived, unseen, to cut a small piece from the tapestry hangings of the bed – and if you were to go to Hatfield, where was the Princess Elizabeth, you would find that a certain bed there in a certain room had a piece cut out of its hangings.

At this point the narrative, told invariably by someone who had met – well, not the midwife herself, but a most reliably unimaginative applewoman, laundrymaid, housekeeper, or, in the best instance, one of the new parsons' wives, not of the flighty young kind that were setting their husbands' parishes by the ears, but quite a respectable body, who knew the said midwife intimately – at this point the narrative in a lowered voice would draw to its impressive close in the firelight, followed by an awed silence and a few shocked 'Ohs!' and 'Ahs!'

'I always liked that tale,' Henry had said when they turned to him.

And to their protestations of its truth as testified by the aforesaid parsons' wives, housekeepers, laundrymaids, and applewoman, he would only add, 'Ar. Reckon feminine kind have always known it for true.'

His turn came at last. He was led into a small room where three men sat at a table, and the centre one was his eldest brother, in a dark velvet coat with a broad fur collar, his face longer, thinner, and more lined than Henry had known it, the lips more tightly compressed within the drooping moustaches that flowed down into the little pointed beard. The narrow, rather hesitating glance the Protector gave at the sturdy countryman who had just entered flashed into disconcerted surprise; his eyebrows shot up into his forehead, making a network of new furrows; the liverish yellow-whites of the eyeballs swerved like those of a shying horse. Henry felt an instant's most unusual satisfaction, that there was no one he could meet who could make himself look like that.

'He-ey, brother,' he said, on exactly the note he would have said, 'Whoa there, whoa.' 'Well met, brother, at last.'

'But why – why – what have you come for?'

As if to stave off the real answer to this question, the Duke hurriedly followed it with others: 'Is it the Purbeck stone or the conduit? I've told you about 1,600 feet is not an inch too long for it – if I want water brought to my house I must have it, whatever the cost. I said you need not try to recover the French workmen—'

'It's not the Frenchies,' came the answer, slow and sure as doom, '*nor* the conduit, *nor* the marble, that I've come to see you about. Reckoned I'd better come, as I never had word from you.'

'But this is the Court of Requests.'

'Can't a brother make a request?' asked Henry a trifle grimly.

'I'll see you later, you can't stay here now. There are people waiting their turn.'

'I've been waiting *my* turn. Now I've got it.'

And Henry planted himself on a chair as four-square as a billet of wood, quite unaware of the gasps round him at his seating himself before the Lord Protector. But the Protector himself did not seem to notice. His tone became hesitant, almost apologetic.

'The fools never told me it was you. Did you say you were my brother?'

'Why, no. I reckoned it might be easier to see you if I didn't.'

The Protector hastily suggested their talking in private, and led the way into another room, where he offered Henry refreshments after his journey, and Henry had to remind him that that had been over three weeks ago. Pitiful the way living in London dulled the wits.

He thought so the more when Ned remembered to ask after his wife and children but had obvious difficulty with their names. Henry then asked after Ned's good bedfellow and Ned's nine children, one by his first wife and eight by his present, by name, from the eldest to the youngest. He mentioned that his sisters, Elizabeth Cromwell and Dorothy Smith, were in good health, and he then asked after Brother Tom.

Again there came that startled swerve of the yellow eyeballs. 'But – you know about him!' exclaimed Ned incredulously.

'I know he's in the Tower. That's not to say he's well.'

'It's not indeed. You'd best know it at once. There's no chance for him. There are thirty-three charges of treason against him.'

'What did Tom say to the witnesses?'

'The prisoner under Bill of Attainder is not allowed to speak in his own defence.'

'Hey, what's this? Thought you'd abolished the new treason

laws and gone back to the good old laws of the Plantagenets – aye, and better. Haven't you brought it in that there must be two sufficient witnesses against a man, and that they must be confronted with the accused?'

'Yes, yes, but you don't understand. That is for the ordinary prisoner at law. This is a Bill of Attainder.'

'And why deny to your brother the justice you'd give to the ordinary prisoner?'

'Attainder is a perfectly constitutional proceeding. It is part of the course of the law.'

'Then dang and blast the law! I want justice.'

The Protector shifted his ground.

'You asked me what the prisoner has said. The whole Council waited on him in the Tower, with the exception of Archbishop Cranmer and myself, and told him the charges against him, and he refused to say one word in answer to them – except in open trial.'

'Why didn't you go?'

'I? But – naturally – it would have been too painful – for both of us.'

'Not as painful as getting beheaded.'

There was a stunned pause. Then Henry added, 'Why won't you give him a fair chance in open trial?'

'I? I? It is not my doing, I took no part in drawing up the articles against him. Nor at his examination in the Tower – I told you I was not there.'

'And again I say, why not? Tom might ha' spoken to you.'

'I spoke to him before. I gave him full warning again and again. So did others. Old Russell warned him. He wouldn't listen.'

'I'm not asking what was said before the trial—'

'I tell you, it wasn't a trial.'

'And in God's name, brother,' roared Henry, rising slowly to his feet and leaning over the little table behind which Somerset had entrenched himself, '*why not?*'

'The Council decided against it, for the better avoidance of scandal. It is doubtful whether an open trial would have given him any better chance. Anyway, the Government decided against it.'

'The Government – the Council—' Henry repeated slowly. 'What then are *you*? You sit on a high seat above all the rest of the Council. You act at times without consulting them. This Court of Requests is set up by you, and judged by you alone. You try cases without any other judge. You reverse decisions made by other judges. Yet, when it is a case of life and death for your own brother, you make as if to wash your hands of it, like Pontius Pilate. It can mean but one thing – that you want Tom's death. You alone gain from it. No one else gains anything.'

'The whole country gains, if the country is at peace.'

'It will not have peace. Nor will you. Hark'ee, Ned, this is but a feather of your own goose. Kill Tom, and you'll put a rope round your neck. The country calls you the Good Duke. They won't if you kill your brother. No one will stand by a man who doesn't stand by his own kith and kin. They've heard how your guards took him at Mother's house, with her there. They don't like that.'

The Duke looked at him as though he neither saw nor heard him. Henry spoke a little louder, but gently, for his brother's face was white and piteous. 'Taking him at Mother's house, and she standing by. You shouldn't ha' done that, Ned.'

Ned sat quite still, staring before him. What was he seeing? Henry felt anxious. Was Ned, as they say, himself? There was a queer look on him, the look, it might be, of a man whose horse was riding straight for a precipice, and he with no power and perhaps no will to stop it.

When at last he began to speak it was in a different voice, no longer low and measured, disdainfully impersonal. It was sharp and querulous, the voice of a complaining schoolboy who at any minute will burst into tears.

'Mother this and Mother that,' he cried. 'Is Master Tom always to shelter under her petticoats? Precious little mother's darling, *he's* shown how he stands by kith and kin, hasn't he? Working against me all these two years, doing his best to pull me down, and she – *she* never sees it. Oh no, she wouldn't! Tom can make mincemeat of me for all she cares. All she cares about – all – all – is that he shall be safe, her spoilt brat, and that is all she's ever cared about. You know it too. *We* were never anything to her, as soon as she'd got Tom.'

It was utterly bewildering. There was Ned gone clean back to being a child again, sobbing his fury under the old apple tree in Broom Close because he had been blamed for something that he said was all Tom's fault. These clever fellows who came to the top and ruled the Kingdom didn't ever know how to grow up, seemingly.

'Well, but in nature she loved him best.' Henry spoke carefully, as to a child. 'He was the youngest and always gave her a deal more trouble than the rest of us. Feminine kind are like that. And they like Tom. Men do too. It's in nature.'

He wished he could make it plain to Ned. He had always seen it so plain.

All of romance he had ever known had been bound up in that babbling baby creature who had always rushed into danger as soon as he could toddle: into the green duck-pond or the bright fire, straight up to the fierce stallions or mastiffs or the ring-nosed bull, all of which Henry had always known he must not touch, and at once dragged Tom away. But so soon was Tom standing up to Henry himself or to anyone who opposed him, so soon he shot up taller and handsomer and livelier than any of them, so soon he had darted away from home out into the world, and brought Henry back a whiff of the scent and colour of strange countries and foreign wars, had talked with the Sultan and cracked jokes with the King of France, and sent Henry strange treasures fashioned by dark heathens who wore petticoats.

Henry's hunting-cap at home rested on a round hat-stand of blue and white pottery with Arabic inscriptions; on his sideboard was a Persian dish five hundred years old, with a gay little bird on it sprouting into a serpent's tail at one end and at the other a smiling woman's face in jaunty cap and collar as modern as a lass of today. Tom had told Henry with a dig in the ribs that he sent him his rarest finds for the pleasure he had in hearing him say 'Ar, mighty feat and pretty.'

If he lived as long as Methuselah he'd never cram as much into his years as Tom had done in even one of his dazzling kingfisher flights across the Continent.

Henry had always been rather awed by his elder brother, had adored his younger, and taken it for granted that he himself was the stupid one who did not count – but not so stupid that he couldn't see that the women would love Tom best. Odd that the clever ones should be so stupid.

But nothing of this could he say to Ned, for the poor fellow was fair beside himself, mouthing his face all awry as he talked, and it white to the lips, rolling his eyes round the room and grabbing at one unhelpful thing after another on the table, just as he had done in those queer unchancy rages he had had as a boy.

But now he was not a boy, and Henry felt deep in his bones that he was witnessing that terrifying thing, the rage of a weak man in mortal fear.

It was a case of Tom's life or his, Ned said; there could not be two Protectors, nor even two brothers in power; for himself he cared nothing – but Tom would ruin his great work for England. He worked for the future and for others – but Tom only for the present moment and himself. Tom would always undermine his authority; the country was not big enough for them both, and that was the plain fact of it – and why should he show any consideration for Tom, who had never in all his life shown any for him?

Henry waited till the storm spent itself out and a shaken yellow-faced old man had shrunk back, cold and exhausted, into his huddled furs.

Then he said, "'Tisn't right, Ned, that's all that matters. Take it that Tom's not done right by you – well, you can't help that. But you can help this. Bible says you should forgive your brother, not seven times only, but seventy times seven.'

The Protector passed a feverish hand over his brow. It came away damp. Mechanically he murmured, as he had often found it well to do, 'That may be a mistake in the translation.'

'It's God's holy word, isn't it?' persisted Henry.

'Oh yes, yes, and a dozen fellows at work on it. Miles Coverdale isn't the only Hebrew and Greek scholar in England. Miles acknowledges himself that he's used five other translations in it.' He began to wonder wearily if he had been wise to push forward this business of the English Bible – you couldn't tell where it might lead to, when every ploughman, however simple and ignorant, started quoting it to suit his purposes, profaning the Sacred Word in every ale-house and tavern, just as the old King had complained, and rightly, Ned now thought.

He *would* not doubt it; he would not lose faith and hope in himself, nor yet in the humblest of his brethren – but how could he believe in himself or anything else while this clod stood and gaped at him and preached to him, yes, to *him*, of his duty to his brother?

'Go back,' he shouted suddenly, 'back to your stables and your pigsties! What can such as you understand of me, and of the work I have been called upon to do?'

As if in answer to that hoarse strained shout, a servant entered hurriedly, looking rather aghast. But it was to announce an unexpected visit of King Edward, and with him John Dudley, Earl of Warwick.

They came in, leaving their gentlemen-in-waiting outside, and with only Barnaby Fitzpatrick still in attendance at the royal elbow. The Protector rose in haste, and bowed very low, so Henry did too, though – dear Lord! – it seemed a queer way to go on to a small boy who was your nephew when all's said and done, and in a private room and no affair of State.

He took a good look at the lad, who was complaining about something in a high fretful pipe; he wasn't shaping as well as Henry had hoped, not much taller nor sturdier than at his Coronation two years ago, and he'd been small even for a nine-year-old then. Peaky too. Kept too hard at his books by the look of him. Young plants never grew well indoors. He'd like to turn him out to grass for a year or two to kick up his heels and run wild, and loosen that set small mouth that shut like a trap as he finished speaking.

By which time Henry had heard what his nephew had been saying.

'It's intolerable. Why don't you stop it? The people shout at me in the streets, they yell "Justice for the Admiral!" A woman called out that I was an unnatural nephew, and she wished she had the jerking of me – *me*! And look at that!' He stuck out his foot and the Protector backed as though suspecting a kick. 'Mud! Mud on my stocking. Someone threw that – at *me*!'

'One cannot prevent people calling out in the street, Your Grace.'

'Why not? My father would have. Is this your freedom of speech for all? There's been too much of it.'

John Dudley's cool voice slid between the child's angry treble and the exasperated answer that his uncle was just beginning. 'Indeed, my lord, His Majesty has grave cause for his annoyance if the people are encouraged to think they can insult the Crown with impunity.'

The Protector's hands began to twitch with nervous rage – (How well Henry knew that clenching of the fists, blue-white at the knuckles. If you touched them they would be as cold as frogs.) 'What does Your Lordship suggest I should do?' he rasped. 'Order out the guard to fire on them because some street urchin, who's probably no longer there, threw a clod of mud some time before? Will that impress them with the royal justice?'

He turned sharply on his nephew, 'I have yet to learn how it is Your Majesty is out riding with the Earl of Warwick when you should be at your Hebrew with Mr Cheke?'

Edward drew back from him. 'There's the match of Rovers and Prisoners' Base in ten days' time. How am I to have a chance of winning if I never practise?'

He looked appealingly at Dudley, who smilingly said: 'Mea culpa! Let me be His Majesty's whipping-boy instead of young Barney this time. The day was fine, the royal head ached, and it is certain the King needs practice to give him a fair chance in the match I've arranged. He draws no strong bow as yet, though a very pretty shot.'

Edward flushed with pleasure, then turned to his uncle with his upper lip sucked in and his under stuck out. For two pins, it seemed to say, his tongue would follow it.

It began to dawn on Henry that if the King had been turned against his youngest uncle by his eldest, he did not like his eldest any the better for it.

The Protector burst out, 'Am I the King's guardian or am I not? How can I have any authority if the moment my back is turned every Tom, Dick, and Harry works against it?'

'My name is not Tom,' said Dudley softly. 'I trust you will not confuse the matter. It is not I who am in the Tower on charges of undermining your authority.'

'With as little reason, maybe,' came an unexpected voice.

Something had boiled up in Henry's head, and boiled over. They turned and stared at him, those fine gentlemen, as mum and mim as a couple of calves. As for the little lad, he looked at him as though a piece of the furniture had given tongue.

'Who is this – gentleman?' Edward asked with a slight emphasis on the last word.

As Ned didn't seem able to collect his wits or his words, Henry answered: 'Your Uncle Henry, Your Grace, up from Wolf Hall.'

'Another uncle!' The boy turned away.

But Henry wasn't going to let go of his chance. 'You've a finer uncle than me in the Tower. Have justice done to your own flesh and blood. Give him a fair and open trial. You are the King. Show it.'

The King and the Protector spoke at once. But Henry only heard the boy's voice shrilling hysterically above the man's expostulations.

'Uncles – uncles everywhere – always quarrelling – bullying me – keeping me from my bow, wanting to make me a butterfingers. And Uncle Tom's a bad man, he's dishonoured my sister, he poisoned my stepmother so as to marry her, he—'

'Christ have pity!' shouted Henry, silencing both boy and man. 'Are these the lies they've been telling you? Even a child should see their falseness. The Queen's own brothers are almost the only loyal friends to stand by Tom now. Would they do so if he'd poisoned their sister? Let Tom confront his accusers. Give him the chance you'd give to any common thief or murderer.'

The Protector had got his hand on his shoulder and was trying to shove him out of the room, while the Earl of

Warwick stared with an expression of detached interest.

Henry knocked off the hand as though it were a fly. 'Hark'ee, brother, you shall hear me, aye and the lad too, before you're rid of me. "Whoso causeth one of these little ones to stumble, it were better for him that a millstone were tied about his neck and he were cast into the uttermost depths of the sea."'

Then he went. The Earl of Warwick's eyebrows rose slightly as he looked at his colleague.

'Is that another mistake in the translation?' he asked.

Edward, alone with Barney at last, was fuming at him. Barney had shown him respectfully that he hadn't liked Edward's manners to his Uncle Henry. Edward said that he was sick to death of all his uncles, a lot of nobodies who wouldn't be anybody but for *him*, but just lumps of Wiltshire mud and he wished to heaven they'd stayed there – 'that oaf, that clod, to thrust his way into my presence and speak to me like that – *he* my uncle! They're all alike – knaves, bullies, upstarts. *These Seymours!*'

Barney felt it better not to stress the King's own half of Seymour blood. He said, 'In my country the lords of the land treat humbler people, even peasants and servants, with as much courtesy and friendliness as those of their own kind.'

'Yes, dine at the same table, feed out of the same dish, don't they? We English had to pass a law against it. In your country they live like savages.'

The King swung out of the room and slammed the door. Barney stood looking after him.

'*These Tudors!*' he said.

CHAPTER TWENTY-THREE

Lady Tyrwhitt had been appointed by the Council as the Princess Elizabeth's new governess: an awkward position for the lady, for the Princess herself flatly refused to recognise her as such. Haughtily she declared that Mrs Ashley was her governess; she had not so demeaned herself that she needed any other set over her. In fact, she would rather have none at all. Sir Robert Tyrwhitt's opinion was that she needed two! But he had to admit to his master that 'she cannot digest such advice in no way'.

His wife told him that the girl sulked all day and wept all night. It was all the result they could boast, though she had now been under their constant supervision for more than a month. The confessions of her servants had led to none of any value by herself. She wrote a deposition that echoed theirs, and went no further – except for her bright assurance at the end that this was all she could remember at the moment of her dealings with the Admiral, but if anything came into her head that she had forgotten, she would promptly add it! It sounded far too good to be true. So did the close resemblance between her account and that of her servants. 'They all sing the same song,' wrote Sir Robert glumly, 'which they would not do unless they had set the note before.'

But he grew more hopeful as he reported, 'She begins now

to droop a little'; this when he had let her know that things were going badly for the Admiral, his horses already given away, his property plundered, his servants discharged.

But she did not droop if anyone spoke against him; she flared out then in his defence as passionately imperious as a reigning Princess. Could nothing teach her that she was a helpless prisoner, in danger even of her life?

The Protector wrote to impress her with the fact, and demanded an answer; Tyrwhitt wrote a rough draft for her to copy and send as her own, admitting her faults and submitting herself to his merciful forgiveness.

She scarcely looked at it. She would write to the Protector, certainly, but she needed nobody's suggestions as to what to say.

She sat down, pen in hand, a tight determined smile on her face, the smile of a fighter. And not in mere defence. She would carry the war straight into the enemy's camp.

'Master Tyrwhitt and others have told me that there are rumours abroad that I am with child by my Lord Admiral. My Lord, these are shameful slanders. I shall most heartily desire Your Lordship that I may come to the Court, that I may show myself there as I am.

Written in haste, from Hatfield,

Your assured friend to my little power,

ELIZABETH.'

The Protector blinked as he read the upright beautifully shaped hand. Never surely did a fifteen-year-old Princess dispose of so base a charge in so brief and businesslike a manner. Nothing here of the proper outraged modesty and ignorance of a very young lady – but a sound medical knowledge, and the courage to stand upon it. They said she was with child. Let them prove it then; she was perfectly ready to come to Court to be medically examined and to outface all the prying whispering gossip of the women who would know why she had come.

The Good Duke was scandalised. Why, at her age his sister Jane would not even have known such things. And the bold accusation (for it plainly accused him too), 'My Lord, these are shameful slanders', was like a blow straight between his eyes. Almost he could hear it thundered out in King Harry's voice with one of his tremendous oaths.

There was finesse in the letter too; she thanked him at the beginning for his 'great gentleness and goodwill' to her, and told him that she was only writing to him because he had told her to. (So whatever he got from her, he had asked for it!)

She even insinuated a subtle defence of the Admiral by quoting an almost too innocent question of his, 'Why he might not visit me as well as my sister?'; and of Mrs Ashley, by declaring that her governess had always said 'she would never have me marry without the consent of the King's Majesty, Your Grace's, and the Council's'.

And the only pathetic note in this letter from an utterly friendless child in a desperate position, was that she had altered the conventional closing, 'Your assured friend to my power', with the addition 'to my little power'.

It did not impress the Duke, who wrote in sharp retort that she was too well assured of herself; as to these shameful slanders, let her but name the author of them, and the Council would take up the matter.

Again he got more than he bargained for. She was very sorry he took her letter 'in evil part', but coolly observed that 'I do not see that Your Grace has made any direct answer'. As to naming the scandal-mongers, 'I can easily do it, but I would be loth to do, because it is mine own cause', and she had no wish to punish anyone in that cause, 'and so get the ill will of the people'.

But she told him with uncompromising directness what *he* ought to do, and that was 'to send forth a Proclamation declaring how the tales be but lies'.

The Duchess, reading it over the Duke's shoulder, gave a squeal of exasperation. 'Telling *you* what Proclamations to issue! Who the devil does she think she is?'

The letter told them. She was 'The King's Majesty's sister'. It would be well for the Protector and the Council to show the people that they remembered this, and that they had some regard for her honour.

The Duchess screamed. This bastard, this wanton, was giving herself all the airs of a future Queen. All her talk of the people (it was a marvel she did not write '*my* people'!) and their will towards her, good or ill, showed her sinister intentions. She was determined to play for popularity, to work up a following in the country, as her seducer had tried to do. There would not be a moment's peace in England till she met the same fate as he.

And why, she demanded, was that fate so long in coming to him?

It was over a month now since the Admiral had been sent to the Tower, and every week, day, hour while the Duke delayed, hesitated, prevaricated, hummed and hawed and made tedious speeches, was giving his equally traitorous brother Henry time to work up more and more opposition to the execution.

She swept out of the room. A servant entering just after was surprised to get an inkpot thrown at his head, and hurriedly departed, to tell his fellows that the Protector was not the same man since he had started hounding his brother to the scaffold. He was growing quite irritable.

The Protector raged round the room, hurling books on to the floor, flinging papers into the fire. The airy, erect handwriting of the Princess looked up at him as he was about to destroy that too. It was very like her; the fantastic looped lines of the signature that twirled into a little arabesque at the end were those of an artist longing to draw rather than write; even the two large sploshy blots on the other side of it, which she had ignored rather than write her letter again, were characteristic. But the words were quite unlike the hard frivolous young thing he believed her to be.

'They are most deceived that trust most in themselves.'

That had been in answer to his reproof of her overconfidence; but seeing the sentence apart from the rest, it sounded a warning to himself. Had he, after all, trusted so earnestly in his fine resolves, his noble desires for humanity, only to be deceived by a traitor within his own breast?

He looked again. He saw, 'I know I have a soul to be saved as well as other folk have.' Its simplicity seemed utterly forlorn; yet there was a true pride in it that no humiliation could crush.

Was this girl indeed a contemptible wanton? Her dealings with him and his servants were showing sparks of unexpected greatness. He laid down the letters, still looking searchingly at the writing as at a portrait then inward at himself.

He too had a soul. What had become of it? Always he had regarded himself as morally superior to the run of men. He never swore, nor drank too much; nor felt any temptation to lechery; his greed for money and property was too cold a lust for him to recognise it as that. How should it be a personal lust when he was building his possessions for the future, laying up treasure, honourable position and power for his sons' sons rather than himself?

That sophistry had crumbled. It would not even be his true heir who would inherit his titles, his eagerly grasped lands and gold – a little mud and metal, that was what it had turned to now in his eyes. Yet he had been no greedier nor more ambitious than many others; and no vices stained his private character.

But for all that, he knew now that for many years his soul had been in hell.

He hoped that death would release it.

Bess got her Proclamation. The Protector issued one as she had requested, stating that the scandals against her were lies, and forbidding the people to repeat them, on pain of severe punishment.

Whereupon she promptly made another request: that the Protector and the Council should be good to her governess in the Tower, 'because she has been with me a long time, and has taken great labour and pains in bringing me up in learning and honesty'.

There were many tales of poor Ashley's pains in bringing Bess up; the Protector almost suspected that baffling smile of the Princess behind the words. Yet it was a touchingly loyal appeal. It made no reference to any other subject, though she wrote it only three days after the Bill of Attainder against the Admiral had passed its third reading in the House of Lords. She could make no appeal for him; it would only harm him, since his courtship of her was one of the chief charges against him.

She could only plead for her old Ash-Cat, a poor substitute, and in her agony of anxiety she did not think at first that she could drive herself to do it. But Cat was her old friend and she must do the best she could for her. She did.

The letter was full of a faithful and passionate tenderness – perhaps not all for Ashley. But Ashley was the only person for whom she could admit it.

She walked, these first cold days of March, under the great oaks of Hatfield Park, where she had been so glad to run out and listen to the nightingale on the early summer evenings when she had first come here with Mr Ascham – and Queen Catherine was still alive. There was the old tree scarred with her arrows where she had shot at a mark and her tutor had told her she drew as pretty a bow as the goddess Diana.

Was she indeed walking in the very same place, under the self-same trees? Was she here at all, and was she the same self? Or was there nothing round her, the world nothing, and she herself nobody?

'Thus in no place, this nobody, in no time I met
Where no man, nor naught was, nor nothing did appear.'

The world seemed to have dropped into a vast silence, and yet there were birds shrilly piping their first songs, dogs barking, and the chatter and rustle of female voices and movement all round her.

Lady Tyrwhitt and her women walked with her, talking, talking, watching her, trying to make her talk too. Of what was Her Grace thinking? Why did her lips move and yet say nothing?

'Because I can say nothing,' she said.

And still she said, only to herself:

'He said he was little John Nobody that durst not once speak.'

CHAPTER TWENTY-FOUR

In those first days after his arrest, Tom walked up and down his room in the Tower and talked, while his friend and servant Sir John Harington sat by the fire and stared at it in silence. He listened sympathetically to every word his lord was saying, while the back of his mind, which was irrepressibly given to statistics, computed the number of miles Tom must have already walked that day. He would verify the measurement of the room presently, but he must be doing a good average of twenty-five miles a day. At this rate he could have walked to the South Coast by now and got on one of Jack Thompson's ships for France; in a fortnight he could walk across the Border to Scotland and freedom.

But at every few steps the Tower walls turned his footsteps sharp round and back again. Would he ever walk straight on, out into the air, except to his grave?

The subject of these gloomy fancies was far from indulging in them.

Tom was blazingly angry, but he still had no notion that there was anything to be really afraid of – except of the shock that his sudden arrest must have given his mother. He'd never forgive Ned for that – he'd let him know it too, the damned clumsy heavy-footed brute, so full of his own importance that he'd got blunted to everything and everyone else – 'he can only think in terms of Council speeches, he's forgotten that the People are made up of persons. No wonder his wife is sick of the sight and in especial the sound of him – much good it does her to have a fellow like that in bed with her – if it weren't for the loathing I've got for the bad-tempered bitch I'd cuckold Ned myself to show her what a Seymour can do.'

Three turns in silence, only two steps off four, then out he broke again, 'This is to give me a jerk, that's all. They've not a thing they can really hold against me. I'll be out in no time, and by God if he thinks I'll keep the peace the better for this brotherly hint, he'll soon find his mistake! I'll make him sorry he ever did such a damn fool thing as to clap me into the Tower. *Who* can be behind it? That's what worries me. Ned would never have done this of himself.'

Another turn, then a sharp swing-round on his heel and a thump on Harington's shoulder that nearly spun him into the fire. 'By God, Jack, I've got it! I always knew it really, but I was too hot with Ned to think of anyone else. I'll swear this is Dudley's doing. I've always distrusted that fellow. Didn't I say he's a dark horse, hasn't shown his form yet, but I'll bet a thousand pounds he's keeping something back that will show when it comes to a race for power. And that blind jackass Ned doesn't see it, for all his conceit about his brains – but you know the Spaniard Chapuys always said Ned was "not very intelligent and rather haughty"!' He interrupted himself with a roar of delighted mirth. 'Sure enough, our Ned isn't intelligent enough to see that this dainty fop the Earl of Warwick is making trouble between us for his own ends – the old tag, "divide et impera", and so come in for the pickings. Isn't it clear as mud?'

'Clearer,' said Harington, 'if it's clear that Dudley is in this thing. There's nothing to show it yet.'

'But someone must be, and if not he, who is it? Who else would gain?'

Harington hesitated. Then he said, 'Your brother would gain, or thinks so, or he wouldn't have done it.'

Tom stared at him, really shocked. 'You bloody-minded old cynic, you don't really think Ned did this of himself!'

'I don't know. What is the use of thinking, till one knows?'

'There's the mathematician! But we'll soon know, for it's bound to come out at the trial. That's the best of a trial, everything comes out at it – you can see who's against you, answer their accusations and show how piffling they are. And by God, I'll show 'em a few things on the other side! I'll bring it all out in the open about Ned stealing my wife's wedding ring! And Fasterne – her own family lands. What's he got against me compared with *that*? He'll wish he'd never given me the chance to speak in public. And mark you, I'm going to get that chance. I'm not going to be let out with a warning after a few weeks in the Tower and told to take my medicine like a good boy and go quietly and not make a fuss. I shall insist on a trial. I'll make it so hot for them all, they'll wish to God they'd never touched me.'

And for several more miles he went over and over all the things that he would bring up against Ned at the trial.

He had walked nearly as far as the Welsh Border before he heard that there was not going to be any open trial; but not because he was to be set free without one. It was because they were bringing a Bill of Attainder against him.

He stopped walking. He stopped talking. He stood dead

still and stared before him. It was Harington who could no longer bear the silence, though a man discreetly trained to it. He had married a bastard daughter of King Henry's, oddly named Ethelred, and with masterly lack of snobbery in a snobbish age never let it be supposed that she was anything but the bastard of Henry's tailor. And in these last weeks the Council had tried their utmost by bribes and threats to get out of him any incriminating evidence on the Admiral's relations with the Princess Elizabeth – but all in vain.

Short and sturdy, he glanced uneasily up at that magnificent figure of his patron, like an unhappy dog, and at last murmured, 'I'm afraid this looks bad.'

But Tom did not hear him.

A Bill of Attainder was the surest and deadliest weapon they could bring against him. Thomas Cromwell had used it again and again to rid King Henry of anyone he wished out of the way without the inconvenience of an open trial – until the King turned it on Cromwell himself. And now the Protector had turned it on his brother.

'So – Ned – *is* in it!' He spoke as though he had seen a ghost.

Harington looked at his watch. It was twenty-five minutes since the Admiral had last spoken. And still he had not moved.

Ten minutes later he said, 'Then there'll be no trial. I'll not get a hearing.'

Five minutes, and he said, 'Ned *must* be in it.'

Two minutes, and he moved in a mad rush across the room, sweeping everything off the table with a stroke of his arm, kicking over a heavy chair, and gripped Harington by the shoulders till the fingers seemed to meet through his flesh.

'He *can't* do this thing. He's my own brother, he's stood by me again and again – in a damned superior priggish way if you like, but – he *can't* mean to kill me.'

'Let *go*!' said Harington.

Tom dropped him. 'It would kill Mother. He must know that. If he doesn't mind killing me, he'd mind *that*, wouldn't he? Answer me!' he roared.

'He won't let himself think he's killed her,' Harington replied, feeling his shoulder tenderly.

'By God, I believe you're right. He has my head under his belt.'

But still he could not believe that Ned would keep it there – still less, put it on a spike. From his nursery days he had been brought up to think of his eldest brother as good. Why, even the common people were now all calling him the Good Duke.

There must be some compensation for being good, and now he would find out what it was: a good man did not cut off his brother's head. Ned would still stand by him, somehow or other. Ned would find a way to get him out.

But then the Governor of the Tower, who was very friendly, especially after sharing a bottle or two of Tom's wine, brought him news of the proceedings in Parliament. There were many who objected to a Bill of Attainder being brought instead of an open trial; there were speeches against it in both Houses, especially in the Commons.

But the Lord Protector, 'declaring how sorrowful a case this was for him, did yet regard his bounden duty more than his own son or brother'.

'"His own son" – the Roman father, hey? He's getting on his toga for the rôle. By Christ's soul, he means to do it! Once Ned starts talking about duty, anything may happen. He'll talk himself into being good enough to kill his brother, yes, and his own mother. And never see that he's an unnatural monster – only a man who does his duty – the damned inhuman conceited swab of dirty cotton mopping up the mess that his own injustice has got him into, mopping it with his own flesh and blood. "His bounden duty" – "Foy pour devoir" – that our father used to preach to us, the fine old man, shouting the family motto out like a battle-cry – and Ned the good boy of the family lapping it up like a cat with cream – to see what use he could put it to. If he were living now, he'd have strangled Ned in his cradle to prevent it coming to this – to kill me and "my Margery" as he always called her, and used to say the verse that was written to her, and watch her blush –

> "With margerain gentle,
> The flower of goodlihead."

"To Mistress Margery Wentworth" – yes, old John Skelton wrote that to her when they were both young.

> "Benign, courteous and meek,
> With wordes well devised"—

She's using them now, no doubt – on her Ned. And small good they'll do her – or me. For she's using them on a stone, a clod of earth long since fossilised, a man who's never known what it is to be one, who's wrapped himself round with a cloud of "wordes well devised" so that he sees and hears nothing but what he says himself. So that he can call it his bounden duty to kill me! My God, I'll kill *him*! Just let me get my hands on his scrawny throat when I get out!'

He forgot that he would not get out.

The Council came, to remind him.

His eyes like a hungry wolf's sought Ned among them. But he was not there.

They read him the thirty-three charges against him. He demanded to hear them from the witnesses themselves, in open trial. He was told he could have no open trial, he could call no witnesses in his defence. He could answer to the charges against him now, by himself, or not at all.

'Then not at all,' he said. What was the use if he could not answer the men who made them? They had risen up against him as fast as daws rising up from corn at the shot of a gun – 'Caw, caw, caw,' they cried, flapping forward, croaking their accusations, clawing and pecking at his eyes – and nearly all were those he had thought his friends, fellows he had dined and drunk with and talked to freely, who had nodded in agreement and then chimed in with lists of their own grievances. But now they had all come forward to quote his words as heinous treason, and not a hint of the eagerness they had shown to join in the intrigues they now exposed.

Even Henry Grey whose debts he had paid, whose daughter was under his roof, even Grey had pulled his long melancholy moustaches and turned informer against him.

And Tom could not answer back, to him or any of them. But talking over the charges afterwards with Harington he was cheered again.

'There's not enough to hang a cat among the lot of them. Their worst charge is slackness in dealing with pirates. But they've not attempted to prove it, and if they did, the punishment can only be dismissal from my post as Admiral, with a large fine. There's not a thing that amounts to treason. It's not treason to want to marry the Princess Elizabeth, and they've made that the principal charge. But they've got no change out of it – not one word to help them from the girl herself, bless her stout little heart!'

Bess would prove a match for Ned any day; she had done so since she was four years old. Hilariously he reminded Jack Harington how she had to bear the christening robe for the baby Prince Edward when she herself had been too small to walk all the way in the Procession, and so Ned had been given the doubtful honour of carrying her – to his intense discomfiture, for she had grabbed off his cap and plucked at his beard and all but wriggled herself out of his arms, and everybody had laughed at him – him, Ned – who could not bear to be laughed at!

'And still she's as slippery as an eel. "Wild for to hold" – she'll always be that.'

His pride was sharpened with regret, for he himself had not yet held her, only begun to do so, only enough to know how exquisite would be the triumph when he did.

He swerved sharply to other charges against him – plentiful as blackberries, but as waterlogged as those picked in November.

'Was there ever such blether as to call it treason because I married Cathy so soon after the King's death that *if* she'd had a child at once, it *might* have been thought to be the King's.

Confuse the issue, hey?' he suddenly shot at Harington, who gaped in amazement that he could still joke. 'Well, if that's treason, why did no one say it then, instead of waiting two years? Because no man thought such piffle – nor does now. It's the cloven hoof of the Duchess kicking that bit of mud out from her petticoats!'

'There's more mud from the pulpits,' murmured Harington.

For the preachers were carrying on a furious campaign to work up public opinion against the Admiral. The Bishop of Worcester, Dr Latimer, thundered out sermon after sermon to prove his wickedness. But his proofs could not be said to justify the death penalty.

Imprimis. A woman executed for robbery nine years ago had said her bad life was due to having been seduced by the Admiral about ten years before that.

Item: The Admiral had not attended family prayers regularly twice daily when at home with his wife, but was apt to 'get himself out of the way like a mole digging in the earth.'

Item: He had said this brand new Prayer Book was not really God's holy word, but old man Cranmer's.

Item: He had tried to get his King away from his lessons and out to sports in the open air – 'Now woe,' cried the Bishop, 'to him, or anyone else, that would have my Sovereign not brought up in learning, and would pluck him from his book!'

This list of his crimes brought the heartiest roar of laughter Harington had heard from his master since he entered the Tower. 'What's the use of turning the pulpit into a dung-heap if that's the worst they can rake up against me? They nose out muck near a score of years old, and all they can find is a drab's word for it. And it's treason to care for the King's health and pleasure! Just wait and hear what the boy himself will say to that!'

He still held his trump card – the King himself. They could set justice and even the law at naught, but they could not carry out the death-warrant without the King's own signature. It did his heart good to describe the miniature roar from the lion cub when told to sign away the life of his favourite uncle – he could be as royal in his rage as his father, a chip off the old block as he had called him, and as he would prove. The living spit of his mother too – loyal little Janey, who had stood by her friends, stood up for them even against Old Harry himself.

And he reminded Harington of those days a dozen years ago when King Hal was visiting Wolf Hall to woo their Janey and complain of Nan Bullen – 'I was seduced into this marriage' – and little Jane, while so sorry for him and certain that he could never have loved That Woman, was still devoted to the memory of his first wife, Katherine of Aragon, whom she had served, and her daughter the Princess Mary, Jane's best friend at Court, and insisted that he should reinstate her.

'You are a fool,' King Hal had growled. 'You ought to plead for the advancement of the children *we* will have, not any others.'

But 'Foy pour devoir' was really Jane Seymour's motto; she even risked her neck for it (and so he threatened her) when she implored him to restore the Abbeys and told him the rebellions against him were a judgment on him for seizing them.

'A woman who could do that,' Tom said proudly, 'would stand up for a blind puppy against a tiger.'

And he remembered her nice kind little ways to the people at home – making endless babyclothes for the wife of John Wynbolt the undergrubber ('her fifteenth, isn't it, Janey,' he would tease her, 'or have I lost count?'); compounding lozenges of 'Manus Christi' in the stillroom, of white sugar and rosewater and powder of pearls, as a sovereign remedy for the old shepherd John Gorway's quotidian fever, the daily ague, and explaining with flushed earnestness that she was not really being extravagant as they were only the seed pearls off her old blue bodice. Kind, prim, serious, tactless little Janey; nobody thought she had much beauty, and that cynical Spaniard Chapuys marvelled that an Englishwoman should have been so long at Court and still a maid (she was twenty-five when she married the King). But she was true as steel; she was the only one of his wives to do her duty to the King, she gave him a son and died of it – and he forgot her in a week, 'as merry as a widower may be,' one of his Councillors said slyly. And as if to mock her demure memory, all the College of Heralds disgraced themselves getting dead drunk after her funeral – Clarencieux falling downstairs on top of the Garter King-at-Arms, Chester trying to ravish a maid of the house and all but strangling her, and Rouge Dragon, with his three wives all living, the worst of the lot.

So Tom poured out his memories of his sister to John Harington as he walked up and back again, up and back again, and Harington said a word here and there to keep him thinking of her – and not of her son King Edward.

But back and back again Tom came to Edward.

'Of course her boy will stand by me – just as I've always stood by him, given him pocket money, helped him cut a dash with his fellows, taken his side against his domineering old bully of a guardian. Hasn't he said a hundred times – shown it anyway – that he wanted me for his guardian and not Ned? He'd never let me down.'

Less than a mile away the Lords of the Council listened to a clear monotonous voice, as dispassionate as if it were saying a lesson, telling to his uncle's enemies his uncle's hopes to make it the 'blackest Parliament ever,' with the King's complaints.

'The Lord Admiral came to me and desired me to write a thing for him. I desired him to let me alone. Cheke said afterwards to me, "You did best not to write."…

'The Lord Admiral said of the Lord Protector, "Your uncle is old and I trust will not live long."

'I answered, "It were better that he should die."…

'Then he said he would give Fowler money for me, and so he did. And he gave Cheke money, as I bade him; and also to a book-binder; and to others at that time, I remember not to whom…

'The Lord Admiral said I was too bashful in my own matters and asked me why I did not bear rule, as other Kings do; I said I needed not, for I was well enough.'

They then produced his servants' account-books of 'such sums of money as I Fowler have disbursed by the King's Majesty's Commandment.'

* * *

First. Delivered to His Highness to give to Mr Cheke, at sundry
times.   £xx

Item, to Mr Barnaby by the King's commandment at sundry
times.   xxs

Item, at Greenwich, to certain tumblers that played, His Grace
looked out upon them.   xls

Item, to my Lord Privy Seal's trumpet at Hampton Court when
his Highness skirmished in the garden at sundry times.   xls

That account-book had been Tom's answer to his own jocular
comments, 'You are a very beggarly King; you have no money
to play with nor give to your servants.' He had given him the
money to play with, to give to his friend Barney, to his tutor,
to the tumblers that the child had watched, delighted at their
skill and daring, to the trumpeters of old Father Russell of the
snowy beard at Hampton Court when Edward had
skirmished in the gardens, playing at soldiers with his
favourite uncle, the Lord High Admiral.

But now the source of all these childish games, this royal
boyish generosity, was revealed – in the guise of treason. He
who had helped the King to it was a traitor. Why then was the
King not a traitor also, who had said of the Lord Protector of
his realm, 'It were better that he should die'?

But Kings were not traitors – not yet.

'If this goes on,' said Tom when he heard of it, 'in another
hundred years they will find the King himself guilty of high
treason and cut off his head.'

'A hundred years?' said Harington statistically. 'That
would be in 1649.'

'God damn your dates, you old mathematician!' Tom had

stopped walking, he had actually sat down, to take it in.

So, then, the boy was handing him over to his enemies as coolly as Henry Grey, as Ned himself. Tom had bribed him, as he had bribed the bankrupt Grey, in vain. Owing to him, they were both now 'well enough.' And so they could now do without him.

His nephew would not lift a finger to save him.

His head sank into his hands. At last he had broken down.

'The rat, the rat!' he sobbed. 'The little white rat – with Janey's face. And I loved the boy. I was sorry for him.'

His own fate was as yet nothing to him. It was his betrayal by Jane's own son, a boy of eleven and a half, that had crushed him.

But sitting there with his fingers pressed against his eyeballs so that red suns came whirling up out of the blackness, he began to know that the impossible nightmare was coming true. The walls of his prison were closing in on him, as they did in that torture-chamber of the Inquisition, taking forty days to crush their victim out of life.

It had taken about as long with him. One hope after another had died, and now he knew. His brother intended his death. And his nephew consented to it.

He leapt up, his arms flung high about his head, his fists clenched, his laughter hurling about the little room.

'A chip off the old block, I said, and so he's proved it. He's handed me over to my enemies as Hal handed Crum, whom he called the best of his servants. I loved the boy and he knows it, yet he's handed me over to Ned whom he hates – hates – and will bring to death, as he has brought me. He said it were better Ned should die – he'll do it too – God, let him do it, let him kill Ned as he's killing me. Let Ned kill him too! The rats will devour their own flesh and blood down to the ends of their tails. God, if I could kill them myself! – but I'll do it, alive or dead. I'll drag Ned down, down. He'll curse the day he killed me – he'll long for death – and he'll get it, the same way as he's killed me.'

He would go down fighting and drag his brother with him. England would never stand being ruled by a man who had killed his own brother. King Hal killing his wives was another matter. But to kill one's own mother's son, that was against nature. He himself would raise revolution against Ned.

He sent Harington away, and his voice was surprisingly calm. Then he sat down on the stone bench by the fire and pulled off his shoes. There was paper secreted in them; he drew it out, and pulled a quill from their aigrette ornament. He had ink as cunningly and secretly prepared. He wrote two letters, one to the Princess Mary, the other to the Princess Elizabeth. He told them that his brother the Protector was murdering him in killing him without a fair trial; he told them what the Protector would do to them if they suffered him to live and work his own ends against them. Let them rise up against him while yet there was time, and make the throne safe for their brother, perhaps for themselves. Let them raise the country against this usurper.

He wrote faster and faster, and then in the midst of the second letter, to the Princess Elizabeth, he stopped. He saw her in his mind as clear as if she were there before him, saw her sitting up in bed with that startled, suddenly awakened air that made her look like a wild deer standing at gaze for an instant before it fled into the forest. So he had seen her a dozen times when he had woken her for a romp on those bright mornings in Chelsea Place when she had been a rosy sleep-tumbled child – not quite a child. But never had she looked at him so, in this strained agony and terror, as though awakening from a ghastly dream of him, to find it true.

She must know by now that it was all up with him. Soon there would be no more to know but that he was dead. She was very young, very impressionable, as wild a coquette as her mother. She would forget him for others – but oh, not yet, not yet!

He finished the letter, but no longer saw the words he wrote, for still he was dazzled with his vision of the slight figure sitting up in bed, the red hair rippling over the bare shoulders, the small white face aghast, with staring eyes, staring at him, and open mouth that shrieked, calling his name.

He sent for his valet, gave him the letters, told him to hide them in his shoes and immediately after his execution to give them in secret to the Princesses.

But all the time that he was pushing forward his last desperate project the refrain was echoing in his head, 'Forget not yet.'

Tom Wyatt had written that song; a gay reckless lover like himself, he had written it to that black-eyed witch, Bess's mother, and been imprisoned in the Tower along with the five other men who were executed for her, but Tom Wyatt had been let off.

'Have you such a thing as an apple about you, my sweet Tom? Lord, I have such an incredible fierce desire to eat an apple! Do you know what King Henry says? He says it means I am with child!'

And the child was Bess, the love-apple for whom he himself had had such incredible fierce desire.

There was no more to do. He sent away his valet. He refused to have a jolly supper with the Governor to drown the fact that it was his last night on earth; he would not even spend it with his old friend Jack Harington.

It did not matter now that death was waiting for him on the morrow. Death had always been there waiting for him, ever since he had been born, as it waited for every man: to strike him down, in battle or on the block, of the plague or moribund old age, at the height of the Christmas feast as it had struck down King Hal, looking out with glazed eyes at his vanishing greatness.

And through all the dancing whirligig of his own life, his feasting and fighting and jollity and popularity with women and kings; through all of it that grisly skeleton had been coming nearer. Now, after the mocking, torturing delay of weeks, days, hours, he could feel on his cheek the cold breath of his pursuer in this relentless game of Blind Man's Buff.

Music was going from him, his lute, his magnificent voice. In so few hours it would be dumb for ever; dust would choke his mouth and close his eyes. He would see no more of pleasure nor sing its praise. The hour had come when he must die.

He had loved a Queen, he loved a Princess, he had loved his little King, and put his trust in him. Put not your trust in princes. He had forgotten God. And now there was so short time to remember Him. So soon would no living man nor boy nor girl matter to him any more, but only God.

He dipped the quill again into the ink and wrote on a torn off scrap of paper:

'Forgetting God to love a King
Hath been my rod.'

That had been his own fault, not the King's. He wished now he had not cursed Janey's boy; he was frail like her, and would have a hard time of it now.

He wrote,

'Yet God did call me in my pride,'

but though he tried hard to think of God and how He would judge him, he was still thinking of the King. Rhymes did not come easily with him as with Tom Wyatt, but he must leave something behind to wipe out that curse. He wrote:

'Lord send the King in years as Noe,
In governing this realm with joy,
And after this frail life such grace,
That in thy bliss he may find place.'

He flung down the quill in relief. Rhymes were the devil, especially to 'Noe.' But he had got down what he wanted; he had wished long life and happiness to Janey's boy, Now he was free to die.

But he went down fighting. He refused consolations of religion from Dr Latimer, and even from any other preacher. He refused to make a penitent speech on the scaffold acknowledging his crimes and the justice of his punishment. The executioner, frightened by the defiance of that towering figure, struck a feeble blow with his axe so that it slipped on to the victim's shoulder and a great spurt of blood gushed up.

Tom saw red; this was Ned himself striking at him, as Ned had always wanted to do. He leapt up and grappled with the man, dragging him down, down, but it was Ned he was dragging down with him to hell. A dozen hands tore them apart and flung him on to the block, and again the axe hacked at him, but, not yet dead, he struggled to rise again.

The third blow killed him.

CHAPTER TWENTY-FIVE

The bright late March sunlight shone into the King's garden where Bishop Latimer was preaching his next Sunday's sermon to the King who sat looking out of the window at the end of the gallery, and to the lords and ladies and servants of the Court, who walked up and down in the garden, an annoyingly restless practice, apt to distract the preacher.

Dr Latimer shouted suddenly, 'This I say, if they ask me what I think of the Lord Admiral's death, that he died very dangerously, irksomely and horribly.'

It worked. The shuffling and whispering stopped; no more of his congregation slid away up side-paths; some who had begun to, turned back. Old Latimer was off again on the Admiral, even though he was now in his grave in the Tower.

'He was a covetous man, a horrible covetous man.' The preacher's eyes rolled round his congregation and his voice dropped a semi-tone: '*I would there were no more in England.*'

Now, whom did he mean by that? Sly glances slid among the crowd, at the elegant Earl of Warwick whose blank ironic stare was fixed upward at the preacher; at the Protector himself, who was gnawing at his lip.

'He was an ambitious man. *I would there were no more in England.*'

'He was a seditious man, a contemner of the Common Prayer. *I would there were no more in England.*'

('Latimer's new Litany!' murmured the Earl of Warwick to his neighbour.)

'He is gone. *I would he had left none behind him.*'

And with this generic curse on all men still left alive, the Bishop stepped down from the pulpit. There was no doubt about the effectiveness of *this* sermon.

But the effect was not what he intended. People were soon saying that these snarling curs of the clergy worried even the dead in their graves. And if one did attend to his text, why then it was true enough that there were more men left alive in England as covetous, ambitious, and seditious as ever the Admiral had been – yet he had had to die, while they still pranked it.

Immediately after the execution, men who had been paid by the Council ran among the crowds of waiting citizens, crying that a traitor had died. But they had met no enthusiastic response and many had turned away. 'The man died very boldly,' they said. 'He would not have done so had he not died in a just quarrel.' The Protector himself must have thought so, they said, else why did he not let him be heard in his own defence? There were mutterings about the curse of Cain. The Good Duke had killed his brother. It would do him no good. Soon people were quoting a verse, made, it was said, by one of the Duke's own Council:

'But ever since I thought him sure a beast,
That causeless laboured to defile his nest.'

And the following line exonerated the Admiral (though not the poet), declaring:

'Thus guiltless he, through malice, went to pot.'

Poetry was not what it had been a few years ago when Surrey and Wyatt were writing; there were no coming young men to take their place, said the critics. Sir John Harington's Muse did only a little better, when praising his patron's 'strong limbs and manly shape,' his 'sumptuous generosity' and 'in war-skill great bold hand.' That last was in actual and vivid touch, it called up the Admiral at once to those who knew him.

His servant had been searched; the letters to the Princesses Mary and Elizabeth discovered in the soles of his shoes and instantly burnt; the man himself hanged.

They told this to Bess, still a prisoner at Hatfield; they told her how her lover had died, 'very dangerously, irksomely and horribly'; to the last instigating her to rebellion against his brother.

They asked questions. They were watching her. She had to speak. At last she said,

'This day died a man of great wit but little judgment.'

After that there was no more for her to say or do.

They had burnt his last letter to her; she would never know what he had written. The nightmare she had dreamt had come true; and she was living it.

She went to bed and did not get up again for a long time. For many weeks she was too ill to know clearly what was happening in the country round her, certainly too ill to care –

so ill that the doctors thought at first she would not live, though they could find no definite cause of disease. But she had lost the will to live. She had lost the only two people she had really loved in her short life; and perhaps Cathy's death as well as Tom's had been in part due to her. She had lost her good name; she was beggared of love, of character, and of her health; before she was sixteen, it seemed there was nothing left to live for.

But one thing no fate could take from her, her fierce loyalty, not only to a person, but to an intention. The first got Cat Ashley out of prison and back to her side; the second set her to work, with the almost blind force of instinct, to recover the ground she had lost; to win 'the goodwill of the people' that had been so jeopardised by scandal. They thought her a wanton; they should see that she was not.

There was still, then, something for her to do, and at once; it just saved her nerves, perhaps her reason, from shipwreck. As soon as she could leave her bed she began her lessons again, though her hand was still so shaky that she had to dictate her letters to a secretary since her wilting was 'not now so good as she trusts *it will be*.' In those last three words lay all her indomitable resolution. Her handwriting '*will*' be good again. She '*will*' work; and with a fury that now allowed itself no alleviation of flirting with Mr Ascham, not even when her always ready jealousy was roused by his admiration of little Jane Grey's industry in learning.

For there were three children in England just then driving at their lessons with ferocious intensity, and with the same object, the Crown of England.

Edward must work to make himself a good King. Jane, though herself working for sheer love of it, was being urged by her parents in order to make herself a suitable consort for him.

Elizabeth was working to fit herself for her far more remote chance of becoming Queen. Now that there was nothing left for her to live for, she was free to live only for that. She did. She worked – or someone else did, whom she had ceased to recognise as herself.

She saw this other self sit at her books and write, heard it give the right answers, a shadow moved by some strange mechanism, while all the time she stood apart. Very rarely her own self stirred; once it took up her jewelled pen and wrote words that had nothing to do with her lessons:

'I love and yet am forced to seem to hate,
I seem stark mute, yet inwardly do prate;
I am, and am not – freeze and yet I burn,
Since from myself my other self I turn.

My care is like my shadow in the sun –
Follows my flying – flies when I pursue it;
Stands and lives by me, does what I have done

Or let me live with some more sweet content
Or die and so forget what love e'er meant.'

She stared astonished at the lines. Why had she written them? She had no need to pray to forget what love e'er meant. She had forgotten.

She worked not only at languages ancient and modern, insisting on beginning to learn Spanish as well as Italian (was not Spain the most powerful country in the world and therefore the most important to understand in all the finer shades of political meaning?); not only at history and mathematics and music and dancing; but at acting a part completely alien to her nature. She wore dresses of nun-like severity, refused to wear or even look at jewels, strained her hair straight and smooth, avoided company whenever possible, and in the presence of men kept her eyes downcast and spoke scarcely at all.

But she listened. In her secluded shell of quiet she heard echoes of the world without, and brooded over them, at first in a dull despair that tried to pass as indifference, for what could anything matter now?

Yet it did begin to matter a little when the sun shone more brightly at her archery practice, and her fingers as she drew her bow were no longer stiff with cold inside the long elegant gloves. The silly shout of the cuckoos in the towering trees in Hatfield Park only mocked her unhappiness.

But then came the time when she first heard the nightingale in the hot bright silence of noonday in early June. It mattered too much; she flung down her bow and rushed headlong into the house in a passion of tears.

The sun must not shine, the birds not sing, or she would never dare go out again. She would sit always in a cool dim room, drowning her heart in dead languages. She pulled the books towards her – but a wild leaping tune of the Tartar tribes that Tom had often whistled came into her head; she beat her hands against the table to shut it out, but they were beating to the same rhythm. It was no use to try and read, to deafen her thoughts.

It had all come back, the agonised longing for the sound of Tom's voice, of his quick firm step that made the world his own; for the touch of the 'great bold hand' on her shoulder, on her face, lifting it to meet his – but here the pain became unbearable, she uttered little sharp cries aloud to herself, she seized the papers before her on the table, all the careful work on which she had been laboriously engaged for the past weeks, and tore them into shreds, her hands shaking, her lips trembling, muttering, 'Fool, fool, fool!' to herself, and to him; all her unwilling anger against him burning up again, scorching and withering her heart to ashes.

Why could he not have managed things better, plotted more secretly, played his hand more cunningly, as even she could have done?

He had loved too much, hated too much, talked too much – thought too little. 'Much wit but little judgment,' so little – less than a child's, a young girl's. Why couldn't he have been more like herself?

But if he had been, she would never have loved him, as now she did; loved him just because he had been so gaily reckless of consequences, because, though they could kill him, no one could make him cautious; loved him so that the thought of him was tearing her in two – tearing – tearing – as she tore these senseless scraps of paper.

Why couldn't she forget him?

But she would never forget.

* * *

'No, she'll never forget,' said Mrs Ashley to Mr Parry (for the two of them were both out again). 'Love someone else? Why, yes, I should hope so, and she all but a child still. But mark my words, she'll only love men who'll remind her of the Admiral.'

Wherein Mrs Ashley showed that, though lacking in prudence she had her own wisdom.

Something else woke in Bess in those June days, the hope of revenge.

The house was a-buzz with reports confirming the vague rumours of weeks past, rumours of discontent, of insurrections coming to a head in different parts of England against her rulers. Bess's interest, which she had curbed against hope (the people were always rising, and it led to nothing but their own hurt, poor wretches), now galloped forward into fierce excitement.

The mills of God were grinding, not slowly, but exceeding fast. Retribution was coming quickly on the man who had killed her lover and her good name. Within only three or four months of Tom Seymour's death there were rebellions all over the country against the Lord Protector.

This time they had found a leader: a man called Robert Kett who preached 'communistic law' from the branches of an oak tree, and told his followers to keep the peace and harm no man, and share all property in common. As they themselves had none, this meant sharing other people's property; they tore up the palings of the gentry's parks, levelled the hedges, and drove off their deer and cattle to feed on. The Council sent the German and Italian troops against the rebels, under near a score of noble commanders. But Kett's rabble defeated them and took some of the noble commanders prisoner.

So this, said the Council, was the result of the Protector's Reform measures!

He had to forswear them all; to enforce the Land Enclosures that he had tried to abolish, and follow the hated policy of his colleagues. But he still told them what he thought of it – and of them: it was their covetousness that had caused the revolt, and though it must be put down, he would not himself lead a force against it. Characteristically he ended his bitter speech to all those sneering faces, with a crumb of still bitter comfort, to himself. 'Better that they should die fighting than live to die of lack of a living.'

Death was beginning to wear a desirable aspect to him; no grisly pursuing skeleton through the dance of life, but an angel with welcoming arms and a smile of infinite understanding. When he himself was dead, then only perhaps would the people begin to know how he had wanted to help them. But now a quick death instead of a slow one was the boundary of his hopes for them.

So John Dudley, Earl of Warwick, marched against the rebels, hanged Kett from his Oak of Reformation, put the landlords firmly in power, and returned in triumph, strong enough to move openly against the Protector.

Danger is the best antidote to despair. The Duke at once retorted with a far-flung attack of pamphlets; they were scattered among the people, most of whom were unable to read them at all, and those who began were too bored to finish.

He descended upon Hampton Court, barricaded it, got the little King, who had a heavy cold, out of his bed, and made him address the uneasy populace through the bars of the great gates, with a petition to them 'to be good to me and to my uncle.' Edward did not like it at all. His dignity was ruffled and his cold got worse. And the pathetic effect of his childish appeal was entirely spoilt by the Protector's speech which followed it, asserting that if he went down, the King would go down with him.

The people did not see it. Nor did the King.

And the next night his uncle made him get out of bed again, this time at midnight, and go on a long cold tiring ride through the autumn river mist. They rode out of those gates where Nan Bullen's initials, intertwined with King Hal's, had been defaced for Jane Seymour's. Now the servants at Hampton Court were saying that Jane Seymour's ghost came out from the doorway on to the Silver Stick Gallery with a lighted taper in her hand. And Nan Bullen's cousin, pretty Catherine Howard, beheaded in her teens, was heard at nights shrieking in the Long Gallery that led to the Chapel. Bloated red spiders five inches wide had appeared in the Cardinal's palace, which King Henry had looted from him for his own pleasure, and from which his enormous body could not be moved in those last months of his life without the help of machinery. He who had boasted that he never spared a man in his anger (he might have added, in his greed) or a woman in his lust, was no longer spared.

From this haunted pleasure palace on the river his little son rode away at midnight, frail as a feather on his pony, and coughing fretfully in the dark dank October fog. He had to ride all the way to Windsor – for his safety, the Protector said, though of that Edward was sceptical. It seemed to be entirely for his uncle's safety.

There at Windsor the Earl of Warwick found him, more disgruntled and becolded than ever.

'I bight as well be in prison,' he said; 'there are do galleries here or gardens to play in.'

Dudley took him out of prison. He gave him his friends to play with again, especially Barney. He gave him sports and Christmas parties and mummings, he took him hunting and shooting and made him feel that soon he would be a man among men. The boy was delighted at the change; he flung himself into sports and exercises – with rather too sudden energy in fact for his delicate physique; and sometimes even cut his church attendance so that the Court preacher was disgusted to find himself preaching to an empty royal chair.

But still that nasty cough, that Edward had caught on the long cold night-ride to Windsor, hung on. Dudley told him not to bother about it, he would soon shake it off, as he had at last shaken off his oppressive guardian uncle.

For the Duke of Somerset was no longer the Protector. Dudley, now created Duke of Northumberland, reigned in his stead.

The Seymours' mother, the poet Skelton's Mistress Margery Wentworth, the 'flower of goodlihead,' died only a few months after Tom's death. It was decided not to give her a royal funeral. This was done in order to insult the Duke of Somerset's mother; nobody seemed to notice that it also insulted the King's grandmother – not even the King. He did not even record her death in his Journal. And the Duke himself took it meekly, as he took most things now; people said he was a changed man since his brother's death, not now in his increased nervous irritability but in his broken spirit.

There was enough, without remorse, to break it, for he had to stand by and watch the utter ruin of all his hopes of social and economic reform, of liberty and religious tolerance, destroyed by the greedy tyranny of Dudley and the new landlords. He had lost not only the power, but much of the will to act. But whether he acted or not, he was naturally the focus point of any opposition to the new rule. And the common people, who had been shocked by his executing his own brother, could now consider that he had paid for it in his swift downfall from power, and remember that the Good Duke had been on their side. So were they now on his side. But they had no power; it was all in the hands of the rich, who were on the side of Dudley, a sensible fellow, especially in his sense of property. And Dudley had the sense to see that an ex-Protector was a danger. Even if he didn't do anything, he was always stirring up the people with his talk of liberty.

To secure his position, Dudley had to strike again, this time to kill. And so, less than two years after Tom Seymour was beheaded, his brother Ned laid down his head on the same block. There was a trial of him on some flimsy charges; he was accused, rather oddly, of trying to secure his position against possible enemies; and of plotting against Dudley, even as Dudley had plotted against him. Dudley himself dared not call this 'treason.' But it made no odds. From the first it was clear that the Duke would share the fate to which he had sent his brother.

He met it very differently. Tom died like a tiger, Ned like a gentleman. He behaved perfectly throughout, thanked the

Council on his knees for having given him the open trial that he had denied his brother – though indeed it was only the show of justice that was granted him, for the House had been carefully packed. And he made a beautiful before-execution speech which moved all the watching crowds to a passion of pity, both for him and for themselves.

They surged forward; a deep muttering growl rose and thickened the air. He had them in his sway in this hour of death as he had never had them in his life. They knew now whatever his faults, crimes even, he had taken thought for them, had wished them well; as none had done of the pack of greedy wolves who were now pulling him down. He had but to lift his hand in sign to them and they would rescue him.

But he did not do it. Why should he give the signal that would lead many of them to their deaths, in order to escape his own? It was little he had been able to do for them, prevented by the greed and ambition of others; but also by his own. 'Let me alone' – yes, alone to die – 'for I am not better than my fathers.'

And he did not even remember in that hour that he had at least wished to be better.

Jan. 22. 'The Duke of Somerset had his head cut off upon Tower Hill between eight and nine this morning,' wrote King Edward briskly in his Journal.

Earlier he had entered all the charges against his eldest uncle with considerable satisfaction, especially his 'following his own opinion and doing all by his authority.'

He had shown indifference over his Uncle Tom's fate; this time it was an active animosity, for the Duke's execution was both suggested and warranted under Edward's own hand. The whirligig of time had brought a strange revenge for King Edward V and his brother, the two small princes murdered by their uncle in the Tower, whose fate King Henry had remembered with dread for his own son.

Edward VI, nearly seventy years later, brought about the death of his two uncles.

It did not weigh on him. At a shooting-match shortly after, when Dudley shouted, 'Good shot, my liege!' the boy brightly answered, 'Not as good as yours, when you shot off my Uncle Somerset's head.'

He was painted standing with his legs rather apart, both thumbs in his belt and the fingers of one hand resting on his dagger, in exactly the same stance as his father, with the same argumentative stare, the same thrust of the dogmatic under-lip. This conscious likeness between the slight boy and his tremendous sire gave amusement to many, but also some alarm.

He was enjoying life: the matches and tourneys that his new guardian arranged to dispel any 'dampy thoughts' about his former guardian's fall (but after that shooting-match Dudley realised he need not have worried); the visit of the little Queen of Scots' mother, the stately and gracious Queen Dowager, whom Mr Knox in his rugged fashion called 'an old cow,' and Edward with schoolboy wit amplified it to the Dow Cow. He showed off his music and dancing to her, and, which he enjoyed still more, his performance on horseback at Prisoners' Base and Running at the Ring, and in shooting, where he was able to record proudly that though he lost at Rounds he won at Rovers.

To Barney he wrote gleefully of musters of a thousand

menat-arms, 'so horsed as was never seen. We think you shall see in France none like.'

For now that his little King seemed free at last to enjoy life and apparent health, Barney too had felt free to follow his ambition and go to France. Edward had generously done his utmost for him in this, got him appointed as one of the French King's Gentlemen of the Bedchamber, and made up for his absence by writing him long eager letters into which he put far more of himself than into his Journal.

To Barney indeed he showed what he had never done to anyone else, an affection that could rise to sympathetic imagination. For while Barney went to the French wars, Edward went a delightful royal progress round the country, staying at the houses of his chief nobles, fêted, entertained with dancing and sports and hunting, and 'whereas you have been occupied in killing your enemies, in long marches in extreme heat, in sore skirmishings, we have been occupied in killing of wild beasts, in pleasant journeys, in good fare, in viewing of fair countries...and goodly houses where we were marvellously – yea rather excessively – banquetted!'

And Barney wrote back about Romish processions with crosses and banners in Paris, and street rows between French and English soldiers; and soothed Edward's anxiety for his morals by promising that 'as for the avoiding of the company of ladies, I will assure your Highness I will not come into their company unless I do wait upon the French King'; and always ended, 'Other news have I none.

The meanest and most obligest of your subjects,
Barnaby Fitzpatrick.'

* * *

Then the young man got a letter from the boy more reassuring than any other, in the casual cheerful pluck with which Edward dismissed a recent illness: 'We have been a little troubled with smallpox which has prevented us from writing; but now we have shaken that quite away.'

But it was his death-knell. It left him weakened; his persistent cough, that ill legacy from his last ride with his Uncle Somerset, had come back worse than ever; it got no better as summer came on, and it was evident that he was gravely ill. Barney instantly threw up his promising career abroad to hurry back to him.

He found the fifteen-year-old boy, who had had to give up his new-found triumphs in sport, indomitably interested in all the recent marvels of scientific discovery. He had been studying the cause of comets and rainbows; he showed Barney his geographic and astronomic instruments, the magnetic needle and astrolobe which had been explained to him by old Sebastian Cabot, the Emperor's Pilot-Major of the Indies.

Once again Edward was not going to be outdone by the Emperor; he proposed to make Cabot the Grand Pilot of England.

'The New World ought to be English,' he told Barney indignantly; for it was the Sheriff of Bristol, Richard Ameryk, who'd paid a pension to Sebastian's father, John Cabot, for his voyages of discovery, and that was why people were calling the place America, and *not*, as foreigners tried to make out, because a wretched ship's chandler called Amerigo Vespucci had happened to get there too, within a fortnight of old Father Cabot. 'I'll publish the whole facts to the world – the exact sums my grandfather told Ameryk to pay him—'

'Ah, I wouldn't do that,' said Barney with a careless glance at the accounts that Edward was flourishing at him from his bed, '£40, over three years, doesn't sound much these days for a royal pension!'

The boy gave him a weak thump on the arm. 'All you Irish are cynics. I can't help it if my grandfather was a skinflint. My father made up for that. So will I. And I'm showing what *my* discoverers can do to rival the Emperor's.'

This very day he was sending out three ships under Sir Hugh Willoughby and Richard Chancellor to find a North-East passage through the Arctic to Cathay. It would be a voyage through 'perils of ice, intolerable colds,' but years ago the merchant Robert Thorne had told King Henry that it was possible, for a man might 'sail so far that he came at last to the place where there was no night at all, but a continual light and brightness of the sun shining clearly upon the huge and mighty sea.'

'And,' said the sick boy, flushing with the triumph of man's unconquerable spirit, 'he told my father "there is *no land unhabitable nor sea unnavigable.*"'

He spoke only of Robert Thorne, whom he had not seen. He did not wish to remember his uncle the Lord Admiral and the sunlight flashing on the gold lacing of his coat as he stood there by the window of this very room in the palace of Greenwich, and pointed at the river Thames flowing down below towards the sea; and said, 'There lies the path of England's glory. Take it, and you'll travel far.'

The Admiral had gone, with his great laugh and promise of splendour and power; but the river flowed on.

From its shores a murmur was rising that grew into a

distant roar; it came nearer, louder, ripping out in great tearing gusts of sound, echoing up from the water like a drum.

'They're coming downstream. Look out of the windows. Can you see them yet?' Edward was leaning forward from his pillows.

His old nurse Mother Jack came up and patted them and pressed him back on to them again. 'There, there now, don't you get excited. They won't be here yet. Your Highness will know all about it when they come, the brave fellows, though indeed I think they'd better have stayed at home.'

Barney put his head out of the window, rested his elbows on the sill, and looked upstream, the wind behind him from the sea blowing his hair before his eyes. In the brilliant early summer sunshine the Thames glittered like a diamond ribbon, between its shores that were dark with the swarming crowds thronging to see the start of this wild venture into the terrors of the Outland ocean; where no night was, and rocks of ice as high as mountains and gleaming like sapphire and emerald came drifting down to crush the ships that were no bigger than walnut shells beside them.

Nearer and nearer came the hurly-burly of that mighty cheering as the three ships hove into sight, towed downstream by small boats rowed by mariners in sky-blue cloth. And in answer, more sailors were running up the rigging and shouting till the sky rang with the noise. Now the guns of the Palace were booming out their God-speed to them.

The Courtiers were already clustered on the tops of the towers, the Privy Council had run to the windows of the other rooms in the Palace.

'Hurrah! hurrah!' they all shouted, even old Father Russell of the snowy beard, even the douce quiet secretary Mr Cecil. The King was all but sobbing, 'I *must* see them. It's my venture. Their chief ship is called after me, the *Edward Bonaventure*.'

Barney carried him to the window; it was terribly easy, his weight was so light. Mother Jack tut-tutted and fussed with blankets, but they stayed there till the crowds had swept shouting on, leaving the river banks green and bare; and in the distance the three ships grew misty on that sparkling river, broadening out towards the sea. They sailed out on it, to discover, not the passage to Cathay but the White Sea, and then Moscow, where the great Tsar Ivan the Terrible waited to do them honour in a long garment of beaten gold with an imperial crown upon his head.

But only one of the three ships, the *Edward Bonaventure*, was to achieve this and return to England.

The other two were caught in the ice and there found by the Russian fishermen the next spring, the crews all frozen in their transparent coffin, their gear and belongings intact, to be carefully returned to England by the Tsar.

But now it was still the summer of 1553, and the three ships still sailing out, while the two friends by the Palace window strained their eyes into the future.

'When next they go,' said Edward, 'I will go, too. Old Thorne said he "wondered any prince could be content to live quiet within his own dominions." I am not content. I will—' his cough interrupted him.

Barney laid him down again in his bed.

* * *

The roses were like lamps filled with the level light of the sunset. Beyond them the river shone dark through the bright trees and their long slanting shadows.

The lawns and flowerbeds of the Palace gardens glowed iridescent and unreal like the transparent scene reflected on the surface of a soap bubble – a bubble floating on a ripple of tinkling music that drifted from a boat, clear as sounds can only be on the water; lutes were playing and boys' voices singing to comfort the young King lying sick in the Palace.

In this idyllic scene, screened by the trees from any watching windows, Barney met his Princess once again at last.

He did not in the least want to do so.

Alarmed by the serious reports of her brother, she had ridden in haste to Greenwich to see him, but she had not been allowed to do so. Ever since the Admiral's death she had been carefully prevented from seeing anything of her brother in private, and as she had been living a deliberately retired life she had had only an occasional meeting with him even among the crowds of the Court. Now her desperate attempt to force a meeting had failed, and all she had been able to do was to arrange this semi-clandestine interview with his reluctant page.

It was just five years since that night in early summer when Barney had partnered her for a few moments in the Hungarians' Palace-Dance at the Admiral's house and she had swung him aside into the window seat – to take off her tight shoes, she had said, but surely it was for more than that? She had let him take her hand and speak his love for her; she had smiled at him, and her glorious eyes had opened on him as though he alone were there in all the world; she had – he never could believe it afterwards – but she had sprung up into his arms and kissed him.

And later he had learnt, through tittering deviations of backstairs gossip, that she had gone out that very same night alone with the Admiral in his barge.

Scandal had blackened her far more deeply in the months that followed; and the grudging Proclamation that the Council had at last issued to clear her name had, in the opinion of many, only confirmed it. 'No smoke without a fire,' was a good, knowing proverb. But nothing that he heard later, not even the confident assertion that the Admiral had been beheaded for getting the Princess with child (the clear proof of it being that none of the open charges against him merited the death sentence), nothing that he heard later could hurt Barney as did the memory of that summer night when she had kissed him – and then crept out in secret to the Admiral.

Even at the French Court it had hung about him, giving him a contemptuous distaste for the gay young women who would have been ready enough to flirt with the grave handsome youth. But he had found it easy to obey his little King's anxious injunctions 'for the avoiding of the company of the ladies.'

Now he had to meet the Princess again. She was nineteen by now and had changed, much, so he had heard on all sides; she had lived retired from the Court; she was often ill and, though no one could say what exactly was the matter with her, the doctors sometimes despaired even of her life. Yet she worked like a Trojan, she devoted herself to her, studies; she had become a paragon, not only of learning and theology, but of maidenly modesty and discretion. If she had been a Roman Catholic like her sister Mary, she would undoubtedly have gone into a nunnery, so they said; and as it was, her dress was so simple and severely plain that it was almost that of a nun's. Even when Mary of Guise, the French Queen Dowager of Scotland, had come to visit King Edward with all her ladies from the French Court, and set all the English Court ladies on fire to follow the French fashions, causing a complete revolution in feminine dress and hairdressing, the Princess Elizabeth had not changed her style one jot, had refused to wear jewels or even to curl her hair.

This had brought loud praise of her 'maiden shame-facedness' from the Reformers, who were busy condemning the new fashions, especially the 'hair frounced, curled and double curled' – a hit at the Lady Mary, who, a devout Catholic, could never resist new finery, however unbecoming.

The two sisters were regarded as the rival heroines of the two religious creeds. Little Lady Jane Grey, an ardent admirer of her now austere cousin, had flung herself into the controversy with all the eagerness of a schoolgirl in taking sides; she had refused to wear a cloth-of-gold dress that Mary had sent her, 'It would be a shame to follow my Lady Mary's example, against God's word, and leave my Lady Elizabeth's example, who is a follower of God's word.'

The speech, duly reported, had infuriated (and alarmed) my Lady Elizabeth a good deal more than my Lady Mary; but Barney could not know that; nor would it have altered his firm opinion that in whatever way she dressed or did her hair she did it of set design, for her own ends – and those far from spiritual. Since in all Papist eyes she was illegitimate, she would naturally plump for the Reformed Religion.

And the total abstinence from coquetry was too good to be true; he had the word of others for that. The new Spanish Ambassador to England had spoken of her as 'a creature full of beguilement.'

Let her be! She would never again find it possible to beguile *him*!

So he waited on that glimmering golden evening that was filled like a crystal cup with light and music. The boys on the river were singing the song that the young Earl of Surrey had composed in his scarlet-coated pride and joy in a sportsman's life. Barney hoped the sick boy would not recognise it, for he never cared to be reminded that his father had cut off Surrey's head.

> '*Summer is come, for every spray now springs,*
> *The hart has hung his old head on the pale,*
> *The buck in brake his winter coat he flings,*
> *The fishes flit with new repairéd scale.*'

A slight figure was coming towards him through the trees with swift and resolute tread. Barney found himself looking at a pale girl in a plain dress of dull green, which for all its sober hue showed up marvellously the whiteness of her long bare throat, uncovered by any necklace, and the red-gold glint on her straight, demurely parted hair that was brushed as smooth and shining as satin. Her mouth was wide and the thin lips shut fast as if not to let any secret escape them; she looked sad and strained, a pale girl, rather tall, with no especial beauty, so he kept telling himself – but then he had to admit that her eyes were really beautiful. They were the colour of the blue dusk in the shadow of the trees; he remembered now how they reflected the lights and colours round them, the pupils contracting or dilating till sometimes the eyes seemed pale almost as water, and at others nearly black.

And they were looking into his eyes, sinking into them, as once they had done on a night of early summer years before – and suddenly he knew that there was only one reason why he had consented to meet her thus; only one thing he wanted to ask of her: had she, that same night that she had kissed him, given her body to the Admiral.

He had no chance to ask it. In that same instant that he looked at them, those deep blue eyes changed again, the pupils narrowed, they were the colour of steel as she asked the question that she, not he, had chosen.

'What the devil is this foolery of Dudley's? He has just married his son Guildford in hugger-mugger haste to Lady Jane Grey, to her little liking, and to his own purpose only. You must know of it. It can mean but one thing – that he intends to rule England through her; get the King to alter the Succession and appoint Jane his heir to the throne.'

'It must be for the sake of the true religion, Your Grace,' said Barney uncomfortably. 'If the Lady Mary came to the throne now, it would wreck the course of the Reformation.'

But it was difficult to explain why the Lady Elizabeth, so widely regarded as the representative of true religion, should also have been set aside.

She saw his thought and laughed. 'Yes, he approached me first, all in the cause of the true faith! He quickly found I would have nothing to do with it. So he will set both Mary and myself aside, as declared bastards, which is absurd, for if either is a bastard then the other must be legitimate. Jane's a child for all she's sixteen – and a little fool for all her learning. Her villainous parents are pushing her into this – to her ruin.'

She spoke the more emphatically as she saw the young man's face settle into resistance to her argument. How wooden and conceited and disapproving he had grown – and she had once thought him so charming!

Barney on his side, having stiffened himself against any attempt to beguile him, was annoyed to find none made. Did she not think it worth while? Frigidly he put Edward's view to her: he disapproved of his sister Mary; all his reign had been clouded by quarrels with her over her observance of the Mass in her private household; it had nearly caused a war with the Emperor, since she had got him to take her side. That was the danger – Rome – foreign interference—

'I think,' she interrupted crisply, 'you must have been listening to Dr Latimer's sermon last Sunday. In his opinion, "God had better remove both the Princesses from this Earth," since we *might* marry foreign princes who *might* endanger God's Church. But if Godly Dudley takes that hint, he'll pull a hornet's nest about his ears. He'll do it in any case by putting Jane on the throne. The throne of England depends ultimately on the consent of the people. And the people will never stand it if the rightful heir is set aside.'

'The consent of the people? Yes, Your Grace, and the people have given their consent to the new religion. Which the Lady Mary has rejected.'

'So that they will reject her? Never think it! I know more of them than you do – you've been abroad,' she added, to soften this. 'But indeed I know them, the commoners, well. Creeds don't matter to them as much as people – or as the simple standards of right and wrong. Some of them may think it fun to toss a priest or two in a blanket, but they won't stand seeing an innocent woman done out of her rights. And they like Mary all the better for standing up for them and insisting on her own form of private worship. They tell dozens of good stories about her pluck – how she roared at the Council, "My father made the best part of you out of nothing!" How they bawled back! It could be heard in the street outside! But so was the story. When the English tell stories about anyone it means they've taken him – or her – as their own. And she is not only comedy to them, she is romance. For so many years now she has been a legend, a princess cruelly shut up in Dolorous Guard. I will tell you something I saw myself only this spring; a simpleton of a girl who wandered the countryside, believing herself to be the Princess Mary! She told me that King Henry's sister, the lovely Mary Rose, had appeared to her in a dream – she was sitting in a silver bath! – and told her, "You must go a-begging once in your life, either in your youth or in your age." "And so," said the poor fool, "I have chosen to do it in my youth." You will think this not worth a straw – but straws show the wind – and the hold that my sister's sad state has had on the people's imagination.'

On hers too, it seemed, with such eager sympathy she told the queer little tale – until it occurred to Barney that she too, as well as Mary, had had to go a-begging in her youth; and might well see herself as another ill-used princess in Dolorous Guard.

For the first time it struck him that he himself had not been the only person to be pitied in the affair of the Princess and the Admiral.

He knelt and kissed her hand. 'I will do what I can with His Majesty for Your Grace,' he murmured.

For answer she flicked him on the nose. 'You are impertinent. Who said it was for *my* Grace?'

'For my Lady Mary's then.' At last he was smiling.

But she sighed. 'Why not say, for my Lady Jane's? It's she who would come off worst.'

She went back to Hatfield and wrote telling her brother how she had come to see him and been prevented. It is doubtful if he ever got the letter. He was fast getting worse. Dudley was having to work madly against time. He had married Jane to his son almost as quickly as one bought a cow (but Jane was still refusing to consummate the marriage).

Now he bought quantities of arms and was manning the Tower; twenty ships fully manned and gunned rode at anchor in the Thames on the thin pretext of an expedition to Barbary and the Spice Islands, which everyone knew would not take place.

Only one thing remained to secure his position; he must seize the persons of the two Princesses.

Two bodies of horsemen were sent to bring them to London in answer to urgent messages from their dying brother.

Mary started from Hunsdon. Elizabeth, just about to start from Hatfield, had a sudden suspicion that these pathetic appeals might be a trap to take them prisoner. What if they had been sent, not by the King, but by Dudley in his name?

Edward Seymour had kept King Henry's death a secret for three days while he snatched the supreme power. Was John Dudley now playing the same trick?

She promptly went to bed and declared herself too ill to ride to London. It would gain time, but only for a few days, perhaps hours, and sooner or later she would have to declare herself either for Mary or Dudley.

It was an appalling dilemma, for she knew nothing of what had happened to Mary, and if she continued to disobey the summons to London, it might well lead to Dudley sending an armed force to carry her to the Tower, perhaps the block. On the other hand, if she threw in her lot with him, it would bring her into open enmity with Mary, who might even now be fighting his army – and winning.

She lay back on her pillows and knew that she could do nothing more but wait for the next move.

It came with the public announcement of the King's death. The heralds proclaimed Jane as Queen at street corners, and their printed Proclamations, stuck up in market squares and church porches all over the country, justified her succession on the ground that the King's sisters were both bastards.

It was Sunday, and preachers all preached the same doctrine: Jane alone was the true and rightful Queen. A servant rode back from Amersham where he had heard a little man with a beard like a billygoat thump the pulpit and scream, 'Woe! Woe to England!' if she allied herself to the enemies of the Gospel – by which Mr Knox intended Mary.

No one could tell Bess where Mary was – alive or dead – free or a prisoner – in England or escaped – (as she had often planned) to the Netherlands.

But there was far more that no one could tell her about Mary. She lay by the new open windows, and the clang and peal of church bells acclaiming Jane as Queen of England floated in on the golden early July air. Would the country tamely accept her, or would they rise on behalf of Mary, as she had so boldly assured Barney they would?

She had not felt as bold as she had sounded. Dudley held whatever army there was, and the navy (all those ships lying off London all ready to attack! 'Spice Islands my nose!' she had exclaimed. It had smelt gunpowder, not spices); he held the Tower and all the great nobles in his pay. He was the greatest soldier England had had for years; he had succeeded in Scotland where Somerset, a sound and ruthless general, had failed; he had succeeded against the revolution.

Would he succeed now? Or would that inveterate bungler, Mary?

And if Mary did succeed, what then?

Dudley was the only man Mary had ever feared, except here father.

Nobody feared Mary. Her gruff good-natured laugh; her overdressing coupled with her simplicity and utter ignorance of the world, ignorance that had begun as a secluded girl's, devoted to her deeply religious mother, and had fixed into an old maid's; her inability to say anything she did not mean ('to be plain with you,' it was always accompanying some fresh gaffe); all these things had made her, among those who knew her, a figure of fun, certainly not of any mystery or alarm.

But Bess, lying in the warm July sunshine, shivered as she thought of her half-sister. Would it be better for herself if Mary won instead of Dudley? Dudley was utterly unscrupulous, ruthlessly bent on his own ambition, and would sweep anyone who interfered with it out of the way without remorse.

But Mary was unpredictable. She would never do anything that she did not feel to be right – but what might govern those feelings? Her starved emotions, her bitter broodings on the past and the wrong her father had done her mother, had twisted her judgment, of which she had never had much. She could not see nor reason clearly, but acted on impulse, letting her heart govern, and not her head. That ought to be well, since Mary had a good heart. But a female heart rampant could be a terrifying thing.

Under Mary's essential goodness of nature there lay the sickening uncertainty of hysteria. That quagmire, that welter of shifting angry unhappy emotion, blind, bottomless, a bog on a black night, was always there, waiting to engulf her, and anyone who was so unfortunate as to be having any dealings with her at that moment.

Jane might well turn out to be as much of a bigot as Mary.

But Jane was not an hysteric. Jane's fury of righteous indignation would be a deal less dangerous than Mary's sobbing paroxysms of grief over her sainted mother,

'May God preserve me from good women!' sighed Bess.

But there she had to lie, on the horns of a dilemma, between two very good women.

The church bells broke out again into a peal of joyous triumph. A white butterfly fluttered in and flapped about the room. She got out of bed, caught it and let it fly out of the window, watching it join a cluster of its fellows and go dancing all together, up, up, like flecks of light against the green glory of the sunlit trees, until suddenly she remembered she might be seen at the window.

She jumped into bed again, and looked at her face in the little hand-mirror. It was sufficiently white not to need any rubbing with chalk. Her teeth were chattering with fear; but she laughed.

Something in her that had lain numb all these four and a half years, since Tom Seymour's death, was quickening her pulses to a terrified yet heartening throb.

Now at last again, when at any moment she might lose it, she knew how sweet life was, and hope; yes, and fear too, since it had made her want to keep that life, want passionately, with all the wild excitement of a young lover's desire, to live, and to be Queen.

Elizabeth,
Captive Princess

PART I

CHAPTER ONE

The fields were deep and ruddy with uncut corn, the orchards heavy with ripening fruit. Set in their coloured ring, the courtyard of the great house at Hatfield lay quivering in the dancing light reflected off stone and brick and smooth cobbles. The waiting horses stamped and champed their bits, clanked their harness, tossed their heads, shook off the clustering flies that rose in angry clouds only to sink and settle again, sent their shrill whinnyings spinning up into the sunlight, complaining to each other that yet again their young lady was late.

The subdued voices of the men standing at their heads grumbled in concert with them and the buzz of the disturbed flies; the men had scurried and sweated to get themselves and their mounts ready on the instant they had been ordered, and here they had been banging about in this courtyard for the past half-hour at least. What could the girl be doing to keep them all dangling like this? Surely she didn't need to titivate all this time in order to ride and see her brother before he died? For most of them there knew or guessed by now what message had been brought by the rider in Duke Dudley's livery who had urged his spent horse into this courtyard an hour or so ago, slid from the saddle rubbing his sleeve across a face dripping with sweat, and demanded to see the Lady Elizabeth.

She had seen him, she had given order that an escort was to make ready on the instant to ride with her to London; she herself, but just returned from riding in the great park, would not wait even to change her dress. Had she changed her mind instead? since she did that almost as often. But would a girl of nineteen be so heartless, and one so fond of her young half-brother, and he the King? No one had said openly that King Edward lay seriously ill in his palace at Greenwich, but that was the noise in London, and noises from London travelled fast.

The noises in the courtyard hummed and heaved; they killed off King Edward easily enough, a sickly boy who was always having colds and had been worked too hard at his books, though some murmured sympathetically that it was a pity, for the lad had shown a great keenness for sport since Duke Dudley had taken charge of him. Some of them put his much elder half-sister, the Lady Mary, on the throne, and supposed she'd down the Duke and bring back the old religion. Some thought the Duke would make a bid to keep his place by setting up her cousin, the little Lady Jane Grey, instead as Queen, in the name of the new Protestant faith; he'd just married her off to his younger son, Guildford, which looked as though he had been planning some such move. Others again said if England must keep a Protestant sovereign, why not their Lady Elizabeth, own half-sister to the King instead of mere cousin? and a likely lass with a fine taste in horseflesh, for all she had kept them stewing and sweating in this leaden cup of a courtyard where the sun poured down like molten brass.

The murmurs and questions buzzed in the hot air, and then at last there was a stir within the silent house.

A door banged somewhere. A voice called. Steps were heard running up and down the stairs. The great doors were flung wide, opening a dark cool hollow in the glare of white heat. The Steward of the Household, Mr Thomas Parry, came out puffily, blinked like an owl at the sunlight, turned his back on it and bowed low.

The men in the courtyard could just see a slight figure moving towards them like a shadow through the dim recesses of the hall; a girl in a grey dress came out to the top of the steps and there stood still, the sun beating down on her sparkling red hair and the winking jewels and buttons of her cap and riding-dress. There she stood and stared, her eyes narrowing in a face grown suddenly thin and white; stared, not at the brilliant coloured scene before her, but at a hidden danger just come to light in the sun. Her eyes closed against it, her face shut into a mask.

Suddenly it flashed open. 'Take away the horses,' she called out in a clear and ringing voice where the note of command could not quite disguise an undertone of terror. 'Take them all away. I'm not going.'

There was a rustle of amazement, of alarm. Mr Thomas Parry asked with obsequious anxiety if anything were wrong.

'I – think – so,' was the baffling reply.

'Is Your Grace not feeling well?'

She turned her eyes towards him with a look that might mean gratitude. She paused, then nodded, then swayed, then put out a groping hand, and the long fingers clutched his arm so sharply that he winced.

'Yes, that is it. I feel giddy. Take me back to my room,

Parry. Tell them I am ill. I cannot ride to London. I am going to bed.'

She turned and went back, leaning helplessly upon his arm, and their retreating figures disappeared within the dim cool cave of the hall. The great doors were shut to.

The men in the courtyard looked at each other, nodded, swore softly. Their young lady had changed her mind again. What did it mean? Was she ill? Was it a sham? She could always be ill if she'd a mind to, they fancied. But why should she have a mind to, now, when her brother who loved her best in the world lay at the point of death?

'A hard-hearted young bitch,' the Duke's messenger muttered as he took horse again to ride back with the news – and no doubt the Duke would give him small thanks for it. 'The boy longed to see his sweet sister once again' – that was the moving message he had brought. But it had only moved her for a moment – and then she had gone to bed.

He cursed and rode out of the courtyard. The men left it to lead their horses back to the stables. Soon it was emptied of all life and noise, even of the flies, and became a barrenly blazing cup of silence, and sunlight reflected on the stones, until the shadows lengthened over it and the dusk deepened into dark and the moon rose.

And next day, and the day after, the sun rose hot and bright again, and there was the noise of men and horses again outside the house. But the Lady Elizabeth stayed in bed.

CHAPTER TWO

The room was filled with silence and the July sunshine. No birds sang in the midday heat outside the many windows. All those made to open were pushed wide; the small leaded panes of the others threw a chess-board of shadow on the gleaming floor. One was clouded by a tall fir, blue as thunder; not a leaf fluttered its carved shadow.

Suddenly the bright hush was shattered into fragments; an uproar crashed in through the windows, pealing, clashing, ringing, echoing, carillon after carillon of rejoicing bells.

With that, came a furious movement from between the white and scarlet bed-curtains, drawn back like the furled sails of a ship. The creature who had lain there motionless and wary, breathing an eager life into the stillness, sprang forward, tossing a cloud of fiery hair, fine as blown silk, round her white face and thin shoulders. Rage compressed her lips; the pupils of her pale eyes narrowed like a frightened cat's, but rage conquered fear, she lunged sideways across the looped curtain, snatched up a little silver bell and shook it. In case its tinkle should not have the required effect, she yelled.

There came the clattering uneven sound of tight shoes running in a monstrous hurry. In came a tall angular woman of about forty. Her long nose was inquisitive, her mouth anxious, but her eye irrepressibly lively.

'Hell-Cat!' said a voice from the bed, vibrant as the twang of a lute, 'what the devil is the meaning of that din?'

'The Hatfield church bells are all ringing too,' stammered the Hell-Cat; 'we thought – we didn't dare not to ring them in the house-chapel—'

'We? Who are "we", you Ash-Cat?

The Ash-Cat did not answer.

'Stop them at once.'

'Your Grace – is it safe? Duke Dudley is sure to hear of it. And by the same token, was it wise to yell – I mean, to call so loud? I have told everyone that the Lady Elizabeth is practically at death's door.'

The Lady Elizabeth ducked abruptly over the side of the bed, snatched up a book that had slid to the floor of the dais and flung it against a closed door. Cat Ashley knew when to go.

'Ding dong, ding dong,' rang the bells.

'Ding dong, ding dong,' sang the girl in a spasm of desperate merriment, and she chanted in time to them,

> 'Long live Queen Jane,
> Will Jane long reign?
> Long live Queen Jane,
> How long—?'

The bells stopped in the middle of a peal. The abrupt silence quivered over the sunlit room with an effect disruptive and shocking, like sudden death.

Mrs Ashley had carried out her orders, and the bells in the house-chapel had ceased to ring for Queen Jane. That made no odds; they were still ringing for her all through the countryside, proclaiming her Queen as soon as King Edward was proclaimed dead.

But had he really only just died, today, as announced? Had he really sent that sweet, compelling message to her two days ago, using his old childish nickname for her? Why had she suddenly felt certain, as she faced the blaze of sunlight in the courtyard, that her brother was already dead, that the message was a trap, baited by his guardian Duke Dudley, to get the King's sisters into his power before he had to announce the King's death?

Had Mary swallowed the bait and obeyed *her* summons to her dying brother? It would be just like her! Poor Mary was always gullible. Elizabeth with smug thankfulness snuggled beneath the sheet. But it could not protect her long. And everything depended on what had happened to Mary. Was she, the rightful Queen, now clapped in the Tower? If so, how long would it be before her rightful heir, the Lady Elizabeth, would be made to join her? All these questions tossed to and fro, ding *dong*, ding *dong*, as though the bells were still echoing through the silence.

The silence grew; it weighed on the aromatic air like a thundercloud.

Elizabeth flung herself back on the pillows, plucking nervously at the gold threads embroidered on her linen night-shift, saw that she had unpicked half a butterfly and jerked forward again, pulled out a gold box from the back of the bed and began to eat sweets voraciously. Crisply sugared rose-leaves, primroses and violets, fruit suckets, sticky cloying marchpane, she crammed them all into her mouth indiscriminately; then when they got too much even for her sweet tooth, she helped herself from a dish of wild strawberries by the bed, her long pointed fingers pouncing on several at a time and dropping one on the linen sheet so that it made a small stain like blood, at which she chuckled. How Cat would grumble under her breath!

The footsteps were coming back again, tiptoeing almost as noisily as they had pattered before. They were being followed by a heavy shambling tread. 'Is there a bear in the house?' Elizabeth demanded of herself, and thrust the box back well behind the pillows. 'Come in,' she breathed in an all but extinct voice. The door opened softly.

'The doctor!' was sounded on a solemn note.

Mrs Ashley stepped warily into the room, followed by Dr. William Turner. He began in a blurring north-country voice on what he had evidently prepared: 'I grieve that my Lady Elizabeth's Grace should find herself indisposed. Youth, health and summer should travel hand in hand.'

It was too much for the Lady Elizabeth's logic. 'On the contrary,' she whispered, 'the plague is rife in summer.'

'Plague?' Dr. Turner stopped dead in the middle of the room, petrifying into a black pear-shaped block. From over his head Mrs Ashley opened aghast eyes.

'Have you any swelling under the armpit?' asked Dr. Turner presently, quite forgetting the 'Grace.'

'Swellings all over me,' Elizabeth replied promptly.

One of Mrs Ashley's eyes shut quickly, in time to a slight shake of the head.

The invalid tossed feverishly, and turned her head away. 'Sometimes it's in my throat, sometimes under my jaw. My whole face has blown up like a swine-bladder for a football – it's gone down now,' she added hastily as she felt Dr. Turner's protuberant eyes revolving over her pointed profile, thin as the slip of the new moon. She varied the symptoms. 'I am hot as fire – it is the fever.'

'It is the sun,' grunted Dr. Turner, now advancing, but still rather cautiously; 'this room is transparent to it. More glass than brick!' He looked round disapprovingly on the new-fashioned shining room. 'No tapestries, bare walls, bare floor! These pale oak panels and straw matting reflect all the light. What's wrong with strewn rushes?'

'Lousy,' said the Lady Elizabeth.

'Then you pay for your skin with your eyes. All these new fantods will make the rising generation go blind before they are forty, blinded by the perpetual glare of the sun they are brought up in.'

She pointed at his horn-rimmed spectacles. 'Never tell me you are over forty,' she said archly. 'In what glare were *you* brought up?'

'In the murk of my father's tanning-shed at Newcastle in the ancient Kingdom of Northumberland,' he replied simply. 'But,' he added, 'he owned twenty-two roods of land.'

He leaned over the bed and felt her armpits and drew a sigh of relief; her pulse, which was certainly throbbing, and her head, which was certainly hot.

'No rich nor roasted meats,' he commanded Mrs Ashley; 'let Her Grace touch nothing but a sow pig boiled with cinnamon, celery, dates and raisins; a hedgehog stewed in red wine and rosewater; and jelly, coloured purple by Scorpion's Tail as the vulgar call Turnsole, that flower that turns toward the sun – but you, most learned Princess, would take the Greeks' word for it, Heliotrope. And take two calves' feet and a shoulder of veal for the jelly, boiled in a gallon of claret.'

'I vomit at the sight of any food,' said the invalid. 'My head is too hot.'

'All that hair had better be cut off,' he replied. 'Will Your Grace put out your tongue?'

Her Grace put it out with vehemence.

'Ah, I see Your Grace has been eating sweets. You should not take so many, or your teeth will go black and fall out in old age.'

'Who cares? – as long as I live to old age. Though it's a poor prospect you offer for it – blind, toothless.' Suddenly she flashed a smile that made him blink. A young wild animal snapping at his hands had turned into a charming princess.

'You must grow tired of sick people talking of their ailments. Tell me, have you been writing anything lately? Your *Herbal* and *Dictionary of Plants* has soothed my sickness.'

She turned to lay her hands on the book. It was not there. Mrs Ashley smiled maliciously as Dr. Turner went heavily back to the door and picked up a book that lay on the floor near it.

'It does not seem to have soothed you much,' he mumbled. 'Did Your Grace find a fault in the Latin?'

Elizabeth searched for an explanation and gave it up. She decided to burst out laughing.

'You were the Duke of Somerset's physician as well as mine,' she said. 'We must have taught you that patients have none. It is the doctor who should be called patient.'

'And the herberist and writer,' he burst out, 'and preacher and father of a family, all of which I am. I have fed full on patience and my children on hope, so long that they are very lean. I would they were fatter – and further off. For we are all penned up together for lack of a house. Dean Goodmin, the craftiest fox,' he eyed the girl on the bed, 'yes, or vixen either, that ever went on two feet, won't give up the Deanery to me and my poor childer. 'Tis that that brought me to London to complain to King Edward through Mr Secretary Cecil – but only to find your royal brother dead, poor lad, and Mr Cecil so busy signing letters patent with "Jana Regina" that he can attend to nothing of importance.'

No doubt now that it was a vixen in the bed. A low snarl came from the bared white teeth. 'So – o – *that's* what Mr Secretary Cecil is doing!'

But the murmurous voice rumbled on imperturbably, 'Yes, Queen Jane's new seal leaves him no time for sealing old friendships. I wish I had trained my little dog to leap at lower game than a bishop's square cap – he'll snatch one off at sight. But it should have been deans. That Dean of the Devil, Goodman, nay rather, Badman, is the cause that I cannot go to my book for the crying of childer in my chamber. Never bear childer, gracious Princess. They cry to you to provide their sustenance – and prevent your doing it.'

He shuffled over to the silver mugs of flowers. 'You have a fine tussie-mussie here, what is the newfangled name for it – a "posy"? a word of naught, a chambermaid of a word – no reason, nor rhyme neither in misnaming flowers as poesie. Aha, here are outlandish rarities – Damask roses, my old colleague Dr. Liniker brought you from Syria. But what's this gypsy gang doing from the heath outside?'

'The village children brought me wild flowers and wood strawberries when they heard of my sickness,' said Elizabeth with something of a smirk. 'They know my love for harebells. beautiful even when they fade and their blue turns white, Eke the eyes of the children murdered by Gilles de Rais, that foul sorcerer. Yet once he rode with de Gaulle to fight for Joan of Arc, and did not betray her as did others, her own countrymen. Civil war is the curse of France.' She slid him a sharp glance from under her tawny eyelashes but he was impervious. Obtuse? Or merely cautious? She tried once more, sighing piously. 'Pray heaven it will not be that of England yet again!'

But he was touching the thin flower stems, tossing their whispering bells. 'Yes, they are Your Grace's flowers – fine-drawn as hairs but wiry, upspringing when trodden. Your eyes at times have their blue. Here is one faded white indeed but with a line of blue rimming its edge, carrying beauty into death – as you will do, Princess, at whatever age you die, for your bones are delicate, yes, their shape will shine with noble understanding in a death-mask, even in a skull.'

'You pay a grisly compliment. You may soon prove it.'

'No, Lady, your sickness is not so grave.' (The old rascal must know her mortal danger was not from sickness!) And there was an odd glimmer behind his thick spectacles as he humbled on among the wild flowers, now twirling a dog-rose from the hedges. 'Impostor, you won your name falsely! I have proved you no cure for a mad dog's bite.'

'The mad dog has not yet bitten me. I have snatched my hand back from his jaws,' she added boldly.

But now he was looking at a small pansy. 'Here's a wanton, Love-in-Idleness, though some call it Johnny Jump-Up, which suits these upstart days of the new gentry.'

And he must know that Johnny Jump-Up was the nickname that the common people gave to John Dudley the lawyer's son who had jumped to Sir John, then Viscount Lisle, then Earl of

Warwick, and now Duke of Northumberland, Duke Dudley as he was always called. But his globed eyes did not turn in her direction. 'Aha, my gay fellow, Ragged Robin! Many a Johnny Jump-Up's son may become that, and so may you, my bold Cock Robin, if you ride too fast on your father's errands.'

An oath snapped out from the bed. 'Stop your teasing, you ancient villainy. Tell me what young Robin Dudley has done.'

'Ridden out from London at the head of three hundred horses, as fine a troop as you could see on a summer morning clattering over Tower Bridge, with my bold Cock Robin at their head, and the sun just coming up over the house-tops to glint on his scarlet waistcoat. Aye, I saw 'em all go past with these old eyes at four o'clock yesterday morning, and, thinks I, there's a gallant company of young men, all for one old maid! – For my bonny sweet Robin was riding to fetch back my Lady Mary a prisoner.'

'And has he?'

'Not yet.'

'Where is Mary?'

'Nobody knows.'

Had Mary been as astute as herself? Impossible, she decided, somewhat piqued. Mary must have had secret warning that their brother was already dead. It flashed on her that it must have been Mary's refusal to come to London that had forced Duke Dudley's hand; that he had had to come out in the open before he had intended; declare the King dead, and Jane as Queen.

'And with Jane as Queen,' she said, 'your bold Cock Robin will be no ragamuffin but an elder brother to King Guildford, God save the mark!'

'Not so,' said the doctor placidly. 'They had a to-do persuading little Lady Jane to be Queen,' ('Mighty modest of her!' came with a snort from the bed) – 'but when it came to her young bridegroom as King, she refused as flat as my foot. Who was Guildford Dudley to be King, says she, and he with not a drop of the blood-royal in him? She'd consent to his being made a Duke so as not to demean herself through her husband – but never King! Phew, what a family squabble! Both the old cats yowling their heads off, *his* mother and *her* mother, and the boy bursting with rage at being downed by a girl. Off he goes in his tantrums, he and his mother, to sulk in their own house, and if they think that will bring the bride to her senses, they're clean out, for she can't abide him. 'Tis said she's not yet gone to bed with him, for all her mother's thumps. Little Miss 'Seventeen come Sunday' – nay, she'll not be that for some months yet – has a good dollop of the Tudor blood in her!'

''Tis no news to me. Give me fresher.'

'Fresh as hot bread. For she was proclaimed Queen Jane – a newfangled name, but Joan is now held to be coarse and homely – yesterday at five in the afternoon, and walked in the procession to the Tower, clattering on cork-soled wedge shoes a foot high under her long robes, for she's so small no one could see her else – and the heralds cried "Queen Jane" to the crowds as I rode down Cheapside – I saw all their heads waving this way and that with the sun slanting on 'em like a field of waving corn, but, lord! they stayed as mum as that field – not a cheer raised among 'em, only the archers of the guard to shout "Long live Queen Jane!" Eh, lass, but her proud mother had to bear her train – think of that now!'

'Eh, lad, I'll swear it did more than all else to make Jane consent to be Queened!'

Dr. Turner stood abashed at his familiarity. 'I forget, I forget,' he murmured. 'I grow an old man now, and you be a sharp young thing, sharp as a needle. Don't be so sharp as you'll cut yourself. Your Grace has a hard row to hoe, whichever way it goes now, Queen Jane or Queen Mary.'

Jane the gentle, studious schoolgirl, Mary the modest, simple, kindly old maid, far more akin to each other than to herself; both so conscientious, so anxious to *do* right, so rigidly certain they *were* right, both were of the stuff to be martyrs – and to make them! A duel between those two quiet women would be to the death – and of many.

Aloud she said coolly, 'Do you put their chances as equal? But Johnny Jump-Up holds the Tower, manned and gunned; he still has an army from putting down the last rebellion; he has ships—'

'Aye, a score of 'em riding at anchor in the Thames, been there three weeks past now, all ready, they say, to sail for Barbary and the Spice Islands.'

'Spice Islands my nose! It smells gunpowder, not spices.'

'Sharp as a needle, I say. But Your Grace has left out one thing, the hearts of the people.'

'Are they for Mary and her Mass?'

'They are for fair dealing. They'll not have an innocent woman done out of her rights, and after all the long years she's been bullied and put upon. It's a shame, they say. As I rode here this morning there were copies of the Proclamation all new-printed, still wet and smelling of printers' ink, being stuck up at every cross-road and market square, saying the King's sisters were both bastards – if you'll excuse my saying so! – and that it was King Edward's will and testament that Jane should be Queen.'

'Edward's testament – but Dudley's will!'

'Not the people's. Now I must jog on my way back to Wells, and do you stay still. Do not go to London, it would not be healthy for you. I will write out some prescriptions for your worthy governess to make up in the still-room.'

There was a sharp rustle from the window-curtain as Mrs Ashley's alert and wary back swung round from her pretended scrutiny of the garden.

'Some draughts of rhubarb and water-lily roots to cool the blood, and of acanthus leaves whose subtle parts dry up the moisture of a cold brain and cut ill humours, dispersing them to their appointed places. And let Your Grace,' his voice dropped an octave, 'take the advice of the Latins, *A fabis abstineto*.'

'Abstain from beans – why beans?'

'"Bean-belly Leicestershire" they say, and your cousin Jane is a Leicestershire lass, the more's the pity, for her. You have only to hold up a Leicestershire man by the collar to hear the beans rattle in his belly.'

'Have you tried it with my Lady Jane?'

'Tut, child – and Your Grace a scholar! Have you forgot that the ancients gave their vote by casting in a bean? So that to tell us to abstain from beans is not merely to say they are windy and discompose the tranquillity of men's minds by their flatuous evaporation. Nay, it gives a graver warning: "Do not meddle with affairs of state".'

'That's special pleading. Pythagoras said he might have had calmer sleeps had he totally abstained from beans.'

'That is to say, from affairs of state. So do you sleep as calmly as you can, fair Princess?'

The fear came back into her eyes. 'With Dudley coiled like a snake about to strike?'

'Then take the sour herb of grace, the strong and bitter rue—'

'Rue? Ugh!'

'—for when,' said he, impressively, looking down on the slender tawny head and pointed face, 'that swift creature of enchantment, the weasel or Dandy Dog, is to fight the serpent, she arms herself by eating rue against his might.'

'Have you proved that too?'

'No, Lady – but *you* may do so.'

He took his leave, ducking his way backwards to the door in a succession of clumsy bows, the last of them towards the window.

'See to it, good Mrs Ashley, that Her Grace takes full doses of all I prescribe, for I know well her habit of obedience to you.'

Then finally out he flumped and 'good Mrs Ashley' swung forward in a passionate crackle of skirts. 'What a clown, what a clod! "Bean-bellies" – is it possible! And he as good as called Your Grace a weasel!'

Elizabeth flung herself back on the pillows, laughing uncontrollably as a schoolgirl and mimicking the bell-like whimper of young weasels in chase. 'How do I know they sound like that? How do you know I am not one? Watch me at night and you'll see me slip out to hunt the hare in the dark with a Chime of Dandy Dogs!'

Ashley crossed herself inadvertently. They said Nan Bullen had been a witch – was her child one too? She recovered herself with an uneasy giggle and a reminder of the other parent. 'Fie on your royal father's daughter! You should scorn to belong to less than a Pride of Lions.'

'Oh, the cub can roar too.'

'*That* she can!' muttered Ashley, adding hastily, 'Is that old man to be trusted?'

'Is any man? There's my very good friend Mr Cecil busy writing "Jana Regina"!' She laughed again with, to Ashley, a maddening insouciance. 'I liked his training his dog to fly at bishops' caps.'

'Yet he gets ordained so as to get a Deanery, the old hypocrite!'

'I think I have seldom met an honester man.'

Mrs Ashley pursed up her lips as if to prevent herself bursting with exasperation.

'At the least it shows what King Edward's tutor, Sir John Cheke, has always said, that the fellow's no gentleman.'

'Cheke should know. His mother kept a small wine-shop in a back street in Cambridge.'

Cat Ashley exploded out of the room, to inform the steward, Mr Parry, that when it came to a man, however elderly, ill-favoured or ill-bred, the Lady Elizabeth—

CHAPTER THREE

'There's a man coming to the Lady Elizabeth now,' said Mr Parry, wheeling a heavy eye towards the little turret window. 'I think it's her former tutor, Mr Ascham.'

'*He* back again! I thought he was in Germany. How these ambassadors' secretaries do gad about!'

'His master probably had an early secret wind of the crisis here and came hurrying home. Ambassadors, even abroad, know most of the game.'

'And what's Mr Ascham's? He'd cooled off the Lady Elizabeth, left in a hurry – *and* a huff-and was all for the Lady Jane. So what's he doing here unless to crow over the success of his precious little bookworm in snatching the Crown from her?'

'From her elder sister, the Lady Mary,' he corrected, patting his belly.

'A Papist! The people will never have that now. And she was bastardised after her mother's divorce.'

'So was the Lady Elizabeth after *her* mother's beheading.'

'Be hanged to your logic. The bastardy is only the thinnest excuse for Duke Dudley to seize the Crown for himself, in the person of that undersized brat with the freckled nose. There go the church bells now again for her in the distance. Pray heaven Her Grace does not hear them on t'other side of the house or I shall get another wigging.'

'Mr Ascham is dismounting in the courtyard,' said Mr Pray over his shoulder. 'A pretty nag!'

'I'll never let him in on her. It's not safe.'

'Best find out what Her Grace wishes first. "When it comes to a man," however faithless in transferring his devotion to another, the Lady Elizabeth—'

'Oh, to hell with you!' said Mrs Ashley.

She ran out of the room to the top of the great staircase and stood listening to voices in the hall below. Dr. Turner, going out, was speaking with Mr Aschim coming in.

'It's too late,' she hissed to Mr Parry, who had followed softly at his discretion; 'that old busybody has told him she may receive a visitor. Look, for the love of heaven, at Master Schoolmaster's short cloak in the Spanish fashion! He's put your new sleeveless coat clean out of date. And one of those little Austrian caps like an oyster patty at the side of his pate, glued to it, I'll swear, or it would never stay on. How fast they climb, these rising young men!'

Through all her gibes she was busy adjusting her own dress and hair in a wall mirror of polished steel, the size of a sixpence she complained, as she smacked her cheeks and sucked in her lips to redden them, then shot them out again in a succession of sharp comments like peas from a pea-shooter. 'What's *he* think of the whole queer business I'd like to know, and I will know, too, in the shake of a posset cup. Send for some of that cooled Tokay, Parry, from the lower cellar that the Lord Admiral laid down, God rest his soul! That will loosen his tongue as to which of the three young women – one not so young, and one so young she's scarce a woman – is most likely to sit on the throne of England. And after all King

Harry's efforts to get a male heir, and no one can say he didn't do his best, with six wives, two divorced and two beheaded! Yet after all there's got to be a woman on the throne, is it possible!'

'It is not possible,' pronounced Mr Parry as though from the seat of judgment; 'all the best legal authorities are agreed that it will be declared against the laws of England to have a woman sovereign.'

But Mrs Ashley had not waited to hear the opinion of the best legal authorities. With a pleasant excitement flushing her already smarting cheeks she was pacing in impressively stately fashion down the great staircase into the hall to play the gracious hostess on Her Grace's behalf and the welcoming old friend on her own.

The bells had swung through the lime-scented air as Roger Ascham rode up the long avenue.

> *'Long live Queen Jane,*
> *Long may she reign.'*

That was what they sang to him as he thought of her and of the Lady Elizabeth, but, like nearly everybody else at the moment, not of the Lady Mary.

Two crowded years he had spent in Germany, in Spain, in Italy, learning to be a courtier and a diplomat and a statesman, and here he was embarking on the most important test of his new career; he must cross swords in diplomacy with the Lady Elizabeth, with whom as her tutor he had crossed swords so often, and then once too often.

What had happened? He had never been sure. You never

could be sure with Elizabeth. *Which* Elizabeth?

A lively precocious child had stood beside him at the archery butts and shown off the gay colours of her long shooting-gloves while she bent her supple body as he had taught her to the bow; had laughed, yes, and flirted with him across the schoolroom table. Would he find her now at Hatfield? – or the ghostly stranger who had taken her place after the Admiral's execution and her long illness – a stranger who sat white and tense in a nunlike gown, her eyes only for her book?

Yet even then there had still been a hint of something fiery and provocative, dangerous and baffling, of the wild charm that her mother had swayed over men, to her own destruction. Elizabeth had surely inherited that, together with the vein of poetry from her mother's brother, George Lord Rochford, who had been beheaded for his supposed incest with Nan Bullen. Ascham remembered the lines of broken verse like a torn-off cry of pain that he had found among a mass of papers Elizabeth had destroyed in some frantic fit of nerves or temper:

> '*I am and am not, freeze and yet I burn,*
> *Since from myself my other self I turn;.*
> *My care is like my shadow in the sun,*
> *Follows me flying – flies when I pursue it;*
> *Stands and lives by me, does what I have done.*'

Yes, she had become her own shadow. But she would not stay so; the fire still burned beneath the frozen face, within her ash-grey shroud.

As he had found to his cost when it blazed out against him for no apparent reason.

The Lady Jane would never have so treated her tutor, Mr Aylmer. 'Oh happy Aylmer to have such a scholar – so divine a maid – best adorned virgin!' So he had written to Aylmer, the very words he had once used for his own happiness in teaching Elizabeth – 'but to *you* I can repeat them with more truth.'

All through this long hot ride from London, when he ought to have been rehearsing his approaching interview with Elizabeth, he had found himself remembering instead that letter he had written to Aylmer about Jane. He had written it in the midst of the hotbed of international politics at the Council of Trent, the air seething with the tumult in Africa; with the attempts to organise all Europe into a concerted front against the invading onrush of the heathen Turk, already far advanced into the Christian States; with the expected march of the German Emperor into Austria, which Ascham himself was to attend. Yet in the thick of it all, and the welter of his secretarial duties, and his eager efforts to make himself as good a statesman and courtier as he was a scholar and sportsman, he had sat down late one night and written till two in the morning all about the last visit he had paid to little Lady Jane just before leaving England.

He had ridden to her father's new mansion at Bradgate, the finest house in Leicestershire, and in the great park he had met her parents, and a chattering laughing crowd of young guests, and all the huntsmen glittering in their harness and green livery, out hunting in the early autumn sunshine.

But not the daughter of the house. He had found her quite alone in her study, a girl who looked like a small child, curled up in her chair with her head bent over a volume of Plato in Greek, 'with as much delight,' he wrote to Aylmer, 'as gentlemen read the merry tales of Boccaccio.'

He asked Jane why she was not out amusing herself with all the rest of the household at their sport. She replied, 'Alas, good folks, they have never felt what true pleasure means. All their sport is but a shadow to that pleasure I find in Plato.'

And her great grey eyes shone as she raised them to his. It was too much for Roger Ascham. 'You are so young, so lovely,' he blurted out, 'how can you prefer to sit all alone and read the *Phaedon* – even when your tutor is absent?'

The grey eyes clouded over, but they looked at him with the same clear candour of spirit that prevented her first answer from sounding pretentious, or her second harsh. 'I will tell you,' came after a pause in low, measured tones; 'the reason is that my parents are so sharp and severe to me that whether I speak, keep silent, sit, stand, go, eat, drink, be merry or sad, be sewing, playing, dancing or anything else, I must do it as perfectly as God made the earth – or else I am so sharply taunted, so cruelly threatened, yes, *persecuted* with pinches, nips and bobs that I think myself in hell while with them.'

His furious exclamation cut her short. It looked as though he, not she, would burst into tears. But without any alteration in her deliberate tone she presented the reverse side. 'One of the greatest benefits God ever gave me is that He sent me, with such parents, so gentle a schoolmaster as Mr Aylmer, who teaches me so pleasantly that I think all the time of nothing while I am with him. And when I am called from him I weep, because, whatever else I do than learning is full of great trouble and fear to me.'

The sad little monotone ceased on that note of prophecy – as it now struck him, now when the Crown that was being forced on her might well prove 'full of great trouble and fear' to this child who had become a scholar before she had learned to be a woman.

The contrast with her cousin Elizabeth struck him as strongly. He admired Elizabeth's brilliant wits, but he worshipped Jane's disinterested love of scholarship for its own sake. It had once been his own ideal and when with her he felt guilty at having forsaken it in his pursuit of the full and complete life.

But Elizabeth could never hold it even as an ideal. She had worked as a schoolgirl with the fiery untiring concentration of a grown man, but always, he was certain, for an ulterior motive: to fit herself for the chance she might one day get to be Queen of England.

Jane, now Queen, had never wanted it. Her love for learning was as pure as he, sometimes, wished his own could be.

Elizabeth teased, intrigued, defied, fascinated him.

But Jane was his guiding star, an image that he did not even think of connecting with the grave beauty of her oval face and steadfast eyes.

He envied Aylmer, but he was not jealous of him.

And so he wrote to Aylmer what was really a love-letter to Jane, describing that last delicious meeting with her in the cool shadowed study where the green light came filtered through the great trees outside, and the silence was very still after the blare of horns and shouts of the huntsmen in the park; he had proffered to him his 'entreaty that the Lady Jane may write to me, in Greek, which she has already promised to do'; his prayer that she and Aylmer and himself should 'keep this mode of life among us. How freely, how sweetly, how philosophically then should we live, enjoying all these things which Cicero at the conclusion of the Third book, *De Finibus*, describes as the only rational mode of life.'

> '*You and I and Amyas,*
> *Amyas and you and I,*'

the bells were now chiming in his head to that old song by William Cornish of the perfect trio,

> '*You, and I and Amyas,*
> *Amyas and you and I,*
> *To the greenwood must we go, alas,*
> *You and I, my life, and Amyas.*'

(Why 'alas'? Why, to rhyme with Amyas!)

But the only rational mode of life could not be the only mode for him. If only he could live six lives at the same moment! He had them all in his capacity; but he had not the time. One life was not enough. It had not been enough to make himself the finest Greek scholar in England, to set all the Cambridge students acting the new glories of Greek drama, and with brilliant modern stage effects, instead of gabbling their tedious old-fashioned Latin plays; not enough to shape the new beauties of English prose into an instrument as fine for scholarship as it was vigorous and flexible for common life, for his books on sport, hunting, archery, even the cock-pit. Not enough even to mould the mind of the young Princess Elizabeth, that cynically practical, strangely poetic mind, incarnating in itself the daring spirit of the New Learning that had flamed up all through Europe, springing phoenix-like from the ashes of the new-found ancient classic lore; not enough to invent new methods of education that should make learning a delight to her.

No; one life was not enough. He had wanted, not the study, but the world for his province.

Now, thinking of Jane in the deep shadow of this avenue where he rode so far below the still green branches that he seemed to be riding at the bottom of the sea, he had dropped out of the world, out of time. He forgot his feverish demands on it. He wished instead that he were single-minded, bent only on one pursuit noble enough to fill a man's whole life.

What then was he doing here, riding towards the advancement he had hoped to win?

CHAPTER FOUR

He stood in the hall and Mrs Ashley swept down the stairs towards him, hands outstretched, a welcoming smile pinned on her face, her inquisitive nose all ready to probe his secrets, a host of flattering exclamations and inquiries fluttering from her.

Once he had flattered her and given her presents, pulling strings to help him become the Princess Elizabeth's tutor. Now he must give her another present. He gave it. He staved off her questions. He would not drink the heavy sweet Tokay.

There was nothing for it but for her to lead him off with many protestations of Her Grace being too ill to see any ordinary visitor, but that she knew she would never forgo the pleasure of meeting her former tutor, if she were awake. Only let him tread softly as he approached her room, for Her Grace was very drowsy, had had no rest at all these last few nights, and had signified her intention of going to sleep the instant the doctor left.

Roger Ascham followed her out of the sunlight from the open doorway of the great hall. The sound of bells in the outer air became muffled, then drowned.

In the cool corridor, secluded from the sultry afternoon outside, he heard music dropping in small faint notes like the drops of water from a fountain splashing into the basin below. The instrument was modern, either the virginals or clavichord such as he played himself and had taught his pupils to play. But the tune was ancient, barbarically wild and simple, in a mode long since neglected by the musicians. He thought he had heard it before, he tried to think where and when, and stood still to listen while Mrs Ashley harried on, her steps now clacking noisily with, he fancied, a deliberately warning note, and as she advanced the music swung abruptly into another tune, the popular air of 'My Lady Greensleeves.' It stopped as Mrs Ashley opened a door and went through, shutting it behind her. Presently she returned and admitted him to the Lady Elizabeth's bedroom. A lady-in-waiting was sitting at the end of the room and went out through a door at the end as he entered. Mrs Ashley took her place.

The Lady Elizabeth was leaning back on the pillows with a green brocade bedgown thrown somewhat carelessly, he thought, across her shoulders. True, the day was very hot. But if the glimpse he got of the young rounded breasts under her thin shift was inviting, the glance she gave him was cold as steel.

He flicked some invisible dust off his fine new cloak, hoping she would notice its impeccable cut; she had always liked him to be well dressed and not like a musty pedagogue, she used to say, wrinkling her nose. He flattered himself he was now a long way from the pedagogue as he flung back his head after his courtly bow and squared his broad shoulders that even his frequent practice in archery could not entirely cure of the literary stoop he had acquired from years of study. He felt uneasily that she was summing it all up; he did not guess her answer to the sum – that his mild brown eyes were just the same as she had known them, eager, ingenuous, the eyes of a man who had dreamed of life through books, and wanted to wake up.

He apologised for intruding on her illness, made polite enquiries and, a trifle breathlessly, as though to gain time, he congratulated her on having kept up her music – he hoped she still composed her own songs, words and tunes, as every performer should – he was glad, anyway, she was not too ill to play.

'That was my woman playing,' she said curtly.

Was it? He had remembered by now the tune he had first heard as he came down the corridor, a lament for some savage mountain chieftain killed centuries ago, which King Henry's old Welsh harper had sometimes played at Court; and he remembered, too, the Princess Elizabeth as a little girl listening to it, her small face pale and fierce in its intentness. He did not believe it was her woman who had played that tune.

'Cat,' said she, 'you can follow Mag into the next room.'

Mrs Ashley stared. It was nothing for a man to visit a princess in bed; balls and receptions had been held before now in state bedrooms with the hostess in bed; but for him to be left alone with her there, that was quite another matter!

'Cat!' repeated her mistress.

She went.

'Why have you come?'

The question was shot at him so suddenly that he found all the careful answers he had thought out for it evading him.

'I come from Court—' he began.

'*Whose* Court? My sister's or my cousin's?'

So there it was. He had got to declare himself at the first instant, on whose side he stood. He struggled for a moment's respite.

'I went straight to London, naturally, with my master on his return to this country. I have seen the little Queen.' The sheet jerked from a kick. 'Believe me, Madam, she has no love for the title. She has sobbed and prayed them not to force the Crown on her – she is but a child of sixteen. She could not withstand her parents.'

'She could when she chose. They could force her to wear the Crown, but not to share it with her bridegroom. Queen Jane, oh yes! But King Guildford, oh no!

> '*When I am queen, diddle diddle,*
> *You shan't be king!*'

So she sang on a high note, and ended in a peal of wild laughter.

There it was again, that sudden levity, that pale flash of the eyes, that baffling mockery that had disconcerted him when she was his pupil. Girlish hysteria he had thought it, and that she would grow out of it, but there it was again after two years' absence from her, and he badly disconcerted in his uncertainty as to what the laughter might hide, or bode. She was what the song sang, 'a lady bright,' but 'strangeness that lady hight.'

He had to pluck up all his courage to say what he had resolved. 'Your Grace, the – your cousin – is utterly ignorant of the world. She has lived her whole short life in the schoolroom, intent only on her Greek and Hebrew studies. She has been persuaded by all those elders whom she has been brought up to believe so much wiser than herself, that this is the only way to save the country from the horrors of another civil war, worse even than the Wars of the Roses. You, too, love this country. You saw it in danger of invasion as a child on board your royal father's flagship, *The Great Harry*, you remember. Even then you swore no foreigners should bring havoc to our shores. But worse may come from within. Will you not help to avoid the horror of internal strife-even at the cost of laying aside your ambitions?'

'And so furthering your own! I take it you have been sent by Duke Dudley to exercise your new trade of diplomacy on me. Well, what's your message from him?'

Not much chance to exercise diplomacy after that! And he had prepared such persuasive arguments – he might have known he'd never get the chance to use them. Gulping them back, he blurted out:

'To offer you what you will, riches beyond any man's in England, if you will resign your claim on the throne, and consent to that of your cousin.'

Well, he had said it. He looked at her and saw her as a white flame of wrath, tipped with the red fire of her hair.

But she did not speak. The silence hung over the room. He would have welcomed now any outburst of mocking laughter, even of rage. Once she had thrown a ruler at his head. Would she do that now? He wished she would, that she would do anything rather than lie and look at him with eyes that seemed to be turning to glass, in a face and body already stone.

Then it came on him what the moment must mean to her. Not only her chance of the throne, but her life or death might hang on her answer. She must speak, but utterly in the dark. She could know no more than he what had happened to her sister Mary, who might well by now have been taken prisoner by young Robert Dudley. And if Elizabeth refused Duke

Dudley's offer, she too was certain to be imprisoned and most probably beheaded. Yet if she accepted it, she would declare herself his open partisan against Mary, who might even now be fighting Dudley's army – and winning.

There was the horrid silence of suspense, not only in this room, but in all the quivering sunlit air outside it, all through England.

At last he heard her voice, and with a shock of surprise, for it was low and indifferent, almost nonchalant. 'Why should they try to make any agreement with *me*? My elder sister is the only one concerned. As long as she is alive I have no claim whatever on the throne.'

She had done it again! She had given the only answer that could safeguard her from either side. So had she answered her jailors through weeks of torturing questioning when she was an utterly friendless girl of fifteen, fighting for her honour, her life, and the life of the man she had loved. He felt an absurd impulse to cheer.

But it would never do to take back such an answer to Duke Dudley. He replied judicially, 'The people of England will never accept the Lady Mary as Queen, and with her the old foreign tyranny of the Pope and the priests. They have done with all that, they are Protestant now to the core.'

'You speak very certainly of England after being out of it for two years, Mr Ascham. Did you ever know much of it beyond London and Cambridge, the centres of advanced foreign ideas? But the English do not care for ideas.'

He drew himself up, and spoke stiffly. 'I may not know much of England, Madam, but I know something since I last saw Your Grace of what is happening in Europe.' (Did he sound offended, or, worse, like a pompous schoolmaster? He tried a lighter, though still impressive note.) 'It is even betting there as to whether this country will become the satellite of France or of Spain, both of which are eager to enslave her under the Papal yoke on ideas. The English may not care about ideas – but they care very much about the yoke. We may yet have another invading armada from France or Spain, sailing against these shores. I have come from the Council of Trent – it was to have been a league of nations to settle all questions of religion and policy in friendly discussion between Papists and Protestants – but I heard more of repressive counter-measures against the Protestants than of fair dealing with them. And now it has broken up and fled helter-skelter at the fresh outbreak of war in Germany. If this country is not prepared—'

He broke off, hardly able to believe his ears. The incurable levity of this wild creature trapped in a satin bed (he could hardly think of her as a woman) had broken out again – she was whistling a tune like a schoolboy. And then sang, rolling out the words in a solemn chant as she made them up:

> *'The Council of Trent*
> *It came and it went.*
> *No one knows what they meant*
> *At the Council of Trent.*

Only Mr Ascham, who knows everything. But—

> *All his money was spent*
> *At the Council of Trent*
> *And he borrowed more than be lent*
> *At the Council of Trent!'*

'How the devil did you know that?' he burst out, knocked completely off his guard and his manners. She fell back on the pillow in helpless laughter. He ought to be thankful, but he longed to shake her.

'Was it the dice or the birds?' she demanded. 'Confess how much. Come, I've helped my good tutor out of my pocket-money before now, when *his* good tutor only sent him long lectures that play and cock-fighting would be his ruin. Let Cheke look down his handsome nose at your follies! As purely Greek a nose as Alcibiades, so befitting the Greek Reader at Cambridge! But he'd never understand as you do, Alcibiades Ascham, how Greek it is to love sport and play as well as learning. So how much?'

'About £50 still unpaid,' he said. 'It was the dice, soulless little monsters. I could no more be mistaken over a cock than over a fellow at the long bow. But Your Grace mustn't think of it,' he added confusedly.

'I'm not thinking of it. Parry will see to it.'

'Parry back again!' he exclaimed, then tried to cover his astonishment by expressing his gratitude. But beneath it his thoughts would go racing on in question – and suspicion. Parry had betrayed to her enemies the confidences of her governess, Mrs Ashley, concerning the familiarities between the Princess and the Admiral, Thomas Seymour.

Why then was Parry back in his former position as steward in her household? Was it to show that she disregarded all the scandal he had aided, as beneath her notice? Or was it because there was further, darker scandal that she feared he might divulge if he were not kept favoured and propitiated?

What *was* the truth about her; which the real Elizabeth? This was not the one – or two or three – that he had known.

Even her hair was different from when he had last seen it, then strained back, brushed as smoothly as a tight-fitting satin cap down on either side of her strained face. He could not believe it had been of the same texture as the fiery cloud of gossamer that now tossed loose about her head. The very bee that had been crawling up and down the silver mirror seemed to share his doubts as to its nature, and investigating became entangled in its shining net, buzzing furiously. He dashed to the rescue, praying heaven she would not shriek and so bring her women running. What woman would *not* shriek with a bee caught in her hair? But she did not. She lay quite still and smiled up at him as he disentangled the insect.

Once he had thought her smile that of a pagan goddess carved centuries ago by some man who had never heard of Christ. He thought so now. He still bent over her head; he felt dizzy, a little drunk. What would happen if he kissed her?

The bee stung him and he swore. The pagan goddess hooted.

'Let that teach you to be a knight-errant rescuing distressed damsels!' she said ungratefully. 'But you will be revenged – it's the bee who will die of it.'

He could believe anything of her, say anything to her. Was it true that Duke Dudley's eldest son wanted to divorce his wife to marry her, and take the throne together? That, he had heard out in Austria, had been the first plan, and the Duke had proposed it, but on her refusal had hastily married a younger son, Guildford, to the Lady Jane Grey and substituted her as Queen. He asked her if the first plan had been true.

'Young Jack Dudley? What if he did? That's never the one I'd choose.'

'You'd fancy jolly Cock Robin rather, like all the other women?'

'*What* women?' she demanded quickly.

'His marriage to Amy Robsart hasn't stopped them,' he answered evasively.

'That melancholy insipid semi-invalid! How can he look at her!'

'He's looking for another at the moment, the Lady Mary.'

'He'll be luckier if he fails to find her,' said Elizabeth grimly.

The dazzling moment of intimacy had slipped. He wondered what had possessed him. Yet the next instant she invited it again by her flippant questions of that nest of foreign refugees, with the dreadful names, scholars who had had to flee from Germany because of their opinions, and were harboured by Jane in her parents' home – 'Messrs. Shturmius,' she stuttered, 'and Bull – Ball – no, Bollinger – it makes one bubble at the mouth to say it. Even the English ones are called Skinner or Wallack. What a Lost Tribe they look in their moth-eaten black gowns and mouldy beards like last year's nests!'

'Yet we owe them a debt,' he reminded her. 'If Italy brought us the New Learning, Germany has brought the New Religion. The German mind may be ponderous, but that it is profound—'

'Profound as a bog. Dull as a fog. And I suppose we'll have a profoundly guttural-speaking German for chief minister, since Mr Bollinger has dedicated his new work on "Christian Perfection" to Jane and her father, and she's returned the compliment with thanks for such 'little books of pure and unsophisticated religion.'

'Did she show you that?' he asked with a faint uneasiness, he did not know why.

'*And* her filial excuses for her father, who "as far as his weighty engagements permit is diligently occupied in its perusal." "My most noble father would have written to you had he not been summoned by most weighty business." Well, hunting and gaming are very weighty!'

Her reckless joking flattered Ascham, it showed her trust in him as an old friend and implied the contrast between him and these fusty scholars; but it made him wince for poor little Lady Jane, too innocent to realise how odd her taste in men must seem to this mocking girl three years her senior. He tried to show her Jane as he had seen her in that last interview that had so absorbed his mind on the ride here, to tell her how she had answered him, as Plato himself might have done, on earthly pastimes as the mere shadows of heavenly pleasures.

'I'm sure my cousin's answers to you were platonic,' Elizabeth observed drily.

He tried to engage her sympathy with Jane for her cruel treatment by her parents, 'things which she would not name for the honour she bears them.'

'Much honour it does 'em to hint at things too dreadful to name! Is *that* "Christian Perfection"? My cousin's such a scholar that she seems a saint, but scratch that saint and you'll catch a Tartar – or a Tudor! Some would say it's the same!'

He inwardly agreed – for some Tudors.

And Jane's straight little nose was prettier than Elizabeth's – you could see what an authoritative beak *hers* would be in old age. He wished he could tell her so. He wished she could have seen that letter of his to Aylmer comparing Jane so favourably with her.

A sudden awful notion struck him – *had* she seen it?

He had written it ostensibly to Aylmer but really to Jane; and Jane seemed to like showing her correspondence – this then was the reason for that uneasy quiver he had felt just now when Elizabeth had quoted from it. If, as was more than likely, the two girls had ever had a tiff, that letter of his would have provided Jane with some trenchant weapons in the complaints he had hinted against Elizabeth after a furious quarrel with 'his most illustrious pupil,' complaints 'which prudence makes it necessary I should conceal even to myself. I have no fault to find with the Lady Elizabeth, whom I have always found the best of ladies.' (Poor praise compared with that of the 'divine maid,' etc.!) 'But if ever I shall have the happiness to meet my friend Aylmer again, then I shall repose in his bosom my sorrows abundantly.'

Were those words standing out as sharply in her mind now as they were in his? He looked at her and she looked back at him, smiling, inscrutable – the pagan goddess? Say rather an imp of Satan! A wickedly teasing magic was at work; under its dancing light all his ingenuous enthusiasm for Jane, and Jane's for her tutor, stood revealed as calf-love. It was suddenly plain to him that he was in love with the Queen, and the Queen with Mr Aylmer, and that there was not the smallest chance of the three of them 'keeping this mode of life among them.' however 'freely, sweetly and philosophically' they wrote about it.

> 'You and I and Amyas,
> Amyas and you and I,'
> Not 'to the greenwood,' but 'to London
> must we go, alas,
> You and I, my life, and Amyas.'

No the only rational mode of life did not seem in the least rational now.

And it dawned on him that it had not been the height of worldly wisdom to praise one rival lady to another.

Suddenly he confessed his defeat with a shy, charming smile. 'I thought I was a very clever fellow, but learning is not wisdom. Your Grace has had a dunce for her tutor.' But he had to make a last attempt to assert himself as a man of the world.

'I dare say I had my head a trifle turned with all my business at the Emperor's Court,' he added airily. 'Within only three days I had to write letters to forty-seven different princes, and the meanest of them a cardinal!'

'You have an exquisite discrimination as a scholar,' she said softly. 'Not forty-seven princes could rob you of it.'

She, so much younger than he, seemed older than the Serpent. And he was blushing like a schoolboy, chaffed for showing off. She took pity on him and said quickly, 'What o'clock is it?'

He stared at the elaborate structure of wrought-gold and enamel made to show the phases of the moon and ebb and flow of the tides as well as the time, but did none of these things.

'The clock is stopped.'

'True. I could not bear to hear time's footsteps hurrying past.'

'You will have all time!' he exclaimed, suddenly seeing her as immortal.

'Nevertheless I want an hour now to rest.'

He took his leave, and, at the door, remembered.

'And – Duke Dudley?'

'Say to him what I say to you too, Roger Ascham. Abstain from beans.'

CHAPTER FIVE

'How travel improves a man! I'd never have thought it could do so much for young Master Schoolmaster whom I'd always thought a conceited head-in-air. But now—'

'What's he given you this time, Cat? Another silver pen?'

'Nothing, a mere toy from Venice such as the ladies there carry against the sun.' Mrs Ashley flirted a painted fan. Elizabeth grabbed it.

'That's meant for me. He'd too much diplomacy to give it outright. All the same, I'd say old Dr. Dodderer's got a sounder grasp of affairs here than the cleverest scholar in England. He's got his finger where a doctor's should be – on the pulse of the people.'

'The people, faugh! What power have they?'

'£50?' said Mr Parry, rolling the white of his eye up at the former tutor. '£50 is a tall order!'

'It's Her Grace's order.'

'Ah, but she doesn't know the state of her coffers.'

'Why not?' (She must have changed if she did not. Ascham had seen the household books signed by her at the foot of every page.)

'It's not a lady's concern. I am here to save her such irksome toils.'

'Devil doubt you!' muttered Ascham. They had never got on well. He submitted himself to the inevitable. 'Well, if you rake off £5 for your trouble—'

'Twenty,' said Mr Parry.

'Then I shall tell Her Grace you demanded a score.'

'And I that you demanded a hundred.'

Mr Ascham gritted his teeth, then smiled.

'Come, Parry, remember old times and take a dozen – a baker's dozen,' he added, as the jellied eye coldly crystallised.

'Thirteen,' said Mr Parry, 'is an unlucky number.'

'Make it fifteen then. Why, with twenty off I only get thirty.'

'Thirty pounds is thirty pounds,' said Mr Parry unanswerably.

And with thirty pounds in his purse Mr Ascham rode back to London and the palace-fortress-prison of the Tower. The setting sun had turned the Thames to copper as he clattered through the gateway.

In the royal apartments of the Tower, Duke Dudley sat in his state room with three of his fine sons; they turned at Ascham's entry with a cry of 'Robin!' 'What news?' then muttered in disappointment that it was 'only the tutor.' But the Duke did not stir; nor did he raise an eyebrow at Elizabeth's message, but swore softly, melodiously, as though repeating a sonnet.

He did not look like a desperate adventurer; his slender form and delicate eyebrows, arched as in amused surprise, made him seem much younger than his age. And he still affected the dress of a young dandy in a subdued and exquisite taste – no jewels, not even a ring on his fine hands, and clothes of dark and subtly contrasting colours, cut with startling severity of line, in conformity with his dislike of any seams. Stuffs had to be specially woven for him so as to avoid the crude necessity of a seam, which set his teeth on edge, so he said, to the affectionate amusement of his beautiful wife and the seven children out of thirteen who had managed to keep alive, a fairly high rate of survival.

The three who now hung about the room, Jack, Ambrose and Guildford, were tall stalwart young men, the youngest of them, Guildford, not yet eighteen, his round rosy face still wearing a look of sulky astonishment at his bride's failure to appreciate him. To make up for it he sat at a table in the window, to catch the light that was already dim within these massive walls, and busied himself with scribbling a rough draft of a dispatch recalling 'his' English Minister to the Netherlands. That would show them abroad, at any rate, that he was really King. His elder brothers stood in the other window-seat chattering in low tones with an occasional burst of excited laughter which made Guildford's ears burn red in the sunset light lest they should be laughing at him.

Jack the eldest whistled admiringly when Ascham gave Elizabeth's perfectly non-committal answer. 'There's the lass! You'll never catch *her* out! "My elder sister is the only one concerned" indeed! As if Mary counted for anything! Robin should be bringing her in tow and a flood of tears by now. Can't think what's delaying him.'

'Aye, Bess is the one we have to reckon with, sir, mark my words,' Ambrose growled importantly. 'We'll have to send a body of horse for her too and fetch her in here by force.'

'Her Grace is far too ill to be moved,' said Ascham hastily. 'I had a word with her physician, Dr. Turner.'

Duke Dudley's fine eyes, brown, glossy and rather blank, like chestnuts, fixed themselves on the former tutor in a disconcerting stare.

'The girl's always ill – when it's convenient to her,' he remarked.

'My lord, she was dangerously ill for many months – the doctors despaired of her life after—' Ascham's voice faded out.

'After the death of her lover, the Lord High Admiral,' the Duke finished pleasantly. 'Well, I've no doubt Tom Seymour made many women ill for months – nine to be exact. But as that was four years ago, she's had time to recover.'

Ascham flushed. Nor did Jack Dudley look pleased. To revive a scandal that even her enemies had denied by public proclamation was a shabby way to wage war against a woman.

'It's women we have to fight now, and with their weapons,' said his father, guessing the young man's thought with the uncanny sympathy that made his family adore him. He rubbed his hand back over his head, rumpling the smooth hair with a comically rueful gesture. 'D'you think after all my years of soldiering, fighting off the French from our shores, scarifying the Scots on the Border, that I want to march against a tiresome old maid? Not that Mary will show any fight; how could she? Who'd ever follow her? Who knows her or cares about her? She's lived in a backwater ever since childhood, and for my part I'd be only too glad to let her stay there.'

He was lolling back in his chair, turning his jewelled penholder over and over on the table with a faint metallic click every time it met the polished wood. So he would loll when rattling the dice for the highest stakes, in affectation of perfect indifference as to the result of his throw. He chose his words with precision, as if considering a subject that was of no personal importance to himself. 'She's never had any requirements or capabilities beyond those of any simple country squire's or parson's wife. Let her have her Mass in the privacy of her household, give her pocket-money to buy gaudy clothes for her scraggy little body, presents for her women friends and jellies and baby-clothes for the country women round her, and she'd make no trouble on her own account.'

With a placid eye he watched the effect of this astonishing tolerance on his sons, and signed to Ascham to go. Ascham stole a look at them as he went. Were these gorgeous greedy young men in their lust for money and power really going to swallow such plausible self-deception?

Ambrose swallowed it whole. His round bullock eyes were glazed with astonished alarm. Beefier and stolider than his brothers, he could have no appreciation of such maunderings, nor any suspicion that they might be put up for a cockshy.

'God's body!' he burst out, 'you'll never let her live, sir? Think of the danger to all of *us*! She'll agree fast enough to forgo any claim to the throne, no doubt of that – but think of others who'll make the claim for her and rise in her name, even if it's not with her consent. As long as the King's sisters are alive, our heads will sit loose on our shoulders.'

'No need to wag yours as if it's already coming off!' cried Guildford with a shrill hysterical crow of laughter, but chimed in on the same note: 'Think, sir, she may run to her precious cousin the Emperor and get him to come here and fight for her.'

'She'd never have the wits nor the guts,' said Jack. 'She's been trying to get aboard that ship for the Netherlands for years, and always bungled it. And the Emperor doesn't want her – objected long ago that if she ran away to him he'd have to pay for her keep!'

'But, God's body, *where* is she? She sets out for London in answer to our summons—'

'To her dear dead brother's summons,' his father corrected softly.

'Well, yes, then!' Guildford flushed, not caring to remember that ruse. 'Anyway, she sets out, gets as far as Hoddesdon, and then all we know is that she there met a passing stranger who appears to have been a travelling goldsmith – and after that she's disappeared off the face of the earth. Where? Why? What *can* have happened?'

'What must have happened,' said Duke Dudley, his deliberate voice quietening the excited lad, 'is that she got wind somehow that the King's dying message was a false lure, and fled. It's exasperating, for I've had to come out from ambush, send Robin to arrest her, declare the King to be dead and Jane as Queen – all prematurely before we've secured the Princesses.' He bit back the unpalatable admission that as long as he failed to secure them he had failed to make the chief move in the game.

But Guildford had got a taste of it. 'Mary may be on board ship to the Netherlands even now! Wherever she is, she's a danger.'

'Hardly that. Only a nuisance. And she's not aboard ship yet, and won't be. I'm setting a watch on all the ports along the East Coast. Either abroad or here in England, she must not escape.'

In the same even tones as before he explained his apparent *volte-face*. He had only wished to make it clear to them that he would, of course, have to put Mary away. It was only common sense. He bore her no ill will – 'no more than I bore any to her father King Harry for executing my father as soon as he came to the throne. My father, as a clever lawyer, was very useful in procuring money for the Crown by somewhat sharp practice, which made him unpopular – so the new young King, having benefited, put him out of the way. Purely a popularity measure, no ill-feeling on either King Harry's side or on mine. In fact, he looked after my interests as an orphan child and advanced me steadily in favour and power at the Court. Both of us understood that these matters of political expediency are a necessary part of public life.' He blandly concluded, 'As I hope you all understand that it is of course impossible to allow a potential claimant to the throne to live.' And he let the penholder fall flat.

Ambrose whistled. It was plain that Mary's goose was cooked, and *that* was flat.

Mr Secretary Cecil came in, a youngish man who had never looked quite young. With an air of quiet competence he laid some papers before the Duke that required to be stamped with the royal seal made for the new Queen. Dudley nodded his approval, but with a curious sense of irritability such as some show at the approach of a cat; then, as the Secretary moved to a corner to stamp the papers, his master shot at him, 'What do you know of the Lady Elizabeth's change of plan?'

'Your Grace, I did not even know she had a plan.'

'What! Do you not know that she had ordered her bodyguard, dressed for the journey, and had all but set foot in the stirrup to ride to London in answer to her dying brother's tender appeal?' The Duke had taken particular credit to himself for the wording of that appeal; no woman's heart could have resisted the old nickname the boy had for her – 'to my sweet sister Temperance.' He burst out, 'But she has no heart – and she changed her mind.'

'She is always changing it,' said Mr Cecil; 'it is a feminine infirmity grown to excess in her.'

'Then she's made good use of it.'

'Mary changed her mind too,' piped Guildford.

Duke Dudley had sent her an even more pathetic message in the dead boy's name; the messenger saw her weep, and she had sent word by him that she was thankful that her young brother 'should have thought she could be of any comfort to him'; she had instantly set out.

But she had never arrived.

Guildford flung back to his table and buried his head in his hands. 'If only Robin would send word!' he groaned.

His father's cool stare at him concealed some anxiety as well as annoyance. It was a pity he had had to choose the boy for his throw against fate. Robin would have made the better adventurer, but Robin was already married to that moody lass Amy Robsart. Even the thick-witted Ambrose would at least have more stamina, but he too was married, as was Jack. All his plans were being cluttered by young women in every direction; and the figurehead for those plans not even a woman, but that squeamish little schoolgirl Jane, who gave trouble whenever she could, refused to go to bed with her young husband, quarrelled with her mother-in-law, and now had come out in spots since her arrival at the Tower and complained that the skin was peeling off her back – as it certainly should if she got the treatment she deserved.

Here he was at the pinnacle of his wild flight towards sovereign power; for years he had manoeuvred his way up with consummate skill, first catching his sovereign's eye by his horsemanship in the tilt-yard (King Hal loved good sport), and winning the highest command in the field by his brilliant qualities as a soldier; and then at Hal's death he had got rid of the new boy-King's uncles by egging on the conflict between them until Ned Seymour killed his brother Tom, and Tom's death helped to destroy Ned. '*Divide et impera*,' – and he had by then won entire empery over King Edward.

No longer any need for the private door that he had had made in the royal bedchamber, so that he could slip in unobserved and instruct the lad overnight in how he was to act and speak the next day. The boy openly looked to him for guidance before speaking to the ambassadors and awaited his signal before dismissing them. Dudley's power was then absolute, and it delighted him to see how his flagrant show of it infuriated all observers. Ned Seymour had spoken of him as one of the 'Lords sprung from the dunghill'; the Lady Mary at bay had roared at him and his fellow-councillors, 'My father made the most part of you out of nothing.' Well, he had shown what can be made of nothing; he had sprang to a Dukedom, the first Englishman with no drop of royal blood to take the title; he made the Lords of his Council wait on him every day to learn his pleasure and kept the highest nobles waiting for an audience.

And now the boy had died on him, and he had to make do with the girl Jane. He felt himself a lion with his paw on England's neck – but everywhere he had to deal with mice. He found that he was gnawing his penholder so hard that it hurt his teeth; in exasperation he snapped it between his hands.

The door burst open. A servant, pop-eyed with excitement, ushered in a dusty messenger in riding-boots – 'From Robin!' cried Guildford again, and was told by his father to stop his parrot squawk.

The messenger did not come from Robin. He handed a letter to the Duke, who stared closely at the superscription in the dimming light before he broke the seal. His three sons surged forward. Who is it? Is there news of her? 'Is she – ?'

He burst in to a roar. 'Get back, you cubs! And you, you grinning fool,' to the servant, 'bring a light.'

His sons stepped back quickly and stood stock-still. Silence quivered over the room as the servant brought candles and went, and the Duke read the letter, and read it again.

'By God!' he shouted suddenly. 'She shall pay for this!'

He crumpled up the letter in a tight ball in his fist, then unfolded and smoothed it out and stared at it again as though the words must turn into something else.

'This,' he said at last, 'is from Mary herself. She writes' – he gulped and drew a deep breath, then adopted a mincing old-maidish archness of tone – 'that "it seems strange" – there's a dainty piece of sarcasm! – that we "should have omitted to inform her on so weighty a matter as that of our dearest brother the King dying upon Thursday night last—"'

'Devil doubt her!' muttered Jack.

His father glared at the interruption and went on, '"Yet," says the bright lass, "we are not ignorant of your consultations to undo our preferment – nor of the great bands and armed force you have prepared – to what end, God and you know, and nature can but fear some evil." But she will graciously forgive all my plots if I instantly relinquish them and "cause *our* right and title to the Crown," says she, "to be proclaimed in *our* City of London." Further, she intends to proceed herself to London to see to it.'

He leaned back, feeling as though a sheep had bitten him.

Ambrose broke into a blare of laughter. 'Let her proceed herself to London! She'll do it faster than she thinks, and in worse company. We'll have her here now in no time. Where is she?'

'Written from Kenninghall in Norfolk,' his father read out.

'It looks as if she's given Robin the slip,' said Guildford.

'It does,' said his father drily.

So she had turned aside from the London road after meeting the goldsmith at Hoddesdon, and gone to Kenninghall secretly, perhaps in disguise. Who was that mysterious goldsmith, and who had told him to give her the hint? He eyed the Secretary.

Mr Cecil was at that moment stamping another letter patent 'Jana Regina'. He looked up with mild eyes as the Duke spoke, commanding him to call a Council on the instant.

CHAPTER SIX

'This is nothing,' the Duke said at the Council table, 'a silly woman's flourish, that is all, but it must and shall be stopped instantly. I shall at once proclaim a muster of men in Tothill Fields, not mentioning any rebellion but telling them that the object is to fetch in the Lady Mary. As it will be such a brief affair I shall offer high pay – 10d. a day.'

The Council gasped. Even the little Queen saw it must be fairly serious to offer such pay. But she only sat and twisted her fingers while her mother, that hard-riding, hard-tempered woman whose stout frame and high colour proclaimed her King Harry's niece, burst into noisy sobbing. So much for the Tudor courage, thought the girl, wincing in contempt, and then her mother-in-law must needs follow suit, though more quietly, the tears running down her still beautiful face. The Duke put his hand on his wife's shoulder, and she instantly stopped crying. He eyed the startled faces before him.

'A mere nothing,' he repeated coldly, 'not worth calling a rising even. If some few hundred wretched peasants are fools enough to flock like sheep after that woman, well, they will be sheep to the slaughter. Haven't I put down three rebellions in this last reign, and of far greater force than this one will ever have time to gather? Remember how I hanged the canting Kett from his own Oak of Reformation!'

The Queen's father, Henry Grey, lately created Duke of Suffolk, nodded solemnly over his stiff collar. 'True, true,' he said, 'the Emperor's ambassadors say they wouldn't give a fig for Mary's chances. I find she's written to them asking them to keep in touch with her – the last thing they want! They are calling her attitude "strange, difficult and dangerous" and give her four days at most before she's in the hands of the Council. Her messenger has had to go back without a word from them. Why, they daren't even go out in the street for fear of being charged as her supporters.'

That was very encouraging. Everyone felt better at the thought of Simon Renard the Fox not daring to poke his nose into the street – 'Wise fellow!' said Dudley, smiling; 'these ambassadors are good straws to show the way the wind blows. Here's the draft of a letter that I've written at once in answer to her insolence, for one must speak her fair.'

He read out his 'fair' speech, reminding the Lady Mary that she had been 'justly made illegitimate and uninheritable to the Crown Imperial of this Realm'; commanding her not to vex and molest any of our Sovereign Lady Queen Jane's subjects; and assuring her that 'if you will show yourself quiet and obedient, as you ought, we will bid you most heartily well to fare.

'Your Ladyship's friends, showing yourself an obedient subject – And now sign, all of you,' he commanded, pushing forward the paper under the line of unwilling noses.

But they signed, Cranmer first, to give it Archiepiscopal authority, then the Bishops of London and Ely, the Dukes of Suffolk and Bedford, the Lords Arundel, Shrewsbury and Pembroke, Mr Secretary Cecil and his College friend Sir John Cheke, tutor to the late King. As the paper passed from one slightly hesitant hand to another, its writer encouraged them with arguments even more forcible than it contained.

'I've three hundred horses already hunting for the Lady Mary; in a day or two it will be three thousand. I've sent ships to Yarmouth to cut off her escape by sea. I hold the navy and the army; I hold the Tower here and all its armoury, and who holds the Tower holds London; who holds London holds all England. Mary is quite alone, skulking with her women and a few old Papist serving-men in a lonely country house. No man with a grain of common sense would dare go to her help. Long before the week's out I'll have her here, captive or dead, like the rebel she is.'

There was a burst of applause. Only the sixteen-year-old girl for whose sake ostensibly were all these armaments and threats, looked rather more unhappy than before. Jane did not like to hear of Mary being quite alone with no one to dare help her, of her being brought in captive or dead. Mary had been kind to her in her fashion, had given her a pearl necklace and gown of cloth of gold, mere worldly toys such as Jane had been right to despise; but captivity or death was a poor return for them. She wished with all her heart that her cousin could have been allowed to be Queen instead of herself. Mary might even think that she was doing right to insist on being Queen, even as Jane herself had been told that she was doing right to be Queen. It was very puzzling.

She sat as still as a mouse among the company of great cats in all their fur and claws, their gleaming staffs and jewels, and here and there the wicked narrow streak of a dagger. She sat with her hands crossed demurely over her wide velvet cuffs, her hair tucked away out of sight in a big white kerchief, and another folded over her narrow shoulders. A small nosegay of jasmine and heliotrope was tucked into the front of her bodice where it opened into the fluting white embroidered collar, and she kept her straight little nose bent down to sniff at it.

The candlelight flickered on the faces round her, for the windows had been left open in the heat of the summer night, though they admitted foul smells from the river, and moths, midges and mosquitoes as well as the faint breeze. The faces round her were those she had known all her life as her elders and betters, ever telling her incessantly what it was right for her to do; yet at this moment they looked more like the faces of conspirators.

A white moth flew straight in from the night outside into the candle before her eyes and fluttered to its death in the molten wax. And Mary was to come to the Tower to die. They were all planning it. How could it be right?

But then she remembered Mary was a Papist, so it could not be right for her to be Queen. That settled it.

She drew a breath of relief, but it fled as she heard that her father, the Duke of Suffolk, was to lead the army that was to bring back Mary. That would mean she would be left alone, here with these Dudleys. Her mother did not count. She would be at the mercy of that dark terrible man at the head of the table, who cared nothing for what was right, whatever he might pretend; and of his callow son, who talked about his rights as a husband and swaggered about the other women who admired him, in loud boastful tones so different from Mr Aylmer's gentle voice, and gave himself the airs of a man when he was only a nasty boy; and of his mother, who seemed gentle but could become a fury on behalf of her precious son.

Her heart felt as though it were bursting; she struggled for speech and instead collapsed into tears.

Duke Dudley's look at her was enough to justify her fears. 'The Queen is overwrought,' he said in a voice like steel snapping. 'She is not well and had better retire. No doubt it is past her bedtime.'

Her mother was pulling her out of her chair, telling her furiously to come away this instant.

Jane stood up but did not budge further. She hung on to the back of her chair as though afraid of being dragged from it; she panted out, 'I won't be left alone here. My father must stay with me.'

Suffolk looked pleased. He had always known the girl was fond of him. It wasn't true she was an undutiful daughter without any heart.

'Perhaps it might on all counts be better,' he began, glancing nervously to right and left, and was encouraged to see the Earl of Arundel nodding in assent while Archbishop Cranmer pulled the two prongs of his long beard approvingly.

But Duke Dudley broke in with a roar that made Suffolk's long face sink rapidly into his collar.

'Are you so mad as to listen to the whine of a crying child? Wants her father to stay here and hold her hand while we're at this crisis! Who but her father *should* ride out to defend his daughter's right as Queen? *Who*, I say?'

'You,' said Jane.

She was not crying now. Her fear of Dudley had boiled up into rage. How dare he shout like that at her and her father?

'I am Queen, aren't I?' she said. 'I didn't want it, but you made me be. Then you must obey me. I won't let my father go to lead this army. If he goes, I won't go on being Queen. I'll tear the crown from my head when you put it on. I won't – I won't—' The strangled sobs surged up again and choked her words; they only heard as she clung to the back of the chair, 'I won't – I won't be Queen.'

'It's against all common sense. Here I hold the capital and its citadel the Tower. Here I can direct all things from the centre. All that you have to do is to ride out in the Queen's name and quell a small rabble of the common people.'

'They are not all common. Sir Henry Jerningham has joined Mary, and they say the High Sheriff for Suffolk and the Knight of the Shire are on their way. Sir Henry Bedingfeld is already there and half a dozen other country gentry, all bringing supplies of bread, beef and beer to feed her followers, as well as money or plate.'

'Bread, beef, beer, butter, what in God's name is there in that? Have they got guns? Answer me that!' roared the Duke.

But Jane's father actually protruded his neck a little further from his collar instead of hastily retreating into it. 'And beside them,' he continued as though he had not even heard his master's voice, 'innumerable small companies of the common people as you so lightly call them – but they pulled down the chivalry of France at Agincourt.'

'God's blood, man, when will you or any English fool recognise that Agincourt is an old song and Harry the fifth is dead – all the King Harrys. We are living *now*, in this year of grace 1553, and no bows and arrows, but the great guns are even now rumbling out through the Tower gateway for the army towards Cambridge.'

Duke Dudley paused for those carts of artillery to give point to his words as their thunder echoed out over the Tower

Bridge through the dead silence of the night. 'What country gentleman and his following of shepherds and swineherds is going to withstand *that*?' he demanded. 'War has changed, and with it the whole world. Whoso commands the guns commands the world. It is I who command them. We,' he hastily corrected. Maddening that he had to remember to be conciliatory once again! But after all, this foolish mulish fellow with the long weak moustaches was the Queen's father.

The Queen's father also tried to be conciliatory. 'You are the best soldier in the Kingdom, you have reminded us of it often enough. You have put down three rebellions – why not a fourth? At Norwich and Dussendale you bound all hesitating officers to swear to conquer or die by the knightly ceremony of kissing each other's swords before the fight. So even you believed, so short a time ago, in the motive power of chivalry, despite the great guns. Believe in it now. Ride out and make them conquer or die, as I should have no power to do, who have never been a soldier. All the Council are agreed that that is the best course.'

'To hell with the Council! What are they but my creatures? They're eager to see my back, are they? Why? That they may act against me the better behind it?'

'Such suspicions are unworthy of Your Grace. I shall be here to guard your interests – and my daughter. What should you, the Captain General of all the royal forces, have to fear from enemies in the field?'

'More from friends at home,' muttered the Duke.

Queen Jane woke with a cry. 'I hear thunder!' She had always been terrified of storms, the thunder was the wrath of God speaking, the lightning His eye, 'Thou God seest me.'

Kind Lady Throckmorton came to her bedside. 'No,

Madam, it is no storm. It is only the carts of artillery leaving the Tower to accompany the great army into Cambridge.'

'My father shall not go with them, I have said it. I am the Queen.'

'Yes, Madam, yes. No, Madam, no. Your father is even now persuading the Duke.'

'The Duke! The Duke has been King for years. He shall not be now. I am Queen.'

'Yes, Madam, yes.'

At the sound of voices the Duke's wife and son Guildford came unannounced into the bedchamber. The Duchess wanted to know why Queen Jane refused to consummate the marriage, to recognise her husband's title as King Guildford, refused even to let him sit at meals with her at the royal high table. It made it so marked.

The Duchess would have no more of it. In future her son must share the new Queen's bed, crown and table.

The new Queen sat up very small and childish between the heavy curtains. Guildford in his long white bedgown, looking like an uneasy chorister, told her that *he* did not want to go to bed with her – there were plenty of other women who wanted it of him. But he was King and he needed a son.

Jane, clasping her hands tight under the counterpane, replied, 'The Crown is not a plaything for boys and girls. If the Crown were my concern solely, which it is not, I should be pleased to make my husband a Duke. I would not consent to make him King.'

There was a storm at that. The Duchess, her nerves worn to breaking point by the agitation and tension of the last few days, raged up and down the room, telling Jane she was an unnatural little monster, a changeling with no human feelings, to be so unkind to her son whom everybody else had always loved. Could Jane not see that he was as good and clever as he was handsome? Whom, pray, did she want for a husband – the Emperor, or the King of France? Or some musty old scholar with his nose in his books?

Jane was stung by this last into an answer. 'I don't want any husband. I didn't want to be Queen. But as I am, I will do my duty as one. I will not put an upstart on the throne of England. And now I am going to sleep.'

She lay down and pulled the sheet over her face.

'Upstart!' shouted Guildford, advancing threateningly to the bed. 'Upstart did you say?'

But there was no stir under the sheet. Guildford suddenly sat down on the edge of the bed and began to cry.

His fond mother could not believe that this would not soften the hard-hearted bride, she herself had never been able to refuse anything to Guildford when he cried.

'Perhaps if we leave you alone together now—' she murmured encouragingly to him.

The sheet was suddenly pulled down again. 'I've got spots all over my chest,' said Jane firmly; 'it's probably measles and catching, or perhaps you have poisoned me.'

The Duchess had already snatched her son from the bed. 'Come away, my poor boy, come with me. I'll not leave you with an ungrateful wife.'

He went with her.

'I can't sleep now,' said Jane. 'Is Cheke still up?'

'Yes, Madam,' said Lady Throckmorton, 'he is with my husband and Mr Cecil.'

'Bring him here, and tell him to bring pen and ink.'

The late King's tutor, grave, handsome and austere, entered
the royal bedchamber, and stood before his former pupil in
her grand new bedgown. So lately, it seemed, he had been
teaching Greek prose to her and her cousin Edward; so lately
had he been telling a story to those two children, only nine
years old, on the stormy winter's night old King Harry died;
and so little change was there since that night, seven years
ago, in this slight childish figure and small determined face
that awaited him.

'Cheke,' said Jane (neither she nor Edward had ever been
able to call him by his new title, Sir John), 'do you believe that
it is right that I should be Queen?'

'Madam, how else should right be done? Only by you and
through you can the Church of England continue, and the
Prayer Book of King Edward of blessed memory. Your
accession to the throne is not a thing conceived in a corner,
nor brought to birth in a night. It was planned before you
were born, long years ago, by King Henry the Eighth himself,
when he disinherited his daughters, both the Lady Mary and
the Lady Elizabeth, then a toddling infant, as bastards. Years
later he restored their rights to the succession by Parliament,
but provided that if they and King Edward died childless the
Crown should go to the issue of his sisters, of whom the
younger, Mary Rose, was your grandmother.'

'But – King Henry's daughters are then true heirs to the
Crown. And they have not died—' she bit off the last word,
'yet.'

'Heirs to the Crown – by their father's ruling. But what
King Harry did without question, his son surely had the right
to do, and with far more reason. King Edward's will and
testament has merely restated that early one of his father's,

and removed the Ladies Mary and Elizabeth once again from the succession.'

There was one enormous gap in this lucid exposition; it gaped too wide for the transparent honesty of Jane's logic. 'My grandmother, the Princess Mary Rose, was the younger of King Harry's sisters. The elder, Margaret, would bear first claim to the throne, and her granddaughter is the child Mary, Queen of Scots.'

'That is true, Madam – but it is unthinkable. As soon as she is old enough the little Queen of Scots will be married to the Dauphin; she will become Queen of France as well as Scotland. For her to reign here would amount to a conquest of England by France, and still worse, by the Romish Church.'

'But – it is her right—'

'Her right would be England's wrong.'

'How can right be wrong and truth unthinkable?'

Cheke all but groaned. Jane was his best pupil, but it was impossible to explain compromise to her. '*This* is true, and right,' he told her firmly, 'that King Edward has declared you his cousin to be his rightful heir; so that you might preserve the New Religion pure and undefiled by Popery and the heathenish superstition of the Mass.'

'Cheke, do you remember his laughing when you told us the story of St George and the Dragon?'

'Yes, Madam, but he was then a very little boy.'

'Well, later on he removed St George from the Order of the Garter. Why?'

'Perhaps he thought it an old-fashioned mummery.'

'But some old-fashioned mummeries – only some, I say – may be good. Cheke, do you think my cousin King Edward was always right?'

'Madam, King Edward of blessed memory has died while still a boy. It is not given to any man, let alone a boy, to be always right.'

There was a long silence, broken at last by a long, long sigh.

'I see,' said Jane, 'he may have been right to make me Queen – and he may not. But we must abide by it. You think he was right, and so does Mr Ascham, and if you both do, then so must Mr Aylmer, who loves you both more than any men in the University of Cambridge, which is to say the best minds in England. I wish he were here too with us, but I will try to act as though he were. Take your pen now and write.'

'To whom, gracious Lady?'

'To the Lord Lieutenant of Surrey, who is doubtful on this matter.' She pulled a scribbled note from under her pillow. 'Tell him this: "We are entered into our rightful possession of this Kingdom, by the last will of our dearest cousin King Edward as rightful Queen of his realm. We have accordingly set forth our proclamation to all our loving subjects, not only to defend our just title, but also to assist us to disturb, repel and resist the feigned and untrue claim of Lady Mary, bastard daughter to our great-uncle Henry the Eighth of famous memory."'

'No,' said Mr Cecil, 'I won't copy the letter. I won't write "bastard".'

'Then,' said Cheke, 'His Grace the Duke of Northumberland will write it himself.'

'Then let him.'

* * *

'Heard the news? Mary set out at nightfall and rode through the darkness all night with only half a dozen men of her household. They took the Newmarket road for Yarmouth, so she's aiming at the Netherlands after all.'

'Your news is stale as old fish. She went on to Hengrave Hall, covered sixty miles without stopping, and the last part of them in disguise, riding pillion behind a servant. She has guts.'

'She's no wits.'

'My Lord Duke of Northumberland, I bear a message from the Imperial ambassador.'

'I'll stand no more threats from him, and so you can tell him. Let the Emperor send but one troop of his foreign swine here and he'll knit all true Englishmen together. Besides, two can play at that game. If Mary sends to the Emperor for help I'll send to the King of France – and offer Calais as bribe. Tell the Fox that.'

'Yes, Your Grace. But it's no threat that Simon Renard sends. The Lady Mary has appealed to him again, in desperation. She sees destruction hanging over her unless she receives help from her cousin the Emperor.'

'Well, will she receive it?'

'Your Grace, Monsieur Renard considers it wiser not to forward her message to his Imperial Master.'

'You coming to this farewell dinner too, my lord? Are all the rest of the Council?'

'Most, I fancy. We've got our way in getting Dudley to lead this expedition instead of Suffolk. So now the Duke's taking this chance to tell us all to be good boys in his absence.'

Pembroke's loud laugh made Sir Thomas Cheyne glance round nervously as they went up the stairs to the banqueting hall.

'Pooh, man, I can afford a family joke, we're blood brothers now, with my boy Hal marrying his girl. Heard the latest of Mary? She's raised the Royal Standard as Queen of England and Ireland, and where d'you think? At Framlingham Castle.'

'Hmm, at Framlingham, is she? That's a strong fortress, my cousin old Norfolk built it for wear and tear, it was his chief pride.'

'Your cousin, hey? Never knew that. Well, anyway, much good his chief pride's done him, imprisoned in the Tower all these years! Or will do Mary. It might stand a siege, but they'll soon smoke her out like the doe rabbit she is.'

Sir Thomas Cheyne, Warden of the Cinque Ports, looked sideways at the Earl of Pembroke, wondering if he were quite as confident as he sounded. He had more money and power than any other of Dudley's noble supporters. It would be extremely useful to discover just exactly what was his private opinion of the situation. But that was just what one could not do while mewed up in the Tower with eavesdroppers at every corner. If only they could slip out even for an hour or two across the river to Cheyne's house in Chelsea or to Barnard's Castle, that splendid London house of Pembroke's. But it was impossible for the moment, and they even considered it wiser, simultaneously and silently, to separate on the stairs instead of entering the banqueting hall together.

The Duke greeted his guests with a rather defiant geniality, reminded them with urgency that they had to send more troops after him as soon as they had collected them, to catch up with him at Newmarket, and jollied them to keep faith with him in the manner of a huntsman cracking the whip over his hounds.

'You've heard what her best friends think of her chances? The Papist ambassadors are trailing round dolefully "deploring her rashness in proclaiming herself Queen"! They neither answer her appeals for help nor forward them to the Emperor, the one ally she has – had, rather – in the world. But *he* knows as well as his servants that Mary can't win. They said it themselves – and why? Because of her religion. That touches not only your consciences, all of you, but your pockets. She'd demand the Church lands and revenues to be given back, and which of you would care to do *that*, my friends?'

They seemed to find this rather tactless. There was a murmur that the heathenish abomination of the Mass was sufficient cause against Mary. But he only cracked the whip still louder.

'Don't you leave us, your friends, tangled in the briars and betray us! Two can play at that game; remember, I have just as much chance to betray you, as you me.'

Somehow this did not ring quite in tune with the chivalrous commander who had set his followers to kiss each other's swords before a battle. He remembered that he should be setting out, not on a wild fling for his and his family's fortunes, but on a crusade for the only true religion.

'This is in God's cause,' he said, 'for the preferment of His word – what the devil is that?'

It was the servants bringing in the first course. The Duke's nerves were on edge to start at so obvious an interruption. The Earl of Arundel, a family connection, boldly took the chance to tell him that there was no need for him to distrust them, for they were all in it together, 'and which of us can now wipe his hands clean of it?'

'I pray God it be so,' said the Duke. 'Let us go to dinner.'

And so they sat down.

And so they got up and went into the courtyard, where Sir John Gates, the Captain of the King's Guard, was waiting for them with all his men. The Duke and his sons mounted their horses to ride at their head. The Earl of Arundel came out for a final leave-taking, and standing at the Duke's stirrup he said how he wished he were going with him, 'to spend my blood, even at your foot,' said he, patting the stirrup and looking up with the wistful brown eyes of a faithful spaniel.

The Duke's youngest son, Harry, still a schoolboy, rode with them, and let a halloa out of him from sheer high spirits as they trotted through the little huddled streets of Shoreditch. 'Faugh! but it's good to be clear of the Tower air – not that there is any, for it's thick with river mist and foul stink!'

'It's thicker with fair speech,' said his eldest brother sourly. 'Must you crow in the street like a half-fledged cockerel?'

Harry went pink and he drew himself up in the saddle to look as tall as he could. Curse old Jack, cross again! But Jack was thinking of Arundel, who four years ago had helped Dudley oust the Protector, Ned Seymour, and then found himself in the Tower for his pains and had to buy himself out with £1500.

'He's small reason to be so devoted to you, sir, after all you've lifted from him!'

'Who? What? Oh, Fitzalan! He's a safe dog, never fear, knows his master. Besides, he's one of the family.'

The Duke was turning his head this way and that, looking at the crowds of people who were peering over each other's shoulders in the low doorways, craning their necks out of the tiny windows, running, jostling each other up the narrow lanes, pressing each other closer and closer to the horses till they were all but under their hoofs. It was the sight he had seen every time he rode out for many years past, the Cockney crowds pushing and pressing to see the Great Duke go riding by – but never as now.

For all those dense crowds were silent. No cheer was raised, no cry for largesse; the people muttered and whispered together, but passed no word to him. They were not hostile, scarcely sullen even, but so alien was he in his isolation, they might have come to stare upon a ghost.

He could bear the ill-ease no longer. He said, 'The people press to see us, but not a voice among them cries "God speed!"'

'What do the people matter?' said Ambrose.

His father shrugged himself free of the surrounding silence. 'Not one jot,' he replied. 'Mary can't win.'

CHAPTER SEVEN

They rode north and east through flat fields and fens that were a shimmer of corn or reeds and here and there the sudden gleam of water in the marshlands under the hot unchanging sunshine. Always he seemed to have been riding through this golden dazzle – towards what mirage?

He was not used to such fancies, but the heat, the wide still landscape, made him feel he was riding in a dream. The few grey stone castles that he passed looked impalpable as shadows, the woods a blue mist that smudged the horizon and wavered in the heat-haze but never seemed near enough to cast their grateful shade on him and his troops. Always the thick white dust of the rutted cart-tracks choked their throats, and the trees by the wayside were shrouded in it, white as ghosts.

Over the pale countryside came the sound of bells pealing – pealing for Queen Mary or Queen Jane, they never knew which. Often they would ride into a town or village where the Mayor or beadle had just read out and posted up the Proclamation of Queen Mary and ordered the bells to ring for her; then at the coming of the Duke and his army he would tear it down, stick up Queen Jane's and read that; and the bells would ring afresh for her; and after they had passed, would stick up Queen Mary's yet again and ring for her once more:

'*Long live Queen Jane,*
Will Jane long reign?'

'*Long live Queen Mary,*
All things contrary.'

There were no reinforcements to meet him at Newmarket; he could hear no news of them. He was carrying out a zigzag course to Cambridge, to raise the country as he went, before marching on to Framlingham. Some noblemen came to join him, but with disappointingly small forces; they complained that many of their own tenants had refused to follow their lords and masters against Mary. Nerves and tempers were taut as overstrung fiddle-strings in this white-hot suspense.

'Victory was certain,' but the only sign of it was the smoke of burning houses and barns hanging heavy and acrid on the lucent air. Dudley had ordered that the property of Mary's known friends should be destroyed and pillaged; the younger men, meeting no enemy in the field, found it amusing to ride off on such forays.

Lord George Howard returned from one of them tossing a silver chalice which had been used at Mary's own Mass a few days before; Jack Dudley jeered at him for a common looter, George sneered that it was because Jack coveted the pot, and rode off, with his followers to join Mary at Framlingham. Duke Dudley could hardly keep his hands off his son in his rage at the result of this squabble; but within a few hours he himself had exploded into one even worse. Lord Grey, a distant cousin of the little Queen, told him angrily that to burn and lay waste the countryside was no wise course; the Duke, so long unused to criticism, flared into an uncontrollable passion and actually struck him in the face. Grey hit back, the noble lords had to be pulled apart as though they were a couple of schoolboys. Grey flung out of the room with a bloody nose, summoned his followers, and, staunch Protestant though he was, rode off also to Framlingham.

Political parties and the new religion, even the sacredness of new-won property, were in fact beginning to seem less and less important; what the nobles were increasingly inclined to murmur was that they had stood enough from this jumped-up son of a shady lawyer, and that Mary was true Tudor and King Harry's daughter.

'Let the fools and traitors go!' said Duke Dudley as he marched on to Bury, burning now without any hindrance, 'I'll get my foot on their necks yet.'

He had 4000 troops, and a quarter of them horsemen, and had got them into a good strategic position to cut off the forces in Buckinghamshire who had declared for Mary and were marching to join her.

And, as he kept telling himself and his supporters, he had the navy.

If only he could feel as sure of his Council that he had left back in London, a pack of shifty self-seekers who had sent him no reinforcements, only letters of discomfort!

Two days after leaving London, he reached Cambridge, that foster-nurse of the new religion, where Cranmer as a young Fellow had drunk small beer at the Dolphin with Erasmus and planned to reform the world.

It was Sunday, and the sermons were all sound on Queen Jane. He heard one from Dr. Sandys in the beautiful chapel that King Henry VI had managed to build for King's College in the midst of his civil wars – a shocking waste of money the Duke calculated, especially now all those superstitious frescoes were decently covered with a coat of Protestant plaster. Afterwards he dined at King's College and the dons praised his daughter-in-law to him; her wisdom, her learning, her modesty, her gentleness, above all her passionate zeal for Protestantism, would make all England thankful to have her as Queen. The Duke listened absently while he sent messengers to discover where were the reinforcements that he had again sent for from London.

The weather had broken at last; a strong easterly gale was driving scuds of rain and torn leaves across the pleasant College lawns leading down to the river. He looked out at them, wondering what chance might lie for him in this change; weather should be one of the chief factors in a campaigner's calculations – but then this *was* no campaign as yet; that is what was frazzling everybody in a tangle. So he thought as he watched the wind and rain tearing the green summer garden to pieces, and sipped the College malmsey of fine vintage, and bit into the peaches that had ripened early on the south wall.

Old Dr. Bill, a sturdy pillar of the Reformed Church, was telling him with a chuckle that he had found the Lady Mary an honest woman who always paid her debts, for she had once paid him as much as £10 that he had won from her in an idle bet that few people would have bothered to remember – but for all that, there was no chance at all for her against the new world and the new ideas; she was for ever remembering the old days when her mother and King Harry had heard Mass together; 'She has never learnt, poor soul, that men's minds march forward and not backward.'

There was sense in that and solid comfort, and he repeated it determinedly, for the Duke was not attending; he was staring at the door as it swung open, and his eldest son stood there an instant, splashed with mud up to his thighs, wiping his sleeve over his face, which ran with rain and sweat, and looking round with haggard eyes for his father. In a couple of strides he was beside him, pulling him away from Dr. Bill, who had just begun to repeat his moral for the third time. It dawned on Bill as well as the other dons that he must tactfully retire.

The Duke turned savagely on Jack.

'What the devil is it this time?'

'Sir, it's this gale – there's one at sea—'

'So I should suppose! What of it?' He leaped at it. 'My ships are all sunk!'

'No, sir, no. They're safe in harbour at Yarmouth – put in there for shelter from the east wind.'

'Safe, are they? Then why do you gape at me with a face as long as a wet week? For Christ's sake speak – and wipe the sweat off your nose!'

'They're safe,' Jack stammered, 'but—'

'But *what*?' roared his father as the young man mopped his face again and said nothing, then gasped—

'Sir, they're safe but – sir – Sir Harry Jerningham – you know—'

'I know. Mary's creature – what could he do against my navy?'

'He went to Yarmouth, with what men he had been able to get together in Mary's name. He rowed out into the harbour in a little boat and stood up in it and shouted a speech to the crews, inciting them to desert to Mary.'

He came to a, pause, then said, 'Can I have a drink?

'No, by God's blood, till you tell me the rest! What happened – they had the guns – didn't they shoot him down in his cockleshell?'

'No, sir. They said – they said—'

'What did they say?'

'They said, "Will you have our captains on your side too? or not?" He said yes, if they would come over willingly. Then the crews said, "You shall have 'em, or else they shall go to the bottom." So the crews brought the captains up on deck and they said they would declare for Queen Mary and gladly. Sir, they had to – it was rank mutiny,' Jack added, in terror at the look on his father's face.

'Take your drink,' said Duke Dudley, shoving the bottle over to him.

Rank mutiny on the part of the common people. It was happening everywhere. Queen Jane had learning and wisdom and zeal for the new ideas. But her backing was that of a lot of old grey-bearded doctors and dons.

The navy had guns, but it had gone over to Queen Mary. The crews had told the captains what to do, 'or else they shall go to the bottom.'

Duke Dudley rode out from Cambridge the next day, towards Bury again. He rode east and he rode west through the mud, his cloak weighing heavier and heavier from the wet; he gained no new followers, and his old ones were drifting away on the wind, deserting right and left, slipping away by one and two and tiny companies of men, drifting in a zigzag course across country to avoid the dykes and marshes, all drifting away towards a missish, determined little figure with sandy hair turning grey who sat perched upon the top of one of the towers of Framlingham Castle.

There Mary sit, peering out of her short-sighted blue eyes at the men coming to her by various ways across the wide countryside, by twos and threes and a few more – men who cared nothing for ideas, new or old, men who had no property to lose, and no guns (except the navy), but who said, 'Tisn't right.'

'It's a shame.'

'We won't see a poor woman done out of her rights.'

The Duke still had close on 1000 horse, he still had all the guns of the Tower's armoury, but what use would they be to him at the latter end?

'Their feet march forward,' he said to his son Jack, 'but their minds march backward.'

England was failing him. Well, there was still France. He had won his spurs in France, and all his early honours. King Henri II was as much a Papist as the Emperor, and Dudley had no illusions; he knew all about the French plan for the future conquest of England through the little Queen of Scots. But the time was *now*, July 17th, 1553, and he would give all the future for an ally now against Mary Tudor. He sent his cousin Henry Dudley off to France with a desperate bid for foreign troops; if the French King would send them, now on the instant, Dudley would yield him Calais, the last English foothold on French soil, that had held firm for two and a half centuries.

That done, he had only to wait, trailing here and there to collect forces that if they did come in to him only vanished again within a few hours. And wilder and wilder reports raced out to him from London.

Old Lord Winchester had slipped off in secret to his own house and had to be brought back by force to the Tower at midnight.

Then the Treasurer of the Mint had escaped with all the money in it and could not be found; he was probably on his way to Mary.

Bishop Ridley of London, after preaching against Mary, the idolatrous rival of Queen Jane, at St Paul's in the morning, had set out to ask her pardon by nightfall, and actually got as far as Ipswich, where he was arrested.

The whole Council was ratting, scuttling off from the Tower, some to their several holes, but the most important members with Lord Pembroke to Barnard's Castle in the Strand. The conclusion to that followed in a few hours; heralds from Barnard's Castle proclaimed Queen Mary at Paul's Cross, and all London was running mad with joy.

It was late at night when the news came to Duke Dudley as he sat at supper at Cambridge, to which he had drifted back again from Bury. He was at King's College with Dr. Bill and Dr. Sandys and Dr. Parker, who had waited seven years for King Henry to die before he, an ordained priest, had dared marry his patiently waiting Margaret. Queen Mary was now proclaimed, and so Dr. Parker was no longer lawfully married.

But the dons still sipped their wine and talked theology and made an occasional Latin pun.

The Duke left them and went and sat in the window-seat, staring out at the thick raining night. All his life he had ridden towards a brilliant future, and as fast as he had made it the present, another still brighter shone before him. But now the mirage had vanished; he saw nothing ahead of him, but stared into a future thick and dark as the night outside the window. He could see into it only as far as tomorrow morning, and what he must then do.

The heavy rumbling voices round the table fell silent one after the other as the speakers glanced uneasily at the silent figure at the window; finally they took their leave of him and he rose and took their hands in his and asked each of them to pray for him, 'for I am in great distress.'

'That,' said Dr. Parker as they went, 'was the hand of a spent man.'

The dawn was white and misty when into the marketplace came the great Duke of Northumberland, alone with the Mayor of Cambridge. He had looked for four trumpeters and a herald but could find none. With his own hands Duke Dudley tore down the Proclamation of Queen Jane, and himself read the Proclamation of Queen Mary, waved the white truncheon that he bore as Captain General, and then threw up his cap as though he were glad and shouted, 'Long live the Queen!'

People were running into the square, gaping and pointing at the tall figure by the market cross who waved his cap and shouted as if with joy, but on a harsh raucous note, while the team ran down his face. He threw gold coins to them as they came nearer, but nobody cheered.

That evening Jack Dudley heard that another Proclamation had been drawn up by the Council in London; it offered the reward of £1000 in land to any noble, £500 to any knight, £100 to any yeoman who should lay his hand on the shoulder of the Duke of Northumberland and arrest him in the Queen's name.

He galloped to King's College to find his father.

The Mayor of Cambridge had been before him. He also had heard of the Proclamation, and went to win easy money.

But the abject figure of the rebel recanting at the market cross had vanished; in its place sat the great Duke of Northumberland who had ruled England with a rod of iron for these four years. The Mayor stretched out his hand – and withdrew it. £500 lay beneath his fingers for the grasping. But the courage ebbed out of his finger-tips; he backed out, stammering and excusing himself.

Jack Dudley rushed in to find his father still at liberty.

'Thank God, sir, you're still here. Sir, we must start at once. There's been a Proclamation.'

'Another?' said his father. 'There's one every five minutes.'

'But this is for your arrest.'

'I know.' And as his son stared he added, 'The Mayor came just now to arrest me. He didn't dare. Which of the rats – the mice – will dare put a paw on me?'

Jack had no use for these questions. 'Well then we've still got a chance. I've horses outside. We must start on the instant.'

'Where to?'

'Why, sir, the coast – anywhere but here.'

'What odds? What odds?' said the Duke; then as he saw the young man's impatient agony, 'Very well, we'll start – in the morning.'

Those few hours of the July night might still hold some strange chance for him. His luck had always held. All the rats in the country might desert him, but he could not believe his luck would desert him. And he must sleep. He could do nothing till he had had some sleep. He had had so little these list nights. In the morning things might be different.

He went to bed, and his son Jack, still booted and spurred, with his riding-cloak still over his shoulders, ready to start the moment he could get his father to do so, looked in on him, and was amazed to see him dead asleep. Had he gone mad, or suddenly old and childish, that he could not stir himself in this hour of his greatest need? What had happened to that demonic energy that had made him like Lucifer, Son of the Morning, hurtling from plan to plan, no swifter in thought than execution?

Then he wished he had not thought of Lucifer, who fought God and fell, and crossed himself before he remembered that the action was a crime, and worse, a folly.

He went away to see what few followers he might still get together by the morning.

Before it was quite light, the Duke was woken by a knock on his door.

'I have heard that knock before,' he said aloud, but still half asleep. There was more knocking, louder and louder. He dragged himself awake and out of bed, began to put on his clothes, then, with his boots half on and half off, he went to the door.

His brother-in-law, Fitzalan, the Earl of Arundel, stood there. He stretched out his arm and put his hand on the Duke's shoulder.

'My lord,' he said, 'I am sent here by the Queen's Majesty, and in her name I arrest you.'

The Duke gaped at him, stupefied. Less than six days ago Arundel had stood at his stirrup and wished he could ride out with him and spend his blood for him 'even at his foot.' He wanted to say that; to remind Arundel that he himself had said that they were 'all in it together and which of them could now wipe his hands clean of it?'

But what odds, what odds would it make? He found his knees giving under him, they were sliding to the ground, he was down on his knees clutching at Arundel's coat, praying him to 'be good to me for the love of God' – and then, in oblique but desperate reminder of what he dared not say outright, 'I beseech you use mercy to me, *knowing the case as it is.*'

'My lord,' said the Earl, 'you should have sought for mercy sooner.'

CHAPTER EIGHT

Time took twice as long in the Tower as elsewhere, Jane found. She had more than enough means to tell it by. For she had sent for her personal belongings to make her feel more at home, especially her books, and the stupid servants had brought few books, but a mass of things she did not want; among them, mufflers of purple velvet and sable (in this heat!), black velvet hats, ostrich feathers, three pairs of garters, a dog-collar with gold bells (none of her dogs was here), a box with a picture of her mother inside the lid, which Jane opened and shut firmly down again, and an extravagant number of clocks – striking clocks, alarm clocks, and one with the figure of a little man who held a sphere on his head and an astronomical device in his hand.

Her cousin King Edward had given it to her. There was also a small image of Edward carved in wood. It had a real look of the delicate eager boy. She looked at it and listened to his clock ticking. It was strange they should still be here with her, when he had now lain dead for more than a week. So short a time ago he had played cards with her.

She had always been told that when he was a grown man as well as King, she would be his Queen. Now she had to be Queen all alone. But Queen alone she *would* be. No upstart should usurp the Crown that he had left to her.

Edward was dead; young Guildford Dudley stormed and sulked; Queen Jane lived on and on alone, so long it seemed, while all the clocks struck or rang their alarms, and the heat-wave melted, and a gusty east wind blew up the Thames which cooled her hot head but only a little, for it ached all the time and she felt sick and feverish and worried about those spots. Was it some fever, or were Guildford and his mother really poisoning her? Or was it, as Lady Throckmorton said, only the Tower fleas, more venomous than other fleas because they had bred on the bodies of traitors?

The Tower itself grew less and less like a royal palace-fortress and more and more like a prison, whose walls closed in nearer and nearer to her, shutting her in more and more alone.

Other people were trying to escape from it, she knew that. Lord Pembroke and Sir Thomas Cheyne the Warden of the Cinque Ports had wanted to slip out unobserved that they might talk somewhere else in private, so her father told her, proud of having circumvented them. She heard how old Lord Winchester had had to be brought back at midnight; that Bishop Ridley had gone, and the Treasurer of the Mint with all the money in it.

She heard – worse than any ill news – the howling of the mob outside the Tower, yelling like wolves through the night for Mary as Queen, and death to the rebels. Was it possible that they thought of herself as a rebel?

She stayed at the window listening, trying to pray, until the river glimmered with a cold light, and streaks of white appeared between the clouds downstream; and in that first light of dawn she saw a short dark figure riding out of the Tower gates towards Lambeth Palace. Archbishop Cranmer had also left her.

Archbishop Cranmer, the Arch-Reformer, the exquisite architect of the new religion, who had built it up in phrase after lovely phrase in Edward's Prayer Book, he too then was recanting. What should she do, what faith could she find anywhere in this world of new ideas that he had helped build, and was now deserting? She sank to her knees by the window and clutched the little wooden image of King Edward. 'What would you do now, Cousin, what *could* you do?'

Then it struck her that this was worse than Popery, to take a graven image of the dead for God, and ask help or comfort from it. She must ask help from God alone. She stayed on her knees asking it until she fell asleep.

She woke remembering that Cranmer had left the Tower.

After that it did not seem to matter much that next day nearly everybody who was still in the Tower found it imperative that they should go with Lord Pembroke to Barnard's Castle to arrange, they said, about the French troops that would soon be coming into England in answer to Duke Dudley's summons for help.

Lady Throckmorton had to go to a christening as proxy for Queen Jane, who felt far too ill to go herself, though she would have been thankful to leave the Tower even for a few hours.

Her father was still with her. But men kept coming in to speak to him, urgently, privately. At last he went to his daughter and said, 'I am but one man. What else can I do?'

She did not answer him; he did not wait for any answer. He left her without another word. It was late evening when he returned, and she was sitting at supper alone, except for the attendants who served her, since she still would not allow Guildford at the royal table. Her father came straight up to her without speaking and began to pull down the royal canopy above her head. She exclaimed at what he was doing, and he only answered, 'Such things are not for you.'

Then he sent the servants away and told her that when he had left her he had summoned all his men who were still left in the Tower and told them to lay down their weapons. He had said to them, as he had said to her, 'I am but one man,' and he had led them up on to Tower Hill, and there, leaning over the walls, he had proclaimed Queen Mary. He had then gone on to Barnard's Castle, and signed the Proclamation. 'One man,' he repeated, 'against them all. What else could I do? Against *them*, did I say? No, but against all London. The Proclamation for Mary has been read from Paul's Cross – and London is a howling, dancing, bubbling frenzy; bonfires blazing; gutters running with wine; the people have dragged tables out into the street – they are feasting and drinking, the best way Englishmen know to show their joy. They are shouting "Long life to Queen Mary and death to the rebels!" People are throwing money out of the windows in their madness, and my sweet Lord Pembroke, the turncoat rat, flung away his cap stuck all over aigrettes and diamonds – saw him do it myself! All the belfrys in London are clanging and caterwauling, the din's so loud it deafens you, there's not a man dares go to bed in London tonight lest he be dragged out and made to drink Queen Mary's health on his knees. I had fine work I can tell you to make my way back here through the press though I had my fellows with me and all of us on horseback, but we were as near as may be pulled off our horses, we had to stop and drink at the hands of pretty near all we passed and shout "God bless Queen Mary!" Only the Tower is dark and silent as the tomb in the midst of the burly-hurly,' – he considered the word askance, then carefully corrected it.

His voice was thick and his eye bloodshot as he dramatised his heroic journey, but his daughter did not recognise these symptoms as any but those of distress. 'Then, sir,' she said in a small appealing voice, 'oh, sir, can't we leave the Tower too and go home?'

He began to cry, and at that Jane was really frightened, and cried too on a loud wailing note. Her head was spinning. Everything went wrong here, everyone was different – 'Oh, why, why can't I go home?'

He pulled himself together, put his arms round her and tried to comfort her, though it was little comfort that he gave.

'You can't go home, my child, not yet in any case. We're the Queen's prisoners now.'

'But why? It's not my fault. I only did as I was told. I never wanted to be Queen.'

'Tell her that!' he urged on a sudden note of inspiration. 'Go to your writing closet now, this instant, and tell her the whole thing – how you were forced into this – by the Dudleys, mind you, not us. We've been as helpless as you, my poor innocent child – almost. Your mother, of course, is a masterful woman, never stops reminding one that she's half a Tudor – but she'd never have done this of herself. It's all Duke Dudley.'

'But, sir – I thought it was King Edward.'

'Of course, of course. But he was a sick, a dying boy, and Dudley had all the power. But none of that concerns you – you knew nothing of it all.'

'No,' she said, trying to check her sobs, trying to think through his hot rush of words as his square brown chin-beard wagged up and down, with the light of the candles shining through it and showing hardly any chin beneath. 'No, I did not know any of this, till three days before you told me to come to the Tower.'

'Not *I*,' he cried angrily, 'it was Dudley, I tell you.'

'Well then, he told you to tell me. And as I have always been told to obey my parents, I obeyed.'

The Duke of Suffolk gave up trying to get the wording right. There was something of the mule about his daughter; she got it of her mother. 'Anyway,' he said, 'it will clear *you* of any wilful intent and purpose in it. Bring my grey hairs to the block if you will, so long as you go free.'

Jane burst into fresh tears. Why should she be accused of bringing his grey hairs (not that he had any) to the block? It was unfair. It was all so unfair. They had made her do what they wanted, and now they blamed her.

'Don't cry, don't cry,' he urged, 'it may yet come right. Mary can't last. The Londoners are mad and fickle. They think they want her now, but, in a few months even, they may turn against her.'

His face grew suddenly long and cunning as he sucked in his cheeks and laid a finger against that big important nose of his that always looked as though it were trying to be twice as big and important as any round button of a Tudor nose. 'Given time,' he said, 'and Dudley safe out of the way, if we win only a few months' grace, we may even yet get another chance.'

But at that Jane became quite wild and hysterical. She did not want any other chance. She would never let herself be made Queen again, never, never. She did not want anything but to go home.

* * *

Lady Throckmorton returned from the christening party that night. The crowded rooms that she had left so full of bustle and agitation a few hours before were now empty, silent, stripped of all sign of royalty. She asked a servant where was Queen Jane, and Lord – King Guildford. She was told they were both prisoners.

A letter patent had been left out on a table, either by accident in the wild scurry, or else of intent. Across the royal stamp Mr Cecil had written 'Jana non Regina'.

CHAPTER NINE

Mary had won. Everyone else thought it a miracle; Mary knew it was one.

Only ten days before, she had set out on her desperate adventure, riding all night with her tiny company of six gentlemen; then in disguise as a peasant woman behind a servant, twenty miles at a stretch through the darkness; then on, with a pause only to change horses and snatch a meal in a quarter of an hour, first to Sawston, the house of a Catholic friend, Mr Huddleston, then to Kenninghall, then to Framlingham; looking back to see the flames of Huddleston's house rise flaring across the sky behind her, in revenge for having sheltered her; knowing that her pursuers were within a mile or two of her, that if they had the sense to leave their burning and looting of her supporters' property they had only to follow and catch herself.

But she rode on, still free, and 'I'll build you a better,' she cried to John Huddleston, who now rode with her.

Could this be herself, a prim old maid, as she was sure her critical young half-sister Elizabeth always thought her; who had had nothing to do for twenty years but wage an endless nagging petty warfare of words, words, words with her father's and then her young half-brother's evil counsellors?

Her only chance of adventure had been the hope of slipping

away in disguise one night to a boat that would take her across the sea to the Emperor's dominions where she would be safe from persecution. But she had never taken it – because she feared to? or because she knew the Emperor did not really want her on his hands? or because deep down in her heart she had always hoped that she would get this chance of another, far more glorious adventure? To be Queen of England! It seemed an all but impossible presumption to the woman of thirty-seven whose only opportunity of governance till now had been to visit the cottagers near her, sit down and take a cup of milk or ale while telling them to go on with their meal, seeing what they had for supper, asking after the goodman's job, his wages, the temper of his master, and the health and schooling and prospects of the children, patting those on the head who could still repeat a Paternoster, despite the opinions of their schoolmaster; and then sending them money or help afterwards incognito.

But now she had set out on an adventure more desperate than that of her Spanish grandmother, Isabella of Castile, who had driven the Moors from Spain; or of her Welsh grandfather, who had landed in England to kill the tyrant Richard III and make himself Henry VII. Their deeds had become the romances of the last century, not possible in these modern days, when money and vulgar opportunism ruled all things. Yet her enterprise was wilder and more forlorn of hope than theirs; she had set out blindly into the night, into a countryside where armies were marching against her, to raise to her side a Kingdom that knew nothing of her.

And she was doing this quite alone, except for the half-dozen gentlemen of her household who rode with her; without any money, any arms, any promise or assurance of support that might come to her, and above all without anyone to advise her.

This last was the worst of all to Mary. Till she was seventeen she had always depended on her mother to tell her what to do; and then, at her death, on her mother's nephew, the Emperor Charles. But there had been no time to ask his advice, and the behaviour of his ambassadors showed that if there had been, he would have advised most urgently against it. So that added to the excitement was the anxiety lest, instead of acting like a heroine for the first time in her life, she was only behaving like a naughty troublesome child.

Charles V, the solemn young man with the huge chin like a slab of cheese whom Mary had not seen since she had been betrothed to him at six years old, had represented God to her ever since her father had so brutally toppled himself off his divine pedestal. Always her mother had told her the Emperor was the greatest monarch on earth, Lord of the New World and the ancient Holy Roman Empire of Charlemagne, head of all temporal power, as the Pope was of all spiritual. Dreadful as it would be if she were taken prisoner and killed (and she had no illusions as to what her fate would be in Dudley's hands), it would be still more dreadful if the Emperor thought it was all her own fault!

But she rode on and reached Framlingham safely, one of the strongest fortresses in the Kingdom, where she could keep a line of escape open across country to the little Suffolk seaport of Aldeborough, so that if things went too badly she could even yet slip down to the shore and on to a boat and away to the Netherlands and their master, the Emperor – and even if he scolded her, she would still be alive and free.

Her first command was to keep a line of retreat guarded

from the Castle all the way to the shore. That showed true
generalship, said the country gentlemen who were now there
to advise her and to whom she listened as respectfully as to a
group of Field Marshals. ('Hush, my dear, the gentlemen are
talking,' had been a frequent admonition of her mother's.) So
from the top of one or other of the Castle towers she looked
out towards the sea, and constantly inspected the defences of
her bolt-hole. But it did not prove necessary.

The miracle had begun to happen. Men were coming in to
her side. Sir Henry Bedingfeld with 140 of his Suffolk
tenantry, fully horsed and armed, and Sir Henry Jerningham
with his men of Norfolk had already joined her before she left
Kenninghall, so that her six gentlemen-in-waiting had become
the nucleus of a tight little force of cavalry. But within two or
three days at Framlingham her army had swelled to 13,000,
all volunteers; they demanded no pay, but instead brought all
provisions with them and, to help her cause, money, plate and
jewels. Here was a contrast to Dudley's beggarly hirelings, at
tenpence a day! they said proudly when they heard of the
muster against them in Tothill Fields.

Not only were there more and more gentry and some
nobles coming in at the head of their tenants, but there were
bodies of tenantry, some small, some quite large, without any
leader, who had flatly refused to follow their lords and
masters to fight for Duke Dudley, and marched off of their
own accord to fight for the Lady Mary instead. Some had
good weapons of war, shot-guns or the long bows and arrows
or cross-bows, others only hay-forks, bill-hooks and other
farmers' implements such as they had marched with a couple
of years ago against the New Prayer Book and the Enclosing
Act that cut off the land from free grazing for all, as it had

been for centuries, and turned it into private parks for the pleasure of the new gentry.

They had been smashed then by the new gentry. This time they might beat them, they might come into their age-old rights by bringing the Lady Mary into hers.

They knew little of her. To most of them she was only a name and a legend, a Princess shut up in Dolorous Guard, oppressed by all these jumped-up gentry because she stuck to the good old ways as her mother had done before her. She was being done out of her rights as they themselves had been. But she had often given good answers to her oppressors.

'My father made the most part of you out of nothing!' So she had roared at Dudley, that robber son of a crook lawyer – as any one of her followers would have given his ears for the chance to roar.

'I know not what *you* call God's truth. That is not God's truth as it was known in my father's day.' (That was the way to treat 'em!)

'I pray you send me back my steward from prison, for I wasn't brought up as a baker's daughter to know how many bolls of meal are needed for a dozen loaves, and I cannot start to learn now.' She had called that out of her window to the Council as they rode off; she'd had the woman's last word there sure enough!

Old Ridley had had the new clergy's last word down in her hall when he drank the stirrup-cup she'd sent down for him and then dashed it from his lips, declaring that no true servant of God would drink in such a house.

'But he'd taken a good sup of her wine first, and made that fine gesture only to her servants after he had been well worsted in argument by herself – mind that!' said they, nudging each other, chuckling with delight at the Bishop of London's discomfiture. He himself gave all he had to the poor, but it didn't alter their opinion of these new clergy as a lot of dry husks, lickpennies to the new landlords – 'As for the new landlords, why, even one of those greedy-guts will pillage a countryside and never be satisfied, where fifty tun-bellied monks might fill their paunches, but there was always something over for a bite and a sup for anyone who cared to call at the monastery gatehouse.'

All these tales went round and lost nothing in the telling. The Lady Mary had her father's pluck and humour, her mother's charity.

'Ah, good Queen Katherine, she was a saint, *she* was – would take the clothes off her back to give to the poor'; but they were glad, too, to know that her daughter was not as careless of her dress as Queen Katherine, who had indeed been apt to look like a charwoman. But Mary had always loved to dress up in gay finery. That was right and proper, and some old men remembered the long fair hair that her father had been so proud of that he'd pulled off the child's cap to let it tumble down to her waist and show it off to the foreign ambassadors.

They marched to join the ranks of this lady of legend, the oppressed golden-haired Princess of Dolorous Guard.

They found a little woman with a big voice, surprisingly it even recalled that of the obese giant her father – but that was all to the good. They heard her laugh, they did not see her cry. They saw her review her troops on a horse that, startled by their frantic cheering, reared and all but threw her. She was not a good horsewoman and dismounted to finish the review on foot, a meagre little body who bustled along the ranks and showed her almost unbelieving joy and pride in them. She was no princess of fairy-tale after all, but she was old Harry's daughter right enough and true Tudor. That counted for more than all the rest. The Tudors were a dynasty only two generations old, but they had brought peace and stability to the country after long years of ruinous civil war.

And there were moments these days when one might almost see Mary as beautiful when her rather dim peering eyes lit up at sight of all the new followers, and the sea-wind off the Suffolk coast whipped fresh colour into her faded cheeks, and even her hair, that had begun to grow grey and dull, shone bright again in the high July sunshine. To the women who had been her devoted companions for so long, it seemed that yet another miracle was coming to pass, and that the fair-haired Princess whom her father had petted and adored as a child would now shed the long sad years between, and come into her own as freely and gaily as though she had never despaired of it.

For there was no time now for Mary to have headaches, or to cry, or to remember what her mother had said, and wonder what she would wish her to do.

There was only time to live every moment to its utmost; to review her troops, to inspect the mighty fortifications of her Castle, three moats with a walled causeway, and thirteen square towers; to superintend the mounting on these enormous walls, forty feet high and more than eight feet thick, of the navy's guns, her first artillery, and as juicy a windfall as ever fell into a lady's mouth, said the proud gunners. She appointed Sir Henry Bedingfeld Knight Marshal of her army and gave tactful directions that if any of them went short of food or clothing his captain should provide it as from himself and charge the amount to her. She appointed 500 men as her personal bodyguard. She ordered bakers to be sent from Norwich for her host, and malt to be brewed for it at Orford. She commanded all prisoners in Suffolk and Norfolk to be freed – they were mostly political prisoners and therefore safe to be on her side. She went on welcoming new arrivals.

Young George Howard rode up without the chalice he had looted from her, and very angry from his quarrel with Jack Dudley; and Lord Grey rode up with a swollen nose, and still angrier from his quarrel with Duke Dudley. The Earls of Bath and Sussex slipped away from the Council in London and rode to her. The Bishop of London rode to her to ask her pardon but got arrested at Ipswich.

And then Mr Secretary Cecil rode to her, sent by the rest of the Council to explain that they were all hers to a man, and had been so all along in their hearts; only Duke Dudley's terrorism had made it necessary for them, 'in order to avoid great destruction and bloodshed,' to tell a certain amount of 'pardonable lies.' Mr Cecil explained so well that Mary told his sister-in-law, Mrs Bacon, that she 'really believed he was a very honest man.'

Finally, the representatives of the City of London rode to her and gave her a red velvet purse that clinked with £500 in half-sovereigns.

It was all over. The miracle had happened. Well before July was out, her enemies had melted like snow in the hot sun; the all-powerful Duke was a prisoner, and all his sons had been rounded up and arrested. Mary had been proclaimed Queen in every town in England, last of all in London. The reign of Queen Jane had proved to be literally a 'nine days' wonder.' And having begun to disband her army within a fortnight of its assembling, Mary rode in leisurely state to London to be Queen.

CHAPTER TEN

She rode through cities and a countryside alive and ringing, singing, shouting mad with joy in her triumph. Crowds ran for miles beside her horse, called down God's blessing on her, wept for happiness. To them, hers was a personal triumph. She had come into her own after being so long done out of her rights, even as her mother, Good Queen Katherine, had been. Many in those crowds would gladly have risen and fought for Katherine of Aragon when, after she had been twenty years his devoted wife, King Harry put her away like any wanton and then hounded and worried her until she died. She had lain cold in her grave nigh on a score of years; but now her daughter, who had been bullied ever since, branded with illegitimacy, now she had triumphed for them both.

'Eh, but your poor mother would have been glad to see this day!' was the cry that many gave aloud, and was echoed deep in Mary's heart.

But she did not see how entirely personal was their feeling.

To her, their joy was a clear sign of their faith in the old religion and their thankfulness that she would now bring it back to them.

God had chosen her, stupid, weak, backsliding as she had been, for she too had not dared withstand King Henry to the uttermost, she too had been forced to truckle to him, to her own and, far worse, to her mother's shame. She had never forgiven herself for it; but now God had shown that He forgave her, He had chosen her for His servant, to do His work in England. His victory was not a reward to be selfishly enjoyed; it was a holy trust, His instrument to build God's Church anew.

She would be harsh to no one, for she too had been guilty, but she would free this unhappy country from its crime of cowardice in following a King's command into heresy, and bring the prodigal son happy and repentant back into the arms of the loving Father.

'Look at her!' exclaimed young Mistress Frances Neville to the Mistress of the Robes. 'She looks ten years younger and really almost pretty.'

'I can remember when she was really very pretty. You should have seen her on her eighteenth birthday listening to John Heywood's poem in praise of "her lively face", and it's true again today, thank God, that it's like "a lamp of joy".'

'But why choose that violet velvet?'

'That, ' said Lady Clarencieux severely, 'is the colour of our Blessed Lord's coat.'

'Ah, but our Blessed Lord did not live to be thirty-seven!'

'I hear Frances' laugh as usual,' said the Queen, looking back at them; 'what's making you merry this time?'

'Oh, Madam, who would not be merry at this time? We'll never sing of 'Jolly June' again, but jolly July shall be the Queen of the months from now on for bringing our Queen, Merry Mary, to the throne.'

Mary's quick flush of pleasure answered her gratefully; in contrast her laugh sounded gruff and husky, it creaked a little from disuse.

'You managed that very cleverly,' said Susan Clarencieux a trifle sourly as their horses fell behind again.

'Oh, anyone can do that, she is so good-natured and easy-going. I hope she gets as kind a husband. I suppose she will marry – even now. Who do you think it will be?'

'Well, her dear mother always hoped it would be the Lord Reginald Pole. And so did his mother. I often heard the poor Countess of Salisbury talking of it with Queen Katherine at their embroidery, when she was the Lady Mary's governess.'

'But he is a Cardinal now.'

'He only took minor orders. The Pope could give dispensation. And it would redress a great wrong. King Henry put the old Countess of Salisbury to death for little other reason than that she was a royal Plantagenet, daughter of George Duke of Clarence.'

'Well, *he* was put to death for the same reason by his brother Richard Crookback – and in a butt of malmsey wine! It is all so long ago, what does it matter now? *I* hope she'll marry a great foreign prince.'

'True, she was betrothed once to the Emperor himself.'

'What, that old man!'

'He is only fifty-two,' replied the elder lady stiffly.

'Oh, dear Clarencieux, don't think of the years – think how he's crippled with gout, and has to suck a green leaf all the time for his parched mouth. Heaven defend our poor lady from marrying Nebuchadnezzar! Besides, he's talking of abdicating.'

'Well, there's his son Prince Philip.'

Frances Neville made no comment this time, but her eyes shone. Prince Philip, young, handsome, heir to half the world – what luck for a greying old maid!

Women's voices laughed and chattered, horses' hoofs squelched the leaf mould, wet from the recent squalls, the sunlight pierced the heavy summer foliage of the great trees in Epping Forest, knocking sparks of light from the jewels and bright metalled harness of the leisurely train.

The Queen rode with Jane Dormer, her favourite lady-in-waiting, beside her, a handsome young widow, clear-cut in her opinions and bold in expressing them. Lady Dormer asked her what they had all been wondering, what must happen to the Lady Jane Grey?

Mary did not see why anything should happen. Jane had written to her and explained everything. It was obvious that she had been a mere tool in the hands of the Dudleys ('A dangerous tool,' murmured Lady Dormer). Why, she had known nothing about the whole business till two or three days before, and had been practically forced into the Crown, as into her marriage – she had written that she had been positively ill-treated by her young husband and his mother. 'I am sorry for her, though I admit I have never really liked the girl since –.since—'

'Since Your Majesty sent her that cloth of gold dress she never wore, because "it would be a shame to follow my Lady Mary's example in finery, against God's word, and leave my Lady Elizabeth's example, who is a follower of God's word!"'

'Now, Jane, you know they had no right to tell us what she said, and indeed it was not that that I was thinking of' (though her deep flush showed that she was), 'but of that which should grieve all of us far more, that – that – I mean, about the baker.'

'The baker?' Lady Dormer was bewildered, then remembered and, devout though she was herself in her practical way, with some amusement that Mary could not bear even to repeat the story.

Jane Grey had been paying a Saturday-to-Monday visit to Mary at Newhall with her parents, and passing through the private chapel with one of Mary's ladies noticed her genuflecting and asked if the Princess had come into the chapel.

'No,' was the answer, 'the Host was on the altar, and I did reverence to Him who made us.'

'Not so,' said Jane, 'the baker made *him*!'

And that too, of course, had been duly repeated.

'But,' said Mary, 'it is all the fault of her upbringing. She has been taught to think so.'

'She might at least have been taught not to speak so, and in your house. These Reformers have no manners.'

'At least she is honest. And my poor little brother was very fond of her. There is something so pathetic in a childish love-affair.'

Lady Dormer thought her unduly sentimental. 'King Edward would never have married her. Don't you remember, Madam, how he wanted a grand foreign princess "well stuffed with jewels and rich provinces"?'

Mary laughed with her at his boyish conceit, but insisted on his romance. 'My Jane,' he used to call her when they played cards together. 'Now, my Jane, you have lost your king, so you must take me for your King instead.'

'Oh, but, Madam, he said that to *me*. It was *I* who was "his Jane" at cards, not Jane Grey! Of course I was older, but you know what children are like.'

Jane Dormer was so determined to claim the story that Mary let her have it. And it had stopped her worrying about what was to happen to Jane Grey. She herself was not worrying; she had made up her mind to have no more bloodshed than was absolutely necessary. Her reign should be as happy, as free from fear and hate and revenge, as she felt herself to be.

For now her soul was coming out of the dark forest of fear into the sunlight, even as she and her cortège rode out from under those dark ancient trees into the dazzle of golden fields. They were nearing the great house of Wanstead, where she would break her journey before entering her capital.

Another large company was riding towards them down the road through the bright corn, many ladies and gentlemen in glittering clothes and harness, and then hundreds of horsemen in white and green, their satin and taffeta coats shining like the waves of the sea. At their head rode a tall slight figure all in white, straight and gleaming as a drawn sword, whose hair blazed redder than the ripe corn.

The Lady Elizabeth had ridden out from London, with all the nobility attached to her household and all its horsemen in the Tudor white and green livery, to greet her sister and help escort her into her capital.

At sight of her, Mary felt a little cold shock, as though Fate had knocked at her heart.

CHAPTER ELEVEN

'You have made a quick recovery from your severe illness, sister!'

'What better cause of recovery, Madam, could I have than the news of Your Majesty's glorious, and, thank God, bloodless victory?'

'And what was the cause of the illness?'

'I must have eaten something,' said Elizabeth demurely, and then with a side-glance at her half-sister from under downcast eyelids, 'or was afraid that I might come to do so if I went to London.'

'Who warned you that the King's summons was a false lure?' asked Mary sharply.

'No one, Madam. I guessed – but not until I had all but started.'

'You are very wise.'

'Not as wise as Your Majesty has proved herself.'

'I? Oh, *I* had a message.' There was a tinge of bitterness in Mary's voice. She herself would not have guessed.

Elizabeth longed to ask from whom the message came. But it was safer not. Mary's tone to her had sounded a little tart. It would be better to go on congratulating, which she could do with complete sincerity. 'I was not thinking only of our reasons to suspect that summons,' – and her voice rose from its low tone to a proud and ringing note – 'but of the extraordinary wisdom and courage, if I may say so, of every move you have made since then. The greatest general could have done no better – to advance intrepidly even before you had any army, but always to guard your line of retreat. The greatest monarch can have no more glorious triumph than yours – to be brought to the throne by something stronger even than your unquestionable right – the will of the people.'

'It was the will of God,' corrected Mary.

There was a brief silence that seemed to quiver on the air. Each sister had stated her creed, and with it the gulf that lay between them.

To Mary it brought a pang of discomfort, and fear. The will of the people was the will of God, in her sister's eyes. Would Elizabeth be loyal to her? It was a question she had already pondered; it had even occurred to her just now when talking of her cousin Jane, that she might not have felt so leniently disposed had it been her sister Elizabeth. But why?

Jane was the white hope of all these 'hot gospellers' as they were called in the odious new phrase. But Elizabeth had always been extremely cool to them, though she affected their severe plainness of dress – no doubt from policy.

Jane had been downright rude to herself behind her back, but she must have known it would get round to her, and had not cared. She had only cared about saying what she felt to be right, regardless of whom it hurt – not surprising, perhaps, in anyone who had been so much snubbed and rebuked herself. Mary could understand that. But Elizabeth was never rude to her, wrote frequent charming letters to her 'very dear sister' full of kind enquiries and sympathy about her bad health, sent her her own favourite servants for any special purpose that

Mary required, generally medicine or music.

Yet she never could feel sure of Elizabeth, never quite knew what she meant. You always knew exactly what Jane meant, however little you might like it. Jane was honest in every sense, not only truthful, but a pure and virtuous maiden. Was Elizabeth? Mary tried not to ask the question, to which she knew she could never give a fair answer, but only another question – how could the daughter of Nan Bullen, who had corrupted her father, lured him from his long allegiance to his true wife and true Church, so that he himself complained of her, 'I was seduced by sorcery into this marriage,' how could the daughter of Nan Bullen – whom the rough Cockney crowds had seen in her true colours, mobbing her for 'a goggle-eyed whore,' – be pure and virtuous?

Behind the flaming hair of Elizabeth she saw always the raven-smooth tresses of Nan Bullen, the Night Crow, as Cardinal Wolsey had called her, brushed glossily back from the bold clever forehead; behind those downcast white-lidded eyes of Elizabeth, sometimes pale as green water, and sometimes blue as the heart of a flame, she saw the black sparkling eyes of Nan Bullen that, as the ambassadors had discreetly said, 'invited conversation'; behind the quiet grey or white clothes, all but those of a nun's habit, which Elizabeth elected to wear, the outrageous dresses of black satin and velvet in the latest French fashion, each of them costing three times as much as a whole year's dress allowance for the Princess Mary, which Nan Bullen had flaunted as a setting for King Henry's most costly and ancient jewels.

Elizabeth had then been an infant; she was not responsible that she had then been declared heir to the throne, and her sister Mary, nearly eighteen years older, illegitimate and uninheritable. Nor was she responsible for taking precedence over her elder sister, who had had to walk behind her and bear up the baby's 'train'; nor for her mother Nan Bullen's message to the maids she sent to wait on the Lady Mary instead of Mary's own devoted friends: 'Give her a box on the ear now and then for the cursed bastard she is.'

But Nan Bullen had been responsible for Elizabeth, even as Katherine of Aragon, the daughter of Isabella the Catholic of Castile, Crusader against the heathen Moors, had been responsible for Mary. And Mary, knowing something of what she herself had inherited from her mother, could not fail to see the sorceress and seductress Nan Bullen in the downcast glance, the demure demeanour of this slim girl in virginal white, about whom scandal had whispered such shocking things over four years ago, when she was but fifteen.

And there again Mary knew another reason why she could not be fair to Elizabeth. Not only distrust, not only horror lay between them, but curiosity, yes and envy. This girl little more than half her own age, held behind her cool gaze more knowledge and experience of life than Mary had ever touched. Useless to disclaim all wish for such knowledge; to vow, as her mother had told her to do, that she would keep herself pure as any nun, not even desiring man's love and marriage till it should happen of God's will to her. She had desired it; she did desire it; she had never come within even speaking distance of it; and she was thirty-seven. How much had Elizabeth, at nineteen, already known?

She looked at her half-sister across the widespread gulf that this instant's silence had made visible; and a question struck at her heart like an adder. Was Elizabeth even her half-sister? Was King Henry indeed her father? – or was Mark Smeeton, the handsome young musician who used to play the lute in Nan Bullen's chamber?

Her voice came at last in a strained husky whisper, 'A great while ago this story began.'

What did she mean? She herself did not know. She had a way of dropping out these unconnected, disconcerting sentences, and then hearing them hang on the air as though they had been uttered by someone else. It was one of the bad habits of a solitary. She must shake them from her; hold her first royal Court at Wanstead, kissing on the cheek each of the ladies presented to her by Elizabeth; reform her procession and ride on in state to enter her capital.

She left all that remained of her armed forces at the gates of the City, in accordance with their ancient statutes, and in spite of much cautionary advice that it was scarcely wise to disband her army completely when London had only a few days before been so full of turbulence and rebellion. But Mary was determined to show her trust in her people.

It was seven o'clock as they entered the City of London. The sun was setting in a fury of flame and storm-clouds. All the dark rickety wooden houses leaning top-heavily across the streets as though they were nodding to each other, all but rubbing each other's foreheads, all seemed to have put on scarves and petticoats, so many bright cloths fluttered from the windows, while the gaily painted shop signs flaunted and creaked and clattered in the breeze. The streets below were a sea of dim white faces surging forward from all the dark corners and alleys, blackened with swaying shadows cast by the leaping flames of the bonfires and tossing flicker of torches. And like the sea in a great storm came the roar of welcome from all those grinning gaping mouths.

Mary had to put a tight hold on herself to keep from bursting into tears. It made her face go wooden and she held herself as stiffly as possible in accordance with all she had been taught on the proper behaviour of a Queen.

It annoyed her that her half-sister, whom she had graciously placed only a horse's head behind her in the procession, seemed to have no such companion notions on the proper behaviour of a Princess. In the tail of her eye she could see Elizabeth sitting her horse as upright as an arrow, and nearly half a head taller than herself; but otherwise her whole behaviour lacked dignity, not to say decorum. She was looking to right and left among all those faces as though she knew them personally; she held her reins with hands drooping from exaggeratedly raised wrists, in order to show off her long white fingers and rosily gleaming nails, and Mary was sure that it was with the same intent that she patted her horse's neck or waved, smiling at the crowd as though their smiles were for *her* – as perhaps many of them were. Her ears caught the laughing applauding murmurs,

'Look at the lass!'

'There goes Old Harry's own!'

'*That's* the Tudor red-head!'

These murmurs were not for Mary and her greying head.

An extraordinary elation was mounting in Elizabeth as she rode through this roaring City in the sunset light, knowing that it crowned her hair with a halo of fire, that she was alive and free, instead of in the Tower under Duke Dudley's dread thumb, that she was not yet twenty – and that anything might happen!

These people were greeting their Queen loyally, but they

laughed with gladness as they looked at herself. They looked to her as next heir to the throne; they threw flowers at her and she dexterously caught a red carnation and flourished it – another opportunity to show off her long white lovely hands, and how clever of Cat Ashley to have discovered that new stuff for the finger-nails just in time! But her excitement was far deeper than the mere personal vanity of a girl showing herself off to the crowd.

It was the crowd itself that intoxicated her; the queer sense that she was part of them, that she and they lived at their fullest when in conjunction.

All these long, desperately quiet years when she had worked in solitude at her books and music, danced only with her dancing master, seen hardly anyone outside her household, all through that nunlike retirement, when Time crawled on leaden-soled boots, she seemed to have been waiting, living for this moment when Time would gallop for her yet again. Always it had shone at the back of her mind, lighting her loneliness, sometimes her despair.

And it had not been a hope so much as a memory. They said she could not have remembered what had happened in her infancy, she could only have imagined it from what she was told later. But she did remember; or dreamed of it so often that it was as vivid as if she did. From the very day she was born, and again and again through the first two and a half years of her life, a gigantic glittering figure would swoop upon her, hoist her up in his arms and hold her at an open window above a wavering sea of faces that flickered white, red and black in the flamelight and shadow cast by the torches, and roared 'Long live the princess!' 'Long live Elizabeth!'

Until one day the giant, clad all in yellow satin like a towering toad, with a white feather in his cap at which she clutched from her perch upon his enormous padded shoulder, went prancing through his Court, showing her off to his English nobles and foreign ambassadors alike, shouting, 'Thank God the old harridan is dead! And this is your future Queen Elizabeth!'

That had been the last of Elizabeth's royal progresses on the shoulder of her dread sire, King Harry VIII.

The old harridan had been Mary's mother, Good Queen Katherine, who died in January. But in May, Elizabeth's mother Nan Bullen was dead too, not only in accordance with King Harry's desire, but by his command.

January and May were dead; their daughters lived on. And all these things now cast their leaping flickering light on Elizabeth's mind, throwing a strange glow of exhilaration on the present huge untidy turbulent crowd of people thronging out of their obscure homes, jostling and struggling to get near her, stare at her, grin at her, toss flowers to her, shout silly joking intimate things in welcome to her. These people, rough, poor, ragged and drunk, tramps and drabs, and respectable shopkeepers and their wives in their Sunday best, all these people whom she could never hope nor probably want to know personally, all seemed a close and integral part of herself. She could delight in their delight and know what caused it. The fear and horror of civil war, of ruin to their homes and death to the men-folk, must have hung heavy on them these past two weeks; and now they saw the shadow lifting. They could go back to their work and carry on their multitudinous little lives and loves and activities in peace and safety. What intricate network of custom, law, business, work and payment, supply and demand of food and goods and clothing, held all this thrumming, passionate, rough-tempered, good-humoured swarm together, so much more complicated than any hive or ant-heap whose workings were a miracle of nature? But *this* miracle, of order among the tangle of humanity – who could work it?

From deep down in her unremembered infancy came the answer, '*I* could.'

This human hive, this swarming ant-heap, had so nearly been kicked over. These hot grinning faces bobbing round the triumphal procession of their rightful Queen and her heir might so easily have been shrieking in terror, trampled by advancing troops of rebels; these bonfires might have been the flames of their burning homes; the gutters might have been running with blood instead of wine.

What hand could be both strong and sensitive enough to wage rule and harmony among these wild and discordant elements? Once again she raised her own.

CHAPTER TWELVE

The grim gates of the Tower stood open. A little group of captives stood there awaiting them, dark in the dimming light of the courtyard; and at the approach of the Queen, fell on their knees.

There was the Duchess of Somerset, widow of Edward Seymour the late Protector whom Dudley had executed two years before – a handsome haggard woman whose ravaged face showed none of the softening of grief but only a fierce determination to grab what she could from life.

There was Gardiner, the Bishop of Winchester, rugged, indomitable, with his blunt nose and humorous eye, whom King Harry had cut out of his will and the place he had expected to find on the Council because, 'though he himself could manage Gardiner, nobody else could.'

There was the old Duke of Norfolk, under sentence of death, no one quite knew why, ever since King Harry, whom he had served as faithfully as any savage mastiff ever served his master, had died six and a half years ago, just before his failing hand could sign the death-warrant for his most doggedly devoted servant.

And there was young Edward Courtenay, son of the Marquis of Exeter beheaded fifteen years before; he was tall and handsome, with pale transparent skin, like a fine plant grown in the dark; the only reason for the imprisonment that had dimmed his lot since childhood had been his Plantagenet blood, which gave him too dangerously near a claim to the throne.

In the last flush of the sunset Mary dismounted and advanced with her quick-short steps towards the huddled group of kneeling figures in the shadow of the Tower wall. She raised them one by one and kissed them, saying, 'These are my prisoners,' while the tears ran down her face. 'You shall come back into the Tower, but as my friends and guests, to stay with me in the royal apartments until my Coronation,' she told them laughing through her tears.

To the Duchess of Somerset she said, 'My good Nan.' and to Bishop Gardiner, 'You shall be my Chancellor,' and then she came to the Duke of Norfolk, who had bullied her into compliance with King Henry and told her that if she were *his* daughter he would have beaten her to death and knocked her head against the wall till it was as soft as a baked apple.

She raised him too, and kissed his grizzled cheek, and then for an instant she stood silent, thinking of his cruel words to her all those years ago, and thinking too of his son, the magnificent young Earl of Surrey, the finest poet, soldier, sportsman of his day, swinging down in his scarlet coat to the tennis courts at Hampton Court – whose death-warrant her father had lived just long enough to execute.

Then she said, 'Your castle at Framlingham has done me good service, my lord.'

He answered, 'Madam, when King Harry confiscated it, I asked that it should go to no lesser hands than those of his children, for it is stately gear.'

'My lord, the stately gear is yours again.'

And she turned to young Edward Courtenay, calling him 'Fair Cousin,' but it seemed he hardly heard her. His wide eyes were fixed on the slight commanding figure behind her, on the face like a white flame of pride and glory beneath its red-gold crown of hair. Youth and gaiety of living, from which he had been debarred, now shone before him; he knelt, not to Queen Mary, but to the Lady Elizabeth.

CHAPTER THIRTEEN

To beget a male heir for England had been the one persistent purpose through all King Henry's murderous philanderings and six marriages, cut short only by his death. But now that his one male heir had died, a woman had become the Sovereign of England for the first time since, four hundred years before, the savage Norman Queen Matilda had provided good reason why there should never be another.

But no gloomy comparisons with Queen Matilda seemed likely to be justified. 'Merciful Mary' was what everyone was calling her, and declaring that

> *'Her honest fame shall ever live*
> *Within the mouth of man.'*

John Heywood's birthday poem to her had come back into fashion as fast as the sturdy playwright-poet himself had returned to London (for, being a Papist, he had found it convenient to travel abroad during King Edward's reign) and presented himself before her with, he said, two objects: 'the first, that I should see Your Majesty; the second, that Your Majesty should see me!'

She guffawed in answer to the hint and promptly reinstated him in his appointment as manager of the children's theatrical companies at Court, and moreover insisted that she should claim no royal privilege but always pay for her own seat in the audience.

Everyone was delighted with her; except her supposed ally, the Imperial ambassador. His master Charles V had instructed him to advise the new Queen to go slow on the executions of the rebels so as to ensure an easy start for her reign. Mary's immediate response, as eager as that of a schoolgirl anxious to obey fully, was, 'Would the Emperor like me to forgive Duke Dudley?'

Forgive Dudley himself, arch rebel and traitor of the whole revolt, who had tried to sell Calais back to the French (and indeed Mary found that hardest of all to forgive) so as to bring foreign troops into England to help overthrow the lawful Sovereign! It was going beyond the bounds of reason, even of possibility.

But the Duke himself thought otherwise. The Dudleys were not good losers. He had been utterly crushed at first. The crowds that stared in silence as he rode out from the Tower had surged round him on his return to it as a helpless prisoner, hooting and howling their jeers of hatred, throwing stones, spattering him with filth. His son Jack, who rode behind him, broke down and cried. Duke Dudley himself had been almost too dazed to realise the nightmare. His health, never strong, had cracked under the strain and he was in a high fever.

But when quiet in the Tower he began to struggle for life like a drowning fly.

He had climbed so high above all others, he had helped pull down the powerful Seymour brothers to the block; it could not be that he should now share their fate.

He set to work to pull every string he knew; his beautiful

wife sent round to all their influential friends (it was surprising how they all declared now that they had no influence whatever) with what presents of jewels and sables she could muster. He changed his religion, of course; he said he had always 'certainly thought best of the old religion; but seeing a new one begun, run dog, run devil, he had let it go forward.' But he did not put it like that to Queen Mary.

His behaviour at the trial was noted as 'very obsequious,' though he politely pointed out that the judges were as guilty as he; and his fellow-prisoner, Sir Thomas Palmer, not so politely, roared out the unpalatable truth – 'The judges are traitors too – they deserve punishment as much as me and more!' It did not help them.

Even after he had been sentenced and warned that he would be executed the next day, Dudley made a last frantic attempt and wrote to Arundel imploring imprisonment, confiscation, banishment, anything as long as it was life. 'Oh my good lord, remember how sweet life is, and how bitter the contrary! – An old proverb there is, that a living dog is better than a dead lion. Oh that it would please Her good Grace to give me life, yea the life of a dog, that I might but live and kiss her feet!'

The lion had fallen very low. But he fell lower on the scaffold when he turned to his second-in-command, Sir John Gates, and holding out his hands, told him, 'I forgive you with all my heart. Although you and your counsel was a great occasion of my offence.'

Sir John Gates promptly offered his forgiveness in return, with the reminder, 'Yet you and your authority was the cause of it altogether.'

Old connoisseurs of decent scaffold behaviour shrugged

contemptuously and reminded each other that the Duke had acted just like his father the lawyer, who had laid all the blame on others in his before-execution speech.

Tom Seymour had died like a tiger, and his brother the Protector like a gentleman, both victims of John Dudley, who now died like a craven. The London crowds had wept and groaned for the first two; they cheered themselves hoarse for the third, shouting, 'The dog is dead!'

One of the connoisseurs, Sir John Bridges, the Lieutenant of the Tower, dropped in to dinner at Mr Partridge's house in the Tower, where the Lady Jane Grey had been lodged ever since her eviction from the royal apartments, but with as much respect and deference as if she were an honoured guest. She happened to come down to dinner that day instead of having it in her rooms, and they all apologised for the intrusion of a chance visitor. Jane was gracious, told the men to keep on their caps in her presence, and asked for the news of the town – was it true they were already hearing Mass in the churches?

They told her yes, in some places, and there had been some riots against it, a priest nearly killed in the pulpit at Paul's Cross, and anonymous leaflets blowing about in the gutters telling people to rise against 'the detestable Papists who follow the opinions of the Queen.'

But the Queen's Proclamation against all this had been surprisingly mild, exhorting her subjects to give up 'those new-found devilish terms of papist or heretic and apply instead their whole care to live in the fear of God.' Since then things had quietened down a bit – with the help of 200 guards to keep order at the Paul's Cross sermons. One or two London churches had even begun to give Mass at the people's own wish, without any command, and there had been no disturbances.

'It may be so,' said Jane, and then, bitterly, 'it is not so strange as the sudden conversion of the late Duke. Who would have thought he could have done that?' she demanded, opening wide astonished eyes. It was an awkward moment; she evidently did not know that her own father had also just got converted – at a price of twenty thousand pounds.

Mr Partridge coughed judicially and said that no doubt Dudley had hoped to get his pardon by it.

'Pardon – for *him*!' she flashed out, all her grave composure shattered – 'he has brought me and our stock into most miserable calamity. His life was wicked and full of dissimulation, odious to all men. So was his end.'

Sir John Bridges cheerfully supplied further details of his odious end; the executioner limping up, for he was lame in one leg, in a white apron like any common butcher; the scarf slipping from the Duke's eyes as he laid his head upon the block, so that he had to get up again to have it refastened, and in that minute 'surely he figured to himself the terrible dreadfulness of death; then struck his hands together once as if to say "this must be," and cast himself down again.'

The connoisseur told it well, but Jane was not attending. No scarves nor white aprons were needed to impress on her the true dreadfulness of Dudley's end. Her lips moved as if in silent prayer, and then aloud, though very low, she said, 'I pray God that neither I nor any friend of mine shall die so. I am young, but would I ever forsake my faith for love of life? God forbid! But to *him*, an old man of fifty who had not long to live in any case, to him life was sweet it seems! So long as he might live he did not care how – perjured – captive. He would have lived in chains if he could!'

The company of elderly worldlings sat abashed in the

sudden white-hot flame of the little creature, who knew nothing yet of life except that she scorned to find it sweet if she could not keep her integrity of spirit.

They could only answer her by giving assurance of that life. Queen Mary, it was now generally known, had resolved there should be no more executions than those of Duke Dudley, Sir John Gates and Sir Thomas Palmer. Jane's father had not only been granted his life but all his property, and let off his fine of twenty thousand pounds in reward for his conversion. He and his wife had already been set at liberty, and it was Mary's firm intention that Jane should be too, though she had had to give her counsellors assurance that she would take all proper precautions first against any further outbreaks of rebellion. Bridges told Jane this in frank amazement, for Mary's advisers, even including those who had so recently been Jane's own supporters, were all urging that her innocence was beside the point, but that the safety of the Kingdom depended on the death of the rival who had been actually proclaimed Queen.

Jane listened, looking straight in front of her, but seeing only her own study at Bradgate in the green shadowed light from the great trees, and Mr Aylmer putting her books for that morning's work upon the table; hearing the deep hush fill the room that would be broken only by their two voices when they read aloud; a quiet eternity that would be interrupted only by the next meal.

She would be going back to that, after all.

Mary was a Papist, but she had been good to her. She said, 'I beseech God the Queen may long continue. She is a merciful Princess.'

CHAPTER FOURTEEN

Item. A large leather box marked with King Henry VIII's broad arrow, containing two old shaving cloths and thirteen pairs of old leather gloves, some of them worn.

Item. A fish of gold, being a toothpick.

Item. Three old halfpence in silver, seven little halfpence and farthings.

Item. Three books, a girdle of gold thread, and a pair of silver tweezers.

Item. Sixteen pence, two farthings and two halfpence. Three French crowns, one broken in two.

Item. A little square box with divers shreds of satin. A piece of paper containing a pattern of white taffeta.

Item. – Mary stopped writing with a start, as she felt her half-sister's eyes upon her.

Elizabeth must have entered the room a few minutes ago. How silently she moved, just like a cat – but Mary could hardly blame her for coming so promptly when summoned, nor yet for keeping quiet while the Queen was writing. So her annoyed exclamation had to be transferred to something else, and she went on quickly, 'I cannot understand it. Lord Winchester says he put all the Crown jewels into Jane's hands on the 12th of July, together with various other articles belonging to the Crown, and that some of them are now missing. He actually hints that Jane must have sold them.'

'Even our father's old shaving cloths?' asked Elizabeth demurely.

Short-sighted herself, Mary had had no idea that her big square handwriting was clearly legible at the distance where Elizabeth stood.

'That is merely to identify the box,' she explained hastily. 'But it is not a question of the value of the goods—'

'No?' asked Elizabeth, glancing down at the list of half-pence and farthings.

'But it is the principle of the thing that matters. These things are Crown property, delivered to Jane as the pretended inheritor of the Crown. I should have thought she would have been careful to guard and restore them.'

And she went on saying what she thought Jane should have done, while Elizabeth forced back her look of amazement. How could Mary, who was so generous and used to give away nearly all her beggarly dress allowance, sit poring over lists of rubbish like any cracked old cottage woman counting her broken treasures? Where could she get it from? A horrid thought flashed upon her, their grandfather, Henry VII, had started life as a splendid adventurer and ended it as a miser. Could it ever be that she, Elizabeth herself—?

She brushed it away and spoke hastily, putting all the trouble down to Winchester, 'I'll swear that old vulture's hooded eyes never lost sight of anything he handed over – or didn't hand over. Depend on it, Madam, he stuffed the shaving cloths into his own basin.'

Even as she said it she wished she hadn't. Mary was peering sharply at her. She used rather to enjoy being teased; but that had been when she was glad of any attention that was not a threat or a snub. Had power changed her already?

Elizabeth immediately looked sympathetic, and murmured that it was indeed tiresome of Jane and/or Winchester, and then with a swift stroke of what she felt to be genius she pointed to the item of the pattern and said, 'Surely I remember that white taffeta. Wasn't it a dress that our father liked you to wear?'

'It was,' said Mary discouragingly, for she remembered other things about it; how she had written to King Henry asking if she might leave off mourning for the latest wife he had beheaded, young Catherine Howard (a badly brought up girl whom Mary had never liked); on his somewhat ungracious message, that she could wear whatever colour she liked, she had ventured to write again demanding whether he would like her to wear that same white taffeta edged with velvet 'which used to be to his own liking whenever he saw it.' And to that tentative filial request he had sent no answer whatever.

'Why do we talk of such toys?' she demanded in the harsh deep voice that so surprisingly recalled him. 'No doubt you'd like to see his jewels that I have now inherited, yes, even those robbed from the tomb of the Blessed Martyr Saint Thomas à Becket, his tomb, that was the glory of Christendom, rifled to make thumb-rings and necklaces for the King – and Queen – of England. Look!' She pushed a tray of enormous rubies and emeralds set in antique gold towards her sister. 'Saint Louis, King of France, sent this great ruby to the English Saint's tomb before he went crusading with the Coeur de Lion, more than three hundred years ago. Your mother wore it on her Parisian black dresses. Would you like to wear it, sister, the "Regale de France", on those delicate fingers that you are so anxious the world shall notice?'

Elizabeth flushed scarlet. 'I care nothing for such gauds,' she cried, turning away her head. 'When have you ever seen me for years past wear jewels or bright colours or even do my hair as—'

'As you would like, sister?'

'As *you* would like, Madam, is all that matters now. Do you like my style of hairdressing?'

'No. I don't.' said Mary bluntly. 'The Scriptures tell us that a woman's hair is her crowning glory, and I see no point in stuffing it all under a net or cap as you do – except when, by some strange accident, it flies out into a flaming aureole as on our entry into London.'

Elizabeth murmured something about the wind, and that stupid Ashley.

'As you will,' Mary said abruptly. 'But I sent for you on matters more important. You have said you need instruction before entering the true Church, you ask for books, as though religion were an intellectual exercise. But what of your conscience and your soul? Are you playing at conversion out of policy? Why did you not accompany me to Mass last Sunday?'

'I had a stomach-ache,' said Elizabeth simply, but added wickedly, 'like Erasmus, who refused fish on Fridays, saying, "my heart is Catholic, but my stomach is Protestant".'

Mary, as an admirer of Erasmus, had to smile, and answered almost indulgently, 'You were always of a high stomach.' But she was eyeing her intently, seeing her again as the baby not yet four, who had asked indignantly how it was that she had been called the Lady Princess last week but now only the Lady Elizabeth. 'There's early showing of a high and haughty stomach!' the Court had murmured in amusement, but Mary, despite her grim satisfaction, had only felt sorry for the child who did not know that she had been bastardised in the past week.

She did not feel sorry now. Elizabeth needed reminding. She set about it.

'My first Act of Parliament will, of course, be to reinstate my mother as the lawfully wedded wife of King Henry, and myself therefore as his only surviving legitimate child. Is that plain?'

'Your Grace could not be plainer.'

'Have you any objection to make? You look as though you have.'

'What objection could I make? I had a mother – as Your Grace has had. She was done to death – more violently and publicly than yours. I do not remember her as you, Madam, have the good fortune to remember your more worthy – your sainted mother. I can have no public reason to object; but at least you may give me leave to regret in private the slur cast upon my mother's memory.'

It touched Mary on a tender spot. 'It is true,' she said almost apologetically, 'we cannot both be legitimate.'

'But, Madam, we can – if only it is not defined too closely and caged down in words. Think how wise our father was! He came to know he was mistaken to declare either or both of us illegitimate. But did he ever revoke what he had said and so admit that be had been mistaken? No, he let the past go, and merely replaced us both in the Succession after his son and heir King Edward, you as the elder, I the younger, without opening up again any question as to the which of us was born legitimate. You of all people will not question our father's wisdom when – when his passions did not lead him astray.'

Mary hesitated, hated it – it was compromise, casuistry, no clear-cut definition between right and wrong, but just the sheer Machiavellian doctrine of expediency. But there was no question but that it was what her father had said, and what he said was always right except in those cases at which Elizabeth had so tactfully hinted, above all the case of Nan Bullen.

But at the thought of Nan, something in Mary that she could not control rose up and cried aloud to be revenged upon her daughter. She heard it cry, not in her own voice but one strained and wild as a lost soul – 'You think then to be declared as our heir, my Lady Elizabeth? Are you so sure I shall not be able to provide a better? Yet women older than I have married and borne children. I am not yet thirty-eight, though that must indeed seem withered to one who is not yet twenty.'

'Madam, I—' all the colour had drained away from Elizabeth's face. She who was so clever, who thought out everything, had not thought of this. For so many years now, she and all her entourage had considered Mary a confirmed old maid. 'Madam, I – forgive me for being so silly as to have left out the thought of marriage at the moment. It is only because I never think of it for myself—'

'No?' asked Mary drily.

'No, Madam. I have had small reason to do so these past four and a half years.'

Mary suddenly felt ashamed of baiting her. How was it she was always at her worst with Elizabeth?

'Well,' she said, uncomfortably trying to ease her way on to a more gracious and friendly footing, 'I can assure you I have not thought of it either, but now all my councillors seem determined that I ought to marry. The trouble is, they all offer me young men of about half my age. Their favourite is Edward Courtenay at twenty-four, so as to bring back the last drop of Plantagenet blood into the Succession. No, Bishop Gardiner has another reason; he has grown so fond of the poor unjustly treated lad in the Tower that he actually cried when I thought the match unsuitable. He looks on him as his own son – Courtenay has always called him "Father".'

'But that's no reason for you to make Courtenay one!'

Was Mary shocked? But luckily she did not seem to have heard – or perhaps not even understood. She was peering at Elizabeth with more than her usual short-sighted intentness. What was she trying to see? Suddenly the question was shot at her – 'And what do *you* think of him, sister?'

She answered quickly, lightly, 'As you do, Madam, a handsome lad but scarcely suitable.'

'For *me*. But he is five years older than you. I have seen the way he looks at you. And I have heard him say,' she added with an unexpectedly malicious smile, 'that if you were not a Court lady you would make a charming courtesan.'

'That hardly sounds like matrimonial intentions,' said Elizabeth calmly.

Her shot having failed, Mary was quickly ashamed of it. 'He did not intend an insult. He is utterly ignorant of the world.'

'He seems to be improving his knowledge rapidly.'

'The poor lad is at a disadvantage. He is eager to take his natural lead at Court, and he has learnt accomplishments in the Tower, but knows nothing of sport. He cannot even shoot with the long-bow—'

'He can draw it, though!' muttered Elizabeth.

'—and he has never ridden since he was a small boy. How he must envy all the other young men at Court caracoling on their great horses!'

She must be in love with him after all; – or was she thinking of her own bad horsemanship, due to her neglected girlhood?

The cynical young sister decided that the sympathies of women were apt to be a mirror to their self-pity. But she bit back any disparagements of Courtenay; Mary might take a fancy to him and would then remember them against her. There was an agitated silence while she rejected all the things that she might say. Better not. Too emphatic. Would only make her more suspicious. Wait till she speaks next.

But Mary seemed to be waiting for her to speak – and not about Courtenay. In a flash Elizabeth saw that she had forgotten him, that her mood was no longer dangerous but shy and eager, like a young girl who wanted to be asked about her lovers. But the indiscretion must come from Elizabeth. So she mentioned other possible suitors.

Mary looked wooden.

Elizabeth then remarked casually that doubtless the Emperor would welcome a match with his son. Mary instantly reacted, half turned away her head and blurted out gruffly, 'But then he too is much too young for me – and so I kept telling Signor Renard. Only a year or two older than Courtenay.'

So the Imperial ambassador was already pushing it! Elizabeth felt cold with anxiety but had to reassure her. 'That is quite different – he has had so much experience,' (perhaps that was a mistake!), 'so much power. Why, he is the greatest Prince in Christendom.'

'That is what my mother always said of his father, the Emperor,' said Mary happily.

Her shining eyes encouraged Elizabeth to a wicked reminder.

'Wasn't there a plan when I was a small child to marry you to the Emperor and me to Prince Philip?'

It worked. Mary laughed with her. 'But it came to nothing as usual. Why?'

'Because we'd both been declared bastards,' Elizabeth reminded her, 'and when the Emperor demanded our reinstatement, our father would not unsay what he had said.'

To Cat Ashley twenty minutes later she was raging – 'She is mad, I tell you, mad! One moment she is laughing with me as though we were two milkmaids on the village green – and then I catch her peering at me as though she's seeing, not me, but some dreadful thing of long ago that has never escaped her mind. Oh to run away from her endless "friendly arguments", her probing, nagging attempts to get at my conscience! God, how I hate all women! I know, I know, all my stepmothers were very kind to me – and my mother was a hateful stepmother to Mary. Well, my mother hated women and so do I. Once I'm free, I'll have only men friends.'

'And plenty,' murmured Mrs Ashley.

'The time I've had to spend making friends with women – all those kind stepmothers – how I've had to truckle to them, curtsied – bobbed – cast down my eyes when spoken to – wrote 'em letters in Latin, in Greek, in French, in Italian, all full of fine moral sentiments and dutiful affection – made 'em little presents at Christmas, pricking my fingers to the bone embroidering those damned violet leaves on the "Mirror of a

Guilty Soul" – and could any soul be guilty of a more colossal piece of dullness than that interminable poem I translated – at ten years old – to show off to my last stepmother?'

'Poor Catherine Parr!' sighed the governess. 'But Your Grace was devoted to her. That showed true love between women.'

'True, till a man came between!'

She brooded, bit her fingernails, then pulled them away, remembering it would spoil their shape. 'Jealousy – the curse of all women's love. Women cannot love, they can only clutch, grasp, hang on till love turns sour. They choke, they smother and say it's maternal – "I'm a mother myself," said the sow when she sat on the eggs. They break in, they try to violate your secrets, they demand windows to peer and pry into the soul. Mary will do that with her husband, she will do it with her country. She loves her mother, who was a saint and a Spaniard, and so was her grandmother, whose reign was a crusade against the infidel. So Mary's reign will be a crusade – against England.'

Her eyes narrowed as she stared into the future. She added darkly, 'The virtues of the mothers are visited on their children, even unto the third and fourth generation.'

'Her grandmother?' repeated Ashley comfortably, without raising her eyes from the seed pearls she was busy sewing on to a bodice Elizabeth had given her, to cover a rent in it. (Her Grace was a bit on the mean side in her presents of clothes.) 'Wasn't that Isabella the Catholic who vowed not to change her linen till the siege of Granada was raised?'

'Just so, dear Cat, which is why we have the colour "Isabella brown".'

'Well, Her Majesty won't take after her in *that*. Such a fuss and to-do as there is now over her wardrobes! I am sick to death of hearing of all her Coronation clothes – first the blue velvet and ermine (may she sweat in it, that's all, if it's as hot as now!), and then her crimson Parliament robes, and then her cloth of gold and skirts furred with miniver – the bellies only, mind you. What is Your Grace doing to keep up with all this?' (There might be some better pickings if Elizabeth had an entire new wardrobe.)

'I?' said Elizabeth with elaborate indifference. 'Oh, it doesn't matter what I wear, as she has all but promised to cut me out of the Succession. I shall just wear a simple little white dress as usual.'

'*What?*'

'Something quite plain, all in cloth of silver. With long hanging sleeves, "angel sleeves".'

'Ho!' said Mrs Ashley.

CHAPTER FIFTEEN

'Cousin, will you dance with me?'

'You have danced with me already, my lord, too often.'

'I could never do that.'

'You should ask the Queen again.'

'She dances so badly, strutting up and down like the water-wagtails in the Tower garden. But you, Cousin, you move like the flight of a swallow. When first I saw you against the sunset I knew what freedom was, what life could be. Will you not dance with me?'

This was going a deal too fast, Elizabeth told herself. But she never could resist a good partner. They touched hands and swung into the pattern of the dance in perfect timing with the tinkling, twanging thrumming little music like the music of birds and insects on a summer's night. Another hum rose through it, the spontaneous half-laughing murmur of voices in applause.

'Do you hear what they say?' whispered Courtenay.

'They whisper that you are true Tudor, and that I am the last of the Plantagenets.'

She gave a faint groan. 'Shall we ever hear the last of the Plantagenets?'

He flushed as he swung away to complete the measure, then back to take her hand again. 'You heard *that*? Someone said we were made for each other – youp!' His smiling partner had dug her long finger-nails into his hand as a sharp hint of discretion.

But she too was glowing at what that ripple of praise from the onlookers implied. 'The old stock' of English Kings, tall and fair and perfectly moulded as a curled Norman knight on his tombstone, coupled with the red-gold, the quick-changing white and red of the new Celtic blood that had leaped to power and transformed English sovereignty – yes, they might indeed have been made for each other, to rule England together – 'if only,' sighed the cold old strain of Visconti blood that twined like a serpent deep within her, 'if only he were not such a fool!'

Others did not see that so clearly. They saw a fine young man of the blood royal, and if the Queen refused to marry him and so missed her best chance of securing her throne, then why should not the Princess take him? More and more people were asking these questions; Edward Courtenay asked them alternately.

He wooed Elizabeth whenever he got the chance to, and when jogged by Gardiner he remembered to woo the Queen also, in an insouciant absent-minded fashion, like a schoolboy making up to an aunt at odd moments in spasmodic hopes of a tip. He got a good many. She gave him one of her father's huge thumb-rings with a diamond in it worth 16,000 crowns, and he stuck both his thumbs through it and waggled them at her, telling her she had handcuffed him as her prisoner for life. She laughed indulgently at the silly lad, and appointed one of her gentlemen as his bear-leader, to guide him through the world that was so new to him and keep him out of mischief – in which he was unsuccessful, though he had orders not to leave him alone for a moment – clear sign to de Noailles the French ambassador of the frantic jealousy of a frustrated female for the beloved object.

There were pleasanter tokens of her solicitude for Courtenay; she gave him the choice of whatever house he liked best in London for his own mansion; she reinstated him in his Exeter estates and created him Earl of Devonshire, in a most splendid ceremony when he wore robes that made him look about nine feet high and all the women stared and smiled at him.

All but his cousin the Lady Elizabeth, who unaccountably denied herself this glorious sight on some flimsy pretext of not feeling well enough. Courtenay was certain she only did it to annoy him. Who was she to give herself such airs? A bastard, and of an upstart House, two upstart Houses (some day he'd tell her that!). Mary was at least worthy of him on the distaff side. And there were plenty of other women only too eager for him to play the fool with them. He did so, with the hectic excitement of a colt getting his head for the first time. He had met noble ladies in prison, for the society in the Tower was of the best in England, but their restrained and melancholy company had been poor sport compared with the Cockney wit and freedom of the women of the town that he now enjoyed – whenever he could shake off his bear-leader.

Gardiner scolded him; Mary gave him motherly reproofs; the French ambassador, who was backing him for a royal consort against the Imperial ambassador's suit of Prince Philip, warned him that he had already spoiled his chances of being made Duke of York and would ruin those of being King. Of course he must amuse himself, but let him do so in discreet privacy. But Courtenay's notion of discreet privacy was to leave his house at midnight in a 'disguise' that was very becoming and strikingly conspicuous; and Mary declared in public that it was not to her honour to marry a subject.

After that the French ambassador decided that Courtenay had better give up any hope of Mary and concentrate on Elizabeth instead, and the two of them make a popular combined head for the discontented Protestant party. So de Noailles had him to dinner one Sunday in order to coach him in this role, tell him to be bold and resolute and he might yet get himself a crown, and with a young instead of an old woman attached to it. It should be an easy matter for him to go down and raise his peasantry on his behalf 'now that he was the Earl of Dampshire,' – a combination of Hampshire and Devonshire that the French Ambassador persisted in using even in all his dispatches.

Courtenay showed small inclination to visit Dampshire. He seemed to prefer France, for he asked de Noailles what welcome he was likely to get from his master Henri II if he found it necessary to leave England.

De Noailles then asked Roger Ascham to dinner on the Monday and told him that his previous evening had been engaged in trying to train a young game-cock who had been fed on chicken-feed instead of raw meat and wine; Courtenay could crow and flap his wings with the best of them and strut round the hens, but de Noailles doubted whether it would be much use to sharpen his talons and fasten the steel spurs to his legs.

'Your true game-cock in this case is the hen,' Ascham told him.

But de Noailles had to confess that though he had danced with Elizabeth, flirted with her (and she had done both charmingly), when it came to talking politics he had found himself utterly unable to sound her. Her old friend and tutor should have better luck.

'Abstain from beans' was still ringing in Ascham's head. He declared himself more interested in the New Learning than in high politics.

De Noailles, leaning back and picking the gleaming teeth in his thick black beard with a silver toothpick, asked him blandly whether his hopes for the New Learning were likely to be realised under a Queen who had cried, 'As for your new books, I have never read any of 'em – nor ever will do!'

Young Dr. Dee had come back from his triumphant career abroad – where he had created a furore in Paris by the first lectures on Euclid ever given – expressly to induce her to found a National Library that would be the glory of England. But she would have none of it, and he had begun to collect his own instead.

'Poor lady, she is born fifty years too late. She cannot see that the world will never go back to the dingy old-fashioned ways of thought to which she clings. She has never taken in the new doctrine of our modern Copernicus, that the world is a round ball rolling through space; it makes her dizzy, for why then should it not drop down through space and crash to nothingness? Ha ha! So she prefers it flat, a safe platform with Heaven above and Hell below, all firm as a rock.'

'Do you think that makes much difference to belief?'

'But, my friend, why else did the Church oppose the idea? The Church knows that all that is happening in science now will alter men's minds for the rest of time. And not only their minds. Life is sweet, is it not? all the more when it may turn out to be the only one. But the Queen's senses have never had any opportunity to know it; she has never seen that the world is holding out its eager hands to the present life that is so well worth living.' His rings flashed as he spread his own fine hands in illustration. 'The dresses she is introducing at Court, they are gorgeous indeed, but my God, do they render the women desirable? What has happened to the lovely necks, down to the breasts, that we saw in King Henry's reign? They are covered under a canopy of stiff silk or damask.' He shrugged in despair, cast his eyes to the ceiling, and saw his argument escaping him. So he compared Mary's antiquated provincial outlook with the enlightened attitude of his own Most Catholic Sovereign of France, Henri II, and his wife Catherine de Medici, who loved to encourage reform and free thought – within reasonable limits.

'Within financial limits!' Ascham remarked drily. 'The French Monarchy may toy with heresy as a fashionable mental exercise, but it will always have to remain Catholic, for the simple reason that it would be bankrupt if it did not. It still draws its chief revenue from its ecclesiastical patronage, and its best paying vested interests are in the Church.'

De Noailles quickly parried the thrust. 'Just as those of England are in the Reformation. Yet Queen Mary actually hopes to restore the Church property, filched by practically every one of the English nobles and gentry, to the "poor dispossessed monks and nuns" – many of whom made quite a good thing out of its sales, and most of whom are now married and unwilling to part with their wives and husbands. How is she going to do it? Answer me that.'

But it had already been answered and flatly in the negative, at her first Parliament; all the nobles and gentry had confessed their error against the Pope and begged his forgiveness upon their knees in a most moving scene, but refused point-blank to give up one scrap of the Church property they had amassed.

Mary had been bitterly hurt; and even more by the changed attitude of the common people at her Coronation, where it had been necessary to take all sorts of precautions to guard her safety from those very crowds that had roared themselves hoarse with joy at her entry into London. She could not see how even the notoriously fickle Cockney crowds could have so changed towards her in a few weeks.

But in those weeks she had had the Mass said in public (against even the Emperor's advice), and while it was still illegal by the existing law of the land.

Many were glad to hear again the old accustomed chanting that had meant religion to them since childhood, where the New Prayer Book only meant a lot of fine-sounding sentences that they understood little better than the unintelligible Latin drone. And then one year there had been a New Prayer Book which everybody had to believe in by law – and then two years later there had been another New Prayer Book which everybody had to believe in instead, and it had suddenly become as illegal to believe in the first New Prayer Book as in the old Mass. It did shake your faith up, a lot of people had complained, to have the form of religion altered every two or three years, instead of sticking to the same one for nine centuries as their fathers had done.

They wanted to hear again the chime of the chapel bell comforting the black silence of the night; to see lights again in the windows of the monastery guest-houses that had long been blind, giving no welcome to tired travellers.

But the people who wanted this were mostly over thirty-five.

The younger ones were agog for change, for release from everything they felt to be stuffy and old-fashioned. The world, to them, had come out of its dark schoolroom; they were not going back into it to be scolded and frightened like children with old tales of hell and purgatory and the unseen figure of the Pope of Rome always behind them like an invisible headmaster. Rome was the interloper, the secret invader, the prying fingers of a distant hand, itself unseen, that groped into every man's affairs, picked every man's pockets, even the poorest, for 'Peter's Pence'; taking money out of the country, putting foreigners into it.

So they said, in the flush of their new-found national pride that King Henry had given them, not by any spectacular foreign conquests or military victories, but by cutting England loose from the centralizing European power of the Church into a splendid isolation, so they felt it; while to Mary it was merely cutting the ship of state adrift to float rudderless on the high seas.

To the younger generation, England had leaped ahead in one vast stride.

To Mary, England had slid back into lonely darkness. It was her mission to recall it to 'my father's day,' when he and her mother had gone to Mass together, with herself as a little fair-haired girl beside them, and he had not yet broken with Rome.

She intended to bring back not only the Mass, but the old allegiance to Rome. She intended an even worse thing, so ran the growing rumours, and that was to marry the Prince of Spain, to bring thousands of insolent foreigners into the country, spying, interfering, cruel priests, the Spanish Inquisition itself.

While Mary herself still coyly imagined that she had not yet made up her mind, the French ambassador was spreading the news everywhere that the marriage was as good – or bad – as settled. Bad it was, from de Noailles' point of view. His best hope to prevent it lay in the will of the people of England, and their best hope of a figurehead lay in the boy Courtenay and the girl Elizabeth, a romantic couple, untried, unknown, but good-looking, charming, above all, young.

It was the young who were beginning to group themselves to a man – especially a man – round Elizabeth.

She was the bright crescent slip that might eclipse Mary's already waning moon. Some of them wrote poems about it. Roger Ascham forgot that he had written letters about Jane Grey. Her pale star was in eclipse; she was happy, he heard, with her books in the Tower and the promise of liberty in retirement. But would Elizabeth ever retire, however meek and obedient her demeanour?

She stood in the full gaze of the Court, she stood very stiff, but her stillness was bright and aware, she could move as swift as a meteor. Watching, he drew near her; he found himself standing by her, looking on at an absurd Interlude acted by John Heywood's company of boy players.

'You are the darling of the people of England,' he whispered to her, 'and do you know who has said it? No butcher's or baker's wife, but Commendone, the Pope's own envoy, writing in despair to the Papal See.'

'The devil he does! And so puts me between the devil and the Papal See!'

Ascham laughed on the queer note of rising excitement that

Elizabeth's repartees always it up in him. 'Yes, he has written that not the Queen, but "her heretic sister is in the heart and mouth of everyone".'

'And "her head on the block" will be the corollary – which is no doubt what Signor Renard is suggesting at this moment to the Queen.' And she nodded to where the Imperial ambassador was bending his head down to Queen Mary's stiffly resolute little person. 'But on what possible charge?' she added complacently; 'I have done, said, even thought – nothing!'

'That is the charge. You have done nothing about going to Mass – or nothing much! Your example is giving strength to all London. The royal Chaplain's sermon has been shouted down with yells of "Papist!" and he had a dagger thrown at him. He was lucky to escape with his life.'

'And is that due to *my* example? God's death, you'll convert me to the Mass better than any Papist! Rank rebellion and attempted murder, do you think I stand for *that*?'

'Your Grace stands for the people. Can you, any more than they, bear to see a foreign despot in power here, England a mere province of Spain, and the Inquisition rooting out all freedom, so that no man shall speak carelessly in his cups without it being reported by his neighbour and he himself cast in a dungeon?'

'No. Nor can I bear that the Queen's Chaplain shall not speak in his pulpit without having daggers thrown at him. What freedom of speech is that? And *is* it the will of the people? Of how many of them? Since you have not abstained from beans, will you tell me how many make five? If the people are divided, is every sermon to be the occasion for a free fight?'

The Interlude was over; it was time for the banquet. Elizabeth swept a deep curtsy as the Queen passed, and rose from it to follow her in the customary order – then froze to the spot. Mary had held out her hand, not to her sister to take precedence of the Court, but to her cousin the Duchess of Suffolk, the mother of Jane Grey.

By this gesture the Queen stated publicly before all the Court that she regarded a convicted rebel as the first lady in the land, next to herself, rather than her own sister; that she refused to acknowledge that sister as her heir.

What would then be the Queen's next move? It would never be safe to disinherit Elizabeth and yet leave her at large. Would the next step be to put her in the Tower?

The eyes of all the Court were on her. She could not hear their whispers; she could guess.

With her head high, her face white as stone, she followed the Duchess of Suffolk through the doorway. But no further. Once outside, she broke away from the stately procession – and rushed to her own apartments. All prudence and restraint were flung from her, the meek role that she had played so patiently all these weeks. She was in great danger, the Queen's insult had shown it clearly, but she cared nothing now for the danger; it was the insult that goaded her to a mad ecstasy of passion that caught her hot by the throat, that blinded her with fire in her eyes, that throbbed hot, hot in her hands with the longing to smash and stab and kill. She raged up and down in a tornado of rustling silks, swearing with shocking and surprising blasphemy, striking at anything in her way – no person dared come in – like a furious swan hissing and swishing its wings across the water – like a lioness raging in her cage, like – like her dread sire Old Harry himself in one of his rages, thought Mr Parry, mopping his damp forehead as he cowered behind his writing-desk in the attempt to make himself invisible.

The attempt was in vain. She pulled up sharply in front of him, her arm raised, her fist clenched. He ducked his head instinctively as it crashed on the table.

'Write. Write my sister. Write this. That I will not see her again. That I will leave the Court. Take tip your pen, blockhead. What, does your hand shake? Her "*permission*," do you mutter? By God's most precious soul, she *shall* give her permission, whether she will or no.'

CHAPTER SIXTEEN

'SIR,

If it were not too much trouble for you, and if you were to find it convenient to do so without the knowledge of your colleagues, I would willingly speak with you in private this evening. Nevertheless I remit my request to your prudence and discretion.

Written in haste, as it well appears, this morning of October, Your good friend MARY.'

What a note, thought Renard, for a Queen to write to one of her ambassadors! This meant another secret interview, creeping at midnight, slipping through back doors 'muffled in a cloak,' for that she fondly believed to be sufficient disguise, to be shut up alone for a long feminine heart-to-heart talk with a girl grown old, who had never learnt to be a woman.

Yet Mary's naivety had served him well. He had only had to leave it to her to play into his hands, to angle openly for the Emperor's proposal of marriage for his son Prince Philip, to ask him guileless questions to which he knew all the answers.

It was true that Philip was betrothed to the Princess of Portugal, but this was already being broken off. It was untrue that he loved her.

It was true that Philip was a mere couple of years or so older than Courtenay, but then he was grave and wise in judgment; he had the steadfast safety of middle age and the vigour of youth.

It was quite true that Philip was of an austere and handsome dignity, as she would see for herself when Signor Titian's portrait arrived – only she must be sure to look at it from a little distance, as was necessary with all his pictures (perhaps also with Philip).

It was quite untrue what the French ambassador, de Noailles, had brutally declared, that once she were married to Philip she would probably not see him for more than about a fortnight in all their wedded life; Philip was devoted to Spain, but he would make England his second home; Philip would be Emperor of the World, but he would never dream of making England a mere province.

It was true that his master's family had a motto, 'The Hapsburgs do not need to fight; instead, they marry'; but that did not mean a conquest of England, only a peaceful alliance.

He had a complicated course to steer, but the Queen was making it unexpectedly easy.

He saw through all her fears as to whether Philip were too young and experienced, and she too old and innocent – Philip too ardent, she too cold (Cold? these chaste old maids? God, he could pity Philip!) – saw through her, through and through, he told himself, smiling with complacent pity, to the last frantic strivings of her frustrated womanhood to clutch a lover to her before it was too late.

Now in this secret midnight interview he must be sympathetic, tactful, but above all firm, gentling this nervous mare with a soothing hand so as not to start and shy at every obstacle in the road. But, lord! thought he, carefully trimming bits of greyish fluff from the drooping moustaches and thin fringe of beard that edged his face and ended in two little tufts (that fellow never shaved him properly, always removed the brown and left the grey), what man could ever do that? The Queen was utterly incapable of holding to the same course for two minutes together, so irresolute was she, weak, vacillating; her nerve must have been permanently broken by her terrible father's treatment of her as a girl. Yet she had shown unswerving courage all through Dudley's rebellion; no weak woman had held that course. Must it always need a major crisis of war to knock a spark of sense as well as a great heart into her?

It seemed so, for he found Mary in a distracted state of fidgets, pacing up and down the room that was so like a chapel with the lamp burning always in front of her prie-dieu in the alcove. She had evidently been starting to do half a dozen things at once. Sewing had been taken up and flung down again in the corner. Letters strewed the table, including a few lines of one in her own writing; a couple of books lay open beside them.

'You see me,' she said with a tremulous smile, 'making an act of sacrifice. They say the vanity of an author is worse than that of any woman. Yet to be fair I cannot condemn Protestant works and make exception of my own. Bishop Gardiner says that it would be wise to suppress the Paraphrases of St John that I helped to translate from Erasmus some years ago, to be read in the churches as a companion volume to the new Bible in English.'

'I had no idea that Your Majesty was a Protestant author!'

'Only a translator, but in company with the Protestants

Udal and Cox. Archbishop Cranmer thought my work the best exposition of the Gospels,' she added with wistful pride. 'But Bishop Gardiner was always against their use for the common people, and now I am recalling them from publication to be destroyed. "Reform" has hardened into heresy. The Church is a beleaguered city that must guard her gates and allow no compromise. No doubt it was presumption on my part to think I could serve her by my halting translations. So let them go. Compromise is the devil's weapon.'

'Yet, Madam, are you free from compromise in the most crucial question of your reign? I speak of your sister, the Lady Elizabeth.'

Mary swerved like a startled horse. 'Why do you speak of her? Have I to be for ever considering my attitude to my sister?'

'You gave many people, Madam, the opportunity to consider it, when you so pointedly transferred the precedence from her to the Duchess of Suffolk the night before last. It places the whole Succession in question, by publicly proclaiming her bastardy.'

Mary was trembling from head to foot, and to Renard's alarm the ready tears began to flow down her cheeks. 'Is she indeed even my father's bastard?' she cried in a shaking voice. 'I do not know what to think of her. I do not know *who* she is. My father's child – or of one of the Night Crow's lovers? What proof have I that Elizabeth is connected with me in blood?'

'Then you deny her the Succession?'

'My conscience denies it. Illegitimate, heretical, unscrupulous, she would ruin this country as her mother did before her. How could I then leave it in her charge with a clear conscience?'

Mary's conscience was final, Renard knew that. He wanted to make his next point, but she would go on about Elizabeth.

'I do not know what she is in any way; she is a mask, not a human face. She was twenty last month, yet she is as old as the Sphinx and as inscrutable. She has pretended to be wax in my hands, to plead ignorance of the true religion; asks for books and learned priests to instruct her; is willing, she says, to go to Mass, though she invents one pretext after another to avoid it when the time comes; yet when I expound religion to her she will listen to me by the hour together – "marvellous meek", that is her reputation.'

Renard felt, not for the first time, a certain sympathy with the girl he was so relentlessly seeking to destroy.

'Is she then proving herself a docile pupil, anxious to learn the truth?'

Mary looked blankly at him through her tears with the candid gaze of a bewildered, disillusioned girl.

'How can she be so docile if she were true? Has she no loyalty to the religion in which she was brought up? It is my belief she doesn't care a fig for it, nor for anything that may work against her interests. I might respect her if she were a heretic, but she is even worse – a hypocrite. She pretends to obedience, to loyalty, even to affection for me – when all the time I know she is hating me, hating – as indeed she must,' she added ingenuously, 'for she must know how I hate her.'

'It does not necessarily follow,' said Renard. 'I should much doubt that her feelings for you are as strong as Your Majesty's for her. Nor have they ever had the same reason – insulted, ill-treated as you were for her sake by her mother and the King, her—' he hastily corrected himself, 'your father.'

'I will not bear her ill-will for that. She was a helpless child.'

Renard, twirling his tufts of beard into sharp points, murmured that these conscientious scruples should not be allowed to affect the real issue. The one thing that mattered in her relations with Elizabeth was for her to decide what to do with her.

'You can't have it both ways,' he said; 'hate her if you will, distrust her, disclaim her as any relative of yours, but do not leave her at large to make capital of all this against you. If she does not, others will. As long as people are satisfied that she is your heir it will keep them pacified—'

'In the hope of my early death,' she interrupted ruefully. 'That indeed is very likely. I told the Council four years ago that I should not have long to live. I have still less reason now to alter that view.'

'Madam, you have every reason to alter it. You were ill because you were unhappy.'

'And am now.'

'Then stir yourself to action. Let your heart guide you to happiness and health – and a new heir. Make up your mind as to the course you mean to follow. You distrust Elizabeth; very well, then, place her under arrest in the Tower.'

'But she has done nothing to justify it.'

Renard groaned. 'Circumstances justify it, Madam. The need for safety, not only for yourself, but for one whose safety I hope will be even more dear to you. How can Prince Philip come to a country that is seething with discontent which may break out at any moment into plots to reinstate the Princess in the Succession – and perhaps on the throne? You *must* remove this danger from him. Her death is the only safe course.'

Slowly, with the look of a patient, sorrowful, and at this moment rather beautiful mule, Mary shook her head.

'Not for anyone in the world could I again be brought to do what my heart tells me is wrong. I did it once as a young girl; I betrayed my mother's memory. Under pressure from my father, I acknowledged that I was illegitimate, that he acted rightly in divorcing my mother.'

'You were a prisoner, you could have done nothing else.'

'I could have died. It seems now so simple a thing to have done; but I didn't. I did as he willed me. He gave me a thousand crowns, and Thomas Cromwell, the infamous minister to his pleasures, gave me a horse. These were my rewards.' Her laugh had a harsh and terrible sound. 'No, there was another; my father showed me affection as he had not done since I was a little girl. That counted with me more than the fear of death, for which I have longed many times.' She beat her hands together. 'It is done, it is done, and it cannot be undone. At least I will never do it again. I will never again betray my conscience.'

It was a great pity, thought the ambassador, that women would always remember. The past had passed, let it pass.

He firmly brought her back to the present. 'Then, Madam, you must dissemble your hate for Elizabeth. If you will not put her out of harm's way, do not at least make her the centre for disaffection, her own and others'. Continue to encourage her conversion, even if you do not believe in it; give her some few toys, tokens of friendship.'

'She has just demanded leave to retire from the Court.'

Renard was not surprised, after the open blow at her position. He remarked that Elizabeth's caution was no less than her pride would make her want to get out of the way.

Mary laughed bitterly at the word 'caution.' Elizabeth's demand had been bold to the point of defiance, she said; it was more like a command.

'Might be as well to grant it all the same,' Renard considered, 'it would get her out of mischief. But she'll never be that until she is out of England. If she is not to be' – he coughed back *beheaded* – 'imprisoned, at least she can be married.'

'To Courtenay?'

'Impossible! And she appears to like his company – as do most women. Is there any serious danger, or is it mere coquetry?'

'Everything she does is coquetry,' Mary cried. 'She flirts with every man she meets – and with policy – with religion – with danger, with life and death itself. In that, as in all else, she is the daughter of her mother, who laughed even on the scaffold. Ann Bullen was a savage, many thought her a witch. Her daughter, for all the modest mask she puts on at times, is the same. Nothing is sacred to her, not even her own soul – least of all a man's heart.'

These women! thought Renard. Could nothing keep them to the point?

Quick as always to feel displeasure, Mary flushed with shame at her outburst and made an effort to speak dispassionately. 'Their marriage is what everyone in the country seems to want – and de Noailles too – I suppose as a consolation prize for Courtenay!'

'For him to prize you from your throne, rather!'

Could she really not see that de Noailles, having failed to marry Courtenay to Mary so as to keep her from the Spanish alliance, would now try to marry him to Elizabeth so as to destroy her?

He told Mary firmly that the only possible match for Elizabeth was some useful satellite of Spain. 'The Prince of Piedmont, now, would be a convenient match.'

'Oh yes, we make plans for her! Do you think any of them will make any odds?'

She flung open a window and pointed across the dark courtyard to where a window opened a square of golden light; music and laughter and the merry sound of voices and dancing feet came pulsing out into the quiet night. Alone in the sleeping palace the Lady Elizabeth's apartments were alight and awake with young life.

Renard gasped at this boldness, opening his fringed mouth in an indignant round. Had she taken no warning from her public disgrace of her imminent danger? 'I heard – but could scarcely believe – that she had flown into a royal rage and openly defied Your Majesty. She must be mad!'

'We both have tempers,' said Mary uncomfortably. She nearly said 'we get it from our father' before she remembered that she had denied him to Elizabeth.

He made an impatient gestate at the excuse. 'I presume that Your Majesty confined her to her apartments?'

'No,' she answered drily. 'She herself has refused to leave them since the night before last. She has never been to see me, though she knows I am ill – always am in the autumn,' she added tearfully. Amazing woman, she seemed really hurt that Elizabeth should not have concerned herself at this moment with her fits of weeping and palpitations of the heart.

'If she has disobeyed you, Your Majesty has full occasion to put her under arrest.'

'And half the Court, the younger half? For they are all disobeying me. I forbade anyone to visit her, but all the young men and some of the young women have been thronging to her, some of them staying with her all day long, making merry with her, as you can hear. My friends were delighted in her discomfiture, but she has managed to discomfort me instead, set up what is practically a rival court here in my own Palace, and a much livelier one. What *can* I do? Imprison all these gay young people and brand myself a jealous old maid? An old maid,' she repeated softly as though the words were echoing back to her.

She slammed the window to, and Renard, obeying her gesture, pulled forward the curtain, shutting the sombre room into itself again, but gave a last lingering glance through its heavy folds at the shining open window that framed the rival court. They must be having a masquerade; he could see fantastic head-dresses bobbing to and fro in the dance, and a wild dishevelled figure swung laughing away from it to the window where he could see her clearly, a Bacchante or Maenad of the woods, he thought, his pulse quickening at sight of the rounded arms and shoulders, the neck bare right down to the milky curves of the young breasts. A loose mop of fiery curls tossed light as gossamer round her excited face, which now he saw suddenly unbelievingly, to be Elizabeth's.

He swung round to tell the Queen of this singular metamorphosis of the decorous young lady reputed so 'marvellous meek'. But something in the tired patient little figure of the Queen checked him. He would not tease her further with the contrast of her flamboyant, possibly disreputable young sister, now that she had forgotten her.

For Mary was waiting to ask him something, peering up at

him with her intent, short-sighted gaze that had now turned shy and wondering, evidently longing for him to reassure her.

'You said—' she began tentatively in a gruff voice like a bashful schoolboy, 'you spoke of the possibility of another heir. God has already worked a miracle for me. May He not complete His work by yet another miracle?'

'Why should it be a miracle, Madam? Many women older than you have borne a child for the first time. Your ill-health will vanish like snow in the sun, once you have known happiness.'

'You think I should know it with Prince Philip? He is much younger. He has loved, he has married other women. If he wants passion he will be disappointed in me. I am...' she hesitated, 'of that age – of that age you know of. I have never given way to thoughts of love. I have never even taken a fancy to any man. Give me your hand. Will you pledge your word on it that all you have told me about Prince Philip – his even temper, his balanced judgment, his kindly nature – is indeed true? Tell me again what you think of his character.'

'Madam,' said Renard solemnly, 'it is too wonderful to be human.'

She gripped his hand tighter and said, 'It is well!'

There was a silence that was rather uncomfortable for Renard, hardened politician as he was.

The thin hand that clutched him was that of the English Alliance; he would not think of it as a woman's; he would not think of other women; he would not think of Philip's first wife, the little bride of sixteen, whom Philip, barely a year older, had gone in disguise to look on for the first time, waiting among the noisy jostling crowds in the streets of Badajoz to gaze with them on a small figure in a silver dress under a tower of black hair. He had straightway fallen passionately in love with her; within a year she had borne him his son Don Carlos, and died of it.

No, he would not think of her; nor of Philip's devoted mistress, Doña Isobel, who had borne him several fine children; nor of his latest affianced bride, the Princess of Portugal, who was his cousin and talked his own language, figuratively as well as actually. Least of all would he think of the slender supple white hand with the rosy pointed fingernails of the young woman who danced and sang and held her laughing court out there on the other side of the dark Palace, a frivolous, perhaps an abandoned young woman, who was now the greatest danger Philip had to face in England, but who might come to be – who knows – a closer ally than this ailing, failing woman whose clutch might soon be loosed in death. If she should die in childbed—

But he had to attend to the restive Queen, who had shied again, all but galloped away.

'How can I face the Council? Gardiner keeps urging that the country will never accept a foreigner, willingly. Englefield has said definitely that Courtenay is the only possible marriage for me; Walgrave says that if I marry Philip it will mean war with France; Wotton writes from abroad that the French are doing all they can to prevent it. If the two great Catholic powers are at war, how can we hope to preserve the true Church?'

Renard stiffened and withdrew his hand. 'I am amazed, Madam, that you can allow your subjects to command your choice. Are you really going to let them force you into marriage with your servant?'

'No, oh no. I have no liking for Courtenay, though some

pity. But I do not want to give my word to Spain until I am sure that I can abide by it. I do not wish to be thought inconsistent,' she added pleadingly, all too aware from Renard's face what his own thoughts were on the matter. 'I *believe*,' she said timidly, 'that I will agree to the proposal, I cannot say more now or I shall burst into tears.'

'And I *believe* I understand what that means.' Renard's tone was arch but tenderly soothing.

It unloosed the tears, and with them a torrent of words. 'I have not slept since the Emperor's letters came. All through the night I have wept and prayed for guidance, argued with myself, weighing all that others have said against my own heart – for always my heart has been with Spain. I was betrothed as a child to its Emperor – for years I thought I was to return to the country of my own dear mother, sacrificed here in England. Only Spain then tried to protect her – only her nephew the Emperor and his ambassador then offered me sanctuary. Oh, those black nights when I tried to escape! – I waited shivering on the riverbank for the boat that should take me away from prison, and worse, from perjury – from the dangers that threatened my body, from the false prophets that would blind my soul – to be safe in Spain. I shall never go there now.

'But now the Emperor offers me another sanctuary, his son may come from Spain to save me yet. I have kept myself, as my mother urged me in the very last letter she ever wrote me, from even wanting the love of a man, for well she knew it would not be possible for me to have it with honour. In that at least I have kept faith with her. It is not in any loose desire that I now long for a husband, but because I do not know how to order my affairs without his help and advice. I have no one to whom I dare even speak of them, except yourself. I can bear no more questions and arguments. Let us pray to God to show us what is right – pray now, here, to the Holy Sacrament.'

She turned towards the alcove where the Sacrament bad been placed on her little prie-dieu with a lamp burning before it, its yellow light flickering on the hollows of her eyes, on the tragic downward curves of her pale lips that now moved in the ancient rhythm of the Latin hymn, 'Veni, Creator Spiritus.' Renard knelt too, and presently there was silence.

Did she hear God speak in the silence? He felt cold, uneasy; the taste of all be had said turned sour in his mouth. What if he should now say aloud, 'Don't! Don't listen. It is only your own voice that you hear.'

He did not say it. He remained piously upon his knees.

She rose and came to him and held out her hand. 'I believe that God, Who has worked such miracles for me, has given me word here in the presence of the Sacrament to be Prince Philip's wife. I promise to love him perfectly. You need not fear that I will change my mind again. It will never change.'

CHAPTER SEVENTEEN

Elizabeth had won. Mary had at last graciously allowed her sister to leave London, and as though it were merely to satisfy her desire for rural solitude.

So now the sisters met to say goodbye.

Seventeen years stood between them, but it might have been a century. Both were aware of the enormous gulf in time; Elizabeth knew she would have to choose and comb her words as though to her grandmother; Mary felt how hard and baffling were these young women of the modern generation, so terrifyingly self-assured. Elizabeth looked so neat and well groomed with her hair strained back under the absurd little riding-cap as flat as a plate on top of her high bold clever forehead where the fashionably plucked eyebrows made two thin half-moons. Her waistcoat was buttoned up tight to her throat; a narrow double ruffle of white lawn billowed crisply out from the high collar and at the close-fitting wrists of her sleeves. She wore no earrings, no rings, and carried a handkerchief twisted round her fingers (was it to refute Mary's accusation of showing off her hands?).

She looked so young, spruce, new-minted, as though she would never remember, never regret, never weep nor wish for impossible things, never sap her taut vigorous life in all the useless ways that Mary had done. 'She thinks me a muddle-headed old maid,' thought Mary, and it was no consolation that she thought Elizabeth a brazen young adventuress.

She sought to retrieve her superiority by a spate of parting presents. This was by Renard's instructions, but it was also her natural outlet, the act in which she had taken her most spontaneous pleasure since her starved girlhood.

'The year is going fast,' she said, 'and soon we shall have Christmas upon us before we know where we are. You must let me give you my Christmas presents now.'

The first one was embarrassing; it was a book of gold with a diamond clasp containing the miniature portraits of Henry VIII and Queen Katherine of Aragon. Had Mary chosen this deliberately to put her yet again in her place? But her manner gave no hint of it, she seemed to think Elizabeth should be as pleased to have a memento of Queen Katherine as if she were her own mother instead of Mary's. 'The likeness is excellent,' she observed complacently, and Elizabeth murmured politely that she wished she could have known the original. Her face had frozen into wary immobility; but it thawed into pleasure when Mary fastened an enormous brooch on her dress; on it, carved in amethyst, was the story of Pyramis and Thisbe, the lovers, in translucent purple, peering at each other through a wall of diamond. And the next moment she flung a sable wrap round her shoulders.

'There,' she said; 'look at yourself in the mirror, it is becoming to your fair colouring, isn't it?'

'One moment she scratches, then she strokes – I can never make her out,' thought Elizabeth as she stammered out her thanks, abashed by the generosity of this odd woman whom she had begun to think wholly her enemy.

'You gave me yellow satin once for a skirt when I was a

child,' she said. 'Do you remember, Madam? And a gold pomander with a watch in it to tell the time. I treasure it faithfully.'

'Treasure time too!' said the Queen. 'It may be on your side.' She gave an acid little laugh.

It was safest not to answer her.

Instead, Elizabeth looked in the mirror. She saw her bright defiant head framed in the soft depths of the furs, and the gleaming purple of the carved jewel on her breast made her eyes look a clear green in contrast. She saw a young woman fashionably dressed, who could be dashing, gay, recklessly attractive – and who must at present be none of these things. The charming picture before her was her true self – and must be hidden. She would not wear Mary's gifts again – and not only because they were Mary's.

The frivolous flamboyant creature that had broken loose at her masquerade must go back into the stable. That self could wait; her turn would come. But now once again the demure scholar, the near nun, must be trotted out – God, how sick she was of her after all these years of restraint, of living down the scandal of her love-affair at fifteen! She must still live it down, and more, she must represent a positive ideal – the opposite in all men's minds to the gorgeously dressed females at Court, and above all to the Queen herself, who 'takes more pleasure in clothes than almost any woman alive.' In appearance as well as behaviour she must show herself the white hope of the austere spirit of the Reformation.

So might any girl just twenty look in the glass and wonder what style of dress would suit her character, and in what character she would face the world. But Elizabeth's reflections sprang from no such untried speculations. They radiated from the centre of her being, which remained fixed and constant as the lodestar – her belief in herself as the future Queen of England.

And then she saw Mary looking over her shoulder.

Though she knew her sister was just behind her, the glimpse she caught of her in the mirror turned her cold. Mary's watchful gaze at Elizabeth's reflection seemed to pierce deeper than when she stated at her face to face. Was the old belief then true, that the reflection is the soul, stepped naked and defenceless from the body? Did the Queen, looking at her mirrored face, now behold her true thoughts?

She shivered and muffled the sable wrap close round her face as if to hide it. But only the mouth with its secret close-shut smile was covered. The eyes of a wild animal facing its enemy peeped out through all her suave submission.

Then Mary spoke. 'I have had no answer from you to the message I sent asking how you liked the Prince of Piedmont's offer of marriage to you.'

Elizabeth took fright and it flared into rage; her hands caught at the fur, tearing it off her. This kindness was a bribe, a trap. An insignificant foreign marriage was, then, the next attempt to oust her from her rights. An angry laugh flew out of her mouth, the words followed before she could stop them.

'Madam, I liked both the message and the messenger so well that I hope never to hear of either of them again.'

Then she knew what she had said and stood ice-cold, waiting for the answering burst of rage from Mary. She could roar too, as loudly as their father; Elizabeth had once heard her two rooms off. And the roar would be an order to the guards to come and arrest her and lead her away to prison. She looked at the fur lying at her feet, another trapped – no, dead animal, and wondered that she had thought it beautiful. 'Oh God, to be free, and free of fear!' she sighed to herself in the silence.

At last she heard Mary's voice, gruff, undoubtedly grim, but not a roar, not an order for imprisonment.

'So you openly admit it – your fixed purpose to stay on here, on the chance of the throne?'

With a physical effort Elizabeth unclenched her hands and looked at her sister with a calm untroubled gaze.

'No, Madam,' she said quietly, 'but I admit that I am mere English, and wish never to leave my country.'

'Mere *English*! And what of your French friends? Do you think I know nothing of what goes on? More than one young friend of yours overheard de Noailles' repartee to you at my Coronation when you complained of the fit of your coronet – "Have patience, you will soon get a better!"'

'"Have patience" indeed!' cried Elizabeth, with as free and natural irritation as if she were speaking to Cat Ashley. 'May Heaven send it me and save me from my friends! Am I responsible for a few giggling young fools?'

'You have entertained a great many of them in your chamber lately, where their giggling has been plainly audible. No, do not apologise—' (though Elizabeth had shown no sign of doing so) – 'I prefer laughter to whispers, and at least – at last – you were frank with me just now in your reply to Piedmont's proposal. If you would only be so always! What is the truth about you and the French ambassador? Does de Noailles visit your chambers, not as one of a crowd of silly young things, but in secret, at night, disguised as a French refugee priest?'

Elizabeth swung round, her irritation more frank than ever

in her relief at having something tangible that she could honestly deny. 'Of all the gibberish!' she began, then checked sharply. 'Madam, I beg your pardon, I was startled out of my senses. Who on earth could have accused me of such a thing? It can be no one who knows anything of me. Would I do anything so preposterous – so utterly insane? Were I the most criminal plotter in your kingdom – which, God hear me, I am *not* – I could not do anything so farcically inept.'

The words that were rushing into her head had to be bitten back: that Mary's own passion for mysterious midnight interviews had led her to suspect it in others; that Mary could only see politics in terms of persons, and since she had taken the ambassador from Spain as a combination of confidant, dearest friend and father confessor, so she thought Elizabeth must be playing the same silly game with the ambassador from France.

She forced herself to keep calm, to wait before she spoke again, and then only to beg the name of her accuser.

Mary would not tell her, she would only murmur a trifle shamefacedly that it was obvious that Elizabeth and Monsieur de Noallies were close friends, should she say allies?

Elizabeth summoned all the appearance of candour she could muster, staring her sister full in the face and speaking so forcibly that she sounded as though she were barking. She was honest enough now in all conscience, but could she make this stupid woman believe it?

'That, Madam, is what he has desired, naturally, from the moment that he has suspected your future affiance with Spain. England is the deciding factor in the balance of power between France and Spain. Whichever of those two countries is allied to England will rule the world, and the other will sink to a secondary power. The moment you wed Spain you make France your enemy – and mine, for she will try to stir up strife against you in my name. But she is no more my friend than yours. She is working only for herself, to restore the balance of power, which you have tipped over on to the side of Spain by throwing England into the scales with her, instead of keeping the balance even,' – 'as *I* shall do if I ever get the chance,' she added to herself, but dared not look in the glass even as she thought it, lest her bared eyes should tell her thought to Mary.

She had been unbelievably bold, but it worked. As she had seen, it was her only chance to impress Mary; and, offended, sad and angry as Mary was at the criticism of her purpose, which she remained determined not to alter, she yet felt rather less distrust of Elizabeth, and even a grudging respect. But she could not be gracious to her. 'You are very wise about politics,' she said with a snort that relegated the upstart chit back to the schoolroom.

'I have had some reason to be,' said Elizabeth patiently. 'My enemies – no, ours – are doing their best to make you destroy me on one pretext or another. As soon as I am gone they will invent other lies against me.' She stood looking down on the stiff, meagre little figure, the ageing unhealthy face; then forced herself to kneel to her. 'Promise me one thing, Madam when I am gone.' She put out her delicate hand with reluctance (but it looked like timidity) and touched the stumpy pale brown fingers with their heavy rings. 'Promise me you will never listen to any ill tales against me without giving me the chance to answer them, myself, to you in person.'

Mary looked down in her turn on the graceful arrogant

young figure now so consciously humble, and tried not to feel satisfaction. 'Once I had to walk behind you and bear your train' she said to herself, staring in a way that Elizabeth found terrifying, for she could not know that Mary was seeing her as the squalling infant with fluffy red hair who had been declared heir to the throne instead of her seventeen-year-old sister.

'Why do you look so at me, Madam? Will you not promise this? Is it too much to ask – that you will not condemn me, *unheard*?'

'Oh, you will be heard,' said Mary, trying to speak lightly while still remembering the enraged squeals of that infamously royal infant. 'You were always very good at that!'

What did she mean? Never mind. The interview was over and on her feet again, all but staggering with relief. And she had won her point; Mary would not condemn her unheard.

It was a pity she rather spoilt her success by then taking her farewell with the gentle and forgiving air of an injured innocent obliged to leave the Court in disgrace after the insults she had endured; she was aware that this irritated Mary profoundly, but she could not help overplaying her part out of sheer bravado and thankfulness that she would soon not need to go on playing.

She rode out on a brilliant frosty day with five hundred gentlemen in white and green like heralds of the spring. Their horses whinnied in the keen air. She felt like whinnying herself. She had triumphed. She was still in danger – but who wasn't these days, unless one was a milkmaid or a ploughboy? To be out of danger was to be insignificant, to be humble, to be dull (God forbid!), to be dead. But she would rather be dead dull.

'I am alive, Cat! I am free! I am young!' she cried in ecstasy.

'Well, don't make too sure of any of them,' was the governess's admonition.

'Not even the last? No one can take away my youth.'

'Time can.'

'Oh, but Time is on my side. Even the Queen says so. And I will treat him as carefully as an old uncle from whom I have expectations – as indeed I have! He'll never let me grow old – when I am, I won't be, or at least no one will think so. Look at me and tell me honestly, can you believe I'll ever be old?'

'No,' said Cat honestly, then turned away her head. It might well be that her young mistress would never be given the chance to grow old! Did she herself understand that? Yes, she did, but she seemed to glory in it, so headstrong was she, so wild and ungovernable. Cat told her that she seemed positively to revel in tempting Providence.

'What, that frail lady! She can never resist temptation. How unlike my poor elder sister, who has resisted temptation so long that now she has no chance to do so!'

'Don't be too sure. She might be tempted to cut off your head.'

'She might. And she has been. But she's resisted that too, with my help. I've won the first joust with Mary. And I've impressed her. I might even have impressed her rather more,' she added pensively. 'One can't do a good thing too thoroughly.'

Mrs Ashley looked sharply at her charge's face, which was alight with sheer devilment. Too well she knew the signs of her wicked love of teasing.

'Now what by all the imps of Satan does Your Grace intend now?'

'Don't blaspheme to me, woman!' (This from *her*, thought Cat, and her pretty mouth full of the sailors' oaths she learned from the Admiral!). 'I intend nothing but pure religion.'

'*Which* religion?'

'Both. I am the white hope, not only of the new, but of the old.'

And she halted the cortege to send back a messenger to ask the Queen to let her have some holy books of instruction in the Roman Church, also a rosary and some copes and chasubles to accustom her to the true faith at Ashridge, which, as she reminded her sister, had been a monastery dedicated to 'the extirpation of ignorancy'.

But Mary sent none of them, nor any reply. A dead dog had just been thrown into her Presence Chamber with a halter round its neck and a label saying that all Papist priests should be hanged.

PART TWO

CHAPTER EIGHTEEN

'There is no adventure nowadays,' said Tom Wyatt. 'England is growing smaller and smaller, a tight little island buttoning herself in, ever tighter. She used to be an empire, but now all her conquests in the fair land of France have shrunk to the single seaport of Calais. And, with it, the minds of Englishmen have shrunk. We are no longer part of Europe, no longer continental. We are growing insular, prejudiced, narrow-minded, we have forgotten how to travel. For centuries every generation of our young men, lords and peasants, used to go abroad, at first to the East to fight the dark heathen for the Holy Land – then, until lately, to the French wars. But both are over. I fought at Boulogne myself before old King Harry died, but nothing happens there now. Nothing happens anywhere for Englishmen, but internal squabbles as to whether an old maid or a young one shall sit on the throne. A New World has been discovered on the other side of the Western ocean, but what odds does that make to us, for all that it was an Englishman, Richard Ameryk, who gave it its name? Yet we've let the Spaniard get in first and take possession of its gold and pearl – while 'Here I am in Kent and Christendom' as in my father's poem! And we let old Harry's fine new ships rot in their harbours while we sit at home and hug the fire. Throw another log on it, Ned – not that way – put it upright so that the flames will catch it.'

His small son did as he was told, soberly, for he had asked for a tale of adventure and been fobbed off with a lecture about the world getting duller and duller, which he knew already as well as all the other boys at school – that there were no Crusades now, nor wars in France, and only old Davey on his seat on the village green to tell you how he'd gone North as a boy and seen all the Scots lords, their fine young King at their head, mown down like hay on Flodden Field.

He looked reproachfully at the fair handsome young man whose small forked beard now no longer wagged up and down, whose eager eye no longer flashed in indignant animation, but rested once again on the broad page of manuscript in the book that lay open on his knee. Seeing it upside down from where he knelt on the hearthstone, young Ned saw the handwriting like the design on the damascened blade of a sword, strong as it was fine, like that sword, the magnificent unerring strokes going straight across the page without any slant. 'There go the long l's,' thought young Ned, 'and the swoop of the tailed y's, and oh,' he sighed, 'I wish my grandfather had not written so much!'

He pulled the ears of the old spaniel that lay sleeping with his nose thrust as near as possible to the burning logs, then swung backwards and forwards squatting on his heels, stared hopelessly up at the dripping grey windows with all their looped and scrolled latches of wrought iron fastened tight against the wild January weather, stared higher still at the plaster-work on the domed ceiling which depicted in bas-relief a man in a lion-skin carrying another man in nothing at all, stared further and further back at the other plaster pictures above and behind him, until he felt himself toppling over, but instead executed a backward somersault in solemn silence and left the hall to find a few of his nine brothers and sisters.

His father, Sir Thomas Wyatt, continued to look through the writings of *his* father, Sir Thomas Wyatt. He meant to have them printed, particularly the poems. His father had had no time to attend to such trifling business, a diplomat, ambassador to France and Rome and Spain, courtier at King Henry's Court, soldier at one time and commander of a man-of-war at another, Steward of Maidstone, and Knight of the Shire for Kent. And Sir Thomas Wyatt the younger was even more of a man of action than his father; he had been described as 'a born soldier' in dispatches to King Henry before he was twenty-three. Yet as be turned these pages of beautifully designed handwriting, while the wind rattled the new glass panes and flung handfuls of sharp rain and sleet against them like pebbles flung by a rude boy, the conviction slowly grew on him that his father would be remembered chiefly, not for his brilliant public life, but for his poems; and for the belief in most men's minds that he had been Nan Bullen's first lover before she met King Henry and her doom.

There was a poem his father had never written, but that his father's sister Margaret had often told him, how on the night before the 1st of May, when Nan had been just on three years Queen, she was beset by unknown terrors, and, unable to sleep, had risen and wandered about the garden; and there, in the first white light of dawn and the shrill bird-song, Margaret her lady-in-waiting had found the Queen standing under an apple tree in full blossom, a ghost within a cloud. 'The Duke of Norfolk has come to see Your Grace,' Margaret had said, and in a whisper the Queen answered, 'He has come to arrest me.'

But no poem did he ever write of that tragic Maying, only a guarded sonnet on the chances 'most unhappy, that me betide in May.' He never wrote directly of Nan Bullen, though again and again between these lines of verse Tom Wyatt could see the young Queen he had gazed at as a schoolboy, the quick hands and pointed face and dark eyes where the flashing laughter was often chased by the startled look in the eyes of a deer.

> 'They flee from me that sometimes did me seek
> With naked foot, stalking in my chamber.
> I have seen them gentle, tame and meek,
> That now are wild and do not remember
> That sometime they put themselves in danger
> To take bread at my hand.'

Who were 'they,' and why did that same image of a deer haunt his father's poems – a deer in a diamond collar where,

> 'in letters plain,
> There is written her fair neck round about,
> 'Noli me tangere,' for Caesar's I am,
> And wild for to hold, though I seem tame.'

'Noli me tangere' – but had he never touched her, before Caesar put his mighty foot in the stirrup and 'list her hunt' – to the kill? King Harry had killed Nan Bullen whom he had made his Queen, and with her five tall handsome young men, the finest of them her own brother, accused as her lovers.

Wyatt, the poet, also arrested, had been set free. Had she then never sought him in his chamber 'with naked foot'? Never come to him

> 'In thin array, after a pleasant guise,
> When her loose gown from her shoulders did fall,
> And she me caught in her arms long and small,
> Therewith all sweetly did me kiss
> And softly said, 'Dear Heart, how like you this?'
>
> It was no dream; I lay broad waking:—'

Tom Wyatt closed the book with a bang.

He would read no further, peer no longer into his father's secrets. That last magnificent line, in the open-eyed wonder invoked by its slow-paced monosyllables, had brought back too vivid a picture of his father's finely carved head bent lovingly to his lute as he sang the words. He had never spoken of their hidden meaning, only of their purpose, written in English 'for Britain's gain,' to rescue their native tongue from the dull drudgery that had beset its verse ever since the splendour of old Chaucer two hundred years before. 'These modern poets, pedants rather, think only Latin or French worthy of their lyre, but I'll show them!' And well he had, for he had adopted the very same formulas of the Latin poets that were in fashion on the Continent and shown that a plain Englishman could use them as well as or better than any foreign poet.

He had given the world an English Wyatt for their Italian

Petrarch, had proudly turned his back upon proud Spain, 'for I with spur and sail go seek the Thames,' to sing in praise of London and

> '*My King, my country, alone for whom I live.*'

And with that trumpet-call of his father's ringing in his mind, Tom Wyatt sprang up and began to stride up and down the room.

'Proud Spain' had been the nightmare of his boyhood, when his father had been imprisoned by the Inquisition. He had escaped, to be honoured later in a diplomatic mission to Spain from whence he had written many affectionate letters full of good advice to his schoolboy son. But the earlier horror of the boy's anxiety, lying awake night after night to wonder – and picture – what tortures his adored father might even then be enduring, had ever since haunted his mind.

Spain was the evil spider of the world, spreading her web over the vast circumference of the globe, to ensnare all free men. Now the net was stretching over England. If Queen Mary were so besotted as to persist in taking Philip of Spain for her husband, she would be putting her country in chains.

Was this the moment, then, to think of escape? It was a boy's, a coward's way to dream of adventure on the high seas, to think with longing of the three ships he had watched this summer sail down the Thames under Sir Edward Challoner, sail out across the ocean to discover a new North-East passage through the Arctic to Cathay, sail out away from England and all her internal worries and restrictions, her eternal new regulations regarding the new religion and whether fish days should be held on Wednesday and Friday (religious and therefore superstitious) or on Thursday and Saturday (economic and therefore sound) – all to be reversed in a few short months under the new return to the old religion.

No true Englishman could now afford to seek escape to a freer life across the world. If England were in peril of conquest by a foreign foe, under the insidious mask of a peaceful royal marriage, then she would need all her sons, she would need *him*.

He had laid his plans against it, together with his neighbours at home and his friends at Court. The next move was in their hands, and not merely those of his friends. The Council were presenting the Queen with a public petition, headed by Gardiner, her staunchest ally, but staunchly against her in this. Wyatt himself could do no more until he knew its result.

If that were failure – well, then he was prepared for what he must do.

Liberty was not to be sought abroad, but here 'in Kent and Christendom' where till now

> *'No man doth mark where I do ride or go,*
> *In lusty lees my liberty to take'*

– liberty to hunt and hawk, 'and in foul weather at my book to sit,' as he had just been doing; liberty to finish building the house his father had begun and replace with clear glass the draughty wicker-work that still filled some of the windows to save expense; liberty to bring up his sons in the faith that they should have the liberty to choose; liberty from the subtly encroaching spies who cast their webs abroad from the dark centre of a foreign power, and ensnared men's minds before they enslaved their bodies.

'It's the hares!' he exclaimed aloud. He had shot them, the cook had baked them in a pie, and so he had eaten them at dinner along with a fine brawn and some salted mutton ham, though hares were known to nourish melancholy. He'd soon stop worrying about England for a bit if only the weather would clear up and he could get out with his gun or cross-bow – and shoot more hares.

But the rain was rattling so loud it sounded like horses' hoofs on the cobbles in the courtyard.

It *was* horses' hoofs.

There came a loud knocking on the door. Tom Wyatt sprang towards it. A tall young man entered, muffled up to the eyes in a dripping cloak which he dropped to the floor in a wet heap as the servant left them, and stood dramatically disclosed. Wyatt looked curiously at the fair hair ruffled up from a high-bred, finely cut face, whose ancestors had done all they could for it without much help from its present owner.

'The Council have drawn blank,' were the stranger's first words. 'The Queen is furious with the whole pack of 'em. They say she's sworn to have Philip of Spain or no one.' And then, as Wyatt led him to the fire, 'You know who I am, the Earl of Devonshire.'

Yes, Wyatt had known it, though be had never met young Courtenay, and he seemed much younger than his twenty-five years. But time stood still with lives in retirement; prisoners, like nuns, were apt to look young until suddenly they looked old.

'Earl of D-d-dampshire,' the young man corrected, shivering as he spread his long blue hands to the fire, shaking his wet gloves that sent little spitting showers on to the blazing logs. 'That's de Noailles' version of the name. And how true at this moment! He's told me to come to you now all else has failed. Poor old Gardiner, he did his best, beetled his shaggy eyebrows like a bull about to charge and spoke out like a true Englishman – trust a Gardiner to call a spade a spade!' He crowed with mirth and finished at a gulp the wine just handed to him (not the first he had had on this ride, thought Wyatt), then suddenly looked solemn and shook his head. 'But she spoke out too – how they roared at each other! Says she'll take away his office as Chancellor. She'll do it too. Told him her father was the only man who could manage him, and so would she. Said she'd as much right to choose her own husband as any of her subjects, but that's not right, you know, not for Kings and Queens. We can't choose. Look at me – not bad-looking, hey? and "a man may not marry his grand-mother," yet I was willing to sacrifice myself to a skinny old maid for the sake of England.'

'And its Crown, my lord.'

'Why, yes, it's crowns that count. Else I'd have plumped earlier for that sly minx her sister, as I've now come to do, thank God, or rather Venus, which is her votary saint, I'll swear. Between her and me and the bedpost, we'll get the Crown yet.'

Looking at his high fair brow with the damp gold curls plastered on it and his startled blue eyes flickering with excited pleasure like those of a schoolboy out on an adventure, Wyatt thought, 'If this lad has one spark of true courage in him we are bound to win,' and then in the same breath, 'but why the devil did he start drinking before he ever got here, or had even seen me for the first time?'

Aloud he said, 'Has Your Lordship won her consent, then, to marry you?'

'Elizabeth consent? Don't you know her better than that? She's a lady, a Court lady. She doesn't say yes and she doesn't say no. But I know a better answer. Surprise her when she's out riding at Ashridge, marry her by force and carry her off down to Devon.'

Wyatt gave a short, rather savage laugh. 'I fancy it's you who'd be surprised, my lord!'

'Oh, she's wild as a cat of the woods! But I know she likes me.' He preened himself like a wet peacock. 'Rape,' he murmured in the tone of a bemused boy, day-dreaming of lust, 'could anyone make sure of that one without it? I fancy the Lord Admiral found you couldn't, *he* could have told us how he'd handled her.'

Wyatt struck sharply across these nauseous fancies. 'Did de Noailles suggest this?'

'Well, he may have said it first – what odds? He's written to his master the French King that all that's needed is for us to marry and go together to the West and the whole country will rise for us to a man. They say in Devon that if Philip of Spain lands there he'll get as well barked at as ever man was. They say in Cornwall, "We ought not to have a woman bear the sword," and *then* they say, "If a woman bear the sword, my Lady Elizabeth ought to have it first!"'

Again he gave that odd little high crow that sounded more scared than pleased. 'And look at this letter from the Mayor and Aldermen of Plymouth – they beg me to come and take them under my protection against the "outlandish men" from

Spain – look at it! They'll put the town in my hands and whatever garrison I place there, "being resolved not to receive the Prince of Spain nor obey his commands in any way." So there it is – and Croft has promised to answer for the Welsh Borders, and you for the men of Kent—'

'Wait, my lord. *What* garrison do you propose to place in Plymouth?'

'De Noailles'. He's sworn to conduct us, Elizabeth and me, down to the West, with French troops and money and even the French fleet to stand by in case of need.'

'French troops fighting Spanish on English soil! And a captured Princess for support! Such an action would mean utter ruin to you both. Fight for yourself, my lord!'

Courtenay blinked. 'Without de Noailles – or Elizabeth?' he stammered.

Wyatt was walking up and down to quiet the sudden astonished rage that had risen in him. He was thinking of the girl he had watched riding like a white flame through the smoky sunset city last summer; thinking of the delighted murmurs around him in the crowd greeting her, rather than the Queen, as 'true Tudor' and 'old Harry's own.' The people were already welcoming that fiery spirit as their leader. But in alliance with this weathercock? He could not welcome that last at all.

And Courtenay's anxious stare, following him like a dog's, seemed to perceive it, for when he spoke again his voice was quite different, it had a shy, dreamy appeal.

'Have you noticed how bright her eyes are? That is because they have stared at danger since she was a child, and never withdrawn their gaze. Those long slow grey hours in the Tower, she knows nothing of them – only of bright life, and blood-stained death.'

But as Wyatt did not answer nor cease his steady tramp up and down the room, Courtenay drank again and took another pull at his thoughts. If he could not count on de Noailles nor yet Elizabeth to carry things through for him, what should he do? Cut adrift from it all? It might be best.

'I'm in Kent now,' he said, 'it's not far from Greenwich. I think I'll ride on to the Palace and try the great horses King Edward left there.'

That pulled up Wyatt. 'Why?' he asked blankly.

'I need practice. It doesn't do to have a Prince who can only ride a palfrey. It's the worst thing the Tower's done for me. I've been saying for days I must get down there,' he added, elaborately off-hand.

Wyatt puzzled over it, then suddenly saw. 'You mean to slip away in the darkness of the night on a ship to France!'

'Why not? I'd be among friends there. The French King said so. I'm sick of all these schemes, I only want to be free.'

'Go, and be damned to you!' was the answer Wyatt longed to give. But to have him babbling of their plans to Henri II would be as bad a danger as any. France would work against Spain, but she would work against England too.

'I wouldn't go if I could be sure of my backing here,' Courtenay continued on a faint note of reproach. 'They said I could count on you at any rate. You will come in with us, won't you? They say you are heart and soul against Spain.'

Yes, that still held. The one thing that mattered now was to prevent Philip taking possession of the country. Wyatt found himself giving his marching orders as though to a subordinate. 'Nothing can be done yet, and above all,' he said sternly, 'nothing *said*. The signal for revolt against Spain must be the moment that Spanish troops land on our shores – and not a day earlier. But when that happens I can answer for every true Kentish man to rise and resist them. Sir James Croft can do the same for the Welsh Borders. And you, my lord, should go down at once, on your own account, to your estates in Devon and Cornwall – to show them that they can trust you,' he added, not without a suspicion of irony. It would, in any case, get him safely out of the way from his friends the enemies: the ambassador, de Noailles, on the one side, with his doubtful promises of French support, and, on the other, Bishop Gardiner.

'Do you still see much of Gardiner?' he asked abruptly.

'Oh well, you know, we were friends in the Tower, it was a small world there, one was glad of anyone, and the old boy can be quite good company for all he's a bishop, full of good stories in spite of his appetite for work.' Courtenay had seemed surprised by the sudden question, but with his usual eagerness to please was hurriedly explaining the answer. 'He *would* see to my education, looked on himself as my tutor, worse luck, and my father too. I still call him "father",' he added on a note of boyish sentiment that filled Wyatt with foreboding.

'And confide in him as one?'

'Oh no, not really. But I have to be grateful to the old man,' he added virtuously. 'And besides, he is all against this marriage of the Queen's.'

'But not against the Queen. Go to Devon, my lord. For God's sake,' he urged, leaning forward and trying to hold those restless glancing eyes with his steady gaze, 'go down to Devon.'

CHAPTER NINETEEN

Now she had gone into winter quarters, Elizabeth told herself, like a squirrel burrowing into its lair to conserve its life and energies for the spring, and indeed she looked very like a squirrel as she cuddled Mary's furs round her in the privacy of her room, her bright eyes peering out from them at the snow-clouds marching over the Chiltern Hills beyond her window. Winter had closed in on her, but she was safe and snug here at Ashridge, she had gone to earth, or if it were not quite as good as that, she had burrowed into a cave in the rocks where she would be safe – but only just as long as the tide did not rise and flow in on her.

She could build her own pleasures better than at Court, removed from the daily fear of a royal snub, as much danger as disgrace. She read Italian and French romances, and with her tutors the Greek plays that had become the rage at Cambridge, and of course she must not forget to keep up her Latin also, since it was the one common language of diplomacy that held Europe together – though somehow it had acquired a musty monkish flavour from its long usage in the old Church and had none of the excitement of discovery to be felt in reading Greek. She composed verses, and tunes to sing them to on her lute or the virginals, and she liked still better to compose ballets to dance to her own tunes.

She could do all of them very prettily for she had inherited her father's turn for composing verses and music, and playing it, and her mother's for dancing to it. In the ice- or snow- or rain-bound solitude of the old monastery built on the site of the Black Prince's hunting-box, she could practise her charms and talents, let her hair curl into crisp ringlets, try on the jewels and gay dresses she dared not wear in public.

She could even have her picture painted in the dress she had worn as Diana at her private masquerade. (The Dutch artist on giving her the brawny neck and arms of an athletic huntress!) It was a daring dress for the current fashion, and you might have taken her for a Bacchante or wild Maenad until you noticed the small pearl crescent of the moon goddess crowning her cunningly dishevelled curls. Her face too was off guard, for the only time she was ever to let it so appear, giving full rein to the imprisoned freedom and daring of her spirit.

But Elizabeth was not left entirely free from the outside world. Her worst trouble from it was one that should have delighted her particular vanity, for it was due to proposals of marriage. The Prince of Piedmont's offer was still being urged on her, almost with threats; and the Prince of Denmark, who had been so eager to marry her a few years ago, was now renewing his offer privately and must not be offended, nor encouraged.

Another proposal, even more embarrassing than matrimony, was continually reaching her through de Noailles from the King of France, in cipher, assuring her of a warm welcome at his Court, where he and his wife, Catherine de Medici, would be delighted to treat her as their own daughter. 'And what can we say about that?' demanded her secretary, Mr Parry.

'That he has one too many extra daughters already,' answered Elizabeth viciously. His only reason for offering her a home would be to remove her as a future rival to his other 'extra daughter,' Mary, the child Queen of Scots – and 'a long home it would be,' she said, 'whether in prison or the grave.'

'But we must not say that,' said Parry, smiling discreetly so as not to reveal the loss of a back tooth.

'Oh no, we dare not offend him, we must be very grateful and polite and never let him know that we see through him. God's death, if I could but once shout the truth out loud and shame the devil!'

Instead she called the fiddlers and lutist to play the tune she had made up the night before and tried her dance to it while she thought out her answers. No time was better for that than while she practised the intricate manoeuvres of the dance measures she had invented, threading them with hand and foot while her busy mind, soothed by the rhythm of the music and of her swaying supple body, spun its own casuistic subtleties.

Two steps to the left and slide, two to the right and glide, here hold out your hand to your partner – which partner? Edward Courtenay danced well, a graceful lad, had had good masters in the Tower, but there was no magic in his movements to call out the music of one's own; he was Narcissus dancing with his own shadow. Robin Dudley danced well, he was bold and gay, 'Hey, Robin, jolly Robin!' as the country song sang. But there had once been a partner more gay and bold whose touch had thrilled her more nearly, who had swept her off her feet and danced her to his death, and all but hers.

Dancing here alone in the firelight, while the shadows

deepened in the corners of the room, and the short winter's day faded against the chequered window-panes, she felt that she was dancing with a ghost. The ring of a mighty laugh that she had not heard for five years echoed through her mind, shattering the discreet tinkling of the music; a smouldering log flared up and glinted on the bright tapestry, but for an instant she thought it was on the towering gold-laced figure of the Lord Admiral, Tom Seymour, whose magnificent head had been struck from his shoulders for making love to the Princess Elizabeth when she was all but a child.

She could dance no more alone – and what use had it been? She had not thought out a thing more than 'Your most Christian Majesty has shown the kindness of a loving father to an unhappy daughter.'

She turned towards the window where the little group of musicians sat to catch the last of the light, three shadows whose faces were dim white as they turned towards the darkening room.

'One of you come and take this movement with me – I cannot work it out alone.'

The lute-player sprang up first, and as he came towards her down the long room she noticed that he was strange to her, a tall fine-looking man with a short fair beard.

'Since when have you entered my service?' she asked as the fiddlers struck up the tune again and she led him into the measure of the dance.

'All your life, Madam,' he answered low.

Heavens, the man was another secret agent, and this another trap! She froze with fear and anger, was about to call out, but his hand tightened on hers. 'Wait, Madam, till I have told you. You are in danger—'

'From you! If you give me any message from Courtenay or de Noailles I shall expose you here on the spot.'

'I bear no message. I have news you must hear. Dance on, Madam, and I will tell you. The fiddlers cannot hear us.'

He spoke with such calm authority that she obeyed, pretending to show him the movements of the dance while his low rapid voice told her, 'The case is desperate. You must get away from here. Courtenay has betrayed all to Gardiner, and Gardiner to the Queen.'

'And what has that to do with me?'

Her whisper was cold as death. Her lithe quick figure danced in and out of the firelight, the hair a-shimmer, but the face a still shadow. Could nothing quicken her into life, not even the fear of losing it? He spoke with angrier urgency.

'They will seize the chance to strike at you. Gardiner will have your head if he can. Leave this place and go to Donnington – it is further from London, it is a strong house. Fortify it well, man it against attack, and do not leave it on whatever summons, above all do not go to London.'

'Who are you?'

'Thomas Wyatt, Your Grace.'

'I knew it. God's death, did I not say I would take no letter from you?'

'So I had to come in person.'

'And bribe my servants!'

'Your lute-player is well known to me – I have told him all that was necessary. The case is altered. We must strike at once, within the next three days. Suffolk has already left the Court.'

'Suffolk again! He will declare his daughter as Queen Jane while the West cry "Courtenay!" and the rest "Elizabeth!"'

'But all will cry "Down with Spain!" Philip's landing was

to be the signal, it would have shown we were against him, not the Queen. But now we cannot wait. You will not join us?'

'No.'

'Then you have two days to move your household, with all the guards you can muster, and secure yourself in Donnington. Will you go tomorrow?'

'No.'

'When?'

'Never.'

'You will not save your life?'

'By all the means I have – if any. But to admit that I am in the conspiracy – that I know of it even – I will not do that.'

'The rising is not to place you on the throne – only to secure your succession to it.'

'You may shout that to the troops, but no one will believe it, least of all Mary. She too is Tudor. She'll not take her throne on terms. Nor will I fight against her on it – or what peace should I have in my own reign if I had rebelled against my Sovereign?'

'What *will* you do then?'

'Nothing. I wish that you would too. Your plan has miscarried. Let it go.'

'It must go forward. At least say you wish me well.'

She was looking at him at last as a person, a man, as they moved towards each other in the dance, and a faint smile slowly lightened her shadowed face. 'My mother's daughter could surely say no less to your father's son.'

He took her hand to lead her forward in the final movement – and said in time to the last notes of the music that fell clear and precise as drops of water:

> '*I promise you*
> *And you promise me*
> *To be as true*
> *As I will be.*'

'So – nearly so – my father wrote – was it to your mother?'

'If it were, then *absit omen*! But I will never show you "a double heart".'

'Nor I you, my Lady Elizabeth, God give me grace!'

Hand in hand they paced in the stately measure of the pavane down the hall, out of the firelight into the shadows. The music died on the air. Their dance was finished.

That was on the 22nd of January, the day after Courtenay had sobbed out his confession to Gardiner, having first obtained a promise from him that whatever happened he should not be beheaded.

On the 25th, Wyatt marched on London at the head of his Kentishmen.

On the 26th, Elizabeth received a politely urgent invitation from the Queen to come to Court and avoid the dangers resulting from 'an unnatural rebellion' induced by certain 'malicious and seditious minds.' But the most disturbing thing in the letter was the mention of Donnington, 'whither, as we understand, you are minded shortly to remove'!

And how, in God's, or Satan's name, did she understand *that*? Elizabeth demanded of herself, but could find no answer, except that she was beset with spies and most probably with potential assassins. 'Look over your shoulder and you'll see Death waiting for you,' – who had said that? Was it the Admiral, laughing despite of death – or Sir Thomas

Wyatt the poet who had loved her mother and so narrowly escaped death on the scaffold for her? The fishermen had a superstition that if a life were saved from the sea, then it had to be paid for with another. Was it the same with the scaffold? Did it now wait for another Sir Thomas Wyatt?

She refused the invitation of her most dear sister. It was the old pretext, she did not feel well enough. But this time it became more and more true. The waiting game she had forced on herself was more terrifying than any daring action. She did, it is true, set an armed guard round her house both inside and out, but this was because Suffolk was known to be on the march not far off and, as he had proclaimed his daughter Jane as Queen, there was very real danger that he would attack Elizabeth as well as Mary. She took care to announce this publicly as the reason for putting her house in a state of defence, but knew well that her enemies would only interpret it as an act of rebellion against the Queen, and do their best to make her believe in it as such. 'Elizabeth and Courtenay,' those two names were being proclaimed everywhere as the true instigators of the rebellion, and its true motive to supplant Mary with them as King and Queen.

On that same day, the 26th of January, the report came flying from London that all the gates of the City were being watched 'in harness' because Sir Thomas Wyatt and Sir George Harper and Sir Hare Isley and Mr Rudston and Mr Knyvett and divers other gentlemen and commons were up, and already held Rochester Castle and its bridge.

But Elizabeth was not 'up.' She went to bed, as she had done in the high summer weather at King Edward's death, to watch the icy rain shoot down in grey sheets outside her windows, and shiver with fear and cold. Nothing could warm her, however huge the logs they piled on the fire and however many hot bricks wrapped in flannel were placed in the bed and quilts of goosefeathers on top of it. All the nerves in her head throbbed with pain, she had tooth-ache and swellings in her jaw and neck, and her body swelled too, probably with nervous indigestion and wind, though Mrs Ashley warned her not to mention this symptom, as her enemies were sure to say again she was with child. They did.

She woke at night crying that she had been dancing with a ghost – 'his hand turned cold in mine,' she cried. She had this dream more than once.

She heard that 15,000 Kentishmen had gathered round Wyatt's standard, furnished with arms and ammunition by the Venetian ambassador, and were encamped in the fields bordering the highway from Dover to London, harassing the Flemish and Spanish merchants from the coast. A generous leader, he had given all his followers good leave to depart if they willed going on to London.

'But why haven't they started for London?' asked Elizabeth.

She heard how the Duke of Norfolk had marched against the rebels at the head of the City bands in their white coats, quickly grey with rain, and was urging the Warden of the Cinque Ports with his troops in Sheppey to 'come in on Wyatt's backside.' But the Warden complained of 'the weather being so terrible yet no man can stir by water or well by land.' The Duke's Whitecoats were deserting. Wyatt besieged and stormed Cooling Castle in six hours, and its owner, his uncle Lord Cobham, sent a frantic letter subscribed:

'To the Queen's most
excellent majesty
haste haste
post
haste
with all diligence possible
for the life
for the life.'

The household at Ashridge was wild with excitement. Lord Cobham's sons had all gone over to Wyatt, they saw what their cousin could do, since he could take the massive fortress of Cooling, with its moat and inner and outer wards and drum towers forty feet high and walls six feet thick, all in six hours.

'Six hours wasted,' said Elizabeth.

Then Mrs Ashley came running into her room with news that Wyatt's army was at Southwark, only just across the river from the Tower, and the Queen not even fortressed there but in her Palace of Whitehall, with only 200 archers for guard. She had ridden to Guildhall and appealed herself to the citizens, ordered all the London bridges to be cut to keep him out, but it could make no odds.

The Government had already sued Wyatt for terms. The Court had panicked, and the citizens; the streets were a pandemonium of terror and confusion, and so was the Palace, where armed men stood on guard in the Queen's bedchamber, and her women ran shrieking through the corridors, and Gardiner was begging the Queen on his knees to fly for her life. The Imperial ambassadors had already fled disguised as merchants, all except Renard, who had refused to leave the Queen in her hour of utter defeat.

And now Wyatt was across the river. He swam the swollen Thames himself at Kingston, got hold of a boat, and with a few of his men worked to restore the bridge until he got 7000 of his troops across at night, and by half-past two in the morning was pressing up the Strand towards Fleet Street, driving back the Queen's forces to Lud Gate, and cutting off Whitehall from any help.

A man drenched to the skin came flogging his horse through torrents of rain to say he had seen a wild mob surging round St James's and Whitehall and that they had broken into the Palace. Wyatt had stopped their looting and put the Queen under a strong guard. Her battle was broken and he had the mastery.

The rain-soaked messenger, a younger brother of Sir Hare Isley, asked to kiss the hand of the Princess Elizabeth and assure her of the devotion of every man in their ranks. But she would not see him.

'What more does Your Grace want?' cried Cat Ashley as she leaned over the bed and chafed the long hands that were still blue with cold in spite of this glorious news. 'Are you not as good as Queen of England?'

'I will wait,' said the chill whisper from the bed, 'till I am Queen of England.'

'But, my love, my lamb, Your Grace, Your Majesty, you have only to stretch out your hand—'

Elizabeth withdrew it from her governess's warm compelling grasp and replaced it in the bed.

'Tell Mr Isley to go away, tell him that I refused to receive him or any message from him. Tell him that I am too ill to hear of any business. Go out of the room, Cat, put out the candles, and leave me alone.'

Cat Ashley did as she was told. Elizabeth was left alone, at the leaping flames in the fire. She did not believe the tale had ended. She knew her sister.

She was right. Mary was Tudor too.

She had already rallied the citizens by her magnificent appeal at Guildhall when in movingly simple words she told them, 'I cannot tell how naturally the mother loves the child, for I was never the mother of any – but assure yourselves that I do as earnestly and tenderly love you, and cannot but think that you as heartily and faithfully love me – and then I doubt not but that we shall give these rebels a short and speedy overthrow.'

They had thronged to her aid after that; they had closed the City gates and cut the bridges; the very lawyers on their way to hear their legal cases had flung off their gowns and seized arms to go to her help.

But she herself was her best ally.

When arrows were shooting in at the Palace windows and her officers came crying to her that all was lost to Wyatt, when her guards forsook their posts and hid in the pantries and out-houses, and her sobbing women implored her to escape by boat to the Tower, she stood her ground; or rather, she advanced, and coming out on to a balcony cried to the people below, that rather than surrender, she would come down into the battleground and die with those who were still faithful to her.

Wyatt was indeed within an ace of capturing the Queen, but neither he nor any of his men actually got inside the Palace, though in the howling confusion round it many people thought at one moment that he had done so.

That was the moment when young Isley rode headlong to Ashridge to be the first to give the glad news to their future Queen.

But from that moment came the rebels' overthrow, and the moment had been lost by the day wasted earlier in taking Cooling Castle. If Wyatt had reached London a day sooner, the Queen would have had no chance to make her appeal at Guildhall; it was that, and her stand at bay in the Palace, that won the day.

A charge of the loyal troops shouting the cheerful battle-cry of 'Down with the daggletails!' drove down on the drenched disorderly mob and cut off Wyatt from his followers. With a handful of men he straggled towards Fleet Street, and a few hours later was found, with only one follower left to him, sitting on a bench by a fishmonger's stall near Lud Gate. The rain sluiced through the links of his mail shift, his clothes of velvet and yellow embroidery were torn and muddy, his face was covered with blood.

But in his dilapidated lace-trimmed hat was something that showed him his father's son, for, knowing a price was on his head, he had put a label on it with his name, so that anyone could sell him who had a mind to. No one took the opportunity.

The Norroy Herald, Sir Maurice Berkeley, came to arrest him and stood looking down on the exhausted figure, abusing him for a rebel and traitor. Wyatt did not seem to hear him; he got slowly to his feet and his dulled eyes looked grimly at his captor.

'It is no mastery now,' was all he said.

* * *

Mary had won, and gave thanks to God in a Te Deum sung the next day in St Paul's, and the church bells rang for joy all over the country. But it was not the happy victory that her first had been. She had then shown such mercy as had never been seen after a rebellion to put a usurper on the throne. Only three people had been executed. And look at the result! exclaimed Mary's advisers – another rebellion within six months, and far more widespread and dangerous than the first! Useless to expect gratitude; the people did not understand it, only the simple law of reward and punishment. Her mercy was cruelty, since it had been so abused and led to worse crimes which must now be punished with the utmost rigour.

Her bitterness made it easier for her to agree. Dudley's revolt had been for ambition only, impersonal to herself. But now she had become known to her people, had been as good to them as she knew how, and they had repaid her by attacking her through all that was most dear to her: her faith, and the husband she longed to marry while she could yet bear him a child.

Already his coming had hung fire through all the disaffection openly shown, the rumours and threats of revolution. Now it would have to be delayed much longer before the country could be counted as settled and the Emperor and his indignant Spanish nobles would consider it safe for their Prince to venture into this barbarous island that had shown so violent a hatred of him. Mary wept tears of humiliation at the thought, and was only too ready to believe it was all her own fault for having been too obstinate in her leniency before.

She promised she would not be so again.

She quite understood that all the ringleaders would have to be executed, including the Duke of Suffolk, who had so foully repaid his free pardon by yet another attempt to usurp the Crown for his daughter Lady Jane Grey. And Jane herself, though innocent, was far from innocuous.

Reluctantly the Queen was made to understand that, for the safety of the Kingdom and of the man she hoped to make King of it, the daughter too must die.

CHAPTER TWENTY

So now it had come to this; it was Jane's last evening on earth and nothing awaited her on the morrow but the narrow grave dug for her within the Tower grounds. Her enemies had done their best for her, Mary had tried to save her; it was her own flesh and blood that had betrayed her, her own parents who had used her remorselessly as a tool to further their insensate ambition. It was not fear but anger that Jane had to fight in these last days, to keep her spirit pure for its final ordeal. For death was common, it came to half the population far earlier than to herself. A brother and sister had died by the will of God before she was reared. But her death was by the will of unjust man. 'It isn't fair,' had been the constant cry of her childhood against the harshness of her parents, their eternal complaints that she was 'stubborn and needed a strong rein.'

But what could have exceeded her father's stubbornness in raising rebellion yet again in the name of his unwilling daughter and sending her to the block? Yet he could not be stubborn in defeat. Jane had heard with sheer disgust how he had been scented out by a dog – his second treachery too rank even for a cur! – from a hollow oak where be had hidden for three days in icy February rain. And that was the last of the 'daggletails,' when the sodden wretch that had been Duke of

Suffolk was hauled down through the slimy branches and fell on his knees in the mire.

Surely the daughter then had the more cause to complain that the parent 'needed a strong rein.' Her strong sense of justice could not forbear writing to her father that her end had been hastened 'by you, by whom my life should rather have been lengthened.' But now that her last night on earth was drawing in, she wished she had not written that. The thing was done. Nothing could lengthen her life beyond these few hours; it was feeble to reproach as to pray for mercy. She could even feel pity for him who was so soon to die himself. She wrote now again a letter to be given him after her death – 'the Lord comfort Your Grace,' telling him to 'trust that we have won immortal life.'

She did not write to her mother.

She wrote to her young husband, Guildford Dudley, who also was to be executed on the morrow just before herself, refusing his request to see her again, though the Queen had granted it. But Jane wrote that she would rather wait till they could meet in Heaven. He might be different then.

She might have thought him different now, if she had known that at that moment he was chipping away at the last letter of her name, which he had been patiently carving night after night with his penknife on the hard stone of his prison wall. JANE – his mute appeal to her would remain as long as the Tower should endure; thousands of eyes would look on it with pity; but not hers.

The living lusty youth who had tried to bully her into loving him had nothing to do with her lonely childhood. That belonged to herself alone, and alone she would go to meet its end.

She wrote a long letter to Sir John Bridges, the Lieutenant of the Tower, sending him some books, and a far longer one to her sister Catherine, sending her own Greek Testament and telling her 'it will teach you to live and learn you to die.' All her learning now had come to that. She must do her last lesson perfectly.

So she wrote on and on, giving all of herself that she could in these last moments, to the world that had known her so little; like a very young plant grown in the dark reaching out eagerly towards the sun, before she went where she would see neither sun not moon. The world did not know her. The world *should* know her. 'God and posterity,' she wrote, 'will show me favour.'

It was growing dark. Her women brought candles for her and shut out the oncoming night. She asked to be left alone again, and they spoke to her gently through their tears, but though her lips moved she did not answer them. She was saying to herself, 'O Lord, support us all the day long of this troublous life, until the shades lengthen and the evening come and the busy world is hushed, the fever of life is over, and our work done.' Her work was done.

She took up her lute to sing the psalm that went with the evening prayer. She found she was not singing it, but a song that Mr Ascham had sung to her and her tutor Mr Aylmer.

> 'You and I and Amyas,
> Awyas and you and I,
> To the greenwood must we go, alas,
> You and I, my life, and Amyas.'

She did not know why she remembered that strange pagan song now, which had nothing to do with her, nor with her tutor Mr Aylmer, who was safe abroad, long miles from her, nor with Roger Ascham, who was once again knocking at the door of her cousin Elizabeth, that bright strange creature whom Jane had adored since a child and vainly tried to follow as one might follow a will-o'-the-wisp, never knowing what it was.

> 'The portress was a lady bright,
> Strangeness that Lady hight.
> She asked him what was his name,
> He said, 'Desire, your man, Madam.'
> She said, 'Desire, what do ye here?'
> He said, 'Madam, as your prisoner.'

Yes, that was Elizabeth, whom men desired; who held the hearts of men in thrall, as she now knew, and bewitched them to her service.

'You will live on,' she cried, striking the wailing notes on her lute,

> 'You and Amyas will live on,
> But I shall die alone, alas!'

Her lute slid from her grasp, tears came hot and heavy into her smarting eyes, they would not keep open, like a child she was crying herself to sleep. What need had she of sleep who so soon would sleep never to wake again? But her head slipped down on to the table among all the letters she had written, and there lay while her exhausted spirit rose out of the small tired body and wandered back to her home.

She passed round the great palace of red brick at Bradgate that her grandfather had built to show how rich and proud he was and how secure against his neighbours – no moat, no drawbridge, only warm red walls enclosing orchards and pleasure-gardens full of scented flowers, for this was February but her dream was summer. And her spirit did not stay in those trimly ordered gardens, nor on the terrace where she had played with Catherine, the younger sister so much smaller than herself that it was like playing with a doll that had come alive.

She wandered down the trout stream that went tumbling and tossing over the smooth boulders to the Wishing Well where once for a few moments she had sat with Mr Ascham and Mr Aylmer and all had wished and none had told their wish, but she had had a notion that it was the same – that all three should continue in their friendship, and in their common purpose, to promote both the advancement of learning and the worship of God in the true way, divested of superstition. That was how her mind had put it into words as she leaned over the clear water that her two friends told her was the image of herself, a well of water undefiled – that was how her mind had put it, but her heart had sung,

> 'You, and I and Amyas
> To the greenwood must we go, alas.'

Why 'alas'? Why, now she knew, for now she was walking all alone under the tall trees, and they were no longer tall, they were writhing and twisted, stunted like mighty dwarfs that should have been giants. She cried aloud, asking what had happened to her beloved oaks, but nobody heard her, nobody saw her, though there were people walking all round her, and then she heard one of them say, 'They cut off all the heads of the oaks hundreds of years ago. They say it was when Lady Jane Grey was beheaded.'

CHAPTER TWENTY-ONE

'This morning at 8 o'clock the Lady Jane was beheaded on Tower Green, and the body still lies there.'

Elizabeth heard this as she stood on Highgate Hill, forcing herself to lift her foot and step into the litter that was waiting to drive her down into the smoky dark smudge of the City below. The Queen's invitation had turned to a command enforced by armed troops; if she disobeyed she was to be carried by force. It had all been of no use to snatch at straws, to struggle and resist, to feel very ill and exaggerate her illness, to prolong the journey because of it so that she only travelled four or five miles a day and finally rested for a whole week at Highgate. But every time she had looked from her window there, she saw London below, waiting for her, and now she was driving down into it, on the very day that Courtenay had been committed to the Tower, and Jane Grey executed.

She tried to pray for Jane's soul, though Jane would have forbidden it. Her last words on the scaffold were already being repeated: 'Good people, pray for me, as long as I am alive'; faithful, even in that last moment of fearful loneliness, to the Protestant faith that forbade prayers for the dead.

But Elizabeth could only think of Jane and herself as two little girls at a Christmas party, and Mary the kind elder sister and cousin giving her five yards of yellow satin to make a skirt, and fastening a gold and pearl necklace round Jane's thin little neck – and today Mary's executioner had cut through that neck.

All her life she had thought of her sister as 'poor old Mary,' always in bad health and badly treated, tearful and tactless but kindly, always trying to do the right thing in the wrong way – and now she had acted as swiftly, boldly and terribly as ever their dread sire had done. 'Off with his head!' to right and left, and even 'Off with her head!' for Jane. No doubt it was expedient, perhaps necessary. But how had Mary come to see it as right?

After that, anything might happen. One was no longer walking on firm ground, but a quagmire. She herself had split nuts and played 'Bon jour, Philippine' with Mary and won a valuable present from her, and said, 'You will win next time, won't you?' and Mary had answered with a bitter laugh, 'Oh no, you will always win.'

But now Mary was winning.

Elizabeth's journey was over, she was driving down from Highgate into the night, diving down into that deep pit of darkness where lay her doom.

For it was already evening and the chill February mists from the river made the streets shadowy and the silent faces that lined them all pale as ghosts, thronging thicker and thicker, stretching up and peeping over each other's shoulders, peering and gaping, aghast and staring, and tears running unchecked down their long worried faces – but not a sound from them, not a groan nor murmur of indignation among those quickly stifled sobs, not a voice to cry aloud, 'God save Your Grace!'

These mice would never save the lion. The springing hope with which she saw their pity changed to contempt. Gibbets stood at street corners, hung with grinning corpses, some many days dead; heads were stuck on spikes on the public buildings; not a hand in all this weeping crowd would be raised to save her from a like fate. It was a funeral procession, they were all sure of that; nothing they enjoyed so much as a good funeral! Her lip curled with scorn as she sat well forward in her litter with the curtains drawn back so that all could see her upright body in its white dress, her pale proud face that never turned nor looked at them, nor flinched at the ghastly sights she passed, all through the City, now Smithfield, now Fleet Street. She was suspected more deeply than any of these dead traitors; 'but nothing can be proved,' she told herself again and again.

They entered Whitehall Palace through the garden – to prevent a rescue? Elizabeth asked herself ironically. There had been little fear, or hope, of that, with two hundred guards close round her, among all those tearful but tame herds.

Now she was in the great hall, bracing herself to stand erect, to smooth her face from any over-anxious lines that might look like a guilty conscience, seeing Mary's face in her mind so clearly before her that already her eyes were searching it for signs of hysteric rage or cold and bitter determination; already her lips were beginning to move to say the things she had rehearsed. But they all flew out of her head, all the convincing clear-cut proofs of her innocence, all the dignified implied reproaches of her sister's unworthy suspicions.

There were no thoughts left in her head, only words running round and round in a circle like rats in a trap, words chasing a silly rhyme as barely, crudely defensive as a rat showing its teeth.

> *'"Much suspected of me,*
> *Nothing proved can be,"*
> *Quoth Elizabeth, prisoner.'*

She need not have troubled. She could have nothing after all these frantic searchings to say to the Queen, for the Queen refused to see her.

For three weeks she waited in her rooms at Whitehall with guards set close about them, to know what Mary would do with her. She knew that the Queen was being urged to take this heaven-sent opportunity to cut off her sister's head; that ambassadors and bishops alike were telling her that she was 'too busy chopping at the twigs of the rebellion when she ought to chop at the root,' and that the root was her own long white neck. Her only hope lay in the fact that Bishop Gardiner would find it difficult to get the Princess beheaded without his beloved protégé Courtenay being beheaded with her.

But Mary did not seem anxious to behead her, at any rate in a hurry. She would have to go presently to Oxford to open her Parliament, since that was now a safer place to hold it than London so soon after the rebellion; and asked which of her lords would undertake the charge of the Lady Elizabeth in his household to keep her out of harm's way – and out of mischief, was the clear corollary. Elizabeth drew her first easy breath at that. But she drew it too soon, for she quickly heard that not one of the lords would risk such a responsibility.

'I'll make them pay for that!' she cried. 'When I am Queen I'll stay with every one of them, and if the expense of my gracious royal visit ruins them, so much the better!'

'*When* I am Queen!' She hastily touched wood, crossed her fingers and muttered 'In a good hour be it spoken!' to propitiate the jealously listening fates. *They* knew what would happen to her. It was incredible that she could not know. The future was dark as the night all round the sleeping Palace and her wakeful bed. At any moment the curtain of the dark might crack into a splinter of light, widening to show the black shape of an assassin – the surest service Mary's friends could render her, to rid her of her dangerous rival thus quietly without her responsibility.

She strained her eyes against the thick dark that pressed upon her eyelids like a palpable weight, till she could bear it no longer, called for lights and began to read again. History should help. It gave one a sense of continuity, made one believe that life went on. Yes, but whose life? Her own; as Queen Elizabeth? Or Queen Mary's? Hall's *Chronicle* could not tell her.

There lay his list of chapters before her:

I.   The unquiet time of King Henry the Fourth.
II.   The victorious Acts of King Henry the Fifth.
III.   The troublous season of King Henry the Sixth.
IV.   The prosperous reign of King Edward the Fourth.
V.   The pitiful life of King Edward the Fifth.
VI.   The tragical doings of King Richard the Third.
VII.   The politic governance of King Henry the Seventh.
VIII. The triumphant reign of King Henry the Eighth.

How would it go on? What would the future historians have to say?

IX.   The brief reign of King Edward the Sixth.
X.   The pitiful life of Lady Jane Grey.
XI.   The merciful and religious? – *or* the bloody reign of Queen Mary? (Depending on her success or failure.)
XII.   The triumphant reign of Queen Elizabeth?
Or

The tragical brief life of the Lady Elizabeth?

One or other of those two was going to happen, and no one could tell which, certainly not 'this rude and unlearned history' written to extol her father and grandfather for bringing a golden age of peace to England. But would she ever have the chance to continue it? Were the Tudors finished? Mary was none of them, she was all Spanish; if she should ever bear a child, it would be Philip's of Spain.

Hall was dead, and all the kings he wrote of; his book was to be burned by order of the Queen for upholding the new religion; worse, it was criticised severely by modern taste and Mr Ascham had accused it of being written in 'indenture English' with its high-flown tropes such as the 'cankered crocodile and subtle serpent' of rebellion that 'lurked in malicious hearts and venomous stomachs.' But modern authors and authors not yet born would continue to write the chronicle of history yet to be lived; and no one knew what it would be. She could not see a year, a month, a day, even an hour ahead, as she waited in the night.

All around her England waited too, stirring uneasily in its sleep, aware of no such 'inevitable trend of events' as the histories would come to chronicle, but only of a breathless uncertainty. For the world was turning topsy-turvy and nobody knew from day to day what was the law and what was a crime.

A tradesman had just said in the street, 'That jilt the Lady Elizabeth was the real cause of Wyatt's uprising,' – it seemed safe enough but you never knew – people had been whipped last year for saying Archbishop Cranmer had two wives now living, and punished this year for saying he had none; both were false but if the lies had been reversed in time, both would have been commended.

Old Goody Crickle had been burnt to death a few months ago for approaching the Cross on her knees, but young Tom of Ramsden had just been flogged for refusing to kneel to it. Parson Plucky had been heavily fined for letting his village girls play before the image of the Virgin, but Parson Manly put in the stocks for throwing her image on the dunghill. Images were being thrown down and put up again all over the country, and Mrs Tofts, who never could keep up with the times, thought it sound to say 'They be devils and idols,' whereupon she found herself in jail and threatened with burning alive unless she instantly recanted. Little Lady Jane had been proclaimed Queen last summer and now lay headless in her grave, and the woodsmen at her home rose up and took their axes and cut off the tops of the oaks to show their grief and anger at her death for as long as the trees should stand.

But her mother, the Lady Frances, who had forced her into the course that led to her death, was so little dashed by it, still less by her husband's, that within a fortnight of their executions she flung off her brand-new mourning, put on a bridal dress of scarlet taffeta and married Mr Adrian Stokes, 'a smart red-headed young gent,' twenty-one years old, who had been a servant in her household, some said a footman, others, more kindly, an equerry. The Duchess of Suffolk was so well pleased with her exploit that she had their portraits painted by Lucas de Heere immediately after the wedding, a memorial to last as long as the sad dwarfed oaks of Bradgate. There young Mr Stokes still stands today, looking very dapper, with no hint of nervousness, beside his large and elderly bride whose hard grey eyes, with their alarming likeness to her uncle's King Henry VIII, show a bright indifference to the fact that while they were being painted her recent husband's head was rotting on a spike of the Tower gates.

She was only following the new fashion for tragically widowed duchesses, for Anne Duchess of Somerset, whose intolerable pride had helped drag her husband Edward Seymour the Protector to the block, had married her groom, Sergeant Newdigate, as soon as Queen Mary had released her from the Tower; nor did Mary show any disapproval of these matrimonial jaunts: the Duchess of Somerset was still 'her Good Nan,' the Duchess of Suffolk continued to take precedence at Court, and her now eldest daughter Catherine was given the post of lady-in-waiting to the Queen, presumably to make up for her sister Jane's death. An element of horrible farce hung about the family's tragedy ever since the Duke of Suffolk was nosed out by his own dog from that wet hiding-place in a hollow tree. The world had gone mad, a monstrous anarchy now held sway in thought and feeling, as in politics and religion.

A deputation of nine grave members of the Queen's Council came and questioned Elizabeth for hours; they told her that Wyatt had accused her and Courtenay of being the instigators of his rebellion. Could that be true? She remembered his voice as they had danced in the firelight and shadows,

> 'I promised you
> And you promised me
> To be as true
> As I would be.'

No, he would never have shown a 'double heart', he was true, and this report a lie, the usual common ruse to make her confess; she remembered the tricks they had tried for that purpose when she was fifteen – 'They have told all. Confess, and you will be forgiven.'

But she had given nothing away then. She was determined to give nothing away now, but it was harder, in spite of her added years and experience, for the long suspense and her illness made her shaky and uncertain.

She made a bad slip when they accused her of receiving a warning from Wyatt to go to Donnington; in the confusing terror of the moment she declared she did not even remember she had a house of that name, then saw it would not do and tried desperately to cover it. 'Donnington – Donnington? Oh yes, *Donnington*! I *have* heard of it, but never been there, even when, so you say, Wyatt warned me I would be safer there, so of what are you accusing me? Of *not* going there?'

Was she overacting her petulant stammering? But it was impossible to keep her hands from shaking, so it was better to twist them nervously together and seem innocently perplexed by all these pointless questions, to push her hair up off her forehead and hold an ice-cold hand to her hot head as she turned wide bewildered eyes from one grim bearded face to another. There was more behind those faces than what they were saying; soon they would say something worse, something she had been waiting through weeks and months of dread to hear, and now she heard it.

It was the Chancellor speaking, Bishop Gardiner, his shaggy eyebrows working up and down – if he did not shave them soon they would meet in the middle over his jutting nose. She did not hear a word he said, but she knew what he was telling her; she was to go tomorrow to the Tower.

She shook her head. 'Oh no,' she said softly, 'no, no! Not after all this – no, no, it can't be so.' She did not know what she was saying, not even that she was crying, until a warm tear splashed down on her cold hand. Their faces made a blur round her; some gradually came distinct, looking at her sheepishly, Winchester's with a smirking satisfaction, taking an evident pleasure in making a pretty woman cry. That pulled her up sharply; she rounded on them and there was the ring of a threat in her voice as she told them to remember who she was; it was unwise to go so far in trying her loyalty. This royal defiance in cold measured terms, though the tears were still running down her ashen-white face, had yet another effect from another of the ring of dogs baiting the young lioness.

One of them she had noticed as hitherto more sturdily impassive than his fellows, more determined not to be led astray by any feminine wiles, but he was now regarding her with a baffled expression, trying to conceal an emotion that she had forgotten any of these men might still be made to feel. Who was he, the tall burly elderly fellow with the rubicund face, now slightly purplish, who stood four-square with his thumbs in his belt as if defying any softer impulse to get the better of him, quite unaware that his large round eyes were scanning her with rueful tenderness?

'My lord of Sussex' (his name came to her even as she turned to him), 'surely Her Majesty will not – surely she will be too gracious—' She turned quickly from him, as he pulled a thumb out of his belt to rub his nose in embarrassment, to one after another of all those shut faces, imploring them to intercede for her to the Queen not to commit a true and innocent woman to – she could not say 'the Tower' – 'to *that* place.'

Some of them promised to do so, with expressions of pity for her sad case. The Earl of Sussex said never a word. But it was at him that she looked in yearning entreaty as they left her room.

She waited an hour but gained nothing. Sussex came back with a hangdog look, and Gardiner and Winchester with him, to order the discharge of nearly all her attendants on the instant. Guards were placed against both the doors to her bedroom, an armed force in the hall and another two hundred strong in the garden beneath her windows. Elizabeth rushed to look out at them in a sudden frenzy of hope. Did it mean that they suspected some plot to rescue her at the eleventh hour, before the Tower gates shut on her tomorrow, perhaps for ever?

She stayed awake and fully dressed all night, straining at every creaking night-noise that might mean the beginning of such an attempt; but the raw daylight came and the Earl of Sussex came and Lord Winchester and the guards, and told her the barge was ready to take her to the Tower and she must prepare to leave at once, 'for the tide is now right, and time and tide wait for no man.'

'The tide. The tide,' she repeated stupidly. She had told herself so short a time ago that she would be safe as in a cave in the rocks, if only the tide did not rise. But the tide had risen, the roaring waves of the rebellion had flowed up into her cave and washed her out, to be swirled away on its flood and stranded at Traitors' Gate.

If only she could contrive that they should lose this tide it would gain her, well, twelve or perhaps twenty-four hours' respite certainly, and who knew what might happen in twenty-four hours?

'The Queen promised me,' she cried, 'the very last time she saw me, she gave me her word that she would let me speak to her in my own defence. By the Queen's own word I demand to see the Queen.'

'No use,' grunted Winchester. 'Her Majesty says that at all costs she'll not see Your Grace.'

Sussex, looking like a worried bulldog, confirmed this with an unwilling shake of his massive head.

'If I am so dangerous she can at least see my writing. I can send no letter to her from the Tower – once there I shall be as shut off as in the grave, perhaps soon in my grave. Let me send her but one word before I leave this outer world.'

'The tide!' Winchester interrupted. 'We daren't risk losing it.'

'At least six lines. It will not take me five minutes.'

'I tell you, Madam, in my opinion it is inconvenient.'

A sudden roar from Sussex cut across Winchester's boorish irritation. 'By God, I say she *shall* write. I'll answer for it to the Queen. Aye, and I'll see to it, Your Grace, that she gets the letter. Write, and I'll take it to her myself.'

Heedless of Winchester's grumbling protests, he bundled

him into the anteroom and left her to write her letter undisturbed, with only one word of admonishment, 'Hurry, Madam, hurry.'

Now her brain must move like the wind, snatch at all she had planned to say to her sister in these past weeks and cram it into a few words – but for an instant her head whirled in a dull void and no words would come. Then she remembered those she had spoken just now, 'the Queen promised me.' *That* was the note to strike. She struck it, hard, right at the top of the sheet of paper, without any preamble or opening address:

'If any ever did try this old saying "that a king's word was more than another man's oath," I most humbly beseech Your Majesty to verify it in me, and to remember your last promise and my last demand that I be not condemned without answer and due proof. Without cause proved, I am by your Council from you commanded to go into the Tower, a place more wanted for a false traitor than a true subject. And therefore I humbly beseech Your Majesty to let me answer before yourself – and that before I go to the Tower (if it be possible), if not, before I be further condemned.'

Would this move Mary? Would anything that came from her young sister? Mary hated her and was glad of this chance to put her out of the way. But she was conscientious, she would not do what she knew to be wrong. 'Let conscience move Your Highness to take some better way with me.' That was bold, but she had written it now, there was no time to start again.

Sussex was putting his great head round the door – 'Madam, the tide! We must—'

'One moment!' she cried, her pen scratching furiously, yet

still keeping the bold upward strokes well formed and even. 'I have heard in my time,' she wrote, 'of many cast away for want of coming to the presence of their Prince.' Did she dare mention the man she had loved? Mary had never forgiven her the scandal that had made his own brother condemn the Lord High Admiral to the block. But she dared. 'I heard my lord of Somerset say that if his brother had been suffered to speak with him he had never suffered. I pray God that evil persuasion persuade not one sister against the other.'

A great blot spread over 'evil' in her haste to turn the page and give more assurance of her truth. 'And to this truth I will stand in till my death.' But now Sussex was by her chair and she must stop with three-quarters of the page still blank.

'If I leave it like that, some cunning rogue might get hold of it and add some forgery to my hurt.'

'Does Your Grace suspect—?'

'Not you, you fool! The only true friend I've made in my troubles.' She glanced up at him with a quick look of compelling intimacy as she rapidly scrawled lines all down the rest of the page to prevent a possible forger thus using it; they slanted wildly downwards from left to right towards her signature at the bottom in the right-hand corner, and another dreadful blot must needs come and smear the flourishing twirligigs of the 'z' in Elizabeth. Sussex had seized the sand-castor and was sprinkling the page, laying hold of it to fold it.

'One word more, just one!' she cried, snatching it back, and scribbled in the bottom left-hand corner, 'I humbly crave but one word of answer from yourself.'

CHAPTER TWENTY-TWO

She had won her twenty-four hours' respite, she had beaten the tide, and the night-tide too, for they dared not take it lest there should be an attempt to rescue her under cover of the dark, though every hour of delay increased that danger.

But it was all no use. Mary was moved only to rage against Sussex, she roared at him that if her father were alive his servants would never have dared treat him so; and looking on that pale sandy-browed little face suddenly darkened and distorted by passion, Sussex wondered that he had dared so treat the daughter.

He had learnt his lesson and turned up obediently the next morning just after nine o'clock, with Winchester, to carry the Princess by force if need be into their boat, resolved to stuff his ears with cotton-wool rather than listen to the siren's pleas.

It was Palm Sunday and pouring with rain – two safeguards, since everybody would be in church or indoors.

Elizabeth knew their fears; as they hurried her through the Palace garden between the files of soldiers on guard she looked back up at all the windows in a last vain hope, and cried out in a loud voice that she wondered the nobles would let her be led away into captivity.

But all the streaming windows looked blankly back at her, not one was flung open, no voice called in answer to her appeal, and the cold rain cut her face. Sussex seized her arm and urged her into the waiting barge, its floor already waterlogged, and now there was no chance for her, the rough grey relentless river was bearing her fast away, so fast that they nearly capsized at the bridge, where the tide was not yet high enough and the fall of water too great to shoot it without appalling risk. So the boatmen urged, but to Winchester, and now even Sussex, no risk could be worse than the presence of Elizabeth still outside the Tower.

She all but escaped it by drowning, for in shooting the bridge they struck the stem of the barge against the starling and there were frenzied shouts and curses while the water went swooping round her, splashing over the boat's side, and 'Which of us, my lords,' she asked in hysterical mirth of the two elderly faces before her, both grey from fear, 'is born to be hanged?'

For now the boatmen had succeeded in clearing the barge and she was caught and borne away again, swirled along by the tide, after all her struggles and clutchings at straws, at a sister's promise, a Queen's word, at a scrap of paper that she scrawled with lines – after all these, here she was carried away in the current, only to be washed up now in this supreme and dreadful moment at Traitors' Gate.

Here in this sodden moment – or on a shining morning in May seventeen years ago, when all the birds were singing and her mother, a young and lovely woman, had landed, to her death? The moment had waited for her ever since, and now it was in her mother's rooms that she was to be lodged.

She looked up at the dark gates frowning at the head of the water stairs, and as she looked they opened and she saw the warders and servants of the Tower drawn up to receive her. Lord Winchester was holding out his hand to help her step from the barge on to the stairs; the river was sloshing up all over the lower steps.

'I'll not land here,' she cried wildly. 'I'm no traitor – and I'd be over-shoes in water.'

'Your Grace has no choice,' said Winchester gruffly, and threw his cloak over her against the heavy rain. In a fury she dashed it from her and stepped into the swirling water and up the stairs to where that grim body of men awaited her. 'What – all these armed men for me!' she almost laughed.

But a strange thing was happening among them, some were falling on their knees and some cried out, 'May God preserve Your Grace!' Their Captain was trying to check them and threatening them with punishment, and they froze into iron again as Sir John Bridges, the Lieutenant of the Tower, appeared from behind them and advanced towards her.

At sight of him her knees gave under her and she sank down on to a wet stone. She would not – could not go further, she would not enter those gates, whence, it was muttered, none came out alive, and many had died without trial. Sir John was standing bare-headed before her, begging her to come in out of the rain or she would get ill.

'Better sit here than in a worse place,' she answered dully, 'for God knows where you will bring me!'

There was a sob behind her. A young gentleman usher had lost all his rigidly correct, self-conscious composure and fairly broken down and burst into tears. That pulled her up, literally, on to her feet, and she swung round on him with a wry smile. 'That's a fine way to cheer me, to cry like a baby when you ought to be giving me courage!'

But no one, she knew, could do that but herself.

She went resolutely up the stairs, staring up at the dark bulk of the Tower looming over her.

There was a face looking down at her from behind one of the rain-blurred windows. She could not see who it was but it was a pair of very bright eyes that looked down on her, and something was moving to and fro – was it a hand waving to her?

Was it Courtenay's hand?

He had been sent to the Tower the day she had driven down from Highgate into London. She supposed, without interest, that it was Courtenay's, and then forgot it as she heard the gates clanged to behind her, the bolts shot fast.

The thing had come to pass. She was shut in the Tower. Her servants crying and praying round her on their knees made it clear how little hope there was of her ever coming out of it again, except to her death.

'But not by the axe,' she muttered. She would not suffer that clumsy butchery. Already her frantic thoughts, chasing each other in terror of the dark stillness of this place, were busy composing her final plea to Mary, that an accomplished swordsman should be sent over from France, as had been done for her mother's execution, to strike off her head with a single stroke of his elegant long blade. Mary, who had not vouchsafed 'but one word of answer from yourself,' could not refuse her that.

There were various signs that she had little else to hope for: the confinement in which she was held, never allowed to go outside her room; the delay in executing Wyatt and the leaders of the rebellion, so as to try and extract further information against her; worst of all, the continual brow-beating examinations of her by different members of the Council. Hour after hour they questioned, argued, tried to catch her out.

Strangers were appointed as her servants; only pretty Isabella Markham was left of her friends, and there were threats that she too would soon be parted from her on account of her Protestant beliefs.

The Tower was closing in on her; her prison narrowing until it should take the shape of her grave.

There was still a window. She gazed out of it continually, at the bare trees tossing in the March wind, and the river where once she had floated at night with the Admiral in his barge, and felt his urgent desire for her and tried to fend it off with the crude coquetry of a very young girl, and they had seen a light in Lambeth Palace and supposed, laughing, it was Cranmer writing another Prayer Book.

And then one day she saw Cranmer.

A heavy black barge was drawn up at the foot of the stairs to Traitors' Gate, and a body of armed men marched down on to it, and in their midst the Archbishop of Canterbury and the Bishops Latimer and Ridley. They stayed up on deck, three forlorn figures bunched in rusty black robes that flapped in the breeze, among all the showy soldiers guarding them; they were looking round them on the busy, noisy river-banks, 'boisterous Latimer' still the one most easily distinguished, clapping one or other of his companions on the shoulder, flinging out his arm as they pointed out the familiar landmarks to each other. They passed the Archbishop's Palace at Lambeth and the gardens down to the water's edge, where King Henry had loved to walk with his friend in their 'singular quiet.' and where one night in May the Archbishop had walked alone all night, waiting for the dawn when Nan Bullen was to die.

The oarsmen pulled with long swift strokes, singing as they rowed, and the barge passed quickly upstream out of sight round the bend of the river, on past Somerset House, the palace of Edward Seymour the Protector, Duke of Somerset, and Seymour Place, the palace of Tom Seymour the Lord Admiral, those princely brothers both of late beheaded. The Thames should run blood, not water, the Princess said to herself, and turned to ask where the three priests were being taken. She was told, to prison in Oxford to await their trial for heresy.

It seemed superfluous. There was quite enough against them as traitors to behead them – nobody could understand why Cranmer especially had not been executed long ago for giving the full weight of his Archiepiscopal authority to Dudley's rebellion.

What a bungler Mary was to confuse the issue and win public sympathy for the offenders by bringing in charges of heresy! Treason against herself she could forgive, but 'heresy,' she was fond of saying, 'is treason against God.' Elizabeth, following her sister's argument in her mind, suddenly saw to what dark end it was leading.

Cranmer and his fellow-bishops were being spared execution in the Tower, to meet a worse fate in Oxford. Those three figures on the deck of the barge had looked their last on

London. The first Act of Mary's Parliament would be to bring back Henry VIII's laws against heresy, condemning those who denied the doctrine of Transubstantiation to be burnt alive. They were to be kept alive till then, so that the Pope of Rome should condemn the Archbishop of England to death, and so reassert his authority over this country. This was to be Mary's triumph, her expiation of England's turning away from the Faith!

'Fool! Fool!' cried the girl, beating on the thick glass of the window-pane between its heavy bars, her rage rising hot from a new cold fear. If Mary could not catch her out as a traitor, would she make sure of her death as a heretic?

A service of the Mass was given every two or three days in her room, and she had noticed that the examinations of her by different members of the Council were growing more and more theological. It was to this end, then, that they were leading.

The very next day the test question was suddenly hurled at her; did she or did she not believe in the transubstantiation of bread and wine at the Mass into the actual body and blood of our Lord? To say 'Yes' was to declare herself a Papist, and, by Papist belief, a bastard and no heir to the throne; to say 'No' was to declare herself a heretic; and that, she now knew, would condemn her to be burnt alive.

The dark room swam round her, the cruel watchful faces of the men surrounded her like hunters' drawing in for the kill. They peered at her through the squinnying windows of their eyes into her soul, but they could never get a glimpse of it. They saw her narrow face whitening, sharpening with animal fear, the startled brightness of her eyes scanning them in turn, flashing the thoughts she did not speak.

She thought – was this religion? – a snare to make one fall into the hands of one's enemies? Were holy things always to be abused, and words of love and worship turned into a death-trap? Should one man's belief be set up against another's, and men kill each other for not holding the same ideas, it would mean wars without end throughout the world, for it was the glory of men's minds to hold different thoughts, and the only thing by which they could be judged was their actions, right or wrong.

She could not say this; she could make prayers, especially of late, but never a creed. But she could make a verse; in urgent stress like this, lines and rhymes came into her head, keeping her panic-ridden brain from reeling into insanity. A line, and another rhyming to it, and then another, slowly, so low she almost whispered them, the brief monosyllables dropped one after the other from her lips, as though she were listening to a voice these men could not hear, and repeating the words one by one:

> 'His was the Word that spake it,
> He took the bread and brake it.
> And what that Word doth make it,
> I do believe and take it.'

There was an uneasy silence among her questioners; they had looked for some clever evasion from her, but this sincerity, the utter simplicity of the hushed voice inventing and speaking those few lines, disconcerted them, and put them clean off their guard. Gardiner cleared his throat, began to say something sneering about woman's wit and neat answers; but before he could get it out, the Earl of Arundel astounded everybody by going down on his knees before that slight, still figure.

'Her Grace speaks truth,' he cried in a harsh voice, so hoarse and rasping that it seemed something he had long tried to smother was now forcing and tearing its way out of his throat; 'I am sorry to see her so troubled by us all, and, Madam, so help me God, I hope for my own part never to trouble you more.'

This from Arundel! who had been so merciless to his old associate Duke Dudley and sought ever since to prove his new loyalty to Queen Mary by urging loudly in council that the first safeguard for her reign must lie in putting the Lady Elizabeth to death! None of his comrades could believe their ears, nor could Elizabeth; she looked at him anxiously, seeking for some sign of a fresh ruse, to snare her by a false security.

But she saw only a stocky elderly gentleman gazing up at her with the wistful eyes of a spaniel that knows he has done wrong and promises to make up for it by a lifetime of devotion. She held out her hand to raise him, checking a mad desire to rap the bald head below her, and giving him instead a faint sweet smile of forgiveness.

Volleys of angry protest from Gardiner and Winchester cut across each other as Arundel stood up; was this the way to conduct an examination of a prisoner suspected, all but proved guilty of treason and heresy?

But a louder roar silenced them as Sussex shouted, 'Take heed, my lords! This is King Harry's daughter and the Prince next in blood.'

'We have the Queen's commission to deal with her,' barked Gardiner, his eyebrows bushing up almost to his hair.

'Don't go beyond it, then! We'd best take care how we deal with her, so that we may not have to answer for our dealings in the future.'

Here was plain dealing with a vengeance! Some of them had an uncomfortable qualm, recalling that Queen Mary had been feeling ill just lately; they stole uneasy glances at 'the Prince next in blood,' but she cast her eyes demurely on the ground while the men wrangled round her, and gave no hint of her feelings, certainly not of the throbs of wild merriment that were now shaking her in her relief, so that it was all she could do not to shriek in hysterical laughter. First Sussex and then Arundel, who had been one of her worst enemies, now her true knights! She should start a Round Table of Grandfathers vowed to her service!

As they took their leave of her, with more courtesy than when they came, she raised her long white eyelids as slowly and dramatically as the lifting of a curtain, and let her eyes dwell on Arundel in a look of grave sweetness that made him feel himself a young man.

He had once tried to marry her to his son, but now the notion shot into his head, why should not himself be the wooer? If Queen Mary died he would have won himself a throne as well as a handsome young woman, who already looked as though she could learn to love him. Her eyes were of remarkable beauty, he noticed, now that they shone on him.

And it was to him she spoke, though she began, 'My lords,' but faltered timidly and waited for his look of encouragement before she could summon enough confidence for her request. 'You have shown me you would not willingly have me die undeservedly. I have been ill, and if I do not soon get a little air and exercise I think I shall die. You will go out now from this dark room and breathe the first sweet air of April. I beg you think if some way cannot be devised for me to breathe it too, if only for half an hour.'

CHAPTER TWENTY-THREE

Two small children were hiding in a corner of a narrow garden enclosed by the high walls of the Tower. Only a few windows overlooked it, but there was no one to look out of them, for anyone who might do so had been sent away to prevent any possible danger of communication with the Princess Elizabeth, now that she had just been allowed to take the air every morning, guarded by Mrs Coldeburn, the lady-in-waiting newly appointed by the Council.

But Harry Martin, the five-year-old son of the Keeper of the Queen's Robes in the Tower, had made up his mind to see the imprisoned Princess and see for himself if her hair were really like the bright silk embroidered with gold threads of one of the Coronation waistcoats. His father had said it was. Harry, having stroked the waistcoat, did not think any human hair could be like it, but it might be that the Princess herself was not human, as she was shut up in a Tower, a thing apt to happen to fairy princesses. She was therefore of far more interest to him than the boy-King had been, but then King Edward had suffered from always being held up as an example; from the age of three he could, and generally did, turn everything he said into Latin, word for word as he spoke it – 'Why – *cur* – so fast – *adeo* – do you ran – *curris*?' – though Harry never wanted to ask such a question and was sure Edward only did so because he had learnt it at the beginning of Erasmus' Latin grammar for boys.

That was the way King Edward had accustomed himself from the earliest age to speak Latin as easily as English, and later did the same with Greek. But Harry had thought he looked pale and cross, and what had been the use of his spending all that time in learning those languages when now he was dead and could not speak heathen tongues in Heaven?

But nobody held up the Princess Elizabeth as an example, not even to his friend Susannah, who was a girl. In spite of this drawback, and that of her age, for she was a year younger than he, she was his most constant playmate, and whatever, he did, that she must do too.

So when Harry decided that he would give a present of flowers to the imprisoned Princess, Susannah helped him to pick them, and when Harry enlisted his mother's help to let him into the 'secret garden' as he called it, and she agreed (for no harm could come of it, and possibly good, if the old sister died and the young one came to power, and might well remember the pretty childish act of service to her in adversity), Susannah bore him company. They hid together behind a waving bush of green broom, studded all over with little tight buds not yet in flower, until suddenly Harry said, 'Now!' and stood up manfully, with his bunch of drooping primroses tightly grasped in one of his round pink fists, and Susannah holding firmly on to the other.

In front of them stood a tall young lady in a dull coloured dress, which was disappointing for a fairy princess or even a real one. But at that moment the sun came out and glinted on her hair, and Harry saw that it was indeed like the gold threads in the waistcoat but softer and flying about, and he wanted to stroke it to feel the difference, but he knew he must not ask to do that, so he held out the primroses instead.

And at that he saw a real enchantment, for her eyes opened wide and looked down into his, and they were flecked with green lights and smiling, and she said, 'You have given me the first pleasure I have had in my prison, you have given me wild flowers which I like better than any, and when – if ever, I mean – I am Queen, I will always have them in my palace. Yes, I will have primroses in my palace and tall swaying harebells.'

'What are harebells?' asked Susannah.

'She is not old enough to remember,' said Harry in excuse. 'She was only three last summer. But I remember harebells.'

'So do I,' said the Princess, 'last summer, when my brother King Edward died, and Susannah was only three, and I was nineteen. I am twenty now.'

It was a pity she was so old, as much too old for him as Susannah was too young. But she could still play Touch Wood with them, as there was no hall to play with, Susannah toddling about in the chase with some difficulty in her long skirts, which the Princess presently looped up for her through her belt, and then Susannah must needs stop the game to point out to her with pride all the toys that dangled from it, the coral on which she had cut her teeth, the rattle hung with silver bells, the gold pouncet box, the little ivory hand to scratch her back.

At all this display Harry grew boastful too, and told the Princess that be had just been given a small young ger-falcon to tie to his wrist and keep till he could learn to fly it at game.

Who had given him this treasure?

No. That he would not tell, he said importantly, but it was a very fine gentleman.

She looked down at the resolute underlip sucked like a red button into his mouth, at the eyes that confronted hers so squarely, and the high round ball of a forehead beneath the close-cropped hair.

'As fine as you will be, Sir Harry Martin, my true knight?'

'No. I will be the finest, truest knight to you of them all.'

She kissed him for that. They laughed a great deal. The early April sun was warm and the grass newly green; a blackbird sang and they could hear the shouts of boatmen passing each other on the river.

She was amazed to find she had not forgotten she was young.

Mrs Coldeburn, a stout body with a shining bluish face like a glazed puff of pastry in the raw spring air, walked angrily up and down by the garden door and paid them as little attention as if she were the bored governess of all three.

Next day Harry Martin was there again and his faithful Susannah, and yet another little girl who stood stiff and silent until Harry said, 'She wants to set you free.'

'And how will she do that?' asked Elizabeth.

The child held out a bunch of little keys, probably to writing-desks and store-boxes, which she had found in her mother's kitchen.

'I have brought you the keys now,' she said, 'so you need not always stay here, but may unlock the gates and go abroad.'

Elizabeth stood looking down on the three small conspirators and the keys so confidently held out to her in promise of her freedom. She could not tell them that they were not the keys to her prison. She took them and thanked them – 'You have made me free,' she said, and then she handed them back again. 'Put them back where you found them, and when I want to go abroad I will ask you for them!'

'Don't you want to go now?' asked Harry.

She looked at him, and for a moment he thought her face had been covered over as though a piece of fine gauze had dropped over it. Then it opened and her eyes flashed. 'No,' she said, laughing, 'I would rather stay now and play with you,' and she held out her hand for the bunch of white violets he had brought her.

It was thicker than his bouquet of yesterday and securely tied, obviously not by him. She asked who had tied them for him, and once again he told her, a very fine gentleman.

'A prisoner?'

He answered yes, but he had promised not to say anything about him to anyone.

'You can tell me this – was it he who gave you the ger-falcon?'

Harry nodded with vehement importance.

So that was it! The child was being used as a stalking-horse for her by some bold intriguer – Courtenay? – Wyatt? – Who? She would have thrown the flowers away but would not hurt Harry's feelings, any more than those of the strange little girl who had presented her with those miniature keys to open the mighty gates of the Tower. Well, why not? A toy could set the fancy free, and these infant allies had brought back youth and hope to her. Excitement and curiosity were alight in her again though she did not know it, she took them only for alarm and anger as she hurried back to her room and, as soon as she was sure she was alone, untied the bunch of violets.

It was just as she had suspected. A tightly rolled pellet of paper was twisted among the limp green stalks. Her hands trembled; to still them, she would not unroll the paper till she had filled a small silver jug with water and plunged the flowers into it up to their frail white heads, which they seemed to lift again towards her almost at once in thanks for their refreshment, breathing their delicate scent towards her.

She stood very still a moment there alone in the shadowed room, a thin girl in a dull coloured dress with a silver jug of white flowers between her hands, her face still and pale, with her eyes downcast at the flowers, but the breath coming quickly from her high, finely cut nostrils. At last she laid down the jug and unrolled the small strip of paper.

There were only a few words on it, asking her to arrange her walk an hour earlier the next morning. And it was signed, not 'Edward Courtenay,' not 'Thomas Wyatt,' but 'Robert Dudley'.

'So – Robin!' she breathed.

Robin Dudley clattering over Tower Bridge at the head of his horsemen on an early morning last July, when the sun rose glinting on his harness and his scarlet waistcoat, and he had been sent out by his father the magnificent Duke Dudley 'to fetch in' the Lady Mary – how was it she had that picture of him as clear in her mind as if she had seen it? Then she remembered the burring north-country voice that had told it to her, Dr. Turner who had come to see her when all England lay under the shadow of death and rebellion. and had talked to her of wild flowers. 'Johnny Jump-Up' he had called Duke Dudley, who had been laid low by the axe, and his son 'Ragged Robin' ever since a prisoner in the Tower.

She had known Robin and liked him, played with him in childhood and done lessons with him. He was gay, handsome, and a friend. She had felt a prick of sharp interest, of hope and fear for him, when she had heard that hot July day of his part in his father's rebellion.

But now she did not think she dared, nor even cared to do as he asked; a day or two ago she would not even have considered it, and why should playing with three small brats in the open air have made any difference to her?

Her life hung by a thread; she would attach no further weights to endanger snapping it asunder. If there were any plot afoot, even for her escape, she did not want to get embroiled in it. 'Heaven preserve me from my friends!' she had sighed that so often lately. Those nearest to her had shown most power to hurt.

> 'My mother has killed me,
> My father has eaten me.
> My brother and sister sit under the table
> Picking my bones,
> And they'll bury them under the cold marble stones.'

That queer riddle-me-ree that Mother Jack, her brother Edward's old nurse, used to croon as she spun the flax on her humming wheel at Hampton Court, had come into her mind with the insistence, not of memory, but of prophecy. For mother, father, brother, sister had spun the web of her fate into this intricate and dangerous pattern, so that now her life hung by a single thread of it. She stood here in the prison where her mother had been killed to set her father free to beget his one male heir, her brother Edward, and now, of them all, only her sister still lived to wreak vengeance on Elizabeth for what they had done against Mary.

Then let no other, no friend nor possible lover, add his coil to the tangle.

She burned the note, and that night she went to bed resolved to pay no attention to it.

But she woke to the sunlight on the river and the noise of cheering as a great ship sailed up it, returned from a voyage of discovery, and she altered the time of her walk.

CHAPTER TWENTY-FOUR

Everything was the same in the little garden except that it was an hour earlier and a good deal colder, with the sun only just coming over the wall, and a sharp early April wind blowing up the river, rocking the newly returned ship, the *Edward Bonaventure*, that lay at anchor below them invisible behind the high walls, but she could hear the men on board singing chanties at their work.

Harry Martin had brought his new ger-falcon to show her, tied by a thin silk cord to his wrist, but did not, after all, pay much attention to it, for he was too full of the tales he had heard this morning of the travellers in the ship below, and their voyage into the White Sea. They had discovered a strange land of endless snow where the people lived on horse-flesh and mare's milk and had taken them in sledges to their Emperor, who welcomed them in a robe of beaten gold with a crown on his head as high as the Pope's; he was called Ivan the Terrible, but in spite of that he had been very kind and given them presents of furs and jewels to take back to their young King, for they never knew that King Edward had died just after the three ships had set sail last summer to explore the terrors of the Outland Ocean – they never knew till now, when one alone sailed back, to find Queen Mary on the throne. The two other ships had been lost in the frozen mists, caught between floating mountains of ice that were transparent as glass and green as emerald, and were there imprisoned till all on board had died of cold and starvation.

'It was a pity they died,' said Harry, 'but I wish I could see the glass mountains. I shall go one day to this new land of Muscovy. It is at the topmost end of the earth, no one has ever gone so high up before. I shall take my sledge. Will you come with me?'

'To the top of the world,' said Elizabeth, and she chased him round the garden to keep warm for she was shivering and she supposed it must be from cold though she did not feel it.

Mrs Coldeburn said she would get a cloak for her; Elizabeth said she did not want one, but Mrs Coldeburn then said she would get one for herself and hurried away, declaring she would be back on the instant. The children were now chasing each other, for Elizabeth had tired quickly and was walking up and down, watching the garden door, wondering why Mrs Coldeburn should be so long, wondering why she should feel so strange and excited, for whoever came through it when at last it opened could make no difference, no possible difference to her.

It opened at last and a tall figure stood there an instant in the dark mouth of the doorway, looking out, and it was not Mrs Coldeburn. She tautened and flung back her head, bracing herself as if to meet an attack. A young man came quickly towards her, dropped on one knee and kissed her hand, then looked up at her for a long moment; his bold dark eyes grew grave and he said in a low tone, 'I wonder, by God's truth, what I have done till now!'

She told him promptly, in a voice like the snapping of crystals against the deep bell of his voice. 'You married little

Amy Robsart because you fell in love with her, or she with you. And you helped your father in the rebellion to put Jane Grey on the throne instead of my sister, or myself. So never tell me, my bonny Cock Robin, that you've done nothing till now but wait to see me again!'

She flicked him on the nose and he sprang to his feet with a crack of laughter. 'You have not changed one jot! The very sight of you is a challenge, my prince of rapier play. Does your sword never rest in its scabbard? But never stab me for a family affair! With my father and brothers all raising rebellion, would you have had me such a snudge as to keep out?'

'Snudge?' She had not heard that new piece of slang. She had grown out of things, mewed up with plots and terrors, but now they were all winging out of her mind, a bat-winged flock of screeching shadows frightened by the coming day. Its light shone on her face and a young man was looking at her, for no other reason than that she was a young woman and good to look at.

'I saw Your Highness land at Traitors' Gate,' he said, almost as though it were a joke. 'Those elegant long feet must have got very wet. But one doesn't worry about one's feet here as long as one keeps one's head.'

'Was it you who waved from that window? I thought it was Courtenay.'

'Are you betrothed to him? He says you are.'

'He says a deal more than is good for him.'

'Or for others. But he's got a Gardiner who won't prune him. Too busy cutting down his old Cambridge friends. How these fellow dons hate each other! He'll get the Archbishop yet. Even Cranmer can't recant all he wrote only last autumn against the "horrible abominations of the Mass"!'

'Oh, but he can! He can cant and recant. He'll prove himself for all time as the Archbishop of re-Canterbury!' Her laugh was wild and cruel as the sudden wind; she hated Cranmer, who had helped pull down her mother to death and herself to bastardy – 'he'd good reason to meddle with other men's wives, with his career all but wrecked twice over by two of his own!'

'*Two*? There's his Gretchen that he brought over from Germany—'

'In a box, the King my father always said, and a fine way to smuggle such contraband! But there was the landlady's niece at the Dolphin in Cambridge long before that, who served him and Erasmus with small beer, Black Joan they called her, and a black day for Cranmer when he had perforce to marry her and so lost his Fellowship – but then lost her in childbed, and so won it back again. Did you never know our Archbishop's scutcheon was blotted by a barmaid sinister?'

'More, I beg you, tell me more. I've never heard you talk before.'

'A lie! And you say it in rhyme to prove it! You've heard me talk since I was seven or eight – what you'd never heard before was the silence of these stone walls.'

'But it's true. I'm hearing you, seeing you for the first time.'

And it was true also of her. They had known each other from childhood but they had not met for a couple of years or so, and at their age that makes a deal of difference. Now each took delight in the discovery of the other. A twinge of exasperated pity shot through him at the thought of Amy probably now crying her eyes out for him on their bleak windswept estates in Norfolk – but then she *was* in Norfolk, and here beside him was a Princess, subtle and sophisticated, who yet evidently admired him even while she mocked him; treated him with the outspoken camaraderie of a boy and the maddeningly teasing coquetry of – no, not a girl, but a woman of strange experience. What had been the truth about her and the Admiral? He had already lain awake at nights guessing, but in almost everything to do with Elizabeth he found himself still guessing.

He was asking her questions now as venturesomely as he dared, as discreetly as he knew how, while the children in their stiff bunched-up clothes played behind them with shouts of excitement on a plank of wood that they had turned into a see-saw.

But she did not answer his questions; 'I am not on examination now, so what reason have I to?'

'No reason – and no rhyme neither? If I write you a sonnet—'

'You will sing it first to your wife, who will praise it.'

'That's how wives are made. Dame Disdain was never wedded.'

'Nor will I be, if I have my will.'

'Then half mankind will lose theirs.'

'Only if they lose their wits.'

'Oh, they'll lose wits and will and more for you. Why are you laughing?'

'I don't know. Am I laughing?' But she found she was shaking with mirth and tears from it were trembling on her eyelashes, making a rainbow dazzle against the sun.

'Here we go up, up, up,' shouted Harry on the see-saw, and Susannah shouted back, 'Here we go down, down, down!'

> *'Sing up, heart, sing up, heart,*
> *Sing no more down!'*

sang Elizabeth in time to their shouts. 'It is all mad,' she cried, 'here are you and I meeting like this, two prisoners under shadow of death, after all this time, and talking blather-skites just where we left off, where was it? – at Whitehall Palace or at Greenwich, where those ships sailed out to discover the Curdled Ocean where "there is no night at all, but a continual light and brightness of the sun shining clearly upon the huge and mighty sea."'

'What is it you are saying?'

She had flushed so suddenly, her eyes shone with so strange a light that he laid his hand on her wrist, fearing to feel it throbbing with fever.

'Why,' she said, 'did you never hear the Lord Admiral speak of the Merchant Venturers – or the pirates if you will – and their hopes to discover yet another world? *We* never spoke of them, did we, my bonny Cock Robin, nor do we now – we are talking nonsense just where we left off – at Greenwich Palace was it, or Whitehall? We were dancing, I know, or were we fencing in the long gallery, and the little black-bearded Spanish master calling 'Riposte! Riposte!' And here we are talking it in the Tower, and either or both of us may be dead tomorrow.'

'Is that all? Why, I thought you were ill! You'll get used to it,' he told her comfortably. 'Here are all of us, my brothers and I, under sentence of death ever since last autumn, but only poor Guildford has suffered it, and even he would not have, nor his wife Jane, if there had not been this new rising. The rest of us may still have to pay for it, but every day that drags by raises our chances that we'll cheat the hangman yet.'

How strange it was to talk and listen without measuring every word lest it should touch danger! To look up at a face that was young and handsome, that looked at her with delight instead of narrowly watching her above a grey beard or under bushy brows for some sign of guilt.

She had even found it amusing that she could make some of those old men fall in love with her, could watch them from beneath her demurely lowered eyelashes as they pondered their chances in wooing her hand now when it seemed not worth a rush, and thus possibly winning a rich prize in the future.

Old men dressing up their self-interest in a gallant's swaggering cloak – and in the past a tutor or two eyeing her across his books with desperate but fearful hunger, letting his hand rest on hers for a supposedly forgetful minute, speaking Latin or Greek into her eyes, in passionate accents but a dead language – these had been her only lovers since the man who had declared his love for her, and died of it.

All since then had been haunted by his memory, and scared away from her. But here at last one stood boldly, who looked at her without calculation or fear.

He had taken her hands in his, and so warm and strong was their grasp that for a moment she noticed nothing else, and did not hear his words. Then their sense fell on her, hot and fierce as the thrust of a sword.

'Will you sup with me tonight?' he said. 'Oh yes, it can be done – you do not know the Tower yet as I do. But – sup with me tonight. I will have good wine and my cook is a clever fellow, you would never guess what he can do with £2, 3s. 4d. a week! And I have my lute and we will sing again as we did when your little brother used to plague us for "the Puddy in the Well" – do you remember, my "Merry Mouse in the Mill"? But you were never a mouse – say, rather, a flashing kingfisher by the mill-stream – and you are not so merry now and you are so thin you stand like a spear in the sunlight – but you will be merry again, if only once, if you sup with me tonight.'

A forgotten magic was at work again. She heard his laugh ring back through the years on this keen high wind of April. She felt herself once more a child on a gusty spring day in a high red brick-walled garden by the river, when crocuses were blowing this way and that in translucent flames of purple and gold, and standing in front of her was the tall arrogant figure of the man who had pulled her forward so gladly, recklessly into womanhood.

She had forgotten she had ever felt like that for the Lord Admiral – or for any man. She had not believed she could ever feel like that again – for any man. She did not believe she felt it now – but then Robin Dudley bent his head and kissed her.

The April wind was blowing, the sun was shining, a young man had kissed her. Life might end tomorrow, but while it lasted it was sweet again. He had asked her to sup with him tonight. There was something to look forward to, something else to hope for, rather than a French executioner's sword.

CHAPTER TWENTY-FIVE

'Farra diddle dino,
This is idle fino!'

Robin Dudley had whistled the refrain so often that he had to
sing it for a change, till the meaningless words palled and he
swung into a verse of the latest song to become the rage at
Court before the young King died and Robin saw the Court
no more.

'Therefore my heart is surely pight
Of her alone to have a sight
Which is my joy and heart's delight.
In youth is pleasure, in youth is pleasure.'

He sang it all the time he supervised the setting of the supper-
table and the arrangement of the room with the new
tapestried hangings his wife Amy had brought him from
Norfolk (showing Diana bathing and Acteon turned into a
stag for looking at her) and bowls of small spring flowers
making flecks of colour and sweetness in the dark mouldy-
smelling corners. He brushed his hair so hard that his head
tingled, looked out his finest jewels, put a dab of scent on his
spruce upturned feather of a moustache, pulled up his head

and pulled down his doublet and, while his face was still passionately in earnest from the importance of these occupations, his feet suddenly flicked out in the pattering steps of a jig.

Here he was plunging into new life after months of agonizing boredom. Oh these endless dark evenings this past winter when he had read all his books and taken to carving his name, ornamented with roses and oak leaves, on the stone walls! Amy had been allowed to visit him two or three times but was awkward and miserable, not knowing the right thing to say, sobbing as she clung to him instead of cheering and amusing him – a stupid little thing, as he had began to discover even before he had gone to the Tower. He had been glad to slip away on long visits to the French and English Courts, to take up his appointment at the latter as Master of the Royal Buckhounds, to become a practised courtier and famous sportsman before he was out of his teens, while Amy stayed at his Manor of Hemsley near Yarmouth – for she was terrified of public life, but no good at country life either, hated housekeeping and was extravagant without anything to show for it, buying quantities of showy clothes she proved too timid to wear, and devoted to him without any sense of how to arouse a like devotion in him. Yes, poor Amy was a 'hoofer', he had decided, clumsy of foot, inevitably putting it in the wrong place. He had thought he was deep in love with the shy delicate nervous girl who adored him, and was also, conveniently, her wealthy father's heiress; but they had married when they were both only seventeen, mere children he now considered, and he had grown up since, but she had not.

He had grown to long for an equal mate in courage, wits and knowledge of the world, a woman of complicated and baffling charm, yet as young as he or younger – and he not yet one-and-twenty. An impossible combination, he knew; but then on a dreary March Sunday, when the stone walls of his room were reeking with damp, and his legs chill from lack of exercise, and the grey skies were pouring down in floods of rain on the gaunt fortress and the sullen rushing river, and it was Palm Sunday but with no hope of spring, and he in prison with no hope of freedom, no hope anywhere, then by pure chance he looked out through the bars of his narrow window and saw a slight girl whose hair flared like a torch in the dripping gloom, saw her step out of a heavily guarded boat on to the flooded stairs of Traitors' Gate, and with a fierce gesture strike from her the cloak that one of her attendant nobles offered her; then sink down in collapse on the wet stones and sit there in the heavy downpour, apparently refusing to move.

Armed men surrounded her, the Lieutenant of the Tower came out towards her. At last she rose and lifted a white stricken face up to the towering walls above her; and swept her draggled skirts on through the prison gates with the haughty bearing of a great prince, or rather, thought the young man watching her, of a wild creature of the woods surrounded by its captors, desperate but untamed, defiant to the end.

His dulled heart leaped and he told himself, 'This is she!'

He had been long enough in the Tower to have grown clever in knowing whom and how to bribe; he could get money from his estates through Amy, and one could do almost anything with money in the Tower, short of escape from it. So he laid his plans with his friend and fellow-prisoner Jack Harington, who had long been in love with one of Elizabeth's ladies-in-waiting, Isabella Markham, and through her got in touch with Mrs Coldeburn the guardian of the Princess's walks, and even made good use of the friendship he had already struck up with little Henry Martin.

He now awaited the fruit of his labours. What would it be?

An amusing interlude? A lifelong love-affair? A king's crown? Or death?

'Damn the fruit!' he muttered as he lit the tall candles before the polished silver mirror. 'Why look ahead to it when the moment is in flower?'

The flames flickered in the draught, then raised themselves in pale yellow pointed shapes that lit up unexpected threads of crimson and blue in the tapestry. Diana's hair now gleamed more gold, her naked body more white; a rabbit that sat up on his haunches to look at her suddenly shot into prominence so that his sharp pink-lined ears seemed to quiver into life. A perfume of musk and rosemary stole from the scented wax as it melted; Robin was using his most expensive candles. He stepped back from the mirror, which was convex, so that at a little distance he could see his whole figure, and stood gazing at his reflection, adjusting it by a lift of the eyebrows, a careless posture of the hand upon his belt, until he was satisfied.

The room was now still, after all its bustle of preparation, and only the husky ticking of the clock made any sound in it, a strangely slow one in the ears of the young man before the mirror, who could hear his heart beating fast as if it would race ahead of time and hasten the moment for which he waited.

Time brought it at last in a flurry of footsteps and swishing skirts, of whispered voices – that must be Jack Harington greeting his Isabella. There came a low excited laugh that made his blood tingle. So she *had* come! And now they were in the next room. The door between clicked open and then the air was hushed again.

A shadow stood there, a figure wrapped in a dark cloak that she held before her face and let trail upon the ground. In silence he approached and knelt beside her and slowly raised the cloak to reveal a pair of jewelled shoes, and remained for an instant thus kneeling before the shrouded figure with bright feet. Then he rose and led her before the mirror and unwrapped the cloak from her so that her satin dress was first glimpsed here and there between the darkness of the cloak, and then flowed all over her like a waterfall, and the candlelight gleamed on her bare neck. Last of all, and looking, not at her but her reflection, he lifted back the hood from her head, and her mirrored face swam out of its obscurity as the crescent moon out of a cloud.

And still in silence he watched, as he would watch the working of a spell, how the green eyes in the silver pool raised themselves to the reflection, first of her own face, and then of the young man who stood behind her and still held the cloak.

A spell there was, binding him who had worked it with such instinctive cunning as well as her, for in that first moment alone together they both seemed to be looking, not at the image of their present selves, but into a magic mirror that reflected something far away – was it in times past or in the years to come?

'They are passionately met in this grey moment of their lives,' Sir John Harington told himself, and wondered what lasting fire might not strike from it. He watched them with a ghostly interest as he talked and laughed with Isabella Markham. He was by far the eldest of the little company, and love no longer seemed to him a race with time and death.

The years he had spent in the Tower gave his mind the leisured space to follow more than one thread at a time, even when the upper web was his own love for the pretty girl beside him. But the woof, spun by the loves of her young mistress the Princess, was as deeply personal to him, for it gave the reason that he had been here in prison ever since he had entered the Tower with his friend and master the Lord High Admiral, beheaded five years ago almost to this day, for his love for the white red-haired girl now singing a catch with young Robin Dudley.

> 'Sing we and chant it
> While love doth grant it,
> Fa la la!'

He was well paired with her, as dark as she was fair, as obviously handsome as she was fine-drawn and variable, visited by sudden gleams of beauty, as wary as a cat, yet unquestionably royal; while he wore like a splendid cloak his careless air of arrogant ambition, as of one born in the purple, yet knowing it to have been achieved only by reckless adventure.

Did she not feel she was sitting with a ghost? Especially when Robin laughed with her and sometimes even at her – as Tom Seymour had done – and looked into her strange light-coloured eyes, looking to her not only for his delight in this present moment, but for his advancement in the future – no doubt Tom had also done. Had she forgotten him now he was cold?

No, Tom's friend conceded, she had not forgotten the man who had first shown her how to love; she would never forget. For she would only love one who would remind her of the man that Harington's own verse had praised for his 'person rare, strong limbs and manly shape,' and 'in war-skill great bold hand.'

Whom did one ever love but the image of the lover for whom one dreamed? Once that had taken the 'manly shape' of the bearded Admiral twice her age; and now another 'person rare,' rivalling him in stature, but of her own age this time, laid his bold hand on hers.

The lover was dead, but 'Long live love!' said Jack Harington, lifting his glass and looking into Isabella's soft brown eyes as she shyly raised them from a sonnet he had shown her. He had written it remembering 'When I first thought her fair, as she stood by the Princess's window.' Isabella had then been a young girl in a new dress, and he had been married to a bastard daughter of King Henry's and had not much liked it, for Ethelreda (what a name!) had something of her father's temper and nothing of his charm. But she had two virtues: she had brought him the royal gift of a fine house at Batheaston and had died early. It was odd to think she had made him a sort of half-brother-in-law – or out of law – to the Princess, who knew nothing of the relationship, for Sir John's discretion, with remarkable lack of snobbery in a snobbish age, had never admitted that his wife was any other than the illegitimate daughter of King Henry's tailor.

His discretion showed itself now in his humorously tender wooing of the timid Isabella, noting with amusement how she responded to his lines—

> 'Why thus, my love, so kind bespeak,
> Sweet lip, sweet eye, sweet blushing cheek,
> Yet not a heart to save my pain?'

Poetic licence had to maintain the lady's coldness, but it was perfectly plain that Isabella had a heart, and that it was delightfully fluttered at meeting her old friend. But there was no need for such licence over the 'blushing cheek' for Isabella could still show it, whereas her mistress, the younger by five years, had learnt to blush, and leave off blushing, five years ago.

Shocked at the scandal then about the Princess, Sir John Markham had hastily recalled his daughter, who had but newly come to Court, to her home at Cotham, where she had grown tired of wearing a big bunch of keys and being called her mother's home-bird, tired of the still-room and the stables, of simples and samplers, of large bucolic suitors in whom she took in interest only because she longed to mimic them to the Princess and see her laugh. 'Markham!' Elizabeth might exclaim in unflattering astonishment, 'You are a wit!'

Nobody at Cotham seemed alive in comparison with the Princess, and she made everyone about her alive too. Isabella felt she had been asleep ever since she had left the younger girl, whom she had feared and adored and found a mass of contradictions, straightforward and secret, bold and cautious, her self-mastery as tight as whip-cord when need be, but a spitfire in her sudden rages.

Then, as if to show she could do everything, she became a model of propriety, everybody heard about it, and so Isabella at last won permission to return to her service, but unfortunately just in time to land herself in the Tower.

But at least, so her parents consoled each other, there was no danger now to morals, for their daughter's letters home were full of the 'sweet words and sweeter deeds' of her Mistress, who was setting her such a heroic example of constancy to the true religion.

At this moment, however, the Princess's example was in another field.

> 'Not long youth lasteth
> And old age hasteth,
> Fa la la!'

she sang with her new lover, knowing they had less reason than most to fear old age.

'If I lived till then, should I have a paunch?' asked Robin.

'And would my teeth go black from eating so many sweets, or my hair fall out so that I'd have to wear a wig?'

They rocked with laughter at such impossibilities, but Robin suddenly grew grave in that arresting way he had. His gay mood dropped from him as he looked at her as if for the first time.

'Age will forget you,' he said; 'though no one else will.'

She wanted to cry. But she laughed and said, 'I have forgotten how to answer pretty speeches.'

'I could make other kinds to you.'

'That sounds like a threat.'

'It might even be that! I never know what I might say to you, or—' he paused, drank his wine at a gulp, and whispered, 'or what I might do.'

He dared no more than a glance after that. There was a

diamond brightness in her smile that told him nothing. He must speak on quickly. 'There's never any knowing what you will be or do next. You swear like a sailor, sing like a siren, smile like a sphinx. God made a thousand women and threw them all away before He found the mould for making you. I can say what I please, for you can't punish me – you and I are only fellow-prisoners now!'

The term pleased them both, it showed them equal, more free together in prison than ever they could be outside it. They shared the danger as well as the pleasure of this secret supper party, so informal and regardless of rank, served for safety by only one trusted servant.

They shared their lot in the Tower, its stolen April hours snatched out of the proper order of their lives, its intrigues and messages entwined in knots of flowers, its knowledge that each meeting might be their last.

And they shared its humdrum commonplaces, its comic and tiresome money problems.

The whole quartette shared those, and drew their heads together again in the pool of candlelight over the table, Harington's thick greying hair at the same level as Isabella's brown curls; Robin's close-cropped head, as glossy as a blackbird's wing, bending close over the gleaming gossamer of the Princess's hair.

Isabella was too shy to speak of her practical problems (she had not brought enough clothes to the Tower and this had somehow grown much more important since she was meeting Sir John), but Sir John told them how he had spent close on £1000 to date in his efforts to pull strings that would hoist him out of prison and, since bribes and flattery had failed, had in desperation written an impudent lampoon in verse on Bishop Gardiner, which he had just despatched to him.

You never knew with Gardiner, if it made him laugh it might win his release, Harington thought, and Elizabeth agreed. 'He hates me, but my father liked him. At least he does not want to bring back the Pope over us, though he would rather have England a Roman Catholic country than not Catholic at all.'

'A Spanish Catholic country is what it looks like being,' said Robin.

'Not if the country can prevent it,' said Harington. 'Nor does she want the Pope.'

'She doesn't know what she wants,' growled Robin, whose family had been badly let down by the country's change of mood.

'She's not a she,' said Elizabeth, 'the country's a young giant, a crack-brained one if you will, determined to launch out in new ways into the future – it's not going to be tied and bound and told to go back and be good by an equally crack-brained old maid, equally determined to cling to the past.' She leaned forward and tapped Harington over the knuckles with a spoon. 'Speak up, Jack, are you going to give up the home my father made for you out of a monastery?'

Harington hastily put his hand under the table. 'Not I, Madam! Nor will any honourable Member who swears in Parliament to follow the Queen back to Popery, but will stick to that far more sacred thing, his Property. But I'll stick to the Protestant faith too.'

Isabella and Robin also protested their Protestantism. Elizabeth had an exasperated sense of their all doing so by way of protesting their loyalty to her.

'Never mind about your religion,' she said to Robin, 'that is to say, your politics, Tell me how it is you have £2, 3s. 4d. a week for your food.'

'Government grant,' he answered complacently. 'But it's fourpence less than for my eldest brother, Jack – do they think he eats a pennyworth a week more for each extra year of his age?'

He was also allowed 13s. 4d. for each of his two servants, and as much again for firewood, coal and candles.

Elizabeth fumed, 'The Government does that for all of you – declared and condemned rebels as you are! while I, on whom they can fasten nothing, have to supply my table at my own cost for myself and my servants – no, spare your sighs, Markham, everyone knows you eat like a sparrow, or Sir John would say a sylph. But may the devil fly away with all the rest of 'em!'

Servant worries – they plunged into them together with gusto as another thing to share. Robin's servants were a low lot who stole from him and levied blackmail on his friends when they got the chance; Elizabeth's a high and mighty lot who turned up their noses at the 'common rascal soldier in the Tower' and objected to any food for the Princess passing through such base hands, though she swore at them that she would rather eat like a scullion than starve like an Empress, and the vice-chamberlain threatened that 'if they frowned or shrugged at *him* he would set them where they should see neither sun nor moon.' But he was induced to settle the squabble more profitably to himself, by giving them permission to cook and serve the royal meals and getting a full share of them; so that he now boasted that 'he fared of the best and Her Grace paid for it!'

And paid heavily, for in decency she could not be served by less than two of her yeomen of the chamber, two of the robes, two of her pantry, two of her kitchen, one of her buttery, one of her cellar and one of her larder. But she was often at her wits' end how to pay, for there were continual delays and hitches in getting her money through to her.

All this she now poured out to Robin, who insisted that he would help her by lending money from his estates; it put her on a very homely, intimate footing with him.

It also put her on a footing with Amy, the agent for his finances, which she did not so much like. Such a silly insipid name, and sentimental – Aimée – the Beloved! *Was* she, by this splendid young man? 'You are married,' she said in accusation.

'Indeed you would hardly know it.'

'Indeed I hardly know her. Tell me of her.'

'She is safe, as we are not. Yet she is afraid of everything – as we are not.'

'Afraid of what?' asked Elizabeth, rising and going over to the fire, where she stood and poked the logs with her toe, less for the warmth than for the pleasure of seeing the leaping flames sparkle on her jewelled shoes. Some of the flames burned ice-blue and green from salt; the logs must be driftwood that had floated on the open sea.

The candlelit quartette round the table had dissolved into shadowed duets, Elizabeth and Robin standing by the fire while Harington had moved judiciously with his partner to the window-seat at the end of the room and, picking up the lute in his turn, began to improvise a tune for his sonnet to Isabella.

'Afraid of what?' repeated Elizabeth softly, absent-mindedly, as she looked at the blue flames and thought of ice-mountains a mile high floating slowly towards a ship no bigger than a nutshell beside them, and the figures of men like ants going up and down the rigging, vainly trying to steer her free.

'Afraid of ill-health,' he answered. 'Of her servants. Of company. Of solitude.'

'She must live in a dream,' said Elizabeth; she forgot Amy and her eyes grew bright, staring at the fire. 'Only danger is real and difficulty. Yet we live to make our lives safe – and those of others. That is what I will live to do for my country – if I live to win to it.' (But at this moment she knew she would.) 'She shall never go to war if I can prevent it. I will fight my own people to keep them from fighting, for as long as can be. Never fight, until it is unsafe not to fight, unsafe for our souls as well as our bodies. Then fight for their safety – but when it is won, remember that safety itself is unsafe. For what is safety? It is a sleepy thing. It does not make one happy. It does not remind one that it is good to be alive. Life is taken for granted, so it is no longer a surprise. It grows dull and monotonous, one lives as a tree or a cabbage or a cow in the straw of the byre. Our forefathers scorned 'a straw death.' A straw life is worse.'

Her face looked beautiful at this moment with the firelight leaping up on it, and her talk of danger inflamed him, for he felt her to be dangerous as well as beautiful. To love her would be a wild adventure. He longed to essay it, as a young knight might long to prove his manhood in some desperate action. What a trophy her love would be! Yet how difficult to begin to make it when she talked thus, like one young man with another.

He had brought over the wine flagon and their glasses to a little stool, and now held hers out to her.

'You think too much. Don't think. Drink.'

She motioned it away. 'I don't want any more.'

'It will make you let go of yourself.'

'The last thing I wish, or dare.'

'You've nothing to fear from me.'

'I am not sure.'

'It would warm your eyes,' he said, trying to laugh, for her cold glance made him shiver. Her careless gaiety with him had masked an icy self-control that would always give her the whip-hand over others. But God's blood! could she not hold rule and yet be human?

'Your father was the greatest King England ever had, and he drank deep, God rest his soul!'

'It did not rest his mind. It was observed that he frequently held quite different opinions after dinner from those he had expressed before. No, I fear drink as I fear death – who came nearest to catching me in a jug of brandy posset drunk by a faithful friend.'

But she did not tell him how Cat Ashley had once betrayed her. He said almost casually, 'Do you fear death much?'

'Lying awake at night, yes.'

'If I were with you then, you should not fear it. Our love would kill death.'

It had come so simply, inevitably, that instead of excitement a hush fell on both their spirits, stilling the quick stir of antagonism roused by their dispute over the wine. He was still holding out her glass and looking at each other, they did not notice that it had tilted and was spilling over the floor.

'Stay with me here,' he whispered, 'if only for an hour or two. Harington will take back that little brown mouse and I will tell them we are following.'

She gave no sign in answer; her eyes were inscrutable. He hurried on in a low urgent voice, 'Give me one hour of life, one golden hour, and death may take all the rest if he will – and maybe he will not. We'll make Fate our spaniel – spurn her, and she will fawn on us.'

'And maybe she will not. I'll not lose the rest of my life for the sake of an hour with you, my sweet Robin. Your love may last an hour, or your lifetime, but I want to live—' and in a gasp she added, 'as long as England shall last.'

'Oh Queen, live for ever!' he laughed, ' and if you take me for your lover, why should that prevent it?'

'It would have only one degree less danger than to take Courtenay.'

'Did you ever wish to?' he asked quickly. She shook her head, without coquetry, then saw the wine dripping on the floor and gave a high strained laugh. He put down the glass in annoyance and recovered himself by mocking her. 'That is because you would not drink it – a waste of good wine! And love is the wine of life – will you waste that too?'

But she had turned away, and he saw, unbelievingly, that she was not listening to him. She called to Isabella, who rose with meek reluctance. They muffled their cloaks round them so as to be unrecognizable, and Harington said it would be safer if Isabella and he went in front to guard against any possible encounter.

They slid through the door, Robin stepped quickly after them with Elizabeth beside him, and closed it in her face. She dashed forward to open it again, but he flung his arms round her and beat savage kisses down on her hair and face, searching for her lips. Suddenly she raised her head and gave them to him in a hungering kiss. They clung together, swayed, fell back upon the long hearth-seat. He had her now to do with as he wished, and he since last July had been a monk.

Her eyes in the shadow beneath him had softened to a pale gleam of desire; they opened wide upon him in wonder that was all joy, but even in that instant a change flashed into them, she seemed to be looking up, not at him but at someone behind him. A cold fear shot across him even as he bent over her, blotting out that look with his kisses, and surely he had conquered it, for her body leaped towards him, answering his passion with as fierce a flame.

Yet as he held her, too close to see her, he felt her spirit escaping him; he was having to fight for her, who had just now been his perfect conquest; his arms enclosed an empty shell, she was no longer there. Desperately he tried to force her back into that wild moment of surrender, and now he was having to fight her body as well as her spirit, a losing fight, for this was not how he wished to take her, and his strength was of no avail against her mind.

'Why do you turn from me?' he cried. 'You were mine this moment, all mine, and now—'

'You are not the only man here.'

'Have you gone mad? What are you looking at?'

Was it the Admiral she saw behind his shoulder? He dared not ask her, but she guessed his thought. 'Yes,' she said, 'I see him – but not with my waking eyes.'

'You have gone cold – cold as ice. You were like a flame just now. Oh, come back to me, my leaping flame, come back and let me love you, bring you such joy as you have never dreamed of.'

'No, no, love brings terror, agony, endless suspicion – not a soul one can trust – all spies, a thousand listening, whispering spies opening a thousand little secret spy-holes to peer into one's very soul and whisper about it and mutter all together and then shout foul charges, proclaim them through the land and howl, howl for blood.'

She was shivering uncontrollably as in an ague, she pressed her hands to her head, which swam in sick revulsion as the past came whirling back upon her. At fifteen she had been betrayed unwittingly by her closest friend; had demanded to come to Court to show she was not with child, had insisted on it being proclaimed by Parliament through the whole country; had been watched month after month by enemies wearing the guise of guardians and servants, so that even when she heard of her lover's execution she had had to force herself to speak quite coolly, without emotion; the icebergs had closed in on her soul while it ran like an ant up and down the rigging to seek escape. Was she to go through all that again?

'Never, never!' she cried. 'Give myself to you here in the Tower, where he was done to death, horribly, savagely, for me?'

'As I would die for you! As men will always long to die for you. Life or death, I'd take them both from your hands, and you'd make them glorious.'

He tried to woo her again, to coax and crush down her resistance, but it was no use. A dead man won that fight.

CHAPTER TWENTY-SIX

Nothing was the same next day in the little garden. Nobody was there, no children were playing in it, and nobody came through the garden door. Mrs Coldeburn made no pretext to leave, and Elizabeth dared not ask her if she felt cold and would like to fetch a cloak, she dared not ask her anything, she made a little perfunctory conversation about the weather, about the prospects of this new Northern sea route – how odd that one never finds what one seeks! Ameryk and Columbus were looking for Cathay and discovered the New Indies, and so was the *Edward Bonaventure*, and found Muscovy.

'Truly the world is fall of surprises,' remarked Mrs Coldeburn. Her tone was very dry. Elizabeth thought it safer to say nothing; she walked up and down in silence; her hour of exercise seemed to last a day, so pulsing and long-drawn-out was her suspense.

Next day and the next, nothing happened, but on the fourth, just as she was turning to go in again, she heard a shrill childish voice calling, 'Madam – Madam Elizabeth!'

It came from the door that led to the residences of the officers of the Tower, through which the children had come. She ran to it and tried to open it, but it was locked. 'What is it, Henry?' she cried. 'What has happened?'

'I can bring you no more flowers,' he called back through the keyhole.

'Why are you locked out? What is the matter?'

'No – more – flowers—' Henry repeated in a loud wail as a woman's footsteps came running on the other side of the door. There was the sound of a scolding, a scuffle, a yell of rage from Henry, a slip, and it was plain that he was being borne away protesting.

There was nothing for Elizabeth to do but to go indoors with all her questions unanswered. Isabella knew nothing and was incoherent with anxiety about Sir John Harington.

The silence thickened. The garden remained still and empty. There were no longer any children playing in it, no more visits nor messages from Robin Dudley, no more flowers.

Elizabeth's heart seemed to have stopped dead during these endless spring days of cold sunshine and east wind and harsh light evenings and the shrill mockery of birds singing, free to mate and fly where they willed. Poets were heartless fools to write of spring as a season of hope and joy; its brightness was cruel as a sword's. And all the time she walked in silence or tried to read or embroider (she was allowed no pens nor paper with which to write) the question thumped within her – 'Am I to go through *that* again?'

At last she heard reports of what had happened, through her servants who brought food for her household into the Tower. Gardiner had got wind of her meetings with the children – and with anyone else? No, only the children, but the Chancellor was fully alive to the danger of conspirators of three to five years old. Why should Henry Martin carry flowers to the Princess whom he had never seen, unless suborned to do it by some traitor who had grasped this means of sending notes to her concealed in the bouquets?

The child was closely questioned but gave nothing away. He was promised sweets and a painted hobby-horse, he was threatened with a whipping. Neither could move him from his statement that he had wanted to see the Princess for himself to see if her hair were like a waistcoat, and it wasn't, and now might he have the hobby-horse? But he was only given more threats of punishment if he tried to see the Princess again – which, however, had so little edict that he ran straight from his ordeal to the garden door to tell his new friend he could no longer come to her.

Gardiner, still hot on the scent of the flowers, suspected that old fool Arundel, who had lost his head so completely over the Princess that he too was now committed to the Tower. He drew blank there, and then thought that of course it must be that young fool Courtenay. But that ungallant lad swore hotly that he never wished to have anything to do with the Princess again and would fly England rather than marry an icicle and a firebrand combined, who brought trouble to everyone. Look at Wyatt! Easy enough to do so now his head was stuck high over Traitors' Gate!

Wyatt, executed at last, had made a speech on the scaffold declaring both Elizabeth *and* Courtenay – a surprising, even cynical addition – free of any complicity in his rising. Weakened by long torture, he yet made his statement of their innocence defiantly, carelessly, as though half amused by the uproar it would cause.

For the Londoners rioted with joy at the exoneration of the Princess, they trooped through the streets shouting defiance to the Government, telling them to deliver their darling from the power of the dog – or, as some said, of the bitch.

They lit bonfires and danced round them and drank healths to 'the young one – the red-haired one – Old Harry's own!'

The red-haired one shivered when she heard of it and thought what the grey-haired one must be thinking.

Mary was ill with thinking. She had shown mercy beyond reason, and her people had repaid her with black ingratitude. They had struck at her heart; delayed and darkened the hopes of her marriage. The Emperor said he could not endanger the life of his beloved son in a country that had shown such hatred of him. She had done all she could to make it safe for him – all those executions, gibbets at every street corner, heads on every gate.

Yet still the bridegroom delayed, making elaborate preparations for a sort of farewell tour through his own country, as though to look his last on all he cared for, before embarking for an alien and hostile land and an elderly bride. And every day she looked more elderly, her hair more grey, her face more lined, and felt more ill, and below her Palace windows drunken revellers shouted 'Long Live Elizabeth!' and the night sky was reddened with rejoicing bonfires, and wild stories were afloat of ghostly voices proclaiming Elizabeth as Queen, and the Mass idolatry.

Had she done all she could? No, not all. There was still 'that jilt, the Lady Elizabeth, the real cause of Wyatt's rising'; the chief danger to Philip's security. She could not leave Elizabeth in the Tower till Philip's arrival without continuing these uproars – and what a shameful welcome they would make for him!

She could not set her free without precipitating a revolution to put her on the throne.

She could not cut off her head – but why could she not? demanded her friends, who seemed to think it the least she could do to clear the way for her prospective bridegroom. But Mary still could not feel it was right to do so without proof of her guilt. She had sworn when she took her marriage oath in Renard's presence that never again would she betray her conscience; not for anyone in the world, no, not even for the man she was to marry, would she again do what her heart told her to be wrong.

But the effort to keep this resolution tore her heart in two. Of what use to do good if she could not feel it? Again and again she read her mother's last letter to her, telling her that whatever troubles God sent to prove her, to accept them 'with a merry heart.' But her dumpy dowdy little mother had been a saint as well as a heroine. Mary had shown she could be heroic, but she knew she was not saintly when she felt sick with baffled rage and hate because the jury acquitted one of the suspected rebels, Sir Nicholas Throckmorton. A dozen tailors, fishmongers, etc., humble insignificant citizens from the streets of London, had dared withstand the will of a Tudor monarch, and won. It was the first time such a thing had happened since the Tudors had come to the throne.

'I spend my days shouting at the Council,' she sobbed, 'and it makes no difference at all!' If only her father were alive to deal with them!

Though she read her mother's letters, it was of her father that she thought most now, and it was noted that the shrunken little round of her face was beginning, for all its physical difference, to look very like his. And she did in some sort 'deal with them' by fining and imprisoning the jurymen; but she found herself powerless to reverse their verdict. She was neither good like her mother, nor strong like her father. 'I am nothing, nothing, nothing,' she wailed to herself, and indeed every day she seemed to be shrinking, dwindling, becoming the mere shadow of the woman who, only two months since, had rallied her people to her side by her sheer courage.

If life could always be a crisis, Mary Tudor would have been great indeed. But life fell back, became petty, nagging, anxious; an interminable wrestling with an ungrateful changeable, turbulent people; in intolerable waiting for a man who could not want her, she knew, as she wanted him.

'But one thing especially I desire you,' said that tear-stained letter, the last she had ever had from her mother before she was hunted and harried into her grave, 'for the love that you do owe unto God and unto me, to keep your heart with a chaste mind, and your body from all ill and wanton company.' She had done that to the very utmost of her powers all these long drab years, and to what odds now at the end of them?

An utter weariness of her own body beset her, of all the dressings and undressings of it, and all, she sighed, to no purpose. It was thin, and yet it sagged and was flabby. She could tell Philip she had kept herself pure for him, but to what odds, what odds? If she had kept herself beautiful that would have been more to the purpose. No young man could desire her now.

He was prolonging his departure from Spain to the last moment, on the pretext of these disturbances in her country, of multiform business in his own; but the plain fact was that he could be in no such hurry to come to her as she was in for him to come.

So listless had she grown, so devoid of any desire to get the better of her mysterious illness, that they were afraid that she would die.

Gardiner had especial reason to fear it. He could have nothing to hope, not even his life, from Elizabeth's hands if she should now come to the throne.

Elizabeth herself knew the danger of such fears and watched her household double their precautions against poison. But there was no way to guard against assassination. It was only seventy years ago since the two small brothers of her grandmother had been secretly murdered in the Tower, so that their uncle King Richard III should sit safely on the throne.

There was yet a third way for her to die, and many in the Tower were convinced that Gardiner attempted it; rumours scuttled like rats along the walls, telling of a warrant from the Privy Council for her immediate execution, of furious disputes between the Chancellor and Sir John Bridges, the Lieutenant of the Tower, who had noticed that the Queen's signature was missing and refused to carry out the warrant until he had sent to enquire her exact wishes in the matter.

And small thanks he'd get for that, was the common opinion. The Queen would surely have been thankful to have her worst enemy removed without having to lift a finger in the matter, without even knowing of it – and now her too honest servant had shoved the onus all on her again! So Elizabeth argued to herself, thinking she knew exactly how Mary must feel.

But she did not know all about Mary.

She did not know whether Mary praised Bridges or blamed

him, she did not know what was happening, the days stretched themselves out ever longer and lighter, and she heard the throbbing and thrumming, the shouting and laughing of the Maytime dances and revels on the river-banks far down below the Tower. Her mother had died in May, and with her the five men reputed to be her lovers.

If she too were to die this May, it was a pity she had not taken Robin Dudley for her lover, she thought. It would, after all, have made no odds, except to give sweetness to life before she lost it.

Then one sunny morning she saw armed men in bright blue coats come marching into the inner courtyard of the Tower, and a sturdy elderly knight with a bushy beard riding at their head. More and more of them came through the arch till the courtyard was a pool of blue, spattered with shining halberds and brown weather-beaten faces, more and more till there must be a hundred in the courtyard. She knew that they had come for her. In panic she sent for Bridges and demanded, 'Is the Lady Jane's scaffold removed?'

'Yes, Madam.'

'But have these men come to lead me to execution?'

He quickly denied it. He told her there was no need for fear. They had come in the service of Sir Henry Bedingfeld, the knight on horseback, and he, Bridges, had had orders to hand her over into his charge.

She stared at him with blank eyes and he could only just catch the words she whispered – 'His name was Sir James Tyrrel then.' He thought she had lost her wits, until he remembered that Tyrrel had been given charge of the Princes in the Tower before they were murdered, and in horror he began to stammer reassurances. She cut him short. 'I know nothing of Bedingfeld. What do you?'

'A most worthy and respected knight, very devout, and a man of honour and conscience.'

'Yes – a devout Papist. And would his conscience approve of murder, if such an order were entrusted to him?'

'Madam, you wrong him, and the Queen. She has shown that she will not have your life taken by foul means. Sir Henry and his men have come to have guard of you and take you out of the Tower.'

It sounded like liberty, but she knew better. ' Where am I to go?'

'To Woodstock, Madam.'

'Where Queen Eleanor killed her rival, Fair Rosamond!'

'Well, Madam, they thought first of Pontefract, but remembered that that was where King Richard II had been done to death. It is difficult to find a place without a murder.'

He spoke testily as though combating a foolish girl's fancies. Elizabeth was just about to flare up at him but remembered the service he had done her and never taken this chance to tell her of it. She held out her hand to him 'Do not blame me for my fears, now I am leaving your guardianship. I know what reason I had to trust it.'

He went red as he kissed her hand and silently called himself an old churl, and then, as he saw her smile at him, an old dotard.

She stood very still as he took his leave of her, a model of maidenly patience and dignity, and then the instant he had left her she swung round and whirled away to find Mrs Coldeburn.

'Fetch Robin Dudley here without fail some time in these next few hours!' And then, as the lady-in-waiting stammered expostulations, her utter inability to carry out such a command, Elizabeth let out a roar:

'Do you think you can deceive me as you do the Council? I know that you have taken his bribes, that it was through your agency he came to me in the garden.'

'Madam, I beg you – not so loud—'

'Loud enough to reach the Council, you think? So it shall be, if you do not obey. Go and do so.'

She had no fear of her now. She marvelled that she had ever had any as she saw the plump white face before her shake like a blancmange, the sharp nose thrusting out of it, greenish with fear, like a stick of angelica.

But Mrs Coldeburn's fear could not work the impossible. Sir Henry Bedingfeld's charge of the Princess made itself felt instantly in a far stricter guard than even in these last days since the Council had suspected the children's visits.

Elizabeth raged, Mrs Coldeburn sobbed and shook her pendulous cheeks, and then Isabella Markham, so gentle and timid, became the storm-centre by declaring that no power on earth should force her to leave the Tower. Sir John Harington had asked leave of the Council to marry her, and Gardiner had been so much amused by the 'saucy sonnet' the indignant prisoner had sent him that he declared it would get him out a year sooner than he deserved. They were to be allowed to marry, and they would soon be free, though Isabella's earnest Protestantism was held against her, and her stout refusal to hear Mass.

'Oh, Bell,' sighed Elizabeth, 'I would much sooner hear a thousand masses than cause the least of the million villainies that are springing out of these disputes.'

CHAPTER TWENTY-SEVEN

She was leaving the Tower, and nothing could alter that. Every step she took down the stairs of the Tower wharf was taking her away from that old grey pile of hidden iniquities. The barge was waiting for her, rocking slightly on the ruffled sparkling water. She would step into it and be rowed away upstream in the fresh air, rowing over the swift-running water past fields and woods where people moved in freedom, away from these mouldering stones that bred rheumatism in winter and plague in summer.

Three wild swans came skimming over the water, beating up from it, and flew over her head, the mighty strokes of their wings making a steady triumphant noise, their necks stretched out like spears, pointing the way that she would go. Her eyes followed them as she stood before the barge, then turned back and looked once more at the Tower, scanning the windows for a hand that might be waving, a face that might be looking out at her. But there was none. She was leaving the Tower, and with it any chance of seeing Robin Dudley for a long time, perhaps for ever. To her own amazement she found herself passionately envying Isabella, who remained.

Sir Henry Bedingfeld was waiting to hand her into the barge. She gave him her hand with a quick glance that found his face as impenetrable as if it were carved on a tombstone.

She would have small chance to get her way with him.

But she received a gallant compliment as she was rowed upstream, three cannon shots fired in royal salute from the offices of the Hanseatic League. The Government were trying to smuggle her out of the Tower as secretively as they had brought her into it, by water, so that no one in the streets should see and acclaim her. But here was a foreign power recognizing her princely quality and the virtue of her release from the Tower, and how furious Mary would be!

They never paused to land till they reached Richmond, and there, for the first time, Elizabeth learned that she was to spend the night and see the Queen, who was staying in Richmond Palace.

She was not even allowed time to change her dress as she instantly asked to do, pleading that it had got splashed and crumpled on the barge and her hair untidy, and that it would show disrespect to Her Majesty to present herself in such a state.

But— 'Your Grace's appearance is immaculate,' Sir Henry informed her, averting his eyes. Was there the slightest emphasis on the word 'appearance'? She could not be certain but was convinced to her dismay that his feelings to her were worse than fear or hatred – a cold dislike. He probably guessed that her reason for wishing to change was that she had dressed and had her hair arranged with as gay a show of beauty as possible, in the hopes that Robin would see her thus for his last sight of her – and that she now felt this out of character with the role of the pitiful suppliant for the Queen's mercy. But indeed she felt pitiful enough, unable to swallow anything at supper, and a sick cold throbbing at her heart as she went to the interview.

The Queen was in bed between curtains of purple velvet. She looked very small, and her shrunken face seemed to have a spider web spun over it, so grey and lined it had grown. And the Princess, rising from her deep curtsy at the door and timidly approaching her, felt herself to be a long gaudy fly being drawn irresistibly towards the little spider.

If only she had not put on the white and scarlet! If only she had not let her hair fly loose in tossing curls! If only the Hanseatic League had not shown their sympathy in a royal salute! Had Mary already heard of it?

A glance at her face convinced her that she had.

What was to happen now? Questions on her religion? She had heard the Mass several times in the Tower, it had been forced on her, but she had not much protested. Would that go in her favour for obedience? or against her for insincerity? She could not answer Mary about the Mass as she had done to Isabella. But she could answer nothing, till the Queen spoke. The silence spread and flattened down the air, it was crushing down on her head until she could no longer keep upright and sank on her knees by the bed, closing her eyes.

When she opened them again, she saw Mary looking at her, but not only Mary. Another face was looking at her out of Mary's eyes, the face of their father, in those moments when he had become a monster of suspicion and cruelty.

'I have sent for you,' said a thin hollow voice, scarcely more than a whisper, 'to offer you a free pardon, without further question; your life, which has been forfeit, and your full liberty.'

'My – *liberty*, Madam?' faltered Elizabeth. This could not be true, but could Mary, even in this mood, be so cruel as to tantalise her with such a promise?

'As much liberty,' the dreadful little voice went on, 'as is consonant with the bride of a young man who passionately desires to marry you.'

The blood flew up into Elizabeth's cold face. God's death, what was this? Did they plan to marry her to Robin Dudley? Even in her wild uprush of joy at thought of it, she knew her answer would be 'no.' If they intended this, it was to put her out of any chance of the Succession, as the wife, not only of a subject, but of a younger son of a disgraced family of upstarts.

Mary's short-sighted eyes were watching her so closely that they seemed to be devouring her thoughts. 'So you can still blush, sister, at mention of a young man.'

Elizabeth did not answer as she rose from her knees at the Queen's signal. This cat-and-mouse business was to make her ask who was her intended bridegroom, an unwise move; it would be safer to show complete indifference as to any choice. So she stood silent, and not an eyelash fluttered as she heard that Philibert of Savoy, Prince of Piedmont, was again making offers for her hand, having, said Mary, fallen in love with her portrait and with all – yes, *all* – that he had heard of her.

But Elizabeth knew well there were more substantial reasons for the match from Mary's point of view. Philibert had been expelled from his own principality and was protected by the Emperor. As his wife she would be an exile from England, a dependent of Spain, penniless, powerless, with very little hope of ever getting back to her country, still less to the throne of it.

'I gave you this offer before,' said the Queen, 'but the case has altered, there has since been a rebellion – in your name. Before you again protest your desire to stay in England, think whether you would not rather enjoy your liberty abroad, than stay here in an English prison. What have you against this handsome young Prince to make you prefer such an alternative?'

'Nothing, Madam.' She was shaking with fear but also with a sudden aching longing to be free, to sail across the sea into strange lands, to meet new people who would talk with her and admire her, with no need to guard every word, to ride and hunt and hawk again and hear the arrow whizzing from her bow, and feel her horse's willing muscles spring beneath her and the wind rush past her face – to dance again in halls glittering with lights and crowded with gallant figures and musicians thrumming in the gallery, spinning their enchanting harmony over all the scene, instead of just practising steps by herself or with her ladies to the playing of one thin lute – yes, and to dress her finest and even paint her face and deck her hair with jewels that should bring out the brightness of her eyes.

All this she would be free to do at last and spread her butterfly wings, after years immured like a chrysalis in a tightly swathed cocoon of Protestant propriety.

No, she had nothing to say against such an alternative to prison – except her hopes and fears for England. And those she could not say. So she said, very low, 'Nothing except – that I shall never marry.'

Suddenly Mary shouted at her – 'You still think to be Queen!'

Elizabeth panicked. 'I would rather be a beggar and single than a Queen and married.'

'You! You stand there and tell me you desire perpetual spinsterhood! What possible reason can you advance? Answer me that.'

'Natural inclination,' said Elizabeth, hardly knowing what she said.

'Out of my sight, you lying harlot!' roared the Queen.

Elizabeth fled to the door.

'Come back!' said the thin hollow voice this time.

She came back, not too near.

'What is it you do to me?' said the thin voice. 'I am not like this with anyone but you. It must be that you are evil, to make me so at odds with my true self. I am like this with no one else – no one – no one but you. It is because you are evil, false all through. You stand there and talk of eternal spinsterhood and doubtless chastity, when I know that you have seduced honourable men from their loyalty to me.'

A horrible thing happened, she began to sob and wail. 'Only tell me how you do it and I will pardon you everything. What is the secret of this power you have over men? People say you have only to look at them! Yet there are many women far more beautiful who have not got it – and you are not womanly, for all your sly wantonness and pretence at meek airs and embroidery, you are not all woman, there is much of the man in you, like myself – I too live best in danger, in action. But I have no power to win men to me – and you, who have, dare to say you would rather be a beggar than marry. Holy Virgin, if only I could feel that! Virgin – and that is what you call yourself! But it's not true, it's not true. You are what I have always known you to be – you are your mother's daughter.'

She beat her fists upon the velvet pillows, the tears ran down her distorted face. Elizabeth stared in disgust. This was the woman she had thought like her father, even at his worst! How could she – dared she – lower herself to this? Her anger was shot with terror – for more than herself; she seized her sister's wrist, never knowing that she gripped it so hard as to hurt. 'You are driving yourself to madness,' she cried. 'For your own sake, for all England's, take care of what you do.'

Mary screamed in rage. Her women rushed in, calling on the guards, who quickly surrounded the Princess.

'Take her away,' shrieked the Queen – 'remove all her servants from her, double the sentinels about her rooms, make sure that there is no chance of escape or rescue. I have given her her last chance and she has denied it, she has defied me, attacked me, she is false as Judas – he also had red hair!' she cried on a wild sobbing peal of laughter; and fell into a weeping storm of hysterics.

The sentries were doubled; the Princess's servants, huddled together like a flock of frightened sheep, had to take their leave of her. 'Pray for me,' she said to them, 'for this night I think I must die.' She was too tired to care; that last horrible half-hour with Mary had left her sick even of life itself, and she knew that it had done the same with Mary.

What was it that flared up and took shape like an evil genius between them, so that neither was capable of acting or speaking as she wished? She had been mad to try and warn Mary of herself, to grip her wrist and speak urgently, forcibly, as man to man, instead of trying to soothe a hysterical woman. She would never have taken such a risk with any other enemy – and Mary was her worst enemy. But she was not only that. She was her half-sister, and even while she asked, she knew what was the evil genius between them, for it lay deep in both, the murderous jealousy of their father.

CHAPTER TWENTY-EIGHT

'It's the Gab of May,' said Dr. William Turner as a gust of wind and sleet blew off his cap and sent it bowling down the rough grassy cart-track of a road, 'always cold and gusty at this time in the month, I've marked it many a year. Hey, Billy-boy, fetch him out now, there's a good dog!'

The wind took the cap over the hedge, the dog yapped and pranced after it, but in no serious pursuit, and the piebald pony, that Turner was leading beside the shaggy rough-haired one he rode, kicked up his heels and tried to follow the dog. Turner managed to drag him round the bend in the road and then pulled up short. There was a fine to-do going on there; he had thought he had heard the shouts and clatter against the wind, and here was the cause of them, a litter lying on its side in the ditch with one wheel off, horses stamping and champing, men scolding and shouting orders, more and more men he saw as he rounded the bend, and he'd no mind to ride into their midst. Men asked too many questions these days, they could not let a man alone to go about his business. A narrow lane branched off to the side of the road, be decided to pursue it and his cap together; a sharp shower in the Gab of May was no time in which to leave one's nearly bald head. uncovered.

So he turned down the lane instead, and hadn't ridden

many yards when he checked again at sight of another cluster of people, but this time they were all women, their hoods fluttering like banners, their petticoats blowing and billowing like sails, their voices squawking and chattering like a flock of starlings, and then a voice he'd know in a thousand ringing through their toneless clatter – 'Away with you, all of you! I'm sick of the sight and sound of you! Be off to your shelter if you've really found one, your shed, hovel, pigsty or what not, and leave me alone. *Alone*, I say,' as there shrilled another uprush of exclamation, expostulation, 'I'll not have *one* of you stay with me, shoo! shoo!! shoa-oo!!!'

She had scared them off at last, there they were all sweeping off towards the little barn farther down the lane.

'Gee up, my beauties,' said William Turner to his ill-assorted pair of steeds, 'far may ye travel and farther may ye go, but it's not every day you'll come on a Princess crying under a hedge.'

For she was crying now that she was alone, and doubtless that was why she had wanted to be; the tears ran down her pale, rain-spattered face, and her hair, which had fallen down to its full length, was blown across it in long twisting strands darkened by wet to a purplish copper, like the shining dark red of the willow branches that had not yet burst their buds this late cold spring. Her dress was splashed with mud and had a great rent in the front of the skirt, her head-dress lay crumpled on the ground beside her. The hollow of the hedge where she sat could have given her more shelter, but she did not crouch back under the hawthorn branches that were scattering snow showers of blown blossom over her; she sat leaning forward and, behind and above her wet dishevelled head, an army of grey clouds swept towering and swirling up over the ice-blue sky.

With an angry gesture she swept her green sleeve across her face, wiping away her tears and the teasing hair in the same movement, then looked up startled from its clammy folds at the slow squelching sound of approaching hoofs. She saw two ponies and an old man bunched up on one of them, huddling his bare head and rusty black shoulders against the rain. A smile fought its way through the tears.

'There must,' she said, 'be a special Providence watching over me, for you are the one man in the world that I could bear to see me now.'

'My Lady Elizabeth's Grace,' he said, 'is the Herb of Grace, not to be crushed by a storm of cold rain. And the wind's blowing it away while we speak of it.'

It was true, the sleeting rain was stopping even as he bundled himself out of the saddle and slithered to the ground beside her, and the cloud that brought it sped away on the crying wind over the endless sky.

He stood there in front of her, clumsily trying to disentangle the reins of the two ponies that were passively humping their wet backs against the wind, and lucky for him they were so passive, thought Elizabeth, her smile growing wider and brighter as she looked up at the queer face of her old friend, discoloured and gnarled like the bole of a tree, its peering eyes almost hidden behind the rain-blurred spectacles – what a blind wet old mole he looked fumbling with the reins – 'Here, give them to me, butterfingers!' she commanded, suddenly springing up beside him and pulling them out of his hands, 'and put on your cap – was it your prophetic sense bared your head before I'd even seen you?'

'No, Lady, it was the wind, which has also bared yours, no doubt. Princess or professor, it's all one in this weather. What happened to the litter?'

'Overturned with a loose wheel spinning off it. The Queen – she didn't kill me, I don't know why – but she gave me the oldest and shabbiest litter that could be found, so as to disgrace my progress. So deeply disgraced that I may not even take shelter from this storm in a gentleman's house on the road. He came out to offer it, but the curmudgeon Bedingfeld refused, lest I plot treason with him, so I had to shelter in a ditch to do up my hair.'

'You have not done it,' said Dr. Turner, plucking away a long strand that had blown across his face.

Her laugh answered his growling chuckle, but hers was shrill as a bird's cry, a young laugh, a schoolgirl's laugh, as it should he for one who was only sweet and twenty, and so he told her, but she mocked him for it, there was no sweet in her twenty years, she said. 'There is more for you in your fifty, sixty, how many years of life? For you have your two little horses and you are going to leave this sad frightened country, with yourself on one of them, and I only wish I were on the back of the other. Where are you going to, my learned old friend?'

'I have no notion,' he replied happily.

'And no money either?'

'Enough to leave home.'

'But no home to go to!'

'God keeps open household in all places, and provides for old bustards as well as for young eagles,' he said, smiling at her. 'And wherever I go there will be flowers, fishes, birds and stones to be observed. As one grows old one has time only for the things one cares for. There is still a little time for me, and many flowers still unknown, many too that do not yet grow here, but shall when I return.'

'When will that be?'

'When your sad sister lies dead, Lady, and you sit young and golden on the throne.'

'A pretty prophecy! Did you never hear I'd been in the Tower since Palm Sunday?'

'When the lying priests say "Bless these palms" to their congregations who are all carrying branches of sallow willow!' he answered in hot indignation. 'It is a lie to call a sallow a Palm.'

'You old purist! I see why you became a gospeller!'

'*And* a herberist, for the truth is as necessary in the one as the other. But yes, I knew Your Grace had gone under Traitors' Bridge and come out again alive, which none is apt to do. What better augury that you can keep your head? Yes, and a steady hand, as it is now among this tangle of wet leather. Never cloud the sunshine of your eyes with weeping – make a verse of your sorrow instead.'

'I made one lately.' She wanted to tell him the verse she had made on the spur of the moment (and a very sharp spur!) when her questioners in the Tower had tried to catch her out in heresy by commanding her to state her belief in the miracle of the Last Supper.

But it had gone clean out of her mind. She could only remember the desperate little rhyme that had chattered on and on in her head like a rat running round in its cage all these past weeks in the Tower, as she fought again and again for her life against her tormentors.

> '"*Much suspected of me,*
> *Nothing proved can be,*"
> *Quoth Elizabeth, prisoner.*'

'Humph, you've made better, and will again.'

'No, it has all dried up inside me. I have fought too long a fight.'

'And you have won that fight. It is not your sister you'll have to cross swords with now, for she will no longer be herself, she will see all things only through her husband. He will be an adversary far more worthy of your steel. It is a young man, the most powerful Prince in the world – who is now preparing to advance against you.'

It was an odd way to encourage her with further and worse fears, but he knew his Princess. And in spite of herself she flushed with pleasure. It would be much more exhilarating to fight a young man than an old maid! She swung up the reins which she had finally disentangled, and tied them over a stout hawthorn branch that was sticking out from the hedge. The two ponies began placidly to tear up mouthfuls of the coarse grass in front of them. She leaned against the piebald, resting her elbows on his load, a heaped bundle of a few clothes wrapped round piles of books and tied precariously with rough straw rope. She propped her chin in her hands, and her face grew grave again as she stared over the scrawny wind-swept fields and the dark fringe of forest that overhung them.

'Philip of Spain will be King of England,' she said, 'and half the country are his already, for a country is no longer the land that it holds, but the opinions of the men within it. Many of those in England owe allegiance to foreign powers, to the Papacy and Spain. Less than a fortnight ago Mary brought back the laws against heresy. Her new Parliament passed them without a murmur. Have you heard?'

He chuckled. 'I have indeed. That is why I have become a Newcastle grindstone yet again, that travels all the world over, since no ship's carpenter would sail without one. And so I, a Newcastle man, will heal myself of the stone by Rhenish wine where it is cheap at Bonn, for that is the best cure.'

'What, will you give thanks to my sister for turning you out of the country?'

'As I gave to your father for doing it the first time; else I would never have found new plants in Germany, Holland, Switzerland and Italy. Nay, I would never have taken my degree as Doctor of Medicine at Ferrara, nor', his eyes goggled at the dreadful thought, 'studied botany from Luca Ghini under the leaning towers of Bologna.'

'And what of your crying childer who kept you from your book – have you strangled the lot?'

'Dean Badman has now won back his own name, Goodman,' he replied blandly, 'for he has taken charge of them. He has compounded with the Queen's laws, he will run no risk of charges of heresy and as a Popish priest he dare not marry. But he is fond of children and will salve his conscience by caring for mine. It is well that man is both good and bad, for if he had been all good he would not have compounded and would be fleeing the country like myself.'

'Are you "all good", all you flocks of black-robed crows now flying abroad? Eight hundred of you already have flapped away, I hear, and Messrs. Knox, Foxe, and Cox squawking their loudest at their head. Mr Knox is safe across the Scottish Border, writing furious pamphlets to all his luckless brethren here, inciting them to rebel against the

Queen and so inciting her to revenge against them, while he sits snug in his Edinburgh house. An easy way to be a revolutionary!' She spat.

'But what faith do you hold yourself, Princess?' he asked, and for the first time there was anxiety in his voice.

The thin face framed in the long hands turned its intent gaze from the countryside towards him. It looked like that of a wild young nymph with the wisps of red hair blowing loose across it, and the eyes reflecting the stormy sky with flecks of blue light. Yes, one could see her as a pagan nymph, never as a Christian saint or martyr. She belonged to the Renascence of beauty and splendid life that he had seen in Italy, and she would bring that to England if she could and make the country a glittering palace for the arts. But what of the Reformation? 'What of your faith?' he cried.

She answered slowly, 'Little doctor, do you seek a window to peer into my soul? That is what I will never do to the meanest of my people. But I will say this – that there is only one faith, one Jesus Christ, and all the rest is dispute about trifles.'

'God's true worship—' he began, but she cut across his words as quickly as the crack of a whip.

'Every man jack of you now thinks he is God's spokesman. Let's not talk of God when men are wrangling about Him in every alehouse, in every pulpit, some of 'em struggling into it two or three at a time, each bawling a different sermon against the other. The world has grown grey with dispute, there's a bitter east wind blowing over it, the breath of millions who teach the love of God as shown by hatred of their fellow-man.'

'No,' said he, 'let us not talk of God. Let us look at Him instead.'

'Where?' she asked. 'There?' she asked turning, laughing, to look into his face.

But he answered seriously, 'Yes, you will get a glimpse of Him in this shambling body He has created though not perfected. But look at his perfect creation, the heavenly harmony that binds the life of earth in unity and knits it together into the round globe, so that, though the several parts of nature war against each other, yet they are one whole. Look at this stone, this lump of clay, these bluebells and primroses that spatter the blue sky and shining stars upon the mud for a few fleeting hours, but leave their thousands of seeds to spring towards eternity. Here is life made perfect – here in this *fleur delice*.'

He pulled up the long stem of a wild yellow iris growing in the ditch beside them and handed it to her, touching its nine petals one by one as reverently as a priest handling the pyx upon the altar.

'Here is God made manifest, the Three in One and One in Three, three times over, the flower of the Trinity in Unity, all the delicate veins tracing the same completed pattern of His purpose. What this is, we too could be, if we followed the law of our true nature. But we lost the way to that when we ate the fruit of knowledge of good and evil.'

'And argued about it ever since!'

'Because we struggled to know more. When we know all, we shall need to struggle no more than the flowers, who do not know nor need to know. We shall have reached the harmony that is perfection. And if even one of God's works has reached perfection like this bright flower, then why not all, in God's good time? But His time is not ours. We can only see an hour or two ahead, where He looks through eternity.'

'But think of this hour ahead! Think of Philip's triumphal procession so slowly but surely approaching us. Some of his nobles are even selling their lands and houses in order to take up rich new estates in this country – as much the conquerors as if they had come with fire and sword to lay waste the land. England will be a Spanish province and fight Spain's wars for her, give her the wealth of her trade. And worse, for in the past conquerors might enslave men's bodies – but now their very souls are to be in subjection. Men must think as they are told, or face ruin and death.'

The dog pranced up to them in fantastic gyrations as though wagging five tails instead of running on four legs; coyly, ingratiatingly he wriggled up to his master and deposited a muddy object at his feet, then barked loudly in demand of thanks.

'Is that a bishop's cap?' asked Elizabeth.

He gave her an astonished glance from the corner of his globular spectacled eyes. 'You remember I'd trained him to fly at a bishop's cap! That will make you a true Queen. Men will put their souls in subjection to you of their own free will, a greater triumph than Philip's procession here. He'll get as much profit from it as men shear wool from hogs! But the country will follow you like St Anthony's pig, yes the true country, not just the London lickpennies and the sweet-lipped courtiers. Do not fear for the country.'

She was pulling a draggled wet curl between her teeth and answered despondently, 'There is no order anywhere in the world. The new dogmas have undermined it. Everywhere a hideous discord instead of harmony. This must be our darkest hour since the fall of the Roman Empire.'

'And now we may be seeing the fall of the Roman Church.'

'With the same result. Once again the civilised world is torn in pieces. Christendom is split, country against country, and, worse, a country is split against itself, and fellow-countrymen hate each other as much as they hate the Papacy and the Papacy them. God knows what can ever knit the world together again. It needs to live and let live. But it chooses death – for the sake of Opinion, that bloody Moloch, that self-conceited idol that seeks to make all the world think the same, and so tears it asunder into chaos.'

He was silent, frowning abstractedly, and when he began to speak she thought at first that he had not heard what she had said. 'When I was a small boy there was an old man used to come and sit in my father's tanning shed who'd tell me what he'd heard as a child of the Black Death. Whole villages were wiped out in a few days, and the few that were left in others ran mad and would do nothing but dance through the land, dancing to forget and escape from death, or rather, I say, from life, and all that they might still have done with it, even if only a few hours were left to them, still they were there to be used and thank God for. For only one thing lies ahead for all of us, and that is Death, and what does it matter if it come from what cause, or now or later, or to a whole town together or one by one? So use life while it is here and unfold your petals to the sun, without thinking how they will fall to the ground, for when they do you will have the seed of eternity in you.'

'And what am I to do, pray, till then?' she demanded bitterly.

'Pray till then. Pray as in your father's primer that "we may labour and travail for our necessities in this life, like the birds of the air and the lilies of the field, without care".'

'Oh no, you do not know for what I would pray!' and she

tossed back her head and flung out her hands in a savage gesture of impatience. The birds were shouting with joy that the rain had stopped and the sun come out; a cuckoo hooted derisively from the wood; a milkmaid, crossing the fields behind the hedge, with her pails dangling from the yoke on her shoulder, was singing a country song at the top of her voice,

'For bonny sweet Robin is all my joy.'

'I wish I were that milkmaid going to meet her Hodge. My sister shows me what I shall be like, if I do not have my youth in its true time.'

Why had she not given herself to Robin that night in the Tower? she asked herself, beating her hands together. But a fierce and lonely pride told her, even in this moment of passionate regret, that he was not the mate equal to, no, greater than herself, who must compel her to the ultimate surrender of herself. Had she ever met him? No, and most probably never would.

'But you will have your youth both in and out of its true time,' the old man was saying to her, 'so take it for the things you care for most.'

'And what are they?'

'Your lovers.' And as she exclaimed, he added placidly, 'All England will be your lovers.'

A rustle of feminine voices rose in the air.

'Here comes the gaggle of geese again!' He unhitched the reins from the hawthorn branch, and she held his stirrup while he bundled himself into the saddle and told her by way of thanks, 'Put hawthorn and may among the wild flowers in your palaces, Lady, and never heed the vulgar who say they are unlucky.'

Her women flocked round her, exclaiming in inquisitive astonishment at sight of her companion, explaining and apologizing for their delayed return – a bull had come and stood directly in front of their barn and it was suicidal to try and pass it until a milkmaid had opportunely passed that way and shooed it off.

Dr. Turner rode away, his hunched back dwindling down the narrow lane, the tails of his two little horses flicking their rumps, the one rusty and shaggy, the other a polished piebald. He was off on his travels again, ill, old, homeless and without money, but Elizabeth heard him singing as she went back with her women to the patched-up litter.

CHAPTER TWENTY-NINE

The clouds blew away and the cold crisp sunshine flickered out over the newly green world. She was driving towards Windsor and passed the King's College at Eton, its warm red brick glowing in the late afternoon light. Some boys coming out of school set up a yell and ran out through the gates towards her litter, shouting 'The Princess!' and a cluster of them playing marbles on the steps of a corner house sprang up cheering at first sight of the cortège.

Word of her coming had evidently sped in front of her during the delay of the litter's breakdown, for more and more boys were running up from the side streets, cheering and calling her name, 'The Princess!' 'The Lady Elizabeth! Floreat Elizabeta!' These must be the Oppidans, who lodged with the Fellows or the townsfolk, in accordance with the growing fashion among the gentry of sending their sons to share the free education of the scholars in College, but with fat allowances for their board and lodging.

She leaned forward, looking with interest at this new type of schoolboy and cried her thanks in Latin for their greeting, hoping, she said, laughing, that they always spoke Latin at their play in accordance with the rule.

'Only when there's a *lupus* among us!' called out one of the Scholars, a thin hungry-looking lad who had outgrown his shabby clothes. A dandified Oppidian, his yellow doublet slashed to show an embroidered shirt, told her, '*Lupus*, a wolf, means a sneak, Princess. Beware of wolves!'

A grubby cherub chimed in, 'There's a pack of 'em round you now!' and shot his hand out from his ragged sleeve in a very vulgar gesture at Bedingfeld's back.

Sir Henry gave a sharp command to the troop to hasten their pace, and the horses trotted on, leaving the boys running after them. The litter jogged and jolted over the bridge and the glittering river to where Windsor Castle towered above the town. But here it was out of the frying-pan into the fire for Sir Henry, for all the people in the town were prepared for her coming. They had hung gay cloths and rugs out of the windows as for a royal progress, they had come out into the streets to greet her, the crowds thronging thicker and faster every minute round her litter, their cheers swelling louder and louder in the increasing volume of a mighty welcome. Men were shouting in a deep-throated roar – 'God save Your Grace!' 'God bless our Princess!' 'Long live our Lady Elizabeth!'

A blue-aproned butcher with a thrust of his enormous bare arm flung a bunch of daffodils into the litter with a shout of 'God bless your pretty face!' and a grinning chimney-sweep, his white teeth splitting his black cheeks, roared 'Cheer up, sweetheart, you'll soon be out of prison!' A farm labourer returning to his supper, with his wooden spoon sticking up in his hat all ready for it, waved both hat and spoon so furiously that they flew out of his hand and landed in her lap.

Women fought their way through the men, their white napkins flapping about their heads like a flock of pigeons.

They were laughing and crying with joy, throwing more and more flowers into the litter and little loaves and cakes and sweet biscuits until she was almost smothered, interspersing their respectfully loyal cries of 'God save our Princess – our Lady Elizabeth!' with such homely adjurations as – 'Eat that, my pretty!' 'Don't let 'em starve you in prison!' 'You'll soon be out!'

The soldiers guarding her tried to push them back, but not very roughly, they only grinned as their commander yelled himself red in the face – 'Traitors! Rebels! You are defying the Queen!'

But the crowd shouted rudely back, booing and calling him 'Old turkeycock!' and 'Traitor yourself, ill-treating the Princess!' And then the church bells started ringing in vociferous peals of joy and welcome, a treasonable act indeed since it was an honour reserved for the reigning Sovereign alone. Sir Henry shouted to some of his men to go and arrest the bell-ringers and put them in the stocks, and a small body of them marched off, not too fast, thinning the ranks round the litter.

Suddenly they were met by a fresh attack. The Eton boys had mustered their forces together and came charging in a young army across the bridge from the College. Their concerted roar of 'Floreat Elizabeta!' cut across the seething turmoil, they swarmed through the crowd and the gap in the ranks, they were all round her, stopping the litter and holding the frightened plunging horses. She was looking into a sea of schoolboy faces, flushed and many grimy, grinning from ear to ear as their Latin greeting warmed to more personal cries of 'Our Lady Elizabeth!' 'You'll be our Queen – our Queen Bess!'

Bedingfeld, looking desperately worried, could not command his troop of horse to ride over a crowd of schoolboys, he shouted instead to know why the bells hadn't stopped ringing.

'Yah! Wolf!' they yelled in answer, 'Lupus the sneak!' and a big lad called out, 'You can't stop the bells from ringing or the boys from singing,' and in a moment they were all singing at the tops of their voices,

> '*Sing up, heart, sing up, heart,*
> *Sing no more down,*
> *But joy in Elizabeth*
> *That will wear the crown.*'

It was the Coronation song they had sung for King Edward on high days and holidays, and since last summer for Queen Mary – sheer treason now to substitute Elizabeth's name. She was in terror lest Bedingfeld should complain to the College authorities and get them all flogged; she cried to them to stop and let her pass, but those nearest her had joined hands and were dancing in rings round her. One sprang up on to the step of the litter and flung his hoop, which he had twisted round with sprays of periwinkle in an enormous wreath, over her shoulders.

'Floreat Elizabeta!' he shouted.

'And you have made me flower,' she laughed in answer and held it up to her chin. 'Shall I ever wear a ruff as big as this?' she called to them.

A strapping lad, not to be outdone, thrust a grubby fist on to her lap and opened it to leave his best marbles rolling over her skirt.

She threw to them some of the loaves and cakes that had been showered on her. 'Do you get enough to eat?' she called. 'No!' they shouted, and scrambled and fought for the cakes, scattering a little as she had hoped. The litter was able now to move on, though very slowly, but at that they all came swooping back and ran along beside it. 'Come back!' they shrilled. 'Come and see us when you are Queen.'

'And bring more loaves,' she cried. 'Floreat Etona!'

They were leaping round her in a goblin multitude, and all the townsfolk waving and shouting with them in a tremendous rhythmic chant, 'Our Lady Elizabeth! Our future Queen!' The late sunlight slanted on to the soldiers' helmets and halberds that tried to keep a steady course through the crowd, and behind them rose the huge thunder-cloud of Windsor Castle. Stone walls, armed guards still held her in thrall, but at this moment they counted to her for nothing. She sat amazed, almost stunned with elation, her bright unbelieving eyes gazing at all these loving people, *her* people.

'This is the happiest moment of my life,' she breathed to herself. Here was she a prisoner, an outcast, disgraced, yet in spite of it she rode crowned with triumph, and by the will of the people. She who had been utterly alone, a shivering solitary among the icy terrors of the Tower, was now 'one of a crowd', but more, she was the burning heart of the crowd.

They felt for her with all the rugged chivalry of their nation, their affection for the dispossessed, the unfairly treated, for the younger son or daughter despised and turned out by the family, who became the hero and heroine of their fairy-tales. All these people who did their daily chores and found life a drab painful racket from cockcrow to the next night's snores, all who ever felt injured, downtrodden, put upon, who complained 'They never give me a chance,' and wondered if life would ever open suddenly for them like a door into Heaven, and turn everything topsy-turvy so that they would be on top of the world and all who oppressed them would be down-trodden in their turn, all these could identify themselves with the flame-haired Princess now riding in her shabby old broken litter among her prison guards.

And she knew herself at one with them, as she had not been even at that glorious entry into London when they had taken her for their own; as she would not be even in that day when she would have become a great Queen – and well she knew at this moment that that day would come. But it was now, when she was young and powerless and dispossessed, that she was winning her tenderest place in their hearts; now, when she was travelling only from one prison to another, that her journey was as royal a progress as any that she would ever enjoy.

As she drove on, the cold wind brought the sound of bells from all over the countryside; everywhere the church bells were clashing and flashing in the golden air, winging among the startled birds, singing and ringing as they should only ring for King or Queen.

They had rung before for Queen Jane.

> *'Long live Queen Jane!*
> *Nine days to reign.'*

They had rung, and should be ringing now, for Queen Mary.

> *'Long live Queen Mary!*
> *All things contrary.'*

Now they were ringing for herself, 'Elizabeth, prisoner';
but the Queen to be.

> *'Long live Queen Bess!*
> *England says "Yes".'*

CHAPTER THIRTY

Philip of Spain had set sail with a hundred gilded ships fluttering with scarlet silk standards thirty yards long.

Philip of Spain had landed in England and married the Queen.

Philip had been unfailingly polite. The English had been very rude.

The Lord Admiral Howard had compared the gorgeous Spanish ships to mussel-shells. Philip had said he would endeavour to build bigger ones.

The Spaniards were impressed by the English display of gold and silver plate, a hundred huge pieces on a single sideboard, fountains rimmed with pure gold, a glittering clock half as high as a man. But they were disgusted with the coarse and excessive food and the natives' habit of putting sugar in their wine; they were shocked that their gentlemen greeted strange ladies by kissing them on the mouth. The stout Earl of Derby nearly caused an uproar by thus saluting the stately Duchess of Alba, who bounced back off his stomach in furious indignation and told everybody later that he had only managed to touch her cheek.

The visitors wrote home that 'We Spaniards are miserable here'; that they were being robbed and insulted; that the English had not begun to be civilised like the rest of Europe

but were 'such barbarians that they do not understand what
we say, nor we them'; that their palaces, though very large,
were overcrowded, and with 'such a hurly-burly in all the
kitchens as to make each a veritable hell'; that the gentlemen
wore too many ornamental buttons and the ladies showed too
much leg, in black stockings too; moreover, they were not at
all beautiful. The Queen, though a saint, also dressed badly,
not to say vulgarly, and committed the further solecism of
showing that she was madly in love with her husband;
nevertheless she took precedence over him – the greatest
Prince on earth! – and this wretched little island, lost in the
fogs and rains of the northern seas, refused to acknowledge
the lord of half the world as their superior.

To crown all, it never stopped raining, and they were
always having to hide the splendour of their wedding
garments under cloaks of red felt.

But Philip, to the indignation of his followers, was as much
determined to please as if he were wooing a country equal in
importance to his own. He left off his favourite sober colours
and wore Mary's presents of purple velvet with silver fringe,
and white brocade with gold bugles; he was lover-like in
public to the wife whom he wrote of as 'our well-beloved
aunt'; he was affable to everybody; he practised smiling so
frequently that he asked his friend Ruy Gomez to massage his
jaws at night; he drank beer, which he detested.

Through all this, Elizabeth stayed quiet at Woodstock,
though not secure. She was guarded as closely as in the Tower,
with sixty soldiers on guard by day and forty by night, and
when she walked in the gardens half a dozen locks went click-
clack after her, to remind her, she told Sir Henry Bedingfeld,
of her invisible chains. For even now she could not resist

teasing her jailor. She kept him in agonies of apprehension by demanding liberties he dared not permit without first applying to the Council for a form of leave.

First she wanted a volume of Cicero, and then a Latin version of the Psalms, and then an English Bible, and then leave to write to the Queen (whom she teased in her turn so that Mary said she would 'have no more of her disguised and colourable letters'), and then leave to write to the Council, and then that Bedingfeld should act as her secretary, which was awkward when she insisted on his writing to them that she was worse treated than a prisoner in the Tower, and on second thoughts, worse treated than the worst prisoner in Newgate.

Bedingfeld's bull-dog tenacity on his conscience was strained to breaking-point. He could never make out what 'this great lady' was at, or would be at next; nor what all her rather shady friends were at, when they stayed near by for weeks together down at the local inn at the sign of the Bull – Parry and young Verney and hosts of others whose business was never properly explained.

Yet Elizabeth knew only too well the danger she was in: that English councillors were advising the Queen that 'there would be no more peace for England till the Lady Elizabeth's head were smitten from her shoulders' – and by how much the more must her Spanish counsellors now be urging it? Renard had always wanted her death; and surely the new young husband, whose every wish Mary longed slavishly to obey, must now be doing the same. How then was she still alive?

There came a day when she thought she would not have to ask this much longer, for the King and Queen sent for her to be brought to them, still a prisoner, at Hampton Court. She was lodged at the Gate House on the river at a little distance from the Palace, and for some days heard no more. Then one night late, when she had begun to go to bed, there came a summons for her to go at once to the Queen's chamber in the Palace.

To get such a command at this hour of night, without any warning, must mean only one thing, and it was plain that Sir Henry Bedingfeld thought so too; his plump cheeks had gone a bluish-grey above his bushy beard, and his round eyes looked at her in rueful astonishment.

'It looks,' she said coolly, 'as though your disagreeable duties as jailor will soon be over.'

To her amazement he sank slowly, heavily upon his knees. 'Your Grace,' he begged, 'do not give me that harsh name. I have, rather, been your guardian, if you did but know – and more than once from secret murder.'

'I know that. Get up and spare your gout, man. I wish all my foes were as true friends as yourself.'

He seized and kissed her hand and she felt his tears upon it. 'God's death, but I must be in a bad way!' she said, trying to laugh, and then to her horror found she was crying too, and shaking so much that as he rose he put his bulky arm round her for support.

Then he led her through the thick darkness of the gardens with the torches of their attendants flickering now on the black running river below, now on the tall trunks, the forked branches of the waiting trees. Torchlight, firelight, burning, wood and faggot light, this would be the light of a sacrificial pyre. Two or three weeks ago the burnings for heresy had begun. She wished she had not asked for that English Bible.

Now they were going through the Palace courtyards, and the light struck up on to the red brick arches that had once been crowned with her mother's initials intertwined with King Henry's, and then her initial had been erased to make way for others. And now they passed the great stairway to the Chapel where another wife of her father's had been dragged shrieking from him to her death. They said you could still hear those shrieks sometimes at night even now. She might well hear their warning tonight.

But no sound came through the darkness but their own footsteps (would later years hear those too?), and now they were inside the Palace and going up to the Queen's apartments. And now she was in the Queen's own room, and the Queen sat huddled on a low seat at the end of it, alone. So her chief enemy was still hidden. Would she never see him?

The Queen spoke and went on speaking, and, as always, asking questions, but Elizabeth could not tear her thoughts away from the invisible figure that stood behind all these words, the prince of Mary's every thought and action. What he willed, that would Mary do. What then did he will towards herself?

Mary was now commanding, now almost imploring her to confess her guilty share in the plots against her. Elizabeth denied it. 'Then,' said the Queen, 'you must think that you have been wrongfully imprisoned.'

She could not collect her wits against these snares. Something was distracting her, some sense that what she or Mary said was not the important thing in this interview, that there was some other mightier power to be placated. She ceased to protest her loyalty, her orthodoxy; she fell silent listening, she did not know for what, and suddenly she exclaimed in a voice ringing and vibrant as a girl's pleading with a lover, 'Oh, I beseech you to have a good opinion of me!'

There was a faint rustle somewhere in the room. Elizabeth started and looked around her, but the Queen paid no attention, she continued to accuse and question, and now Elizabeth spoke in answer, but not to her sister. Someone else was listening to her, she knew it, and all her future depended on the impression she might make on this unknown audience. What she said might matter little, might not be fully understood; but how she said it mattered above all. Her voice could be beautiful as the throbbing of a lute, young, eager, passionate, and she made it so now.

The Queen grew uneasy, she tried to check her sister, though she had before been urging her to speak; she walked restlessly about the room, moving near to a gilded leather screen in a corner. She said on a forcedly kindly note, 'You may be speaking truth – God knows! *Quien sabe!*' she added loudly, striking her hands together.

Why should she speak in Spanish? It must be a signal – the signal for her death? Elizabeth's control broke. She cried out, 'Someone is there behind the screen!'

A young man stepped out from behind it, with such majesty that instead of eavesdropping he might have been a god now choosing to manifest himself to human eyes. The candlelight flowed over his smooth fair head and pale golden beard, making his black velvet dress a glistening shadow. He was slight and small, but no one would have dared to notice it. He said in slow and careful English, 'It was the Queen's wish that I should hear you, Madam, before I met you. It is the wish of both of us that you should attend our Court. You are our dear sister, no longer prisoner.'

He bowed low, and she, forcing herself to conquer her trembling, sank to the ground in a deep curtsy, her bright head bowed till it all but touched her knee. Then as she rose, so slowly, with such exquisite balance, her downcast white eyelids rose also, with no timid fluttering but as slowly and steadfastly as her now upright body.

Their bared eyes met like swords at the salute before a duel.

A duel, both knew it, had begun between them, though whether of love, or of enmity and hate, or of all these, they knew nothing; only that from this moment a link of fierce passion would bind them together, inexorable, inescapable, till death alone should sever it.

It was to last for nearly half a century.

Elizabeth and the Prince of Spain

PRELUDE: THE BOY

'My father has fought bulls singlehanded in the arena,' said the boy. 'He is brave as a lion. He has never been defeated. He is the Conqueror of the World. How could he be conquered – by a pirate fleet of heathen Moors?'

'The East is Europe's worst danger,' said a dry voice in dusty answer.

'It *was*. But my grandfather drove all the Moors out of Spain after they'd ruled and ravaged here for seven hundred years. And he was not half as great a man as my father.'

'No, but his wife was,' the tutor muttered, all but sniggered, and covered it with a hasty cough, his precise tone at once correct again. 'My Prince, it is not the heathen who have conquered the Holy Roman Emperor, the "Invincible Emperor". It is the winds and the waves of the sea. Listen to the storm raging even now against this tower.'

He stooped eagerly forward, his sharp nose peaked against the light, his black-sleeved arm swooped to draw back the heavy curtain and in a dramatic gesture pushed aside a wooden shutter.

Outside the small panes of glass a jagged landscape leaped into shape against a frantic sky. Those were not the Guadarrama range that Prince Philip knew, but the mountains of hell.

'Look at the lightning,' insisted the tutor, a stiff man but now curiously gloating, as many a peaceable man will do in a scene of violence in which he need take no part. 'Hear the rain flailing down on the stones of the courtyard far below. *These* are the enemy who conquered the Emperor Charles V at Algiers, smashed his great ships to splinters against the rocks, blew his tents away like dandelion clocks on the sea-shore.'

Something chilled his enjoyment in his descriptive powers. He turned from the window and saw his Prince looking at him. Philip said coldly, 'The storms show the wrath of heaven. It is God who directs the winds and waves. "He spoke and His enemies were scattered." Do you tell me that God fought for the Moors against the Emperor my father?'

Another flash, a long rending crash tore the sky across as he spoke.

'This is blasphemy,' said the boy. 'God himself denies it.'

Dr. Siliceo hastily snapped the shutter to again and pulled the curtain over it, shutting out the enormous scene from the stuffy glittering little room. Candle flames in the draught, which even glass, wood and tapestry could not suppress, winked against the silver figure writhing on the crucifix, flickered over the livid blood-pink and blue in a Flemish picture.

'Certainly,' said Dr. Siliceo severely, 'it is blasphemy for Your Highness to deny victory to your illustrious father. That is exactly what I was explaining. You must write and tell him that you understand his defeat was caused by no human agency; it was by the command not of God but of the Devil.'

As so often, Philip felt himself rebuked without quite knowing why. 'I will write,' he said heavily.

Yes, he must write. Yet again.

Pen, paper and ink. More and more paper, more and more

ink, yet another pen. He was always doing it. 'He fights and I write,' Philip muttered. It was all he could do, while his father fought battles, risked his life in them. 'Emperors don't get killed in battle,' Charles V had often scoffed to those who tried to restrain him, but he had very nearly disproved it this time. His wretched troops had been mowed down in a surprise attack in the drenching night, some had broken and fled; the whole army might well have been totally destroyed if the Emperor had not seized his sword and rushed into the front ranks, rallying them by his courage alone to drive their attackers back into Algiers.

If only Philip had been there at his side! But he would have been no use; only an added responsibility and anxiety to his father. His common sense saw it clearly though bitterly.

One day he would be a full-grown man, he would be a great soldier like his father; he would have more and bigger ships than any in the world, and his armadas would avenge this defeat suffered by the armadas of Spain.

Yet the hope of doing what his father had failed to do lay heavy as lead upon his spirit. Lethargy fell on him like sleep; he longed to sleep, to die, and never to be called upon to prove himself as great a man – no, greater even, than his father. 'Let me alone for I am not better than my fathers.'

'Let me alone,' he said aloud. That of course could not be taken literally. Dr. Siliceo retired to a corner of the room and bent his head over a book, low, lower, as his breathing grew louder. *He* could sleep.

To sleep, to die, to lie for ever carved in marble like the beautiful young Prince Juan on his tomb at Avila, who had never had to live to be King of Spain but had died instead at sixteen. Philip would not be afraid to die. But to live; to take over the mastery of more than half the world; to make swift decisions in the heat of action; to break the power of his arrogant nobles and then seem to make friends with them, while always distrusting them; to trust no one, depend on no one, to listen to advice and take none of it – yes, Philip was afraid to live. How could he ever do it all?

He was small, he was not very clever, and two great Kings would hem him in on either side, his father's lifelong rivals, older than his father and much bigger, two crafty wicked giants, but his father had outwitted and defeated them, outrun them in the race for the Empire. They were Henry VIII of England, huge as a bull, with a bull's brutal inimical stare, in the full flush of his career of murderous matrimony; and the sly 'Foxnose,' François I of France, also well over six feet, whom his father had conquered and captured in battle and held as his prisoner for two years in Madrid. The French would never forgive it, watched always for the chance to attack Spain with every ally they could muster, even the heathen Moors.

Yes, the Very Christian King of France had actually joined forces with the fanatic enemies of Christ, with the Sultan, Soliman the Magnificent, and his slave-born sea-captain Barbarossa the Red-beard, and helped them to build up this pirate fleet at Algiers with the Moors who had been driven out of Spain. From that ancient port on the North African shore they raided the seaports of Spain, destroyed Spanish shipping and trade, and drove the wretched coast-dwellers further and further inland to the safety of the mountains.

'Three things from which no man is safe,' said the old

Moorish proverb. 'Time, the sea and the Sultan.' And now the sea and the Sultan had defeated his father, and no man was safe. No man was safe until he was dead.

The boy laid down his pen on the blank sheet of paper and stared at the tortured figure on the crucifix. Yes, even He was safe in spite of His sufferings, since there had been nothing more to do but suffer unto death.

He rose and walked to the window, making no sound even when he drew back the curtain and the shutter. No lightning now pierced the dreadful night; nothing could be seen. Yet he saw something, the pale glimmer of a face framed in a nun's coif, and it was looking at him.

It could not be; the tower rose sheer from the rock, no one could be there, floating in space fifty feet above the ground. He was seeing a vision, a nun's face. Relief surged over him in an engulfing wave; God had sent him the answer to all his fears and doubts of himself in the world; He meant him to renounce the world and become a monk.

The nun's lips were moving; speaking to him; he could hear no word through the thick glass, nor could he do so, if the window were open, against the roar of the tempest. Yet he knew what she was saying to him, dead contrary to his thought. 'Go back,' she said, 'back to all you have to do.'

'I have not the strength.'

'You will have all the strength you can bear.'

'How *can* I do it all?' But he knew her answer even as her face drifted into darkness. 'As it comes. One thing at a time.'

At this time he could write a letter of condolence to his father.

He shut out the now empty darkness and stood remembering where he had seen that face before. A few months ago at Avila he had stared with the curiosity of a boy at a young woman who some years before had run away from home to become a Carmelite nun, and now proposed to reform the Order and bring it back to its ancient austerity. She was mad, some people said, others that she was a witch; she had visions, or else she was tempted by the Devil; she was a hopeless invalid, paralysed at times, unable to move hand or foot; yet when she prayed, her body sometimes floated up into the air. Her family had complained of her and now her convent was doing so, her confessor had ordered her to make rude gestures of repudiation when visited by beatific visions; she had been warned by the Church, even threatened by the Holy Office of the Inquisition.

Philip stood so still that Dr. Siliceo blinked, sat up, stood up.

'Your Highness requires—'

'Nothing. Yes. What is the name of that nun – the "ecstatic" who is causing trouble at Avila?'

'Teresa of Avila,' replied Siliceo; 'a tiresome woman. Why does your Highness ask?'

Philip did not answer. A little shakily he went back to his desk.

The tutor repeated drowsily, 'A very tiresome woman. Her Superior has told me that she prays for suffering. That is doubtless a way of ensuring that one's prayer shall be granted.' His chuckle rustled like a dead leaf across the room, but there was no sign that his pupil had heard him. Philip was writing. Siliceo took up his book, but his eyelids dipped lower, lower, then flicked open on the desk inlaid with gold and mother-of-pearl, at the jewelled quill scratching at the paper, and the smooth flaxen head ducked over it like a fledgling chicken's bending to peck. A good-looking boy, drowsed the tutor comfortably, perhaps not so good a scholar as one would expect from a pupil of his, but every inch a Prince, especially on horseback where you didn't see how few the inches were; silver fair, his veins showed the blue blood, pure of any taint of the Moor, a rarity prized among the proudest Spanish families, and prized above all by Siliceo, who believed passionately in racial purity and preached that not only all infidel Moors and Jews should be expelled from Spain, as had been done, but all those also who had been converted to Christianity, and even all who had ever had a Moor or Jew, however far back, in their ancestry. Conversion could be feigned; the only sure test was pure Spanish blood.

But Prince Philip, alas, had more of Flemish blood. Siliceo had been engaged to correct that error; the boy had grown into a typical well-bred Castilian, respectable (outwardly at least), grave, reserved, and austere in manner, even more a Spaniard than many who were pure bred, since so much conscious effort went into being it – 'a *converted* Spaniard,' Siliceo chuckled to himself in malicious somnolence. So contrary is even the best regulated mind, particularly when half asleep, that he felt almost peevish at his success. Well, he had trained the Prince to be a gentleman, which was more than his father, the Holy Roman Emperor Charles V, that gross Fleming, could ever be. 'These Hapsburgs!' he muttered on a faint snore that startled him awake. At that instant an eyelid flicked open for a second in his mind; could training be carried a shade too far? That small figure before him, grimly plodding away at his squeaky quill, was a strange silent boy; it was most unlike him to speak even as much as he had spoken just now.

Something there was in him that seemed to check his imagination, his motive power; just as the uproarious rejoicings at his birth had been checked, broken off by his father's command and the whole Court ordered into mourning, sackcloth and penance, when the appalling news reached Spain that the Holy City of Rome was being sacked, and by the Christian troops of the Holy Roman Emperor himself. Outrage, murder and ruin, more horrible even than that wrought long ago by the heathen Goths, ravaged and all but destroyed Rome. It was the most shocking conquest in history, also the unluckiest, for every man who had taken active part in it was said to have met since then a violent or disgusting death.

The Emperor Charles himself was not there; it was not his doing, as he had frequently explained, but that of the other fellows, the subordinates who had let the men get out of hand; slack discipline, starvation rations, they had caused the rot.

True, he had ordered the march on Rome, but he was never one jot the worse for it; his appetites were as huge as ever, whether for food and drink, for bouts of boisterous jollity or an equally unrestrained melancholy; for more power over at least half of the Old and all the New World which, as fast as it went on being discovered, had long ago been decreed by the Borgia Pope to belong to Spain 'to all eternity.'

Unabated, unsated, the old ruffian appeared to savour every moment of his invincible career, for all that he talked at times of his need to 'make his soul' and repent of his sins – but never with any mention among them of the Sack of Rome. In spite even of that, his luck had held, till now.

But it had been no good omen for his son, born in that hour

of hideous victory over the Pope and his Church, to be the Very Catholic King of Spain; to have the high festival at his birth turned into bitter penance, as if he were doomed to an inheritance of guilt. Was the boy indeed haunted by a sense of guilt and need of atonement?

He was. But what haunted Philip was the fear of not behaving himself correctly in public, and every moment of his life was public, every natural function had to be conducted as a solemn ritual. Even at four years old, when he was breeched, it was a religious rite as well as a gorgeous ceremony; he had been perched high up on a mule and led across a vast plain where rocks as big as houses lay tumbled on top of each other in the burning sunlight; he came to red walls that reached up to the sky, and was told this was Avila, and shown the tombs of Torquemada the Grand Inquisitor, and the handsome marble youth who like himself had been Prince of Spain. He had been taken out of the quivering heat into a cold dim chapel where psalms were chanted round him, and long black-robed nuns took off his baby petticoats, touching him with unaccustomed hands, some podgy and clammy, some knuckly and sharp, but all strange; they put on his new manly breeches and black Court dress. Then he had to stand and face a long procession of lords and ladies and clergy, and then a vast cheering crowd below the stone balcony where trumpets blared in his ears and heralds shouted, proclaiming him the Prince of Spain. Very tired, bewildered, half deafened, frightened, he did not flinch, he bowed when told to, he behaved perfectly.

So he did even when he had been naughty and his mother, that serene beauty who seemed to him the Queen of Heaven, whipped him in front of her Court ladies and they shed tears at such cruelty to the tiny fair princeling. But Philip had not cried before the ladies when he was four. He had not cried when two years ago his mother died, and he had to lead her funeral procession out from the gaunt rock city of Toledo down through Spain, riding day after day across the vast tablelands of Castile and La Mancha and Andalusia, down towards Granada, down into the tomb of her grandparents Ferdinand and Isabella. There they lay at Granada, where they had forced the last surrender of the Moors; and there she, young and lovely, now must lie. The great vault was opened, her coffin lowered into it before the weeping multitudes; but Philip did not cry.

And he did not cry now when he was alone, and fourteen, though his whole world lay shattered before him, and his father, the Invincible Emperor, had been conquered by his enemies. No, *not* by them, never that. What was it old Siliceo had said, now blinking like a sleepy black cat in his corner, so little did he care? 'By no human agency,' echoed young Philip in a whisper, staring at the devils that his father found so amusing in that picture by Hieronymus Bosch. Birds swallowed men, toads danced with women, a lean thoughtful face looked out dispassionately on them all, wearing a pink hat, and on its brim yet more devils. The colours were like torn flesh, but unreal. Nowhere on earth could one see pink so violent, so vile, so virulent.

'No human agency,' repeated Philip; and was answered by the wind that flapped the edges of the heavy curtains, rattled the shutters of the turret room in the alcazar that towered defiantly on its rock above the Castilian plain.

The room became filled with the patient persistence of the

boy in proving to himself that the heathen hordes had not conquered yet again, that it was not the infidels' fleet who had defeated his father's ships at Algiers, but 'all the elements that had conspired against Your Majesty's prudence and greatness.'

BOOK I: THE PRINCE

CHAPTER ONE

1554

'I am going, not to a marriage feast, but to a fight,' said the young man.

'And what else is marriage?' grunted his father.

The young man stamped his feet down into his new silver-laced boots while the tailor reverently pulled them up higher and the trunk hose of white kid lower, till they fitted skin-tight round the slim and shapely legs, except for a wrinkle near the knee. The shaggy old man huddled by the window at a table that was covered with the inner mechanisms of a quantity of clocks, flicked up a red eyelid to scrutinize his son's legs. 'The hose are too long,' he said, 'or rather,' with a wheezy chuckle, 'the legs are too short.'

'An inch off just here,' the tailor whispered to his second-in-command. The legs tautened as if to stretch themselves, they balanced momentarily on the tips of the toes, striving for an unavailing instant to deny the sombre truth uttered by his father.

If only he were a few inches taller! It was important that he was a small man, because it was so important that he should be a great one. His father was old and ill and seemed at times half childish in his frantic preoccupation with his clocks, trying to make them all keep exactly the same time; although he knew well he should now concentrate on eternity and have done with time, and was threatening to retire to a monastery and do so. Yet his father, the Emperor Charles V, was still by far the greatest man in the world, and he would bequeath to him the greatest task that any man could undertake; nothing less than that he, his son Prince Philip, should be master of it.

'For it must come to that,' his father had always told him; 'it is One World now. One faith, one rule, and one man to support it,' so the Emperor had told the solemn boy whose pouting under-lip had mimicked his own in the effort to look portentously important; and he said it again now to the sadly conscientious young man who at his command was trying on before him the wedding garments that were an inch too long.

But this time he varied his formula. 'It is *your* world now,' said the thick guttural voice. 'It is *you* who have got to make and keep it one, under Spanish domination everywhere, for that is coming, mark you – it must come, in spite of those damned Lutheran princes stabbing me in the back from my own land of Germany. Luther – Luther – why did I ever let him live? I had him in the palm of my hand' – his fist shot out (and a startled tailor toppled over backwards on his heels), the gnarled fingers struggled to spread out, but had to twist up again – 'and I let him go!'

'Why did you, sir?' Prince Philip's question was almost an accusation.

'God knows! His safe-conduct I suppose. I'd promised him that. Machiavelli was a sound statesman; a prince who breaks his word is stronger than he who keeps it, no doubt that's true. But even an Emperor must think of his soul – sometimes.' The Emperor paused to consider this paradox, then rejected it.

'But no, I know why I did it. I said, "We'll keep this little monk, he may be useful to us some day." A handy weapon against the Papacy, I thought. There have always been heresies in plenty, and one could always stamp them out in time. But I wasn't in time. Luther's been dead for years, but he's still infecting the world. This plague of heresy is spreading like the Black Death, and what will be the end of it all? The death of society, of the civilized world, that's what heresy will bring. It is an international conspiracy to destroy government in every country, to bring one revolution after another, to divide nations, even families against themselves. It exalts treason into a virtue. Men will betray their country to be true to their "ideas" – ideas of what? That Judas Iscariot is a saint, for he betrayed his Master.'

And this was what Philip had to fight, as fiercely as ever his father had done, in hand-to-hand combat, or even the Cid himself, the hero of Spain, against the infidel. The infidel was again the enemy. The heathen Moor, or heretic English, there was nothing to choose between them, except that the latter were the more dangerous since they still pretended to the name of Christians.

His father's rivals, the two crafty wicked giants that he had dreaded as a boy, had been dead seven years, but their work went on. France was again at war with Spain, as bitterly her enemy as when François I had allied himself with the heathen Sultan and his pirate fleet.

And England, for whom Henry VIII had opened the door into heresy – opened it only ajar, since he had intended to keep the doctrine, and the profits, of the Catholic Church, while ejecting the Pope and monasteries – England had kicked the door wide open, and all through the reign of Henry's son

Edward had had heresy imposed by the law of the land. But now for the last year Edward was dead and his elder sister Mary was Queen, and Philip must go to England to marry her and help her bring back the country to the Church of Rome. It would be difficult, dangerous. The law would be now on the side of the Church, but a great part of the people were still against it; still more were against Mary's Spanish marriage. Protests had been openly made in Parliament and even by Mary's devotedly Catholic Chancellor, Bishop Gardiner; last winter the Spanish Ambassadors for the marriage negotiations had been snowballed by Londoners, who concealed stones in their snowballs; and early this last spring there had been a large-scale revolt headed by young Thomas Wyatt, of a most respectable family of diplomats and public servants, a revolt which had surged in civil warfare through the London streets right up to the Queen's palace and all but succeeded in overthrowing her government. Yet Wyatt had been executed, declaring to the end that he was no traitor since he had fought only for 'true religion'. A very pretty example of the high-minded treason his father was inveighing against, considered Philip, and tried to say so, but the Emperor only mumbled, 'Hey, what's that? Wyatt? You needn't worry. That business was well squashed, I saw to that. Executions in plenty. England's been made safe enough for you to go there for weeks past.'

And he lolled out a bright green tongue that slipped and fell sideways in his mouth. It never failed to startle his son's nervous susceptibilities, though Philip knew that it was only fresh leaf that his father sucked to promote saliva in his fever-cracked mouth. But every time it licked out at him like a lop-sided lizard he wished that his father, in spite of or perhaps even instead of being the conqueror and master of the world, were just an ordinary father. Why should he take more than a dozen clocks to pieces all at once? One or two might be reasonable, even three or four might be excused – but fourteen, perhaps fifteen! It was, like everything to do with his father, extravagant, disproportionate, positively gluttonous.

'*How* many clocks, sir, have you disintegrated there?'

'Why – all there are in the palace,' replied the Emperor in a voice surprisingly mild at the irrational demand. 'Time is important, you know, and you will find it so. Be sure that you keep time on your side.'

'Tick tock, tick tock' they all agreed, for at last he had put them together. They began to strike, some deep and sonorous as a church bell, some tinkling and thin as a child's rattle, some playing fragments of tune, some striking hammers, some slow, some fast, but all measuring out the time, one, two, three, four, on and on to the full number of eleven. 'There!' shouted the Emperor through their discordant din, snatching off his horn-rimmed spectacles and flinging himself back in his chair, an exhausted bear in all his furs, hot though the day was. But presently a smile like Jove's smoothed and expanded his rutted, forward-thrusting face. 'There, at last! They are all striking together at the same time.'

But not all. One, the smallest, came cheeping in at the very end, like a belated chicken out of its egg. The Emperor thrust his enormous jaw at it.

'But in any case,' said Philip's precise, slightly disdainful tones, as he pulled his new round globular watch out of the pocket of his discarded coat, 'it is not the right time.'

He could have bitten his tongue out as he heard his own words, but it was too late.

'What's that? Not the right time? These lazy rogues, these muddlers, bunglers—' and the Emperor Charles roared to his servants to bring again the exact time by the Cathedral clock; would not speak again till he had heard it; would not finish the portentous warnings of this farewell interview; but put on his owlish spectacles anew, and set to work in grim silence to regulate them all over again.

An ordinary father would not have done that. But none of Philip's family were ordinary.

He squared the slight shoulders on which the burden of Hercules was doomed to roll; he looked over the bowed backs and busy fingers of the tailors crawling round his legs, fitting on the wedding garments that were to be his armour for the Crusade that he must lead for Spain, the Empire of the world, and the one true Church to bind it together. And then he looked at the grey silhouette of his father's sunken head against the window, and beyond it the jagged outline of rocky hills, bare and tawny as a lion's skin in the harsh sunlight, that was his home. Yes, one – or other – of them must marry Mary of England. And why not the other?

A tinkling chime went up from one of the clocks. The rest followed in ragged chorus. The spell was broken; they were free to speak. Philip resumed the clothes he had been wearing, dismissed the tailors, collected his words.

'As Your Majesty was betrothed to Mary over thirty years ago –' he began, then gulped and started again rather more hurriedly. 'If the marriage were arranged for Your Majesty, that would be the best course.'

'I am over fifty-four and too old,' grunted the father.

'I am under twenty-seven and too young,' said the son.

'As the prospective bride is thirty-eight, she seems tolerably balanced between the two of us. But not in reality. For no one would call you young for your age – you are quite ten years ahead of them. But I, alas, am at least twenty years older than my age, a crippled wreck whose only wish is to leave the world and become a monk.'

But he was still the reigning Emperor, and knew there could be no gainsaying his commands. He thrust out his underhung jaw, fringed with sparse grey beard like the stubble of dead gorse on a wintry cliff, as he passed sentence on his son. Philip stood condemned.

His indigestible veneration for his father rose in his throat. Not for the first time he was tempted to disgorge it. It had suffered a rude shock in his boyhood when he had learned that the Emperor had been defeated by the Moorish fleet at Algiers. The discovery that no man, not even his father, was almighty, remained a guilty secret within Philip's breast, to be shunned even in this moment when he longed to remind himself, yes, and his father of it; to tell him that his hero-worship had once been shaken; that his father's very presence acted as a dead weight, crushing, paralysing him; that though no man could want the adventure of going into a hostile, heretic and semi-barbarian land to marry a prim old maid nearly a dozen years older than himself, yet he could almost welcome it, since it would at least remove him from his father's influence.

Only once before had he left Spain, and that was to go into his father's country of Flanders, where that influence had been ten times stronger and more all-pervading than in Spain. For the Emperor had never ceased to be a foreigner in Spain, while in Flanders he was adored as a native hero, and what was more a good fellow of the first water, or rather vintage.

Philip's visit to Flanders had been a lamentable failure.

At least in England he would be free of that influence, though it did not make him the less indignant at being sent there. He bowed ceremoniously and said, 'As an entirely obedient son, I have no other will but yours, and therefore leave it to Your Majesty to act as you think best.' He added under his breath, 'Not my will but my father's.'

'Are you seeing yourself as Jesus Christ?' demanded Charles on a spurt of laughter that blew the leaf out of his mouth, and he had to replenish it with another from a bowl of water on the table. But he felt a trifle worried. His eyes, enlarged by the globular horn-rimmed spectacles, scrutinized the pale, stiff young man before him as though he were part of the mechanism of his clocks. There could be nothing wrong with the mechanism. The Spaniards, a race as stubborn and untameable as their cruelly barren land, were taking him to their hearts ('if they have any,' he snorted) as they had never taken himself. Yet, unlike so many heirs to the throne, Philip never attempted to set himself up in rivalry to his father, he was indeed entirely devoted to him and did everything his father told him. Not too good a boy either; even at fourteen he had needed watching with the women, aha! and the sly young dog had shown his sensuality by coupling his demands for Titian's religious pictures with discreetly worded requests for 'poesies,' as he called the Master's voluptuous paintings of naked females with respectably mythological names. And now as a young man, for all his public decorum, he took his private pleasures, but perhaps too private; he could never really lose himself in a debauch, and that was partly why he had been so unpopular in Flanders; the old Fleming his father found in this a trace of satisfaction. He had to bear the weight of the world, but he had not let it cramp him unduly; he had taken his pleasures with Flemish grossness and fairly openly, though not flagrantly; but Philip with all his appetites had no gusto, perhaps not much guts. He had won a prize in the tourneys in Flanders, but it was his affectionate aunts who had been the judges. He certainly did not care for war and fighting, though he had his own sort of courage; put him to the tortures of the damned and it would be his pride to pretend he felt nothing. He could stand anything; but would he move? A rock could stand; but the ruler of the world had to be a deal more than a still, carved face in a marble block. There was after all something wrong with this boy; he had never been one.

And into his mind, as though it had passed there from Philip's, there flashed the unwilling memory of his crushing defeat at Algiers, and the stilted dispassionate letter of condolence that his son of fourteen had written to him. He had hoped that damned dull tutor had dictated it, but no, the construction was too bad; it was clearly Philip's work, and clear proof he never was a boy. He shook off the memory, which often before he had shared with his son; though neither of them had ever spoken of it. It gave an edge to his annoyance with Philip for so obviously being about to do what he was told, and think himself a martyr for it. It was unfortunate that others thought the same; the Bishop of Pampeluna had actually compared him to Isaac, sacrificed by his father Abraham. That must have pleased Philip. It was time he learned how lucky he was.

The shrewd screwed-up eyes peered over their spectacles. The green tongue shot out to strike again. 'Fortune is a strumpet,' he chuckled; 'she keeps her favours for the young.'

'Mary Tudor is the last gift one would expect from a strumpet,' came in slow answer as the young man turned from his father; in no impatient movement, for it was his pride to be patient, but with the deliberate determination of acceptance.

Something deeply, sluggishly inert in his nature welcomed the chance to be heroic through acceptance rather than action, suffering rather than adventure.

Heroically he turned again and strode back towards the table, kicking shreds and snippets of stuff shed by the tailors out of his way, as if to spurn the pleasures he was leaving of his life in Spain. Bare and bright the sunlit scene rose outside the window; a lizard flashed emerald across the white wall of the courtyard below, and some young men riding past on their way to the tiltyards were singing an old song of how they had returned from hunting to find their vineyard stripped by the Moors, and there would be no wine for them. Seven centuries of Spain lay in that song, but to Philip it was too familiar for him to have noticed before; only now, as he heard it jigging away into the distance, he thought that he would not hear it in England.

The Emperor divined the self-pity in his gaze and remarked in affectionate exasperation, 'Take another text to yourself for comfort; it is your father's good pleasure to give you the kingdom.'

'A kingdom whose people rose in arms to prevent my coming! A kingdom whose angry Parliament refuses me even the title of King, and has shorn away every vestige of power from my position as the Queen's Consort.'

'You'll get it back in the night-time,' Charles told him with cheerful ribaldry. 'What more powerful position could you hold than that? A young man in bed with an old maid must be a boor or impotent if he fails to get all he wants from her. You are neither. Win her to you, and she'll do her best to get her councillors to give you all we want. Kings don't count for much now in England. Henry VIII did, but he was a giant, and even he was careful to keep on the right side of the people. But now it's the councillors who rule the country – and rule the Queen too. You'll have to win *them* over – not so easy.' He pushed his horn-rimmed spectacles up high on his wrinkled forehead and leaned back in his chair, talking with greedy enjoyment, lisping sometimes and mumbling often, almost inaudibly, yet greedily savouring his own sound advice, blinking in amused memory of the little scenes it called up of that strange, that incredible country that he had once visited for a fortnight when he was a youth.

'Drink English beer, and praise it. It's bitter, but better than their wine, since Henry sold the monasteries and lost their vineyards. Talk to people as human beings, not as abstractions. Look them in the face, don't squint sideways at their boots, it makes them think you've something to conceal, and so you have, your shyness, but they'll never guess that. So look straight at their eyes. Smile, and when any Englishman tells a story, laugh. It's always meant to be funny. But be serious when you talk of sport. Don't forget Henry was the best shot of his day, and I'm told they still speak wistfully of their bluff King Hal; he might chop off your head, but was equally likely to clap you on the back and call you a useful fellow with the longbow or the tennis racket. Make love to the women with discretion. The English do not make kind cuckolds.

'And don't let our women go with their husbands. They'll

make more mischief than any soldiers. Send them home, send them to Flanders, send them to hell. But don't, as you value your peace, your hoped-for crown, your very life, don't let them meet the Englishwomen!

'If you do all this cleverly, you'll be crowned King in Westminster Abbey in three months and, what's far more important, you'll be shipping English troops to Flanders to fight with us against the French.'

At last Philip had a chance to speak.

'England should do so for her own sake. France will invade her from Scotland as soon as the Dauphin is old enough to marry the little Queen of Scots.'

'That confounded brat!' exploded Charles, spitting yet another leaf across the table. 'King Henry swore when she was a baby in arms that she was the most dangerous person in Europe. And here she is just ten years old and the King of France vowing to support her claim to the English throne and so unite it to the French!'

'Queen of Scotland, England, France,' murmured Philip. 'A combination strong enough to overbalance Spain.'

'If it happened – but it won't. We'll break it, for we'll be in first with England. That wretched little northerly island muffled in her sea-fogs right away from Europe, she's always been able to tip over the balance here. All my life and my father's, we have had to woo England. They say we Hapsburgs do not need to fight – we marry instead. And we married England long before you were born, when my poor aunt, Katherine of Aragon, wedded King Henry VIII and then could only succeed in rearing Mary Tudor. It was her one *faux pas* and she paid for it, but look how we've all paid for it! That florid, exorbitant, terrible fellow, Henry, upset everything, divorcing Katherine and bringing the Reformation into England unawares – brought it in like an imp in a bottle to work his divorce and re-marriage. But it wouldn't go back into the bottle, it rose and swelled into a gigantic genie, beyond his control.

'But now, in you, Spain has her best chance to win a real grip on England.'

'No better chance,' said Philip deliberately, and looking his father in the eyes as he had been told to do, 'than when Your Majesty was betrothed to Mary Tudor.'

The Emperor looked back at his son in irritation. It was more than tactless to remind him that he also had had the opportunity to knit the two countries together, when as a youth he had been betrothed to Mary Tudor, a little girl with long fair hair of which her father had been inordinately proud.

It had been a brief settlement, almost momentary; and the moment had passed, the betrothal had been cancelled, and the two countries had floated apart like ships that passed in the night.

'Leave it,' said the old man tersely. 'You'll never make me twenty again.'

'Nor Mary five. But,' said Philip chivalrously, 'I will undertake my poor, deserted aunt.'

His father floundered. Humour from Philip was apt to be unexpected, it threw you off your balance. Charles talked on in his rapid guttural, trying to recover it. 'What's that, you jackanapes? Your aunt? Drop it, you puppy. She's not your aunt, though her mother was mine. But Henry could never bear me to call him "Uncle", – I had to change it to "Brother". So be careful. You've offended her enough already, never writing to her until at last the poor woman had to do it first. What woman can bear that? Having to write the first letter, send the first portrait. And now you're putting off going to England again and again though I told you weeks ago that you'd damage your prestige if you dilly-dallied.'

He stared, startled. For the first time in their lives he had caught sight of a cold gleam of anger in the eyes that he had ordered to look into his; they were so looking, and the Emperor rather wished they were not doing so. For the first time it struck him that perhaps he did not know altogether what this self-contained young man was like, or might become.

'I am going,' said Philip, 'to fulfil your obligation, your father's, and your grandfather's. I am the fourth generation to woo an English alliance. To do so, I am abandoning not only my pleasure in my faithful mistress of many years' standing, but my duty towards my all but affianced bride. We have already settled a large dowry on the Princess of Portugal which will also have to be abandoned, as a bribe to buy her off, and is therefore a dead loss. My own loss will be a wife near me in blood and talking my language, sharing my way of thought, in order to go to a strange country that is seething with hate of Spain, religion and civilization, and marry an old maid with whom I cannot exchange a word, except in languages foreign to us both. I grant you that my future wife has shown consideration for me in begging me to bring my own cooks and physicians. But it is an uncomfortable hint at the likely danger of poison. I see no occasion for reproach.'

The Emperor decided to change the subject rapidly, and introduce the stimulus of a mild flick of jealousy. Philip had frequently shown an inclination to covet something only when someone else wanted it or was likely to acquire it.

Eyeing his son astutely, he told him, 'Well, if you wait much longer, the English Cardinal, that fellow Reginald Pole, will get there first. I have had the devil of a time holding him back as it is. Take care he doesn't cut you out. Ha ha! He's as much of an old maid as she is, and two of a feather might get together. They've done so already in letters, and *he* doesn't wait for her to write first. Their mothers planned their marriage at one time – Lord, what mothers won't do!'

'Sir, he's a Cardinal—'

'He's a Plantagenet. He's a better right to the English throne than she has. That's why all his family were executed by Henry nearly twenty years ago. What's that – a Cardinal? That's nothing. He could get dispensation, he's never taken priest's orders. But in any case he'll be even more dangerous as her Father-in-God than as her husband, stirring up the Devil's own mischief through pure religion.'

'*Pure* religion? Does that mean he's tainted with reform?'

'Oh no, he's right as rain,' his father assured him testily. 'You'll never find *him* charged with heresy. My fears are all the other way, that he'll be too rigid. I don't trust him, he's too sincere.'

Philip understood this surprising statement very well. 'You think he'll want the English nobles to give back their Church property?'

'Exactly. As if the greedy robbers would give up their spoils after near a score of years! The Queen hopes for it, of course, she's a woman. But he's a Churchman and ought to understand. No, he mustn't set foot in England till he brings firm assurance from Rome that it's the right of every

Englishman to keep what he has stolen. The Pope understands that. But the Pope's not Pole.'

'Nor a Plantagenet.'

'The plant of the Devil! Spiritual pride, beware it. But allied with family pride, beware it doubly. Especially in England.'

'Even with the Tudors?' There was more than a shade of contempt in Philip's tone.

'Especially with the Tudors. They've no shadow of right to the throne – except that their grandfather killed the Plantagenet Richard III and picked his crown out of a thornbush. That makes 'em prickly.'

'Is this Plantagenet, Pole, ambitious?'

'No, oh no, I wish he were. He'd be safer if one could buy him off. No, he's a nice fellow, a good fellow, but he *will* talk Christianity. He's even done it to the Pope. He'll do it –' the Emperor's wheezy laughter choked him for a moment – 'to the English Bishops! Imagine what trouble *that* will lead him into!"

'I can imagine it very clearly,' said Philip grimly.

'Yes, the English clergy are in a ticklish position, both religious and matrimonial. They've changed themselves three times over in the last half-dozen years. First, Catholic though not Roman in the last years of my Uncle Henry, and all the clergy celibate, not a wife for any one of 'em, not even for his precious Archbishop Cranmer, who helped him to divorce my Aunt Katherine and marry Ann Bullen and then helped him to un-marry and behead her – but, oh no, never a wife for his useful dog Cranmer, though he'd smuggled one over from Germany in a box, they say. Well, there they are, all of 'em as good as gold and celibate as bullocks, and then under little Edward they all turn black Protestant and rush into matrimony like the rats of Norway that fling themselves in droves into the sea and get drowned. That's England all over – no restraint. One day, no parson's wives, only an occasional modest mistress tucked away decently in the pantry, all very right and proper, and on the morrow the whole country swarms with parsons' wives, pert and prim, fat and slim, messing up their husband's work, meddling with the parish, setting it all by the ears, and then in a few months it's crawling with parsons' brats and the next year double the number. King Henry always said the reason against the clergy marrying was that they'd breed like rabbits, and so they did, right on until last summer, when the poor boy Edward dies, Mary becomes Queen, and hey presto all the wives have gone to earth with their litters, and once again the clergy is celibate, Catholic, and Roman too this time. All this talk has made my throat as dry as the Sierra,' he suddenly accused his son. 'Where's the sherry?'

He reached for the flagon. 'Ah that's better. Sherry – "Caesaris – the wine of Caesar!" Well what's good enough for Julius Caesar is good enough for me. And now for God's sake let me go to dinner. The pleasures of love, especially in holy wedlock, are apt to be grossly over-rated, but it is impossible to exaggerate the pleasures of the table.'

The grandees of Spain entered and hauled him out of his chair, supported his crippled feet, all but carried his painful tottering frame to dinner. He sat and crammed his mouth and belly with food, poured rivers of the wine of Cadiz and the Rhine down his wry neck, and rolled his parched tongue against his palate to let the heady coolness linger on it as long as possible. The sound of his steady chumping was interspersed with the occasional gulp of a belch, but there was none of his ambling mumbling lisping talk, for his mouth was far too fully occupied. To Charles one thing at a time.

His appetites were huge, and even now in his sick old age his digestion almost matched them. He had always found gluttony the safest vice. Vast meals appeased the craving of his senses, made him satisfied, satiated, stupefied, able to relinquish slightly the clutch of his conscious mind on the problems that beset the master of the world – a world shattered and disordered, with the old order crumbling into decay.

But here on the table was order still, unquestioned, established, sacred, each course following the other in harmony unalterable as the stars in their courses; the beef after the broth, the coney and capon after the carp, the swan after the stork, the peacock after the partridge, the venison after the veal, the perfect progress of one savoury flavour after another leading up to the voluptuous chorus of crowded sweets, grapes and apricots and peaches in tarts and fritters and garnished custards, hypocras and cream of almonds, translucent jellies quivering in the towering shapes of the gods on Mount Olympus, treading on rosy clouds with sugared violets in their saffron-shredded hair.

There he sat cloying his palate, cramming his appetite, mercifully dulling his senses, releasing him from his long, taut task of living.

Was life then but a craving to find death? But he had no need to ask it, knowing the answer lay in his longing to lay down his crown, to leave this vast glittering hall and its crowds of nobles, superb yet subservient, who handed him each fresh dish on bended knee; and to put on the single coarse robe of a monk in the monastery of Yuste, sleep in a bare cell, and never come out into the world again.

Even an Emperor must think of his soul sometimes, he had said; but it was not true, it was not possible, it was not even right, while on the business of being an Emperor. One thing at a time. Statecraft must come before soulcraft, Machiavelli had put it down in black and white, but all sound statesmen had known and acted on it long before. He had kept his word and spared Luther's life – and look what had come of it!

What if, in sparing Luther, he had launched the world in revolution for centuries to come?

He had done it for reasons of State; but he would have felt far more guilty if he had done it just because it was the right thing for him to do. The State must come before the individual soul.

Yet Christ had shown that the individual soul mattered above all else. So how could one be a Christian and a statesman – let alone an Emperor?

One could not, that was the answer; and he had only a little time left to make his soul before he died. He would pray continually, have masses said for him unceasingly, he would do penance, fast – the heaped dishes swam before his blurred eyes, and his sated yet insatiable appetite made an agonized protest against that latest resolve. But would his state of health permit it? Surely his Confessor would feel bound to grant him a dispensation from fast-days. And a serpent whispered in his mind, 'Yes, surely the Emperor's confessor –'

He drowned the whisper in yet another enormous tankard, now of golden Rhenish wine from his Fatherland. A fig for Julius Caesar and his colony of Spain – this was better than all the wines from Cadiz and Jerez! But in that instant's clarity that comes before intoxication, another doubt floated to the surface of his clogged and wearied mind. How was it that in this, their final private interview, he had forgotten to impress on his son, more urgently than ever before, that the chief danger awaiting him in England lay in that enigmatic young woman, not yet twenty-one, the focus if not indeed the cause of the revolution this past spring in England, the half-sister of Philip's bride-to-be, King Henry's red-headed bastard by Ann Bullen (and as much a bitch, he'd swear, as her mother), the Lady Elizabeth Tudor?

CHAPTER TWO

Prince Philip rode out across the sun-dazzled square at Valladolid in his armour of new clothes; crimson velvet, silver lace fringe were all to the taste of the gaudy English. His escort of a thousand horsemen glittered around him, his bodyguard of three hundred in the red and yellow livery of Aragon, with his Teuton Guard close behind, and the highest grandees of Spain, each followed by his retinue. Chief among them, at the Prince's right hand, rode the Duke of Alva at the head of a troop so perfectly disciplined that even Philip tautened his already rigid bearing under the eagle eye of the greatest soldier of his day. Alva was silent, austere, yet magnetic; men and even fate seemed compelled to obey that narrow face and the portentously lengthy prong of his greying beard. Charles had warned his son against his hero-worship of the great General; Alva, he said, was a greybeard from birth; there was too much caution in his courage, and no panache; worse, he needed watching, he was secretly ambitious, a sanctimonious hypocrite who looked like a prophet but didn't lose sight of the profit.

Philip was well used to disillusionment; his father had warned him against all his advisers, even his only real friend, the Portuguese Ruy Gomez da Silva, whose smooth dark profile was now jogging along on his left side. Ruy had been

Philip's unofficial guardian since his childhood, for he was ten years older. He had lately been made Secretary of State and promised the title of Prince of Eboli because the Emperor, though he would not go so far as to trust him, or anyone else, declared that he was at least a foreigner and therefore cleverer than any Spaniard could be. He was even clever enough to be no taller than his young Prince.

They rode out of the capital of Old Castile, past the stone gateway of San Gregorio's College for poor friars, founded by Philip's great-grandmother, whose royal arms were encrusted among its fantastic carving. A less happy reminder of Isabella the Catholic was the end of the little mean street where her devoted servant, Christopher Columbus, having brought to her country a new Empire of fabulous wealth, had died in miserable poverty less than fifty years ago.

Both places were too familiar for Philip to notice, except to wonder when he would see these landmarks of his birthplace again. He rode on towards Tordesillas and Benevente, making a detour down the frontier of Portugal to pay a parting visit to his grandmother. This was the way he would have ridden to meet the Princess of Portugal if only he had succeeded in remaining betrothed to her.

And this was the way he had ridden ten years ago when he was sixteen, towards another Princess of Portugal, Dona Maria Manoela, his first wife, a year younger than himself. Then, as now, he had set out from Valladolid, but not as now through the roar of cheering crowds and the choking white dust raised by a thousand horsemen; and then, but not as now, he had been on fire with curiosity to look on the unknown face of his bride.

It had been autumn on that earlier journey, and the peasants, trampling the grapes in the vintage tubs, their bare legs purple to the knee with the juice, had scarcely turned their heads to look at the little company of travellers with the slight fair boy in their midst, dressed so inconspicuously in a plain hunting-suit. For Philip had then ridden incognito, accompanied only by Ruy Gomez da Silva and a few of his servants. Etiquette forbade his meeting Dona Manoela while on her bridal journey to him, so he went secretly and in disguise to follow her sumptuous procession all the way into his country.

That earlier journey seemed more real than the one he was riding now. He could never smell roses, nor for that matter the whiff of sweat and garlic from a shouting crowd of peasants – as he was smelling it now, mechanically lowering his head from time to time in answer to the cheering – without remembering how he had gone down into the thick of just such a crowd as this and let himself be jostled and his nose and ears affronted no less than his dignity, while he hung about with a suffocating gauze mask over his face, and his feet in the dirt of the Badajoz streets, to catch the first sight of his future wife. He had waited a full hour before there appeared at a window high above him in the deep blue night a slight figure in a silver dress like the slip of the new moon. It had only been for an instant before she vanished, but it had been enough to make him continue to follow her, still in these uncomfortable and undignified conditions; until at last at Salamanca, among a host of grave old people, she stood before him face to face, with pink autumn roses in her hands, and the delicate eyebrows in her round baby face arching high at her first sight of him.

They joined hands and danced; they kissed and came together; for a little time, a year and a little more, the world was their playground and they the only people in it. Suddenly the idyll was over; she lay dead; and he had the rest of his life to remember the curve of her plump cheek, the pout of her lips, like a rosebud opening in the sun. Had she ever known how much he loved her? She could not have done so, for he had been too young to show it, she to know it.

Her childish ghost laughed and chattered in his heart as he rode on to Tordesillas, to meet a living lady who had been a ghost for nearly fifty years. His father's mother, Dona Juana of Castile, was still the nominal Sovereign of Spain, though her wits had fled from her half a century ago, distracted by grief for her handsome faithless husband, Philip of Hapsburg. When at last his death killed her jealousy – of his women, of his boon companions in hunting and drinking, even of his dogs – he had left her with but one clear purpose in her frantic mind, to keep his body in her constant sight. She had borne it embalmed in a coffin over the mountains, travelling only by night for four months, until at last at Tordesillas it found rest in Christian burial. But she never found rest.

She stared through her straggling hair at the fair young man, who flinched under the terrible intent gaze of the crone who had once been the most beautiful of the daughters of Ferdinand and Isabella.

'Who is this young man? Prince Philip, you say? Ah, I remember, he was christened after my husband, but he's not grown into as big and fine a man as Philippe le Bel of Burgundy. You came here lately with your bride, my granddaughter, a sweet child, such a silly mouth. She will grow as plump as a partridge. Where is she now?'

'Madam, she died nine years ago. I am going now to wed another bride.'

'Oh, then you *are* like my Philip. But like all other men too. No man can be faithful, to the living or the dead. You danced with her before me. It was a pretty sight. You are a good dancer. So now she lies still, and you are going to dance with another. Dance, dance, my pretty young man. But one day you will lie still too.'

'Madam, I know it. I think often of death.'

'Then you are a fool. Death is not for you – yet. You will cause many deaths before you come to it; the deaths of those you love and who love you.'

'Of those you love.' His father had warned him that at his early age he must for his health's sake moderate his passion for his bride; he had not done so, and the result had been, not his ill health, but her death in childbed.

He had no need to hide his emotion. His Stoic role would mean nothing in those clouded eyes that saw only what lay beneath. He choked back his pride and said, 'Madam, I am your grandson. I am heir to my father's throne and yours. I shall rule over more dominions than any single man has governed since Charlemagne. I pray you, Madam my grandmother, do not lay a curse on me.'

She laughed, a harsh and desolate sound. 'Who spoke of curses? I speak only what I see. I see a pretty young man who thinks of death.'

Her mind seemed to clear suddenly for a space. She understood that he was going to England to marry the Queen, she even recollected that Mary was the daughter of her youngest sister Katherine of Aragon, who, poor child, had had to be despatched to that remote island in the Northern seas. And Juana herself with her husband had once visited it when they were sailing from Zeeland to Spain, though only because the frightful gales of mid-winter had driven their ship on to its shores.

People said it was that storm, raging and bellowing for two whole days and nights, that had wrecked Juana's wits. But at the time she had been the only calm person on board; indeed, as she crouched, clasping her husband's knees, her wild eyes had shone on his face in peace and joy that so soon the black waters would swallow them and they would go to death together for always.

But the sea had cheated her. The sea had brought them to England and into a forced alliance with that country and its first Tudor sovereign, the cunning upstart adventurer, Henry VIII's father, who had tricked Juana's husband and dared woo Juana when he was dead.

'Those slant-eyed Tudors,' she murmured to her grandson, 'they are not strong, but they make themselves so by guile. Watch them as you would watch the smiling beguiling sea, the cruel treacherous sea. Be careful of the seas round England. They are her strongest allies. But most of all beware of love, which is fiercer than the winds, more cruel than the waves. Love and hate are only the two sides of the same coin, and the coin rings false. All your life, hate will smoulder and whisper its dark way through your love.'

She was a witch, everyone said so, Philip reminded himself as he stumbled out into the sunlight and the glad company of a thousand men. Only her blood and her position, the highest in the land, the Queen of this land, had saved her all these years from being burnt as a witch by the Inquisition. For that Holy Office had first been instituted against the crime of witchcraft, and only later worked against heresy, which at this moment, by comparison, seemed an almost venial sin.

He stood still a moment by a fountain that splashed its cool drops on his hands, and smoothed out his face into the blank mask of icy decorum necessary to a Spanish Prince. A birdlike glance from Ruy Gomez's black eyes did not see that there had been anything disturbing in the interview.

They rode on to Benevente, where his son Don Carlos met him to say goodbye, a boy of nine, excitable and nervous, with a big head and rather humped back and sad eager eyes, who was apt to make Philip depressed and uneasy. Dona Manoela had been Philip's first cousin twice over by both parents, almost as near in blood as if she were his sister; medical critics had considered the marriage not only premature but unhealthy. Philip glanced in furtive anxiety at the queer little boy who had caused the death of his mother; one shoulder was a little higher, one leg a little longer than the other, and his spurts of courage and initiative, of kindness and even of precocious intelligence often seemed uncoordinated, out of focus. That might be natural at his age; so might be his frantic rages and savage impulses of childish nastiness or cruelty.

Philip reminded himself that the Emperor liked the lad and thought he often showed promise of a bright and original wit. But surely Carlos should already be thinking of himself as a man, instead of calling himself 'the little one' in a way any ordinary boy would despise as babyish. Flashes of eccentric cleverness might please an old man who was himself apt to be eccentric, and could afford to be so since he was exceptional, but they didn't clear Philip's mind of the suspicion that in general Carlos was backward. How would he shape when he had to take his place in his turn as master of the world?

Carlos himself had no doubts on the matter; he told Philip

various plans of what he should do when he became 'Imperator Mundi', and then, ingenuously, 'But it's Your Highness who'll be that when my grandfather dies. Perhaps I could go out to the New World and be Emperor of the West instead. I should like to see Red Indians.'

'I shall die, too, some day,' said Philip.

'Then I'll be Emperor of both worlds,' said Carlos, and added with a friendly goblin grin, 'but I hope you will not die yet.'

Yes, there was good in the boy, he had affectionate though childish impulses. He cried that he could not go to England with his father, which was unreasonable; he laughed with delight in the pageants given in his father's honour, the flaming torches leaping against the night; he shrieked at the fireworks and the towering elephants made of painted cardboard, moved by men on horseback inside them. Most of the adults were equally childish; the chroniclers exhausted their adjectives in describing these gorgeous marvels and scarcely noticed a first performance of a first play with comic interludes by a young writer called Lope de Rueda. Philip yawned at the arguments of shepherds and shepherdesses interrupted by a Ruffian, a Fool and a Negress; he listened doubtfully when Ruy Gomez declared this to be a new form of art in which Spain might lead the world; there could not, he thought, be art in crude native forms like plays, written to amuse a mixed crowd mostly of simple folk. He preferred the bull fights, scarlet and black and gold scintillating in the white June dust, but he did not like his 'little one's' unrestrained yelps of joy every time a horse was gored or a man stood within an inch of death.

He embraced the boy goodbye, repressing his instinctive

distaste in having to do so, and thankful that there was no further member of his uncomfortable family for him to see.

His son was an oddity who might become a monstrosity; his father was a hero, but extraordinary; his father's mother was mad. Philip's craving to prove himself ordinary, the only entirely rational and balanced member of his family, had been shown by his choice of his mistress, Dona Isobel de Osorio, when he was only fifteen. By now she had provided him with five children and the settled, rather stuffy peace of an affectionate but unemotional matrimonial household of many years' standing. Dona Isobel always spoke of their union as marriage in the eyes of God, which to Philip were not equal to those of the law; to her friends it was more like their silver wedding, and as middle-class as it was middle-aged. There had never been anything in it of the passion he had felt in his legal marriage to Dona Manoela.

He rode on towards his next marriage, attended rich banquets, listened to long speeches, watched stately processions in the dark churches that opened like tombs out of the white heat. At the holy city of Santiago he met the English Ambassadors. They struck the critical Spaniards as being gentlemen, or at any rate the Earl of Bedford did, though they wore far too many fancy buttons, and in the Earl of Bedford's case every one of them did its duty. Philip entrusted them with a million gold ducats without any sign of unease, though he knew it would cause another financial crisis in Spain. The Lords Bedford and Fitzwalter hastened to write a favourable report of his affable manners, and attended mass with him in the Cathedral, greatly, they declared, to their edification, and did not hear the Spaniards' comment that 'they need it badly enough.'

At last he reached Corunna, where a hundred ships awaited him, and six thousand soldiers who were to protect him against the French and go on to join the Emperor's forces in Flanders. Lancers from Guipuzcoa waved and tossed their lances in welcome to him so that the air seemed full of lightning, and the thunder of the drums rolled along the coast until it was drowned by salutes fired from the muskets and big guns, so loud and long that the chroniclers declared 'the human race has never witnessed such a discharge as this, nor ever will again.' His ship, *The Holy Ghost*, was covered with carved gold and crimson damask and heraldic pennons. Three hundred sailors clad in scarlet were to man this one vessel alone; they climbed the rigging and did acrobatic exercises there, three hundred monkeys in scarlet coats, to amuse him while he waited for a favourable breeze.

On Thursday evening the 12th of July the sea was like silk and the air held its breath, and the captains grumbled that they might be held up here for a month.

Philip walked on the shore with Ruy Gomez and discussed the news brought by a ship that had drifted into Corunna that day from England. Queen Mary was already waiting for him at Winchester, also with a thousand gentlemen, and what was more, with two thousand horses for the Spaniards – most unnecessary, complained Philip, when they were shipping all the horses they needed, but it was too late to alter it now. 'The English Master of Horse will probably lead them into his own stables,' was Ruy Gomez's unkind comment.

The Queen was evidently determined to make unheard-of preparations for her bridegroom. 'To make up, I suppose, for the only really important preparation which she should have made months ago.'

'And that is, Your Highness?'

'Why, to cut off the head of her young sister Elizabeth. Hasn't our Ambassador been urging our demand for this ever since the rising this spring to put her on the throne? And all Renard could do was to get Mary to put her in the Tower for a couple of months – and then let her out!'

'But she is under close guard at Woodstock – as safe as any prison.'

'And what prison would ever make her safe, as long as she is alive? Her red head is the potential head for all the rebels and heretics in the country. It should be lopped off.'

Ruy Gomez felt some alarm; his ten years' greater age and experience, a cool and balanced judgment, and moreover his birth and upbringing in a perfectly ordinary family, had made him apt to feel his young friend unpredictable. Certainly Philip was not prone to be rash or sudden in action, but who knew what he might be if he thought himself personally insulted? But he guessed hopefully that the Prince, alone with his friend as etiquette scarcely ever permitted him to be, was enjoying the rare luxury of letting go his temper. Philip was grumbling, quite naturally, that the English Queen could hardly blame him for not rushing to her with the haste of an ardent lover when she persisted in keeping alive 'that devil's brat to stir up rebellion against me.'

'It might have caused a worse rebellion to behead her,' Gomez said; 'Renard himself seems now to be coming round to that opinion. She has won over many of the people. And some of the nobles too, even old fogies who went to cross-examine her in the Tower, and instead fell head over heels in love with her.'

He watched the effect of this, hoping it would intrigue

Philip, sufficiently anyway to prevent him demanding as a wedding present the Princess's head on a plate immediately he landed in England. But Philip, kicking at a stranded jellyfish, which made a mess on his shoe, only snarled at the low tastes of the English who could set up as a heroine 'a wanton who was smirched in her early teens by her uncle.'

'Her step-uncle, Highness. And it is a moot point if the smirching were actual or only to her reputation. In either case it has rendered her as wary, subtle and alert as a rat that, having once escaped the trap, will know how to elude – or attack – any future adversaries.'

A contemptuous smile gleamed in the Prince's light grey eyes. 'And you think she may attempt to bite *me*?'

Ruy Gomez laughed outright. 'Is Your Highness too high to be bitten by a woman save in the way of kindness?'

Only Ruy could dare thus far, and Philip had always delighted in it when he chaffed him; but Ruy could never feel certain that it was still safe to do so. It added spice to his teasing; he glanced in some anxiety at his young friend's face – though he knew that if it had ceased to be safe, he would see nothing in that face to tell him so. But this time all was well, for Philip was laughing too.

'No, for I can see how dangerous she is, and indeed would be even if dead.' He remembered the little Queen of Scots, even as a baby 'the most dangerous person in Europe.' Elizabeth's death would make that child the future Queen of France, and also the unquestioned heir to England, until he could provide another.

It was a perverse fate for a young man, both susceptible and attractive in his fashion, that he had to marry an elderly virgin in order to strengthen his fight against two charming girls, one twenty years old, the other ten, rivals to each other, enemies to the might of Spain.

Thinking of those two who were his foes, and of the one who must be his ally, he murmured sadly, 'You at least are fortunate. You are wedded to a bride so young that the contract forbade consummation for two years, and now one of them has already passed.'

'Several more may do so before I get back from first England and then Flanders.'

'I hope your Anna will not have grown too tall for you,' said Philip with a spice of malice, but hastened to add with his accustomed courtesy, 'When I saw her at the wedding, I thought her very striking for her age, and', he added, again on the plaintive note, 'likely to become beautiful perhaps, in an unusual way.'

Ruy knew that Philip was most dangerous when he seemed most vulnerable. Self-pity and envy of another's more fortunate lot were the last things to be encouraged in him. He deliberately made his voice casual and dispassionate as he answered, 'She might have become so, Your Highness, if she were not also – well, as you have just said, "striking"! And literally. She has fought a duel with a page in her father's house "to defend the honour of Castile" against some silly jeer, and the boy by accident ran her through the eye. She will always now have to wear a black patch over it, which is naturally a great disfigurement.'

Philip was not deceived by his friend's apparent indifference. Other men he knew had already begun just lately to show themselves far from indifferent to the future Princess of Eboli, in spite of the black patch. Why had Ruy not told him of it before, he asked himself, but not aloud, and turned the question over suspiciously in his mind. What a termagant the girl must be! He felt amused at old Ruy, so placid and reasonable, hoping to tame her, and doubted that he had the necessary qualities. The corollary, of course, was that Philip might himself possess them. With that his discontent surged back over him; Ruy would mate with his tall dark spitfire, a young eagle, blinded though she was in one eye, while he himself must go and marry a poor old tame goose.

He fought down his envy. Ruy was his greatest friend. He would always do his best for him. He turned and smiled at his friend, who drew a deep breath but still felt a little cold as Philip spoke.

'You will conquer your duellist. But do not let her fight a duel with you. Next time it might be her husband who would become blind.'

They walked on along the shore, stepping carefully to avoid the pools of sea water turned to rosy flame in the sunset light. Ruy wished they had not spoken of Anna. He hastened to speak instead of Queen Mary, of her goodness of heart, her simplicity, which Renard had said made her seem much younger than her years. She was good to the poor – Philip yawned. She had been called Merciful Mary – Philip frowned. She had no right to be merciful to her enemies, and therefore his. And Ruy could tell no stories of her. As a young girl there had been wild romantic schemes to rescue her from her cruel father, to steal her away in a boat some moonless night. But she had only bungled it and stayed at home.

Next morning there was a slight wind from the south; the many-coloured ships weighed anchor and spread their towering sails to the breeze, careening before it, dipping and curtseying, as they bore Prince Philip out to sea, northwards to England, with the July sunlight sparkling on the waves.

But the sailors muttered that it was Friday the 13th.

And when they landed in England it was raining.

CHAPTER THREE

How it rained! It would never stop. It came sluicing down, not from clouds carved into torrential shapes that might break up into splinters to reveal an arrow's point of blue beyond the grey, but from a flat sheet of lead that could give no hope of change for the morrow. Their horses squelched and splashed through the mud, the rain stung his face, ran down the back of his neck, down his nose and legs, into his gloves, seeped through his clothes sewn with diamonds, even through the cloak of thick red felt provided to protect their splendour.

His father had been conquered by the sea. Was he to be conquered by the rain? He longed to admit defeat, to turn tail and ride back to Southampton and his ships, draw anchor and sail back towards the sun. But all he did was to stop at the ancient Hospital of St. Cross outside Winchester to be welcomed by kind old gentlemen in mulberry robes who helped him to change out of his black velvet and silver, now looking and feeling like a drowned rat's skin, and into black trimmed with gold, and under-garments of white and gold.

Almost at once they too were clinging damply to him as he rode on again in dismal state through the West Gate of Winchester, through obsequiously bowing and kneeling aldermen, and sulky townsfolk huddled together in suspicious silence and a smell of wet sheep, up to a small host of Bishops that towered like archangels in their mitres and spreading copes on the steps of the Cathedral, but kept as far back as they could in the shelter of the doorway. Not till he and his suite had attended the Cathedral service of rejoicing in his safe arrival, with a particularly long-drawn-out chant of the Te Deum, was Philip free to go on and lodge in the Dean's House, to peel off his wet clothes yet again, and warm his icy legs before a log fire (in July!), to dine comfortably at leisure and in privacy and then, just as he was going to bed about ten o'clock, be sent for to his first interview with his future bride. Her maiden status had to be protected by lodging across the way at the Bishop's Castle, so he was told to come 'secretly,' with only a very few of his gentlemen in attendance. They looked at him in some anxiety, but he gave no sign that his composure was in the smallest degree ruffled by having to dress all over again and sally forth once more into the night, this time on foot.

He put on silver and gold embroidery and the white kid trunks he had tried on before his father – how little the Emperor knew what he was now going through on his behalf! With his chosen grandees he went out into the thick darkness and the Bishop's garden, the torches sputtering ahead of them, their beautifully shod feet slopping through the mud, and the trees dripping down on their heads in the long tunnels of the pleached alleys, the wet leaves shuddering and whispering as they brushed them; until they saw the gleam of lighted windows on the black waters of the moat and went round it to a little back door, up a private stair. It led straight into the Queen's private apartment, or rather a long gallery where several people were standing, and one small figure was moving restlessly up and down, jewels glittering at every turn.

As the door opened she came quickly towards it, hardly giving time to the two torch-bearers who had to precede her. She kissed her hand in the odd English fashion before she held it out to Philip and he, remembering his instructions in another still odder English fashion, kissed her on her lips; dry, rather hard, they met his uncertainly, eagerly. There were no men in England of sufficient rank for her to give even the formal kiss; of any other she had evidently no experience. She was shy and timid as a young girl, and in her heart that was what she was; but he saw a middle-aged woman, whose intent gaze was appealing to him, not as her political ally and partner, but as her sovereign and lover.

He had come, not to a wedding feast but to a fight. But the Queen had come, not to an arranged alliance, but to a love affair. 'These Tudors!' he thought, would nothing, not even a mixture of Spanish blood, teach them manners? Mary's mother had been Katherine of Aragon, of the bluest blood of Spain. But her father had been Harry Tudor, from a line of Welsh adventurers, who had rid himself of one wife after another in his sentimental lust to find himself perfectly married.

A damp chill crept into his heart as his bride's thin hand moved in his; was it holding his, clutching his, saying to his, 'Till death do us part'?

He tried to make his hand answer hers; 'Only remember your manners,' his limp touch told her. 'This is a marriage of convenience; it is bad manners to try and make it a romance; to tell me so plainly that you are a virtuous virgin starving for love; to remind me that I am young and you are old.'

But she was gallantly recovering from her embarrassment;

she became gracious, cordial to his suite, even gay; he noticed that her skin was fair and very clear. Her rather thin hair had lights in it like a sandy kitten's where it had not gone grey. She must have been very pretty, even piquante.

But her little round face and pointed chin which had for so long kept their youthful shape in solitary retirement, as the faces of nuns stay young because there is no worldly stress to make them old, had been suddenly drawn into hollows and sagging folds in this last half year of agonizing action and suspense. Her ungrateful country had rebelled against her marriage to this young man and so had delayed his coming month after month, tearing her empty heart in pieces; and some thought he would never come at all.

And now he was here beside her, he was holding her hand, speaking grave, slow, often incomprehensible courtesies (she had not expected him to speak English, but why should his French be so bad?) – but he had come, he had come at last, the miracle had happened, and she could not be so much older than she had been last August, not as much as a year ago (already she was forgetting what had happened in that year) when she had ridden to London to be Queen, triumphant over all her enemies, and dear Jane Dormer had said she looked as though she were in her twenties. Yes, and even the playwright John Heywood, who had not seen her since her eighteenth birthday, said she had not changed a jot from then, when he had written a birthday ode to her 'lively face' that was like a 'lamp of joy'. If it had been so then, how much more reason had it to be so now!

And so it was. But it was a lamp that gave no spark to her bridegroom's feelings. With a disapproving mind and sinking heart, Philip watched his bride falling in love with him; and knew that others were watching it. As his grandees were presented to her and kneeled to kiss her hand, he could hear all the things they did not say, would not say till afterwards when he was out of hearing.

'The Queen is a saint, a dear, a really nice little woman; she dresses very badly.'

'The Queen is elderly and has no eyebrows.'

'The Queen already begins to make love to her young bridegroom.'

As for the English, the Lord Admiral Howard was already playing the bluff sailor, making jokes that Philip could not understand, but he could see all the English understanding them and laughing, the men boisterously, the women (only a few, and so old – why were they all so old?) shyly and titteringly; he could guess the gist of them and did not care for it.

He suggested that as his gentlemen had been presented to the Queen, he should now be presented to the rest of her ladies who were in the apartment adjoining the gallery. Mary agreed, not very brightly, and was determined to accompany him. They went in together, a resolute little pair, and there were all the English ladies, some of them far too tall, and all showing too much leg, some in black stockings, as they curtseyed. Two by two, they were led forward to him. He stood there cap in hand, and kissed each on the lips as she passed, 'in order', it was translated, 'not to violate the custom of the country.' And in most cases it brought him no better satisfaction than that, but not in all; and to Mary no satisfaction at all.

So when the ceremony was over and he had pointed out to her in his careful halting French that it was getting very late and high time they should both go to bed and get a good night's rest before their public meeting and marriage tomorrow, she took him firmly by the hand and led him back to the gallery and the funny little canopy in front of all the candles (were they arranged so that he should not see her too clearly with her back to the light?) for another chat in her bad Spanish, in his bad English, in their bad French, about the weather, about his journey, about her little dog. But he thought of an unknown young woman of whom no one dared speak, though he suspected that many others were also thinking of her.

The most ominous factor in this official gathering was the absence of the Queen's sister and presumptive heir to the throne. Philip, not a fanciful man, felt that absent figure as an uneasy presence in the minds of all these English who smiled at him with large white teeth and watchful eyes; behind those eyes lurked the image of the Lady Elizabeth, whether as a sinister shadow or an anxiously concealed hope.

There was the Chancellor, old Bishop Gardiner, now installed again in his See of Winchester after years of prison under King Edward's Protestant régime; he had been demanding Elizabeth's death as furiously as one might guess from his fierce black eyebrows, but had now had to follow the Emperor's new policy of appeasement; Philip would like to know his true opinion of it.

Also that of the Lord Admiral Howard, who had had to take Elizabeth to the Tower only this spring, with an armed force, since she had refused to budge on pretext of illness; and they had taken a long time to get there, on the same pretext. What did Howard really think, or know, of his great-niece's probable part in Wyatt's rebellion? Had he secretly sympathized, wished for its success, and his great-niece on the throne? In any case Philip felt it would be pleasant to relieve the boredom, which ached in his every limb, by giving that jocose jackass a twinge of discomfort in his turn, and see how he would be able to hee-haw it off.

So in casual talk with him he asked after the health of Howard's great-niece; he had heard it had caused her, and him, some trouble. His polite inquiry was translated in a rather lower voice than the rest of the conversation, but it reached the Queen's ears and he saw her face pucker and turn pale. Lord Howard on the other hand went beetroot-coloured under his tan as he hastily assured the Prince that none of his family's health gave him any cause for anxiety. His evasion of Elizabeth's name was more significant than any mention of it; it was as though they were all afraid to call up a spirit by naming it.

'What sort of spirit?' he asked Renard in a low tone as they walked to a window to see if the rain were lessening, and his dapper Ambassador opened his mouth in a sudden round O, plucked nervously at his two little tufts of beard, and replied unexpectedly, 'A spirit full of enchantment.'

An alluring description! Yet Renard, too, had always urged her death. Was this intended as a warning? But he could not ask further. Mary wanted to know if he would like the window open, and indeed it was stiflingly airless and muggy, he put up a hand to his damp forehead and firmly held back his jaws from cracking open in a huge yawn.

At last he got away, but he had to learn to say 'Good-night, my lords and ladies' in English, and had to come back to her to learn the uncouth words over again before he could say them to the ladies in the next room, where the giggling was like a gaggle of geese, and some old lady called de Clarencieux thanked God that she had lived to see this day, though she wished she could have brought him a more beautiful wife; and the Queen herself, still more embarrassingly, expressed her gratitude to him for taking anyone so old and ugly.

No language could express his feelings, or evasion of feeling, after that; he said good-night and wished it were goodbye; he staggered out again into the dark and heard the drops pattering on the moat, and the chimes of the Cathedral clock strike midnight as he fumbled through the dripping vegetation; and fell on his bed while Ruy Gomez peeled off his gold-embroidered white kid trunks and praised Mary's fresh complexion and charmingly friendly manner, and then spoilt it when he tactlessly agreed that Mary seemed older than they had been informed, and brightly suggested that if dressed in Spanish fashions she might not look so old and flabby, or was she scraggy? But Philip was past caring. He fell down, down into blessed sleep and forgetfulness, down, down, down, till so late next morning that he was all but late for his wedding.

And then he had to get up and try on two more gorgeous suits sent him as a present from the Queen, one all white covered with pearl and gold and those everlasting diamond buttons, the other all crimson, both all wrong; and visit her publicly in the cruel grey English daylight in her white satin robe and scarlet shoes, still more wrong; with fifty ladies round her and not one of them pretty; and all the Ambassadors and Envoys Extraordinary to give their welcome.

But the one who was absent gave a greater triumph than any present; the French Ambassador, de Noailles, and his gleaming sardonic teeth in the midst of his black beard were not there to grin discomfiture on the proceeding; no, the discomfiture was that of de Noailles, who had never been invited, since Spain was at war with his country – 'and so will England be, as result of this marriage, in a matter of weeks, or at any rate months,' declared the more optimistic of the Spanish prophets and the more pessimistic of the English. And the French Ambassador had to remain at home, gloomily spewing out his ill-natured garbled accounts of the wedding at second-hand from all the anti-Spanish spies he could rake up, for his reports to his master King Henri II of France and his flat-faced Italian wife, Catherine de Medici, who was growing fatter and fatter and must be bursting like the frog in the fable with rage at this clever counter-stroke of Spain in marrying the English Mary, against their blow in betrothing the little Scottish Mary to their son the Dauphin of France. Now France's project to claim England through her was forestalled. Spain had taken over England first. That, to Philip, was the real significance of this tremendous ceremony in the ancient Cathedral of Winchester. 'Check to the King of France' was the whole point of this move, of his stately progress with Mary up the aisle in time to the sacred music. 'France has failed,' it pealed out in triumph in his ears, 'failed to annex England in the name of Mary Queen of Scots. But open your gates, ye everlasting doors, and the King of Glory shall come in. Who is the King of Glory? The Lord of Hosts, Philip of Spain, he is the King of Glory. He has annexed England for Spain and the Empire of the World.'

If Mary could actually bear him a son, that would set Heaven's final seal of approval on the match. But even if she did not, and were to die in childbed (she did not look at all strong, he considered, as they approached the altar), then he as her widower could still make a claim to this country. The Church would support it against the bastard Elizabeth. His bride must understand this sacred purport of their marriage.

Her dry little hand lay in his like a withered leaf, her thin lips moved in silent prayer, her short-sighted eyes, blank and blind in rapture, were fixed alternately upon the crucifix and on the plain gold ring on which she had insisted 'because maids were so married in old times.'

To her, the marriage had another purport. She heard the music throb, boys' voices soar in angelic ecstasy; Stephen Gardiner, her father's old friend, now again Lord Bishop of Winchester, rolled out the sonorous Latin phrases; the incense burners wafted their blue spiced clouds through the damp heavy air, little bells pricked it, tingling, and the congregation sank on their knees; the old times had come again and all the right and ancient ways of serving God through His one true Church and His Viceroy the Pope; all just as it had been in her father's day, when he had gone to mass with her mother, and herself as a little girl holding their hands; all just as it had been then, and was now so again, while she held the hand of a young man as fair as an angel, who was, unbelievably, her husband; all just as it would be now for ever in this happy land, freed by her at last from guilt, and grateful to her, for ever and ever.

There followed a feast where Philip wondered heavily if even his father's Gargantuan appetite could cope with half the dishes served him. The massive sideboard behind his head creaked under its weight of gold plate; a marble fountain on it whispered and tittered, and a clock more than half his size thumped its loud ticking into his ears. Incomprehensible voices shrilled higher, grew gruffer, all but shouted as the wine went round and round. Heralds blared a piercing blast on their long glittering trumpets and proclaimed him King of Naples. This was a happy surprise arranged by his father so that he should not be a mere Prince beside the Queen his wife; but even so he took a lower seat than she and was given only silver plate where she was served on gold, and he was careful to insist that none of his Spaniards should share the honour done to the four English lords who bore the canopy over their heads.

The Spaniards muttered that they might as well be turned out as vagabonds; at the dance that followed, they took their revenge by not giving the ladies any of the Spanish leather gloves that they had brought as presents for them, and by memorizing rude comments on their looks and clothes to write home. The ladies for their part held a poor opinion of the Spaniards' dancing.

The Spaniards consoled themselves next day by going sightseeing in Winchester, and the new King Philip took the chance to escape with them. They were impressed by King Arthur's Round Table with the names of all his knights inscribed on it, but thought it a pity that Henry VIII had had it new painted with a huge Tudor rose glaring aggressively out of its middle. And then one of their English guides, a lamentably would-be conscientious old man, thought he did remember his grandfather saying he did, that there great table there had been made for the old King Edward, and when asked indignantly which King Edward, he thought it might have been one King Edward or it might have been t'other, but no, it wasn't one of the last three King Edwards, so he figured that it rightly was Edward III. But in any case, if not the original, it had been made in *memory* of King Arthur's Round

Table, for King Edward always thought a deal of that King, he did.

'So did Queen Mary's grandfather, presumably,' said Philip drily, when Bishop Gardiner had translated this piece of local colour which he evidently considered comic. He did not at all like Philip's reminder that Henry VII had christened his eldest son Prince Arthur, a name never before chosen by an English King; for both knew it had only been chosen in order to bolster up the Tudors' legendary Celtic ancestry.

Prince Philip's lowered eyelids showed that he knew the Tudors to be past masters at such tricks; Bishop Gardiner's heightened eyebrows showed that he'd never liked this Spanish match and never would, but they'd all got to make do with it now. He did his best. He showed the gardens. The green lawns, the luxuriant masses of roses tumbling over the old walls were a wonderful sight, but one was apt to get a shower-bath in picking them.

'If these are the groves of Amadis,' said one of the disillusioned Dons, 'then give me the barest stubble-field in Toledo.'

CHAPTER FOUR

Mary would wake herself up when she lay dozing in the early morning to make sure that it was indeed true. She was no longer a lonely old maid; she was married, and to a Prince whose nature was as noble as his looks.

'It was no dream; I lay broad waking.'

Who had written that? But no, she would not remember, for it had been the poet Sir Thomas Wyatt, who had loved Ann Bullen, and whose son had risen against her this spring to prevent her marriage and put Ann's daughter on the throne. He had been beheaded, and his father's verse should lie buried and forgotten. But you can give no orders to poetry; the simple one-syllabled line paced slowly into her head and stood there looking at her in wide-eyed wonder like her own flower the Marygold, opening to the sun.

No, it was no dream. She convinced herself of it by writing to her father-in-law that she was 'happier than I can say' in the daily discovery of her husband's 'many virtues and perfections.' The Emperor remarked drily that Philip must have changed a good deal; but then, he chuckled, lovers made poor judges. Soon, however, he received from others almost equally glowing accounts of Philip's affable behaviour. The

English nobles declared 'they had never yet had a King in England who so soon won the hearts of all men.' Panegyric poems composed for London's welcome to him praised his 'grace of speech so frank' and declared England's 'chiefest joy is to hear thee, Philip, speak.' Only a poet could think of such inappropriate praise for one who was taciturn enough in his own language, and apt to go dumb in any other. But it did look as though he were putting a severe strain on himself, and his father hoped it wouldn't make him break out the more violently later.

Mary's tender conscience had been worried by Philip's broken betrothal to the Princess of Portugal, but now even that little wound was healed, for the Princess had been so very understanding and kind and had sent her a most handsome present of dresses, and head-gear a foot or two high in the Portuguese style (had Philip contrived to send a hint to his former bride-to-be of the unbecoming English fashions?) and Mary could not stop trying them on and gloating over them.

At last, after years of scrimping and saving on her meagre dress allowance so as to afford the presents she loved giving to her friends and their children, Mary had as many fine clothes as she could wish to wear; and it was not after all too late, for here was a handsome young husband for whose sake it was her bounden duty to make herself look also as handsome and young as possible. She was already looking younger, the hollows in her face filling out and its colour brighter; even the Cockney crowds noticed it, suspicious as they were of the Spaniards (but there were only a few in the procession, Philip saw to that) when she brought him in triumph to London.

Why shouldn't she have a husband, poor woman, the same

as other folk? It was high time she got a fine young man, so they decided in the benevolent haze induced by the fountains running with red wine, and free banquets set out on trestle tables in front of the wealthier houses as soon as the procession had gone by. They danced in the street to music of their own making on lutes and rebecks, the butcher and baker and candlestick-maker and their wives and children all hopping and shouting and screaming with laughter as they joined hands and dragged each other round and round in a ring, and even the Oldest Inhabitant in Cheapside sitting on a stool and banging time with his stick.

No wonder that for the moment they could speak kindly of Philip and even say that you might take him for an Englishman as he was so fair; but then wasn't his father a Fleming like those big fair weavers from Flanders that had settled in England? This young fellow wasn't near their measure; but as pretty as a picture, a proper Prince in white and gold on his white horse.

And a good sportsman, so they said; had been hunting at Windsor where he'd been made a Knight of the Garter, and he had ridden in a tourney, though the Frenchmen did say (but they *would*!) that they had never seen worse lance-play than his. In any case he had given them all good sport with these shows and pageants and above all the cartloads of American gold, solid ingots from Peru, so heavy that it took near a hundred horses to draw them trundling along on their way to the treasure chests of the Tower.

The shrivelled human heads of Wyatt and his rebels stuck on spikes at the Tower and on the Bridge had all been taken down, also the corpses that ever since the spring had hung dangling on gallows at street corners; another sort of scaffolding had been built up for everyone's pleasure; a young man had danced on a rope attached to St. Paul's steeple and jumped the whole height of it down on to a feather bed. Orpheus sang to his 'counterfeit' wild beasts of prancing children in masks and furry skins (it was Orpheus who had to compare his music, unfavourably, with Philip's eloquence); the giant figures of Gog and Magog stood on guard over the City; and perhaps best of all, for the sly jokes it caused, were the painted figures of the Nine Worthies, and among them Henry VIII with an English Bible in his hand and 'Verbum Dei' on it – 'and God's body! if you could have heard how Bishop Gardiner swore when he spotted it only just in time before the procession, and got the Bible painted out, but by God's soul, the fingers got painted out with it, so there's Old Harry holding up his maimed stump like any old soldier beggar from the French wars asking you to give him a halfpenny. But you can still see the shadow of the Bible, and where's the worry, for no one's going to swing for *that*, I'd say.'

'Not swing! Burn. The Bible, Verbum Dei, the Word of God, that's heresy they say. And they'll make it English law as soon as the Cardinal, that Italianate Englishman Reginald Pole, comes over to hand us all back again to Rome and the Pope.'

'But he's English – a Plantagenet, one of the old stock.'

'Small odds that'll make to him, and he in foreign parts so long. It's as like as not he's forgotten his own mother tongue.'

The Oldest Inhabitant cackled shrilly; 'His own mother didn't forget the use of her tongue when she ran round and round the scaffold, as I saw her with my own eyes, *and* heard, she screeching like a pea-hen with stout butcher Giles after her, for the head executioner was away busy up North, chopping off the rebels' heads as thick as nettles, and young Giles was new to the work – a nasty job he made of it, the bungler, when he did catch her. It took him near a score of strokes to finish her off. Plantagenet blood, my arse or her head! It ran as red from it as any other.'

His granddaughter Mag told him not to be a nasty old man – if he must talk of red heads, then why not their Princess Elizabeth? She should have been riding in the procession, as she had done a year ago beside the Queen, and had clean outshone her sister, as though *she* were the Queen and Mary only her governess. No doubt that was the real reason they kept her shut up far away in the country, especially now the Queen had got herself a young husband.

But Grandfather Talbois, who couldn't keep away from executions, dared swear 'that jilt the Lady Elizabeth' had been the real cause of the rebellion this spring, and all these pesky bodies hanging till now at the street corners to bump your hat off if you weren't careful, 'they should hang 'em higher'; and his son, Will Talbois, the best candlemaker in Cheapside, agreed about that jilt with an admiring chuckle, 'she'll give 'em more trouble yet, mark my words, for all they've tried to mew up the eaglet, but they'll never clip that one's wings. *Mag*!' he shouted to his daughter, 'where are you strolling off to with that black foreign Moor?'

'It was only a poor young Spaniard, Father, who had lost his way and had no English to ask for it.'

'Then how could *you* tell him? I know, by signs and taking his hand and pointing to our house, I dare swear. Let Spaniards alone, I say.'

So said most Englishmen. Diego Valdez of Malaga, who

would have run any man through the body who dared call him a Moor, had learnt his way to pretty Mag Talbois' house in Cheapside; but for the most part, as the Spaniards wrote home pathetically, they found it safest to avoid the English, as the English did them, as though they were strange animals.

The English complained that there were four times as many Spaniards as Englishmen.

The Spaniards complained that they were charged twenty-four times as much as the proper price for everything.

The children in the gutters shouted, 'Spanish apes who steal our grapes,' and threw stones after them.

The Spanish Ambassador suggested to his young master that it would be a good way to relieve the tension if he passed on straightaway to the fighting in Flanders with his Spaniards and a large body of English as well, and thus unobtrusively, said Renard, as sly as his name, involve England in war against France. But Philip had too much to do first.

He had not yet decided whether the Lady Elizabeth were more dangerous dead or alive; he was not yet crowned King of England, he did not yet know if his wife were with child; he had not yet given permission to the Cardinal, Reginald Pole, to return to his own country.

Every man was thinking of that return, and of what it would mean to himself, when the form of religion would be changed by the law of the land, and anyone denying it would be subject to pain of death. No sensible Englishman dreamed of denying it; but a vast number were in terrible fear that their pleasant houses and lands and yearly rents might then be taken away and given back to the monks and nuns.

Even Mary was nervous of Reginald Pole's return, though she had for twenty years been longing for it.

He wrote to her – interminable letters, complained Philip, who had also received some – so long-winded ('so high-minded,' said Mary), so touchy ('so sensitive,' said Mary), so unpractical ('so eager to do God's will and that only,' said Mary).

'And do not *I* wish to do God's will?' asked Philip.

'Yes, dearest, yes.' But Mary, even now, and with another new silent hope springing in her heart, the chiefest, most miraculous hope of all, could see that in Philip's eyes God was a Hapsburg.

And in Reginald Pole's eyes she was no better. He had practically accused her of taking God for a Tudor. God had done her will, set her on the throne, rescued her from her enemies and their devilish conspiracies, given her the strongest country in the world for her support, and its magnificent Prince for her husband. But she had not yet done God's will in bringing this heathen country back to *His* loving care. With every week that she let go by, thousands of the souls in her charge were dying without the Last Sacraments, and so lost to all hope of heaven.

'He is right,' sobbed Mary to the pale impassive face of her young husband as he read the letter. 'We cannot "go easy, play for time," as even you have suggested, and even Bishop Gardiner of Winchester, even your dear father, yes, and even the Pope. But souls dying in sin cannot play for time.'

'Nor can those living in it,' said Philip with a strange smile. He had his own reason now for wishing the Papal Legate's arrival in England. It could be very useful to him.

Yes, he must write. But carefully. Reginald Pole must understand the conditions attaching to Christianity in these days, and especially in this country. So he wrote to him that he and the Queen passionately desired his return to England, that all the English longed for him to bring them Absolution from the Pope for their great crime in following their former rulers into rebellion against the Holy Father, and prayed to be allowed to return into the fold of his sheep – only Pole must remember that they had taken an enormous amount of spoils from the shepherds of it. Those spoils could not now be returned. The Pope's Absolution must therefore be coupled with a Papal decree confirming all the gentry who had annexed Church lands and property as perpetual owners of their gains. Without that decree, the aforesaid gentry would have nothing to say to the Absolution, to the Pope, nor to Pole.

He then returned to his wife, and told her he had written in most cordial welcome to her kinsman, entreating him to come and restore this wretched country to God. 'And if I were backward before in this matter,' he said, with so subtle a smile of his full lips above the pale gold fringe of beard that she did not at once perceive it, and he had to do it all over again, 'then you, of all people in the world, have reason to excuse it.'

'But why?' she asked bewildered, and he, looking down into her eyes (she was, fortunately, seated) saw, unbelievingly, that they must have looked very like that, though brighter, when she was eight or nine – 'why have I in particular, any reason?'

'My Queen,' he interrupted her softly, raising her hand to his lips (what a pity that hands grew old sooner than eyes, for he had always a partiality for beautiful hands), 'have you forgotten that Reginald Pole had been suggested as your husband, years before myself? And – but I do not ask you this, remember – how do I know that he himself has not suggested it? Or, if he had come before me, might not have done so?'

His clear eyes penetrated her, they made her shiver in a delicious sense of guilt that she had never before felt at mention of any man. Was it possible that this glorious young man could be jealous of her?

At that moment she could have worshipped him. And she told him her secret belief that she was with child.

If she were right, then one of the objects was achieved that stood between him and his departure from her; with sincere gratitude he expressed his satisfaction.

Mary wept, for joy, she said, but the resulting tears were as unbecoming as those of grief. He no longer found it intriguing that her eyes had looked like those of a little girl instead of a grown woman's; he found it irritating.

Did none of the English ever grow up? 'I'm nothing but a great boy – a little girl – at heart'; that seemed to be their perpetual covert boast. Mary's idea of duty was a child's, to be kind and conscientious. She had no understanding of the duty of a ruler. He was kind and conscientious himself; but he could think clearly.

He was doing so now while he gently stroked his wife's hair. 'Those living in sin cannot play for time,' she had said, and he had thought of the Lady Elizabeth, that unavowed heretic and hidden enemy, who had continued to play for time. But when the Papal Legate arrived in England, then Papistry would be made the law of the land, and death the punishment for breaking it. That would put an end to her anomalous position. It might even put an end to her altogether.

Yes, Philip had his own good reason for wishing Reginald Pole to come home.

CHAPTER FIVE

And late that autumn he came.

After twenty years of exile, most of them under sentence of death as a proscribed traitor in his own country, and with a price on his head for any private assassin who chose to murder him abroad, he returned home to hold greater official power than that of the Queen's Consort.

He came in the more than royal state of a Prince of the Church, such as had not been seen in England for a generation. In his Cardinal's robes and scarlet hat he stood on the Queen's own barge that had been sent to bear him up river from Greenwich; and before him stood the standard bearers holding up the insignia of his office, the huge cross and silver pillars and pole-axes that glimmered through the misty November sunlight, to announce the arrival of the Pope's Ambassador to all the waving, welcoming crowds along the river shores. The chief Bishops and Nobles of the land with their households in blue and red waited to meet him as he landed, and the London crowds ran to see the gay sight and shout and cheer as madly as though they had been saying mass in dangerous secrecy ever since he had gone into exile.

Philip was dining with the Queen in Whitehall Palace when the news was brought of the Cardinal's arrival. She turned red and then pale and clasped her hands to her side; and the King rose in haste from his unfinished dinner and walked out to do this Prince of the Church more honour than he would have paid to any Prince of this world, except his father. Bareheaded, in the faint but chilly mist from the river, he stood only a little apart from the crowds that thronged down to the water's edge, for Whitehall Stairs had been a right of way ever since the Palace had belonged to Cardinal Wolsey; King Henry had shamelessly commandeered it from the greatest of his subjects, but would not interfere with the rights of his meanest. So King Philip was half deafened by the cheers close round him of the fickle Cockneys who had dreaded the return of the Papal Legate, but now in their inconsistent fashion were hoarse with sudden joy to see a tired old Englishman come home.

He watched a very tall thin man wearily mounting Whitehall Stairs towards him. Reginald Pole's fair, greying head stooped a little, partly from weak health, partly from courtesy, since he so often had to speak with those of lesser height. He looked tired; 'who would have thought this fellow could give so much trouble!' went through Philip's mind at the approach of the languid elderly scholar who had sustained such obstinate conflict with Mary's terrible father, and with Philip's.

He led him up the stairs to where Mary awaited them, surrounded by her ladies; she curtseyed as Pole advanced and knelt to her, then kissed him as her cousin and stood, a moment longer than etiquette demanded, while she held his hand and looked up at the lean face that had aged so much since she had seen him. Yet it had grown the more familiar, for it was now so like the finely cut face of his mother, the Countess of Salisbury, her very dear Governess, who had been torn from her to the Tower and then to the headsman's block. Mary still treasured the portrait of her in all her finery of ermine hood and ruffled sleeves, but carrying in her exquisite fingers a sprig of wild honeysuckle from the hedgerows. And here again was her reflective calm in the deep-sunk eyes that looked down into hers, a touch of her ironic humour in the questioning curves of his long mouth above the forked grey beard.

The intent sympathy of his gaze brought a trembling question into her mind; it had been his mother's wish, and hers, that they should marry; had it been his too? Was it because of her that he delayed so long in taking priestly orders, had been made a Cardinal against his will, had refused to be made Pope?

She flushed like a girl at the thought, and prayed that neither he nor Philip guessed the reason. Hurriedly she turned and led him to a seat beside them under the royal canopy, making polite inquiries about his long and fatiguing journey.

He conversed with them in slow and sometimes slightly tentative English, but glad to be talking it again; 'I have dreamed of doing so, here in England, so often,' he told the Queen, 'that I seem to be talking in my sleep.' He told her of his progress up the river in the royal barge and how he seemed to be returning to his childhood as the banks of the Thames floated slowly past him, the grey-green fields dotted with sheep, the great trees he loved so well, the reedy wastelands of the Kentish marshes, streaked silver with water, the grounds of the old convent in the Hundred of Hoo where as a small boy he had visited the tall black-and-white nuns who had fluttered round him like a flock of clattering pigeons and led him away to pick red plums off an old grey wall.

He asked of the Carthusians' Monastery at Sheen to whose Grammar School he had gone when he was seven. But then he remembered what he had heard of its fate, and was glad that the Queen spoke instead of his later education at Oxford; Sir Thomas More himself had praised his virtue and scholarship, 'as your dear mother told me long afterwards.'

He smiled. 'I chiefly remember the furious mimic warfare between the Grecians and Trojans; we at Magdalen were all hot Grecians like our tutors, but there was one Oxford tutor who proclaimed all students of Greek to be devils and heretics.'

'How insular!' murmured Philip. 'In Spain we encourage the classics. But then we have many universities, whereas here, I believe, you have only two.' But he said it in rapid Spanish and neither of them understood.

'Her Grace's royal father,' Pole said to him in Latin, in the rather difficult attempt at a common language, 'gave us poor "heretic devils" most royal support when he wrote his commands to the University of Oxford to devote itself with energy and spirit to Greek studies.'

Pole's mother had been brutally butchered by Mary's father, and here they were casually mentioning both of them in polite conversation. Pole noticed that she blushed as they did so; there was no need; she had shown there was nothing in her of her father. Except in the button nose, the occasional steely look in the eyes, but that might be from short-sightedness.

He looked down at her tightly tucked-in little face, all bunched and crumpled up in smiles at the moment, but what would it be like when the lines ran the other way, in the deep furrows of a frown?

She was sixteen years younger than himself, a sweet and docile girl when last he had seen her, and the only woman whom he ever might have married, though the possibility had been more of others' planning than his own, and more from motives of policy than of his cool cousinly affection. He had never wanted to be involved with politics any more than with women; yet he who had tried so hard to keep himself disentangled from both, would he ever be free of them now?

Already she was urging him, begging him, she said, but in a voice that had shrilled to an imperious note, to become *at once* the Primate of the Church, the office that had been waiting for him ever since Archbishop Cranmer had been put in prison for his heresy.

'I too have waited,' said Pole gently.

'I know! I know! Oh! if *you* could but know the shame, the agony I have suffered these eighteen months, ever since I came to the throne, in triumph, they said, a conqueror – but what conquest was that, when I could not at once get the cruel Bill of Attainder against you reversed by Parliament? Obstinate, insensate brutes that they are, thinking only of their own stolen property, and so fearing your coming.'

'They were not the only ones to fear it,' said Pole, and turned his eyes on Philip. 'Your Highness and Your Highness's father the Emperor, and His Holiness the Pope have all combined to keep me dangling for months at Dillingen and Brussels, to send me as emissary to France on the pretext of trying to patch up peace with Spain, a ruse only to keep me from England until I would consent to sell God's Absolution to the English nobles, at their own price.'

'But you *have* consented?' Philip interposed, a shade too quickly.

'I have consented. Because I am to be allowed no other way of restoring the many thousands of innocent souls in this country to the Church of God. We sit here and talk at ease, while thousands are dying unabsolved by the rites of that Church, because it has not yet been made law. Your Highness had the power to save their immortal souls – and rejected it.' He added in slow and careful Spanish, 'You have rejected Christ.'

Philip's eyes turned to pale stones.

His anger was shot through with fear. Was this, could this be true of *him*? It could not be. Yet his father had said that one could not be a statesman and also a Christian, as Christ had understood it; his father feared to gain the whole world and lose his own soul; and so was going to renounce the world.

Suddenly Philip remembered that he had wished to do the same, and when he was only fourteen. He forgot that he had been helped to do so by dread of the difficulties he would meet in the world; he knew only that once in his boyhood there had been an autumn night of storm and despair when he too had wished to be a monk. He had had a vision in the tempest-torn darkness of a nun's face, a nun who was now winning a saintly reputation at Avila; but she had denied saintliness to him; she had told him to go back and become the ruler of the world. His father was that now, but he was going to give it up, in order to save his soul.

But Philip could not do so; he would have to carry on his father's work. He had not rejected Christ; but Christ had rejected him. For a moment he was aghast, for he was angry now with God. He had given up his earthly inclinations to do his duty by his father – yes, and God. Was he, for that, to lose his reward in heaven too?

It was blasphemy to think so. This tall fellow was a fanatic; he knew nothing of what it meant to be a statesman. And what had he ever done or could ever do for the Church?

'We are not living now in the days of the Apostles,' he began, but that would not do. He would never admit – and it would never be true – that he could not be a real Christian as well as a wise ruler.

He said quietly and clearly, 'Our latest Holy Order of the Soldiers of Christ has the motto that "the means justifies the end." Parliament refused to restore England to the Church, unless the Pope promised they should keep the private property they had robbed from the Church. The means are bad, but they lead to a good end, in England being once more a Christian country.'

And that 'end,' as Pole saw, would be the means to Philip's own ends. He would find a Roman Catholic England easier to rule. But of what use to say it, to say anything? He had accused the King just now with simple, almost inadvertent courage, and for a moment he thought he had shaken him, so rigid and silent had Philip sat. But no, he had again shown himself the astute politician, and Pole's attack had been of no more use than his futile errand of peace to the astute worldling Henri II of France and his gross, complacent, clever wife, Catherine de Medici. The Emperor Charles had sent him on that mission not as a diplomat, but as a stool pigeon. He had been baulked by all these potentates, until he himself was forced to reject Christ.

For that was what he must do in four days' time when, as Legate and Ambassador of the Pope, he would stand before the Queen's Parliament at Westminster to tell them the Pope had absolved them for their betrayal of the Church, and had confirmed their rights in all that they had robbed from it.

For all the pomp and glory of his return to his country, it was a sleeveless errand he had come on, to strike a base bargain with God.

He turned his head away to hide his bitterness, but as he did so he saw the Queen was crying. She at least had no part in this bargain; she had given back to the Church all the Crown's property from it; and had passionately desired to make her subjects do likewise. She hated compromise as he did, and had been called a bungler for it; as he had been proved one.

He bent towards her, speaking with great tenderness as he took his leave. He tired easily these days; he must go across the river to Lambeth Palace, now his home, and rest from his journey and gain repose in which to think out all that he must say so soon to the Parliament and people of England.

She could not let him go like this, and after the terrible words he had spoken to Philip. What if they were true? And if so, what could she do? Or say?

Surely the future, that she now held within her body, would make amends for the past? She opened her mouth to say goodbye, and found herself telling him, breathlessly, that at the news of his arrival she had felt for the first time the child leap in her womb.

CHAPTER SIX

'So now,' purred Philip, stretching his bare legs to the comfortable blaze of apple logs while Ruy Gomez warmed his night-shirt, 'we have that young Lady within both jaws of the nut-crackers.'

It was four days after the Cardinal's arrival; and he had that day accomplished the greatest work ever done by a Churchman in England since St. Augustine had converted it to Christianity. So all had agreed with awe, which had passed as the evening wore on into somewhat maudlin expressions of self-congratulatory joy over their saved souls. Reginald Pole had preached a very long and deeply sincere sermon, extempore, before the Parliament at Westminster, and all the Members had fallen on their knees and confessed themselves 'very sorry and repentant' for their past heresy; he had then pronounced absolution from the Pope, and the Members wept and sobbed for thankfulness that they had regained the Church, and retained the Church property.

To the two Spaniards now talking in the seclusion of the King's bedroom, it had afforded a scene of exquisite farce, highly gratifying to their sense of superior fine feeling. The English conception of 'honour' was clearly very different from the Spanish *pundonor*. 'Our common soldiers,' said Philip, 'gave up their pay, even their few personal possessions, to meet the demands of their allies the German mercenaries before the battle of Pavia. The English would call them fools.'

So would Ruy Gomez, an astute Portuguese man of business; but he quickly agreed, and gave poignant instances of how the Spaniards were being robbed by their London lodging-house keepers. The famous English hospitality had proved a hard bargain; they were a nation of shopkeepers. Philip, warming to his subject by the fire, declared that 'they may brawl and fight for their "honour", but they will not pay a halfpenny towards it, not even when their debtor is Christ himself.'

And he gave his rare sharp bark of laughter when his friend described seeing Sir William Cecil, who had been Secretary of State during the Protestant Edward VI's and Lady Jane's nine-day reign, ostentatiously fingering a rosary of extra large beads.

'The Queen thinks he is "really a very honest man." I had difficulty in restraining her from making him our Secretary too!'

'Then he should be careful, sir, not to pay so many visits to the public-house of the Bull at Woodstock. Our spies say there is continual secret correspondence between the Bull and the Lady Elizabeth up at the old Palace, and not all her guards can prevent it. So much for a country house as a prison!'

It was then that Philip reminded him that today's Act of Parliament had closed the other jaw of the nut-crackers on the young Lady. 'She's escaped beheading as a traitor, but may now be legally burnt as a Protestant.'

'The Lady does not protest very much,' murmured Ruy Gomez.

'True. She seems most anxious for guidance. Her letters to

her sister are full of the right sentiments. It looks as though she only needs a touch, a firm masculine touch, be it said, to propel her in the right direction.'

He dipped his bare toes in the basin of warm scented water on the floor beside him, then twiddled them over the fire, sending a shower of drops to hiss and splutter in the flames.

Ruy Gomez's small dark face peered curiously at his master's over the white shirt he was holding. Never had he seen something so like a leer at the corners of Philip's voluptuously curved lips. In any other man, it could only mean one thing; in Philip it might mean two. Was he hoping to amuse himself with Elizabeth's love, or her death?

'The Queen would be ill advised to make a martyr of her,' Ruy said. 'It is doubtful if the country would stand it.'

'That would make small odds to her. The Queen can be as much a martyr as a martyr-maker. She would probably enjoy being dethroned, perhaps murdered, for her Church.'

Ruy turned the shirt round and stared over it at the fire. 'There is another point to consider,' he said carefully. 'The doctors are now certain the Queen is with child; they cannot naturally be certain of the result, especially at her age and with her delicate health. She may very possibly die in childbed. Even if the baby lived, the undoubted heir to the throne, yet this turbulent country might easily boil up again in yet another revolution to upset the Succession and make Elizabeth the Queen. Then Your Highness would lose all hold on England, perhaps even your life.'

'The more reason then to make away with Elizabeth, if not publicly, then by private means.'

'I think not, sir.' Ruy was firmly making use of his ten years' seniority that had stood him in good stead since Philip was a baby. 'You would be in an even more dangerous position, with so small a force of Spaniards to guard you against the rebels, and with no one to use in bargaining with them.'

'You suggest I should secure the Princess as a hostage?'

'Or possibly, sir, as an ally.'

'Hmph. I can hardly put these arguments before my wife. However much she desires my safety, she might be unreasonable about my planning it in the event of her death.'

He held up his arms, and Ruy pulled the shirt down over them. As Philip's fair short-cropped head emerged, a trifle ruffled, he told Ruy casually how Renard had described their enemy as 'a spirit full of enchantment.'

Ruy guessed him to be more curious than casual. 'My spies bring me some queer stories about her,' he said, and told them while Philip, reluctant to leave the fire, brooded on this unknown creature who haunted the minds of the English. The more they avoided speaking of her, the more he was aware of her in their thoughts; he himself was apt to avoid speaking of her to his wife as it upset her; but often he had seen Mary's eyes harden and stare as if her sister were actually before her.

But to many that invisible presence was not a shadow but a quickening light; it brought a smile, a questioning shrug, as it now brought to Ruy Gomez while he slyly recounted his gossip.

The young Lady had a reputation for being 'marvellous meek,' yet she could rage like her father and had openly defied the Queen.

A Protestant nun in dress and behaviour, yet, when confined to her apartments in disgrace, she had given a fancy-dress dance for her friends, who had practically amounted to a rival Court, and had danced at it, dressed, but not over-much, as Diana.

Even in the Tower, when the axe, that had just struck the head off her little cousin Jane Grey, swung so imminently above her own, it was said that she had contrived to meet a paramour. Who was he? Probably Edward Courtenay, the young Earl of Devon; it was known that he had once planned to carry her off and marry her by force. And now, released from the Tower, he was writing heart-broken letters to her.

'And why released? *And* his paramour?' exclaimed Philip in a rare burst of impatience. 'After a rebellion to put them on the throne! My dear Aunt' (he still persisted in so calling his wife to Ruy Gomez; he seemed to think it amusing) 'carries mercy to extremes.' It irritated his tidy mind that Mary should have missed her perfect opportunity to cut off two such inconvenient heads at a blow.

But Ruy was right as usual. The Princess's death was no longer, at present, opportune. Therefore the best alternative was to cultivate this impudent and beguiling foe; it might also afford some contrast to the drab duties of matrimony.

He went to work cautiously with Mary and burrowed with mole-like patience to his purpose, through a seemingly endless damp tunnel, for that was what England smelt like, sodden earth and sour beer and boiled puddings and musty clothes and wet dogs, turning him sick with longing for the sharp smell of wine and of small herbs growing in stone paths in the hot sun, and spicy oranges dangling in a grove, and even of garlic. As for green 'resting the eyes,' his own felt tired out by so many heavy trees piling themselves up into the blurred shapeless landscape of never-ending woods. He would give them all for the single minute flash of a lizard across a wall, and the clear-cut cruel line of rocky hills, their tawny earth bare against the blinding sky.

They went to Hampton Court, and the green, now browned by winter, covered them, smothered them with a soggy blanket of moss, lawns, trees, and drifting clouds of dead leaves. The river flowed sleepily between softly waving rushes. Mary loved 'my father's favourite home,' so she was always calling it, and Philip refrained from mentioning that it had been Cardinal Wolsey's before Henry filched it; and that it was Wolsey's genius, not Henry's, that was impressed on the red-brick Palace that rose like a sunset cloud from the river-bed valley where one could never see above the tops of the trees.

Yet even this royal seclusion was considered a right of way by the casually intrusive English. King Henry's own Privy Garden seemed a bitter misnomer when the public were at liberty to hang over its hedges and little gate to watch Philip pacing up and down its paths. He insisted that at least the Palace should be kept immune; and the shocking report went round that 'the hall-door within the court was continually shut, so that no man might enter unless his errand were first known; which seems strange to us Englishmen that have not been used thereto.'

Suspicious, secretive, foreign, that was what it was. King Hal had never minded who strolled through his palace to get an eyeful of him.

Philip, holding a sprig of rosemary to his nose as they walked past the people in the gardens, complained to his wife that the Lion of England had respected these mice more than a pride of lions. In this country it should be a pride of mice.

But Mary liked the common people; she had sometimes

called at their cottages with one or two of her ladies and sat and talked with them about their work and families and often helped them secretly, without letting them know who she was.

It sounded a childish idea of royalty to Philip, who was trying to work himself up to a properly royal command and finding it unwontedly difficult.

'Your sister,' he began, saw her brows knit, and added hastily, 'the Little Bastard, as her father called her' –

'If he *were* her father,' muttered Mary.

Philip had no wish to hear her theories on the possible paternity of Elizabeth. Even if she were, as Mary declared, 'the image of Mark Smeaton,' the handsome young musician who had been executed for adultery with Ann Bullen, along with four others, including Ann's own brother, it had been made plain to him by Renard and Ruy Gomez that the bulk of England looked on Elizabeth as 'True Tudor' and 'Old Harry's Own,' – and all the greater menace for that.

'Whose-so-ever daughter she is,' he expounded laboriously as he launched himself on his carefully prepared speech, 'she is an ever-present factor to be reckoned with, and we must reckon with her. Since you have refused to put her to death, it would be wiser to come to terms with her.'

'*What* terms?' demanded Mary.

'Whatever terms may prove most expedient,' he replied smoothly. 'But it would be safer to have her as an apparent friend than a declared enemy. As a prisoner at Woodstock, she is proving dangerous. Sir Henry Bedingfeld is as trusty a jailer as any bulldog; he plants his troop of soldiers every night to keep watch on the hill above the house; he lets no one enter it without his permission. Not even the cofferer, Thomas Parry, who has to arrange all the housekeeping, is allowed to stay in the house. No, but he stays at the public-house in the village, at the sign of the Bull, and God knows who else with him. Half the disaffected elements of England appear to stay constantly at the Bull, and your bulldog Bedingfeld knows of it, writes, "if there be any practice of ill in all England, they are privy to it," yet he cannot keep them out of it – such is the licence granted to the English public-house! Your bulldog is no good at baiting the bull. Therefore, Madam, let *us* take the bull – or shall I say the cow? – by the horns.'

Mary was shaking all over, a symptom that he found inseparable in her from any mention of Elizabeth.

'It's true, it's true,' she gasped on an hysterically sounding sob. 'She is taking advantage of every inch I give her and stretching it to an ell. First Bedingfeld tells us that she asks for a volume of Cicero and the Psalms in Latin, then for a Bible – an English Bible, mark you, to flaunt her heretic inclinations in our face! – then for leave to write me one of her teasing letters, all innocence and false colours; then for leave to write to the Council, and makes poor old Bedingfeld her secretary to write complaints of his own treatment of her, "worse than a prisoner in the Tower," he has to write, and next day, "worse than the worst prisoner in Newgate." And then she's ill and won't have any but my own physicians, for she is "not minded to make any stranger privy to the state of her body," if you please! Are those the words of the worst-treated prisoner in Newgate? They are the words of – of "this great lady," so Bedingfeld himself, her very jailer, speaks of her! But *that* she is not! They are the words of an insolent traitor and pretender to the throne.'

Philip listened fascinated to his wife's outpouring of furious yet halting Spanish, like a lame dog run mad, he thought, and so strangely old-fashioned. She had quite forgotten her mother-tongue in all the long years of separation from it, but now that she was striving hard to take it up again, it had come back to her in all the out-of-date colloquialisms that her mother had used from the time when she in her turn had last spoken Spanish freely as a child. The result was that Mary's use of the language seemed two generations behind the times, and she herself as not merely his aunt but his great-aunt.

'Will the Lady Elizabeth speak Spanish?' he asked.

'I have no doubt she is busy acquiring it,' Mary replied on a biting note, 'and she can also speak French or Italian to you or Latin or, if you prefer it, Greek. She is very clever.' No wonder her tone was biting; she could have bitten her tongue out for it – after she had spoken. She loved Philip, she hated Elizabeth, yet could not resist using even her and her cleverness as a whip to flick at him, and his placid assumption that everyone should speak his language, and he none but his own.

But he was too certain of it himself to perceive any gibe at his stupidity.

'That is well,' he said; 'it will be well for many here to learn Spanish.'

Even Mary needed a reminder that her country was now a province of his. It amused him that even Mary flushed at it. And it pleased him to conceal from the majority that he could by now understand English pretty well, and even speak a few carefully prepared sentences quite correctly if necessary, though it would have to be a strong necessity to make him risk any possibly ridiculous mistake.

He had his way. Elizabeth was sent for to Hampton Court. But Mary would not have her in the Palace under the same roof as herself. She was lodged in the gatehouse on the river, a square red-brick block of masonry as strong as any fortress, and still under the close guard of Bedingfeld and a picked force of his men.

And still Mary put off seeing her; would not see her with Philip, dreading the effect of her own jealousy; did not feel well enough to see her alone; was afraid that her passive insolence, her false words, her subtle dangerous smile might infuriate her so much that it would provoke a miscarriage.

'You do not know what she is like,' she sobbed angrily to her husband. 'You have heard of her from the Court, no doubt, and they will have told you that she has done nothing down at Woodstock but sit and sew at her embroidery and study the classics – yes, and devout books so as to learn to be a Catholic – and that she knows nothing about all her unruly friends at the public-house down in the village. But I don't trust her an inch – and – and – I don't trust myself either when I am with her! One day I shall do something terrible to her – and then I shall be blamed for it, not her.'

Her head sank in shame. He looked at it, then laid a cool hand lightly on it. She clutched at his fingers before he could draw them away. 'Oh, do believe me. But when you see her you will not, for she charms all men to believe only what she wishes. And you, of all men, she will set out to deceive. But if you could see her as she is sometimes when alone with me—'

'Why not, if you wish it?' he conceded indulgently. 'I could be in the room, behind a curtain or a screen if you like, and hear all she says to you, without her knowing of any witness.'

'You will do that for me? Oh, but how good you are to me! You understand my fear of doing anything without you – and yet I know I ought to see her first alone,' she added hastily.

Philip agreed, but said that if she intended to come to terms with her sister, he must meet her openly some time.

'How do I know what I intend until I see her?' demanded Mary pettishly – at least she thought it was only the natural pettishness of a woman in her condition; but Philip thought she looked and sounded just as her father must have done in his quick rages. To tell the truth he was really afraid of her uncontrollable bursts of temper when her voice, most unexpectedly for such a little mousy-looking woman, would suddenly swell into the loud roar of an angry man's.

She was working herself now into a passion as she walked up and down, twisting her hands together, forcing herself to come to a decision, to be bold and resolute, to be like her father. 'I shall send for her tonight.'

'Without any warning? Then she will surely fear the worst.'

'Let her!' shouted Mary. 'It would be no more than her deserts.'

Certainly she was not to be trusted by herself in that state; it would be very awkward if in a rage she committed her sister to instant execution, or the Tower again, or even if in simpler fashion she threw a knife or something at her, or even, still more simply, scratched her face or tore her hair. One must remember what barbarians these English were. He braced himself, not unpleasantly, for the scene he was to watch that evening.

CHAPTER SEVEN

He took up his position behind the gilded leather screen in which, without mentioning it to his wife, he had thoughtfully cut a small slit. It was a pity the Queen's room was so dark; she said her eyes were too weak for a strong light, but he suspected that even with her sister, perhaps indeed especially with her, she preferred a flattering dusk.

It was after ten o'clock on a chilly night and gusts of wind, smelling of the river below, hurled themselves against the rattling windows. He thought almost with fellow-feeling of the girl now coming towards them in the flickering torchlight through the dark damp gardens, even as he had had to stumble his way at just this hour to his first meeting with the Queen. What a night-owl she was! He put his head round the screen and said on a note unusually imperative, almost exasperated, 'When you have said and heard all you want, give me a sign, say some word in Spanish, and I will come out and present myself.'

Mary was about to expostulate, but at that instant they heard the tread of men's feet on the stairs. Philip moved back behind the screen and Mary huddled herself down on a low seat at that end of the room. Sir Henry Bedingfeld entered the door at the other end, followed by some of the guard, and all stood there at attention.

A tall girl in a dark cloak walked quickly past them with her head held high, and down the long room towards the crouched bent figure of the Queen. Her appearance, after Philip's long waiting for it, was startlingly sudden, like a spirit called up by that hunched grey Witch of Endor on the stool, as she came so straight and swift towards her out of the black night.

She fell on her knees, but with her head still high, her face upturned, seeking, beseeching her sister's answering gaze. It was a transparently white face in the midst of the bright hair that had been dishevelled by the night-wind, and the eyes were wide and wary as a hunted animal's. She looked as though she knew her last hour had come – and so it well might, thought Philip, were he not there on guard.

Mary was speaking in English too fast for him to follow all she said, but the tone told him of the spate of accusing questions. Elizabeth's complicity in Wyatt's rebellion last spring – was she not guilty of it, would she not admit it, would she dare imperil her immortal soul by denying it?

But it was not fear for her soul, it was the sheer bodily fear of a trapped wild beast that darted from the eyes of the kneeling girl. Philip imagined them fixed and staring in death, the red head cut from the body, and the ruby-bright blood flowing from the white neck. Yes, she would make a good execution – and lucky to get it, it seemed, from the turn the Queen had now taken. For it was her sister's heresy that she was now urging her to confess, even more furiously than her accusations of treason; and Philip could see the straight slight body bound to the stake, the clouds of smoke, the long flames leaping up to consume that tossed cloud of flaming hair. He was glad he had thought of slitting a spy-hole in the screen.

What would the girl do now? One look at Mary's shut face, rigid as a mask, must show it to be deaf to pleading. Would she shriek and wail instead, shed floods of tears? He waited in hopeful curiosity. But Elizabeth spoke softly, faltered, fell silent, spoke again, in low scurries of speech, like the gusts of wind that flung themselves against the windows and then, like them, died of themselves. It was almost as though, finding herself unheeded, she sought another listener.

Suddenly, out of silence, there came a cry from her as passionate and tender as if she were pleading to a lover. What was it she had cried? Something that sounded curiously young and innocent, beseeching the Queen 'to have a good opinion of her.' What a way to entreat, when she must have been seeing the imminence of a fearful death as clearly as he had done!

She spoke again, but more continuously and composedly, and he noticed how ringing and musical her tones were now, throbbing like the strings of a lute, and sweet, full of the love of life rather than the fear of death. They seemed to be moving the Queen too, but in a different way, making her restless and uneasy; she tried to check her sister, then rose and walked hastily up and down, passed near to the end of the screen where she could glance behind it and catch his eyes in question. He nodded; she turned back to Elizabeth and spoke in an exhausted, exasperated voice, dragging the words heavily after each other like the trudging footsteps of tired men on the march. How old her voice was, old and tired, after that other! She was trying to make it kindly, but it only sounded despairing, too weary to go on disputing. 'You *may* be speaking truth,' came in grudging, gruff admission, 'God knows!' and then repeated the words in Spanish, '*Sabe Dios!*'

and caught her mottled hands together as if to wash them of the matter.

But it was a signal, and the girl knew it. She was crying out in terrified question, pointing at the screen. He had to answer it, to come out and meet her at last after all these months – or was it years? – that he had been waiting for this moment.

His usual reluctance towards any decided step became enormous, ominous; he could only overcome it by telling himself that it was because he might have made himself ridiculous by this childish device of hide and seek. He had to draw a deep breath, to fill himself with majesty and a sense of power more than human, as he stepped forward slowly from behind the screen, bowed low, and advanced towards the girl.

She gave one startled glance at him, then sank low, lower, down to the ground, her head bent till it all but touched her knee, remained thus while he had time to remember how a swan folds its wings and sinks upon the water; and then rose, as slowly and exquisitely, looking up at him until their eyes were on a level.

Odd that his first fanciful impressions were all of her in death, and by violence, beheaded, burnt, and now drowned, drawn up from the sea, for so pale she was that the candlelight flowing over her slowly rising face seemed blue and opalescent, and ripples of fear shimmered over it in waves of light rather than shadow. The long eyelids, sandy-fringed, lifted themselves at last, with no maidenly flutter, but wide open now. Looking straight into his were the eyes of no dying nor swooning victim, but the eyes of an equal. As a rival? an enemy? a lover?

They were utterly alien from the troubled eyes of her jailer, his wife, those starved eyes shadowed with pain and doubt, afraid of herself, of life, of him, praying for affection like those of a spaniel.

The eyes of this girl, he thought, would never pray to man or God; they were Pagan, perhaps even inhuman; clear as water, the eyes of a mermaid who could lure men to destruction under the cruel, softly curling waves of the translucent sea. He had seen death surrounding her high white brow, her lurid hair; but was it hers, or that of her enemies?

He could not stand looking at her, before his wife, in a moment that had caught them up beyond this present time, on throughout both their lives.

He had to move, to take her hand and bend his head over it, feeling how strong and sinuous were its fingers. He had to speak, and for once he heard his words before he knew what they would be. He bid her welcome to their Court, assured her she was no longer a prisoner, but their dear sister.

And then he had to kiss her, not on the cheek, but on her quivering red mouth.

Why had he thought of death to do with her? To kiss her was to kiss life itself, warm, tingling, and, he could have sworn, laughing. He longed to ask her why she laughed, but his wife was standing by.

CHAPTER EIGHT

Only an hour ago she had come this way under the swaying sighing trees, their shadows leaping forward across her path in the light of the torches carried by her silent guard. She had thought then she was walking, stumbling over sticks or grass tussocks in the dark, to her death, perhaps by fire. But in that hour her life had leaped and shaken itself into another pattern; the time and form of her death had fled away, become distant and unknown. She was not to die now after all, she was no longer to be a prisoner, closely guarded by Bedingfeld and his men; she was to go to Court again and be the Queen's, and her husband's, 'dear sister.'

She had to keep her feet from dancing on the wet grass; she turned at the door into the gatehouse and laughed in Bedingfeld's beard as she bade him good-night.

'You'll soon be free of me. Did ever a guardian have better reason to thank his stars? I've plagued you nearly to death.'

His breath caught in his throat at the sight of her face. 'I know well,' he said huskily, 'that it was in order to plague others.'

'Oh, in part! But in greater part to amuse myself. Prison teaches cruelty.'

He wanted to say that she could continue to tease and mock him without mercy, if only she would always look so at him, breathing the very spirit of young life and hope into him; but he could only clear his throat and bend stiffly to kiss her hand and curse to himself as he heard his knee-joint crack.

She lowered her head near his and whispered with the very devil of mischief dancing in her eyes, 'When I am Queen, I will not bring your rheumatism out in the middle of a wet night!'

'*When* I am Queen!' it was more reckless than heresy, with Mary drawing near her time, and prayers and processions in all the Churches to ensure her and Philip an heir. None of his men were near enough to catch the words, but that only made his enforced share in her criminal levity the more shocking – and just when he had longed for one crazy instant that she might go on teasing him for ever! Let her do it to her husband – if any man should be bold enough to marry her – and he hoped it would be one with a strong arm and no compunction in using the whip.

'Oh yes,' she said, exactly as though he had spoken aloud, 'but there may never be one, you know.' She swirled round on her toes, whistling a tune like a schoolboy, kissed her hand to him and vanished.

Philip was coming to see her. By himself. Mary might well not have been able to prevent it; and doubtless policy demanded it before she should be received at Court – but why had Mary sent a special message telling her to wear her best dress and jewels for the occasion? To do honour to her husband, ostensibly, but many wives in her case would have preferred him dishonoured. Perhaps she 'owed it to herself,' as dear Cat Ashley was always saying, not to appear as a mean jailer. Or, yes, that was the more like her, she was determined to fight her jealousy by being over-generous. In any case Elizabeth was delighted to obey her, and spent the morning trying on all her dresses and pronouncing them not fit to wear.

She tried first her ruby rings and then her emerald to see which made her fingers whiter, and could not bear to part with either. She had her hair dressed in a cloud of curls, and declared it made her one of the vulgar, and then smooth and pure as an angel's in an old Italian picture, and cried out that it made her a milksop, so went back to the curls – but would Philip be alarmed lest they meant she had designs on him? – or amused rather than alarmed? He had had plenty of experience where women were concerned; those pale eyes were very far from a fool's, they were likely to see through any feminine pretence at maiden modesty. Had he also *heard* through her that night? Had he detected when she had guessed his hidden presence, and used all her charms to plead to him, rather than to Mary?

No doubt, too, he knew all the standard tales about her shocking conduct, and dozens more that she herself had never known. Yes, it would be better to be quite natural, she told her mirror, as she rubbed a touch of rouge on her cheeks. In any case there was no time to change, for out of her window she could see a cortège come riding over the Palace bridge between all the stone griffins and dragons, towards the gatehouse.

Now she must go down and be careful not to laugh till he did, and congratulate him on his coming heir and Mary's healthy looks (she had never seen her look so ill) and lead him on to talk of Spain, for which he must be dismally homesick, and especially for his mistress, de Osorio, and all their children. It would not be his fault if Mary did not produce an heir and yet – Mary? – even now Elizabeth could not quite believe it.

She went down with her women and stood by the window with the light on her face, for he must be sick of shadows.

He was. He stood still for an instant by the door, suddenly realizing it. So long he had waited for the sun while weeks lengthened into months, and the weather worsened as an English summer became an English winter, until colder winds and sharper gales proclaimed an English spring. But now the real spring stood before him, bright and upstanding as a sword, with all its flowers spangling the embroidery of her white brocade, and jewels flashing red and green from her elegant fingers; it pleased him to see that they were shaking slightly. It was all rather bad taste by Spanish standards, but he would change all that – or perhaps he wouldn't.

He advanced between his grandees, bowed and looked down on the sunlit head bent low in curtsey, on her young face as he raised her, and then kissed her. England had some good customs.

The rest of the company drew back towards the open door of the anteroom. Elizabeth sat on the window-seat, leaving him the ceremonial chair; she could see him clearly now, as she could not do in the agitation of her first meeting with him.

She thought, 'He is handsome. He has a great deal of majesty, too much. If he were taller he would not need it. And his eyes are like a prawn's. They have grown cold in the study – no, they were born cold.' But his lips had not been cold, nor did they look so now. They were full and sensual. But they gave her a sense of fear. She wished he had not first seen her in that hour of her terror before Mary. He had probably enjoyed it.

They finished their polite enquiries and talked politics, which of course meant religion, and that he wished to sound her on her views. She agreed with him that men were always making some new religion, of earth too, she said, as well as of heaven.

'They preached "Communistic Law" here just lately – that no man should own any property and all should share alike, so they pulled down the palings in the great parks and slaughtered the deer, and said it was following Christ's own words.'

'They should never have been permitted to read them,' said Philip severely. 'Ideas are fertile.' A faint smile caught the corners of his lips as he added, 'They say "Erasmus laid the egg and Luther hatched it." And "Reform" is a bad egg.'

'Certainly it is explosive,' said Elizabeth.

'My father did one wrong thing, which he now has bitter reason to regret, and does. He had Luther in his power at the Diet of Worms, and he did not kill him. He let him go.'

She did not say 'But he had given Luther safe-conduct!' only, 'But then by your own showing he should have killed Erasmus too.'

'Assuredly. He was the father of heresy.'

'With others. The broody hen Luther flirted with a clutch of cocks.'

'Who accused each other. Even your advanced thinker Sir Thomas More called your translator of the Bible, Tyndale, the father of all heresies. Do you agree with him?'

'Oh yes,' she said lightly, 'because Tyndale made such mistakes in the translation. How right More was to complain of that word "charity" for "love". Words derived from Latin are all as cold as – charity.'

She felt his eyes upon her at mention of More, whom her father had beheaded because he would not acknowledge his marriage to her mother. Agreement with More would be slippery ground for her. She slid off it gracefully with a compliment on the new University Philip had just established at Mexico City, the first to be founded in the New World. What a triumph for the civilization, the initiative and enterprise of Spain, to be carrying her faith and learning into the dark and savage corners of the heathen world!

'I signed the order for its establishment,' he replied, 'on the same day that I signed the contract of marriage with the Queen of England.'

As another crusade against the heathen, his tone said clearly. But difficult to congratulate him on it, except personally. So she told him how he had won all English hearts by his affability and readiness 'to put up with our rough ways, for I have no doubt we must sometimes seem to you like savages.'

Quickly, to prevent a return to heresy, she repeated – and invented – some golden opinions of him she had heard, or hadn't heard, while she was at Woodstock. Even in the remote fastness of her country prison, she said wistfully, echoes had sometimes reached her from the outside world.

He was well aware of it, but made no reference to the public-house of the Bull, which had made such a convenient sounding-board for those echoes. He inquired with grave sympathy as to her pursuits in her retirement. She drew him a pretty picture of herself reading Greek and Latin and working at her embroidery-frame, and sprang up impulsively to show him a black-letter edition of the epistles of St. Paul with a cover stitched in a bold design of scarlet and gold thread.

'Who drew the pattern?' he asked. 'Yourself? You are an artist.' He flicked the pages and she had an anxious moment lest St. Paul came within the compass of heresy, since Christ had seemed dangerously near it just now. But he only murmured, 'I dislike this old-fashioned black-letter. Printing has improved greatly. What is this – your handwriting?'

'Yes, on the blank leaf. One should not write in books, but I was not allowed any paper. Please, Your Majesty, do not read it. It was only to beguile my loneliness by talking to myself.'

But in spite of her modest protestations, or because of them, he read:

'August. I walk many times into the pleasant fields of the Holy Scriptures, where I pluck up the goodly herbs of sentences by pruning, eat them by reading, chew them by musing, and lay them up at length in the high seat of memory by gathering them together, that so having tasted their sweetness I may the less perceive the bitterness of this miserable life.'

'"Pluck up the herbs – eat them – chew them by musing –"' he repeated thoughtfully. 'It sounds as though you were a cow.'

'*Oh!*' she flushed scarlet and her hands flew out to snatch the book from him, but thought better of it, and clasped each other instead, with a laugh now instead of an indignant cry, peal upon peal, at first musical as a carillon and then an uncontrollable fit of giggles which she had to choke with her handkerchief while the tears on her light eyelashes caught the sun and turned them to rainbows. 'How cruel,' she gasped, 'and true, for I remember now that I was watching the cows in Woodstock Park when I wrote it. They were moving so slowly through the grass, pulling up the long moon-daisies and munching them, chewing the cud, and I wished I were a cow, never to think of anything else but that, and then a milkmaid came with her three-legged stool and bucket on her arm, and milked them and sang so merrily while the milk poured ting-a-ling into the pail as though it were singing too.'

'What did she sing?'

'Oh, an old country song – "for bonny sweet Robin is all my joy—"'

'And you remember that – from last summer?'

'Prisoners have long memories, sir. I remember the evening going, the summer going, and the shadows of the trees dark and heavy as long-cloaked guards closing in on me. I remember how I said, to one of my own guards I suppose, that I wished I were that milkmaid, for her lot was better than mine and her life merrier.' The laughter had trembled into the note of the pathetic prisoner again.

'Was it raining?' asked Philip.

'It had been, I think, but the sun's last rays had come out and lay red along the cows' white furry backs, and yes, the grass was shining with raindrops. But why does Your Majesty ask?'

'I cannot remember any day last August when it was not raining.'

His tone said clearly that whatever he had to put up with in England from its diet and manners, its politics, its heresy, even its Queen, he would never forgive its weather. She knew better than to laugh about it. But she wished he would notice how strictly she had been kept a prisoner all these months that he had been disporting himself in England.

'Even the rain could not spoil your "tournament of reeds"?'

she asked. 'I cannot tell you how I longed to see your "cane game" as they called it here, surely the daintiest exercise of chivalry, the jousters riding at each other dressed in green and silver, white and gold, and armed with nothing more dangerous than long reeds – all to the music of silver trumpets and drums made of kettles. I pray you, gentle and courteous brother-in-law, to have that game played again for me to see.'

He looked down at her, suddenly suspicious, for he was noticing for the first time that his ceremonial chair was higher than the window-seat on which she sat (had that been of her planning?) and said, 'I do not think that tourney will ever be played again in England. Your countrymen do not care for it. The more cruel the sport, the more popular.'

She felt she would burst if she did not say the Spaniards were at least as cruel as the English. But she did not say it. She looked at him with sorrowful eyes and said, 'No cruelty of raw combat can equal the cruelty of keeping a young live thing cooped up in a cage, as I have been these two years.'

'And with no other consolations,' he said slowly, 'than those of learning and religion? Do you then assure me, my pretty, my very pretty sister, that you had no other consolations?'

Her cheeks had grown pale under the touch of rouge: 'What other could I have had?'

'I have heard of some, and in a stricter prison than an old country house. Did you never receive a visitor in the Tower?'

'No, Your Majesty.' It came with too strong a fervour.

'Nor pay visits – to another prisoner?'

'But what does Your—'

'No, enough of Majesty. I am your brother now, and believe me, more kind a brother than you know.'

'I can believe it well, since my sister—'

'Yes, what of her?'

'I do not think she is always kindly disposed towards me.'

'No. A few nights ago, when you were summoned to her, you thought, did you not, that you were going to your death?'

'Yes.'

'And so did I, or thought you might be. That was why I concealed myself behind the screen. Well, I have saved your life for this once at least. And now have you nothing to tell me of the Tower?'

'Sir, there were two children who played with me in the little garden, and brought me flowers to cheer my captivity. The eldest was a boy of five.'

'And you will tell me nothing more?'

'I have nothing to tell.'

'And never will have,' he thought, scanning those downcast eyelids that had shut her clear face into a mask. 'So, no consolations, though even your jailers would be glad to provide you with them?'

The mask flashed open into frank laughter. 'What! Poor old Bedingfeld! Would you accuse *him*?'

'I accuse no one, my sister, not even your beauty. But permit me to envy him.'

'Then talk with him, sir, and learn how much he finds his lot unenviable. He would be so thankful to be rid of the charge of this nuisance, this plague, this monster, that am I, that only his bounded loyalty and duty to the Queen has made him prevent my murder half a dozen times.'

'Is that true?' he asked quickly.

'Very true. My enemies have tried to set fire to the house at Woodstock, to shoot me as I walked in the maze, to put poison in my cup. All of which Bedingfeld has prevented, through no love of me, but determination that such methods should not dishonour the Queen.'

'You are very certain, my sister, of the motives of others. It must be from your infinite experience of life – you who have been so closely guarded these last few years of it – you who are more than half a dozen years younger than I.'

'What do you mean to say, sir – my brother?' ('The last thing he could ever be to me, or to any other!')

'What do I say? Why, nothing – as you have nothing to say of your brief sojourn in the Tower. But not too brief for love. For love is brief—'

'As breath! Love is brief, and life too. That is why I wish to breathe my life a little space before I die – to see your grave grandees, now gathered in a thunder cloud at the end of this room, so dark and quiet, to see them deck themselves in purple and black and yellow and silver, green and white and gold, and ride a tourney of the reeds before me. And – before I die...'

'What else, my sister?'

'To dance.'

'With whom, my sister?'

'With you, my brother.'

CHAPTER NINE

'Now I am alive again,' Elizabeth sang in her heart in time to the jigging notes of the lutes. 'I am still only twenty-one and I am at Court again, and dancing with Philip of Spain.'

The last three words were oddly exciting; not only because she was dancing with the greatest Prince in the world, nor because she felt that he admired her, and unwillingly, which made it so much the greater compliment. Why did she have this sense of immediate importance in dancing with him, in snatching a few words with him within the formal enclosure of their dance? In their interview he had said nothing that showed originality; but she had continually found herself wondering why he had said this or that, whether he had held back some meaning for himself behind the bare words. There seemed an infinity of reserve behind them.

Did he too find a hidden urgency in their meeting, an importance far beyond this present moment in the brightly lighted room enclosed like a jewel in the surrounding darkness? She laughed at herself. Philip of Spain had none of her reasons to hear this moment ring like a peal of bells within her; it was she, the disgraced prisoner, the Princess degraded from her rank, who had reason to thank her stars that she was alive, let alone free to dance with a handsome young man whose dancing was nearly as excellent as her own.

But for his chin, she thought, smiling sweetly at it as they parted at the end of the dance (it was a bad line, that underhung jaw; would Mary's baby inherit it?), but for that, he was as personable as any man here, except one. 'Oh Robin!' she whispered to a young man who stood among the encircling background of courtiers that had been watching their dance, 'how glad I am that you are so much taller than I!'

He was handing her dropped handkerchief, to her, a square of embroidery and lace, large enough to cover his fingers as they gripped hers. 'Is that the only difference between him and me – a matter of a few inches?'

'No, you fool! There is the difference of more than half the world and the whole mastery of England.'

'He'll never leave a footprint in England – unless you let him.'

'Let go my hand. He's watching.'

'Let him! Let all the world—'

'Let *go*!'

Her nails were sharply pointed. He let go, hurriedly, and she left him, a little too hurriedly. She should touch wood when she touched Robin; it was tempting Providence even to remind that frail lady (for she must be one, as she could never resist temptation) that her worst hour of danger in the Tower had come from none of her enemies, but from this young man who had so passionately desired her.

'Who is that tall fellow?' asked Philip in their next dance.

She did not know which tall fellow he meant. Was it the son of the Earl of Arundel?

'No. Though he, I believe, aspires to your hand, or his father does for him. Or is it rather, now, that his father aspires to it for himself?'

'The aspirants are three times too many. When I was in the Tower, the Earl of Arundel was urgent for my death.'

'Until he saw the light – of your eyes, and swore on his knees never to trouble you more.'

'A chivalrous old gentleman. But marriage to him would trouble me worse – well, almost worse, than death.'

'My sister, you are a virgin. It is quite correct that you should find some things worse than death. But I do not think that the tall young man standing by the door is one of them. And now will you tell me who he is?'

'Oh – *that*! Oh yes, I see whom you mean. But that is a nobody – l only thanked him for picking up my handkerchief.'

'Yes, I saw where you dropped it. And who is this nobody?'

'Only one of the sons of the late Duke of Northumberland, whom the Queen has lately had the clemency to release from the Tower. His father, Duke Dudley they called him over here, was beheaded for his rebellion when my little brother King Edward died, and he, the Duke, tried to put his daughter-in-law Jane Grey on the throne. A very wicked man,' said Elizabeth virtuously, 'he would have killed both my sister the Queen and myself.'

'I know about the Duke. What of his sons?'

'Let me see. There was Jack, Earl of Warwick – no, he died of the plague in the Tower. And Guildford – no, he was Jane's husband who died with her, the only one to be beheaded. And Harry, but he's too young. And Ambrose, or did he too die of the plague? If so, this must be Robert.'

'Robin Dudley. I think I have heard of him by that name. And is "Bonny sweet Robin"—'

'Not "all *my* joy," I assure Your Majesty! He was married years ago to Amy Robsart in a boy and girl love-match.'

'The kind of match that burns out quicker even than the match-tape held to a gun. And he was put in the Tower after the Queen's victory over his father. So he was there when you were, a year ago.'

'Yes, but—'

'But, what? Will you tell me again that it was only a boy of five who gave you flowers in the Tower? And nothing else?'

She looked into his eyes and felt cold. Suddenly she laughed. 'Whatever I say to you will be disbelieved. So of what use to say it? But what, after all, can you do to me? Nothing worse than death. But I have looked at death too often and too long to fear it now. Only – if I were dead, and if by any evil chance the Queen too might die, Your Majesty might have an awkward rearguard movement to reconnoitre before leaving England.'

He could not believe her boldness. She had put it all into open words, the fear of dangers that even Ruy Gomez had only dared to hint at, but that was guiding all his policy in releasing her from prison. *What* was he releasing? A genie out of a bottle, as in the old Moorish tales, rising in a cloud of fiery smoke against him? Even in this country, where men who had never seen her seemed to adore her, there were hints of a cloven hoof in her ancestry, and a prevalent belief that her mother had been a witch. He would have liked to cross himself against this daughter of the Devil. But instead he spoke soothingly.

'What nonsense is this? You must give a brother licence to tease you about your lovers, or else I shall believe that they are all indeed your lovers in good, or bad, earnest; yes, even the bald Arundel and the bushy-bearded old bear Bedingfeld.'

She was laughing happily, not at his badinage, as he

flattered himself, but because she was thinking, 'Now he is playing soft in his turn. It is always safer to attack.' 'Be bold, be bold,' as the nursery tale had it, but in answer to it came a chilling whisper, as from an open grave,

> '*Be bold, be bold, but not too bold,*
> *Lest that thy heart's blood should run cold.*'

'And that,' she said, not knowing she spoke aloud, 'was the end of the story.'

'What do you say, Princess?'

'Nothing, sir. I was thinking of a fairytale,' – 'and of a dance in the firelight with a dead man,' she added to herself, but not aloud.

She was thinking of Tom Wyatt, who had come to warn her before he rose in rebellion to put her on the throne instead of Queen Mary; and was beheaded.

The tinkling music struck its final chord. She curtseyed to King Philip, turned, and saw Queen Mary looking at them.

'The body is a traitor. It is not my mind nor my will that is jealous. I urged my husband to dance, and with my sister. Once she was admitted to Court, I knew that I should have to do this, that I should have to sit on this dais and watch them dance together, since I cannot dance now, and perhaps I never shall again. But that is no reason to be jealous, since the reason I sit here is because I hold his child in my womb. I am blessed among women.'

Mary said this last to herself many times, and, at the same time, that she had no need thus to reassure herself.

But so many were seeking to reassure her. They had

brought a woman of fifty to see her who had just given birth for the first time, and to a hearty pair of twins, and reminded Mary that she herself was not yet quite forty. They had no need to reassure her, she told them. God had already worked a miracle for her in setting her on the throne above all her enemies. It was because He had meant her to be there, to do His work in England, and to bear a child that should carry it on.

The cradle, gorgeously decorated, lay in her room all ready for the day – it was any day now – that the bells should peal out the news that she had reached the triumphant pinnacle of her life, for which God had created her. Baby clothes and swaddling bands were piled high, some of the embroidery worked by herself, but not much, for the fine stitching made her eyes and head ache. Even toys were all ready, a rattle with silver bells, a coral mounted in gold to cut his first tooth on, a jack-in-the-box, and even, from donors with long views, painted hobby horses for him to ride. There was never any question but that the baby would be a boy. The future Sovereign of the World must be a man, and a strong one, to hold the world together. God, having done so much already for her, would not be niggardly in this final gift. If He gave her a child, it would surely be the one best fitted to carry on His work.

And why that 'if'? The child was certain, his birth would come any day now, the doctors said.

Any day. Day after day. And as each day died, then it would come the next. There was no need for her women to fuss and ask her questions so tactfully. There was nothing to do but wait patiently, as her husband was doing in such exemplary fashion, in spite of the supposed eagerness of youth. But then he was able to occupy himself, riding and hunting, and Mary did not dare ask how often Elizabeth was of the party.

More often than she saw; though more than once she saw them ride out through the gates of the Palace gardens into the Home Park at the head of their gaily coloured cortège while she stood behind the window curtains, hoping no one would catch a glimpse of her, and peered out from the dim panelled room to see them ride into the sunlight. Short-sighted as she was, she could see his flaxen head turn towards the deeper ruddy gold of Elizabeth's, and her mind twisted and turned inside itself to try and guess what the two were saying to each other.

But nothing could be more innocent than Elizabeth's opening to conversation – in Spanish, for she had been working night and day to perfect herself in it. She had flung back her head to look at the chestnut trees above them and laughed with pleasure at the strange sculpture of the spring, the leaves bursting from the tight sticky swaddling bands of their buds into shapes as fantastic as the outlandish plants that his sailors had brought back from the New World.

'Or as your signature,' he replied unexpectedly. 'Never have I seen a signature so fantastically designed. I said you could be an artist, but I do not know in what craft.'

'It is pleasant to think so, and I have thought it – that if I were turned out of this kingdom in my petticoat I could yet contrive to earn my livelihood.'

He gave an uneasy glance at her and she gave back a resolutely candid gaze that met and held his eyes. There was something both cool and reckless about her which disturbed all the ideals he had built up for his way of living and thinking; it was such a disturbance as the old often feel in the presence of the young; and that was ridiculous, for he was only half a dozen years older than she. But he was of an older world and way of thought, and in her he confronted a new one, outside his ken; she was of another race, barbaric, he told himself, and even of another sex than he had known; as tantalizing as any woman, yet bearing the challenge of a man.

'And how would you earn your living?' he asked rather lamely, for it was not what he had wished to say.

'I know nothing of that. Only that I would make a fair shift of it. Will Your Majesty try me at it for a wager? Turn me loose in Europe tomorrow and see what comes of it.'

'God forbid! I'd as soon turn loose a young lioness! Your hair and eyes are of the colour of danger. You are not a craftsman but a conquistador.'

'A freebooter? Like your Cortez and your Pizarro who conquered a strange continent?'

Her tone showed her delight in the odd compliment.

'Possibly.' He turned over the notion with grave deliberation. 'My great-grandmother of Castile, Isabella the Catholic, she was a Crusader, a Conqueror, as great as any man, greater than her husband Ferdinand of Aragon, whom she had to urge to join with her in driving the heathen Moors from Spain. They had oppressed our country for seven hundred years – until she conquered them. You too might conquer.'

She turned her head and asked him, 'Whom?' He felt as though he were looking into the sun.

'Myself,' he said, and he could look at her no longer.

They jerked their horses' heads straight again and rode on in silence. They flew their hawks to bring down their quarry; the long grey bodies of herons lay under their talons, and the hawks turned their proud heads up, away from them, never looking at their kill.

They dismounted and sat to rest on cloaks that their attendants spread on the grass and then handed round small silver cups of wine and knacks of stuffed cockscombs on biscuits, and Elizabeth snatched a scarlet radish from the dish and peeled it into a fair imitation of her own spreading riding-skirt over the white petticoat. 'I am the radish that is sown in the new moon,' she said.

'So is rosemary and lavender, but they are too dim for you.'

'No, I'm a gaudy vegetable. You, sir, should stick to the colewort.'

'Which is sown in the old moon, with the sign of the cross.' It angered him that she had not thought he would guess at her reference to the Queen. 'Did you think I would not understand gardeners' talk after nine months in England?'

'Lord no! You must be with child with it! Any day now you may bear a herb plot or a knot garden.'

He caught at her radish-coloured skirt, but she sprang up to pick a primrose or violet she saw, she ran down to the edge of the little stream to watch a water-rat swim across, and the water-beetles spin circles on a shallow pool. How fast she moved! Mary's movements were quick too, but with none of the lithe strength and grandeur of this young wild creature.

Yet both these half-sisters, so unlike each other and unlike him, made him uneasily conscious that they had no need to consider their dignity, as he did. *Why?* he demanded of himself, grinding the heel of his riding-boot into the springy green turf. The Tudors were Welsh upstarts, foreign to the English. The Spaniards had complained of his father as a foreigner, despite his Castilian mother; and he, Philip of

Spain, had determined they should never call *him* that.

But these Tudor sisters had never needed nor heeded such a determination. Their Welsh father and grandfather had bolstered up their ancestry with fairytales, had claimed descent from Arthur in order to make good their precarious claim on the throne. The daughters of their line were the more instinctively royal.

He watched Elizabeth as she came back along the bank and called to one of the falconers, spoke to him about her hawk, asked his advice, as Philip would never do of a servant, then handed the bird to him to see to, whistled in answer to a storm-cock until he whistled back again to her, and sank all in one movement on to the grass again beside Philip.

'My father says that English is the best language in which to call to hawks and other birds,' he told her.

'And in German to horses, I imagine.'

'You guess right, as always.'

'And what is Spanish best for?'

'For God, and the King.'

'Being the same?'

'It is convenient to think so.'

They laughed. Blown petals of wild cherry fell into their laps. She asked him about the plain of Cordova, which she had heard was a vast cloud of white almond-blossom every spring.

'There is a reason for that which might please you, if you would care for a love story.'

'What woman would not! Tell it me.'

'It happened four or five hundred years ago when the Moors ruled the land, if locusts can be said to rule. There was a female mule-driver called Romaiquia – yes, women still drive mules in the South. She was of the lowest birth, a brazen hussy, but a beauty and of great wit – she could cap verses impromptu better than anyone in Seville. That is a game you can still hear played in Seville, the drivers of mules and goats making up verses and calling them to each other as they pass down the narrow streets. It was so that she caught the ear of the Sultan, and then his eye; she became his Sultana, and he her slave. He would have made the world anew for her. One winter it was so cold that for the first time in memory there was snow on the Cordova plain. Romaiquia was so pleased with the sight that she demanded it should be provided for her every year. The Sultan could not command the heavens to fall, but he could command trees to rise. He had white almond-trees planted all over the plain, so that every year in early spring Romaiquia should see the Andalusian plain as white as snow.'

He had flushed at the unwonted length of his speech, and also because, as he had made it, they had both felt it come near to themselves. Of low birth and brazen, a beauty and great wit – she knew he had been thinking of her as he said the words.

'Now *there* was a female conquistador!' she exclaimed. 'I wish I had been a mule-driver to cap verses in the Seville streets.'

'And capture a Sultan?'

'Yes, if for me he would spread almond-blossom like snow in Andalusia. Your Moorish locusts had some pretty fancies. I should like to see their stucco work in Granada, making fine lace out of stone.'

'Dolls' gardens, my father calls them' he replied contemptuously. 'Perhaps you would also have liked the

Moorish Prince Motadid's flowerpots in Seville, that held the skulls of his enemies, with labels to show their names instead of flowers.' The hatred in his voice showed her that she must not mention Moors lightly, and small wonder.

She dared not let their conversation end on that note, though old Lady Clarencieux was watching them out of the corner of an eye acid with disapproval at this prolonged interruption to the hunt. Fortunately Ruy Gomez was entertaining her very well; Philip must find the Portugee an invaluable fellow. And Susan Clarencieux was unlikely to worry her adored Queen at this juncture with any disturbing gossip; Elizabeth had more to fear from that lively forthright young widow, Jane Dormer, but all *her* attention was being engaged by the Spaniard Feria. Most of the company indeed were pairing off like the birds that shrilled above them in the new warmth of this early April day, and what more natural than that her brother-in-law should still be sitting at her side?

She led him on to tell her more of Spain, and so of himself, a subject rare with him, yet he found himself doing it with such unusual ease that he thought she had been talking most.

'Your mind is a dragonfly or a green lizard darting in the sunlight,' he told her; 'you catch ideas as they do insects. But I,' – he hesitated, then took the plunge, 'I am slow. I am not clever. Nor was my father. He has told me that he was stupid as a boy and a young man. Yet he had to pit his brains against the cleverest rulers in Europe – François I of France, that treacherous fox, and Henry VIII of England—' He paused.

'Yes, please say it. You have no need to paraphrase your father's opinion of mine.'

'No, I have no need. For it was an enviable tribute – that King Henry possessed "that nonchalance which is the best secret of politics." Only a rich and rapidly working mind can possess that. My father, on the contrary, has had to work like ten men to make himself a great ruler. And I therefore must work ten times as hard as he.'

A really mediocre mind could surely never admit as much, or rather as little of itself. She was impressed by the dignity, and the determination, with which he recognized his limitations. And for all the frankness, almost simplicity, of this unusual mood, there was still some secret meaning, or perhaps secret power, retained behind the suave voice, which he did not choose to show.

The seed of what strange growth lay deep within him? A saint? A satyr? A great ruler? A fanatic? A frozen monster?

Any of these was possible; but also, at any rate at this present, a worshipping boy when he spoke of his father. Who might develop into a man capable of an equal give-and-take of passion and friendship with a woman? She wondered, weighing the unnatural formula of etiquette and piety which had bound his youth in rigid swaddling-bands long after he had ceased to be a child, and forced him to regard his body and soul as a public institution.

Against such upbringing, compared with which her precarious and often neglected childhood seemed sheer freedom, there was now this moment of springtime when he was falling in love with her.

And she, at this moment, might soon find herself in love with him. What might they not make of it? Might he not shake off his swaddling-bands, his ancient inheritance of a sense of guilt that he must atone, of belief in an angry God that must be appeased by sacrifice; and become a living hopeful force that would wield the future, with her help?

She could see him thinking this too, and believing it more than she. She knew more clearly than he what had already been made of him; how small a chance was left for him to become the partner who could help her in the work she might one day do. There still might be a chance. If not, would she ever again find such a partner? She thought not. She was alone, and must be so always, unless she met her equal; without any conscious pride she knew that to be unlikely.

Playfellows, not partners, were all that she could probably afford. She was playing with Philip now, and knew it, hoping that he did not. Her purpose would probably be always different from his. He certainly did not see that. But she for her part no longer saw his eyes as a prawn's.

A man came riding down the glade and after a quick glance round the company went up to Ruy Gomez and spoke to him. Ruy Gomez came towards Philip, who stiffened and froze as he approached. 'He knows it is from Mary,' thought Elizabeth. 'She has sent word that his presence is urgently required.'

And so she had. They all rode back to the Palace, and this time as they came through the grounds Philip kept his horse at a much further distance from Elizabeth's, and did not once turn his head towards her.

But to Mary, again watching from behind the curtain, the sight brought no comfort, and no appeasement of her rage.

CHAPTER TEN

'I might have died,' she stormed at her coldly wretched young husband. 'I felt so ill, in such pain just now, that all my women feared it. But *you* wish it!'

'Only your illness could make you think it.'

She clutched at his hand. 'Yes, yes,' she sobbed, 'it must be my illness. How could I say such dreadful things of you! You are kind. But you cannot know what it is to feel as desperately ill as I am doing, almost more in mind than body. Questions twist and turn within me, they are serpents gnawing at me.'

She had flung away from his hand, which had been as limp as his glove, and was walking up and down, up and down. Suddenly she threw over her shoulder, 'I know *she* wishes me dead.'

'Very likely,' observed Philip. Obviously Elizabeth would wish Mary's death, since she had everything to gain from it. Why could not Mary see and admit it? But she could see nothing clearly. The room seemed dim and small after the sunlight, and she like a dark bat flitting up and down in it, weaving her way blindly and her words with it, as if she did not know what way she or they would take.

'She may even work my death. It may well be possible. She is the daughter of a witch. Nan Bullen had the beginning of a sixth finger on one hand, a devil's teat for his imps to suck.

And her daughter' (she could not bear to speak Elizabeth's name) 'has a strange look in her eyes at times. I have seen the pupils go narrow and upright like those of a cat.' Her voice had died away into a mutter, ashamed to speak such haverings clearly before his coolly watchful gaze. Yet surely if a witch might overlook her or her child and cause their death, that witch must first be put to death. But there was only her own fancy to prove it.

'What *can* I do?' she cried, and he tried to answer sympathetically.

'Nothing; but wait for your hour and God's will.'

But she could not wait. Was there indeed nothing she could do? Nothing it seemed but to antagonize her husband, call him back from hunting on what he plainly regarded as a flimsy pretext, and then nag at him. She would give her life for him, but he would not believe that, and would not care if he did. She must not say it.

If only she could give her life for the child, if she could die in giving birth to him, then she would accept the sacrifice with resignation – no, with thankfulness!

She jerked herself to a standstill, staring open-eyed at the sudden dreadful knowledge. It would be no sacrifice; it would be a blessed relief. What heaven not to have to struggle on with life; to feel more and more tired and sick of her aching body; to see herself get older and older in Philip's eyes; to see them turn from her to Elizabeth; and, when he knew that she was watching, to see them turn away.

What a fool she was not to have known this before – or had she always known it, even before it had happened, before he had even met Elizabeth?

Being herself, she could not refrain from showing Philip

that she knew it. 'You watch her very carefully.'

'As I would the Devil,' he replied.

Her heart leaped. 'Then – you *don't* like her? You, too, don't trust her?'

'Not an inch.'

As she did not look convinced, he added, 'If you keep a panther in a cage, then suddenly release it, would you trust it?'

'I only released her because you wished it,' said Mary, and, Oh God, there she was crying again. Her sobs turned to hysterical little shrieks. In another minute her women would come running to her and he would be silently accused of endangering her life and their child's. He must stop her crying. He must say something quickly that would reassure her about Elizabeth, for that was plainly the trouble.

'You – and I—' he added hastily, for it would comfort her to link herself with him, 'need not trouble ourselves unduly with that young lady. In England admittedly she is an ever-present nuisance, a possible danger. Then let us get her out of England. We have already considered the plan to marry her to Emmanuel of Savoy and so link her to a Spanish dependency. And moreover give her a husband who, if he is half as forcible in the marriage bed as he is in the battlefield, should be fully capable of keeping a tight rein on her.'

He watched his effect. Mary was looking at him doubtfully. Did she think this too good to be true on his part? Uncomfortably he reviewed the conversation he had just had with Elizabeth in the woods, he did not know for how long; it may well have been longer than he had thought, and someone may already have told the Queen of it. But what he had just been saying to her surely gave good reason for it.

'I have not been merely amusing myself with the chase,' he said virtuously, and to his annoyance caught the echo of the self-exculpatory tone he had so often used as a boy to his rigid tutor. 'I have been putting forward this project to her, as indeed it has been put before, and with your approval – but this time, I think, with greater urgency and persuasion.'

'Indeed,' said Mary. She had quite stopped crying; in that at least he had had the effect he intended. But he was not so sure of this new steely stillness. He had better go before she had time to think of anything else. But she had already thought of it, and before he reached the door she said it.

'A Spanish dependency. And that would place her in most convenient dependency, and proximity, to you when you return to Spain.'

'This, Madam, is ridiculous. Her husband—'

'Is a soldier. So was Uriah the Hittite.'

For the first time he saw a resemblance in her to Elizabeth. What a pair!

But the resemblance was already crumpling up in her now puckered and sagging face. '*You* thought of that!' she cried, 'to have her near you, away from me.'

He had thought of it. But he had not thought she would do so. He would never have suspected her of being so suspicious. These virtuous women were always evil-minded.

For the first time she saw clearly the distaste in his eyes as they opened full and pale upon her. But distaste was not a thing she understood; and she read the look as one of cold hatred.

Her next words horrified him. 'The only safe place for her is where your father long ago wanted her to be – on the scaffold.'

'He does not now.'

'No. You have all changed, all of you. Your policy shifts and veers like a weather-cock, because it is only policy, because none of you care what is right or wrong. I spared her life when all my friends advised me against it, because I thought it right to do so. I do not think now that it is right. If I were to die now she would be a worse enemy to England than all the invading armies of France and Scotland. She would undo all my work for the Church and lead the country back into heresy. I will not risk it. If I should die of my unborn child, at least I shall first rid the country of this subtle canker.'

'Do so, and you will remove my one chance to defend myself here, alone, against your country. If you should die – which God forbid – then leave her to me as hostage – that is all the interest I should have in her.'

It was comfortable to believe it. She felt too sick to fight further.

Philip disliked having been led into a direct lie. Besides, it was unsafe. He decided to make it true at the first opportunity, and soon made the opportunity by walking with his sister-in-law in one of the pleached alleys that led down to the river in the gardens of Whitehall. It was out of sight of the Palace windows.

Elizabeth listened with respectful interest to his proposal of Emmanuel Philibert of Savoy as a husband for her; she had heard it before, she said, and agreed that he was a most worthy and honourable choice, young, good-looking, a good soldier, and so good at mathematics, of which she had always wanted to learn more; 'we could work out Euclid's propositions together,' said she, clasping her hands in girlish pleasure, 'and he could teach me algebra, but perhaps not that, for didn't the Moors invent it, or was it only the alphabet?'

'Is that all that he could teach you?'

'I doubt he'd have time to teach me anything – yes, *anything* – for I hear he sits up all night studying the arts of engineering and mechanical warfare.'

'Well. Would you rather choose a carpet knight?'

'I would not choose to sleep on the floor, but if I did, I should prefer a carpet to a steel plate. Marry him? I'd as soon marry a lobster! They say he lives and sleeps in his armour for as long as a month at a stretch.'

'You seem to know a great deal about him.'

'Naturally, sir. I made it my business, since he has often before been suggested as my bridegroom. But –' her light voice deepened, hesitated, it was a different woman speaking, 'I did not think that you would have done so.'

'Should I not have a brother's care for your welfare?'

'You did not speak of this when we talked so lately.' She sounded wistful, a little hurt. 'Did you have it then in your mind?'

'I had then, and have now, this in my mind – that I must have you near me. If not here in England, then in Spain. Let us speak freely—'

'Good God!' breathed Elizabeth.

'Well then, as freely as any man can draw breath in this heavy air.' He looked around and behind him, but no one showed through the thin lattice-work of the still all but leafless trees. 'The Queen *may* bear an heir to me, and live. What then? Why, then I am tied to her, and to this country, at intervals; but of shorter and shorter duration.'

'Why?'

'As she grows older, there will be the less and less chance of her bearing heirs to our two countries,' he explained patiently. 'And there will be the less reason for my presence here – the more for it in Spain, the centre of the world's government.'

She only nodded.

'In that case,' he doggedly pursued, 'what place would there be for you here, among a minority of suspect heretics? You would have small shrift from your sister, let me warn you. Nor does she choose to believe that you are her sister.'

'Who then, in God's name?'

'Scarcely his, Madonna mia. Yes, I can speak that much Italian. You'll find no Archangel Gabriel among the fathers she suggests for you. But a choice of five others.'

'With my mother's own brother, George Lord Rochford, among them!'

'I think she fancies rather the hireling musician, Mark Smeaton, as the favourite.'

'Tell me, Your Highness, is it your own opinion that my true name is Elizabeth Smeaton?'

'No. From what my father has told me of him, I should say that you bear all the markings of King Henry VIII.'

'I thank Your Highness. But in any case, if King Henry's elder and undoubted daughter Mary continues as England's Queen and your wife, and the mother of your heirs, it matters little to you who and what I am.'

'It matters little – *nothing* – in any case.'

They had reached the bank of the river below. It gleamed silver between the feathery gold of its waving rushes, it slid down below them past their elegantly shod feet, his in white buckskin, hers in green leather, it flowed on through London to the great Tower itself, its gentle ripples lapping against the steps of Traitors' Gate, where just a year ago she had been forced to land and enter that narrow prison from which so few came forth alive.

Well, she had done it – once. But a second time was too much to hope for.

'It matters a deal to me,' she said, 'if the Queen should consider double bastardy as equal to treason.'

'I fancy,' he replied judicially, 'that the truer and nearer your claim to the throne, the greater your danger. It is in your best interests that I advise your leaving England, and if not as the bride of Savoy (or, as you prefer it, of a lobster) then it might be as the guest of my Aunt Margaret, the Regent of the Spanish Netherlands, who has more than once invited you to the safe shelter of her Court.'

'I am greatly honoured by your aunt and indebted to her. But I could never bring myself to leave my country, however dangerous it be to me.'

'Why? Because your highest hopes are rooted in its soil?'

She did not answer. He changed his tack and said carelessly, 'I shall have to give close attention to the Netherlands in the near future.'

'So that, whether with your aunt or with my bridegroom, I can rest assured of Your Highness's continued brotherly care?'

'Assuredly.' He laid his hand on hers, which by a furious effort of restraint lay still under it, instead of flinging up to box his ears.

So this was the lover and possible equal partner she had imagined in the forest glade only two bright mornings ago! No equal, but a strutting little superior, farming out his secret slut with one pander or another! She could permit herself at least to flout away his hand in a show of pique that could not really offend, might even flatter him. 'And I thought you wanted me for myself!' she exclaimed, with an air of childishly brazen frankness.

'I want you for *my*self.'

'But only at second-hand, it seems.'

'How else, at present? Since that is only how I can make offer of myself. I am tied at first hand to the Queen of England, and must be while she lives and gives hope of an heir. But if she should not—'

He waited, but Elizabeth gave him no help.

'It is possible she may not survive childbirth,' he said. 'In her low state of health it is, I am told, even probable.'

Still she did not speak, and the reflected light from the running water below played up and down on the pale oval of her face, making a mockery of its stillness. So it would stay still for ever, while the emotions of others wove their pattern of life and death against it, but left it untouched, a mask hiding the woman beneath.

His words came up against her, each sentence groping, daring a little further, but fell back from her, leaving no mark.

His voice dropped very low. 'Then your hopes might match with mine.'

This time he drew an answer, though only in the form of a question. 'Does Your Highness know so well what mine are?'

'To be Queen of England.'

'And yours?'

'To make the match I spoke of just now.'

'Is this a wooing at first hand this time?'

'As near first hand as "ifs" and "ands" will allow it. We are neither of us free – yet.'

'Nor will you ever be,' she thought, and aloud, 'Spain is indeed a constant lover! Fifty years ago Katherine of Aragon married first my father's brother and then my father, so as to keep England in the family. And now you would marry first one sister and then the other, in the same good cause. But the precedent was unlucky. King Henry annulled his marriage because it was incestuous to marry with his brother's wife. Your deceased wife's sister would stand in no better case. And believe me, sir, I will not claim Mark Smeaton as a father in order to clear it!'

'I think,' he said slowly, 'that your true father is the Devil himself. You affect to know nothing of what I feel for you. But you must know it. I want you, whether at first or second hand, whether in Savoy, the Netherlands, or in England. But you will give me no shadow of a sign in answer.'

'Have pity! Such a shadow may well lead me into the shadow of death.'

'Then – is it only fear—?'

'"*Only.*" Your Highness can never have known what that is. You laid your hand on mine just now. If anyone passing at that moment saw it, would you bet high on my chance of outliving the Queen?'

'No. You are wise, and cautious.' They were the two qualities on which he had most prided himself, and now he hated them. 'Tell me this at least—' he paused.

'What, sir?'

'That if – that one day you might—' he began, then stopped outright. It was not for Philip of Spain to beg for love, when he was so uncertain of the answer. 'I will ask you nothing,' he said. 'But one day I may take.'

He bowed low and formally, turned on his heel and left her.

She watched him go back up the pleached alley. The neat criss-cross pattern of its branches cast a shadow like a gridiron on the slight figure as it walked away from her, with a little more dignity than became a rather small man, but that gave her no amusement, and some fear.

She wanted to call him back, but already it was too late, and then to run after him, but now it was too late for that too. It was always too late to retract, to try and retrieve what one had done. She had dared not encourage, but she need not have teased and tantalized him to such a point. And now he was moving away from her, up into the long tunnel of the trees that cast a shadow on him like a gridiron.

She shivered; she strolled on beside the river and wondered what would happen next.

It happened very soon; a tall young man, who waved his cap, then ran towards her, and her downcast heart flew up when she saw that it was Robin Dudley.

'The Queen has sent a page to look for you,' he told her breathlessly. 'Go to her quickly and be very careful. There's the devil to pay – it's because of John Knox – you know, the Presbyterian Scot, the preacher who gave trouble here even with the Protestants.'

'But he's not here now. Knox fled with Foxe and Cox and the rest of the box.'

'That's the trouble.' Robin was striding back in the direction of the Palace, she could scarcely keep up with him, his long legs went so fast without seeming to hurry. She found them curiously reassuring after the slow determined pace of the smaller man that she had just been watching.

'A tall man is safer,' she told herself.

'Knox sits snug and smug with his fellow Black-gowns at

Geneva,' Robin flung back over his shoulder, '*so* he can safely write a book to attack the Queen and add fuel to the fires at Smithfield. The Bishops have only lately begun to burn a few heretics there, but you'll see, the pace will quicken now.'

'At least slacken *your* pace. I'm out of breath.' (Even to Robin she would not admit that she had gasped for fear.) He slowed down, and she still more, planning desperately how she should answer Mary.

'He's going the best way to foul his own nest,' she called after him. 'His fellow Protestants here must hate him anyway for his quickness to save his own skin.'

'He's still saving it, or thinks so. The dirty coward's published it anonymously, but it's known to be his book.'

'What *is* the book?'

'It's called *The First Blast of the Trumpet against the Monstrous Regiment of Women*.'

CHAPTER ELEVEN

Mary had deliberately allowed John Knox to escape from England together with hundreds of other Protestant preachers at the beginning of her reign. She had believed then that she could lead back her country to the Church of Rome in peace and mercy, and had publicly resolved to use no harshness nor punishment for the error into which it had been led by its former rulers.

Her plan had not worked.

Since then, a priest's nose had been hacked off in Kent, a church full of worshippers set on fire in Suffolk, and in London's own Cathedral of St. Paul's a priest had been all but murdered on the altar steps, and the Host splashed with his blood. Words matched the deeds. Mr. Foxe was including the would-be murderer in his projected Book of Martyrs. Bishop Bale had written to Bishop Bonner, 'What is your idolatrous mass and lousy Latin service, you sosbelly swill-bowl, but the dregs of the devil?' And Mr. Knox had written a book that denied Mary any right even to the mercy she had shown him.

So this was how he returned thanks! This was what came of being merciful. She had tried to be, and her enemies would not let her. They had hardened their hearts against her and rewarded her mercy with hate. God could not have meant her to be merciful. This must be His way of telling her that He had sent her to bring not peace but a sword.

She sat crouched in her bedroom over the book, peering into it with her short-sighted eyes, and stabs of pain running up from them through her head as if the thick black strokes of the printed words were actual knives thrusting into her.

'That horrible monster, Jezebel of England,' they called her – 'a wicked woman, traitoress and bastard who has no right to the Crown.' She turned the page and read his prayer that 'God shall kindle all hearts with deadly hatred against her.'

She raised her eyes and saw Elizabeth standing before her; and in her the answer to John Knox's prayer.

That bright still figure was surely kindled with deadly hatred against her.

'This preacher – John Knox – what do you know of him? Speak honestly, if you can. No hesitation. I want no false abuse.'

Elizabeth answered rapidly, breathlessly, 'Then, Madam, I will say only what his own party said of him when they had made him Court preacher here – "he is neither grateful nor pleasable." The very first of his Court sermons was a long scream against what he called "the hideous idolatry" of kneeling at Communion. Afterwards he preached against his patrons under a thin disguise of names from the Bible; he protested that, even under their violently Protestant rule, no one but himself was Protestant enough. His own Archbishop Cranmer could not abide him; he said he was "a trouble-maker who could never let well alone." This is the character given him by his own allies.'

But Mary was peering at the book as though she had not heard. '"Heresies breed disorders,"' she muttered. 'Sir Thomas More said so long ago.'

Elizabeth tried desperately to distract her attention.

'Madam, there can be no surer proof of it than in this man's disordered mind.'

Mary thrust the book at her. 'Read it,' she commanded, 'read it to me. Do not turn the page. Read it wherever you are.'

Elizabeth read aloud, '"Woman having been accursed of God is to be for ever in complete bondage to man, and daily to humble and subject herself to him."'

'And do *you* agree with that?'

'No, Madam. Nor with any sentence I can see. This is not literature, it is "blotterature".'

'So you can quote too. More and Colet, we are in fine company!' Her laugh was dreadful. She snatched the book again from Elizabeth, bent her head almost on to the page and read out, '"It is more than a monster in nature that women should reign over men." – Ah, that touches you to the quick, too, you who look to be the next woman ruler! It's for *that* that you wait and watch. You stand there looking at me – there's another name for such watching – the overlooking of a witch.'

'Witch – watch,' the words yammered against Elizabeth's brain, thrown clean off its guard by this astounding new accusation. She had plunged into a nightmare, she dared not move nor speak, dared not look at Mary since that was 'overlooking,' dared not look away since that showed a guilty conscience.

She heard a voice loud as a man's, loud as their father's in a rage, telling her that it was of no use for her to wait and watch for signs of the Queen's ill health, to hope for her death and that of her child – 'no use, I tell you,' said Mary's strange voice, 'for you are a bastard twice over, you can never inherit the throne. What if I leave no heir? What even then? It makes no odds to you. For then the true heir to England is, without any question, Mary Queen of Scots.'

Even this was a respite. Elizabeth was not after all being ordered to her death. But she was now as much afraid, though more coldly. This last threat was blurted out in Mary's rage as it swayed uncertainly to this point and that; but it was none the less plain that it was her considered intention. She would hold to it. She would, if possible, carry it out in her Will. Philip would not like it; but that might be an added inducement, especially after one of their quarrels.

Mary cried out, 'Why don't you speak? What are you thinking?'

'That the little Queen of Scots casts a long shadow.'

'Which turns you cold, hey?'

'And will others. When she is Queen of France as well as Scotland – and –' Elizabeth baulked, but said it – 'and England, then Spain will no longer lead the world.'

'Always politics. It is all you think of, yes, *all* of you.' Yes, even Philip, she thought, and hurried on, 'At least that child would keep England's religion safe. She is a true daughter of the Church.'

'She was brought up in it, Madam, as I was not.'

'How should you be, by a mother known as "a spleeny Lutheran"!'

She was hitting feebly now, aimlessly. She would regret such a taunt instantly and be the more amenable. Elizabeth felt safer.

'But I am learning now,' she said meekly.

'You are taking a long time over it. And how do I know you are sincere, since it is for your safety? Life is sweet to you.'

The last words fell on so dropped and sad a note that a sharp pity caught Elizabeth unawares.

'Ah, Madam, and how should it not be sweet, now you have restored me to your favour, at least in part? But you,' she glanced at the cradle in the corner, 'with your great hopes, you must—'

'Find life sweet? Girl, what a fool you are, or would be if you believed yourself. But you are well used to unbelief. And how should I believe your faith in God? *I* forswore Him once, because I too was young and found life sweet, and feared to disobey my father – as you fear to disobey me. I acknowledged him to be the Supreme Head of the Church of England; I did "utterly refuse the Bishop of Rome's pretended authority within this realm"; – the words will stand for ever – I see them before me now in the flickering candlelight – a hot June night, Thursday it was, Thor's Day the heathen called it, and his thunder was rolling in the sky, but no thunderbolt fell to strike me dead. They made me sign each clause, forswearing God and my dead mother. She was hounded to death, but they could not make her forswear herself. It was I who did that to her, I who loved her more than anyone in the world. I acknowledged that her marriage with my father "was by God's law and man's law incestuous." And God has not yet punished me, not *yet*!'

With a blind gesture she groped out towards the cradle.

She had utterly forgotten Elizabeth who stood aghast before a misery so near to madness. Reason could never answer it; though she longed to tell her almost angrily that at least she had not hurt her mother by her perjury, since she had then been dead.

Remorse had been useful while it had helped Mary to be

merciful. But now it had begun to work the other way, what horrors might it not lead to in England? And anyway it was nineteen years ago, and how could one live, let alone rule, if one kept company with ghosts?

But the sagging, hollow face of the forlorn woman, whose womanhood seemed given her only for torment, stabbed her with a painful and unwilling emotion. She flung herself on her knees, and caught at the thin hands that were twisting and tormenting each other.

'God *has* punished you, Madam. Our father treated you vilely. You were a girl of twenty. He had kept you for years in prison. He could break the strongest spirit, but you stood up against all others. You told Edward to take your head but you would keep the mass.'

A little cold serpent of common sense whispered smiling to her that there had been no danger of the boy Edward taking his elder sister's head, it would have been most embarrassing to him – but that would not occur to Mary. The hands between hers had gone numb and dead. In anxiety that was only in small part for Mary, she chafed them, crying, 'It is over and past. You have fought a great fight and won the country to you. You have restored the Church –'

'But not the Church properties!' cried Mary on a cracking peal of laughter, and pulled away her hands.

Well at least she had heard and answered, so was not mad, yet. Elizabeth spoke more coolly, 'You have restored *your* share of them, Madam. What more can you do?'

'What more? You dare ask me that, who are the hope and figure-head of all these rebel Lutherans!' She was trembling, baffled and bewildered by Elizabeth's unexpected sympathy. She did not want to believe in it, and indeed Elizabeth herself was now amazed at it. Why had she been hurt even for an instant by hurt to Mary, who was crying, 'Oh yes, you can protest your innocence, you don't agree with their opinions, you know nothing of their plots, you can fold your hands and purse your lips and pretend that butter won't melt in your mouth, you can deceive all the world, even yourself – but your sin will find you out. God is not mocked. Guilt can only be expiated by sacrifice.'

So the storm's worked round again, was Elizabeth's thought, and as if in answer to it a rumbling, grumbling, thundering sound came bumbling from far off, from the streets behind Whitehall Palace, nearer and nearer, boring its way into this airless room. But it was not thunder. It was a curious animal sound, of many voices, not of an organized march of men, but a sort of muttering growl, now swinging into the rough rhythm of a tune. Involuntarily she turned towards the windows, then turned back.

'No. Go to them. Open them,' said Mary. 'Listen to what the crowd says. That is your forte, I think.'

'They are not speaking, Madam. They are singing.'

'What are they singing?'

'I can barely hear the tune, certainly no words.'

'But you know what they are.'

'No, Madam. London is always finding new street songs. I know very few.'

'Then I will tell you one. Do you know this?

> '"*Mary Mary quite contrary,*
> *How does your garden grow?*
> *Silver bells and cockleshells*
> *And pretty maids all in a row.*"'

'I have heard it and surely it is very harmless. The bells for church services through the day and night, the holy palmers with cockle shells in their hats, the nuns with their pretty faces all in a row, are "quite contrary" to the last reign, and all the better for that, so do many feel.'

She had shut the window and was talking fast to help shut out the sound of that other song. Not for her life did she dare admit that she knew the savage irony of its attack on Mary and Philip.

> '*Spare neither man, woman or child,*
> *Hang and head them, burn them with fire,*
> *What if Christ were both meek and mild,*
> *Satan our lord will give us hire,*
> *Now all shaven crowns to the standard!*
> *Make room! Pull down for the Spaniard!*'

There were louder, angrier shouts outside, shouts, the clash of weapons, a long shrill cry, then a gradual deadening of the noise as the Palace guards dispersed the crowds.

But the swinging rhythm of their song still seemed to echo on in the shut room between the two frightened women.

'Those are your friends,' said Mary.

'God save me from my friends!'

'Go!' Mary shrieked, and Elizabeth fled.

Mary sank her head upon her knees and folded her long-sleeved arms around them, shutting herself in with her dark wings, feeling her knees press against her heavy womb; but could feel no stir within it. 'I am with child with grief, and the midwife is hate.' Her foes, whom she had spared, hated her. Her husband, whom she worshipped, did he hate her? Did

God Himself hate her? Because she had failed Him long ago – or because she was failing Him now, in her weakness towards His enemies?

Her foot thrust out and kicked against the book that was poisoned with a heretic's 'deadly hatred.' Surely he had rent his mother's body asunder when escaping from her hated womb. Would God punish herself in such a way by giving her a son who would also hate her? Could she do nothing to prevent it?

The answer came to her from her answer to that bland and baleful face of her young sister. 'God is not mocked. Guilt can only be expiated by sacrifice.' England must learn that lesson. She harboured many obstinate heretics, but only a very few, and only just lately, had been punished. She must act quickly or her child would be born in sin, the deadly sin of her neglect of the souls of her country. In sudden terror she got up with difficulty and clambered across the room, heavy with child, heavy with guilt, towards the cradle that stood waiting, glittering, empty.

She read again the rhyme carved on its side.

> '*The child which Thou to Mary*
> *Oh Lord of might hast send,*
> *To England's joy, in health,*
> *Preserve, keep and defend.*'

Oh, Lord, give her might to defend him!

Not mercy any longer, but might.

Others must help her. She must consult a man. Not her husband; he was kind and considerate, and she had been mad to wonder if he hated her. But if she asked him now about

English affairs he would only tell her that he could do nothing until she had made the Council give him the Crown matrimonial and an English expeditionary force in Flanders. She had asked, but the Council had refused.

'If it were my father he would have commanded them,' she thought, and then still more bitterly, 'If it were Elizabeth she would manage them.'

But even if she could give Philip all that he asked, would he help her? His own private chaplain, the learned Spanish friar Alfonso de Castro, had just lately preached a sermon declaring that persecution was not a religious duty. Philip must have allowed, even encouraged him to do so, and why? The answer struck on her heart like a blow; because persecution 'was not always expedient.' That was Machiavelli's word; it never should be hers.

Only one man she knew despised expediency. In her mind's eye there stood again the tall scarlet figure of Cardinal Pole dominating the Members of Parliament last November like a messenger from heaven, his arm outstretched over the abjectly weeping, kneeling forms as he pronounced their absolution.

He had rebuked this guilty nation; and herself. His words to her still burned her mind; 'I do not know if your councillors who urge you to set your kingdom's affairs in order first, and *then* restore religion, believe the words of the Gospel.' He had written that to her, and she could not refute it. He was strong and she was weak. She had once renounced God and her mother. He would never have done that. He alone could help her expiate it.

She would confront Elizabeth with Cardinal Pole.

INTERLUDE: THE PRIEST

CHAPTER TWELVE

Reginald Pole had not always wanted to come home. Italy had indeed been his true home ever since he had gone there to study after leaving Oxford. His scholarship was so excellent that when he was still only twenty-four one of his professors in Greek sent him his book to correct and edit at will; the 'immodest modesty' of which his friends accused him, preferred this to any task of his own.

He had not wanted public life, nor any share in the ruling of his country, nor of the Church. He had refused the Archbishopric of York from Henry VIII; he had done his best to refuse to be Cardinal; he had as good as refused to be Pope. He hated politics and the modern cynicism about them. He had been given a copy of Machiavelli's *Prince* by Henry's minister, Thomas Cromwell, who always carried it about with him as his Bible, and thought it would teach the young dilettante some practical sense of the necessity of force and fraud in statecraft.

It did, but not as Thomas had intended, for Reginald declared the author to be an enemy of mankind and that his book was one to poison Christendom for centuries to come.

Nor did he feel any better about the management of affairs by the Church. At Rome he was horrified at 'the abomination of the Cardinals and Bishops, the detestable vices of the city';

he fled from the capital of Christendom to Venice, where on Ascension Day he watched with joy the purely pagan ceremony of the Doge in crimson and cloth of gold flinging his ring into the water to 'espouse the everlasting sea'; then back to his villa at Padua and his friends and their delightful way of life, as near as possible to that of the patricians of ancient Rome.

His friend Cardinal Bembo preached sermons on Platonic love and avowed himself an Epicurean philosopher. His friend Longolius had abjured his French name, Longueil, vowed never to read any book for five years but those of Cicero, and was solemnly created a Roman citizen as of old; when he died in Reginald's house he bequeathed him his classical library.

The influence of his friends lay like sunlight all over Reginald's early manhood.

'Friendship, dear boy,' Bembo had said, twirling the little moustache that followed the disdainful curve of his lip, 'that is the field of your genius, your nation's genius. You are cold to women. Stay cold. You would make neither them happy nor yourself. You love argument, conversation, though never did any man converse in so few words – but that is the cause of conversation in others. You love the rush and swing of Greek verse, the slow measured cadences of Latin prose, things that no woman has ever truly loved. I, too, love these things, but I love others, which women also love. I love to gather my strawberries myself, to spread them in these flat blue dishes of coarse pottery that the Tuscans have made for centuries, and leave them lying within my darkened rooms during the heat of the day so that their cool scent shall awaken appetite before even the first incredulous rapture of their heady savour. And I love to fill my house with roses, freshly plucked each day. You also love these things, Rinaldo mio, as long as you do not have to do anything about them.

'But, like all Englishmen, you are passive about them. Others must provide your delicate pleasures. That, my young friend, is an unfortunate attitude to take up with regard to women. Therefore I advise you to continue to have nothing to do with them.'

Reginald did not wish to have anything to do with them, and he had not. He did not then remember that his mother was also a woman.

His exquisite life in his villa, with gardens laid out to the plan of the aesthetic Lucullus, was provided by the princely generosity of his relative King Henry VIII of England, who allowed him a hundred a year and with no other obligation than that of entertaining the English Ambassador to Venice and all his retinue, a mere nothing to Reginald, who was accustomed to have his house full of guests at all times. Too full, his house steward Bernardino complained, for they treated the house as though it were their own, and did not leave Bernardino nearly enough time off to copy and edit Greek manuscripts.

But then Reginald in his turn paid long visits, chiefly to Cardinal Bembo and his voluptuous mistress Morosina and their three children who were like Raphael's dark-eyed bambini. He sat among gleaming statues of naked goddesses dug out of the dark earth, and portraits of poets and their loves, Dante and his Beatrice, Petrarch and his Laura, of Boccaccio, of Roman maidens by Mantegna, of Bembo himself by Raphael; he explored Bembo's library, his collection of ancient classic manuscripts, Greek coins and vases, and cameos carved into rings for women to wear before the Virgin Mary was born. Bembo's profile was also a cameo, the high domed forehead, the finely chiselled nose and eye-sockets forbidding one to notice the too small chin under its tiny point of beard. He was the perfect example of the modern Italian Churchmen who had survived the Renascence of pagan culture by identifying themselves with it. As a youth he had been passionately in love with Lucrezia Borgia (he always said those stories about the Borgia family were grossly exaggerated); now as a Cardinal and secretary to the Pope, he advised the young deacons in his charge not to read St. Paul lest the saint should spoil their style; he put Plato above Christ; but even with Plato one should be careful to preserve the golden mean, and treasure philosophy not as an aim of life, but as an added elegance to help the refinement of 'delight and play' which was its true purpose.

Reginald listened to him, looked at his Morosina with delight but not desire, played with their children, admired his antiques, followed his advice and wrote a Life of their learned friend Longolius in faultless Latin prose, using no word that had not been used by Cicero, a tribute so appropriate that surely God would permit Longolius to appreciate it even in an all-Christian, non-pagan heaven.

But life could not go on being all roses and strawberries and other men's mistresses. After seven years, the correct term of years in fairyland, he had to go back to England at his King's command. Henry had grown twice as large and loud and terrible. Reginald felt the shadow of fear that lay on all his own family; and the hush that fell on the crowd of courtiers whenever the King's glittering bulk strode into the room and his darting capricious glance put every man in terror lest he be the one whom its lightning would strike next.

The magnificent royal cousin, 'to whose generosity and care I owe my knowledge of letters,' as Reginald gladly acknowledged, now showed that he expected payment. He was busy collecting a bodyguard of learned and ecclesiastic opinions to support him in saying that his marriage of twenty years' standing to his late brother's wife, Katherine of Aragon, was incestuous; that the former Pope had no right to give him a Dispensation for it; that in fact he had been living in sin with her all these years, and their daughter the Princess Mary was a bastard; and therefore, finally, he was free to marry Ann Bullen.

Reginald, finding himself one day unexpectedly created Dean of Exeter, as an obvious step to conscription in this bodyguard, packed his books, musical instruments and fustian mattresses, and left for Paris. But Henry sent after him to consult the University there about the divorce, *i.e.* to persuade them to Henry's view of it. He did so with satisfactory results, and returned home to retire to the Carthusian monastery of his schooldays, not as a monk, but for board and lodging and peace to study.

But Henry dug him out again, threatened to make him Archbishop of York, commanded him to state publicly his own private opinion of the divorce. Reginald must either abjure his mother's friend, Queen Katherine, and his own sense of right, and help to ruin his pathetic little friend, the Princess Mary; or else endanger all his own family as well as himself. His elder brother, Lord Montague, implored him to find a compromise; he desperately sought one, thought he had found it, and went to tell the King.

Henry came on him suddenly at the end of a gallery; huge, overbearing, he stood there like a monstrous apparition of brute power. Reginald was appalled; the jolly kindly kinsman he had adored was now a tyrant who demanded toll even of one's private thoughts. He forgot every one of his perfectly prepared sentences; he tried to speak, gasped, and heard himself begging the King not to ruin his own soul.

Henry's hand flew to the dagger in his belt and jerked it up to strike, then flung it clattering on the floor, turned on his heel and swung out of the gallery. 'There was so much simplicity in his manner,' Henry said later, 'that it cheated my indignation. I could not think he meant me ill.'

He was right. Reginald, left alone, was weeping broken-heartedly, not for the singular failure of his first effort at diplomacy, but for the wrecked nobility of the man he loved.

There was a partial reconciliation; Henry even accepted Reginald's reasons, chiefly economic and therefore sound, against the divorce, which he wisely put in writing this time instead of attempting speech. Henry then added, as brightly as a child claiming a prize for *not* learning his lesson, that if Reginald 'would now only show his approval of my cause, nobody should be dearer to my heart.'

But he let him escape abroad again, and even continued his allowance, and Reginald went back to Italy, this time for more than twenty years. He thought he was going home again. But it was not the same. The game of playing at being Greeks and Romans now seemed childish; Bembo's luscious verses would not last, nor his Epicurean philosophy; it might be original to argue against the immortality of the soul, as the philosopher Pomponazzi had done, but Reginald thought he would back Plato and even the Church against Pomponazzi.

'Even' the Church? He realized how little he had considered its teaching in comparison with classical learning. He began to study theology and divinity, and challenged all philosophy that did not lead to these as its consummation. Prayer came more and more to take the place of contemplation, the New Testament that of Cicero, and even Homer was beaten on his own ground by Isaiah.

He had always hated the active life of affairs; he had grown dissatisfied with the contemplative life of classic scholarship; at last he had come to know that what he wanted was to lead a life dedicated to reform within the Church. The world would never know peace as long as the policies of Church and State were based on selfishness and tyranny. His King had now made himself his own Pope, plundered the monasteries, turned out the monks and nuns, married the Courtesan, as Ann Bullen was called on the Continent, and beheaded the wisest and saintliest scholars in his kingdom, Bishop Fisher and Sir Thomas More, for the crime only of keeping silence.

Then Reginald also was forced to meet that charge. The King demanded his approval of his actions. Reginald asked for time, and took it, more than a year, to answer, not in a letter, but a book, a long book, a very rude book, and sent the manuscript to the King. He told Henry to his face that he had once admired and venerated him more than any other man, but that now he had become a robber and murderer and enemy to Christianity; one who 'never loved the people; – robbed the clergy; – destroyed the best men of your kingdom, not like a human being but like a wild beast.'

His final shot was a suggested epitaph for Henry's tombstone: 'He has spent enormous sums to make all universities declare him incestuous.'

The only hope, he said, of bringing Henry to his senses was to give him a severe shock. It did. Henry swore to make Pole 'eat his own heart.' He proclaimed him a traitor and offered huge rewards for his assassination in Italy. But he found Christendom gathering itself together against him. England rumbled with revolution, a bloodless one, that should bring the King to an understanding of God's law; it was to be called the Pilgrimage of Grace. Europe rumbled too, especially Rome and the Papacy. Reginald was summoned there and started for Rome. On his way he received such urgent letters from his mother and elder brother, Lord Montague, begging him not to go to Rome, that he all but turned back.

But his friend and fellow-traveller, the ferocious old Cardinal Caraffa, prevented him. Reginald had an enormous admiration for him, he was so full of vigour and ardour, though it was a pity he was also always so full of mangiaguerra or 'champ-the-war,' the nickname given to the thick black fiery wine of Naples; it should also have been Caraffa's nickname. Like Henry of England, Caraffa frequently held quite other opinions after dinner from those that he had had before; it was another point of resemblance in the two men most different from himself, whom Reginald had yet most nearly worshipped. He still worshipped Caraffa's fiery zeal for the Church, and it was the old man's violent persuasions that changed his mind again and led him on to Rome and the ruin of his family.

For there, to his consternation, he found that he was to be made a Cardinal. He saw the danger to his relatives, he tried to refuse, but the Pope sent along, not only his Chamberlain to tell him he was nominated, but his barber to shave his tonsure. Mildly protesting, he was led 'like a lamb to the shearer.'

Then, inevitably, he was appointed Papal Legate for

England, to bring the King back into the fold of the Church under threat of excommunication and of moral support to the Pilgrimage of Grace. But the 'Very Catholic King of Spain' noted that the moral support lacked financial support, so gave none. Both he and the 'Most Christian King of France' continued to support their anti-Papal brother of England. So Henry, undisturbed, squashed the bloodless revolution in an ocean of blood, and turned like a tiger on Pole's family. Pole's mother, the Countess of Salisbury, was the daughter of the Duke of Clarence, whom his brother, Richard III, was believed to have drowned in the Tower in a butt of Malmsey wine; her children had a claim to the throne closer than that of Henry; he had been waiting for an opportunity to destroy this branch of the White Rose Plantagenets. Reginald's younger brother Geoffrey, an odd uncertain weakling, was threatened with torture in the Tower and confessed to whatsoever his judges wanted. His mother had embroidered a coat of arms with marigolds, the emblem for the Princess Mary, and pansies, the emblem for Reginald Pole. This was considered a clear indication of a plot to marry them, as both their mothers had always wished, and put them on the throne. So the old Countess was beheaded or, rather, butchered by a bungling executioner, and also her eldest son Montague; and his son, a child, was put in the Tower and never seen again, just as two other little princes had been put in the Tower by their uncle King Richard nearly sixty years before, and never seen again except once or twice in the winter twilight as two small shivering ghosts.

Only Geoffrey, having turned King's evidence, escaped; if it can be called escape to live on, shrinking from all men, starting at shadows, hating to live, and trying in a futile frenzy to smother himself with a cushion, but failing even to die.

'Pole must now eat his own heart and be as heartless as he is graceless,' wrote Bishop Hugh Latimer in exultant congratulation to his King, whom he called the 'instrument of God' in wiping out the noblest family in England.

There was some reason to call Pole heartless. His blood ran thinly in an effete body; no human emotion was urgent in him, neither love of family nor of country, and certainly not of women. But now he was forced to remember that his mother was also a woman, and to realize that her fate had lain at his door.

A villain like Thomas Cromwell, or even Machiavelli, would have managed to avoid it. But he dared not twist the knife of remorse within him. He had to make of it something that should not turn his brain.

So he wrote in a letter that he had been 'the son of one of the best and most honoured ladies in England; but now God has wished to honour me still more, by making me the son of a martyr.' His friends commended his pious serenity; it was also his courtesy that hid his unceasing ache from them.

He showed no rage against Henry. He did not even take the revenge of publishing his attack on him; he had never intended to do so; and Henry's crime against him could not make him change his mind. He had spoken out his blame of the King in it, and so made amends for his cowardly hesitation in not doing so before. That was the importance of the book to him; he had declared his true mind in it, and the consequences were beyond his control; but they left their mark in deep lines on his haggard face. He wrote of them, 'the hatred with which the King pursued me acted on me as the ploughman's furrows on the earth,' and so, he hoped, 'the seeds of faith, hope and charity might take deeper root.'

He seemed almost to welcome the tragedy that made him know he had a heart as well as a soul to offer God.

He still kept his genius for friendship; was still broadminded. He took two young men into his household who were strongly suspected of heresy. Even more surprisingly, he made great friends with an odd, ugly, violent artist whose nose had been broken in a fight with a rival sculptor, and whose loud abuse of other artists struck Reginald as not only un-Christian but ungentlemanly. But then his painting in the Sistine chapel had earned Michelangelo the right to be an 'original.'

And he made close friends, for the first time in his life, with a woman, ten years older than himself, a famous poet under the name of Vittoria Colonna, also a friend of Michelangelo, who gave her drawings of his and they wrote sonnets to each other. 'You, gracious lady, might create me new,' he told her; Reginald called her 'our dearest mother in Christ,' and she called him her 'son and Master.' They formed a group of which she was the 'mother,' and the 'father' was the pious, learned Contarini who had dared tell Pope Clement VII that 'nothing is stronger than truth, virtue goodness, and a right intention.' It was not as witty as the sayings of Cardinal Bembo. But Vittoria, like Reginald, had outgrown her friendship for Bembo: for years she had imitated his smooth verses and it had brought her a great reputation; no literary party was complete without her, and one met everybody at her house, uncouth artists, uneasy poets, and now that interesting austere new English Cardinal who was such an aristocrat that his family had been executed for being too near the throne.

But Vittoria was outgrowing also her taste for parties, and the arid brilliance of the society which she outshone. Like Reginald Pole she felt the need of religion, and he of her motherly consolation. Their new coterie was called the 'Spirituals' by those who liked them; those who did not, like old Cardinal Caraffa, called them 'crypto-Protestants.' Prayer-meetings and theological discussion gave a purifying influence to their companionship; only a new disturbing spirit of criticism made Pole wonder if it were not all rather too pleasant to be much use.

The 'Spirituals' stayed at each others' houses, walked and talked in shady groves, sat by playing fountains for their alfresco meals; almost it seemed that the sunlight of his early days in Italy had returned. But the light was colder, the friends were older. They walked more briefly, talked more lengthily, thought more slowly, and both friends and foes were much more apt to die.

King Henry died, and the gentle 'father' Contarini, and then Reginald's 'new mother'; yes, Vittoria Colonna, noblest of Roman matrons, lay dead; everyone seemed to be dying except Cardinal Caraffa, older than anybody, who swore he would never die.

He was now openly an enemy. He had forced the Pope to establish the Inquisition in Rome, bought a building with his own money to house its dreaded officers, and gave secret information to them of Pole's circle of scholars and 'Spirituals,' both of which were 'plain heretics' to Caraffa. Michelangelo's nudes were an abomination and should be decently covered – or destroyed. Erasmus had been the arch-traitor and all his works should be put on the Index; though Pole reminded him that Erasmus's aim, like Caraffa's, had been the revival of religion within the Church.

Caraffa replied by hounding some of Pole's household to fly for their lives, and calling Pole himself 'worse than a heretic – a heathen cannibal, devouring his own kind.'

Pole's cannibal crime was that he had stated publicly that 'we, the shepherds, are responsible for all the evils now burdening the flock of Christ.'

Caraffa urged reform too, but it must be reform of others, not himself.

Then death struck his worst blow, at the old Pope Paul III, whom Reginald did not like. But his death left the Papal Chair vacant, and everybody said that the English Cardinal was the right man to fill it. All his friends implored him to take up the highest office, rescue it from political tricks and devices, and carry out the work of Church reform as only a man so high-minded and disinterested could do.

The prospect of being the first English Pope for four centuries, and the youngest for nearly as many, the easy winner of a prize that the magnificent Cardinal Wolsey had struggled for in vain, was too showy and vulgarly ambitious to affect him. His trouble was that so few others were disinterested. The Emperor Charles V was backing him with every Spanish Cardinal he could muster, but only so as to thwart French power by defeating the candidate favoured by France. Most urgent of all his supporters were the money-lenders and bankers; they told him the betting was so high in his favour that fortunes would be lost throughout Italy if he backed out of the running.

Was this the race that he must run for Christ?

He did not back out; well, not exactly. But he shrank from the ugly and immoral muddle he had got to clear up if he were once seated on the throne of Peter. The appalling stew of the Conclave of Cardinals shut up in the Vatican to decide his election, so crowded that the stench of the lavatories seemed certain to breed the plague; most of them guzzling and drinking when they were supposed to be fasting; admitting Ambassadors over the roofs and through the windows when they were supposed to be hermetically secluded, and slipping out betting notes to the bookmakers of Rome; and then the reports that what Pole had most to fear was not the rival votes for the French King's candidate, but the alarm of the Papal Court that if he became Pope they would all have to lead a new life; these things revolted him into calling the whole proceeding 'that comedy, not to say tragedy.'

What part could he act in it, even if he were 'called upon to be the ass who should bring Christ back into Jerusalem'? He told himself he would not refuse to answer that call; but every nerve in his body prayed against it. And when the crisis came, those nerves acted more mulishly than Christ's ass.

The Spanish Cardinals tried to push a rush election at night before a reinforcement of opposing French Cardinals arrived. Pole, faced with a sudden and slightly irregular action, took fright, and refused obstinately to enter the Papacy 'under cover of darkness.' But by daylight the other French Cardinals arrived, and the chance had been missed. Pole had lost his opportunity to work the counter-Reformation from within the Church. A safe, easy, worldly man was chosen instead, to compromise between the Spanish and French parties; and Pole tried to excuse his relief by thinking God had not really wanted anyone so ineffective as himself to be Pope.

Inaction yawned again for him in all its grey temptation of 'accidie,' that dull sloth and disbelief in life which is the worst and loneliest of the Seven Deadly Sins. He had escaped the Papacy, but only to find no place for himself anywhere, no true work that he could do for God. Was a monastery the only answer? Debating with himself and in long letters, dipping first with one foot and then with the other, he tried to take the plunge. If he took vows, he would no longer be in doubt as to what God wanted him to do; it could only be what his Abbot ordered him to do. And he would be more free than anywhere of the pitiful puzzle of human relationships. Even among the Spirituals there had been jealousy, criticism, pride in conscious piety; and he had felt impatience at such a refined little heaven of choice souls. Such annoyances in a monastery would at least be free from femininity; and under the discipline of Orders. To be told what to do; there at last lay rest for his uneasy spirit, in the final surrender of his will.

But was it God's will? He had drawn back his foot for perhaps the fiftieth time, and just in time, when he heard that Mary Tudor was now Queen of England; then, within three weeks of her accession, that the Pope had appointed him Papal Legate to his own country. Pole's first reaction was to ask if the Pope could not appoint someone better. But that was only habit. He quickly overcame it. He had at last received a clear call to action; it was, he knew, the last chance God would give him. In a spirit almost of exultation he resolved to take it.

Now at last his path lay clear ahead of him. It led back home, to his own country. His roots lay in that soil, like those of the great oaks that he had climbed as a schoolboy in the playground of the Carthusians' monastery, now dispersed, destroyed.

Many beloved things had been uprooted in that soil. His duty now was to plant them again.

The new Queen wrote urging him to it; she shared his sense of divine purpose in bringing both of them to power in their own country. They might indeed share even more. Their friends had long wished for their marriage; he had shunned the thought of it in his dislike of ambition; but now even his 'immodest modesty' had to admit that he was respected throughout Europe and that none would make that charge against him. He resolved 'not to retire from the busy scenes of life,' nor 'make more account of myself than of the public.' He might well serve the public best by marrying his cousin and Queen, and so keep England balanced between France, Spain and the Papacy. Still more might he serve God best by it. He had not even yet taken the priests' vows of chastity; was it because God had reserved him for the more onerous duty of the vow matrimonial?

Elderly and timid, he shrank from it, but Mary too was middle aged, modest and virginal. They would understand each other, and could work together. He remembered her as a delicate, pretty little creature, simple hearted and kind, a loyal and admiring friend to himself, and deeply attached to his mother, whose dearest wish had been that they should marry. In carrying this out he hoped to make himself believe that he would expiate the doom he had brought upon his mother.

But when at last he met Mary again she was the wife of Philip of Spain.

Pole had done his best to prevent it. He knew Englishmen well enough, even after twenty years abroad, to tell the Pope that a Spaniard as King-Consort would be 'universally odious' to them.

The Pope had replied that 'one could not swim against the stream' – not when the stream was directed by the Emperor.

For sixteen months Pole had struggled to swim against it, before at last the Royal Barge rowed him up the Thames – to take up a position of truncated power, a work deprived of half its value. He had to restore England to the Church without England making any restitution to the Church. His own enforced compromise embittered him as no enemy had done. Bitterness brings weakness. He was the less a man.

The first English winter he had suffered for so many years, at a time when he was far older and colder in blood and the less able to resist it, put him at his lowest ebb physically as well as spiritually. Coughing and sneezing his aching way through the riverside mist and rain at Lambeth, he came face to face with the task most alien to him. The Queen demanded his co-operation in the rooting out of heresy by 'blood and fire.'

He urged her to continue in the mercy she had shown when she came to the throne. Was her name of 'Merciful Mary' to be changed to 'Bloody Mary'?

She answered, 'What does it matter how men call me? I gave my mercy for crimes against myself, not against God.'

He said, 'Are we in our frailty to act as God's judges? My first promise to Parliament when I arrived was that "I am come not to destroy, but to build; to reconcile, not condemn." She answered, 'And what have you built? Whom have you reconciled? The rich keep silent, but hold fast to their thefts from the Church. The poor blaspheme aloud.'

Her eyes were fierce, her voice rasped against his ears. This had been the warm kindly little creature whose work he had hoped to share. As he looked at her the blank fog of his 'accidie' darkened into the night of despair. He could never help her, nor his country, nor his Church, any more than he had been able to help himself, or his family, or his mother. He had had the courage to say openly to Caraffa, the most violent instigator of the Inquisition in Rome, 'I do not like the methods of the Inquisition, even though I agree with its aims.' He did not tell her that, but he said it again now. How hollow it sounded, how feeble, negative! In any case she was not listening, and he found himself wondering what would have happened if she had married Caraffa.

They were the people who got things done. She had all the force of a strongly sexed nature that had been starved of sex, and still was, though she did not know it; and that force was now set on doing what was right for the Church. He was doubtful of her methods, but his doubts led nowhere. Even his defiance of her terrible father had brought about nothing but the hideous death of his own mother.

'She is dead, she is dead, let it go, do not think of it, for you can do nothing.'

But Mary, who loved her, was alive. Mary, who had greeted his homecoming 'as though she were his mother.' Mary, who was the only woman he had ever thought of marrying, who was only not in love with himself because she was so much in love with her husband, who did indeed treat him as a second husband, as furiously, eagerly dependent on his opinion as she was on Philip's will. And Mary was appealing to him, entreating him to help her against her enemies, above all against the enemy who was the avowed or secret hope of every heretic and rebel in the country.

'Who is that?' he asked as his heart turned to lead; he had no need to hear the answer hammered against it, 'Elizabeth, Elizabeth, always Elizabeth.'

So families must turn and rend each other, a sister seek a sister's blood, and all in the name of God. What then had the Devil left to do?

This he thought and could not say, while Mary's harsh voice hurried breathlessly on, deaf to all but itself.

True, Elizabeth now went to mass, but how true was she in that? Elizabeth was slippery as an eel in argument, obstinate as a mule to persuasion. 'I have tried to speak to her, but can make no headway. She is not the sort of woman who can trust other women.'

'Madam, remember only a year ago you put her in the Tower, under constant expectation of death.'

'I released her. It makes no odds. She cannot feel gratitude. I gave her presents when she was a child. I never liked nor trusted her, but I was sorry for her then. I should not be now, whatever happens to her.'

'*What* should happen?' he asked heavily.

But Mary would not admit that she hoped to find justification for her sister's death. She would only urge rather incoherently that Pole must see Elizabeth alone, must make friends with her as he was so well able to do with such different people, that he must discover the secret workings of her supple mind and inflexible heart; and then, and then – well he must decide whether, in leaving her alive, Mary was not undermining all her own work and his for the Church in England.

He said coldly that he was not a spy. But the burst of hysteria that followed showed him that he was exposing Elizabeth to worse danger by his refusal to take part in the matter.

He said he would see what he could do, and left her,

wearied and in disgust at this homecoming to friends that had grown so alien. He had looked on death as the great divider in friendship; now he knew that life could be worse. It was better when friends died; then their memory could stay sweet in one's mind; but friendships that festered, what could be done with them? You could not discard them, put them on the rubbish heap; you had to breathe fresh life into them; and that was the last thing he could do.

'I am not for life but death,' he told himself in despair, his hand on the window-latch, his tired eyes watching the scurry of torn blossom in the cold wind outside, a puppy leaping and barking up at a little boy running against the wind. That child would have to live, grow up, to face worse than a spring gale – but, thank God, not himself! He would not have much more to face, he told himself droningly, longing to lie down by a warm fire – and then at that moment he had to face it.

He was summoned to a Council meeting assembled on the instant, in a fury of haste and alarm. They were ducking their heads like hens, pecking at a torn paper which at last, with difficulty, he learned had been found nailed on a gate of the Palace. Scrawled over it in a botched handwriting was the question: 'Will you be such fools, oh noble Englishmen, as to believe that our Queen is pregnant? And of what should she be, but of a monkey or a dog?'

A chill nausea crept up through his bones. Men could be more vile than devils. He thought of the poor distraught creature he had left; who was, in the last resort, only a lonely, frightened woman, longing desperately for her child; and was made the target for such filthy attacks.

BOOK II: THE PRINCESS

CHAPTER THIRTEEN

Pole did not trust Elizabeth, and needed none of Mary's warnings that he would find her sly, discreet, demure; it was exactly what he had thought her at his meetings with her in public. He was almost inclined to agree with Mary's opinion that she was not even King Henry's bastard; a still, frozen creature, wary as a young cat, begotten of the moon rather than by that huge sun of a man.

She had quoted Aristophanes at him and he felt she was showing off, and told her he had left Oxford without taking his degree. She murmured that with his position it was no doubt unnecessary, and he replied, 'It was uninteresting.'

'Like all achievement – to such Eminence.'

The mocking little compliment annoyed him more than he cared to admit to himself. It would be of no use for him to talk further with her; no one could be worse at it; even his most intimate friends had always told him he had fewer words in speech than any man alive.

'But that,' Mary told him with surprising astuteness, 'is why others say so much to you.'

People did indeed talk to him with extraordinary freedom, it was a part of his 'genius for friendship' they said, and it was often, though they did not guess it, because he knew what was in their minds.

But Elizabeth, he was certain, would never show him hers.

Yet when at last by sheer chance he saw her in private, on the last day of April, she showed it in a way that took him by surprise, even by storm, for she was in a blazing rage.

So he knew the moment he entered the long gallery at Hampton Court and saw a tall slight figure sweeping away ahead of him, then swing round and pull up short. He had entered a cage, and interrupted the headlong pacings to and fro of a young tigress; her tawny hair and eyes flamed before him, her lips compressed in a tight line shutting out the things she had been saying, even shouting to herself in the paroxysm of her rage. But she had not shut them quite in time.

'Fool! Fool!' he had heard her cry before she turned, and thought he had caught the words 'blundering dolt' and 'to presume to rule!'

No wonder she stood still, aghast; but not for more than a second; her skirts came ruffling back towards him like the spread wings of a swan, then swished to the ground in a curtsey that denied its gesture of obeisance and was more of a challenge, defying him to take note against her of whatever he had heard. She rose, and her blackly dilated pupils looked him full in the face, a girl of twenty-one facing a man of fifty-five, knowing that she must fight for her life, and that her only defence now could be attack.

'Listen, my lord Cardinal, if you have listened already and heard that which I spoke only to my own ears – but I will say it again for you, for you to do with what you will. I am angry, not because Protestants are punished, but because the wrong ones are chosen for punishment.'

'It is not for you to choose. Therefore you find it easy.'

'Is it so difficult? Have you not enough real traitors to God and the Queen – the men who made themselves rich by robbing the Church and now make the best of both worlds? Smug in their security, they practise religion as a mere State function.'

She checked on these words, for it was just what the Queen accused herself of doing, and she saw that he guessed her thought.

'That is not a chargeable offence,' he said drily.

'So they use their ill-gotten wealth to buy their immunity from the law, and offer up to it instead such humble victims as are too poor to buy themselves off.' She hurried on,

'Who are these devilish heretics, these mighty traitors to God that are being burnt? Such small fry as the Devil himself might throw back from the fires of hell! A Welsh fisherman who couldn't even read the Bible which he cherished because he had been ordered to do so in my brother's reign. Four washerwomen from Essex who had never known there were seven sacraments to believe in, had only heard of one, and "what it was they could not tell". One was a young girl who had been brought up to think "the mass was an idol". My brother's ministers of State made it law to think that. But *they* do not smell of the pan! Not a single noble has been brought to trial, nor any man of wealth and power. They get off scot-free while they put up the butcher and baker and candlestick-maker, and their wives and widows, yes, even their children, to draw the fires of Smithfield.'

She took breath at last on a gasp. He was watching her closely, and his eyes seemed to have sunk to the back of his skull. He was appalled by what she had told him. He should have known of it. But how should he know of it? The administration of justice in the ecclesiastic courts was not his province.

Then it struck him, how had she come to know of it? He asked her, and she shrugged. 'I? Oh, I have low tastes; I gossip with my servants.'

'You are a friend of the butcher and baker and candlestick-maker.'

'As my father was.'

'Yes, he had the common touch.' But the appreciation in his voice did not beat down her defensive attitude. He tried further.

'Why should you not admit your championship of the common people?' he asked, and saw her thought that he must be a fool not to see how dangerous it would be for her to be acclaimed the Friend of the Poor. 'Yet,' he said, 'your sister has shared that with you from King Henry. Even since she has become Queen she still loves to visit the poor in their cottages. She would be horrified if she knew of such injustice as you describe. Have you told her?'

'I have not dared. To you it is different. And you caught me unawares,' she added with a smile, but felt it glance off him ineffectively. Well, he was old. 'You must teach me how to view heresy,' she said.

'You see it clear enough. It is a plague which if allowed to breed will infect the whole State. No country has ever yet been able to allow a second religion within its borders. When it does, it will do so because its true worship is for a third religion, that of the State.'

'The herd cannot see that.'

'Every effort must be made to instruct them.'

'It is,' she replied in sudden weariness. 'Think of Bishop

Bonner! He will argue subtly with angry ignoramuses for weeks on end.'

'To save their souls and convert their hearts.'

'That is what they fear worse than the stake – to be turned from their belief. So they answer with vulgar abuse, to hurry on their death. Your Eminence knows well that the mental agony of doubt, fear and, above all, hope can be worse than the rack. But our fellow-countrymen are mules for obstinacy. Let the donkeys alone to graze in peace and quiet and they'll not have a thought beyond what to put in their bellies. But put words in their mouths and tell them to speak this and thus, and they'll dig their heels in and bray the contrary, louder than Balaam's ass. They'll rush on martyrdom, they'll long for a chance to "witness to the truth" and abuse a Bishop. They'll show everybody they can go one better than St. Peter.'

The flippancy of her change of front was bewildering. 'You are now mocking what you had championed.'

'Championed – I – those self-conceited fools!' She was doubling on him like a hare. Why? Somehow he did not feel it was only to ward off suspicion.

'Your sympathy is with the common people, not with their opinions,' he considered.

'I hate opinions. They split the world in pieces. They nearly split a pulpit when three or four brawlers clambered into it together to preach against each other! Some sects deny the divinity of Christ; some His manhood; some reject baptism; others churches; others turn the altar table to the west, or north, like apes who cannot tell which way to turn their tails. They call all ceremonies play-acting, all laws tyranny, and nobody ought to own any property, unless it's oneself, or to obey anybody, unless it's oneself. That's what happened in my little brother's reign, under the bigots who thought ideals should govern politics. This country was a football kicked to and fro by their precious opinions. Edward sided with the German Protestant States against Spain, because Spain was "reactionary"' and Germany "advanced". Advanced towards what? God knows! Though in due time He may show.'

Was this attack a feint to safeguard herself? 'What is your policy? Not, I think, the present alliance with Spain?'

'My policy is that policy should be kept free from emotion, from ideas that are valued as "new" and "old" only by those who do not study history. This poor silly football of England has now been kicked over to the other side, allied with Spain and therefore against France. But you, sir, know, as King Henry did, that England's safety and power stands in the middle of the see-saw, to keep the balance steady in Europe and never let it dip too far over on either side.'

Yes, he had known that. It had been the chief reason that he had considered marriage with the Queen, to keep England free of foreign entanglements. He wondered if this girl had guessed it, and did not like her any the better. 'I am not a politician, as you, Madam, so plainly are.'

It gave him an unwontedly malicious pleasure to see her eyes flash open in sudden perception of his view of her as a smart modern young woman, symptom of this modern England he had never known.

'A smart red-headed young gent.' That was the odious description of the upstart groom who had married Jane Grey's mother last year within a month of her daughter's and husband's executions. A feminine counterpart to young Mr. Adrian Stokes – God's death, was that how he saw her? – and how truly? 'You be a sharp young thing, but don't be so sharp as you'll cut yourself,' echoed back in her mind in old Dr. Turner's North Country burr. No, don't cut yourself. She had only an instant to stop Pole's distaste for her turning into a guarded enmity, and how could she, on the instant? Flattery, however subtle, would be seen through and scorned. Only sincerity, however savage, might serve.

It astonished her to find as she spoke how sincere she was.

'Is policy only a term for such as Machiavelli? Should it not be used as a bulwark for the Church against those who would destroy her authority? It is not the cynics, the atheists, the time-servers and State-servers who have the power to do that. Thomas Cromwell destroyed the monasteries, his followers stole from them, but they created nothing.

'It is Bonner and the other Catholic Bishops, it is *you*, it is –' (she gulped, but his eyes were looking deep into hers, seeing all she did not say, so she had better say it) – 'yes, and it is the Queen herself, who is giving Protestantism a soul. It will no longer be a commercial bargain, a vested interest in which half England has taken shares. Nor will it be the half-baked, ill-digested crank-belief of a disreputable rabble. No, the case is altered. The roughs who mishandled the priests, the church-robbers, the iconoclasts who broke all beauty that was held sacred, the atheists who denied God, the anarchists who defied law, they will all be herded under one banner now. The banner of a holy army. You have given haloes to the followers of those who sold their God for thirty pieces of silver.'

'If the haloes are false, they are of no more effect than the rings of gilded cardboard in a Christmas play.'

'They are to others. Think of their audience! Suffering purifies. You have turned this mob into a band of saints. Protestants will be remembered because of the humble folk who chose to suffer for their cause, who glory in the chance to be uplifted out of their drab, ignoble lives and feel themselves at one with the saints of God. Already their own teachers are having to hold them back from the ecstasies of martyrdom. That fisherman called the shirt for his execution his "wedding garment". The little Vicar of Hadleigh danced on his way to the stake, saying, "Now I know I am almost at home – even at my Father's house".'

'Such heroism is of God, but not the belief that inspired it.'

'How should *they* know that?'

'By the teaching of God, through the Church and the tradition of His Apostles.'

'But they deny that, and now the Church has sanctified their denial by their sacrifice.'

Her sincerity had overcome her after all. The tears had stood bright in her eyes and now they ran down her cheeks unheeded. 'Where will it all end?' she cried. 'How can there ever again be one Church in England? Why should there not be as many sects as there are souls, each holding his own opinion to be infallible, and heading to unutterable confusion? Authority is now condemned. Any rebel against it will think himself sanctified, and welcome any lying slander of it. They'll find any stigma good enough to beat a dogma with!'

Her tears broke into hysterical laughter. She flung away from him and leaned against the window, hiding her face against the curtain, stuffing it into her mouth. What had she been saying? She did not know, and dared not speak again. In another moment it would all come out, all that she must never say to anyone – that she was an outcast, that she could never belong to the Church if it remained split in England, as these fools were ensuring that it should be. Her whole position, her chance of the throne, depended on her belonging to the Protestants – and now there would be no hope for her to bring them back gently and gradually into the body of the Church, so as to resume the old worship by degrees, almost without noticing it, and make an English Catholic Church, not Roman. This her father had wanted to do, and others before him. Now it would never be done, and she would always be outside, associated with a rabble of crazy cranks.

'I might as well give up Christianity and worship the Devil,' she thought, and wondered for a horrible instant if she had said it aloud. There was an uncanny silence in this man that made one say things one had never dreamed of speaking. The silence was still going on, it seemed to penetrate even through the back of her head to the thoughts within it. She had to speak in order to break it. She turned back to him.

'I have been too bold.' She was shivering. 'At least tell me what you are thinking,' she said, and her hand flashed out and brushed his, as light and cool as a butterfly's wing, yet he felt as though a flame had touched him. He was still silent. 'Do not be angry with me,' she pleaded. 'You have given me a rare and dangerous pleasure – no, not dangerous' (how she hoped that was true!), 'since I spoke in confidence to a great gentleman. Which is more than can be said of my great father!' she ended on a spurt of astonished laughter. What power was there in this sad, tired old man to draw her hidden thoughts from her? He could not like her. She was raw, crude, vulgar in his fastidious eyes; yet she had never seen disdain in them, for her or anyone. He honoured all men. But what did he think of her?

What he thought was that for all her frankness he knew

little more than before of her religion. But on one point he was at last assured; she was not begotten of the moon. He saw life burning in her as it had done in the enormous sun that had sired her, 'the greatest enemy I had in the world, that King whom I loved above all other men.' He did not know if this his daughter was his enemy. But to watch her, hear her vibrant voice, still more to feel that fleeting touch on his dull hand, was to catch something of King Henry's fire, his sense that one life on earth was not enough, that he needed as many lives as he did wives to compass the overweening arrogance of his desires.

But he must answer her. He said slowly, 'I am not sure you love the Church truly. But very sure you hate her enemies. Perhaps because you identify them with the enemies of the State.'

'Isn't that what they are bound to become – finally?'

'Yes. But that is not the reason one should hate them. One should not hate them at all.'

'No. Only love and pity – and burn.'

'There is love and pity in the judges who wrestle for weeks on end, in the face of their prisoners' furious abuse, to try and save their souls. And not only theirs. The worst danger in false doctrine is in its inverted pride. It cannot rest until it has led others also into damnation. The Church has had to fight through centuries against those who were willing to risk death and torture for the liberty to pervert thought. The worship of the State, Heathenism, Satanism, Witchcraft have all had their devotees.'

Had he indeed seen the passage of her thought just now? She spoke hurriedly. 'They say the Pope has just died.'

'It is true.'

'And your Eminence?'

'They have asked me to go to Rome. I shall not go.'

'Why not, in God's name?'

'Because it is not in God's name. If I do not go, Marcello will certainly be chosen this time, the very man that the Papacy now needs.'

She was not listening to him, but to something else; the flame in her seemed to shrivel and die, her eyes stared dull and blank at him for an instant before they hid under the dropped eyelids. His slower ears caught the sound of hurrying footsteps coming nearer, louder.

A sturdy dark-faced boy came at a run into the gallery; it was Elizabeth's new page, young Humphrey Gilbert, but he ignored her and bowed, panting, to the Cardinal. 'My lord, the Queen's labour has begun – they say already ended happily, with a boy.'

A hand shot out and boxed his ear, almost toppling him over as he rose. 'And what of the boy's aunt, you jackanapes? Do you not greet her too? "Why not?", I think, is the motto of your house!'

He gaped at the merry tone following so instantly on a hard blow, and raised his head to meet her brilliant smile.

'Come, no apologies. Joy can confuse us all, especially that of welcoming a new young master.'

CHAPTER FOURTEEN

It was still the last day of April, but it began to look like being the first, so Elizabeth muttered darkly to her faithful Cat Ashley by the evening, for might it not turn out to have been All Fools' Day after all? The bells had rung, the choirs had sung; Te Deums were already being chanted as far away as Norwich Cathedral, thanksgiving processions had borne their flickering candles through the churches, the shops had shut, the prentices run to light bonfires in the street and put out trestles for public feasting; a new envoy from Poland arriving in the middle of the excitement had publicly congratulated King Philip on his son and heir; and the parish priest of St. Anne-within-Aldersgate had described from the pulpit how fair and beautiful a child was their new Prince, 'as the like has not been seen.'

That was the trouble; nobody seemed to have seen him; messages began to come from Hampton Court contradicting the first report and saying there was as yet no delivery.

And still people went on contradicting the contradiction and dancing in the streets and feasting, for it was a pity to spoil an occasion for holiday; and still Elizabeth walked up and down in the privacy of her room and swore and tore her handkerchief and would not eat her meals, but kept on eating sweets, and felt that time itself had ceased to breathe, that the world had ceased to move, that for all eternity she would hang here in a vacuum between two reigns, not knowing if Mary would die and she be Queen, or a Prince be born to sit on the throne.

Very seldom on it. He would be, not Tudor first, but Hapsburg. A son of Spain, a grandson of Germany and the Roman Empire, three-quarters of his blood Spanish, and only a quarter of him to carry on the ancient British blood that had flowed in the veins of all this island before the Romans and then the Danes and Saxons had driven it away, higher and higher into the Welsh mountains. Never before had Elizabeth, now contemplating her alien, unknown nephew, been so proud of being mere English and half of that Welsh. Proud but panic-stricken.

The future was so near, yet out of reach. So often she had asked herself, would this be the end or the beginning of Elizabeth?

'If only I could see Dr. Dee!' she cried aloud. '*He* could cast my horoscope.'

'They say he's back again,' said Cat Ashley, 'and wants the Queen to buy a library, but she says she doesn't care for strange books.'

'*Back?* Why did no one tell me?'

'My lady, my darling, it wouldn't be safe—'

'Tell me where he is. Never shake your head. I know you know.'

Cat Ashley whispered, 'In Mortlake, by the river. But are you going to—'

'Bed? Where else? It's late.'

Tick, tock, went her mother's clock. It stood on a bracket looking down on her bed, and a rushlight in a silver pan shone on its fantastically inlaid face. The signs of the zodiac surrounded it, the heavy pendulum swung below, the minutes marched on towards the hours. It was still the last day of April. The stars shone bright outside her uncurtained window. The Palace watchman went his rounds and called,

> *'Twelve o' the clock, look well to your lock,*
> *Your fire and your light, and so good-night.'*

It was no longer the 30th of April 1555. It was the 1st of May. The clock struck one, then two. Her mother had lain alone in the dark and listened to it striking those same small hours on the 1st of May nineteen years ago, until she could bear them no longer and had risen and wandered about the garden. In the white light of dawn King Henry's ministers came to arrest her and found her standing under an apple-tree in bloom, and led her away to her death.

'Stop the clock!' shrieked Elizabeth.

Cat Ashley came running to the side of her bed, but Elizabeth was already out of it. 'Cat, Cat, we must go a'-maying. No, never mind the clock. I was riding the night mare. I'll ride my new gelding instead, and you'll come with me. Too early you slugabed? Go to the ant, thou slug! Why, it's May Day, and all the boys and girls of London town are out in the woods of Westminster by now!

> *'"Is't not fine to dance and sing*
> *When the bells of death do ring?"'*

She was whirling round the room in her white shift, her red hair flying loose. Involuntarily Cat Ashley crossed herself. 'What mischancy words!'

'Then we'll have the next ones—

> *"Is't not fine to swim in wine*
> *And turn upon the toe?"'*

She was turning like a spinning top, picking up a garment here and there and pulling it on her as she twirled, finally snatching up a dull, rather shabby old cloak of Cat's and flinging it round herself.

At last Cat was ready, their two most trusted grooms had saddled the horses, and they rode out.

In Hampton village the birthday bonfires were guttering down, and so were the stars, paling fast before they were snuffed out. The river, first to catch the still hidden light, gleamed like the grey steel of a sword behind the huddled shapes of the dark cottages. They rode towards the darker, shapeless mass of the woods, and the trees began to stretch their groping fingers against the lightening sky.

The woods were already awake. People were rustling among the trees, whispering, giggling, in excitement and awe; unconscious worshippers in a heathen rite whose meaning had long been forbidden and forgotten. They knew only that they must be in the woods this night, to greet the dawn and 'bring in May.' The birds, who had cheeped a sleepy questioning note or two, suddenly shrilled into full chorus, and with it there rose here and there young human voices scarcely distinguishable from the birds, so closely they imitated their notes. A band of dim figures trooped past the horses, branches of white hawthorn glimmering like sheaves of moonlight in their arms; one was piping on a flute and the others trilled and gurgled an almost wordless song to it in mimicry of the nightingale –

'*Dug, dug,*
Jug, jug,
Good year and good luck!
With chuck, chuck, chuck, chuck!'

From deep in the wood another human-bird chorus answered back,

'*Then derry come down, derry come derry, come derry!*
Come derry, come down, hey ho!'

The light woke suddenly, astonished, on a cluster of young rabbits in a glade, sitting up and washing their faces with their front paws wet with dew. They leaped up and down opposite each other, then sat suddenly still, upright, their ears cocked at the thud of horses' hooves, and disappeared in a scurry of white scuts into the silver-green grass.

As the light, now pale gold, struck the tree-tops, a chain of young men and girls came crashing out of the undergrowth hand in hand and swung into a many-coloured ring, their flushed faces split open with their shouts. Their bird-song had turned to words;

'*Round-a, round-a, keep your ring,*
To the sun we dance and sing,
Ho ho! Ho ho!'

Those final yells made the horses rear; the ring whirled faster and faster till it broke, and some fell headlong with shrieks of laughter, then leaped up and chased each other back among the trees.

'Disgraceful,' panted Mrs. Ashley, trying to soothe her horse, 'they might be heathen savages.'

'They *are*, on this day!' Elizabeth laughed. 'Papists and Protestants are not the only worshippers left in England.'

Mrs. Ashley wished she would not speak so. 'It's not safe to be out here,' she stammered; but she felt Elizabeth herself was not safe on May Day.

A young man rode down the long ride through the trees with a hawk on his gloved wrist and silver bells on its jesses; he wore a shabby old green velvet hunting-coat and fine white leather riding-boots; his horse was old but a thoroughbred, his saddle was patched but it fitted, his spurs were bright, and at his heels pranced a couple of good hounds. He drew rein at sight of Elizabeth, and from sheer surprise forgot to sweep off his hat and bow.

The light shone full on him, cutting him off from his still shadowed horse.

'The sun is lifting you from the saddle,' she cried to him.

'And who has lifted you from yours, my Princess?' he asked in amazed laughter. 'Not a maid in a hundred who has gone to the woods this past night will come out again a maid.'

'I'll swear I've done nothing but what could be done on horseback.'

'I'll have to believe you – unless you'll give me the chance to disprove it.'

'Too late, Robin Dudley! The sun is up. But I'll see your hawk fly at a heron before I go back.'

'Why back? Come on with me and break our fast at Chelsea. It's the prettiest village along the river bank and you can get curds and cream at the farmhouse. I know Mrs. Ashley there, yawning her head off, is a very Cat for cream.'

'Hush! Don't wake her or she'll say it's as much as her place is worth, won't you, my Cat? Never mind if she nods. My grooms are a very vigilant pair of guards, even against my bold Cock Robin.'

'The hen is bolder. What the Devil took you into the woods at dawn on the first of May?'

'The Devil. And the fear of what he's doing at Hampton Court.'

'Nothing happened last night.'

'Then the chances are it's happening now. Ah me,

> '"*The chances most unhappy*
> *That me betide in May!*"'

'That's not a maying song.'

'No, it's a mourning song. One of her lovers wrote it of my mother. The devil took her in the garden on the first of May.'

He had never heard her speak of her mother, and it frightened him. 'Why think of the past?' he said as they jogged on together.

'I do not. I think of the future, and a Spanish Prince on the English throne. We'll be dragged into war with France.'

'Well, that's nothing new. England always used to be at war with France, it was the only way to get our fellows abroad across the sea.'

'There are other ways now. And other seas.'

'Oh, you mean the New World. But the Spaniards have got that.'

'Not all of it. And they may not keep all they've got.'

He leaned forward in his saddle to scan her face, rosy in the new-risen light. She looked like any milkmaid sallying forth on a May morning adventure, yet she never stopped thinking, planning – or rather straining forward to see into the plans of others. For that matter he could do it too, he was not to be outdone by any clever girl some months younger than himself.

'An expeditionary force might be a good thing,' he said; 'it would take people's minds off religion, which is an unhealthy thing to have your mind on. Philip might give me a company of horse to lead in Flanders. He asked me lately if I wanted employment, and I told him, "Urgently, since all our family is bankrupt!" Not a bad fellow if you know how to handle him.'

'And do you?'

'Not as well as you, Princess. You must give me lessons.'

Their laughter rang out through the shining air where all the birds were shouting with joy. The sun was gilding the edges of the leaves with a rim of wet light, dewdrops were sparkling everywhere, they breathed in the damp delicious smell of new grass and budding may, they were the only pair in the world to be young on a spring morning. She snatched at a branch above her head and brought away a cluster of white blossom. 'The buds are as tight and trim as a page's buttons,' she said. 'There's no embroidery half so fine on the cradle of the new young Prince. But there's no new young Prince in the cradle – yet. There may never be a new young Prince.'

'For Christ's sake, what are you saying?'

'Treason, isn't it? But only your hawk is near enough to hear.'

'There's myself. You can trust me to the death. But you should not. No, not your own shadow.'

'My shadow isn't here yet. The upper air is filled with light like a cup, there's no room for our shadows. But ssh, look, they are there behind us after all, stretching away like ribbons.' She flicked her branch over her horse's ears. 'I fill my rooms with blackthorn and may, though people call them unlucky.'

'Not for you. For they are sacred to Queen Hecate.'

'Do you call me that, Robin Goodfellow? Well, he too is of the Devil.'

'I always said we were a pair.'

But she fell silent. They were riding along the river bank, drawing near to Chelsea village, and she could see the square tower of Sir Thomas More's Church rising above the trees; and soon she would see the red garden walls of Chelsea Manor House, where she had lived as a child, and the postern gate opening on to the reedy marshes through which Tom Seymour had come one early spring day when the wind was high; and that, she now thought, was the last day that she had been a child.

The village street had blossomed white and green with branches stuck before the doors, the village green rang with happy shouts, as the great painted maypole swayed into place, hung with ribbons and wreaths of primroses and wild daffodils. A bagpipe shrilled on a piercing note, a flute answered it like a bird, boys and girls joined hands and capered round the pole.

Never did any banquet taste as good as the curds and cream in earthenware bowls, the sticky buns hot from the oven. But as they turned and rode back out of the village, a horrible thick cloud of depression came down on her as heavily as a curtain. Her high-cut nostrils quivered as she realized why, for into them had begun to steal the smell of burning flesh. She turned her horse's head and struck across the fields. Robin spurred after her. 'Where are you going?'

'Anywhere in the world that will take me away from *that*. And this is to please God! Or her husband!'

'No. His chaplain thumped the pulpit and called the burnings "repugnant to Christianity".'

'So you were there, my Protestant Dudley!'

'When in Rome, or keeping in with Rome, do as the Romans do. Or as my Protestant Princess does.'

'Michaeli's as shrewd as most Venetians. He says England would turn Jew or Mahomedan if ordered by their sovereign. Well, there's one poor devil behind us who didn't. A pest on this wind, it's carrying the stench after us. If Mary herself had ever smelt it – by God I'll get some cunning chemist to manufacture it and give it her as a present!'

'For the christening?'

She swore volubly and pulled up her horse to wait for Cat Ashley, who had been following in a flurry at such haste.

'Robin, will you come with me on an adventure?'

'To the end of the world.'

'It might be that for us. There's some danger. I am going to Mortlake to see Dr. Dee.'

'Then let no one know of it.'

'Cat must know, and keep guard in my rooms.'

She beckoned Mrs. Ashley close beside her and spoke low and urgently. She must go back to Hampton Court with the grooms, and into Elizabeth's apartments, and conceal her absence until she returned and would slip unnoticed into her apartments with her private key, which she had long ago had copied, of the side gate from the tennis courts. No one had observed them ride out so early, and she could pretend that the Princess had a megrim and was keeping her bed. In the meantime Elizabeth would take Lord Robert as her escort to visit a learned Doctor.

Cat was too much troubled by this last to worry over the proprieties.

'O Jesu!' she sighed, 'I knew there was mischief afoot when you took my old sad-coloured cloak that you'd not be seen dead in if you were in your right mind – but sure, to go a-maying was mischief enough. Pray heaven you keep the hood well over your face. To rush off like this without any plan or preparation, on the spur of the moment—'

'The best spur of all. Come, Robin, use yours.'

She had swung her horse's head round again and cantered off.

CHAPTER FIFTEEN

Here he was riding all alone with Elizabeth, the chance of a lifetime, thought Robin, and no chance to use it, even to show his skill in flying his hawk; and far less to make love to her. She seemed scarcely to know that he was there, so intent was she on riding as fast as they could to Mortlake. Besides, it had begun to rain in sharp cold gusts, and who could make love, or even conversation, at this rate, and with wet slaps continually stinging one's face? The villagers huddling off, with cloths and sacking pulled over their heads, had deserted their maypoles, whose gaudy colours were now all dripping in the rain; a melancholy bear had been left tied to his stake, and when Robin thought it would be a good joke to set him free to frighten his intended baiters, Elizabeth did not even answer, but rode on, on, along the sulky sluggish grey river, until at last they came to a small stone house, so near the river it was like a pebble washed up by the tide.

It did not look like a magician's house.

And Dr. Dee was not in the least like a magician. He was young, not yet thirty, tall and fair, with a face as clear and rosy as if he spent his days out hunting instead of poring over forbidden arts. Robin instantly suspected him of drinking the blood of freshly killed children to keep his youthful complexion, like the sorcerer Gilles de Rais.

He wore a loose white artist's coat slit up the back, with hanging sleeves, but somehow looked elegant even in that, and no whit put out at being surprised by a Princess in his workaday garb.

If indeed he were surprised, for he showed no sign of it. He greeted them as a charming host, asked after Elizabeth's tutor, his old friend Roger Ascham, and smiled over some scandalous story of their college days together at Cambridge. Elizabeth wickedly reminded him of another scandal, when he had produced a Greek play with startling scenic effects, and he airily admitted that he had been sent down after it; one of the characters had flown up to the ceiling on the back of a huge scarab, and it had shocked some of the old dons, who suspected him of sorcery.

'They had some ground – or should I say ceiling – for their suspicion!' murmured Elizabeth, with difficulty restraining an hysteric giggle.

She looked uneasily round her at the room, a fortress of secret learning, armed and barricaded by enormous books. There were nearly four thousand of them, he said, and many of them very rare. But books would soon cease to be rare; the Printing Press was not merely another new invention, such as was continually startling this learned and inquisitive age; it was a revolution. The Papacy had recognized it as that from the beginning; fifty years ago they had tried to control the Press – but in vain. No Caesar could again destroy the learning of the ancient world; the library of Egypt had been contained in a house, and burnt to ashes; 'but the library of the future,' declared Dr. Dee, raising his white-sleeved arm like the wing of an avenging angel, 'will have no limits but the world.'

All the same he agreed with Elizabeth that it would be a pity if the Queen would not buy his books to found a National Library; England needed it, and he needed the cash.

Robin asked eagerly of the Philosopher's Stone – did Dee think it was hidden in Cathay or in the undiscovered city of El Dorado? Did it hold the secret of life and death? Could it really transmute base metal into gold?

Dee answered him with a touch of impatience, 'Yes, yes, gold is money now. But money could be anything, however flimsy, even paper. Money is nothing, except that particular substance that men have agreed shall be important to them.'

'And to you, if the Queen buys your library,' said Elizabeth.

But it was evidently too important to laugh at.

'Metals *can* be transmuted, made interchangeable,' he declared, 'and the power released therefrom may remake or perhaps destroy the world. That may well be the secret of life and death that is hidden as yet from mankind.'

'And long may it be so!' cried Elizabeth. 'When would such fools as men are, have the wisdom to use such knowledge?'

This man might look like an archangel, but so did Lucifer, who chose to reign in hell rather than serve in heaven.

Robin gazed awestruck at his crucibles and astrolabes and new scientific instruments; he was eager to hear of the lectures at the Sorbonne that Dee had given when only twenty-three, on Euclid, the first ever given on him in an European university.

'Were you afraid that no one might come?'

'No, my lord. The Parisians, like the Athenians, are always eager to hear new things. Even the herd can guess that higher mathematics hold the highest secrets. But I did not expect the

Sorbonne to be so overcrowded that the rabble of students who couldn't get in fought each other to climb up outside the windows to listen from there.'

'Still higher mathematics,' observed Elizabeth.

Robin whooped in self-justification, 'And your precious Roger Ascham, Madam, said I'd never learn to be a politician because I gave up Cicero to study "Euclid's pricks and lines". That's how he snorted at 'em. But I say they hold magic.'

'That may be,' said Dee, smiling. 'For what charm is wielded by an isosceles triangle so potent as to risk a broken neck on the Sorbonne roof? And does mankind, yes, even the rats from the Paris gutters, so crave certainty as to find a benediction sweeter than the Church in the curt syllables of Q.E.D.?'

There was more scorn than sweetness in his smile, and not only for his ragamuffin admirers, but for the great Duke of Mantua and the Emperor himself, who had come to visit him at Louvain in order to learn from him and his inventions. He let them know this, not with complacency, but a fiery snatch at his triumph, as he offered to show his laboratory and his designs there for an instrument that men had been trying to make ever since Roger Bacon had propounded it three hundred years ago – a glass at the end of a tube which would enable one to see distant objects, even the very stars, as though they were quite near.

'Still more useful to see an advancing enemy on land or sea,' said Robin, all agog to go into the laboratory but already too busy talking about navigation, and why had the Spaniards mastered its art above all other nations?

But Dee had a plan for a Petty Royal Navy to be kept always on guard round the coast of England.

'And will you propose that too to the Queen?' asked Elizabeth.

'Not to this Queen, Madam.'

She caught her breath. She could fend him off no longer. She sent Robin packing off into the laboratory to look at the designs for the magic glass; then sat quiet an instant before she spoke.

'I also risk my neck for certainty. Do you guess why I have come?'

'Do you fear to tell me, Madam?'

'No. I wish you to cast my horoscope.'

'And yours only?'

'No. King Philip's – and the Queen's.'

'That is indeed to risk your neck.'

'And yours. Or it may bring you great fortune.'

He did not speak. He did not move. As he stood there before her he seemed to tower above her, an arrogant archangel, and his eyes plunged down into hers as from a great height. They were the strongest eyes she had seen; they dragged her up out of this dim book-lined room, out of all their urgent scurry of talk that had raced over time and space; they dragged her out of time and space; into a silent infinity.

None of her hopes nor terrors counted here, not even of death. That was not the final extinction. She knew it now.

A veil was closing round her, but through it she could still see his eyes. And now, from a great way off, she heard his voice.

'The future is not ahead of us. It is around us and with us now. Our death is in our life, and our life in death.'

His eyes loosed their hold. She could now see before her the leaded panes of glass in the window, down which the raindrops were running thick and grey. She could see nothing else through the blurred glass. There was no one else in the room.

She sat there alone, staring at the rain, her head light and empty as a blown-up bladder banged by a Fool at a fair; at any moment it might float away from her. Perhaps it was because she had eaten nothing since sunrise, and the light was fading as though it were already afternoon, so she told herself, struggling to get back to today, this morning, this afternoon, to prevent this small stone house on the river drifting off the edge of the world.

Something stood outside the grey window; 'It is a sunbeam,' she told herself, and then remembered that it was raining; 'It is a rainbow,' she told herself; and then saw that it was looking at her. It was the form of a child that shone clear for an instant outside, then glided through the closed window into the room, where it appeared as a coloured shadow, the bright hair rolled up in front and hanging down behind over a long dress that gleamed now red, now green. She was walking upon the bookshelves, where there could surely be no room for her, yet as she moved, prancing, playing up and down, the books seemed to move too, displacing themselves to make room for her. Elizabeth knew she could not be seeing this, yet she was seeing it.

This many-coloured little creature, whose childhood flickered as her own had done in the flame of danger, was herself; a being not afraid to walk through the world alone, a world whose purpose it was to overcome her – and here she was, nearly twenty-two years old, and not yet overcome.

'Shall I then live after all?' she asked, and heard the answer, 'You will live, as long as the name of England lives.'

She knew that whether her body lived on in splendid vigour, or was burnt tomorrow to the dismal smell of ashes that yet clung to her nostrils, she herself would travel on throughout eternity.

The grey air round her slowly darkened; she could see nothing more; she thought that night had fallen, that she was dead; but a strong pair of hands was chafing hers, a hot urgent voice was calling in her ears, calling her back to this discomfortable and anxious life; eager kisses were pressing her cheeks and lips; desire of life, of the body, was dragging her unwilling spirit from eternity into this frightening world again.

'My love, my beauty, come back to me, come back, come back!' cried Robin Dudley's young and furious voice.

She had to come back; she did not want to, she was so tired, but 'I am here,' she thought she cried aloud, and heard it as a whisper. Her eyelids opened an instant on his face, she had forgotten how handsome he was. 'I was dead asleep,' she said, and he answered, sobbing, 'Too dead, dead asleep. I thought you were dead. You shall never die – while I am here.'

'How long will that be?'

'Ever – for ever.'

> '"So you and I
> Will never die?"'

'What a posy for a ring!' she murmured.

'To bind the two of us together for ever. Here it is.'

He was thrusting the ring off his finger on to hers, and then because it hung so loose, on to her thumb.

'So now I'm an alderman with a thumb-ring,' she said,

sleepily, 'and that's well, since my mother had an alderman in the family, a Lord Mayor of London. "Turn again, Whittington, Lord Mayor of London!" Shall I ever get the chance to turn again?'

'You'll turn and turn and turn again, the slipperiest serpent and daughter of Eve that ever coupled under the Tree of Life! But now you'll not turn again. I hold you in my arms now and for ever, my spirit of enchantment!'

Once before he had held her to him like this, a year ago in the Tower. She had eluded him then, she should not now.

The rain lashed against the little windows, the river lapped and roared in the wind like the sea, they were all alone in the dim book-lined room, there was nothing now to keep her from him, only a long pale face beneath his, swooning under his kisses, growing paler and paler. God's breath! was she fainting indeed, perhaps dying? He sprang back with a curse from her cold face. 'For Christ's sake, what ails you?'

'Oh, Robin,' she wailed, 'I am so hungry!'

It never seemed to be the right time for seduction, Robin reflected as they rode back to Hampton Court after a savoury knack of brawn and bread and a draught of ale, taken standing in a hurry, for the sooner she was back, the safer for her. But his disappointment did not weigh too heavily on him, for he was full of this fresh attempt that Richard Challoner was going to make to discover a North-East passage through Russia to Cathay. Robin had been studying Dee's maps, for Dee was geographer to the expedition and held the opinion that it would soon be accomplished, and should take only about thirty-six days, perhaps less. The Tsar of all the Russias, Ivan the Terrible, had belied his name and most courteously invited the English explorers to his Court to arrange a trade agreement with the West, and would send a magnificent present of furs to the Queen of these intrepid adventurers. He had also invited Dr. Dee to Moscow to be his Court Astrologer at a fee of a thousand roubles, 'and that shows you what Dee is,' said Robin with glowing cheeks (he had quite forgotten his suspicions of the probably unholy cause of Dee's fine colour). 'The money would be the least part of it – for even their Ambassadors wear clothes set all over with precious stones – yes, even their nightcaps are sewn with great pearls. They drink a fiery staff out of jewelled goblets and eat the little black eggs of sturgeon.'

'It sounds horrible.'

'No, it is delicious. Challoner gave some to a friend who sent it back, saying they had enough black soap of their own, but it wasn't soap, it's a stuff called caviare. I tell you, I have half a mind to go North myself. England is played out. Her only hope is to colonize. We no longer go to the wars in France. We have let Spain get in ahead of us in the far West – but why call it the New World as though it were the only one? Dee is sure there are others, that there is a vast Southern Continent far down in the globe below Cathay, the Terra Australis he calls it. No man has yet discovered it. How if I should be the one?'

'What, first North and then South?'

'I would sail all round the world if I could. Some man *will*, one day, and why not I?'

'"Why not?" "Why not?" That is the motto of my new page, Humphrey Gilbert, who wants to sail to all winds.'

'Yes, and I'll sail West too, despite the Spaniard, and find El Dorado. Think of that fabled city built of gold and jewels lying hidden in the black heart of the impregnable forest! A sailor told me that the jewels come alive at night and flit through the trees like the burning eyes of witches. But John Hawkins says those are insects that carry fire in their wings. And he said that the most dangerous fire he had met was the light of the African moon. He always made his sailors shut their cabin windows against it. 'Juan de Aquines' he calls himself now since Philip knighted him at Plymouth, but he says it with a wink, and spits out of the corner of his mouth. I tell you, John Hawkins and I will see to it that the Spaniard doesn't have his own way all over the world. Why should England not win a new continent, and you be Queen of it? And Hawkins goes to Dee for his maps too.'

Elizabeth huddled Cat Ashley's shabby cloak about her; she felt cold and old, a hundred years older than Robin, who was less than a year older than she, but was now like a boy, as all men were when they talked of the adventures they wanted. Once, before she was quite fifteen, a man of thirty-five had wanted to lead his fleet to oust the Spaniards from the Western World, and there carve out an Empire for himself – and for her. He had ridden with the Magyars, feasted with the mountain robbers of Hungary, talked with the Sultan, Soliman the Magnificent, cracked jokes with François I of France and Henry of England.

But he carved no empire for himself, nor her.

For her, the Lord High Admiral, Tom Seymour, had laid down his splendid head upon the block.

'Are you listening?' asked Robin. 'I tell you, it's feasible.'

'Eggs in moonshine!' said Elizabeth tartly. 'That is what I say to young Gilbert when he talks as you are doing now. But *he* is only sixteen.'

'Yet you like to talk with him.' Robin's tone was sulky.

'He's a clever lad, though like you he thinks the classics old-fashioned, and studied navigation at Oxford instead. But how could you have had all this talk with Dee? And—' she turned her head quickly on a sudden suspicion, 'how was it you were not ravenous – as I was?'

'Why, I had a knack or two in the laboratory after we had left you alone...'

'For a few minutes only—' she broke off at his stare.

'How long then *was* it?'

'Look at the sky,' he said. 'Now it's stopped raining, can you not see it's growing dark?'

Bewildered, she looked about her. A few wild blossoms in the hedges waved like pale flames through the wet gloom. Where had she been during these hours that had hidden themselves in the compass of a few minutes?

The day had passed without her knowing anything of what it might have brought.

She reined in her horse abruptly, stopped an old farmer trudging towards them through the mud, and asked if any further news had yet been heard of the birth of the Queen's baby at Hampton Court.

He told her at great length all that she knew already of the bell-ringings and thanksgiving processions, while she checked her fidgeting horse in an agony of impatience.

'But for all this great labour,' he ended at last in his broad slurring voice, 'for our yoong maister so long looked for, in the end there's been neither yoong maister nor yoong maistress that any man to this hour can hear on. Eh!' he added reprovingly, while pocketing the coin she gave him, 'there's no call to laugh at honest folk neither.'

And he splashed aside into a puddle, where he stood

glaring at them and muttering about a cackling gaggle of geese, while the two rude young people, riding on, rolled in their saddles and shouted and hooted with delight.

'"No yoong maister." Oh Rob, think of the priest describing him in the pulpit!'

'"Nor yoong maistress neither" – oh Bess, think of the Polish envoy congratulating Philip!'

'Think of Philip *still* not a father!'

'*Still* not crowned King of England!'

'*Still* not getting England into war with France! All "Eggs in moonshine", all of 'em, Robin, and addled!'

'A fine pair you think you are, Maister Cock-up-Spotty and your smart yoong drab,' growled the farmer, well out of earshot, as he trudged away and looked back again and again over his shoulder. 'Splashing me with your horses' hooves and giggle-gaggling about your betters. The Queen's a lady, and that's more than you'll ever be.'

And even Elizabeth might have agreed if she had heard him.

It was quite dark by the time the Palace loomed across the river, the lighted windows glimmering on the rough dark water. She parted from Robin at some distance from the gates, leaving her horse with him, and would not heed his protest that it was dangerous for a female to go on alone through the dark.

'A deal more dangerous for me to be caught with you,' she told him, and he had to admit it; dared not linger for more than a snatched kiss and a whisper; but had to stand and watch her slip away – to become captive or Queen, criminal or conqueror? She slid away swiftly, a shadow lost almost at once in the black dark.

She went down the long alley of the tennis courts, her hood pulled well over her face, then with her secret key through the small square enclosed garden under the windows of the rooms where her little brother King Edward had stayed while at Hampton Court; but there was no one there now, and all the windows were dark. Then into the servants' quarters, the narrow passage of Fish Court, and under the great arch that led to the kitchens, and so, keeping close against the wall, towards the door of the staircase to her own apartments.

There was a torch flickering in a bracket further down the passage, but all was silent and empty. She had only to glide through this arch, open the door noiselessly, she was all but there—

A figure stepped out from the dark archway just in front of her. She had either to turn and run, which was hopeless, or to go on. Desperately she sank her head further under her hood, hunched her shoulders into a low stoop, and set herself to shuffle past. A hand fell like a stone upon her wrist, another thrust back her hood. She was looking into the grey, deep-shadowed face of the Prince of Spain.

CHAPTER SIXTEEN

So this was what Dee had foretold. All the future Dee had shown her had been the spirit of her past self. To see the wraith of herself. What a fool she had been not to recognize in it the sign of her own immediate death. That was what he had meant by all his fine, vague talk of death in life, and life in death; that was why he had said nothing really of the future. What a fool she had been not to see it till now, 'What a fool!' she said aloud, and then instinctively repeated it in Spanish, and was answered so; and was asked,

'In what folly? Or treachery?'

'No treachery.'

But to cast the horoscopes of King and Queen was treason. To cast her own, in her case would be treason. She waited an instant, practising in her mind the tone she would use when she could speak. At last she forced it to her lips, and it did not sound forced, but like that of a reckless wanton.

'And what folly? What other could there be when a woman slips home in the dark hid in a cloak? What else was Your Highness waiting for here, so near the kitchen quarters, but to catch some errant scullery-maid?'

'I was waiting for you.'

'As I said! So you knew of my absence?'

'I knew. I wished to see you. Your governess protested

you were sick in bed. It is a game you have played too often. I walked past her into the room, and you were not there.'

'Is this Spanish etiquette? You shock me, sir.'

'You mock me, Madam. All England is mocking me now. If it had but one neck I could cut it off with a blow. I cannot. But I can yours.'

His hands flew up and fastened in a murderous grip round her throat, then as suddenly dropped to his side.

'I do not believe,' he said, in a quiet, almost casual voice, 'that the Queen has ever been with child. I think she has a tumour.'

Elizabeth, feeling her throat tenderly, gave a gasp that was more of a croak.

'Well?' he said. 'You may speak your thought.'

'Not easily. It hurts.' She swallowed, then began again. 'But the Queen is convinced—'

'Of course she is convinced. Of course everyone has been convincing her. And now they say she was mistaken in the time; she may have to wait another two weeks; perhaps another two months. Do the women here carry their young for eleven months?'

Was it possible she might after all escape death yet again? Philip did not seem to be concerned with the reason for her absence, disgraceful as she had hinted it to be.

'Why did Your Highness wish to see me? I should not know near as much about the Queen as any of her women.'

'I did not seek you as a midwife.'

'Well then—?'

'It seems you have been absent a long time – since early this morning perhaps. Have you then heard nothing of the battle?'

'The *battle*! But where?'

'Here. In the very precincts of the Palace. Five hundred of my Spaniards attacked by near twice as many English. Not another brawl, but a pitched fight.'

'How many killed?'

'Of your English, I suppose? Ask of your own people – who shouted at mine that I am impotent to get an heir.'

'Sir, you did not seek me as a mediator any more than as a midwife. Why then?'

'To tell you that I must leave England. I will not stay here to be insulted, my people murdered, while I am enslaved by the fraudulent pregnancy of a brainsick wife. I am nothing here. I am *called* King only as my wife's consort. To be crowned King, that is denied me. I am no King. I am here merely as a borrowed stallion – to a barren mare.'

'O God,' she thought, 'if Mary could hear him she would run mad.' And if Philip had heard her and Robin on the road, their cruel laughter at his humiliation – but she dared not even think of that, lest he should hear her thoughts.

But he was intent on his own. He was deliberately pulling them together out of the fury of his almost unconscious attack on her, dragging them into sane and reasonable words.

'My father demanded my sacrifice on the altar of this heathen island, and I did his will, for as long as he required it. But now he demands my presence. He only awaits my return so that he can retire into the monastery of Yuste and make his soul before he dies. If he should die before then, I shall have his soul for ever on my conscience.'

'What the Devil!' she longed to shriek, and 'What a family!' The cruel laughter was welling up again within her; she choked it back and said gravely, 'Your Highness's conscience is too tender, and the burdens laid on it too heavy. There is not only the fear for your father's soul – but for your wife's reason.'

'You wish me then to stay? For whose sake? Never tell me it is for your sister's.'

She looked at him for a moment in silence; then said, 'No.'

He gave a short bark of laughter. 'You are wise as usual, my sister. It is very necessary for your sake that I should stay. I have saved you from death at the hands of the Queen more than once. If I stay, I can still save you. But if she dies, as is likely, I would be in danger of death from your English rabble.'

She spoke very softly. 'It would then be my turn to save you, my brother.'

'I wonder if you would,' he mused doubtfully, but without any sign of resentment.

She dared not try to assure him; put a foot wrong now, and the thin ice on which she was skating would crack and plunge her to ruin.

'But the question will not arise,' he said, 'for I shall go.'

Her hand fluttered out in the darkness and brushed past his.

'And leave me to die? Will not my death be also a burden on your conscience?'

'Your life endangers it far more.'

His tone, sombre and relentless, made her fear his love more than his hate. She tried to shrug it off. 'If that is a compliment, I have little liking for it.'

'It was not to pay you compliments that I forced my way into your room.'

'And why did you, then?'

'To tell you, for your own sake, that you must leave England when I do.'

'And go where?'

'To Spain.'

'As your—' she stopped, aware that he was enjoying her stupefaction.

'My daughter,' he finished for her; and she knew that he was smiling. She was glad she could not see the smile.

'My father,' he continued, 'wishes me to marry you to my son, Don Carlos.'

'That – little boy!'

'He will grow. And when ripe for matrimony he will be no younger than you, than I am younger than my wife. And your experience will be more apt than her virtue to ease the situation.'

Blind with rage, she tried to push past him, but he took her by the shoulders, forced her head back against the wall and struck kisses like blows upon her face. She turned her head this way and that, trying to escape them, she cried out, but strangled the cry, knowing that if she were seen in Philip's arms, there would be no escaping death from Mary.

He gave that sharp toneless bark of laughter. 'Are you now showing me your virtue, you who have just blazoned out to me that you have been playing the harlot?'

She cried wildly, 'No, it's not true,' and struggled free. 'But you believed it! Do you want a harlot for your son's wife?'

'Yes. Or any other's, so it bring you near me.'

And he laid his hands on her again, but she shoved them frantically aside. 'Let go. You had better. I am going to be sick,' and was.

It worked. He left her.

* * *

If she had not thought of that – for she *had* thought of it, she had felt sick with disgust and fury, pain and exhaustion, but she could have restrained it, one can restrain anything – if she had not thought of it, she would now be his harlot. Nothing else would have served to prevent it, not even a dead faint.

But he alone stood between her and her sister's hate. It might mean her death if she had driven him away in disgust for good – as she might well have done. How oddly fastidious, she thought, as she lay in bed under the cold wet cloths that Cat Ashley was applying to her bruised mouth, how finically fastidious in a man who wanted to marry his son to the woman he meant to make his mistress! A man who, she suspected, rather relished the spectacle of executions by fire or axe.

But no, not odd, for to him the unforgivable thing was to make him, or what pertained to him, ridiculous. He would never forgive his wife, nor the English people who had milled in the streets today to shout taunts at him and at her.

And how should she be forgiven, how retrieve her position as the object of his fastidious desire? For the first time she saw clearly now what that was – that he did not mind if she were a wanton, he preferred it; did not mind whom she married – the Prince of Savoy, Robin Dudley, even his own schoolboy son, as long as it would enable him to enjoy her in secret, and as a sin. It was that which he wanted of her, not matrimony.

As a wife, she was neither respectable nor safe. She might deceive him, or dominate him.

But towards her as a mistress he could permit himself the luxury of her forbidden dangers.

'I should be one of the "poesies" of Titian that he keeps concealed behind a curtain,' she thought, remembering the swift, bare-breasted Diana pursuing the stag, which he had once shown her so shyly, or, she now saw, slyly; and she began to shake with silent laughter.

'No laughing matter, you'll not be fit to be seen for days!' grumbled Cat Ashley as she took off the cloths and applied cooling unguents, 'My lamb, my pretty, you were mad to go alone with him.'

'Good God, woman, do you think young Robin Dudley made his mark here? What a fool you are!' She laughed a little shakily, to think how Robin had indeed kissed her so few hours before.

But she did not trouble to account for her bruises. She lay in the dim rosy light from behind the velvet curtains; she sank deep down into her goosefeather bed, while the edges of sleep came curling and rippling up around her. With the sudden force of a swimmer, all but spent, striking out in a last determined stroke for life, she shook herself awake, to realize that there was but one way to retrieve what she had thrown away with Philip.

She must show him that for her part she did not care how ridiculous or repulsive she may have made herself to an over-conscious young man who had been paralysed by his upbringing into a horror of natural bodily functions. He had been taught to be unnatural; the cold savagery of his passion for her had revealed that clearly enough. But she would let it have nothing to do with her. She would be true to herself. She would continue to show him all her natural audacity, her carelessness of reputation, yes, and of refinement. 'If *he* is refined,' she said to herself, 'then thank God for the coarseness of the mere English.'

With that she lay back again and let herself wander into the borderland of sleep, that enchanted country where the edges of one's world, of one's very self, become remote and unexplored. Was this still herself, with all the cares and busynesses that had clung to her like coils of tangling rope through the day? Or was she sliding away, gradually freeing herself, a boat slipping its moorings, gliding she knew not where, becoming she knew not who, losing herself – and what could be lovelier than to be lost? If such bliss lay in sleep, then why fear death? She fell deep asleep.

But then she dreamed, and the ropes coiled round her again.

She was telling Robin about Philip – 'He kissed me here, and here, to hurt, where you had kissed me so short a time ago,' and Robin swore to kill him in a tourney; it would be easy, for Robin was the best man with a lance in England since Tom Seymour had borne down all his opponents; he would strike through the opening of Philip's visor at his eye, and the point would drive through to his brain and he would fall dead.

'So die all the enemies of the Queen!' cried Robin in a loud swaggering voice, and that was the first time she knew that she was Queen of England, Elizabeth of England, how new it sounded, and yet she had always known it. She left her throne above the tiltyard and walked over the muddy ground to tell Robin he was her own true knight, and found him sitting there beside Philip, who was not dead at all, but also sitting up, comfortably discussing with Robin how he would help him to marry Elizabeth, and then Philip would invite them both to stay with him.

CHAPTER SEVENTEEN

In that month of May the cuckoos went mad with joy in the belated spring. It had rushed into flower on top of the chilled and sodden world, borne on the wings of innumerable birds that had waited till this moment to burst into vociferous chorus. But loud and shrill as they sang, the cuckoos shouted them all down. They piped from every tree, and some from where no tree was. They called from the street corners, they hooted behind the houses, they whistled up in wild mockery from the crowds that ran to throw stones and jeer wherever they saw a Spaniard. And the bird's cry ran on into new words for an old country song.

> '"Cuckoo!" her singeth as her flies,
> Her bringeth good tidings, and all of 'em lies!'

A ship sailed home from Antwerp up the river, and the sailors told how the great bell of Antwerp had pealed rejoicing at news of the birth of England's Prince, and all the English crews in the harbour had been given a hundred crowns to drink his health. 'May the Prince have a few more false births!' they guffawed, as they clinked their cups on the long bench in the Angel. It used to be the Angel of Our Lady, but they changed it in the last reign, and the inn-keeper wasn't going to spend good money on yet another sign, so just added 'Our Lady' in small letters at the bottom.

The Queen was still lying-in at Hampton Court; the doctors had admitted a mistake in the date, and that her child might not be born for a few weeks yet; but down in London taverns there were whispers that if a Prince were produced, it would be no son of Philip and Mary, but hatched from a cuckoo's egg laid in the royal nest.

An honest woman of Aldersgate, one Mrs. Malt, had been asked by certain lords in disguise (but she *knew* they were lords), if she would give up her new-born son to them, but she would not, not for all the gold in the Tower.

'Another mare's nest in Aldersgate!' cackled Grandfather Talbois on his stool at the door of their house in Cheapside, where he sat all day now it was warmer, to see the crowds go by. 'Did she get her boy by St. Anne's parson? Told 'em all just what the Queen's baby looked like, didn't he? But I'll have no mare lay a cuckoo's egg in *this* house, let our Mag mark that. Them Spaniards do be terrible oncoming with the maidens.'

> '*When Spanish apes*
> *Steal all our grapes*
> *What will Mag do for wine?*'

chanted her little brother Tom, and made a rude sign at her. She hated to be called Mag, her real name was Mary, but they none of them called her that any longer, for they didn't hold with the Virgin Mary now; nor with the Queen. Her mother often didn't hold with Mrs. Malt either (nor for that matter with most other women), but at this moment she chose to hold fast by her; she said that Granddad had no need to doubt Mrs. Malt's word, there were others in Horn Alley who would vouch for the lords' visit to her, and what's more they'd brought a fine lady with them to serve as rocker for the baby. These foreigners would go to all lengths to get their ends; the new Order of Spanish priests had a motto for it. 'The end justifies the means,' and the end of it all might have been that they'd have had young Timothy Malt from Horn Alley for their next King, and how would they all like that?

'Well enough,' objected her husband; for all he was the most prosperous candlemaker in Cheapside, the finest street in London, he'd sooner have a Cockney brat come to the throne than a lad who was three parts Spanish, who'd make them all pay Peter's Pence again to the Pope, another pesky foreigner.

His wife bade him speak low, for the prentices were going in and out, and already the streets were crowded with barrow-mongers crying their wares, and they the worst spies and tell-tale-tits in the town, and why was young Tom still dangling about, his ears growing long with listening, when it was nearly eight o'clock and he late for school and sure to get a beating?

The boy snatched up his satchel and grabbed an orange out of it which he flung at his sister. 'Fine Seville oranges!' he called, imitating the street cry, 'Our Mag will be a Spanish lady, as civil as an orange!' He ran hooting up the street to escape the blow she aimed at him, and she ran after, not to try and catch him but to run away from her odious family – and oh, would she really one day run away for good and all, with Diego Valdez of Malaga?

She couldn't run fast through the hustling crowds; a

spiteful little wind blew her flaxen hair into her eyes that were already smarting with tears, she stubbed her toe on a stone, she splashed her gown with filth, and this was Cheapside, 'the beauty of London'!

The fine buildings in Goldsmith's Row looked down on a filthy dunghill in the highway; the Lord Mayor would get it cleared for the next royal procession when Queen Mary came back to town with her baby, to prove all the unkind Protestants false; never for one moment did Mary Talbois doubt it. But they would find other nasty things to say, just as the dunghill would start growing again at once. The stench of it blew out on the breeze and curled up into her nostrils. She had seen and smelt London all her life, but only now that she loved Diego did she know how dirty London was; and how coarse and stupid her old grandfather, who had come up to it to make his fortune, but had never stopped being a countryman; and how harsh and crude and purse-proud were her parents.

Diego was a poor squire, but he held himself as much a noble as the King, and nobler, for the King was part Flemish. But Diego's family had lived in Malaga when the Phoenicians were there, long before the Romans came, and then the Moors; they had helped drive out the Moors, except those who were converted and were called Moriscos; the de Valdez lived in a white house with a walnut door in one of the former Moorish streets that twisted up the hillside like a white ribbon, and as clean, for Diego had to say that for the Moriscos, the town shone like a pearl above the sapphire sea.

She had never seen the sea.

His house had a little courtyard in the middle with carved arches to keep out the sun, for the sun was so hot that it made this English sun like the moon. There she would sit with a black mantilla over her flaxen head, and see flowers hang in purple bells and scarlet stars against the dazzle of the sky, and smell the figs ripening and the thyme and aromatic herbs blowing down from the mountain, and eat oranges plucked fresh from the tree, which tasted like none you could get here.

She bent her head to the orange still in her hands, so eager to sniff it and forget the dunghill as she ran towards the fields of Holborn that she rubbed her nose pink against it. She blessed her horrid little brother now for throwing it at her; it was a talisman to show that her dream would come true, it glowed like a ball of fire in the sunlight, she tossed it up in the air and caught it, running after it with dancing steps and singing,

> 'Oh Mary, Mary Talbois,
> The candlemaker's daughter!
> But I shall be Mary of Malaga,
> Far, far away in Malaga,
> I shall be far from Da and Ma
> When I go to dance in Malaga,
> With Diego Valdez of Malaga.'

She searched in a thick clump of thorn trees until she found a blackbird's nest, deep hidden, from which the birds had flown. Then from the pocket, hung with coloured tassels, that dangled at her belt, she pulled out a twist of paper, looked at the few words she had scrawled on it, kissed it and tucked it down into the nest.

'No cuckoo laid *that* egg!' she laughed, and took to her heels and ran back into the London streets.

A new crowd was forming somewhere, boys were scampering and calling to each other, she saw the glint of halberds moving slowly along amidst a welter of people; there were now no shrill excited calls, but an angry mutter of questions, exclamations, rolled to and fro:

– 'another prisoner' –

– 'is it another heretic?'

– 'another bonfire soon then!'

Now she could see the cart and a tall man standing up in it with his arms bound. A boy with a basket of turnips threw one at him; the prisoner turned and looked at him, and with a howl the boy dropped his basket and backed out of the crowd and ran away.

'Who is it? Why are people afraid of a heretic?' she asked, and got a shrug for answer and a whispered 'Heretic! If that were all!'

'It's the Lady Elizabeth again,' she heard. 'That's her servant Carey behind the tall fellow.'

But no one would tell her who the tall fellow was. She had to wait till she got home and found her grandfather cackling over 'that jilt again, she's always making trouble! Mark my words she'll be known for always as Bad Bess.' And then Mag heard that the prisoner, who had frightened the boy in the crowd only by looking at him, was a famous sorcerer newly come from abroad, and that the Princess's servant Carey had been arrested with him, no one knew why. But that the young Lady had been mixed up in some devil's work was plain as a pikestaff, plotting the Queen's death by magic as likely as not – 'but when will they get Bad Bess herself in the cart. That's what I'm asking – and she too, I shouldn't wonder!'

* * *

Elizabeth heard of Dee's arrest, and Carey's, who was to have brought her the horoscopes, as arranged with Dee; she did not know if they had been found on him, nor what the charge was against the two men.

Not for some days was she summoned to the presence of the Prince of Spain; not the Queen's. Did Mary not yet know of the matter, and was there in this some ray of hope for her the first after all these quaking days and nights?

She was taken privately to him where he sat alone in the little room that had been Cardinal Wolsey's sanctum at Hampton Court; the oak panels had already darkened with fire-smoke since she had sat here as a child with her father and played with his chessmen; but the gilding was still bright on the carved Tudor roses in the ceiling. Cardinal Wolsey had sat there with her father; he must have guessed his doom long before it took place. How long must she wait before she knew hers?

She could learn nothing from Philip's manner in receiving her; it would have the same chill politeness whatever he had decided to do with her. He had risen and bowed while she curtseyed, handed her to a chair and then seated himself again, all the movements timed with the deliberate grace of the preliminaries to a dance, or a duel. Her hands were icy, but she would not hold them to keep them from shaking, she would not let them shake; her lips were taut and her breath came fast, but she would not speak first; he looked at her, but she would not look away.

Was it herself sitting here, or was it Wolsey, waiting to hear her father say that this palace of Hampton Court was too fine for a servant of the Crown and should be for the King? Wolsey had given it all over to him, lock, stock and barrel, yes, all those barrels in the cellars, and made him a present of the ninety-nine years' lease at fifty pounds a year, and all the furnishings that had put King Henry's in the shade; but that had not saved him from King Henry.

She was mad to be thinking of this instead of what to say. Why did Philip not speak? She still did not look away from him; it was he who turned his eyes from her, towards the window. Was it himself sitting there, slight and pale, or was it a great gross man in scarlet and gold who looked out of the window at the workmen pulling down the initials H. and A., that had been carved over the courtyard gate for Henry and her mother, Ann Bullen? Ann had sat here too with Henry, had played at chess with him and watched the firelight flickering on the panels, and purred, sleek as an elegant black cat, with pleasure that it was now their home and no longer that overweening Cardinal Wolsey's. Ann had been Henry's 'own darling,' his 'entirely beloved sweetheart.' But Henry had ordered her death.

Soon she would run mad and scream at Philip to do likewise and get it done with.

At last she heard his stern, measured voice and had to force her wits to take in the brief words.

'You have been consulting an astrologer.'

Unexpectedly came her answer, pat, before she knew what it would be.

'Your Highness, it is one whom your own father has consulted.'

'But not in the same circumstances. Nor, I think, as an astrologer.'

'How then?'

(He had spoken as a judge. But he had not said, 'a sorcerer'; there was no hint yet of magic; nor of attempted murder.)

Philip shrugged. 'As a remarkable savant in geography and other sciences. Your Dr. Dee is a man of many parts. Too many. He must know, and you, that to cast the nativities of reigning Princes is treason.'

He had passed judgment. Still she spoke boldly.

'No treason was intended. I ordered them, but only to learn of the future.'

'What did you hope to learn? That the Queen would die shortly, and you reign in her stead?'

'I wanted to know what was going to happen next. The probabilities were – and are – that I should die rather than the Queen. It is not treason to wish to know if I should see this next summer. Which now seems unlikely.'

'The horoscopes did not say so.'

'So – you have seen them?'

Was he smiling? Her heart leaped, though she did not trust his smile, 'I'd keep it from the milk anyway,' she told herself with the almost hysterical gaiety that always flared up in her in desperation. And with it there surged back her resolve when she last met him, and fought his lust as now she fought his enmity. She would retrieve her position with him, and in her own way. He should never see how frightened she was.

'Come, tell me,' she said, in as casual and confidential a manner as if he had paid that visit to the little stone house by the river together with her, 'what has he foretold for you and me?'

'For "*you*" and "*me*"? Do you then put us together?'

She lost hope. There had been none for her in that half-smile, only the scorn that now snapped off his words like splinters of ice. But she came back to the attack, and drew her bow at a rash venture.

'Did not he?' she asked, still almost casually.

He stared at her. Involuntarily she put up a hand to hide the bruise that still showed near her mouth, then snatched it away, furious that she felt herself blushing.

His answer came at last. 'He foresaw that our lives would be linked.'

'How?'

He did not answer.

Had Dee said they would be deadly enemies? If so, her position was deadly, for Philip's belief in astrology and sooth-saying was stronger than her own. But surely Dee would have been cautious on paper, and not given Philip cause to fear her as a future enemy. Yet wise men could be singular fools. She braved it out, still on a quiet note. 'If he said that you would be against me, it is unfair that you should have the advantage of knowing it, while I go unwarned.'

'You seem singularly unwarned of the danger in which you have already placed yourself. You have committed a treasonable act against the State, and your associates in it are already in prison.'

'My servant Carey knew nothing of it. He is only the messenger who was to bring me some documents, he did not know what. And Dee obeyed my command, probably without knowing it was criminal, as indeed I did not – only that it was imprudent. There are so many crimes against the State now, it is difficult to keep pace with them.'

'You are overplaying your innocence.'

'But not that of my fellow-culprits. Indeed, Your Highness—'

'You have no need to defend them.'

'Are they already – dead?'

'No. They will shortly be free. Dee's defence had more power than yours. On the day that the informer, Ferys, brought the charge against him, one of Ferys' children fell dead, and the other was struck blind. No judge dares convict Dee after that, not any jailer keep him in prison. He will be allowed to go into exile abroad.'

Elizabeth had risen from her chair, and stood stunned. 'If he had the power – and will – to do this horrible thing—' she stopped, and then, 'He did not seem evil. Can he really be a devilish sorcerer?'

'An effective one, it seems. And when is sorcery not devilish? Have you practised it?'

He looked away from her, then added, 'It is said that you have a familiar spirit.'

She flared into furious denial.

But even as she spoke she thought of a child with long hair who had slid through the closed window in Dee's house and played among the great books on the shelves. Could he have sent that sprite to haunt her, invisible to herself, but not to some other? The terrible fancy broke down her courage.

'It is not true,' she cried; 'I am not a witch. If he has cast spells, I have used none. I went to him only for the horoscopes.'

But her protest sounded in her own ears like that of all who were accused of witchcraft. One could never disprove it. Her mother could not.

The Inquisition had first been instituted to deal with witchcraft; and the Spanish Inquisition was more ruthless than that of Rome. Philip had been her chief hope of protection against Mary. But what protection could she hope from him now? He still would not turn towards her; was he afraid to do so?

With a quick desperate movement she leaned over his chair and caught at his cold hand. 'Why do you not look at me? Do you fear that I will cast a spell on you?'

He looked. He put out his other hand and touched the bruise near her mouth.

'You have already done so.'

CHAPTER EIGHTEEN

The spell kept him in England against his will, against his judgment, against his father's urgent requests for his presence, and his own bitter feelings about the country that had refused him everything he had hoped for; had insulted him in the public streets with taunts at his impotency (he who had fathered more than a dozen children to the best of his knowledge), yes, and even across the Channel, those accursed narrow seas that hemmed this island into a little arrogant, ignorant world of its own. Yet still this witch held him dangling here, to endure the Cockney's disgusting gibes and Mary's damp devotion and his own awful pretence that he too believed in her hopes of an heir.

Once she accepted the fact that she was too old and ill to bear a child, she might run mad in good earnest, Ruy Gomez told him – and why might she not? he asked, shrugging his already rather high shoulders in contempt for her, and all women. How they loved to torment themselves! All save one.

Yet he agreed with Ruy he must stay a little while longer for the sake of the Queen; but knew it was for the sake of that one. The Queen pleaded with him to remain another month, another week or two perhaps, and he would see her hope come true. He hardly heard her. But he listened when

Elizabeth pleaded with him to stay, for her life's sake, that was true enough, yet she never mentioned so small a matter; and it was not her words that he heeded, he did not trust them, but the low, ringing, laughing tone she sometimes used that was like the thrumming of a guitar.

Her voice was an orchestra; he had the suspicion that she practised its various instruments before she played on them to him. But to whatever tune she played he had to dance, so he told himself, bitterly and in enmity, while in solitude; and then while he was with her he could only listen to her in pleasure and in confidence.

How amusing she could make even the Cockney insolence. 'You should have heard them even against my father, the Great Harry, when he could not get himself a male heir to England. The Tudors are a poor lot, they say, as poor in heirs as they're rich in ancestors, as *they* say.

> '"*King Arthur was a noble king,*
> *His breeches cost him half a crown,*
> *But ne'er an heir from them did ring,*
> *With that he called the tailor 'lown'!*"

'So now you know. We *may* be descended from Arthur, but even he can't guarantee our descendants. Who cares if the great bell at Antwerp did ring on a false report? You'll make it ring true on a dozen other births when you go, so soon, alas, to Flanders – but no, you'll keep those muffled! Who cares if the English sailors are rude? They are always rude. Our Lord High Admiral Howard called your glorious Armada a fleet of cockle shells last summer, and look how much bigger your new galleons are already – but our sailors would never see that. Sailors don't care. They say what pleases them – and they have little else to please them. It is the same with the crowds in the street, what else have they got? Scandal, sniggering laughter, we need not grudge them to the low; they have no other compensation against the great.'

'Not even here?' At last his anger fought through the charm of her comradeship, more potent than her coquetry. 'Here, in this country, where every heretic and robber still hopes for Communistic Law that shall make every man a law unto himself?'

'And, therefore, have no law – until all men be glad and wise. Jack Cade himself, a century ago, showed how far off all men still were from making their own law. So did Robert Kett only a few years since. If my poor little brother's Reforming – deforming – Ministers had not hanged him from his own "Oak of Reformation", he would have hanged himself, in despair at the lawlessness of his followers. He had hoped to lead them into the Promised Land and all they saw of it was to break down the palings of the deer parks!'

He looked at her in amazement.

'You pity all men,' he said.

'God forbid! It is necessary sometimes to be pitiless.'

'Then what is it that makes you seem almost to love all men, even the rascal herd?'

'Why, what is it that makes all men kin? I hope to feel that in all – even those I might have to hang.'

'You speak as a ruler – and born to it.'

'I am more likely born to be hanged. It is for that reason I never learned to swim,' she added on one of her sudden wild digressions that left him following her lamely, as with a dictionary. 'And for that very reason,' she hastened on, 'I have a fellow-feeling with the crowd, even when they jeer at me as "that jilt". It's some small compensation for all their squalid chores—'

'Chores?' he repeated, bewildered.

'Oh, that is an old-fashioned word meaning household tasks such as scouring the greasy wooden trenchers after a hot meal, and can you guess what that would be like? No, Your High Daintiness cannot, but I, you see, am a natural kitchen wench at heart. And I can see that, to such drab lives, scandal, especially royal, can be not only compensation but even a rough affection, a sense that the great ones are even as they under their silken robes, that we are all the same under our skin.'

'I have not observed any such affection,' remarked Philip.

No, he was a foreigner. She had gone too far, thinking of herself while speaking of them both. She had sought common ground with him (it would be easier with an English sailor), but she must not go too far. She must restrain her mockery even of her family and herself (God's life, would she ever be able to laugh freely with anyone? – Well, perhaps with Robin – in secret), even though it had been to salve the wounds of Philip's self-love.

At all costs she must keep him here in England until Mary was more safe to deal with. She must not laugh nor go on talking, she must forget her almost unbearable relief that for the moment anyway she was safe with him. The moment was going on, going past her ('tick, tock, said her mother's clock'), and soon, very soon, it would change into something else.

It was changing now. She must stay very still and try to hear what was in Philip's mind behind his words.

He asked her, apparently with some pique, why she had

shown no curiosity about her horoscope, and his.

She answered doubtfully, 'Your Highness seemed displeased at my daring to link them together.'

'At the readiness of your guess, perhaps. That linked you to the sorcerer, rather than myself.'

But no, it was not that, she thought. What should she say? 'Say nothing, nothing. He has not spoken yet.'

He spoke again, unwillingly. 'Yes, the stars foretold that their courses will be in conjunction.'

Again she longed to ask how, but was silent.

'And so,' he said at last, 'I have come to hope. I think you know my hope.'

Well, the last thing she had known of it was that she should be his daughter-in-law! She bit that back; and still waited.

He actually made a movement towards her; but it froze – then, impatiently, he turned away. 'My hope is not of England, as you once accused me,' came on a sudden sour note; evidently he had expected some sign from her and been disappointed; 'I have no hope nor understanding of this ungrateful, stubborn country. You seem to have it; – very well then. I would leave England to you to manage.'

'The Queen does that, sir.'

'Must you pretend for ever? We are alone. The Queen will not live for ever. She may not live very long.'

'Did Dr. Dee foretell that?'

'The Devil take you! And Dee, if he has not taken him already. The Queen knows nothing of the horoscopes, and I will not tell you what he said of her chances of a long life. The doctors could tell you of them as easily as he, if they spoke truly. But he said that you – and I – would live long.'

She could hear Philip's thoughts clearly now. He was

cautiously transmuting the base metal of his dishonourable proposals into the pure gold of matrimonial intentions. Here was alchemy indeed! Equal to Dee's, and partly due to him. The Prince of Spain was translating the prophecies by the light of his desire for her.

It should be easy to fall in love with this handsome young man who would be the master of the world. But could he master her?

'Why do you start?' asked Philip, rising and walking to the window. 'What did you see out there?'

'Nothing. A kingfisher. I saw a flash of red and green.'

'But a kingfisher is blue.'

'Then it was a woodpecker – green in the sunlight, and the flaming crest on its head.'

But it was not a bird she had seen at the window; it was her own thought, that had flashed across her vision in the form of the child that had been herself, a being not afraid to walk through the world alone, a world whose purpose it was to overcome her. And could Philip? 'God's death, no,' she almost exclaimed aloud, 'let him try all his life. He'll never be my master.'

'Come, what were you telling me?' she said aloud. 'That our lives would be long? Did Dee foretell how they would end?'

'In bed.'

'The same one?' rushed out on a spurt of laughter, but was instantly choked with the exclamation, 'If bed's so deadly, I'll never go there.'

'It's saved you from death more than once. And so have I.'

'May you never regret it,' she said tenderly, for a messenger was approaching them from the Queen, and he would have no further opportunity now to ask her if her hopes matched his. But he probably took that for granted.

He did. It was not Philip's way to ask questions.

He gave special injunctions for her safety, tactfully to Mary, commandingly to her principal lords and ministers, before he left England. It was late August by the time he went, after just over a whole hateful year in England, and nothing accomplished in it, not even the assurance that it, and Elizabeth, would be his when Mary died. Ruy Gomez, now to be created Prince of Eboli on his return, assured him of it with confident chuckles, but Philip could not feel sure.

> "*Souvent femme varie,*
> *Bien fol qui s'y fie,*"

he quoted gloomily to himself from that prince of lovers, François I of France, but not aloud, for not even to his closest friend would he admit his fear that any woman should be so variable as to throw him over.

But no woman could equal the inconstancy of the English people, so fickle and light-minded they welcomed any change for the sake of novelty; so said the Spaniards, and with some reason, on their last amazing ride in public with the Queen. She had insisted on seeing off her husband at least as far as Greenwich, though still very ill, but thank God no longer believing it to be from pregnancy. They drove through the streets together, with Cardinal Pole on her other side, in an open litter to show themselves to the crowds that were already packed close as salted herrings in a barrel with all the countrymen who had come up for St. Bartholomew Fair. And countrymen and Cockneys alike yelled themselves hoarse, waved and huzza'd and flung roses all the way before Mary's path, and ran nearly mad with joy at the sight of her after this long weary time. Laughing and weeping like prisoners suddenly set free, they thronged round the litter of the sick woman they had mocked and defied, in almost frantic desire to show her that while they hated her husband, her Church, and all that she loved, they passionately loved and sympathized with herself.

'England likes Queens,' was the Count de Feria's dry verdict as he rode behind the litter with Ruy Gomez. 'They welcome no King except as a Queen's consort. It is a Mother country.'

'If they forsake the worship of the Virgin Mary,' his friend answered, 'they will make up for it with worship of their "Virgin Princess".'

'You surely speak ironically if you call Elizabeth a virgin!'

'I speak officially, since that is what she is to the public.'

'She could hardly be anything else – in public.'

'You know the Queen has had her sent by water all the way to Greenwich, for fear that she should draw an even more rapturous greeting from the crowd. She's already the Queen of Cockney.'

'Prince Philip is mad to interfere on her behalf.' (It was always safer to talk freely when in the heart of a crowd.) 'She will be a danger to him as long as she lives, and so I warned him. But he won't listen. To think that he should be in love with one of this unstable and unruly race.' De Feria's left eyebrow curved up sharply, a dandyish trick that he liked to practise, he had had his portrait painted so; he flicked his riding-crop towards a girl who was struggling, shrieking, fighting her way with fists through the crowds in the open market of Cheapside. 'What woman in Spain would behave so? Here they want *form*.'

'Does your Lady Dormer? Aha, you think I do not know about that? You are a fine one to talk, Feria. And of constancy too.'

For the Count de Feria had fallen so deep in love with an English beauty, the Queen's lively young lady in waiting, the widow Jane Dormer, that he had broken off his engagement to the heiress cousin whose estates marched with his own at Zaffra, or Little Seville as he liked to call it. He had already gone to all the trouble and expense of procuring the Papal dispensation for marrying a cousin, but that could still be used and her estates secured to the family, if he transferred the lady to his brother. He would get it all settled in Spain, and then, when he returned to England as Philip's envoy, he would marry Jane Dormer.

He laughed a little self-consciously at his friend's chaff; he would never permit it in a true Spaniard like himself, but Ruy was Portuguese-born, somewhat nouveau-riche and, like the English, inclined to 'want form.' Which could certainly not be said of the pretty young widow riding so elegantly ahead of them. He looked at her with pride, then with sudden alarm.

Only in England could things happen like this! That mad girl down in the crowd had fought her way even through the guards, and was now hanging on to Lady Dormer's long skirts, shrieking to her for help. The guards laid hands on her to pull her away, but Jane Dormer was stopping them and speaking to the girl, she turned her horse's head away out of the procession, and the two women, together with three or four guards, were now detached from it in a huddled excited knot at the side of the road.

Feria quickly swung out of line and spurred his way through the crowd to the group. His fiancée was calling to him as he came – 'Your squire, de Valdez, we must rescue him instantly!'

The girl, still clutching frenziedly at Lady Dormer's skirts, turned towards him a wild, fair face, spattered with tears, her pale golden hair flying bedraggled about it.

De Valdez had come in secret to her father's house in Cheapside early this morning to carry her off with him, away to his home in Malaga. Her father had caught him there, and her elder brothers and the neighbours came rushing at his call and seized him and pushed him into the boiler with shouts of horrible laughter, and lighted the fire and swore that there he should boil alive, as his Prince had caused true Englishmen to burn. 'Not that they are Protestants,' stammered Mary Talbois through her frantic weeping, for even in these straits she would not betray her family, 'but they will not let me marry a Spaniard. But my Lady Dormer is going to do so, and sure she will help me, and you, sir – but, oh, sir, come now at once or it will be too late.'

It was not too late. By the time they reached the candlemaker's house, Diego de Valdez had not yet begun to boil. The guards pulled him out, dripping, mad with fury, issuing challenges to all concerned, by the duello to the death, but Feria pushed them away.

'You are lucky to be alive,' he said, 'and the Prince sails within three days, and Lady Dormer will speak with the Queen to get your love married to you within that time, and go with you to Malaga. You are luckier than I, who have to wait for *my* English bride.'

He was indeed, for it was four long years before Don

Gomez Suarez de Figueroa y Cordova, Duque de Feria, Governatore di Milano, could take the English widow Jane Dormer to become an ultra Spanish wife in his home at Little Seville.

But his squire was married to Mary Talbois the very next day. The Queen was delighted to arrange it – a happy omen, she said, sobbing, to Philip, that there should be two such happy Anglo-Spanish love-matches in his train.

'But *three*,' he said gallantly, raising her tired, puckered hand to his lips. 'Come back again?' Of course he would, almost immediately. He would look in at the Netherlands, as was essential, report to his father, and be back here again probably in less than a month.

She did not believe him; but she pretended to do so.

She did not like it when he told her that she must safeguard Elizabeth's life; but she promised to do so.

She could hardly bear it when he told her she must not allow any Act of Parliament to be introduced that would declare or imply Elizabeth's bastardy, and so disinherit her from the throne; it was what she had longed to do ever since her father had done it to herself. But this too she promised. She would have said or done anything to win him back to England and herself again.

And for his part he had to tell her yet again that he loved her; had to enter the sad embrace of her thin arms, had to say that he lived only for the moment when he could return to her. But he added somewhat hastily that she was now ill and overwrought with her loyal subjects' rapturous welcome of her, and must take some rest. And having safely despatched her at last, he went down to the river to welcome the arrival of the Princess Elizabeth by boat.

CHAPTER NINETEEN

Smiling and shining in pearl and silver, she alighted from her gaily coloured barge, apparently delighted at having been deprived of her share of the triumphal procession.

So pleasant, cool and restful, she told him her voyage had been, and commiserated with him on the heat and noise and smells of his ride through the streets; how had he liked the hotch potch of enthusiasm spiced with onions, the burr of Bartholomew Fair bumpkins bumbling through the shrill narrow vowels of the Cockney crowds? She mimicked both accents so that others near her doubled up with laughter, but Philip hardly heard her talking on; and in his silence her real self became silent also behind her chatter, aware of the urgency of what he could not yet say.

People were apt to keep a wide distance when the Prince of Spain talked with his sister-in-law; he soon had his chance to speak in a low and private voice. Yet when he took it he might have spoken loud for all to hear.

What was all this he was telling her with such strained urgency about the Troubles in the Netherlands (and when were there not?), and then again about his father clamouring for him to come and set him free to make his peace with God (and why could he not make it while at work?), and about the war with the French, who would never forgive his father for having kept their magnificent monarch François I in a Spanish prison for two years (of course they wouldn't, so why did he?), and now about the next new Pope (there was always the Pope and he was always new); the new one this spring had lasted only a few weeks, and now the Pope was that old firebrand Caraffa, who had never forgiven his father's Imperial troops for their Sack of Rome.

'But that was when you were born!' she exclaimed, 'and you are now twenty-eight.'

'But Caraffa is eighty, and to him it seems like yesterday. He was on the royal council in my great-grandfather's day, he opposed Ferdinand of Aragon as an 'Arrogant Usurper,' and so he calls all our House ever since. As for this Sack of Rome, worse even than Atilla's,—'

'Caraffa remembers that too perhaps?'

'He's mad enough to think so. He takes three hours over dinner, his "frugal meal" he calls it—'

'All Papal meals are. Granted, he drinks more than he eats.'

'Yes, and walks as he drinks, bounding up and down with a step as light and free as a young man's, while he airs his age-old grievances against us. My father never ordered the Sack, was not even there. Yet it's been held against him ever since, and even against me, an infant in the cradle, as a bad omen for my reign. And the instant this mad braggart Caraffa became Pope Paul IV, he vowed a holy war against us both, and against all Spaniards. He swears they are the spawn of Jews and Moors – that he will ally himself with Lutheran heretics, yes, and even the heathen Turks if they will come and help him drive the last Spaniard out of Italy.'

'It looks,' said Elizabeth drily, 'as though Christendom will have to find a new name for itself. Even Europe is a misnomer if Italy calls in the Turks to help fight against Spain. Will Your Most Catholic Majesty march against the Papacy and sack Rome yet again?'

'Never that!' he exclaimed in horror. 'Alva has sworn never to set foot in Rome by force. He is devout as any monk. But I shall have to send him at the head of an army to Italy if our settlements there are attacked. And they will be, if Caraffa lives. But he ought to die soon.'

'Nobody dies when they ought, least of all Popes. Decrepit old invalids are put in to fill up gaps for the moment, and when they put on the tiara they last a decade. But the saintly Marcello, welcomed by all, goes and dies almost as soon as he's elected.'

'Caraffa is full of years.'

'And his carafe is always empty. Even now that he's become Paul the Fourth, the Four Bottle Pope!'

Philip was shocked by her ribaldry. 'The man is my enemy, not the Holy Office.'

'I trust you will be able to separate them. Why do you speak of them to me?'

'To tell you that I do not know when I may return here.'

'That is not what you told the Queen.'

'I must keep her calm, as far as I can.'

'It will not calm her to suffer the tortures of suspense.' She saw his surprise at her compassion, and added, 'She suffers as I could never suffer. I have more sense, or less heart.'

'Your heart may find you out. Have you indeed so little of it – El-iz-a-beth?'

It was the first time he had called her by her name and it made a stillness on the air. Every syllable fell distinct and slow, like the four petals of a flower falling one after the other in the heavy late August evening. She had to brace herself to meet what all this time he had been bringing himself to say to her. Now it came at last, abruptly, and so direct, it could not be Philip; or was he ceasing to be Philip when with her? The words jerked themselves out of him as if against his will.

'I have two days left in England. But only this night can be made free for me. And for you. Will you give it me?'

He flung up his hand as if to ward off a blow. 'Do not answer. I did not intend to say it like that. You do not know what this means to me. This may be the only chance I ever get to prove myself to you as a lover. I have put it in your power to deny it me, but take care how you use that power. My sojourn in this country has been an insult to my manhood.' He broke off. 'Nothing comes as I would say it. You have laid a mocking spell on me that twists my words. Love is cruel as fear.'

So she was to vindicate her country's insults to his manhood, and if she did not, so much the worse for both! She was too angry to laugh, and, as he had warned her, it would not be safe. His terror lest any woman might refuse him was terrifying.

'I can well believe you did not mean to woo me with threats,' she said slowly, 'but it is plain you care nothing for my safety, after all your promises. All that you have done to guard it will go for nothing, if some spy should tell the Queen.'

'No spy shall ever get the chance. I can trust my men. They will keep guard. Can you not trust me as far as I trust my servants?'

Once before she had stood here in these rose-scented gardens on a late summer evening and watched the river shine darkly through the heavy trees and their long slanting shadows, while she talked with her brother's Irish page just before her brother died. Barnaby Fitzpatrick had loved her with a boy's love, unselfish, pure and harsh, adoring, disapproving. What love did Prince Philip offer and hope to win from her?

She drew a deep breath. 'What if I should bear a child to you?'

She saw the light leap up in his pale eyes. 'I shall not let that happen,' he said.

But it was what he wished; it would be the final vindication of himself to England and to her.

'You do not trust me?' he demanded.

'How can I? And how can you? You are young and virile.' Again she saw that dangerous light, but he lowered his eyes.

'Whatever happens I swear it shall bring you no harm. It would only precipitate our marriage. I could get a Papal annulment—'

'From *Caraffa*? Your enemy! Why even easy Pope Clement VII wouldn't do it for my father.'

'Because he feared to offend *my* father. Can you never leave politics and become human? This mockery of my marriage will end one way or other, by death if not annulment. I must have you in the end – but why not now, this night? We shall never be younger. What are you? Not woman only. Not man—'

'God forbid! Do you make me out an hermaphrodite?'

'God forbid again. Yet there is something in you that is of either sex, and of something beyond sex – a goddess maybe – but not holy.'

'No. I am that Other Woman that husbands love to worship in secret. A wedding ring is a yoke ring.'

'Not if it were with you.'

'But *I* might find it so. Could you tame a goddess – an unholy one? Queen Hecate is not for the hearth, but the woods. She turns married women into wild Maenads.'

'And men into monsters. As you will turn me if you drive me too far. I think you wish to drive me mad.'

'I think I do sometimes – Philip.'

It was the first time that she had spoken his name either, and on a note as caressing as his had been. But it was the wrong note. His eyes rested on her, heavy with suspicion.

'Your tone is sweet music,' he said, 'but it withholds the words I've sought from you. You would withhold yourself even in my arms.' The anger mounted in his voice. 'You mean to play me false. You have played with me all these weeks, months, baiting me with false hopes so as to fish safety for yourself and your accursed heretic country, which you *mean to rule*. I see it now. That is why you have kept me dangling on here in the humiliating pretence that I believed the Queen's false hopes. She and you have cheated me between you – the Tudor sisters!'

There was hysteria in his laugh. She dared not show her fear, nor soothe him too obviously. Once suspicion were awake in him it would coil and twist interminably; better to seem to ignore it than do anything to attract its attention. So she spoke stammeringly, nervously, of his plans for their meeting, discussing the difficulties of her escape from her room, as though she were thinking so hard of the practical arrangements that she had scarcely understood his outburst against her.

In whispered, hurried confusion, more convincing than any protestations of love, she told him that if it were humanly possible she would come to him that night.

CHAPTER TWENTY

She had had no intention of keeping her promise. She sat by the open window in her hot room; the tall candles melted and bent over in the heat and their flames flickered as the moths fluttered in out of the dark and danced to death around them. Her resolve began also to melt and flicker as she looked at it now from this angle, now from that. It might lead to escape and freedom for herself; it might lead to disaster and ruin for her country.

The steamy night outside showed no star. A mosquito bit her forehead. Cat Ashley tried in vain to get her to come to bed.

The night was heavy as fate, it held all the years to come in its dark womb, and she was the midwife to help bring them to birth – in what shape? That would be determined by her whim to go or not to Philip tonight. The danger to herself of going was obvious, but the danger to her country of her not going might be far greater. He would never forgive England for another affront to his sexual pride; the worst, since it came from her. His emotion was something growing in the dark; for years you might think there was nothing there, and then it would rear its white head in growth sudden as a fungus and show its poison. It was a horrid image – why a *white* head? Almost she could see it in front of her, pale as the veiled moon hovering in the murky dark outside, waiting for her, either as lover or as enemy. She had sworn no man should win her through fear. But fear of what his revenge might be quickened her senses into curiosity.

And if she did not give him reason for revenge? Then he too might become something very different from the cold implacable image, nursing its secret hate, that she had imagined just now. Already she had seen the change in him when with her – the unwonted directness of speech that sometimes cracked out of him as brutally as an explosion. His fate also hung in the balance. He and she would live out their brief day, England and Spain would go on for centuries, but the course of all might be determined by what she did tonight.

She could sit still no longer, all her nerves were jangled in an agony of indecision. With the spring of a cat, she uncoiled herself from her hunched position on the window sill, swung a cloak over her head and shoulders, and ran down to the door that had been left unlocked and unguarded as Philip had contrived.

As soon as she was moving under the sky, heavy and close as it was, she ceased to feel trapped within an ever narrowing circle of conflicting fears. She was free here, and alone. A livid forked flash split the edges of the darkness and against it the huge trees loomed over her head, but the lightning would not strike them, they would not fall on her. Nor would destruction from Philip, if she played her game well. She and England, now so utterly within the power of Spain, would make a shift to wriggle free, in spite of the wounded vanity of a thwarted young man. To hell with him, she thought and would have laughed aloud if she had not been so careful to move noiseless as a shadow. She stood for a moment gazing defiantly up at the threatening sky, and one or two drops of rain fell heavy as blood on her upturned face. She had been a fool to come. Why then, she would be wise and go.

She turned and moved as fast as she could under the blackness of the trees, half running, stumbling back towards the Palace. She hurried round a huge tree-trunk, tripped over a stick, fell forward, and was gripped by arms that held her in a furious grasp. As furiously she struggled and hit out, without a sound, then suddenly knew the man who held her was too tall for Philip. Nor was it his voice whispering in her ear.

'So you're baulked of him – or had you baulked yourself? You came away before you'd met him – what way then *were* you going. Never trust a fox-haired woman – a vixen fox.'

'Robin, you fool! I was going back to the Palace.'

'You didn't come out just to go back. What happened?'

'Nothing, I've never even met him.'

'You were going to, then?'

'What the Devil does it matter? I haven't gone.'

'And why then, why? Did you quail at the thought of his full lips – cold as a sea-anemone's, I'll swear. Or his arms, long as an octopus? They'd hold you so – and *so* – if you lay dead in his grasp.'

'Let go of me. You talk like the foul fiend.'

'You talk too loud. Come this way. It's safer.'

He led her through an undergrowth of thick shrubs as surely as if he could see in the dark; she had no notion which way they were going until through an opening in the bushes she could see the iron glimmer of the river flowing sluggishly below. 'Safer?' she demanded, 'but we are far further from the Palace!'

'And from Philip and his guards.'

'What do you know about them?'

'Only what I've spied out and guessed. I played scout tonight when I found your door was left unguarded. But you changed your mind? Say you'd changed it!'

'A hundred times. And always will. What's a woman's mind for?'

'I'll swear you never wanted to go to him. You were afraid not to.'

She did not like that. She said coolly, 'Two devoted wives, one passionately permanent mistress, among others, should recommend him as a lover.'

'If you want a lover—'

'What maid does not?' She sang under her breath, but on a note of wild hilarity,

> '"*Then oh, then oh, then oh, my true love said,*
> *She could not live a maid.*"

'No, Robin, no! I don't want you as a lover because of a silly song.'

'Nor because of anything else?'

His caresses were moving her almost unbearably, shaken as she was already by the torment of indecision, dread, and sensual hunger that had worn the guise now of attraction, now repulsion. She *had* wanted to try Philip as a lover, and had hated the thought of it. And perhaps it would be the same with any man. She told Robin this; trembling with desire, she could yet whisper her doubt if she could ever really give herself. 'Even if I lay in your arms and played at love with you, I could never bring myself to that last surrender.' He demanded reasons, and she could find none, but said at last on a gasp, 'It may even be because my father killed my mother.'

'What has that to do with you and me? Do you think I could be cruel to *you*?'

'No. But I could to you.'

He swore that he would not listen. Love could be cruel and shot through with fear, as she herself had found it; violent death on the scaffold had prevented her final surrender to the man she had first loved. That was why she so feared it.

But it was not only fear, as she tried to tell him.

She could not bear to give herself up into the power of any other thing or being. Neither man nor magic, wine nor lust, should ever be her master. However passionately she might desire to be his mistress, she would always want far more to be her own.

He pleaded, argued, but could make no headway against it, and had to fall back defeated.

But a strategist has more than one line of attack.

Very softly, he began to chuckle. In astonished indignation she demanded why.

'I was thinking,' he said, 'what a joke it would be if you came out to go to Philip and stayed instead with me!'

She quivered and a secret smile turned up the corners of her mouth in the dark.

'And keep him waiting – all night?'

'All his life!'

'Yes, that may be.' She was shaking now with laughter. 'Poor Philip! And I told him I'd come if it were humanly possible!'

'Well he's not human, so it's not possible.'

'He said *I* was not human – a goddess, but not holy.'

'Yet men will worship you – always. As I do.'

His kisses stifled her laughter. She sank back into his arms. Surely this would be the final surrender. But even as he swore so to himself in triumph, she was saying with cool consideration, 'But what will happen when I meet Philip again?'

'You may never meet Philip again.'

'He's promised to come back to England within a month.'

CHAPTER TWENTY-ONE

But Philip did not come back to England for nineteen months.

To Mary it was a lifetime of agonized hope; yet human lives do not last as long as their possessions, and after four hundred years her prayer book still shows the stains of her tears at the prayers for the absent, and for women labouring with child. If only Philip would come back soon, she might still bear one.

To Elizabeth his absence was a peaceful though dubious respite. She had not seen him again, even in public, before he set sail, and could have no inkling as to his state of mind towards her. That he was still very careful of her safety was clear from his express commands to the Queen and her ministers for their good treatment of her; but his reasons for it were not so clear.

She was allowed to go back to her pleasant home of Hatfield with a sumptuous escort, and all the countryside turned out to cheer her and give her such a rapturous welcome that in alarmed prudence she hid herself as much as she could behind her guards. It was a strange reversal from the time she had been brought away from Hatfield, by force of arms, through silently watching crowds afraid to show any sign of goodwill. Yet here was her return greeted like a royal progress, and Hatfield soon wearing the appearance of a rival

Court to the Queen's. One of her many visitors wrote of her as 'a jolly, liberal dame' whose hospitality equalled that of her gay and pretty mother, 'one of the most bountiful women in her time and since'; with of course the corollary, 'and nothing like so unthankful as her sister.' Elizabeth could only pray that Mary would not hear such comparisons.

Her friends were her worst enemies, she complained to her former tutor, Roger Ascham, who was there to read Greek and Italian and other languages with her; as he wrote somewhat cryptically to a colleague, 'I teach her words, and she me, things.'

To her fears he replied, 'There is no danger in walking in fields.'

But her rural retreat came to be threatened by further plots and risings in her name. Her household were questioned, some of them imprisoned, but Cat Ashley held staunchly to her declaration that it was 'as much as her place was worth' to speak anything against the Queen. Elizabeth also wrote in exalted strain to protest that 'such misty clouds should obfuscate the clear light of my truth.' She liked that new word of hers; but to Mary her flowery style was only an irritating token of her insincerity and immunity; she muttered angrily yet again that Elizabeth's 'disguised and colourable letters' were no proof of her innocence. But no proof could be found either of her guilt, and Elizabeth did not remain obfuscated for long.

Yet there were other 'misty clouds'. Her suitors were the most troublesome. The young Earl of Devon, Edward Courtenay, now in exile, bored and short of cash, kept on writing her desperately lovesick letters, which made it very awkward for her when rebels declared their renewed intention of putting him and her together on the throne. Then he died suddenly, some said suspiciously, and that it had been arranged by that useful fellow of Prince Philip's, Ruy Gomez da Silva, now the Prince of Eboli. It gave Elizabeth a cold shudder when she heard that rumour.

Philip kept his hand hidden; but no one knew how far the fingers stretched.

The Archduke of Austria proposed (through Philip) for her hand; the Crown Prince of Sweden, son of the great Gustavus Vasa, proposed to herself; she refused them both, and with possibly the greater emphasis because she feared to hear next of their premature demise.

The only suitor Philip favoured was his former choice, Philibert Emmanuel of Savoy, of whom she had complained as a lobster on account of his night and day wear of armour. But she won some respite from him after a gossip-writer had reported that he had 'been observed making love out of a window' to the Duchess of Lorraine. Elizabeth's maidenly sense of propriety declared itself outraged; she could only hope that Philip's sense of property would be as tender, for he was now known to be the Duchess's lover.

He had been enjoying a prolonged spell of violent and sometimes even vulgar dissipation in Flanders; many said, even in England, that he had done something to deserve it after his year of far too holy matrimony with Mary.

Elizabeth heard of it with the curiosity that was always the main part of her feelings towards Philip. It was odd to think of that austere, sometimes terrifying dignity of aspect changing its pale colour for a masked disguise, while rollicking in the streets of Brussels in search of adventure. 'Rollicking Death, I should think!' she exclaimed mockingly;

but she found herself frequently wondering what it would be like to encounter him in such an adventure.

But for her, everything was being very circumspect, placid, cautious and ladylike, in a world that had suddenly become too predominantly feminine for her liking.

Robert Dudley and his brothers had been sternly warned by the Queen's ministers to stay quietly at home in their country estates, nobody quite knew why, but it was rumoured that they had been attending subversive political meetings in London. In any case the Queen had no reason to like the sons of Duke Dudley, and had never appreciated Philip's curious interest in the eldest, Robert, who looked so boldly at Elizabeth. As soon as Philip left her Court she saw to it that Robert did too, and was determined he should never return to it.

'So

> '*This is the way the lady rides,*
> *Nim nim, nim nim,*'

chanted Elizabeth, and could remember a mighty voice shouting it somewhere above her head while she rocked on a vast, warm, satin knee; though that must have been before she was three years old. At least she could say King Harry VIII first taught her to ride! And as long as she rode 'nim nim' now, the road seemed quiet and fair for her.

She was invited by the Queen to Court; she rode to Whitehall through Smithfield and Old Bailey and Fleet Street with a great company of gentlemen in velvet coats, and of men in red coats, and settled at the Palace of Shene, which at once became gayer and more popular than that of the Queen's at Whitehall. But the 'lobster's' claws were still outstretched; she soon found that she had been summoned only to be pressed into marriage with him and that speedily, so that Philip should be gratified with it as *a fait accompli* when he came to England next month. Yes, it was true, he was really coming at last, and everyone could believe in it now that the reason for it was so clear and urgent; that he must at all costs draw England as his ally into the war against France.

He was now the greatest monarch in the world, for his father had carried out his long-promised abdication. Charles V had retired to his monastery and had given over to Philip all his kingdoms and the whole of his vast empire, though he had not been able to pass on the title of Emperor. That went by vote, and to the Emperor's indignation, the arrogant electors had refused to vote for his son. But the Holy Roman Empire was becoming an empty pious relic, said the cynics, neither Holy nor Roman nor an Empire.

To make up for it, and for all the scornful snubs he had received while trying to curry favour in the impudent little country of England, Philip was now, in Europe, King of Spain, Naples, Sicily, and titular (though still uncrowned) King of England, Duke of Milan, Lord of Franche Comté, Burgundy and the Low Countries; in Africa, he was the ruler of the Cape Verde Islands, Canaries, Tunis, Oran and other great ports on the Barbary Coast; in Asia, of the Philippines and Spice Islands; in America, of the gold and silver cities of Mexico and Peru and most of the West Indies.

It was, as the Emperor mumbled with a fair show of content, though still grumbling at the choice of that insignificant fellow Ferdinand as Emperor, enough to go on with.

And his abdication was 'the most impressive scene in history,' people declared; everybody wept; even the iron composure of Philip was melted, and to his annoyance was shown a tentative sympathy by his cousin, Prince William of Orange, a popular, talkative young man of whom the Emperor had lately made a great favourite. He leaned heavily and affectionately for support on William's arm throughout the proceedings, and bade him and Philip keep friends always. Charles was incapable of recognizing congenital antagonism in people, any more than in nations; he had never noticed how uncomfortable Philip always was in the company of his much younger but also easier, more frank and friendly cousin, William of Orange.

'You two dear lads will work together in carrying on my work,' said Charles as he embraced them both goodbye, with tears that he did not attempt to hide. He had had to take off and wipe his spectacles several times as he made his long, exhausting and often touchingly simple speech in farewell to mighty dignitaries of this world, which he was now leaving for a monk's narrow cell.

But he may be said to have enjoyed his abdication.

Mary longed to add the actual Crown of England to her husband's new honours. She tried to lure him back to her with hopes of his coronation; she prayed frantically for his return. Her friends tried to keep from her all the gossip about his infidelities; but once she was found tearing his portrait with her fingernails.

Yet even jealousy was not so strong as her desire to please him. In desperation she now did her utmost to force Elizabeth into the marriage with Savoy. It was the most painful thing that she could do to herself, for she knew that Elizabeth would then be living near Philip, and strongly suspected that this was his chief motive in urging on the match.

'I shall be jealous of Your Highness,' she wrote to him,

'which would be worse for me than death. Already I have begun to feel uneasy.'

Yet against her own wishes she fought like a fury to make Elizabeth obey. Elizabeth was badly frightened, but swore that she would rather die than consent. But the position now was very different from that of just three years ago, and she did not think that the country would let her die. Philip could no doubt have it arranged. But she did not think he wished her to die.

She could find out nothing from himself, for she was sent packing in disgrace back to Hatfield just before he arrived in England. There she waited, walked, rode, read and talked increasingly irritably with Ascham, looked out her jewels, tried on her best dresses, practised different ways of doing her hair, all in readiness for when Philip should send for her to come to Court. But he did not send. She was summoned on one or two occasions to meet the Queen at a Court function, but it was in Philip's absence. He spent indeed little time on functions. He was attending more to the raising of an armed force from England. As soon as he had succeeded in coercing Mary into a declaration of war against France and her present ally Pope Paul IV, he set sail again and went to war, with Philibert Emmanuel of Savoy as his Commander-in-Chief, and Robert Dudley as Master of Ordnance to the Earl of Pembroke, the leader of the English Expeditionary Force.

So now Elizabeth was quit of all three of them. She was amazed, amused, relieved, chagrined. She began to wonder if Robin Dudley's guess had been right, and that she would never meet Philip again.

That would not mean that she had done with him.

* * *

It was surely one of the oddest wars in history, and to all the Spanish explanations of it as 'a good war,' Cardinal Pole would reply, 'War is never good.' He was Mary's chief adviser and had moved from Lambeth into the royal palace so as to be in constant attendance on her. They had need of all the comfort they could give each other, now that her passionate heart and muddled mind had landed them in the worst impasse of both their careers. The crowning achievement of those careers had been their conversion of their country back to the Papacy – yet here they were at war with the Pope! Caraffa, as everybody still called Pope Paul IV, was extending his insane fury to Pole, trying to depose him from the post of Papal Legate and summon him to Rome, where he would certainly be clapped into the dungeons of the Inquisition. And in order to prevent this, the devoutly Papist Queen Mary had to prevent the Papal envoys from entering her country. The climax came when Pole was commanded to go to Rome on charges of heresy.

Elizabeth heard of it with wild and angry laughter. Of what use was it to have a good nature without good sense? Of what use to amble through life like a melancholy mule in blinkers, seeing only the right and wrong of each step ahead of him and blind to everything on either side? For this was the end of Pole's conscientious scruples.

He had refused to let himself be made Pope, so now the Pope was an old barbarian whose most frequent piece of rhetoric was 'Cut off his head! Cut off his head! Cut off his head!' In his arrogance and ignorance, his enmity to all thought, all art and learning that did not subscribe to his conception of religion, Caraffa was doing his worst to crack the unity of Christendom.

But one might say Pole had done it too in standing by and letting such a man step into power; and had helped Mary to do it by allowing her to insist on Cranmer's death by fire.

To Elizabeth that was their supreme crime in blunder.

She had good reason herself to hate the late Archbishop of Recanterbury, as she called him. He had signed the death warrant of the man she had loved when she was a very young girl, and it had been against Canon Law for him to do so, an illegal murder. He had also helped to bring her mother to execution, and had proclaimed herself a bastard, as he had done earlier with Mary. So she had as much reason as Mary to hate him.

But, though seventeen years younger, she had already begun to know that if love is blind, hate is blinder. Mary could have executed Cranmer long ago for treason and perjury; he had signed the Proclamation to make Lady Jane Grey Queen instead of the rightful Sovereign, he had supported Duke Dudley as usurper; legally he could have been hanged, drawn and quartered as soon as Mary came to the throne.

But she had kept him in order to make a martyr of a traitor. Heresy was treason against God, and therefore worse than treason against herself. Her motive was admirable, the result deplorable. Even when it came to the trial for heresy, she threw away all her cards. For Cranmer gave them all into her hands. He had made his supreme recantation, had put Mary and her injured, falsely divorced mother in the right for ever; had declared Elizabeth finally illegitimate, and Protestantism a crime. He had said it all, all that Mary could ever wish – that he had sinned against England as well as against God; against King Henry VIII as well as against Queen Katherine of

Aragon; he had confessed that he was the cause and author of their divorce, and that that divorce was the 'seed-plot of all the troubles in this country,' of heretics, and the violent deaths of good men; of the slaughter of so many souls and bodies.

Yes, he had said 'the souls,' and proclaimed 'the souls of the dead I have defrauded.' Could any man say more to blast himself and his cause for ever?

So Mary won it all – and threw it away. Hate is blind. She could have kept Cranmer alive as an example to all the world of a shameful turncoat, a self-confessed liar and perjurer who had damned his own cause for ever. But she hated him to the death, so to death he must go. But all that he had said had been said in the hope of escaping death; for he had been 'so afraid, he wished to creep into a mouse-hole.' Then he found the mouse-hole stopped; and that he had not saved himself by his recantation, not by so much as a faggot, not even gained a hanging instead of a burning. But a mouse can turn, even a 'Mumpsy-mouse,' as Elizabeth as a child had called him. He had recanted, and all for nothing; very well then, he might just as well re-recant.

He did, in the hour of death, before his judges and executioners and all the populace who were expecting to hear his abject confession yet again. Instead, they heard him call the Pope Antichrist, and say that he had only acknowledged him 'for fear of death, and to save my life if it might be.'

They rushed to hush it up, they hurried him to the flames to stifle his words. But he thrust his right hand first into the fire and called out that it should suffer first because it had written his lying confession. And so his shrinking, terrified flesh gave the strongest testimony of all against Mary.

'She has cut her own throat,' said Elizabeth as she walked

in the fields round Hatfield with Roger Ascham, where there was no danger, for no one was near them. He noted that she hated her sister for her bungling more than for her cruelty. And Cranmer for his cowardice more than for his treachery.

'God never meant the poor mouse for a martyr,' he said gently.

'No. And he could write. Those collects of his, their prose is like the clear music of flutes. He should have stayed a Cambridge don, and it was my father's fault, not his, that he did not.'

'He could stand up even to your dread father, when it came to prose.' Ascham chuckled and stole a glance at his Princess. 'He knew the King did not write the King's English as well as himself, and calmly showed it in his comments on King Henry's corrections of the Bible translation.'

'Did he dare to be critical of my father?'

'Critical? He was barely civil. "This is superfluous," he wrote in the margin. And – "This obscures the sense," and further – "I perceive no good cause why these words should be put in here". Should I dare to write as much to Your Grace?'

'Get out, you devil. I know what you are at – that unlucky word, "obfuscate". Yes, it's true that Cranmer had the courage of a scholar. And Mary a warm heart. And Pole integrity. All good people by nature. Yet look at the Devil's brew they've broiled between them. No one can be everything. I suppose it is too much to ask for a grain of common sense among all these martyrs and saints – yes, and a lunatic who sits on the Papal throne and jangles the keys of St. Peter. They are all of 'em tearing England to pieces.'

'How would you save her, Madam?'

'How? By a touch, not a clutch on the bridle; by a bit, not a spur; by a care-free laugh, by the appearance of ease and confidence in security, even when the reality were never more absent. And when the gulf yawns indeed beneath our feet, to cry "Farewell to such miseries, and to hell with melancholy!" Or as you would say, Master Tutor, "*Valeant ista amara; ad Tartara eat melancholia.*"'

CHAPTER TWENTY-TWO

Charles V's taste for public ceremonies had been somewhat curbed since he had become a monk, though he still insisted on hearing all the news and telling his son's ministers what he thought about it.

'Is Philip in Paris?' he demanded when Philibert Emmanuel of Savoy won a resounding victory at St. Quentin. If not, why not? If Philip, in immediate consequence of it, had ordered his Commander-in-Chief to march direct on Paris, then by now all France would have been at his feet.

Instead of which, he let the war drag on, until even Calais, English for over two hundred years, was lost to England; and Spain had to make a humiliating peace with her implacable enemy the old Pope Paul IV, whom his own countrymen still swore at as 'Caramba! Caraffa!!' The Duke of Alva had to apologize publicly to this old ruffian who had declared war on them, for the crime of having impiously defeated his troops; for Caraffa had sworn that 'sooner than surrender this point I would see the whole world perish; not so much for my own sake as for the honour of Jesus Christ.'

So Alva had surrendered the point, and in return Caraffa had asked him to dinner. The result of the war was that the troops in Italy had died by thousands of the pox; that the prosperous commercial city of Naples was ruined financially, though it remained under Spanish rule; and the Turkish pirate fleet, that heathen devil raised by the Pope, sacked the Calabrian coast and carried off Italian Christians to be Moslem slaves.

It was a severe penance for both conquerors and conquered. But the only penance done by Caraffa, who had caused it all, was to execute two of his favourite nephews and to fill the Inquisition prisons with so many suspected heretics that everyone went in terror of spies and secret police.

All this would have been saved if Philip had marched on Paris directly after his great victory at St. Quentin.

What he had done was to note that it had taken place on the day of St. Lawrence's martyrdom, and, to his remorseful grief, that the beautiful old Church and cloister of St. Lawrence in the city had been sacked, defiled and destroyed. Yet again, it was 'not his fault,' any more than the Sack of Rome had been his father's. But yet again the weight of unwilling guilt settled on Philip's soul. He longed to win a victory unstained by sacrilege; a victory for God, and over himself and his sinful lusts. He found a new hope in his boyhood's vision of a nun's face in the black of the night, as he had stood at a window looking out at the storm that raged along the jagged mountains of the Guadarramas; it had been the face of a nun who 'prayed for suffering.' He too would show the courage of a true soldier of Christ by praying for it, and by building a temple in praise of it; he would dedicate it to St. Lawrence.

He would build it high up to dominate the rugged leonine mountains that he loved; it should be his palace, and also a monastery, and a royal tomb.

And it should be in the shape of a gridiron. For it was on

that instrument that St. Lawrence was burnt in martyrdom. It would be called the Escorial; and it was there that Philip proposed to live eventually until such time as he should come to die and be buried in a superb vault under the Palace, together with all the bodies of his kingly ancestors that he could collect, and all those of his successors in the years to come.

The father's necrophily was challenged by the son's. Philip was taking long views about his obsequies; Charles would show what he could do about his own funeral. He ordered an impressive rehearsal for it in his mountain monastery at Yuste, and watched it from a gallery; some said he even helped to ring the bells for it.

It was an unlucky omen, for Charles had too much gusto for life to wish himself dead; he had only wished to see what it would look like. But in due consequence, some said, he died in good earnest a month later. He had already bequeathed his vast empire to Philip; he now had only one final heirloom to send him, the blood-stained scourge with which he had sought to expiate his sins in these last years.

Philip received the grisly relic at the same time that he heard his wife Mary was very ill, probably dying. She had never recovered, they said, from the blow of the loss of Calais; her letters still besought him to come to her, if only to bid her farewell. He read them, he remembered her, he thought of Calais and her possible reproaches, he looked at his father's scourge, he did not go. It was all too much. After all, he was only just thirty, he was not yet halfway to death, however much he might plan for it, and draw gridirons for the design of the Palace-tomb of the Escorial. Besides, he was very busy.

He sent instead his faithful Count de Feria, who would be

glad to see his pretty English bride-to-be, Jane Dormer, again, and gave him many messages for the Queen – and some for the Princess Elizabeth.

And the matter of first importance in Feria's mission was to ensure that Queen Mary should acknowledge her sister as the undoubted heir to the throne. Feria found her ministers and confessors already hard at work on that, and hard it was to win the Queen's consent, for she was still passionately against it. When they told her it would prevent civil war in England, she still said it would be wrong, since she believed Elizabeth to be Mark Smeaton's daughter; when Feria told her how much Philip wished it, she wept bitterly, for she wondered if this were because Philip would then marry Elizabeth, when she lay in her grave.

She knew now that she was approaching it. The faces of her doctors told her so; and the fewer and fewer faces of her friends. Only her dear Jane Dormer stayed constantly by her, trying to warm her with her fierce affection, to stifle her indignant sobs at 'those rats – *rats*!'

Where were all the other faces, where had they all gone? Why, to Elizabeth of course, to worship the rising sun, now that Mary's dim star was setting.

At Hatfield Elizabeth waited safely away, but not too far away, from London; seemingly passive but preparing her forces, secretly mustering from a distance what armed bands she could raise in case of revolt against her. There she received more and more of Mary's servants who came to swear that they were devoted only to Elizabeth's service. Their changed loyalty reassured her, but a shudder shot through her relief.

'Shall *I* be deserted on my death-bed by my formerly faithful friends?' she asked, and answered herself quickly,

'No, only by those *formally* faithful!' For she must joke, or choke, she said; suspense had her by the throat. Mary was almost certainly dying; but no one could tell what move the Roman Catholic leaders might make at her death.

Cardinal Pole could head a formidable resistance against an anti–Papal accession; he was not only the Archbishop of Canterbury, but of the blood royal, and more royal than her own. The Archbishop of York, Nicholas Heath, was Mary's Lord Chancellor and firmly committed to the supremacy of the Pope. Two Archbishops would be alarming adversaries, with all the Bishops on the Bench behind them. But the Archbishop of York was an amenable man. Elizabeth had been at pains to make friends with him lately, and now he actually invited Cecil to his house, and showed himself most reasonable, a trifle more loyal to the Tudors than to the Pope.

An ally greater than Cecil dealt with the Archbishop of Canterbury.

Reginald Pole would soon be faced with his final chance of action, the chance to strike a blow in deadly earnest for his Church, the Church of the woman he most nearly loved, and of his country as he had known it when he most loved it. The action would be in a form more repugnant than any he had yet had to consider. He would have to head an armed revolution against the young female claimant to the throne, and to lead England into civil war all over again. 'War is never good,' he had said. This action would belie him. And his whole nature would be belied by the appalling possibility that the revolution might compel him to take the throne himself.

But this time he did not have to refuse.

* * *

1558 was a full year for deaths. The Emperor's came in the last week of September, at one end of the scale of greatness; and at the other end came that of a shivering, wretched ghost, whom most people believed to have died long ago, if they remembered him at all.

This was Geoffrey Pole, Reginald's younger brother, who just twenty years before, when under torture, had betrayed all his family to the butchery and undying enmity of Henry VIII. He had tried in his remorse to kill himself, but lacked the nerve even for that. Now he sought out his brother the Cardinal and begged his forgiveness, so that his death, which he felt to be approaching, might come to him as a friend and not an enemy.

He found an ill old man who looked at him with hollow eyes above his resplendent robes. 'You may account me of equal guilt with yourself,' Reginald Pole told him. 'This scarlet bears the stain of our mother's blood. My ordination as Cardinal condemned her to the scaffold.'

'You did what you thought right,' stammered the younger brother.

'And you, what you knew to be wrong. Yet the result was the same. A righteous Nero – do you think that title consoles me?'

Then, for the poor wretch was sobbing, Reginald bent over him and blessed him with his absolution and said he believed that God would forgive them both, and that soon now they would see their mother's smiling spirit again, twirling a sprig of honeysuckle between her fingers.

He did not know if he believed what he had said. But since Mary's illness he had felt (or hoped) that there was little time now left to him; and in that time there was only one thing left he wished to do, and that was to give comfort where he could. He wished he could have given more of it to Mary. If he could have either supported or withstood her more firmly, if he could have led the country truly to the Church, or herself to mercy, she would not now be so wretched in her last illness, crying out that her whole life had been a tragic failure. But so it had been; and so his own would be. For he had begun to believe that he would not have to make the final decision, whether or not to fight Elizabeth. Once again the decision would be made for him, in accordance with his wish, perhaps his will. He had no will to live and fight.

Elizabeth would triumph. Yet he and Mary had aimed at least as high, or higher. Why then had they failed, and failed each other? He had planted fig-trees in the gardens of Lambeth Palace, to grow for centuries to come, and that would be his most notable achievement.

The Queen died before dawn on the morning of the 17th of November, and the Cardinal's household determined to keep it from him, as he was then lying dangerously ill; but a stupid servant let him know of it. He said nothing for some time, and then he spoke quietly to a friend, of her and himself. Their fates, he said, had been akin, and so were their natures. He then fell silent again, 'but,' his friend wrote later, 'though his spirit was great, the blow had entered into his flesh,' and he died just twelve hours after her.

In death as in life they were close together. Both had wished deeply to do only what was right; but she had lacked wisdom; and he, vigour. Her vision was clouded by passion, while his remained clear to distinguish evil from good; but he had the sloth, and despair of his own judgment, to let evil pass for good. So she became known in England as 'Bloody Mary';

and he might well have said to his country the dying words of another Cardinal, one that lived only in the imagination of a poet, 'And now I pray thee, let me be put by and never thought of.'

Nobody was thinking of Pole or of Mary in that autumn sunrise on the 17th of November, as the men of the new reign rode through woods that were burning gold and red up over the high ground to the Palace of Hatfield, to tell the only thing that now mattered about Mary – that she was dead, and Elizabeth was Queen.

But she was not in the Palace; she had walked abroad early this morning, the servants said; no doubt she was somewhere in the Great Park. They found her sitting under an oak tree, reading, with a red-and-white straw summer garden hat on her head to guard her complexion from the strangely hot autumnal sun. She stood up at their approach, and all the branches above her seemed to be lifting their arms like flames. She heard their news, that the 'old Queen' was dead, that she had nominated her sister as her successor; she took from Sir William Cecil's hand the ring that Queen Mary had bequeathed in token of this now undoubted fact.

She stood beneath the mighty oak that their ancestors had worshipped; she looked at all the men's faces before her, at Cecil's, neatly chiselled and cautious, the face of a born lawyer, and behind his the face of Robin Dudley, newly returned from the wars, handsome, eager and ardent, and behind them many others of hopeful Englishmen kneeling on the dead damp leaves to do her homage as their Queen. She too fell upon her knees, and spoke in an ancient tongue, not used for many centuries in the common speech of men, 'A

Domino factum est istud, et est mirabile in oculis nostris.'

But every man there understood what she said; 'It is the work of the Lord and it is marvellous in our eyes.'

Suddenly she rose and sprang towards them; in a flash she was transformed from the priestess to a creature of the woods with the dappled sunlight glinting on her hair, for her hat had fallen off and Robin Dudley, catching it, flung it up among the branches of the oak, shouting, 'You are Queen Elizabeth, you are our Queen!' And she had seized him by one hand and Cecil by the other, crying, 'I am your Queen, and you, Robin, are my Master of Horse, and you, Cecil, are my Secretary of State. Laugh man, laugh, all England will be laughing now!'

And so they were – laughing to see her ride in state all dressed in sparkling white, over roads strewn with flowers, to London to be Queen; and when they told her, tiresomely, that some old man in the cheering shouting crowds had turned aside to weep, she would not listen to any trouble-making but said happily, 'I'll warrant you, it is for joy.'

She knew well that many must regret the old order and 'poor Queen Mary' who had done her best – and worst – to bring the country back to it, but of what use was it to her, or help to them, to think of that now?

Poor Mary – even Elizabeth could feel that, now that she at last was safe from her. She looked at her lying dead, so much calmer and more at peace than ever she could be in life. 'She had a wintry life,' she said; 'her spring was nipped in the bud.'

So had Elizabeth's own been nipped, but not too late, like Mary's, to bear hope of summer.

And now high summer shone on her, now in the late autumn of 1558, though nearly all her onlookers prophesied darkly that it was unlikely she would outlast the winter, and that her little hour of triumph would melt with the frost and snow. The bookmakers of bets throughout Europe gave her six months at most to sit on her shakily balanced throne. Only a speedy alliance with a strong European Power could possibly make her safe. She knew of these gloomy forebodings, but they did not dim one spark of the glory of her present moment.

Its climax was reached when the procession brought her in the triumph of a reigning Queen to her royal Palace – fortress of the Tower, its great guns thundering out their welcome at her approach. She looked up at those dread walls and remembered the most despairing hour of her life when she had entered them, less than five years ago, by the Traitors' Gate, and never thought to come out except to her execution. She turned to all those around her who were thinking of the same thing, and bound them to her by her masterly simplicity.

'Some,' she said, 'have fallen from being Princes in this land to be prisoners in this place. I have been raised from being a prisoner in this place to be Prince of this land.'

She spoke too of God's justice and mercy, but it was her frankness in speaking of the dramatic contrast in her fate that struck them, and gave them belief in her. As the Protestant exiles were proclaiming in joy throughout Europe, 'The Lord has caused a new star to arise!'

But she would countenance no sudden changes in religion, no hard and fast rules 'making bold with God Almighty,' she said, intruding 'as many subtle scannings of the blessed will, as lawyers do with human testaments!'

* * *

That went for both sides of the religious fence, and nobody was yet able to discover on which side of it she stood.

The Count de Feria made a determined effort to do so at his very first meeting with her as Queen. It took place at the gorgeous ceremony of welcome to the new Sovereign at Somerset House, with all her lords and ladies and foreign envoys thronging round her – no moment, obviously, for any discussion of politics or religion. She was speaking now to one, now to another, in Latin, French, Italian, and most often in the 'mere English' that came with the same homely direct ring from her curved red lips as it had done from her father's terrifyingly straight-cut mouth. Her supple figure in the white dress made her look very tall, her usually pale cheeks were flushed (or were they rouged?) her eyes wide and shining; but in the excitement of her new triumph she bore herself as one who had been Queen from birth. Feria's quizzical black eyebrows arched in recognition of this. The grandee of Spain, with the diamond Order of the Golden Fleece around his neck, advanced with some difficulty through the crowd towards her.

She saw him, smiled in welcome, and at once everyone made way for him, and she took off her glove for him to kiss her hand. The correct compliments passed between them; she was delighted to receive her dear brother's Ambassador; and he was there only in order to let her dear brother know how he could serve her.

But he added unexpectedly, perhaps even to himself in the stress of such a moment, that her brother had told him to ask her to be very careful about religious matters, as they were what chiefly concerned him. She had to answer it, and on the instant.

At once a hush fell on the gossiping multitude. Here was an ultimatum with a vengeance! At the Queen's very first public appearance, before she had been given any time to hold her first Parliament, or even consult with her private ministers, she was being called upon, before a host of witnesses, to proclaim what her intentions were with regard to the religion, and therefore the policy, of her future reign.

Would she proclaim herself Protestant or Papist? If she defied the wishes of the Very Catholic King of Spain and the Netherlands, and of rather more than half the world besides, and denied the supremacy of Rome, then she would almost certainly lose the Crown, which was still only hovering above her head.

If on the other hand she plumped for appeasement, and told the Spanish Ambassador that she and her realm would be truly Roman Catholic, then she would throw to the wolves all those who had stood by her so staunchly through the long-seeming years of Queen Mary's reign; who had believed in her, hoped for her, prayed for her; and risked their fortunes and a horrible slow death in doing so.

Which then would she, could she, do? It was a fearful predicament to face, after years of disgrace, imprisonment, and fear of death, in the first moment of her power; which might prove her last, if she answered wrongly.

Yet in all the vast assembly she alone seemed unperturbed. Her lips were still smiling, her hand made only a slight movement, and that was to still Lord Robert Dudley, who had made a quick step towards her. But her light calm eyes never turned from the inquisitorial gaze of the dogged little Spaniard, though they opened a shade wider in surprise at his raising such a question in the midst of this purely ceremonial occasion. And she answered gravely, 'It would indeed be bad of me to forget God, who has been so good to me.'

Well, there was nothing he could say to *that*, everybody agreed in whispered chuckles, and he in silent fury. Her answer was too simple to be straightforward. He would write to Philip that it had been 'equivocal'. But he had to keep on good terms with her, and do his best to further his master's suit in marriage to her.

That also was still equivocal; although everybody in Spain and the Netherlands knew of it. The Venetian Ambassador had stated clearly that the 'whole Spanish Court is full of the King's intention to have her for himself.' Yet Philip had given Feria no free hand with regard to it; and though he knew perfectly well that it was what Philip wanted, he also knew – and perhaps so did Elizabeth – that it was the hardest thing in the world to get Philip to do a thing just because he wanted it. A hundred other reasons had to be found for it, conscientious, pious, and if possible self-sacrificing.

At the present moment Feria had to recognize that he had made a blunder, even rather an impolite one. He hastily spoke of other matters; he tried to arrange another interview. The Queen most graciously promised it, and that she would send two of her Council to summon him when it was convenient. *Which* two, he asked quickly, hoping to find easy channels of communication; and found they would be Sir William Cecil, whom he regarded as the trickiest time-server in the country, and fat old Parry, who had been her secret aid and abettor ever since the bad old days of her disgraceful affair with Lord Thomas Seymour. Certainly she was sticking to her old friends, however shady, with a vengeance.

In the meantime he decided not to pursue the vexed question of religion.

The Bishops, however, were not so prudent. Bishop White preached what many called 'a black sermon' at the funeral of Queen Mary, comparing her successor most unfavourably with her, but admitting that 'a living dog was better than a dead lion'. He was arrested as he came down the pulpit stairs, and seized the opportunity to threaten the new Queen with excommunication, and to glorify himself on his approaching martyrdom. Elizabeth told him she did not care a rush for his threats, and would give him no chance to gratify his hopes, for his only martyrdom would be a short period of house-arrest.

But after that she felt it wiser to forbid all sermons, whether Papist or Protestant, for the time being. She had quite enough on her hands, she said, in preparing for her Coronation, and, she might have added, in fending off her suitors.

CHAPTER TWENTY-THREE

It might seem impossible for a young woman as vain as Elizabeth to have too many wooers, especially when her vanity had had to be curbed and concealed all through the years of its most natural expression. She had been repressing it ever since her first love affair at barely fifteen had brought her imprisonment, shame, and the death of her lover; and she had done so with a self-control which amounted to heroism. Until she was twenty she dressed as plainly as was possible for anyone who was not a nun; she dragged her hair straight, wore no jewels at all, and chose only the soberest and dullest of colours. The end of the ultra-Protestant régime of her young brother and his ministers had brought some respite, since Queen Mary had liked her ladies to make a fine show in dress, and her young sister had been delighted to follow suit; but in behaviour it had been necessary to be more circumspect than ever.

She had been well aware of the malicious gossip circulated by the Venetian Ambassadors concerning her Spanish brother-in-law's particular care for her safety and succession to Queen Mary's throne; she had had to work her hardest to prevent Mary sharing their suspicions that the true cause lay in her attraction for him. And she had not been really successful; the thing had been a race between her and Mary's death; she was fortunate to have won.

Now, on the instant, she was free. There was no woman to stand in her way, no one in England to order her about, no one anywhere to whom she had to give obedience. She was twenty-five last September, but for the first time since her early adolescence she was able, without fear of her life, to behave like a girl. The result was staggering to everybody, sometimes even to herself.

The pale young woman of doubtful position and reputation, with her anxious eyes and compressed lips, who had had nervously to watch her every word and look in public, was instantly transformed to an outrageous coquette, of a gaiety so headlong that it would pay no heed to what others thought, or said, or wrote to their royal masters. She cared not a rap for any of them – let them say what they would and to hell with them! She would now do and speak, look and wear, what she pleased.

Her hair suddenly bubbled up into a myriad of curls; her skirts spread like peacocks' tails, her ruffs like transparent wings. She painted her face; once she wore a light green wig of spun silk. Jewels worth a province sparkled on her neck and breast and on the long fingers that she liked to show off; if one or other of them came in token of love or homage from the King of Spain or some lesser royal lover, she was so much the surer to display the finger that bore it.

She was no longer the well-behaved young lady, she was indeed, said some, no lady at all. She was preposterous, said Feria, she was behaving abominably, she put him quite out of countenance, and also her own ministers. Sir William Cecil, the most discreet of men – and if serving under four such different reigns as Edward's, Jane's (though for rather less than its nine days) Mary's and Elizabeth's, did not prove a man's discretion, then what did? – was evidently in agony as to what she would say or do next. He was about thirteen years older than she, but seemed more than two or three generations. Not that Feria liked Cecil, but at least he was not as irresponsible and imprudent as all the other young people who clustered so thickly about the Court that Feria could never get a proper chance of speaking quietly to the Queen. He wrote to his King that when he tried to send her a message they 'all fly from me as though I were the Devil.'

He complained to the Queen too, and told her he really ought to be given apartments within the Palace; it was due, he said, to his position of honour as the most important of the foreign Ambassadors. She exclaimed, 'What, have they not given you a lodging? My people shall learn how you are to be treated. You shall occupy my own chamber, and I will give you my key!' Then, at Feria's startled look, she made a complete volte-face and declared that on second thoughts it would be improper for them to be under the same roof as they were both unmarried, and he might become her suitor.

He was shocked at such flippancy and the insult to his affianced lady. But Elizabeth could not bear his Countess, an opinionated young woman so conceited as to believe that Edward VI had had a boyish passion for her, and so cruel as to have encouraged Queen Mary to burn heretics.

There were indeed few women that she did like, now that at last she was free of them; certainly not Cecil's learned blue-stocking of a second wife, who had been Mildred Coke; and still less Robin Dudley's little white doe rabbit, Amy Robsart, married to him in his boyhood; but at least Amy had the sense and inclination to keep quietly down in the country. And she was useful in preventing Robin from swelling the already overpowering army of suppliants for her hand in marriage.

For there were as many English suitors as foreign, and all the more obstreperous because they were in her presence, and each other's. Once or twice they actually came to blows in front of her, and she had to pretend not to notice; and there were still more occasions when the elderly Earl of Arundel, now 'very smart and clean,' as Feria sardonically observed, or the young Duke of Norfolk, or the elegant dilettante Sir William Pickering, laid his hand on his sword at sight of some new upstart who dared make pretensions towards the Queen.

If the quarrelsome English were the more immediately troublesome, the absent foreign suitors were the more dangerous. Some of them refused to remain absent; the coloured sails of their ships advanced up the Thames in more and more embassies that needed to be handled with the greatest tact to avoid a foreign entanglement or, worse, antagonism. Lesser lights such as the faithful Savoy's were being dimmed by offers from the Crown Prince of Sweden, from the King of Denmark, who wore a crimson velvet heart pierced with an arrow to proclaim his love for her; also from his handsome brother, the Duke of Holstein, who came in person and was enthusiastically encouraged by her. Germany and Italy entered the chase, a brace of Hapsburg Archdukes and about a score of other suitors, more or less eligible. The bookmakers on the Continent were as busy taking bets on the Queen's lovers as on her chances of survival, and the stakes ran furiously high.

Elizabeth's head could remain cool in spite of her flighty tongue, but even she began to find it tiring to go on finding fresh excuses for not marrying one after another. She would marry no man she had not seen, she said – but then it would cause offence to invite a suitor to her Court and find she did not like him. And she would not trust to portraits, for she could well remember her father's fury when Holbein's charming picture of Ann of Cleves had led him into marriage with her. Unfortunately – or perhaps fortunately from that point of view – there were no painters like Holbein now, for all the portraits of herself made her look a fright.

She did not want to marry a foreigner, as that would take her out of England; nor a subject, as that would make him her sovereign. Though indeed, she asserted, she was at perfect liberty to do so if she chose, 'as my father did – several times'.

The one man she would really like to marry was the Pope. Or the ancient Marquess of Winchester, so she told him, and he regretted that he was not a bachelor and fifty years younger.

The strangest and most subterranean hint at proposal came from Henri II of France, who put out a feeler to let Elizabeth know how much he would like to have her for his wife, if only his own, Catherine de Medici, were conveniently dead.

It almost sounded as though he had access to the secret poison cupboard that his Florentine bride was popularly supposed to have brought over to France as part of her Medici dowry. If so, the plump pug-faced young woman had shown restraint in not using it on her husband's *maîtresse en titre*, Diane de Poictiers, who had ousted her, all her married life, both from Henri II's affections and from her position as Queen.

And now Elizabeth might be given her chance to oust the Medici. Her prompt response to the hint was that if Henri had such a flattering regard for her, he should show it by at once giving Calais back to the English. But naturally these dark suggestions were only whispered (in church, somewhat inappropriately) between the Ambassadors, and were never mentioned in the very long, elaborately affectionate letters from the French King to 'Madame ma bonne sœur' of England, accompanied by an occasional diamond trinket. Elizabeth had at least enough discretion not to send any present in return – but that was a discretion that came naturally to her, especially in the present bankrupt state of the Exchequer. She actually cut down the numbers of the royal household to about half of what it had been in Mary's reign; this showed great courage, as it made for unpopularity – but not with the poorer classes. From the first she made it abundantly clear that to her they were the most important part of the kingdom.

'She is very much wedded to the people and thinks as they do,' wrote Feria to his master in high dudgeon, for he had done his best to make her admit that she owed her crown, and indeed her very life, to Philip; but she had flouted this in the most casual way. It had been nothing of the sort, she had told him ungratefully; she owed her crown to her people alone. No foreigner could have given it to her; it was the free gift of her people's love. And yet, he wrote, 'she seems incomparably more feared than her sister, and gives her orders and has her way as absolutely as her father did.' In short, she was a baffling tangle of contradictions, and Feria was being driven nearly mad by her. And by Philip.

For nothing could be more tangled and contradictory, more tortuous, cryptic, elusive than the mass of directions, instructions, hints and allusions in King Philip's letters to him. They wound themselves through page after page, and, worse still, in and out of the pages, on to the margins. Feria had to ask the King's secretary to leave wider margins for the notes added in the royal hand, for Philip had taken to adding even to his additions, in fact actually 'crossing' them, and Feria found himself getting cross-eyed in his efforts to read them.

He showed his exasperation to the King himself. Why could he not come out into the open and admit that he wanted to marry Elizabeth? Feria even suggested that it would be a good move if he reminded her how jealous Queen Mary had been of her husband's affection for her. Philip was deeply shocked by this. Not in any way should Feria remind her of those horrible scandalous suspicions, nor anyone else, nor himself. He wished never to hear of them again.

Feria cocked an already highly arched eyebrow at such violent protestations; he could almost see that portentous nether lip of the Hapsburgs thrust out over the page as Philip wrote them in his own hand. No doubt they bore witness to His Majesty's good taste as a gentleman, but he thought the gentleman really did protest too much when he declared that there was no fleshly desire in his thoughts of this marriage; that he was indeed undertaking it in the purest spirit of martyrdom, since 'it is difficult for me to reconcile my conscience to it; and it would not look well for me to marry her unless she were a true Catholic... I nevertheless cannot lose sight of the enormous importance of such a match to Christianity and the preservation of religion.' To ensure that England 'should not relapse into its former errors, which would cause to our neighbouring dominions serious dangers and difficulties' (he meant the Netherlands of course, as Feria well understood, where heresy was a growing danger and difficulty under the encouragement of their cheerful, garrulous young Prince, William of Orange) – to ensure this, wrote Philip, 'I am resolved to render this service to God, and offer to marry the Queen of England.'

There followed a multitude of conditions to make it 'evident and manifest that I am serving the Lord in marrying her.'

> *'Was ever woman in this humour woo'd?*
> *Was ever woman in this humour won?'*

Feria had been on the point of sending in his resignation when the letter arrived. But now at last he had a definite proposal to make, and resolved to make it in his own best manner, thanking heaven that Elizabeth need never know how Philip had propounded it.

He went to her, pluming himself in confidence of her awe-struck acceptance of the most magnificent prize that could possibly fall to her in the marriage market. Why, Philip was the master of the world. She had only to do as she was bid, about religion, and a few other matters, and save her poor little country – now all but ruined, lately defeated in the war with France, sought after as an ally only because her odd position as an island made her a precarious point of balance between the greater Powers. Now England would be allied to an empire on which the sun never set, owning dominion over every quarter of the globe – Europe, Africa, Asia and the new-found America – its mighty navies flying the flag of Castile on the Atlantic, Pacific and Indian oceans.

But Elizabeth was not in the least awe-struck. She did not even seem surprised; or if so, only because she had not received the proposal before. There was certainly an amused suggestion in her manner that, in spite of His Majesty's previous hints on the subject, he had been a long time in coming to the point.

She too must take time to think things over and consult her advisers, particularly her Parliament, without whom nothing could be settled. She spoke of gratitude and respect for Philip very prettily but rather perfunctorily; she might have been discussing just any of the odd dozen or so of proposals that she had had to consider lately.

Feria found himself burning with exasperated desire to tell her that even the fortune-tellers, most cautious of prophets, did not give her more than a year to reign.

But he could hint it. If she did not keep Philip's powerful support the Pope would certainly excommunicate her; Mary Queen of Scots would enforce her claim to the English throne, and her father-in-law the King of France would back that claim, send a French army to join the Scots, and invade England.

Elizabeth gave her thanks to Spain and the Netherlands; but tiresomely insisted on playing the mere woman, almost the little woman, whose marriage was her whole life, and must be given time to know her own mind. On a tenderer note she asked him earnestly, but with a charming diffident hesitation, to tell her dear brother 'that if she should ever marry, she would prefer him to all men.'

That cheered him a good deal as he took his leave; it was only afterwards that he wondered if he had not heard her say much the same thing to others.

He would have been appalled if he had heard her first remark to Cecil after the interview: 'What compensation should I claim in the marriage articles for the Lord of the Netherlands' nether lip?'

* * *

Now at last she knew. Philip was prepared to forgive her past behaviour to him; her chief problem now was to see how far and for how long she could make him continue to forgive her future behaviour. As long as she could keep him, and everyone else, in uncertainty, then he would go on protecting her in the hope of winning her consent; and her enemies would be afraid to attack her while they still hoped for her refusal. Nor was she the only one to lose or gain, and she showed Feria she knew it well. The Lord of the Netherlands needed the commercial aid of England and could not afford to lose it. The two were playing a tricky game of alliance and bluff with each other, and the bookmakers might well have laid a fresh series of bets as to which of them would win. But their odds would certainly have been very long against the young woman of twenty-five, half heretic, half bastard, who hoped to stake her wits against all the powers temporal and spiritual of the world that had prevailed till now.

Twenty-five? She seemed a raw lass of fifteen or less to the sophisticated Spanish Ambassadors, who did their best to 'keep her pleasant and in good humour,' as Feria pathetically protested, and then spoilt the effect by bursting out that the country 'has fallen into the hands of a daughter of the Devil.' And even his suave episcopal confrère, the Bishop de Quadra, who had lately come over to help him in the most intricate piece of work that ever an Ambassador had to tackle, even the Bishop followed suit when he exclaimed, 'What a pretty business it is to have to treat with this woman? I think she must have a hundred thousand devils in her body, for all that she is for ever telling me that she yearns to be a nun and to pass her time in a cell, praying!'

Was it in sheer devilry? Nine-tenths of it was, no doubt,

and in sheer delight at watching the frustrated fury in the swarthy, usually smooth, impassive faces, so supremely self-contained and indifferent, of her Spanish Ambassadors. Feria, angrily impatient of all others' points of view, de Quadra, quietly and slyly cynical about them – there was certainly a pleasure in flicking them into a startled awareness of another country, another outlook, another breed of womanhood, than in their own. She was playing for high stakes, but she could not help playing showily, in a bravado of defiance.

But one-tenth of what she admitted was true. At the very outset of her reign and of her high-flushed triumph in arriving at it, she sometimes found it baffling to keep it all up. She was the young Queen of a Court of arrogant men, native and foreign, whose advantage it was, as well as their pleasure, to make love to her. As it was to her advantage and pleasure to pretend to believe in it. But she was no fool nor a guileless maid. She had begun to see that whomsoever she married would land her in terrible difficulties. She saw also that her feints at marriage, and the hopes of it that she held out, could be an integral part of her policy. They were her moves in an intricate game where any false step on her part might mean the loss of her throne and the ruin of her country. Very well then, let it be a game, a pretence at passion, an absurd, sometimes sentimental, but always artificial comedy, in which she would act her part with the best of them, and with more pleasure than most. But an actor has only to play the same part over and over again until he learns a new one, and she had to act a different one every day, sometimes every moment.

For anyone strung on fine wires, as she was by nature, and had been for many years by danger, it was sometimes very tiring. It was in such moments that she sighed at the difficulty of preserving order among her turbulent nobles, knew that she had to go on attracting them to her Court in order to keep them out of mischief, and to maintain its splendour, but sometimes wished she could tell the lot of them to go to the Devil.

And then it was that she talked wistfully of the old ways of worship with Feria; or when de Quadra's softly cushioned hand administered a gently episcopal pat, while sitting beside her in the royal barge as they glided quietly down the Thames, that she could admit, and believe, that one part of her wished only to be a nun.

Even then she could laugh secretly at herself, knowing that this was but another thread in the airy web of diplomacy that she would always have to spin around her, and enjoy spinning.

She did not always enjoy it. Once she herself broke through it, when ill in bed with a feverish cold; the doctors called it the new disease or 'Influence.' She had hoped for a few hours in which to sneeze and shiver in solitude, but Feria had insisted on an interview, duly chaperoned, in order to demand her answer to a question she had forgotten. He had asked it six days ago, he exclaimed, and still he had received no answer.

'And God made the world in six days,' she snapped, 'but you cannot expect lesser folk to follow such an example.'

He did not reply to this blasphemy. He glanced at her ladies, who discreetly understood only English, and assured her that their talk would be strictly confidential and that she could speak candidly. At that moment she could not speak at all because of coughing, so he told her that Philip was very uneasy about her attitude to religion; he must know, and at once, if she intended to become the Head of the Church in England.

She sneezed furiously in answer, but a 'No' struggled through the explosion.

Then, if not in name, did she intend to become its Head in actual fact?

It was too much. Her hands were burning with fever and the desire to box his prominent ears, to slap his indignant, self-righteous face. She burst out that all this was waste of breath. Since Philip thought she was a heretic, she could not marry him, so of what use to go on talking about it?

He stared aghast at her; she sneezed and, he believed, swore. He hurried to reassure her; he did not believe she was really heretical, nor did King Philip. There was a muffled mutter, as she blew her nose, that she did not care a tinker's curse what either of them thought, but before his horrified hearing could make sure of it, she emerged from her handkerchief sufficiently to say clearly that the King of Spain seemed to care a deal more for his Church than for her.

So that was it! The inordinately vain young woman was expecting protestations of passion. Feria promptly gave them. But she paid no heed to them, denied that she would ever be Head of the Church, but declared that all the same she was not going to let tithes and Peter's Pence go out of the country, and that she couldn't bear Bishops.

Her servants came and told him it was supper time, which it was not; he left her with the sad reproach 'that she was not the Elizabeth he knew.'

But she was, the next time he saw her; she was well again, gay and laughing, too much so for Feria, who feared uneasily she might be laughing, not only at him, but at his

Very Catholic Majesty the King of Spain himself. It would be his duty to warn his King in secrecy of this possibility; and of one even more shocking, that Elizabeth might refuse his proposal. In fact she had actually said 'she could not marry him.'

He reproached her for her harsh words at their last meeting; did she mean what she had then said? She asked back, how should she know what she had meant?

'I had a cold,' she added airily.

Such insouciance was suicidal. He warned her that she might keep Philip waiting too long for her answer. She was putting him to a torture of suspense; if he found he could not bear it—

'You mean,' she interrupted, 'that he cannot bear any indecision except his own.'

This was too true to answer.

But suddenly she veered to another breeze. She smiled into his smooth plump face that had looked a shade less self-satisfied of late, and whispered, 'Have patience; and teach it to your master. Remind him of Cesare Borgia, who said he would 'eat the artichoke leaf by leaf.' I have many leaves to eat in this tough artichoke of my kingdom before I can savour the heart.'

His eyes goggled sympathetically. He began to speak a few beautifully rounded Latin platitudes on the heart, the impetuous lover (Philip), the hesitating maiden (herself). She heard them all before he spoke them, and already she seemed to be sitting in a mantilla at the wedding, trying to blush, and confident only that the Spaniards would admire her auburn hair. At the third or fourth reference to her hotly impatient wooer, she choked on what the scandalized Feria took at first instant for a hoot of laughter, but it was at once wafted away on a regretful sigh. Ah yes, she said softly, they were both young. But he was a King, and she a Queen.

'The King would wish me to answer him as a Queen. And I am not yet crowned.'

CHAPTER TWENTY-FOUR

One thing at a time, she had said. Whatever might come later from all the dangers and difficulties that beset her, she would make her Coronation a show to be remembered for generations to come. Those who were not yet born should tell their children, 'Ah, but you never heard my grandfather tell of the Crowning of Queen Bess!' That at least would be secure and true to the heart of her new reign, however brief the gamblers said it would be.

But she too was a gambler, and would take on the longest odds against herself. She believed that she would keep her power; that she would truckle to no man, be he friend or foe, wooer or counsellor, as to how she, a mere woman, should use it. Her strongest desire was of no lover in her arms, nor infant at her breast, but, as she said herself, 'to do some act that will make my fame spread abroad in my lifetime, and, after, occasion memorial for ever.'

Nor should it be only for vainglory. She promised that to herself, even while she gave the order to keep all the imports of scarlet silk in the country, because she wanted every scrap of it for her Coronation. Everything was to be red everywhere for that sunrise of hope and splendour, and if it snowed, then the warm colour would show up all the better.

It did snow at times, and the foul weather made deep mud,

but sand and gravel were thrown down before the procession; and nobody minded the cold and wet in this Crowning Hour.

She herself was all in cloth of gold with jewels on her red-gold head that sparkled brighter than the frost. Sitting in an open chariot on a raised pile that was covered to the ground with gold brocade, escorted by a procession of a thousand glittering horsemen, she was a figure of as unearthly magnificence as any golden image of the Blessed Virgin, or indeed of any heathen goddess from the distant Indies or Cathay. Yet this shining apparition, borne on high through the uproarious clamour of worship in the streets, was also one of the crowd. Her eyes were bright with joy at their welcome, she laughed at what they called to her and what they said to each other – an old man told his neighbour, 'I remember old King Harry VIII,' and she turned and smiled at him with intimate friendliness; she looked now at this one and now at that, so that each felt that he or she had alone caught her eye; she even stopped the procession to speak to some, or, rather, they stopped the procession. Again and again they broke through the barriers and even through the ranks of her guards, and she would not let them be repulsed. She gathered into her arms simple winter nosegays that poor women and little ragged boys threw into her chariot; at the end of the ride to Westminster she was still holding a branch of rosemary that a beggar woman had given her in Fleet Street.

The Spanish and Italian Ambassadors took pleasure in agreeing that her free and easy behaviour 'exceeded the bounds of gravity and decorum,' but it was her Coronation, not theirs – in fact, Feria was so annoyed with her that he pretended to be ill in order to avoid attending it. But he had a good look out of his window, noting in disgust that her new

Master of the Horse, Lord Robert Dudley, rode just behind her chariot on a huge charger, leading her white horse draped in cloth of gold.

'That was an easy bit of jobbery,' he snorted to his friend, the Bishop de Quadra; 'the moment Queen Mary's dead, young Dudley rides to Hatfield on a snow-white stallion, shows off his skill in managing it, and gets himself made Master of the Horse within the hour. And for what reason, I ask you, *what*?'

The Bishop, a plump soft elderly man like a well-padded purple cushion, gazed wistfully after the superb figure of the young adventurer that towered over all around him, and replied more sympathetically, 'His beauty, stature, and florid youth recommend him.'

The Bishop was painfully conscious of his lack of all three qualities. He had some time ago arrived in England after a ghastly wintry crossing, during which his only comfort had been that the English Earl of Arundel, one of the many aspirants to Elizabeth's hand, had been even more seasick than himself, and had indeed cried like a child until their horrid little bobbing vessel had at last bounced them both into port.

Even now the Bishop could not quite believe himself on terra firma; he believed it less every time he met the new Queen of this misty portion of it. He had brought her a priceless ring as a present from his master, King Philip, and she had pocketed it very readily – or rather, wore it on her finger – with a charming smile and expressions of gratitude, but apparently no recognition of its significance.

In the Spanish Court everyone knew the King's intention to marry the Queen of England; but here, in this strange country, which seemed to be entirely given over to raw, new, showy, ignorant young people, they did not seem to think the King of Spain's intentions half as important as those of the Queen of England. Even his superior, the Count de Feria, was not at all reassuring; he kept swearing at the Sovereign they now had to deal with as a 'Medea,' a 'Jezebel,' a 'she-devil' of so many tricks and wiles that there was no knowing where to catch a hold of her.

'Look at her now,' Feria was spluttering as the gorgeous cortège spun itself out beneath their window in an unending glittering ribbon; 'do you see what she is aiming at? The *common people,* the crowds, the apprentices, even the beggars, and their wives, that is the audience she is playing to. She cares nothing for the rest of them – or for us. She is making a new religion for them, she is playing at being a goddess. Think of the Easter processions in my own dear town of Seville – well, it is yours too – think of the image of the Holy Virgin all in gold encrusted with jewels, carried shoulder-high through the streets, with the children singing her praises, and the crowds shouting applause to her, and all the Brotherhoods of the Inquisition following her in their Caps of Invisibility three feet high, with slits for their invisible, ubiquitous, anonymous eyes – think of them carrying her into our vast cathedral, the oldest and largest Gothic cathedral of Europe, adorned with barbaric gold from our new Indies, singing and shouting and dancing, they carry her image, swaying and glittering in the sunlight, into the dark cave of her mysterious worship, the worship of the Mother of God, the Mother of all this queerly mingled world of ours, and as such, they give her honour.

'And this young woman, begotten of God knows whom, of

the son of a Welsh adventurer who made himself King, some say, of a strolling base-born musician, say others – this smart young lass who has a charming appearance and is of a sharp wit, but *has no prudence* – this bright insolent girl, a heathen or all but, is setting herself up to be worshipped like the Virgin herself. For it is that which she is posing as – a Virgin Queen – the rival of the Virgin Mary, to supplant her in the affections and veneration of this God-forsaken people.'

De Feria spoke as one inspired, and so he was, with fury, as he twirled his upturned moustaches. He was longing to return to his 'Little Seville', and might soon have to do so. But the Bishop de Quadra could not welcome any move that would entail another sea voyage during the winter months; he seemed positively to enjoy this spectacle of an impudent, imprudent, cocksure young woman, upheld as a goddess by the ignorant vulgar, with one of her showy lovers *(sic)* in flamboyant attendance; he murmured gentle allusions to her transit as that of Atalanta, who would not pause in her race for glory, no, not even for golden apples (this apparently because she had given him no due recognition of the importance of King Philip's ring) – no, he said, he liked the girl's spirit, and the resplendent show that she was making.

Gentlemen pensioners in crimson damask surrounded Elizabeth, their gilt battle-axes gleaming dully through a light fall of snow; an army of footmen in crimson velvet marched around her, showing 'E.R.' for Elizabeth Regina studded in massive silver on their breasts and backs; pages in crimson satin followed her on their gorgeously caparisoned horses. She had left the Tower for a familiar City now transformed into a fairyland; the windows and wooden barriers before the houses, all the way from Fenchurch Street to Cheapside, fluttered with draperies, with banners and streamers of brilliant silks and cloth of gold. Trumpets sounded, choir boys sang, the City aldermen presented her with a thousand gold marks in a crimson satin purse; and in a quick impromptu speech she promised that for her part, 'for the safety and quietness of you all, I will not spare if need be to spend my blood. God thank you all.'

A mighty roar went up from those who heard her 'loving answer,' and it was shuttled down through the further crowds who could see only her spontaneous gestures and 'merry countenance'. Their cheers swung into a tune, catching up in ragged shouts the song that a boy was singing to her of their

> *'true hearts, which love thee from their root.'*
> – *'True hearts'* – *'skip for joy'* – *'thy happy name'* –
> – *'thy triumph now that ruleth all the game'* –

echoed back to her from thousands of lusty throats.

Another echo followed them in her mind, from her little brother Edward's Coronation when they had sung to him,

> *'Sing up, heart, sing up, heart, sing no more down,*
> *But joy in King Edward that weareth the crown,'*

and she, a child of thirteen, had wondered if that would ever happen to herself. It was happening now; and all these true hearts round her were singing up and up with hers.

There were pageants all along the route; historic or mythological figures greeted her at every street corner.

Under a flowery arch at the upper end of Gracechurch Street, two actors dressed as her grandparents sat in two vast roses, red and white, for the Houses of Lancaster and York, and from them a stem twined up into a second stage, where in another rose, striped red and white, sat the representative of her father, all red and gold between his enormous padded sleeves; and beside him, shown for the first time since she had been beheaded at her husband's command, was a lady of remarkable likeness to her mother, Ann Bullen – a thin white face under an old-fashioned coif like a church window, slant eyes as black as sloes, and long white hands. It was the only moment in the procession when Elizabeth had no appropriate comment to make.

But she made up for it at the Little Conduit in Cheapside where an old man came out of a cave towards her with a scythe and an hour-glass. She lifted her face towards a gleam of sun that shot down on her through the dark blue snow clouds, and exclaimed in delight, 'Time! And time has brought me here!'

Philip had once told her that he and Time together would be a match for any man; but now, in a sudden light of confidence, she felt that she and Time would be a match for Philip. Time should be more prompt at her command, for she stood in the sunlight where his hand moved on the dial, and Philip in the shadow where Time's hand stood still.

Time's daughter, Truth, stepped forward to give her a Bible, and she kissed it and thanked the City for this present of 'the lively Oracles of God.'

At St. Paul's, the head boy of Colet's school spoke in eulogy of her as an example of Plato's philosopher-monarch, and she capped it impromptu in Latin at least equal to his own. The eight Beatitudes (all very pretty children) pranced before her at the entry to Soper's Lane and told her she had been blessed, among other qualities, with meekness and mildness, a speech it was as well the Spanish Ambassadors did not hear. The old gate of Ludgate was more fantastically decked than any maypole; and in Fleet Street, Deborah sat enthroned, 'the judge and restorer of the House of Israel,' to show what a woman ruler could do in spite of Mr. John Knox's shrill 'First Blast of the Trumpet against the Monstrous Regiment of Women,' which he had blown in open publication some months before.

But neither the Presbyterian's sour maledictions, nor on the other hand the old Pope's angry threats of excommunication, could cloud the glory of the Coronation Service the next day, though in some eyes its rites were maimed. But Westminster Abbey had been made 'all glorious within' by Henry VIII's entire collection of tapestries, some of them from Raphael's designs, and of such biblical subjects as the stories from Genesis and the Acts of the Apostles, but others of the secular campaigns of Caesar and Pompey, since it was a pity to leave any out.

The dreamlike scenes, that would last for centuries, glowed and wavered in the draught behind the glory of this present moment. Queen Elizabeth, followed by her peeresses, walked in through the great doorway over a spread purple-blue cloth which the crowd outside cut away bit by bit, to keep the pieces as souvenirs. A little dark Italian writer, hungrily seeking employment in this strange country, feasted his eyes on the procession of noble ladies who all seemed to him tall, fair and beautiful; they trailed their long coloured robes behind them and held their proud heads high under their coronets as they paced slowly past him out of the raw northern daylight into the glimmering richness of the Abbey.

Four earls marched before them, carrying naked swords, one without any point, to signify Ireland, so somebody told the little foreigner, 'because it had never been conquered'; but others said it was because it was Curtana, the Sword of Peace and Mercy. Another sword represented France; but as even Calais had now been won back from England, the sword should surely have been more pointless even than that of Ireland. And why did the Sword of Justice, and its scabbard loaded with pearls, have to be redeemed from the altar for the price of a hundred silver shillings – was that the price of justice in this country? It was all rather confusing to the Italian visitor. Earls, Marquesses, Kings of Arms, which were which? The orb was carried by the Marquess of Winchester; and one of the sceptres by the Earl of Arundel, who had long ago recovered from his seasickness, but still looked as though he might cry at any minute. This, they said, was from sheer vainglorious excitement because he was made Lord High Steward at the Coronation and believed it to be a sign that his young Queen returned his passion for her. There were also two other sceptres, one of them signifying France, as usual; and three crowns, one of them carried just behind the Queen by the Earl Marshal, the young Duke of Norfolk. He was the only Duke left; all the others had lost their heads. How long would young Norfolk keep his? He did not look as though it were much help to him.

And there was as sad a lack of Bishops as of Dukes. There were no Archbishops, armoured in white and gold; no crimson Cardinals.

Oglethorpe of Carlisle, not really important, was the only Bishop who could be got to crown the suspected heretic; and he had had to borrow the robes of 'bloody Bishop Bonner' for the occasion, at the very last minute. He was in a twitter of nervous agitation, especially when Sir William Cecil, the new Secretary of State, passed notes to him from the Queen during the Service, telling him to read the Gospel and Epistle aloud in English as well as Latin.

Some asked behind their hands what business had Cecil, a layman, servant only of the State, in this sacred service; some feared that the Service was not sufficiently Roman Catholic; others, that it was too much so. It was Catholic in form, but did not commit the English Church to Rome, nor promise what course it would take in the future. Elizabeth herself was acutely aware of the anomaly, and of how quickly it might grow into complete division; the exiled Protestant zealots, now swarming back into the country, were pressing hard upon her with their demands that she should lead a revolution to overthrow all the forms of the Church and convert England by force to extreme Calvinism. Force she would not use, least of all for an aim she detested. Her aim was to have simplicity in religious intention, and a wise toleration. If people worked together for God and their fellow-men, it would bring a truer unity, peace and concord than any dialectic. But no one yet dreamed toleration possible, since religion also meant politics.

She must hold the uneasy balance of her reign by favour, and she alone could do it, because she was the Prince the people needed in this hour. Already ballads were being hawked on broadsheets in the streets to tell how wretched England had been under Mary, dulled by fear, disillusion and despair; and how through it all the only hope lay in the refrain that

'*We wished for our Elizabeth.*'

She too had recognized in her triumphal progress through the City that the crowds, for all their jollity and friendliness, had acclaimed her almost as a goddess. She must keep and increase that worship; it would lighten dreary thoughts, restore their confidence in their country and make it great.

The sacerdotal robe of gold was placed upon her, in the same ritual that consecrates a Bishop, and she was dedicated to God and to her people, to whom she had just promised, if need be, to spend her blood. The need might well arise; Philip of Spain still bore the title of King of England, and would till the day he died. He might well try to make it good by force of arms, if and when other means should fail him. But her life, even in this hour of glory, was not dear to her. She now, to herself, promised more; that she would at need spend her happiness. That promise was not made so easily; standing in the stiff archaic gold that might have sheathed a Byzantine priest, she felt that she was decked for sacrifice.

Then her spirit soared as she knew that her life was now indeed hallowed in this most ancient rite of 'the Sacring,' by the love she would give her people. They had been depressed, down-trodden, driven to fight for a foreign Power, and defeated; returned dismayed and forlorn, with nothing to hope for in a world where the old faiths and hopes had become meaningless to many, and a mere excuse for cruelty. They felt that God no longer cared for them, and no man would do so.

Now she had come, and she would care. Once the Sovereign had been a Priest; once he had been a God; but a ruler in Macedon long ago had known more truly when he said, 'kingship is a glorified servitude.' She was here to serve her countrymen; they were her charge, for God had charged her with them. This was the meaning in the heart of these long hours of ceremonial; and no hope of her own happiness, as it might be in the person of her Master of the Horse riding so jauntily behind her in the procession, could compete with this charge that had been laid upon her, and the joy of loving that it would bring her.

No one guessed then at that private hallowing of herself; human as it was, rather than pious, it was too much for her tense nerves; she had to break away from it in mockery, and shocked her ladies who changed her robes after her 'Sacring,' by telling them that the holy oil was 'nothing but nasty grease and stank.'

And as for being their 'undoubted Queen,' as the Bishop of Carlisle had presented her to her subjects, she knew well how many there were to doubt her title; but that was one of the many things one did not say, even in the sudden reactions of flippancy which so often helped her to keep her balance.

Yet it was that moment of her Election and Recognition as 'undoubted Queen' that was the most significant for her. For when she had to mount the tribune and be shown to all the people in the Abbey – North, South, East and West in turn – to ask if they were willing to do their Homage and Service to her as their Liege Lord, she was following the old tradition that a monarch did not reign by hereditary right alone, but was chosen freely by the people.

She owed her crown, she had told Feria, to the will of the people. Now they spoke that will with one voice; they acclaimed their wish for her as Queen in shouts of 'Yea! Yea! Yea!' so tremendous that they drowned the blare of trumpets and peal of bells that proclaimed it to the world outside. It sounded as though the world were coming to an end; and so indeed it was, for better or for worse, for joy or sorrow, the old world, the old ways of worship that Queen Mary had tried to bring back to England, were gone for good or ill, now that this new young Queen had been crowned.

She came into the outside world again, the orb and sceptre in her hands glittering in the wintry light of day, and on her head the great ruby of the Black Prince, which Henry V had worn in his helmet at Agincourt.

She smiled and talked to everyone near her, to the delight of the English and disapproval of the graver Latin observers; she changed her dress again and sat down to a banquet in Westminster Hall at which everybody was dressed in red, and drank red wine in the flickering light of the torches and great log fires. The old world of chivalry came back into the hall when the Queen's Champion, Sir Edward Dymoke, rode into the midst of it on a black charger draped with cloth of gold, and flung down his mailed glove in challenge to fight to the death any who wished to dispute the titles of his most worthy Empress. Nobody wished to do so, and the Queen drank his health in a gold cup worth two hundred crowns, which she presented to him. She sat all through the banquet, which had begun at three in the afternoon and lasted for ten hours; and at one o'clock next morning she went to bed for a week.

POSTLUDE:
THE KING AND QUEEN

Feria stood before his King in Flanders. He had finished his account of his mission in England; that at least was something. Ambassadors were sometimes struck dumb with awe when first confronted with Philip's pale and icy majesty. This was by no means Feria's first meeting; he had known him well (*how* well he suddenly doubted); had always stood up to him in his letters; and the King had never shown displeasure. But could his face ever show anything? It seemed to have crystallized still more of late.

The dark and angry little man who confronted the slighter figure of his King had to remind himself that it was through no fault of his own that he had failed in his mission; to console himself that at all events he had for ever shaken the dust or rather the mud of England off his Spanish-leathered shoes. He squared his broad shoulders and twirled up his aggressive black moustaches. No blue-blooded hidalgo from 'Little Seville' should let himself be overawed by a half-Flemish King who tried to seem more Spanish than all Spain, but gave himself away by the plodding industry of a German clerk. His glance slid down to the gold-inlaid desk at which Philip was reckoned to sit frequently for about sixteen hours a day.

He noted with disapproval that it was covered with the architects' plans for the new palace-monastery-tomb of the Escorial – a fantastic idea, and where was the money to come from, with the Exchequer in its present state? There was too much of this mountain-monastery business. The King had ordered the whole of Spain to collect alms for the building of a great new church at Montserrat near Barcelona, probably all because his father had visited it nine times and said there was a '*je ne sais quoi*' about the place. Armies of workmen would have to scramble two thousand feet up an almost inaccessible mountain with sacks of cement and loads of iron on their backs; Feria resented the expense of effort even more than that of money. Philip was behind the times. Mountains were holy only because they had been the refuge of the past, against the heathen Moors. Now, on the sea-board, lay the future of Catholic Spain.

He thought hard for an instant, then abandoned thought, and his words broke out as explosively as a bubble from a frog's mouth.

'Piety should be practical – and patriotic. All the good workmen in Spain should now be in the dockyards, preparing an armada for the conquest of heretic England.'

He urged Philip to this heroic master-stroke with a few well-placed pinpricks, insinuating the petty details that had revolted him of late in England. Their climate they could not help, poor, sodden, half-drowned devils. Their manners they had learned too late to learn, half civilized as they had been while Spain was leading Europe and discovering America. But their tastes! His eyes goggled, his mouth burst open, as he told Philip how their new young 'Virgin' Queen liked English beer, which Philip loathed; her own was 'so strong as there is no man able to drink it,' and went by such low, uncouth names as 'double-double' and 'hum and huff'.

That, he assured himself, should cure His High Austerity of wishing to feast with the tall girl who looked like a white and gold lily.

'Beer for Bess,' he rubbed it in, was the slogan of the new reign – how different from the life of their late Queen!

He spoke in terms of praise, but tones of scorn, of Elizabeth's extraordinary gift for the unconventional and impromptu – the very gift which Philip would regard as vulgar and ridiculous.

She had stopped a formal procession to call up to a sick friend at a window and ask after his health – oh yes, it was always 'his'; she had no women friends.

She had chaffed her dignified old ex-jailer, Sir Henry Bedingfeld, a devoted adherent to Queen Mary of blessed memory, by telling him that when she wanted any prisoners guarded with extra strictness she would put them in his charge.

She had no dignity, no propriety. Feria could not bring himself to repeat the jokes and innuendoes she had made to himself. But he repeated a good many.

He broke off suddenly. The King's face showed no sign of interest; he had not answered. He frequently did not answer. But Feria felt that a change of subject might be advisable.

So he congratulated him on the recent betrothal he had made for his young son, Don Carlos, with the eldest daughter of Henri II of France. It was a firm step forward, this matrimonial alliance with France, in the project of subduing England; Feria gave it his unqualified approval. And Isabel de Valois, a lovely and gentle girl of sixteen, barely two years older than her prospective bridegroom, would be an added grace, an easily malleable tool for the Court of Spain. She would also make a true man of the eager boy who, said Feria with a spruce smile, was already reputed to be madly in love with her portrait.

The King made a slight movement, but only to bow politely. His servant's thoughts began to course wildly. Could there after all be some truth in the stories he had heard? Did the King really hate his odd, outspoken, backward, yet sometimes precocious son and heir? Philip, like all the Spaniards that he emulated, was respectable. Carlos gave no sign of ever being so. He was vulgar, violent, rude and uncontrolled. But everyone said that since his betrothal he was a changed creature, quiet and modest, walking as in an enchanted dream with the miniature of the dark grave-eyed girl who was to be his bride; when he thought himself alone he kissed it, talked to it, promised it that now he would be good and gentle and worthy of her love.

Just such an idyll had been Philip's own first marriage in his boyhood; Feria wondered if he should suggest this. No flicker of expression passed over the impassive face before him, yet Feria could have sworn that at that moment the King shared his thought. So why not say it? But he did not.

He shot back to the vexed question of England, and answered it in arrogant confidence. The country, once conquered, would be re-converted with ease. The English would always worship as their rulers and their interests demanded. His spies' statistics had proved that only one per cent. of the population were even now really Protestant – and they were only negligible artisans in sedentary jobs that gave time for conceit, such as tailors and cobblers.

At last there was a break in the mask; the faint eyebrows had arched themselves slightly. 'In my father's day,' said the low, even voice, 'a petty cobbler led the revolt of the Communidades in Majorca which slaughtered the patrician families and held out against the Emperor for over a year.'

'And then was conquered only by a dirty Flemish trick,' Feria longed to add, but even he did not dare. He found himself hovering, clinging on with his Spanish-leathered toes to the marble floor, while he desperately propounded that

England was only heretic because of her Queen, who had to be one, or else declare herself a bastard with no legitimate claim to the throne.

It was no use. He found himself dismissed, and with no idea as to what was the King's decision – if any.

Philip himself could not have told then what it was. He needed time to think it over, alone, at his desk. Time, he had said, was on his side. But on which side of him? He knew, to his torment, that he had two sides, and could never be sure on which stood Time. He thought of the rocky peaks in the rare luminous air of Castile, where the castle homes of his boyhood had been built long ago – Segovia, Toledo, Avila of the eighty towers. There his spirit lived, and longed to draw to its end on earth, as his father's had done on the mountain top of Yuste. But his body had to stay now on this soggy plain of Flanders, where his father had blamed him for inaction. Surely that released spirit could not *now* think it better to have marched on Paris than to have planned the Escorial?

He looked down at the designs for the soaring edifice of austere granite that should rise in harmony with the surrounding rocks and pines, but in an urgency of pure spirit. Majesty would be shown as sacred; above the temple a spire would point to the sky, crowned with an orb to signify the power of this world, but on top of the orb would tower a gold cross. He held up the design in his hands, but he was not looking at it now; his gesture was that of offering it to another. He was holding it in self-justification to his father. This was his answer to the Emperor's accusation.

Action meant grasping, seeking for oneself, and therefore ignoble. Self sacrifice, suffering in devotion, was the purest form of action, perhaps the only true form of it. His eyes turned, as so often, to the crucifix on the wall. God the Son had shown the way. In contrast, God the Father had made the world; and, in doing so, a mistake.

'Let me alone,' he had once prayed when a boy, 'for I am not better than my father,'

But it might be that Christ would wish him, too, to prove the contrary.

Not in life, but in death, lay the answer to life. He had known it even when he was still a boy. He knew it better now. What good, even from the view of this world, came out of all this busy planning and self-seeking? He had tried to marry his wife's young sister, a bastard heretic with flaming hair, but eyes as cold as the sea when she looked at him. He had lusted after her while his wife was still alive and tortured by her jealousy of them. And still she had not consented to marry him. God had not only denied him, but cruelly humiliated him through this white witch, this false goddess who now sat on the precarious throne of England. In her arrogance she preened and plumed herself there like a peacock, ignoring the fact that it was he who had placed her there, that but for him she might well be dead. Better dead, since she lived only to flout him; to ignore, even mock his conscientious scruples as those of a fussy little man – yes, that was how Feria had shown that she regarded him – a little man at the mercy of a woman's whim.

Yet again England had wounded him in a personal matter that struck at his masculine pride. It was of no use now to look at his plans for the Escorial, to think of death, the leveller, who made all men equal, even in stature, in the grave. God had used this woman as a sign, to show him that not only must he turn from his longing for her quick, lithe body, her flashes of speech and laughter, all the bright blazing life of her, but that he must turn against her. Her power was for evil; that was now clear from her use of it over himself. Therefore he must withstand it; he must take action, and quickly, hateful as that was to him. Soon she would be boasting throughout Europe that she had refused his offer of marriage.

Philip did not tell himself that at all costs he must forestall that insult; that he must prove to the world that he had jilted 'that jilt, the Lady Elizabeth,' before Elizabeth had jilted him. But he began to see how it could be done. How also, in compensation for his lost false love, God might reward him with a true and docile wife, tender as the opening rosebuds, comparable only with his own first bride, when he had tasted rapture (but for how brief a moment!) in his boyhood.

He thought of his fourteen-year-old son, of Carlos's pathetic belief that when he was married he would be a man, whom no one would dare to scold or order about any more. But how fit was his son to bear the excitements and responsibilities of such early marriage? They might not lessen but increase his abnormal tendencies. It would be terrible to think of a young girl in the power of a crude, savage adolescent.

Philip had already thought of it, but felt that he could not say it; he could not accuse his son, show that he doubted the sanity of his heir. Whatever happened, he would never do that. So he had taken no action; had let matters take their course; had allowed his counsellors to hurry on the betrothal for the sake of the political alliance.

But he could now see another way to secure that alliance, a way that was outrageous to him, contrary to his whole nature – but necessary.

The clock his father had made ticked on. The sky outside

darkened into the Netherlandish night, then grew pale in a watery dawn. Time stepped past at King Philip's side, and his thoughts dragged after it, drawing him slowly towards the only impetuous decision he ever made.

It fell like a thunderbolt on Europe – and on Carlos. The King of Spain proposed to marry his son's prospective bride.

People were shocked, horrified, amused. The King of Spain had chosen an odd way to restore himself to his full stature in his own sight, by behaving like a disappointed lover in a violent fit of pique. Everybody knew now that Elizabeth must have refused him, or that he knew she was going to, since here he was rushing off, without a word of warning, to marry his son's betrothed bride. 'Rushing off' – it was inconceivable in connection with Philip; yet it was true. His dislike of action, his deep-seated fear of ridicule, had led him to the most ridiculous action of his life.

To his son, it was also the worst. The young Prince's burst of frustrated rage was dreadful to see and hear. He uttered such threats against his father, who he declared had always hated him, and now had stolen his wife from him, that people said he really must be mad, and unsafe to be at large.

But the Spanish and French politicians were jubilant. The two countries, after generations of enmity, would now be in the closest possible alliance. With the King of Spain as son-in-law to the King of France, Europe would be united as one Power against the heretics. Nothing now could prevent the invasion of England, to depose Elizabeth and set Mary Queen of Scots on the throne. The French and Scots armies were all ready to march down on London from the North, while the Spanish flotillas would attack the East coast from Flanders across the Narrow Seas.

Spain's greatest soldier, the Duke of Alva, sat at work in Antwerp with maps before him of English harbours, particularly in East Anglia. The Dutch bargees jeeringly called the barge's mooring-post a 'dukdalf' after him, he was so long and thin and wooden; but he was a mooring-post in grim earnest for the Spanish armadas that were thronging to his command.

And his spies came as thick and fast, to tell him how broken were the English armies, how weak their navies and rotten their ships, how frantically busy all their dockyards. Let them build ships night and day, they could not build them in time.

The bookmakers in Europe had given the new young Queen six months at most to keep her throne, and the days were running out.

If you enjoyed this, you may like to read *The Galliard*, Margaret Irwin's enchanting account of the little-known story of Mary, Queen of Scots' great love for her loyal servant, James Hepburn, the Earl of Bothwell, known to all as the Galliard.

Read on for an extract…

Chapter One

He first saw her walking down a street in Paris, swift and shining in the sunlight as though made of Venetian glass. Her tall childish figure so glittered with jewels that it seemed translucent to the hot rays of the evening sun behind her; a halo of pale gold shimmered from the loose threads of hair round her bare head, fine as spun glass. She wore a tiny mask of black velvet which did not conceal the fair skin and broad forehead, nor yet the direct untroubled eyes.

Beside her walked the scarlet figure of a young-looking man, fair and slender like herself and very tall; so lithe, soldierly and arrogant in bearing that it gave a slight shock to the traveller, watching from the doorway of his inn, to perceive that those gorgeous robes were those of a Prince of the Church, and that it was a Cardinal who was swinging down the street like a young Captain of the Guard.

'Who is she?' he demanded, though he had known even before he saw her, from the cries of the people who came running down the street, out of the narrow doorways, thronging round her, throwing up their caps, shouting 'La Reinette! La Reinette!'

So this was their 'little Queen', and his; Queen of France for the last fifteen months; Queen of Scotland for the whole of her short life; Queen of England to all who admitted the bastardy of

Queen Elizabeth. He had known her too from the sight of her, for she had some likeness to her mother, whom he had been proud to account his friend.

That gallant Frenchwoman, Mary of Guise, Regent of Scotland, he had seen for the last time this summer, stricken down with the illness that was to be her death, yet still with the splendid physique, broad shoulders and erect carriage to balance her unusual height, which had led stout Henry of England to offer her marriage, 'since he was so big himself, he needed a big wife'.

'But my neck is small!' she had answered.

Would this girl ever fill out to the same sturdy quality? He doubted it. At this first glimpse, for all she had the height of her mother's family, there was more trace in her of her Scottish father, that delicate racehorse of a king, with fine golden hair and a smile for any lass, but tragic eyes. He too used to walk boldly through the streets among the common people and talk familiarly with them, just as his pretty daughter, whom he had never seen, was now doing, attended only by her uncle of Guise, the Cardinal de Lorraine.

She was wanting to stop and talk to the people who pressed about them; she held out a hand to a ragged woman who had dropped on her knees crying out that she was an angel from heaven. The Cardinal flung a coin to the woman and scattered a few more among the crowd, whereupon a thin cheeky lad, going one better, shouted, 'It's either Jesus Christ or the Cardinal!'

Her uncle hurried her on, perhaps because the sweating, chattering crowd was none too pleasant in this dusty heat. She swung easily into step with his stride; she walked like a boy and as though swift movement were a delight to her.

'A nimble filly,' thought the young man in the doorway of his tavern, 'though still a long-legged foal. If she be anything but a virgin yet, I know nothing of women.'

But the Galliard knew women nearly as well as he knew horses.

And he knew Mary Stewart, and a good deal about her, as soon as he set his bold eyes on her. But 'Who are they?' he asked again, for it amused him to play the ignoramus abroad, one got a deal more information that way.

The thin lad, cheerful, disreputably shabby, with a nose as pert as a sparrow's beak, and a sallow, pock-marked but not ill-looking face, swung round at the question with a squawk of laughter which he instantly checked at sight of the stranger.

Incredible! Did the foreign lord not know Charles de Guise, the great Cardinal de Lorraine, 'the Red Phalaris', the 'Tiger of France'?

The soubriquets shrilled higher and higher off his tongue in a crescendo of national pride. The Galliard took his measure at a glance, balancing the wiry strength of the fellow against his high voice – a lively rascal, nervous, but all the quicker for that, should be useful in a tight corner. Master Cock-up-Spotty (so he named the talkative youth) was telling him that the Cardinal and his eldest brother, the great soldier, Duc de Guise, were known as the Pope and King of France; and 'the Pope', that suave, scholarly courtier, had been the fiercer of the two in quelling the Huguenot rising this summer – 'such a rage he flew into, he tore the biretta from his head and trampled it underfoot!'

My lord was unimpressed. 'The more fool he,' he remarked in easy French, but with a strong Scottish accent, 'hadn't he his brother's hat within reach?'

But if a man must wear the long robes of a woman, it was something that his blood should burn like a man's inside them. He liked also that the Tiger minded the hatred and gossip 'no more than the barking of a dog; he collects all the lampoons against him and keeps them with his rare pictures – and some of *them* ought to be rarer, they say!'

It gave the Scot a twinge of patriotic jealousy that 'the Cardinal's Niece' seemed here a prouder title than Queen of Scotland in her own right, and even of France by marriage; 'La Petite Sauvage' they were actually calling her, though with a chuckling admiration. 'Ah, she's bred from barbaric stock on her father's side!'; so Cock-up-Spotty told him with a grin that split his face and was instantly wiped off as the Scots lord stiffened, for this was not the way for a French gutter rat to talk of the Stewart Kings. But his Border blood answered with a throb of amused sympathy when he heard that the Little Savage's wild blood was not to be tamed even by her severe mother-in-law. Catherine de Medici's own children were terrified of her, but nothing could make La Reinette afraid, she only tossed her proud little head, despised the Medici for her lack of breeding, and even said in one of her naughty fits that she was only the merchant's daughter of Florence.

'Damned careless of her,' grunted the Scot. La Reinette's mother had fondly told him of the Medici's glowing praises of her daughter-in-law; 'this bewitching child,' she had written, 'has only to smile to turn all heads.' With any sense, she'd have smiled at her mother-in-law most of all; but he could not help liking the spirit of the lass, for he had no love for people who remembered to smile in the right direction – as he must now do himself!

And at that the Galliard shrugged and grinned mockingly at the Parisian youth's instant compliment on the shrug, that Monsieur had the air of a true Frenchman, a Gascon *par exemple*. It was inconceivable that Monsieur should not know Paris as well as himself, but if by any chance he required the services of a guide through the streets, he, Hubert, would be enchanted to render them.

'Hubert of what?' It might be useful to know of this fellow some time.

'Hubert of Paris,' replied Cock-up-Spotty with a superb air, and was rewarded with a short laugh like the crack of a pistol.

'Of all Paris, are you? Get out of my way, fellow. I don't need a guide to the Tuileries, *nor* your introduction to the Queen Dowager!'

And thus unashamedly answering boast with boast, the splendid stranger pushed past the street loafer into the mean inn where he was lodging; pulled up his soft leather boots and roared to his page to fetch a brush for them, picked up a pair of gloves embroidered in seed pearls by his latest mistress, and swaggered off to the interview he had been promised with Catherine de Medici, Queen Dowager of France.

He had to save on his lodging, but his clothes were fine enough to bear comparison even with her courtiers, or had been, though perhaps they were getting a bit worn-looking. But his bearing carried that off; his hat was cocked triumphantly on the side of the dominant head; his doublet was rather shabby, but that did not prevent his swinging his short scarlet-lined cloak far back in gay insouciance as to what it might reveal; and his gloves, the only new and perfect garment, he flicked against his knee in rhythm to the tune he was whistling, as though he were urging his horse to the gallop instead of strolling through the streets of Paris.

His stride showed the born horseman, the long, lean-flanked, slightly bowed legs and the easy swing of the long arms from the broad shoulders. His reddish-brown eyes were the colour of bogstreams on a sunny day, alert and quick-glancing, as they had had to be from childhood against sudden danger; but now alight only for the women, scanning each that passed in cool, arrogant appraisement of her points, as he had just now scanned those of a young Queen.

And would he need then to be afraid of an old one? Not he! Here he was again in Paris, which he had not seen since he had finished his education as a boy; he had gone far since then; he would go farther, and Queens, young or old, would be the pawns to help him on his way. His father had tried to work that line, and bungled it, but his father had been a bit of a fool and more than a bit of a traitor; he himself knew better. He had shown he could not only win a Queen's trust, but deserve it.

For that reason he could now be tolerably sure of a good reception from Queen Catherine. The Medici's only possible game at present lay in subservience to those great brothers of Guise who ruled all France between them. And it was their sister, Mary of Guise, Queen Dowager and Regent of Scotland, dead these two months past, who had proved this young man to be the most audacious and loyal of her servants. She had given him the highest office in the land, to guard against England, and this two years ago when he was still only twenty-three. And early this summer, when Mary of Guise lay sick to death and besieged in her castle of Edinburgh, she had sent him to Denmark to enlist the services of the Danish Fleet, the most important at that moment in Europe, against her enemies of England and those of her subjects who were in league with them against her.

Her new Lieutenant of the Border had carried out her mission with as much success as a diplomat as he had shown as a soldier; he had drunk deep with King Frederick of Denmark, undeterred by the three-litre capacity of that monarch's wine-glass, and discussed with him the breeding of horses and bloodhounds; the King and his brother had been so taken with him that they had gone out of their way to escort the young Scottish Envoy across the sea from Copenhagen to Jutland on his way to Germany.

It was on that journey that he heard of his Queen Regent's death in Scotland; heard too that both Scotland and France were now signing a treaty with England. There was therefore no further use in his mission, and he travelled direct to France to lay his sword at the service now of the daughter, Mary Stewart.

Of all this, Catherine de Medici, Queen Dowager of France, showed due recognition when James Hepburn, Earl of Bothwell, Hereditary Lord High Admiral of Scotland and Lord Lieutenant of the Border, was presented to her that evening. She was walking in the midst of a little group of courtiers and ladies and her favourite dwarfs in her gardens of the Tuileries. The sun had not yet set, but slanted behind the late blossoming rose trees and monstrous forms of giant toads and diminutive dragons of green majolica; they threw their squat shadows on the path where that tall stout lady in black walked up and down between two hunchbacks not three feet high.

As she walked, a fretted gold ball containing a pomander, suspended from her girdle, bounced up and down against her stomach – her sporran, the Scot instantly dubbed it in his ribald mind. Her cold and glassy eyes, brown, blank and opaque as chestnuts, took with shrewd accuracy the measure of this tough weather-beaten young adventurer, the swaggering self-confidence of his splendid chest and shoulders and sturdy horseman's stance, as she turned to him with a dirty jest about his amorous career.

It brought back to him with a flash of amusement the gossip he had so lately heard: 'banker's daughter', 'shopkeeper's daughter'? – what was the epithet given by the girl who should wear three crowns to the lady whose family emblem was three gold balls? Whichever it was, it fitted this stout Florentine dame as snugly as her own tight black brocade as she cushioned her beautiful hands in the yielding flesh of her hips in the determined gesture of commercial *bonhomie*, and asked him if it were Scotland, France or Denmark that had most contributed to his reputation as Don Juan. And she followed this compliment with a loud, purposefully jolly laugh.

He'd no love for shrinking modesty in woman, God knows, but there was something in the coarse-grained fibre of that hearty matron and mother of ten that struck him as more unnatural than even the chastity of a nun. Of this he was not really aware, but thought her repellent because her chin fell away like a rat's beneath the sensual lips. But he found himself no whit at a loss in answering her badinage; they exchanged one or two low stories of an ancient pattern, and the Scot was certain that his was the less hoary.

The heavily robed figure pushed its way on through the humming sweet-scented air of the rose-walks, out on to the open squares of chequered marble, her erect head and wide skirts making a wedge-shaped block of shadow, narrow at the top, wider and wider at the base, cleaving its way so purposefully through the late evening sunlight.

Yet she had no fixed purpose; she changed her mind a dozen times a day even in quite small matters; she valued common sense above all things, and was fond of saying that the end justified the means; but she had no end, no aim, except first to win the love of her husband, and second to get power for herself. The first aim had died with the death of her husband a year ago; the second – well, that remained to be seen.

She was a clever woman, she knew how to be all things to all men, she studied medicine, mathematics and astrology because she liked them, but Greek and Latin because they were the fashion. She had encouraged the Reformed religion because it was the fashion, said rude things about the Pope, who was 'no more than a man', and had liked to sing the Huguenot Marot's psalms with the late King Henri II, her husband, perhaps because his mistress Diane de Poictiers had been a staunch Catholic. But, like everyone else, she had to obey the Guises; and though the tastes and interests of the Cardinal de Lorraine all leaned towards these new experimental ideas (he had even attended their prayer meetings for a bet), his policy was firmly Catholic.

Queen Catherine took trouble to explain this to the young Protestant from Scotland; she even, as though she were one of his warmest admirers, quoted the Cardinal's very words on the subject, warning them that the true danger of these new doctrines was that they struck ultimately at the root of all government. And for proof of that, the Lord Lieutenant could furnish only too many instances, since nearly all the other nobles of his faith had banded themselves together as the Lords of the Congregation, in league with England against their Regent.

'But you, my Lord Bothwell, almost alone, have contrived to

reconcile your advanced ideas in religion with a loyalty that is alas now old-fashioned.'

'Madam, my ideas are no more advanced than my boyhood's lessons, where I learned them – such as they are,' he added deprecatingly as he shot back in his mind, trying to remember when he had last attended any service. 'We of the Border ride light, we don't take more religion than we can carry with comfort' but no, that was not too safe even with this old pagan. He was on surer ground as he went on: 'But loyalty is my true creed, as it is the motto of my house – "Keep Trust". I cannot see why men should not worship as they choose and let others do so.'

It was a bold remark to make to the lady who had signified her approval of the executions at Amboise this summer by watching them from the Castle balcony; and so she hinted, with a glance at him from her blank eyes as they rolled round in her fat, flat face.

But he answered the challenge as coolly as he had provoked it. 'Those executions were for rebellion, not for religion. If the Huguenots plan to murder the rulers of the kingdom and kidnap King François your son, what can they expect but to lose their heads?'

She winced very slightly at his reference to the Guises as the rulers of her son's kingdom, but agreed enthusiastically: 'No one can call me a bigot. I have brought up my own children in the doctrine of the Huguenots, and have always said that anyone of intelligence must think much as they do. But one must be practical. It is results that count. "By your fruits ye shall know them," as Saint Paul said, I believe, and if he did, it is magnanimous in me to quote an apostle who paid scant regard to my sex.'

'Madam, you are right. In Scotland, at any rate, religion is being used by rebels chiefly as a decoy duck.' ('And much Saint Paul would care for being quoted by you, you ugly old bitch!' he added to himself.)

Yes, it was good to walk out from that interview, to take a deep breath, remember that he was going to sup with a couple of men, and look round him in free solitude on the familiar town which now looked fantastically beautiful in the September dusk. A single star hung over the piercing loveliness of the spire of the Sainte Chapelle; Notre Dame lay like a couched lion in the dark mass of little buildings round it; the river flowed broad and pale and gleaming under the quiet sky. After this hot day its smell was as exotic as its beauty. 'Edinburgh is as strong but not so rich,' the Scot decided. In the capital of his native land the predominant smell was of stale salt fish; here, of rotting garlic.

But it was for the cool pungent smell of bog moss, of heather and bracken after rain, of dew on the tough hairgrass in these misty September dawns, that his finely cut nostrils were longing. All this summer, and longer, he had been away; what had happened since then at home? What raids had been ridden in spite of the treaty? What mischief had his rascals been getting into?